Legions of Fire

*Based on an
original outline by
J. Michael Straczynski*

THE LONG NIGHT OF CENTAURI PRIME
ARMIES OF LIGHT AND DARK
OUT OF THE DARKNESS

PETER DAVID

SCIENCE
FICTION

Legions of Fire

CONTENTS

CONTENTS

THE LONG NIGHT
OF CENTAURI PRIME

Keep your face to the sun,
so you will not see the shadow.
—HELEN KELLER

prologue

The Drakh felt sorry for him.

Londo Mollari would have been surprised to learn that such considerations went through the Drakh's mind. Had the Drakh's sentiments been relayed to him, he would have been even more surprised to learn precisely *why* the Drakh felt sorry for him.

But he did not know, so he faced the Drakh with his jaw set, his shoulders squared, obviously doing everything within his ability to look cool and confident in the moment when his keeper would bond with him.

The Drakh, however, could already sense the accelerated heartbeats, the forced steadiness of the breathing, the general signs of rising panic, which Londo was pushing back by sheer force of will. All of this was clear, to the Drakh, for the bond upon which he and Londo would operate was already beginning to form on a subliminal level.

His name was Shiv'kala . . . and he was a hero. At least, that was how the other Drakh tended to speak of him, in whispers, or when they communed in silence, having abandoned the need for verbal speech.

Among the Drakh, there was none more brave, more diligent, more pure in his vision of what the universe should be. Nor was there any who was more sympathetic to his fellow creatures. This was what served to make Shiv'kala so effective, so pure, and so ruthless. He knew that in order to accomplish what was best for the galaxy, he had to be willing to hurt, terrify, even kill if necessary. Anything would be justified, as long as he never lost sight of the common good.

Shiv'kala loved the common man. He had the common touch . . . and yet, he had also been highly regarded by the Shadows. With equal facility and consistent equanimity, Shiv'kala was able to walk amid the mundanity and yet move among the gods. He treated the

gods as mundanes and the mundanes as divine. All were equal. All
were of a piece, and Shiv'kala could see all, understand all, and love
all. He loved the cries of creatures at birth. And when he wrapped his
hands around the throat of a creature he was sending to its death, he
could glory in its scream, as well.

He was one of the most soft-spoken of the Drakh, and his mouth
was pulled back in an almost perpetual smile—or at least that was
how it was perceived by others.

That wasn't how Londo Mollari, imminent emperor of the great
Centauri Republic, perceived him now. That much, Shiv'kala could
tell even without the tentative connection that already existed between them. In all likelihood, Londo looked at that curious rictus of
a smile and saw the satisfied grin of a predator about to descend on
its prey. He did not know, he did not understand. But Shiv'kala understood. Understood and forgave, for such was his way.

The keeper was stirring within him. Londo would never have
known it, but the keeper was fearful, too. Shiv'kala could sense that,
as well. This keeper was relatively newborn, spawned from its technonest mere days before. Shiv'kala had attended to this one personally, for he knew of the great fate and responsibility that awaited it.

When the keeper had opened its single eye for the first time,
blinking furiously against the light, it had been Shiv'kala's face into
which it had gazed. It hadn't been able to see clearly, of course; Shiv-
'kala had appeared as a hazy image at first. But full vision hadn't
taken long to develop.

The keeper had been born with a high degree of self-awareness,
but no certainty as to what its purpose was in the broader scheme of
nature. Its tendrils, mere stubs upon birth, had flickered around aim-
lessly, momentarily brushing against its parent. But the parent—as
was always the case with keepers—was already a small, blackened
husk. It had no soft thoughts to offer, no guidance to give as the off-
spring tried to determine just what it was doing and how it was supposed to do it.

"Calmly, little one," Shiv'kala had whispered, extending a grey
and scaly finger. The keeper had tried to wrap its tendrils around the
finger, and Shiv'kala had gently lifted it from its technonest. Then he
had drawn aside his robe and placed the newborn keeper against his
chest. Operating on instinct, the keeper had sought nourishment
there—and had found it.

Shiv'kala had trembled slightly and let out a deep, fulfilled sigh
as the keeper burrowed in, sucking and drawing sustenance from

Shiv'kala's very essence. In doing so, the keeper had burrowed not only into Shiv'kala's soul but into the Drakh Entire. Shiv'kala would always have a special status with this particular keeper, would always be the most sensitive to its needs, wants, and knowledge. And the keeper, now that it was attuned, would be able to commune with any of the Drakh Entire at any given moment.

A magnificent creature, the keeper. It had nursed within Shiv-'kala and had grown to maturity within three days. Now it was ready . . . ready to assume its most important job. Yet as prepared as it was to do so, and as much as its nature suited it for the task, when Shiv-'kala opened his vest to extract it from its nourishing pouch, he was amused to discover that the keeper, likewise, was apprehensive.

What troubles you, little one? Shiv'kala inquired. Across from him, a few feet away, Londo Mollari was in the process of removing his coat and loosening the collar of his shirt.

He is very dark. He is very fearsome, the keeper replied. *What if I do not keep him properly? What if I fail in my task? Can I not stay with you, in the pouch, in the warmth?*

No, little one, Shiv'kala replied gently. *We all serve the needs of the universe. We all do our part. In that way, I am no different than you, and you are no different than he. He will not, cannot hurt you. See how he fears you, even now. Reach out. You can taste his fear.*

Yes, the keeper said after a moment. *It is there. He is afraid of me. How odd. I am so small, and he is so huge. Why should he fear me?*

Because he does not understand you. You will explain yourself to him. You will make him realize what is to be done. He thinks you will control him, always. He does not understand that we will not deprive him of free will. He does not understand that you will simply monitor our mutual interests. You will not force him toward what he must do . . . you will simply help us to guide him away from what he must not do. He fears not being alone.

That is strangest of all, said the keeper. *The one time I felt any fear . . . was when I was alone in my nest. Why would anyone or anything desire to be alone?*

He does not know what he desires. He has lost his way. He moved toward us, but then moved away, then toward and away again. He is without guidance. You will guide him.

But he has done terrible things, the keeper said with trepidation. *He destroyed many Shadows. Terrible. Terrible.*

Yes, very terrible. But he did so because he was ignorant. Now . . . he

*shall learn. And you shall help teach him, as will I. Go to him. See how
he fears you. See how he needs you. Go to him, so that he may start his
new life.*

I will miss you, Shiv'kala.

You will not, little one. You will be with me always.

With that parting sentiment, Shiv'kala removed the keeper from
its nourishment pouch. Its tendrils had grown marvelously during its
sustenance period, and were now long and elegant. Moving with the
grace that was customary for its species, the keeper glided across the
floor and wrapped itself around Londo's legs. Shiv'kala could sense
the tentativeness of the keeper. More, the keeper could sense the rising terror in Londo. Sense it, but not see it. Londo's face was a mask
of unreadability, his brow furrowed, his eyes . . .

There was fury in his eyes. They bore into Shiv'kala, and had they
been whips, they would have flayed the skin from his body. Shiv'kala
decided that it was an improvement over fear. Fear was a relatively
useless emotion. Anger, fury . . . these could be harnessed and directed against an enemy and be of great use to the Drakh. Furthermore, such emotions were far more alluring to the keeper and would
make it much more comfortable with its new host.

Above all, Shiv'kala wanted to make certain that host and keeper
blended smoothly, for they were a team. Yes. That was what Londo
did not yet grasp: they were a team. Although the creature was called
a keeper, implying a master-slave relationship, the reality of their
binding went much deeper than that. It was almost . . . spiritual in its
way. Yes. Spiritual. Others, including Londo's predecessor, had not
understood that. He had not had enough time, or had simply been
too limited in his perspectives.

But Londo . . . Londo possessed a much broader view, had much
greater vision. Hopefully he would comprehend and even come to
appreciate what he was undergoing.

Londo's back stiffened as the keeper crept up toward his neck.
He had potential, Shiv'kala was certain of that. Perhaps the most
potential any associate of the Shadows had ever shown. Perhaps
even more than Morden had offered. Morden had been an excellent
servant and had proven himself superb in carrying out orders. While
he had been capable of actualizing the dreams of others, he had
been noticeably limited. Morden had glowed brightly, but only because he had been basking in the dark light generated by the desires
of Londo Mollari. Now Londo himself was in thrall to the Drakh,
serving in turn the great philosophies and destinies of the Shadows,

and that opened an array of new opportunities and possibilities. What was most important was the dreamer himself, and Londo was just such a dreamer. Yes, it promised to be most exciting indeed. Shiv'kala only wished that Mollari was capable of sharing in that excitement.

The keeper dug into Londo's shoulder, and Shiv'kala sensed the bonding. He smiled once more, reveling in the joy of the moment. Londo's emotions were a snarl of conflicts, fear and anger crashing into one another like waves against a reef, and he shuddered at the feel of the keeper's tendrils as they pierced his bare skin. That was all right though. He would adjust. He would learn. He would see that it was for the best. Or he would die. Those were the options, the only options, that were open to him, and Shiv'kala could only hope that he would choose wisely.

As for the keeper, Shiv'kala was pleased to sense that the creature was calming. Its initial trepidation was dissipating, as the Drakh had suspected it would. Furthermore, Londo's thoughts were coming into clearer focus, the blinders and shields falling away.

Londo stiffened slightly, as Shiv'kala eased himself into the Centauri's mind the way that he would ease his foot into a comfortable shoe. Within seconds, he inspected the nooks and crannies, studied Londo's deepest fears, viewed his sexual fantasies with morbid interest, and came to a deeper and fuller understanding of Londo's psyche than Londo himself had been able to achieve in years. Londo didn't know *how much* the Drakh had already discerned. His mind was still reeling and disoriented, and with a gentle push the Drakh steadied him, helped realign his focus.

Deciding that he would ease Londo into casual telepathy, he said out loud, "You will be all right." He spoke with his customary low, gravelly whisper, which forced people to listen closely. It was an amusing display of his power, albeit a minor one.

"No," Londo said, after a moment's consideration. "I will never be all right again."

Shiv'kala said nothing. There was no point in trying to force a realignment of Londo's state of mind. Sooner or later he would learn and understand, and if it was later rather than sooner, well, that was fine. The Drakh Entire had great and impressive plans, long-term goals that spanned decades. The instant comprehension, understanding, and cooperation of a single Centauri—emperor or no—simply was not necessary. They could wait.

So Shiv'kala just inclined his head slightly, acknowledging Londo's remark.

Londo tried to sneak a glance at the keeper, but then looked away. Instead he started buttoning his shirt, pulling his vest and coat back on. "It . . . does not matter, in any event," he said after a moment. "Whether I am all right. It is my people that matter now. It is Centauri Prime, only Centauri Prime."

"You will rebuild. We will help," said the Drakh.

London laughed bitterly at that. "Unless, of course, you choose to blow millions of my people to pieces with your fusion bombs."

"If we do . . . it will be because you have chosen that path for us."

"Semantics," Londo said contemptuously. "You act as if I have free will."

"You do."

"One choice is no choice."

"The Shadows you killed when you destroyed their island . . . they had no choice in their fate," Shiv'kala said. "You do. Do not abuse it . . . lest we give you as much choice as you gave the Shadows."

Londo said nothing to that, merely glowered as he buttoned his coat. "Well," he said briskly, "we should begin this sham, eh? This sham of leadership. I, as emperor, with you guiding my every move."

"No." Shiv'kala shook his head ever so slightly. Everything he did, he did with minimal effort. "Not every move. Simply keep in mind . . . our goals."

"And your goals would be?"

"Our goals . . . are your goals. That is all you need remember. You will address the populace. They will be angry. Focus that anger . . . upon Sheridan. Upon the Alliance."

"Why? What purpose would that serve?"

Shiv'kala's skeletal smile widened ever so slightly. "The Alliance . . . is the light. Let your people look at it in anger . . . so that they will be blind to the shadows around them." As always, Shiv'kala spoke in a low, sibilant tone of voice. Then, ever so slightly, he bowed, and thought at Londo, *Good day to you . . . Emperor Mollari.*

Londo jumped slightly at that, clearly not expecting it. Reflexively he looked around, as if trying to figure out where the voice had come from, and then he looked at the Drakh. His lips drew back in anger, and he snarled, "Stay out of my head!"

But the Drakh shook his head and, with that same damnable smile, thought at Londo, *We will always be there.*

Then he extended a hand to Mollari. He did so as a symbolic gesture, for he did not truly expect Londo to take it. And Londo did not. Instead he stared at the hand as if it were dried excrement. Shiv'kala then stepped back and allowed the shadows of the early evening to swallow him up.

In a way, it felt as if he were returning home.

PART I

2262-2264

Nightfall

1

When Londo saw the creature emerging from the chest of the Drakh, it was all he could do not to scream.

A half dozen different ways of handling the situation tumbled through his mind. The first and foremost was to attack the Drakh, to grab a weapon—a sword, preferably—and step forward, the steel whipping through the air and striking home. In his mind's eye, he could see the monster's head tumbling free of its body, that hideous smile permanently frozen, perhaps even transformed into an expression of surprise. Then he would take the creature's head and slam it on a pole next to Morden's. He could stand side-by-side with Vir, and they would wave at them and laugh at the notion of anyone thinking that they could strong-arm or bully the leader of the great Centauri Republic.

Next he simply considered running from the room. That, in particular, seemed an attractive notion as he watched the one-eyed creature skitter across the floor toward him.

He thought of crying out for help. He thought of trying to arrange some sort of bargain. He would ask the Drakh what else he could offer beside himself—there had to be some way to appease the wrath of these beings, other than allowing that terrifying one-eyed animal to attach its parasitic self to his body.

He thought of begging, of pleading, of swearing eternal fealty to the Drakh or to the spirit of the Shadows. He thought of reminding the Drakh of all the times that he had been helpful to, and supportive of, their departed masters.

What do you want?

The question first had been posed to him by Morden, at a time that seemed eons ago. It was the question he was now tempted to hurl at the Drakh. What could he offer the Drakh that might suit them better than he himself? A terrifying array of possibilities came to him. He could offer them Sheridan or Delenn, the president and first lady of the Interstellar Alliance. Bring them to the Drakh, make them prisoners, or place keepers on them. Make them servants to the Drakh cause.

Or G'Kar! Great Maker, let them take G'Kar. Granted, he and the Narn had healed the wounds of their relationship, but there was still that vision he had had. The vision that one day G'Kar would be at his throat, primal fury boiling in his one true eye. Yes, he could turn G'Kar over to the Drakh and let *him* serve the collective Drakh will. Or . . . or . . .

He could . . . he could offer them Vir Cotto. That was a possibility. A good one. A great one, in fact. Let Vir lose his free will and independence to the Drakh—he didn't have much use for it anyway. The hard truth was, Vir was at his best when someone else was telling him what to do. So really, there wouldn't be any substantial difference from what his life had been, and it might even show marked improvement.

As quickly as all those options occurred to him, he dismissed them all. These were his friends . . . his allies . . . or at least, they had been. Though in terms of Sheridan, in particular, a deep and abiding desire for vengeance still burned brightly. It was, after all, Sheridan's Alliance that had bombed Centauri Prime back to the Stone Age, leaving the glorious world in flaming ruins. And was not Sheridan himself always quick to condemn the Centauri, in general—and Londo, in particular—for every slight, real or imagined?

But as Londo watched the one-eyed monster wrap itself around his leg and start to draw itself up his body, he came to the hideous understanding that he would not wish such a fate even on his worst enemy. That would most unquestionably *not* be Sheridan, and certainly not Delenn. No, despite their rapprochement, the title would likely still be held by G'Kar. Even on G'Kar, though, he would have no wish to see that . . . that *thing* . . . attach itself.

No one deserved that.

Including him.

It's not fair, he thought bleakly, *it's not right. I have to stop it . . . I can still pry it off me, throw it down, step on it, grind it beneath my boot . . .*

But if he did so, he knew what would happen next. The Drakh would pull out his detonator, as he had before, but this time nothing would stop his thumb from slamming home. And when he did, millions of Centauri would die, just like that. Fusion bombs hidden by the Drakh would detonate, and the victims would never even know what hit them. They would simply disappear in a massive burst of heat and flame, millions of lives terminated.

For a moment, just a moment, he considered it. After all, they would be dead and gone. Their torment would last a brief second or two at most, and then it would be over and done with. They would be placed within the safety of the grave. More accurately, their ashes would be scattered to the safety of the four winds, blowing the length and breadth of Centauri Prime. This, as opposed to Londo's living a life of continual punishment, the keeper monitoring his moves, sitting like a permanent, one-eyed pustule on his shoulder. Watching, monitoring, always there, never giving him a moment's peace . . .

Peace.

Well . . . that was what it came down to, really, wasn't it.

For when he pictured those millions of Centauri vanishing into the instant holocaust of the bombs, in his mind's eye they were battered and bewildered. Covered in soot and ash, clothes torn, looking to the sky in bewilderment and fear and wondering when the barrage would ever cease. They had no idea. No idea that Centauri Prime had been framed—made to appear warlike and aggressive. Framed by the Drakh, so that the galaxy would turn against them, and the Centauri would be left all alone in the darkness. No idea that he, Londo, was the cause for that deception.

No idea that they would still be living in peace, if it were not for Londo.

He had stretched forth his hand to lead his people back to the greatness he felt they deserved, as part of the great Centauri Republic, a term that had once prompted respect instead of snickering. Stretched forth his hand like a shepherd, but instead he had crushed his flock. His victims had cried out his name, and he had brought them to utter ruin. For if he had not desired to restore the Centauri Republic, then none of this would have happened. There would have been no Shadow involvement, there would have been no war upon the Narn. None of the heartache and grief that had permeated the last five years ever would have occurred. It was because of him, all because of him.

That's what this was, then. As the keeper poked and probed, as its tentacles swept across his bare skin and made him cringe inwardly, Londo realized that this was his punishment. A cosmic sentence of justice was being carried out. Because of who he was and the nature of what he had done, he could never be jailed. Instead, his jail would be his own mind and body. They were being taken from him, and he was going to be trapped within them while lease over them was given to the keeper. It was a prison sentence, and the sentence was life.

From where he stood, he could smell the smoking ruins of Centauri Prime. He so loved the world of his birth. All he had wanted to do was restore it to greatness. But he had made a horrible miscalculation. He hadn't realized that the very things that he so despised—the sickly peace that had permeated the society, the sense that its proudest days were behind it—that those things truly *were* great. Peace, prosperity, happiness . . . what prizes those things were, what joys they brought with them.

Perhaps he had lost sight of the truth because of those with whom he had associated. He had spent so much time walking the halls of power, rubbing elbows with emperors, plotting and planning alongside such master schemers as the late Lord Refa. He had lost sight of the fact that they had been hedonistic, scheming, and self-centered. They had cared only for pleasure, and that was usually obtained over the dead bodies of others.

Londo had forgotten that these people represented only the smallest percentage of the Centauri people. That the vast, vast majority of Centauri Prime's citizens consisted of decent, simple, hardworking people who wanted nothing more from life than to live it as simply as possible. They were not decadent; they were not power seekers. They were just decent, ordinary folk. They were the ones whom Londo had let down the most. It was their homes burning, it was their screams he fancied he could hear echoing in his head.

He closed his eyes and wished that he could clap his hands over his ears and, in so doing, shut out the cries that would not leave him.

And the keeper was there.

He felt it sinking its consciousness into his, attaching and intertwining their interests. Then he became aware of the Drakh, watching him—from without, and from within. It was as if the keeper had given the Drakh a viewport into his very soul. It was invasive, it was nauseating, it was . . .

. . . it was just what he deserved.

Despite all the turmoil that roiled through his mind, he never once allowed it to show. They could rob him of his freedom, his independence, his future, his very soul, but they could not remove from him his pride, and the way he carried himself. Whatever else happened, he was still Londo Mollari of the great Centauri Republic. That was why he had not blubbered or begged. He only sighed with inward relief that he had not given in to his momentary weakness and started offering up others to take his place, to be enslaved. For if he had done so, he didn't think he could have lived with himself.

Live with himself.

Suicide. It was an option that doubtless remained to him still. If it came down to a contest of raw will and the keeper tried to dissuade him from that course, he was reasonably sure that he could still overcome its influence at least long enough to do the deed.

But where there was life, there was hope. As long as he lived, there might still be a way of ridding himself of the damnable creature. If he was dead, he had no fallback. If he was alive . . . anything could happen.

He might still wind up waggling his fingers at the Drakh's head on a pike.

That thought led to one, and then another and another, and he couldn't understand it. It was as if every thought that he'd ever had was suddenly tumbling one over the other in his head. A veritable avalanche of notions and recollections . . .

. . . or perhaps . . . it was an overview. Perhaps the Drakh, even at this moment, was seeing . . .

With tremendous effort, Londo shoved away the intrusion, although he couldn't be sure whether it had been real or imagined. He found he could barely stand. He put one hand to his forehead and let out an unsteady sigh.

And then the Drakh said the most curious thing. He said, "You will be all right."

What an odd thing for him to have said. The Drakh were uniformly heartless, evil creatures—Londo knew this beyond a certainty. What point was there in one of their number pretending that he would be "all right."

"No," he growled, aware of the presence of the . . . the thing on his shoulder. "I will never be all right again."

The Drakh babbled some other meaningless phrases at him, and Londo barely paid attention, giving responses off the top of his head that had little meaning, that he didn't even remember moments later. All he could think about was that eye, perched so close, watching him.

The Shadows . . . the terror that they had spread had come in the form of their vast and powerful ships. The only personal contact he'd ever had with them had been through Morden, and *he* had merely been their voice. Now, however, the enemy had a face, in the person of this Drakh who was, even as they spoke, gliding back into the shad-

ows that had vomited him up. And the enemy had established an
eternal, vigilant presence in the form of the keeper, which was settling in, part of him now until he died.

Until he died.

That was the point at which he began toying with the idea.

He held the sword, caressed it almost lovingly. It had been quite
some time since he had been able to look at it. It was an elegant
blade—the one he had used to kill his friend, the companion of his
childhood, Urza Jaddo. Urza, who had come to Babylon 5 seeking
Londo's aid in a political game that was going to leave his family
name in ruins. Urza, who had obtained that aid . . . by choreograph-
ing a duel during which he had died at Londo's hands so that his—
Urza's—family would henceforth be protected by the house of Mollari.

The protection of the house of Mollari. What a ghastly joke. The
Mollari name had certainly afforded Londo a good deal of protection, hadn't it.

Londo's brain hadn't stopped working from the moment the
keeper had become attached to him. He had picked up on the fact
that the creature did not, *could* not read every thought that crossed
his mind. It would report his actions to the Drakh and they, in turn,
might intervene, but it had to be *actions*, actions that ran contrary to
the Drakh interest. Londo had taken no action as yet, but he was
strongly considering it.

Wouldn't it be appropriate. Wouldn't it be just. If the universe
were really interested in the order of things, then what would be
more just than for Londo to die by a thrust of the same sword that
had killed Urza. Something within Londo had died that day. If he
used the same sword, brought an end to the suffering that his life was
to become, then perhaps he would wind up where Urza was. They
would be young together, young and free, and their existence would
lie ahead of them once again. They would spar, they would laugh,
and it would be good.

Servants were quietly boxing up his belongings, preparing to
move them to the royal suite. The sword was the only thing that he
had not given over to them. Londo was simply standing there, staring
at it, examining the glistening blade and wondering how it would feel
sliding gently across his throat. He envisioned his blood pouring from
the cut, turning crimson the white uniform of his office. A remarkable color scheme, that. Most aesthetic.

And when the Drakh found his body—somehow he knew it would be the Drakh—would the creature be smug over Londo's premature demise, feeling that the death of the Shadows had been repaid? Or would the Drakh be angry, or annoyed that Londo's usefulness had not been fully exploited? That . . . was indeed a pleasing notion. The thought of the Drakh being frustrated, knowing that he and his hideous ilk could hurt Londo no longer. Would the Drakh retaliate, by detonating the bombs and annihilating his people? No. No, probably not. The Drakh Entire didn't especially care about the people of Centauri Prime. To the Drakh, they existed merely to act as playing pieces, to keep Londo in line. If Londo were gone, the game was over. With the king fallen, what point would there be in knocking over the pawns?

It would be the coward's way out, yes. There was still so much that needed to be done, and if he killed himself, there would never be any chance to try and make good on all that he had done . . .

Make good?

The blade gleamed so brilliantly that he was able to see his reflection in it, and it reminded him of his reflection in the window of the Centauri war vessel as it had orbited the Narn Homeworld. The Centauri had smashed the Narns into near-oblivion, using the outlawed weaponry known as mass drivers.

Make good? Make reparations? Balance the scales? What sort of nonsensical conceit was that, anyway? How could he possibly make good on what he had done? Millions . . . Great Maker . . . *billions* had died because of him. And he was supposed to set that right somehow? It was impossible, simply impossible. If he had a hundred lifetimes in which to do it, it would still be a hopeless task.

Perhaps . . . perhaps suicide wouldn't be the coward's way out at that. Perhaps suicide was simply the wise man's way of knowing when it was polite to leave. To keep his now-wretched existence going on this war-torn world, in the deluded belief that somehow he could make things better or atone for his sins . . .

Who was he fooling? In the final analysis, who was he fooling?

He became aware once more of the keeper on his shoulder. He wondered if, given enough time, he would become less aware of it. If he might become so used to it being there that he gave it no thought at all. If that circumstance did come about, he wasn't altogether sure whether it would be a good thing or a bad thing.

He placed the sword down.

It was time.

Time to see the farce through. As for the rest, well, if it came to that, there would be time enough. Or perhaps the notion would go away on its own. His emotions were too raw, and he couldn't trust himself to make a proper decision. He had to allow himself time to figure out what would be the best thing to do.

The notion, however, did not go away.

He made his speech to the Centauri people, as they huddled in their homes, cowering in the burned-out shells of buildings that represented the burned-out shells their lives had become. The mental picture of the sword remained in his head even as his own holographic image loomed in the skies of Centauri Prime. What he truly wanted to do was apologize . . . humble himself to his people, let them know that it was he, and he alone, who was responsible for this hideous pass to which they had come.

But such a speech, honest as it might have been, wouldn't be in the best interests of the Drakh. They had their own agenda, and Londo was merely required to play his part. They had made that quite clear. Do as he was told. Be a good puppet. Speak the speeches as were required, and do not for a moment anger them.

"I will walk alone to my inauguration," he announced. "Take on the burden of emperor in silence. The bells of our temple will sound all day and all night, once for each of our people killed in the bombings. We are alone. Alone in the universe. But we are united in our pain."

But that wasn't true. It was as much a sham as everything else about him. His pain was his own, and could never be shared or revealed. His pain was the creature on his shoulder. His pain took the form of nightmares that came to him in his sleep, that tormented him.

"We fought alone," he told his people, "and we will rebuild alone." But was there anyone on Centauri who was more alone than he? And the most perverse aspect of it was that he wasn't alone, not really. The keeper was there, watching him, studying him, surveying him, never allowing him a moment's peace. It served as a constant reminder of his sin. Via the keeper, the Drakh were with him as well.

And more.

There were the voices. The voices of his victims, crying out to him, protesting their fates. These were the people who had gone to their deaths screaming and sobbing and not remotely comprehending why this was happening to them. They were there, too, making their presence known.

It was entirely possible that, of everyone on Centauri Prime, Londo was the *least*-alone individual on the planet. But that didn't mitigate the circumstances of his situation at all. For there was no one, no one, whom he could tell about his predicament. To do so would have spelled death for that person, of that he was quite certain. He existed, and others maintained a presence near him, but he could allow no one to be close to him. He had to drive away those who once had known him as no others did.

The worst would be Vir. Vir, who had stood by his side every hideous step of the way, who had warned Londo against the descent he was taking into blackness. Londo hadn't listened, and Vir had been right. Perhaps that was why Londo hadn't listened: because he had known that Vir was right, and he didn't want to hear it.

And Delenn. After the speech, when they took their leave of him, Delenn stepped forward and looked at him in such a way that he flinched inwardly, wondering if somehow she was able to see the evil dropping on his shoulder. "I can no longer see the road you're on, Londo," she said. "There is a darkness around you. I can only pray that, in time, you will find your way out of it."

When she said that, the image of the sword presented itself to him once again, even more keenly than it had before. Light glinting off the blade, pure and true, calling to him. It was the way out . . . if he chose to take it.

He walked to the temple, as he had said. Alone . . . but not alone.

He took on the ornaments and responsibilities of emperor, and he could practically feel the sword across his throat now. He could almost hear the death rattle, feel the pure joy of the release. He would be free of it, free of the responsibility, free of everything. By the time he began the long walk back to the palace, the sun was starting to set. And he knew, in his hearts, that it was the last sunset he would ever see. His resolve was stronger than it had ever been, the certainty of his decision absolute.

It felt right. It felt good. He had done the best that he could, and his best had not been remotely good enough. It was time to remove himself from the game.

He sat in the throne room that night, the darkness encroaching upon him. Its opulence, with its gleaming marbled floors, lush curtains, and largely decorative—but still impressive—columns, carried whispers of Centauri Prime's past greatness. Despite the ghastly shades of times past that always hovered there, he felt strangely at peace. He felt the keeper stirring upon his shoulder. Perhaps the creature knew that something was in the offing, but wasn't entirely sure what.

The shadows around him seemed to be moving. Londo looked right and left, tried to discern whether the Drakh was standing nearby, watching him. But there was nothing. At least, he thought there was nothing. He could have been wrong . . .

"Madness," he said to no one. "I am driving myself to madness." He gave the matter a moment's blackly humorous thought. "Maybe that is their ultimate goal. An interesting thought. Reducing Centauri Prime to rubble just for the dubious purpose of sending me into insanity. Such overkill. If that was what they desired, they could just have locked me in a room with my ex-wives for a week. That would cause anyone to snap."

To his surprise, a voice responded. "Pardon, Majesty?"

He half turned in his chair and saw a man standing just inside the doorway, regarding Londo with polite curiosity. He was quite thin, with carefully cultivated hair that wasn't particularly high. That was a direct flouting of Centauri standard fashion, for usually the height of hair was meant to be indicative of the rank in society that one had achieved. There was, however, a fringe fashion element that had taken its cue from Emperor Turhan, who had publicly disdained tradition by wearing his hair shorter than the lowest of the lowborn. Some believed that Emperor Cartagia had done so as a way of showing that he wished to maintain a connection to the common man. Others felt he had just done it to annoy people. Either way, the precedent had been set, and some chose to follow it.

Though in the case of this particular Centauri, the one who had interrupted Londo's musings, it wasn't his hair that caught Londo's attention. Nor was it the starched and pressed military uniform he wore so smartly. No, it was his general attitude. He had an eagerness about him . . . but it wasn't a healthy sort of eagerness. Vir, for example, had been cloaked in eagerness from the moment he had set foot on Babylon 5. That had been an eagerness to please, one of Vir's more charming features. But this individual . . . he had the attitude of a carrion-eating bird perched on a branch, watching a dying man and mentally urging him to hurry up and get on with it.

"Durla . . . isn't it?" Londo asked after a moment.

"Yes, Majesty. Your captain of the guards, as appointed by the late regent—" He bowed slightly. "—and continuing to serve at your good humor, Majesty."

"My humor is less than good at the moment, Captain Durla. I do not appreciate interruptions into my privacy."

"With all respect, Majesty, I did not realize you were alone. I heard you speaking and thought you were deep in conversation with someone. Since your schedule does not call for you to have anyone in this room with you at this time of night . . . I thought I would make sure that you were not being subjected to any threat. I apologize most profusely if I, in some way, have intruded or made you uncomfortable."

He had all the right words and expressed them perfectly, and yet Londo, still reacting on a gut level, didn't like him. Perhaps . . . perhaps it was because, in addition to having the right words, it seemed to Londo as if Durla *knew* they were the right words. He wasn't expressing his sentiments, whatever those might be. Instead he was saying precisely what he thought Londo wanted to hear.

Another possibility, Londo had to admit, was that he was becoming so suspicious—jumping at shadows; seeing plots, plans, and duplicity everywhere—that even the most casual meeting brought sinister overtones with it. He was beginning to view the world entirely in subtext, searching out that which was not said, forsaking that which was spoken. It was no way to live.

Then again . . . that wasn't really a serious consideration for him these days, was it? Not on this, the last day of his life.

Durla hadn't moved. Apparently he was waiting for Londo to dismiss him. Londo promptly obliged him. "I won't be needing you this evening, Durla. As for your continuing to serve, well . . . we shall see how my humor transforms with the passage of time."

"Very well, Majesty. I will make certain that guards remain at all exits."

Londo was not enthused at that particular prospect. If he did decide to do himself in—as was looking more likely by the moment—the last thing he needed was for a couple of guards to hear his body thud to the floor. If they came running in to save him and somehow, against all hope, succeeded . . . the embarrassment and humiliation would be overwhelming. And what if he decided to depart the palace grounds, to commit the deed somewhere more remote?

Then again, he was the emperor.

"That will not be necessary," he said firmly. "I believe the manpower may be better deployed elsewhere."

"Better?" Durla cocked an eyebrow. "Better than maintaining the safety of our emperor? Will all respect, Majesty, I do not think so."

"I do not recall asking your opinion on the matter," Londo informed him. "They will leave, as will you."

"Majesty, with all respect—"

"Stop telling me how much you respect me!" Londo said with obvious irritation. "If I were a young virgin girl and you were endeavoring to seduce me, you might understandably offer repeated protests of how much you respect me. I feel safe in assuming that this is not your intent though, yes?"

"Yes, Your Majesty, you would be quite safe with that assumption." A hint of a smile briefly tugged at the edges of Durla's mouth. Then he grew serious again. "However, not only is your safety my primary concern, it is part of my job description. Of course, you could always release me from my job, but it would be unfortunate if I were to be fired simply because I was doing my duty. It has been my understanding that you, Emperor Mollari, are the fairest-minded individual to come into a position of power on Centauri Prime in quite a while. Is that not the case?"

Oh yes, very facile. Very good with words. Londo wasn't fooled for even a moment by his comments. Still . . .

It didn't matter. Not really. All Londo had to do was wait until he retired for the night. Then, lying in his bed, he could quietly put an end to himself. Since he would be lying flat, he wouldn't need to worry about "thumps" alerting guards.

That was it. That was all he had to do. Bid Durla good night, retire for the evening . . . and then retire permanently. That was it. Dismiss Durla and be done with it.

Durla waited expectantly.

Londo didn't like him.

He had no idea why he was operating on such a visceral level. Part of him actually rejoiced in the notion that, soon, Durla would be someone else's problem. But another part of him wondered just what Durla was up to. He was . . . a loose end. Londo hated loose ends. He particularly hated the knowledge that this loose end might unravel after he was gone.

"Would you care to take a walk?" he asked abruptly. He was surprised at the sound of his own voice.

"A walk, Majesty? Of course. Where on the grounds would—"

"No. Not on the grounds. I wish to walk into the city."

"The . . . city, sir?" Durla looked as if he hadn't quite heard Londo properly.

"Yes, Captain of the Guards. I have a desire to see it closely . . ." *One last time.*

"I do not think that would be wise, Majesty."

"Is that a fact?"

"Yes, Majesty," he said firmly. "At this time, the people are . . ." His voice trailed off. He seemed reluctant to finish the sentence.

So Londo finished it for him. "The people are my people, Durla. Am I to hide in here from them?"

"That might be prudent, at least for the time being, Majesty."

"Your opinion is duly noted." He slapped the armrests of the throne and rose. "I shall walk about the city, and I shall do it alone."

"Majesty, no!"

"*No?*" Londo stared at him, his thick eyebrows knitting in a carefully controlled display of imperial anger. "I do not recall asking for your approval, Durla. That is one of the benefits of being emperor: you are entitled to take actions without consulting underlings." He gave particular stress to that last word.

Durla didn't appear to take the hint, however, although he did ratchet up his obsequiousness level by several degrees. "Majesty . . . there are ways that certain things are done . . . certain protocols . . ."

"That will be the exciting aspect of my tenure in this position, Durla. I do not follow protocol. I follow the moment. Now . . . I am going for a walk. I am the emperor. I think I am entitled to make that decision, no?"

"At least"—Durla seemed most urgent in his concerns—"At *least*, Majesty, and I pray I am not overstepping my bounds here, let an escort follow you at a respectful distance. You will be alone . . . but you will not be alone. I hope that sounds clear . . ."

Something about the irony of the suggestion struck Londo as amusing. "Yes. Yes, it is quite clear. And let me guess: you will accompany these 'phantom' guards, yes?"

"I would supervise the honor guard myself, Majesty, if you wish."

"You would be amazed, Durla, how little my wishes have to do with anything," Londo said. "Suit yourself. Exercise your free will. At least *someone* around here should be able to."

And so Londo walked out into the great capital city of Centauri Prime for what he anticipated would be the last time.

His path from the palace to the temple of inauguration had been a fairly straightforward one, earlier that day. In this case, however, he deliberately strayed from any known path. He crisscrossed the city, making arbitrary decisions and occasionally backtracking. The entire time, a small platoon of men-at-arms trailed him, with Durla keeping a close-up and somewhat wary eye upon them all.

As Londo walked, he tried to drink in every aspect of the city, every curve of every building. Even the smell of burning structures and rubble were sensations that he wanted to savor.

He had never found himself in quite this sort of mindset before; looking upon things with the attitude that he would never look upon them again. True, as he had prepared to accept the post of emperor, his life had flashed before his eyes. Each moment that had been a fond memory then was now tinged with pain. Times past and even times future . . . particularly that much-dreamed-of moment when a one-eyed G'Kar would spell his doom. Well, he was certainly going to wind up putting an end to that particular prediction. He took some small measure of comfort in that.

For so long, he had felt as if he were nothing more than the tool of fate, possessing no control over his own destiny. No matter what his intentions, he had been propelled down a dark road that he had never intended to travel. Well, at least he would confound the fates in the end. It wouldn't be G'Kar's hand that ended his wretched existence . . . it would be his own. No one could harm him at this point in his life except, of course, for he himsel—

That was when the rock bounced off his skull.

2

Londo staggered from the impact. It took him a moment to understand fully what had occurred. His first, momentarily panicked impression was that he had been shot with a PPG blast. Odd that he would have been disturbed at such a notion. He was, after all, planning to do himself in before the evening was out, so it would have been almost ungrateful to be angry at someone who might have saved him the effort.

Then the very fact that he still was able to construct a coherent thought was enough to tip him to the realization that what had hit him was some sort of simple projectile. It had ricocheted off his forehead and tumbled to the ground. A rock, and easy enough to spot; it was the only one tinged with red.

Immediately the guards sprang into action. Half of them formed an impenetrable wall of bodies—a barrier against any possible encroachers. The rest bolted off in the direction from which the rock had come. Londo had the briefest glimpse of a small form darting into shadows of nearby buildings.

"Come, Majesty," said Durla, pulling at Londo's arm. "We must go . . . back to the palace . . ."

"No."

"But we—"

"*No!*" Londo thundered with such vehemence that the guards around him were literally caught flatfooted. That provided Londo the opportunity he needed to push impulsively through the guards and run after the group who were, in turn, pursuing his assailant.

"Majesty!" called a horrified Durla, but Londo had already obtained a decent lead.

Nevertheless, moments after the guards set out in pursuit of the emperor, they managed to draw alongside him . . . not a difficult accomplishment since they were by and large younger and in better shape. As for Londo, he found he was already starting to feel winded, and felt a grim annoyance that he had let himself get into such poor shape.

Perhaps, he thought bleakly, he should have taken a cue from Vir. Lately Vir had whipped himself into impressively good shape. "How did you do it?" he once had asked.

"Ate less, drank no alcohol, and exercised."

"Radical," Londo had responded, sniffing in disgust.

Now, as his hearts pounded and his breath rasped, he felt as if it hadn't been such a radical notion after all.

Durla, only a few steps behind, called, "Majesty! This really is most improper! There could be an ambush! It's insanity!"

"Why would it . . . be an ambush?" huffed Londo. "You said it . . . yourself . . . this is insanity . . . So who would . . . create an ambush . . . and have it hinge . . . on the target doing something . . . insane?"

The chase was slowing considerably. There was fallen rubble from shattered buildings, blocking the path. This hadn't deterred the guards, though, as they had scrambled over debris with as much alacrity as they could manage. They had dedicated themselves to corralling whoever had made such a vile attempt against their emperor.

Then they slowed and fanned out, creating a semicircle around one burned-out area. It was quite evident, even from a distance, that they had brought the assailant to heel.

Londo slowed, then stopped, and straightened his coat and vest in order to restore some measure of dignity. Durla, who drew up next to him, looked disgustingly fit and not the slightest out of breath. "Your Majesty, I really must insist," he began.

"Oh, must you," said Londo, turning on him. "On what would you insist, precisely?"

"Let me bring you back to the palace, where you'll be safe—"

That was when they heard a female voice cry out, "Let me go! Let me go, you great buffoons! And don't touch them! They had nothing to do with it!"

"That is a child's voice," Londo said, looking at Durla with open skepticism. "Are you telling me that I must be escorted by armed guards back to the palace in order that I might avoid the wrath of a little girl?"

Durla seemed about to try a response, but apparently he realized there was nothing he could say at that particular moment that was going to make him look especially good. "No, Your Majesty, of course not."

"Good. Because I certainly would not want to think you were questioning my bravery."

Quite quickly Durla responded, "I would never dream of doing such a thing, Majesty."

"Good. Then we understand each other."

"Yes, Majesty."

"Now then . . . I want to know what it is we're dealing with," he said, and he gestured toward the cluster of figures that had gathered ahead of them.

Durla nodded and moved off to get a summary of the events from the guards who had caught up with the "assailant." He listened as he was filled in on the situation, and when he returned to Londo, he clearly looked rather uncomfortable about it all. "It appears . . . you were correct, Majesty. It is a young girl, not more than fifteen."

"There are other people with her?"

"Yes, Majesty. A family . . . or at least what's left of one. They've constructed a rather crude shelter from material at hand. They claim to have taken the girl in because she was wandering the streets and they felt sorry for her."

"I see."

"Yes, and they appear somewhat . . . irate . . . that she has put them at risk by drawing the wrath of the emperor down upon them."

"Really. Let them know that my wrath is not exactly out in full bloom today, despite any untimely provocations," he said, as he gingerly fingered the cut on his head. It was already starting to become swollen. "Better yet . . . I shall tell them myself."

"It could still be a trick, Your Majesty," Durla warned. "A trap of some sort."

"Should that be the case, Durla, and they draw a PPG or some similar weapon that they plan to utilize," Londo said, clapping him on the shoulder, "I am fully confident that you will throw yourself into the path of the blast, intercept it with your own body, then die with praises for your beloved emperor upon your lips. Yes?"

Durla looked less than thrilled at the notion. "It . . . would be my honor, Majesty, to serve you in that manner."

"Let us both hope you have the opportunity," Londo told him.

Squaring his shoulders, Londo walked over to where the guards had surrounded his attacker. They hesitated to let Londo through, though, only moving when Durla gave them a silent nod. For some reason this irked Londo to no end. He was the emperor. If he couldn't even get a handful of guards to attend to his wishes without

someone else validating his desires, what in the world was the point
of ruling?

But move aside they did, giving Londo a clear view into the face
of a wounded and hurting Centauri Prime.

There, in a makeshift lean-to, stood a Centauri family. A father,
hair cut low, and a young mother. As was the style with many young
women, she had a long tail of hair, which most women kept meticulously braided. In her case, however, it simply hung loosely around
her shoulders, looking unkempt and in disarray, the entirety of it
rooted squarely in the middle of her otherwise-shaved head, so its
askew nature made it look like a follicle fountain. They also had two
boys and a girl with them, between the ages of twelve and fifteen.
Even had Londo not known which of the youngsters had decided to
use him for target practice, he would have been able to tell just by
looking at them. The boys, like their parents, were staring toward the
ground, afraid even to gaze into the face of their emperor. The father—the *father*, of all people—was visibly trembling. A fine testa-
ment to Centauri manhood, that.

But the girl, well . . . she was a different story, wasn't she. She
didn't avert her eyes or shrink in fear of Londo's approach. Instead
she stood tall and proud, with a level and unflinching gaze. There was
some redness to her scalp, which Londo knew all too well: she had
only recently taken up the female tradition of shaving her head, indicating her ascension into maturity. She looked quite gaunt, with high
cheekbones and a swollen lip that marred her features. The blood on
her lip was fresh. "Did someone strike you?" Londo demanded, and
then without waiting for reply, turned to his guards and said, "Who
did this?"

"I did, Majesty," one of the guards said, stepping forward. "She
was resisting, and I—"

"Get out," Londo said without hesitation. "If you cannot rein in
a single child without brutality, you have no place representing the
office of emperor. No, do not look to Durla!" Londo continued,
anger rising. "I am still the power here, not the captain of the guards.
I say you are out. Now leave."

The guard did not hesitate. Instead he bowed quickly to the emperor and walked quickly away. Londo then turned back to the girl
and found nothing but disdain on her face. "You do not approve of
my action?" he asked.

The question had been intended as rhetorical, but she immediately shot back a reply. "You discharge a single guard and fancy yourself the protector of the people? Don't make me laugh."

"The insolence!" raged Durla, as if he himself had been insulted. "Majesty, please permit me to—"

But Londo held up a calming hand and looked more closely at the girl. "I have seen you before, yes? Have I not?"

This time she didn't offer an immediate reply. "Answer your emperor!" Durla snapped, and Londo did not remonstrate him. Youthful insolence was one thing, and tolerance certainly could be a virtue, but if one's emperor asks a question, then Great Maker, one answers the question or suffers the consequences.

Fortunately enough, the girl at least had the good sense to recognize those things that were worth taking stands over, and those that were not. "We have . . . encountered each other one or two times before. At the palace. During official functions." When Londo continued to stare at her without full recognition, she added, "My mother was the lady Celes . . . my father, Lord Antono Refa."

The identification hit Londo like a hammer blow. Lord Refa, his one-time ally, whose political machinations had been instrumental in costing Londo everything he had held dear.

Whereas Londo had made many ill-considered decisions that had set him on a path toward darkness, Refa had dashed headlong down that same path, reveling in the lies, duplicities, and betrayals that were a part of power brokering and advancement in the great Centauri Republic. He had been a strategist and manipulator of the old school, well versed in the ways of deceit that had made the old Republic such a morass of power-hungry bastards. And he had been directly responsible for the deaths of several of those close to Londo. Londo had gained a revenge of sorts, arranging for Refa to meet a brutal and violent death at the hands of enraged Narns.

It had only been later that Londo had come to realize just how much both he and Refa had been used by the Shadows. Granted, Refa had been overzealous in embracing the power when it was presented him, but Londo had also held Refa accountable for acts that had not been his responsibility. Every so often Londo would envision what it must have been like for Refa, to die beneath the fists and bludgeons of the Narns. He had taken such pleasure in it at the time. Now the recollection only filled him with disgust and self-loathing.

Looking upon the face of the young girl, however, Londo—for the first time—actually felt guilty.

Then something about the girl's phrasing caught Londo's attention. "Your mother 'was' the Lady Celes? Then she is—?"

"Dead," the girl said tonelessly. If there was any capacity for mourning within her, it had either been burned away or buried so deeply that it could not harm her. "She was one of the first to die in the bombing."

"I . . . am sorry for your loss," Londo told her.

Durla quickly added, "However, the emperor's sympathy for your plight does not excuse your abominable assault on him."

"My assault? I hit him with a rock!" said the girl. "And what, pray tell, should excuse him for his crimes?"

"My crimes." Londo stifled a bitter laugh. "And what know you of my crimes, child?"

"I know that the emperor is supposed to protect his people. You blamed the regent for bringing us to this state, but you were the one who left the regent in place. If you had been here, attending to your people, instead of wasting your time on some far-off space station, perhaps you would have been able to prevent this.

"And where would you take us now?" she added, and she pointed at him with a quavering finger. "That whole speech about Centauri 'standing proudly alone'? What sort of . . . of prideful stupidity is that? We were the injured party here! Instead we wind up having to pay reparations that will cripple our economy beyond endurance? We lick our wounds and sulk in the darkness? We should be demanding that the Alliance help us in any way they can!"

"And what of Centauri pride?" asked Londo quietly. "What of that, *hmm*?"

"To blazes with Centauri pride!" she said with fire. "What of Centauri blood? What of Centauri bodies piled high? I've seen crying infants, looking for nourishment by pulling at the breasts of their dead mothers. Have you? I have seen people, sightless, limbless, hopeless. Have you? You claimed you wanted to walk to the temple alone to symbolize something. What excrement! You didn't want anyone around because you didn't want to have to look into their accusing eyes and feel guilty on your coronation day. You didn't want to have your personal triumph spoiled by seeing all those who suffered because of your stupidity. You didn't want to have to look upon the bodies that you crawled over to get into power."

"Silence!" Durla fairly exploded. "Majesty, truly, this is too much! The insolence, the—"

"Why do you rage, Durla?" Londo asked calmly. "She simply

uses words now, not stones. It is a funny thing about words. They cannot harm you unless you allow them to . . . unlike rocks, which tend to act as they wish." He paused, and then said quietly, "You are wrong, child. Wrong about a great many things . . . but right enough about a few. Which things you are right about, I think I shall keep to myself for the time being. Think of it as imperial privilege. You are quite brave, do you know that?"

For a moment the girl seemed taken aback, and then she gathered herself. "I'm not brave. I'm just too tired and hungry and angry to care anymore."

"Perhaps they are not mutually exclusive. Perhaps bravery is simply apathy with delusions of grandeur."

"Then they are your delusions, Majesty," she said with a slight bow that was clearly intended to be ironic rather than respectful. "I have no delusions left."

"Indeed. Then perhaps . . . we should attend to that." Londo scratched his chin thoughtfully for a moment, and then said to Durla, "See that these people—this family—is fed and clothed and found a decent shelter. Take money from my discretionary funds as needed. You," and he pointed to the girl, "what is your name? I should recall it from our past encounters, but I regret I do not."

"Senna," she said. She looked slightly suspicious and uncertain of what was about to happen. That pleased Londo. Considering that she had spoken with such conviction before, and considering that all of her conviction had been tied up with the utter certainty that Londo was a heartless bastard who cared nothing for his people, it pleased him to see her a bit confused.

"Senna," repeated Londo. "Senna . . . you are going to live at the palace. With me."

"Majesty!" cried a shocked Durla.

Senna looked no less wary. "I'm not flattered. I have no interest in becoming an imperial concubine . . . ."

This drew a bitter laugh from Londo. "That is quite fortunate, for if that were your career goal, I could assure you that you would not have much opportunity to pursue it on Centauri Prime."

She shook her head in puzzlement. "Then what?"

"You have a spirit to you, Senna," said Londo. "A spirit that is symbolic, I think, of not only what the Centauri Republic was, but of what it could be again. A spirit that is . . . lacking, somewhat, I think, in the palace. Too many people with their own agendas hanging about, and I do not exclude myself. You shine with the youthful light of conviction, Senna. I would have that light shining in the palace. Light tends to chase away shadows."

"Majesty . . ." For a moment she seemed overwhelmed, and then her more customary attitude of defiance came back to her. "With all respect . . ."

"You ricocheted a rock off my head, child. It's a little late to speak of respect."

"Majesty . . . those are very pretty words. But I still do not . . . I don't wish to be grateful to you."

"Nor would you have need to be. If you wish, think of it as simply something that I am doing in memory of your parents. Lord Refa was . . . an ally, for a time. I feel some degree of responsibility for his . . ."

Death. For his death.

" . . . family," he continued. "His family, of which you are the only surviving member, yes?" She nodded and he concluded, "So . . . there it is."

"There what is?"

"Senna," Londo said, his patience starting to erode ever so slightly, "I am offering you a home that is a considerable step up from the streets. You will have comfort, the best teachers available to complete your education, and you will want for nothing. In that way—"

"You can purchase peace of mind?"

Londo stared at her for a moment, and then turned to Durla and said, "Come. We are wasting our time here."

Durla appeared rather relieved at this decision. "Shall we punish her, Majesty? She did assault you."

"She has lost her parents, Durla. She has been punished enough."

"But—"

"*Enough.*" There was no mistaking the tone in his voice. A line had been drawn and Durla would cross it at his own peril. It was peril that Durla rather wisely chose not to face. Instead, he simply bowed his head in acknowledgement and acquiescence.

And so they returned to the palace, for what Londo was convinced would be his last night alive.

3

Londo sat in the throne room, staring out at the rain.

It had begun within minutes after his arrival back at the palace. It had been accompanied by almost deafening blasts of thunder, lightning crackling overhead, and it seemed to Londo—who was feeling rather fanciful in what he believed to be his waning moments— that the very skies were weeping on behalf of Centauri Prime. Normally such heavy rains could be viewed as cleansing, but all Londo could envision were streams of red water washing away the blood of all those who had fallen in the bombings.

He could not get the image of Senna from his mind. Such pain, such anger on her face . . . but there was something else, too. There had been several moments there when she had seemed as if she wanted to believe in Londo. To believe that he was capable of serving the people, of operating on not only her behalf, but the behalf of everyone on Centauri Prime. In a way, it was as if Londo had embodied the entire schism between himself and his people in this one girl.

It was unfair, of course. Ridiculous, even absurd. As a symbol she represented nothing, as an individual, she meant even less. But there was something about her nevertheless. It was as if . . .

Londo remembered when he had first met G'Kar. Even before that time, Londo had dreamt of his own death, had envisioned a Narn with his hands around his throat, squeezing the life from him. When he'd actually encountered G'Kar, he had recognized him instantly, had known that this was someone who was going to factor into his future in a most significant way. Most significant, indeed.

The feeling had not been quite as distinct when he'd met Senna, of course. For one thing, he had encountered her before, in passing. For another, she had never featured into a dream. Not yet, at least. Nonetheless, he couldn't help but feel that she was . . . important in some manner. That what happened to her was going to matter, to the Centauri people . . . and to him.

Then again, what did anything matter to him?

He had been drinking rather heavily that evening, as if steeling himself for what he had resolved to do. Originally he had thought that what he would have to do is slay the keeper and then—very quickly—himself, before the action of murdering the small monster could bring the Drakh down upon him. But he had noticed that, in raising his blood/alcohol level to a satisfyingly high degree, he seemed to be dulling the senses of the keeper. The creature's presence no longer seemed so . . . tangible. The keeper was so intertwined with his own neural system that he thought he could actually sense the creature snoring, in his mind.

The notion that he was capable of drinking his little companion under the table became a source of great amusement to him. It was also a relief to him. He wouldn't have to contend with the keeper or whatever unknown resources it might possess, after all. By getting drunk, he was effectively taking the monster out of the picture.

His blade hung comfortably nearby. He still remained concerned about the proximity of guards, outside the doors. But he was simply going to have to take his chances. He had considered the notion of poisoning himself, but somehow that seemed inappropriate. Poison was the tool of the assassin. He should know, having planned enough assassinations in his time, including that of his predecessor, Emperor Cartagia. Besides, the keeper might actually be able to counteract poison, for all he knew. Now the blade—that was the classic, honorable means of dispatching oneself, going all the way back to the earliest days of the Republic.

The early days.

"I was born in the wrong century," he murmured to himself. "To have lived then . . . to have known the Centauri who built the Republic . . . what I would give to have had that opportunity. Perhaps they would have possessed the strength to face that which I am leaving behind. But I do not. All I have tasted in my life is failure, and I think it is time for me to get up from the dinner table and let others sit in my place."

"Majesty."

The voice came so utterly out of nowhere that Londo jumped somewhat. He felt the keeper stir in its drunken slumber, but without being roused from it.

He didn't bother to get up from his throne, but instead half turned to see a guard enter. Thunder rumbled again. It made a nicely dramatic underscoring to his entrance.

"Forgive me disturbing your—" began the guard.

"Yes, yes, get on with it," Londo gestured impatiently. "What is it?"

"There is someone here to see you."

"I left specific instructions that I am not to be disturbed."

"We know that, Majesty. But it is a young girl who stated that she was here at your direct invitation. Given that, we felt it wisest to check with you before throwing her back into—"

Londo half rose from his chair and steadied himself on the armrest. "A young girl?"

"Yes, Majesty."

"Would her name be Senna?"

The guard looked both surprised and a bit relieved, as if realizing that his decision to interrupt the emperor's peaceful evening wasn't going to rebound to his detriment. "Yes, Majesty, I believe it is."

"Bring her in."

The guard bowed briskly and left, only to return moments later with Senna. She was utterly waterlogged; Londo felt as if he had never seen anyone so wet. If she had had hair, it would have been plastered all over her face. As she walked in, she left a trail of water behind her, until she simply stood there with a large puddle forming at her feet. She was shivering, but trying not to show it.

"Leave us," Londo said.

"Majesty," said the guard, "for the sake of your security . . ."

"Security? Look at her," said Londo. "Where do you think she is hiding weapons, eh?" It was a true enough observation. Her clothes were sodden and clinging to her. There was nowhere on her person that she could have been concealing a weapon of any size. "Perhaps she will strangle me with her bare hands, eh? And I, of course, would be incapable of defending myself in such a circumstance."

"I meant no offense, Majesty," the guard said. He appeared about to say something else, but then thought better of it, bowed once more, and quickly absented himself from the throne room.

They remained in silence for a long moment, the only sound being the steady dripping of water from her clothes. Finally she sneezed. Londo put up a hand to hide a smile.

"I wanted to know if your offer was still open," she said after a time.

"Indeed. And why is that?"

"Because enfolded into that offer was shelter and aid for the family that helped me in my time of need. It would be . . . rude . . . of me to turn down aid on their behalf. Furthermore," and she cleared her throat, gathering confidence, "if I am here . . . then I can be a constant reminder to you of what needs to be done to help your people. It's very easy to become isolated here in the palace. You can get so caught up in the gamesmanship and machinations required in maintaining power, that you too easily forget about those in whose behalf you are supposed to be using that power. But if I am here, my presence will remind you of that. You can never turn a blind eye to it, while I'm around."

"I see. So you wish to live here, not out of any desire for comfort and warmth for yourself, but because of the benefit that your being here will render to others."

She nodded. "Yes. Yes, I . . . suppose that is right."

"Did you have any shelter for this evening, I wonder? And do not lie to me," he added sharply, his tone hardening. "You will find that I am a superb judge of such things. Lie to me at your peril."

She licked her lips and her shivering increased ever so slightly. "No," she admitted. "The family who took me in . . . threw me out. They were . . . they were angry that I had turned down your offer. They said it could have helped them. They said that in neglecting the needs of others, I was no different than you."

"Harsh words. To be no different than I—that is no way to live."

She looked to the floor. "So . . . is the offer still open? Or have I wasted your time and mine, and made a fool of myself for no reason?"

He considered her a moment, and then called, "Guard!"

The guard who had escorted her in made his return with all due alacrity. He skidded slightly when he entered, his foot hitting the trail of water that she had left behind, but he quickly righted himself, maintaining as much of his self-possession as possible given the circumstances. "Yes, Majesty?" he said. Clearly he was wondering if he was going to be given another opportunity to throw the interloper out.

"Prepare a chamber for young lady Senna," Londo instructed. "See to it that she is given dry clothes and warm food. She will remain in residence within the palace. Make certain, however, that hers is not a chamber near to mine. We certainly would not want the wrong impression to be given. Proximity to the imperial bedchamber might be misinterpreted by those of a more coarse bent. Is that not right, young lady?"

"It is . . . as you say, Majesty." Then she sneezed once more, and looked almost apologetic for it.

"Yes. Yes, it is. It is always as the emperor says. Why else be emperor? Go to, then. Get some rest. In the morning, we will attend to the family who took you in . . . and, as happenstance would have it, threw you out in their anger."

"They were angry. Very."

"I'm certain they were. But perhaps the more one is faced with anger, the more one should respond with forgiveness."

"That is a . . . a very interesting thought, Majesty."

"I have my moments, young lady. In the morning, then. We will talk, yes? Over breakfast?"

"I . . ." There was clear surprise on her face as she realized what he was saying. "Yes, I . . . think I would like that, Majesty. I will look forward to seeing you in the morning."

"And I you, young lady. As it happens, you see, it appears I will indeed be here in the morning. It would be rude to deprive you of a breakfast companion. And my advisors have informed me that, by morning, this storm will have passed. A new day will be dawning on Centauri Prime. No doubt we will be a part of it."

She bowed once more and then, as the guard began to escort her out, Londo called, "Guard . . . one other small matter."

"Yes, Majesty?" He turned smartly on his heel.

"Do you see that sword hanging on the wall over there?"

"Yes, Majesty. It is quite impressive."

"Yes, it is. I would like you to take it and put it into storage. I do not think I will be needing it anytime soon."

The guard didn't quite understand, but fortunately his understanding was not required. "Very well, Majesty." He bowed, removed the sword from the wall, and escorted Senna out. She paused at the door ever so briefly and glanced over her shoulder at him. Londo kept his face impassive, although he did nod to her slightly in response. Then they departed, leaving the emperor alone with his thoughts.

He sat there for some time more, listening to the rain. He took in no more drink that night, and as the time passed, he could feel the keeper slowly stirring. Lost in his own thoughts and considerations, he paid it no mind. Finally he rose to his feet and left the throne room. He made his way down the hallway, guards acknowledging his presence and majesty as he did so.

For the first time in a long time, he did not feel that he was a sham. He wondered if it was because of the girl.

He entered his private quarters and pulled off the white coat of office, removed the great seal and hung it on a nearby peg.

He'd had a work area set up at the far end of his quarters, and he turned toward it . . . and his heart skipped a beat.

The Drakh was there. How long he had stood in the shadowy section of the room, Londo had no idea. "What are you doing here?" Londo demanded.

"Studying," the Drakh said softly, his hand resting on the computer terminal. "Humans . . . interest you, I see. You have much research."

"I will thank you not to pry into my personal files," Londo said in annoyance. It was, of course, an empty expression of frustration. After all, even if he didn't like it, what was he going to do about it?

"One of our kind . . . studied Humans. Centuries ago," said the Drakh.

That stopped Londo. He made no effort to hide his surprise. "Are you saying you were on Earth?"

The Drakh nodded. "A Drakh . . . took up residence there. Few saw him. But word of him spread. Word of the dark one, the monstrous one who kept to the shadows. Who drained victims' souls . . . and ruled them thereafter," and he inclined his head toward the keeper. "They called him . . . Drak'hul. His legend lives on . . . or so I am told."

It was the single longest speech Londo had ever heard the Drakh make. As if the effort of doing so had drained him, he remained silent for some time. They simply stood there in the darkness, like two warriors, each waiting for the other to make his move.

Feeling bold, Londo said, "And what do they call you, eh? What should I call you—since we seemed to be bound in this living hell together."

The Drakh seemed to consider the question a moment. "Shiv-'kala," he said at last. Then he paused a time further, and said, "The girl."

"What of her?"

"She is not needed."

"Perhaps. But that is not your concern."

"If we say it is . . . it is."

"I desire her to stay. She poses no threat to you, or to your plans."

"Not yet. She may."

"That is ridiculous," Londo said skeptically. "She is a young girl who will become a young woman and take her rightful place in Centauri society. If I left her out on the street, where her resentment could grow and fester, who knows what she might do then, eh? I am doing us a favor."

"Are you?" The Drakh did not appear convinced. Then again, with his constant but chilling smile, it was difficult for Londo to read any change at all in the Drakh's attitude. "We do not like her. We do like Durla."

"Durla? What of him?"

"He has . . . potential."

"What sort of potential?"

The Drakh did not answer directly. Instead he moved halfway across the room, seemingly gliding across the distance. "We are not . . . monsters, Mollari. No matter what you may think," he said. "We are, in many ways, no different than you."

"You are nothing like me, nor I like you," Londo replied, unable to keep the bitterness from his voice.

Shiv'kala shrugged almost imperceptibly. "We will offer a bargain. We do not have to. But we offer it. The girl may stay . . . but Durla will become your minister of Internal Security."

"Never!" Londo said immediately. "I know Durla. I know his type. He is power hungry. And once someone who is power hungry is given power, it whets the appetite for more. The only way to deal with someone like that is to leave him famished before he develops a taste for it."

"He will be your minister of Internal Security . . . or the girl will leave."

There was a popular Human phrase that suited such occasions. Londo employed it now: "Over my dead body."

"No," the Drakh said coolly. "Over hers."

Londo's eyes narrowed. "You wouldn't."

The comment was so preposterous that the Drakh didn't ever bother to reply.

"She is innocent of any wrongdoing. She deserves no harm," Londo said.

"Then see that none comes to her," said the Drakh. "For that matter . . . see that none comes to yourself . . . for her death would quickly follow."

Londo felt a chill run down his spine. "I don't know what you're talking about."

"Good," said the Drakh. "Then all will be well. Tomorrow you will inform Durla of his promotion."

Londo said nothing. There was no need. They both knew that the Drakh had him . . . had him in every way possible.

Shiv'kala glanced out the window of Londo's quarters. The rain was already beginning to taper off. "Tomorrow promises to be a fine day. Enjoy it, Mollari. It is, after all, the first of the rest of your life."

Londo went to the light switch and illuminated the interior of the room, then turned to the Drakh to offer a further protest over the promotion of Durla.

But the Drakh was gone, as if the light were anathema to him. Londo was alone.

Then he glanced at the keeper on his shoulder. It was watching him with a steady eye.

No. Never alone.

From his place of communion, hidden within the darkest shadows of the darkest area of the palace, Shiv'kala reached out and touched the darkness around him. He drew it about himself tightly, enjoying the coolness of it, the peace it brought him.

And within the darkness, the Drakh Entire was waiting for him, attending to his communication so that he could impart to them the progress on Centauri Prime. To his surprise, there appeared to be a bit of annoyance on the part of the Entire. They did not scold him or reprimand him, of course. Shiv'kala's reputation was too great, his status too elevated, for him to be treated in an offhand or condescending manner. Nevertheless, there was . . . concern . . . and a desire to find out why certain actions had been taken, actions the Drakh Entire could not quite comprehend.

At what game do you play, Shiv'kala? You told him your name.

"He asked. It makes no difference."

Why do you bargain with Mollari? Why do you not simply tell him what must be done?

"For what purpose? To show him that we are the stronger?"

Yes. He must know who is the master.

"He knows. He knows. He is, however, unwilling to accept. He resists our hold upon him. He contemplated taking his own life."

Are you certain?

"Yes. I am certain. He thought to hide it from me, but he can hide nothing. He merely thinks he can. And if he cannot live under the stewardship of the keeper, we will lose him."

If we lose him, then we lose him. He is simply another tool. A pawn. Nothing more.

"No," said Shiv'kala sharply. The sternness of his tone drew the Entire up short. "He is more. He is much more. He is not interchangeable, and although he is of course expendable, he is not to be so lightly tossed aside as the others. He is a visionary. We can help that which he envisions to come true. But our task becomes that much easier when our vision becomes his, as well."

What do you propose?

"Nothing except that caution be displayed, as much as possible. That we allow events to play out, rather than force hands. That Mollari be guided in our path rather than be forced. Particularly because if he believes certain things to be inevitable, or that certain ideas are his own, it facilitates our making use of him. It will bring matters to fruition that much more quickly and efficiently."

It does not matter how subtly you wish to influence him. He will never willingly accommodate certain aspects of our plan. His spirit must be broken, not treated gently.

"What will he refuse to accommodate?" asked Shiv'kala skeptically. "This is an individual who aided in the massacre of entire races. From what will he shrink?"

Sheridan. He will never assent to the death of Sheridan. Nor will he willingly stand by while the entire Human race is obliterated. Not unless he is made to realize that he has no choice.

"Do not underestimate the lack of love he feels for the Alliance, and for Sheridan in particular. As for the Humans . . . he had no difficulty in allowing the entire race to stand, by itself, at the edge of oblivion during the Earth-Minbari War. Now, when the personal stakes are so much higher, he will be even less likely to intervene.

"No, my brothers . . . trust me in this. Londo Mollari is at his most effective when he feels that he has some measure of control . . . even though that control is merely an illusion that we permit. One such as he will not be broken immediately. His spirit must be winnowed down. It must be carefully shaped. We must understand his weaknesses and his strengths, and work with both to our best advantage."

Shiv'kala . . . there are moments when it seems as if you actually like this creature.

"I feel he has great potential . . . and I would not see that potential wasted through mishandling. That, my brothers, is all."

Very well, Shiv'kala. You have earned our trust and our respect. We leave it to you to attend to Centauri Prime, and to Londo Mollari, in whatever manner you see fit.

"Thank you, my brothers."

But in the end, of course . . . it must turn out the only way that it can.

"With Londo's humiliation and death, and the final destruction of Centauri Prime?" Shiv'kala smiled mirthlessly. "I assure you, my brothers . . . I would not have it any other way."

With that, he felt the presence of the Drakh Entire slip away from him, like a shadow dissolving in light. And Shiv'kala was left alone, with his own thoughts and own agenda.

No. Never alone.

In the bowels of Babylon 5, the sleeper slept.

He did not know what he was, or who he was. He thought of himself merely as a vagabond, one who had found—if not a home—at least a place that was less hostile than other places in the universe. Down Below had a stench, but it was a familiar stench. The doctors were there every now and then, to deal with the most scabrous. Work could be had, if one wasn't looking to question the legality of it too closely.

Not much of a life . . . but it was a life, and he was content.

He did not know that all his memories were false.

He did not know that his recollections of how he came to reside on B5 were erroneous.

He thought he had a fairly good eye on his world, and understood the ins and outs. He didn't realize that he understood nothing.

But he would. He would. The only problem was, at the point where he understood . . . that was when it would be far, far too late.

4

Senna lay back on the greensward, gazing toward the skies and the clouds.

"What do you see?" came the question from nearby. Telis Elaris lay there.

It was how they always tended to conclude their study sessions, Senna and Telis. Telis explained that it gave him an idea of just how much he had managed to expand her mind in that particular days' lessons. Senna, however, had come to look at it as simply an excuse for creative woolgathering.

As opposed to Senna, who always lay flat upon the grass, Telis had a decorative mat upon which he always reclined. "I am not as young as you," Telis would say to her, which always struck her as something of an odd excuse, because in truth Telis was only a little more than twice as old as she. He was, however, fond of claiming that he was far older than she in experience.

Senna had been assigned a number of teachers since she had first come to live in the palace, eight months ago. She remembered that night as if it were a distant dream. Indeed, she had trouble associating the girl she was then with the young woman that she was now.

The emperor had extended a hand of friendship to a girl who had ricocheted a rock off his skull, and she had had the temerity to slap that hand away. When she had come crawling back to him that night, she had been convinced he was going to throw her out, chortling with amusement over the pathetic young woman who had thought that she was somehow entitled to anything more than contempt.

Instead she had been given everything she could have wanted.

"Why?" she had asked him the next day over breakfast. She had not felt the need to go any further into the question than that. The one word spoke volumes.

And Londo had understood. "Because," he replied, "if I cannot attend to the body and soul of one woman . . . what hope have I in doing the same for Centauri Prime?"

"So I am to be a living symbol?"

"Do you have a problem with that?"

She considered it a moment, and then said, "No, Majesty." And that had seemed to settle it.

What had become more hotly debated was her choice of teachers. Londo had not hesitated to assemble a list of all the very best tutors, scholars, and lecturers to address Senna's education. This, however, had not gone over particularly well with Durla, the captain of the guards whom Londo—for reasons that remained inexplicable to Senna—had appointed to the key position of minister of Internal Security. The main reason Senna wasn't able to understand it was that she was certain—absolutely, one hundred percent certain—that Londo did not trust the man. And if one did not trust the minister of Internal Security, what could possibly be the point in having him in that position?

She remembered one day when she had heard particularly loud discussions coming from within the throne room. Londo and Durla had been disagreeing about something at extremely high volume. Once upon a time, Durla would have backed down immediately, but such was no longer the case. Durla no longer hesitated to tell the emperor precisely what was on his mind, and precisely why the emperor would be a fool not to attend to it.

On that particular day, she had heard several names being bandied about, and she recognized all of them as having been on Senna's own list of desired teachers. One name had been mentioned at particularly high volume, and that was the name of Telis Elaris.

That hadn't been surprising . . . all things considered.

Senna rolled over, and Telis looked at her quizzically. "Well?" he said in that no-nonsense air he had. Telis was another one of those who openly flouted convention; his black hair was long, but instead of wearing it upswept, he allowed it to run down over his shoulders. The style was abhorred by most older men and adored by most younger women, with the latter phenomenon leading to even greater ire among those members of the former faction.

"Well, what?" she replied.

"Well, what do you see in the clouds?"

"Great Maker take the clouds," she answered in annoyance. Telis had been her historical philosophy tutor for some months now, ever since Londo had first sent for him and hired him at Senna's request.

She had been reading treatises of Telis' opinions ever since she was a child, and once had watched as her angered father had tossed one into the trash. She had recovered it from the rubbish, and Elaris had been her guilty, secret pleasure ever since. Historical philosophy specifically covered the various schools of thought that had served to shape much of the Republic's early years, examining how those philosophies interacted with politics. The topic was of particular interest to Senna. "Why must we stare at the useless clouds, when so much of great importance is occurring, right here under our noses?"

With that, Senna gestured toward a section of the capital city that had already been heavily rebuilt. The entire section had been blocked off as being too badly damaged to be safe for the citizenry, so the populace had been relocated and reconstruction had progressed quickly. In some ways, it was breathtaking.

"Why? Because it means nothing," said Telis.

She looked at him in surprise. "How can you say it means nothing?"

"Because that which we build ourselves, by definition, has no permanence. The clouds, on the other hand . . ."

"Have even less," Senna countered. "Look. Even now the wind wafts them away. By morning they will be a memory, but the buildings will still be there."

Telis smiled lopsidedly. "I have taught you too well. Countering your teacher in that way . . . whatever shall I do with you?" Then his face took on a more serious countenance. "I refer to more than those particular clouds, Senna. I refer to nature . . . to beauty . . . to the light. Those things will continue long after you and I are gone . . . long after all memory of the Centauri Republic is washed away, lost in the mists of time."

"That will never happen," Senna said confidently. "We have far more of a destiny to fulfill."

"That—" he pointed at her "—is the emperor talking. Not you."

"Why? Because it's believing in something for once?" She stretched out again, the back of her head cupped in her hands. "You are exhausting sometimes, Telis. Everything, everything is always being questioned. Nothing taken for granted. Everything must be debated, analyzed, debated and analyzed more . . ."

"What is your point, Senna?"

"Doesn't it sadden you? Having nothing that you truly believe in?"

"Is that what you think?"

He actually sounded stricken. She glanced over at him and was surprised to see that he appeared seriously upset at the remark. "Is that what you think?" he asked again. "Because if it is, then in all these months as my pupil, you've learned nothing."

She wasn't happy that she had upset him, for truth to tell, Telis Elaris was her favorite teacher, and she would not have wanted to hurt him for all the world. But having taken a stand, she felt constrained to defend it. "Well, what else am I to think? You dispute every conclusion I make. Even the most fundamental aspects of our life, when I bring them up, you disagree with them. Sometimes I think you'd dispute the existence of the Great Maker himself."

"I would."

Senna visibly blanched at that. "You're not serious."

"I am."

"But why?"

"To make you think, of course," Telis told her. "To make you question, to encourage you to probe. You must accept *nothing* at face value, Senna."

"You're telling me that I should never have faith in anything."

"Am I?"

She thumped the ground in frustration. "There! You're doing it again! Answering questions with a question."

"That should be welcome in a free-thinking society." He looked away from her and said softly, "And I am concerned . . . that it will not be welcome . . . by all."

She noticed that he was looking in the direction of the palace, off on a hill. "Telis," she said firmly, "you can't be speaking of the emperor. He fought to have you assigned as my teacher."

"Yes. He fought. He fought because there are others who prefer not to allow freedom of speech . . . freedom of thought. They don't desire it because it serves neither them nor their purposes. They require you to accept that which is presented you, and for you to question further is anathema to them.

"If, as you say, the emperor fights for freedom, well, that is to be applauded. But, my dear Senna . . . emperors come and go. It is the society that continues . . . at least for a time. And oftentimes those who shape the society . . . prefer to do so from hiding."

"*You* don't. Right there . . ." and she pointed. At the outer edge of the city there was a small building, rather unimpressive. The fact that it was still standing, considering the bombardment that the planet had taken, was impressive in and of itself. "Right there are your publishing offices. Everyone knows it. From there, you publish your papers and articles, challenging *everything* we do on Centauri Prime. You let everyone know that you believe in nothing . . . and yet you fault me when I point it out?"

He shook his head sadly. "And here I thought you were one of my best pupils.

"First, my dear, I do not attempt to shape society. I would not presume to impose my will upon it. I do not even guide. I simply attempt to get society to think for itself—about that which it has not previously considered—and to shape itself. As for what I believe in, Senna . . . what I believe in . . . is believing in nothing."

"You can't believe in believing in nothing."

"Of course you can," said Telis easily. "Child, it's not enough to open yourself to new ideas. Anyone can do that. The problem with that mindset is that usually there is a limit on the amount of 'openness' a person will accept. Sooner or later, the door to the mind swings closed once again. Most will accept just so much, and no more. The truly wise person, however, empties him- or herself of all knowledge . . . and remains that way. Only in that way can you remain open to all new things, all the time. Only in that way can you truly accept the endless varieties and opportunities that the world will present you."

"Those are fine words, Telis," replied Senna. "But words you can easily offer up with impunity, since you are not a leader. Leaders cannot remain open to all things, all the time. Leaders have to lead. They have to make decisions."

"And you believe the leaders are presently making good decisions?"

"Don't you?"

"A question answered with a question," he smiled. "Perhaps there *is* hope for you."

Suddenly Senna felt extremely impatient with what she perceived as constant verbal fencing. Her time with Telis frequently seemed to devolve into such matches. "Tell me. Tell me what you think," she demanded.

"I asked you first," he responded calmly.

"All right." She nodded, feeling that it was a fair enough point. "I think the answer speaks for itself. Look. See the industry that is underway? And the people . . . they have been through so much. Suffered through the bombings, seen their homes destroyed, their livelihoods shattered. There was a time when the emperor's walking among them posed a great security risk because there was so much anger directed toward him. But now, now they are focused on things other than anger. They are focused on re-creating Centauri Prime, achieving the greatness it once knew. The emperor has put forward a vision and they share it. Certainly this is better than anger, or hostility. Better than a sense of hopelessness. The outlook of the people is far better than any would have credited possible."

"And is that of consequence to you?" he asked.

"Of course it is! Why would you ask such a thing?"

"Because in referring to the people, you refer to 'they' . . . and not to 'we.' "

She opened her mouth to respond, then closed it.

"Would you have spoken in that manner six months ago, I wonder?" he continued. "A year ago? Who knows . . . perhaps you would have, back when your parents were people of rank and privilege. It could well be, Senna, that you have the snobbery of privilege so deeply ingrained within you that all it takes is the most gentle of stirrings to bring it bobbing to the surface."

"You think I don't know you, Telis," Senna said. "Well, I don't think you know me very well. Not very well at all."

"Perhaps. I am open to that possibility."

She swung her legs around and curled them up under her chin, pointedly keeping her back to him. "I answered you. I apologize if my answer wasn't up to your usual demanding standards. You, however, have not answered me."

There was a long pause. Then he said, "Why?"

She looked back at him, angling her head slightly, which indicated her puzzlement. "Why what?"

"That should be the first question you ask yourself about everything . . . and once you have the answer . . . keep asking it. Why is there this drive to rebuild Centauri Prime?"

"To reattain our greatness," she said in confusion. The answer seemed self-evident.

"Why?"

"Telis, this is silly. It's like talking with a child. 'Why, why, *why?*' "

"Children are the greatest philosophers in existence. The purpose of the adult is to beat that drive out of children, because it threatens the status quo as created by the adult. Very well, though . . . I shall answer the questions myself, since it seems too tiresome for you."

"It's not a matter of tires—"

But Telis was already moving forward with his train of thought, ticking off the elements on his fingers as he went on. "There is a drive to rebuild Centauri Prime to make it what it once was. Why? To focus the people. Why? Because people of one mind become easier to manage. Why? Because then you can direct them where you want them to go. Why? Because you have someplace specific in mind for them. Why? Because you have a goal for yourself. Why?" He paused and then said, quite slowly, "Because you have decided that the return to the old ways necessitates a return to the expansionism that typified the old Centauri Republic. Because you have decided that no lessons are to be learned from the destruction that befell this planet except that one must be stronger and more focused than one's opponent if one is to win. Because what you truly seek is a return to a time when the Centauri Republic was the preeminent force in the galaxy, master of all it surveyed. Because you realize that times have changed, and that the Alliance now stands in the way. To overcome the Alliance requires new resolve, new weapons, new and even more fearsome allies, and a rededication and rebuilding that presages a new time of war. It's all in the histories, Senna. The so-called Age of Rationality of the Gaim that led to their Great Conquest March, a campaign that left four worlds burning in their wake before it ended. The rebuilding of Germany on Earth after their first World War, which set the stage for an even more calamitous second World War."

She stared at him, wide-eyed. "You're wrong," she said, her voice hushed.

"I spoke to you of allowing yourself to be empty, in order that you might become filled with knowledge. Beware those, Senna, who sense their own emptiness . . . and fill it with ignorance."

"You're wrong," she said again, shaking her head far more vehemently. "And I will tell you why. Because let us look at the history, indeed. In the circumstances you've mentioned, the sort of conversation we are having would never be allowed to happen. Particularly, it would not be allowed to happen between a teacher and a ward of the emperor himself. Such regimes as you describe are the antithesis of thought. Free will is not only discouraged, it is forbidden. Dissidents, intellectuals, writers . . . anyone who can ask the eternal 'why' such as you do, is silenced. And that is not the case here."

"Are you sure?"

"Of course I'm sure! I—"

And then, to her astonishment, Telis reached forward and grabbed her by the forearm. There was an intensity—even a bit of fear—that she had never seen in his eyes before. "You are still a member of the privileged elite, Senna. If it *were* happening, would you truly know until it was too late? I see others, persons such as myself, others who have questioned or probed . . . and suddenly they have changed their opinions. Suddenly they have accepted that which is presented . . ."

"Perhaps they have simply realized the rightness of—"

". . . or else they have disappeared," continued Telis.

Senna became silent for a moment. "Disappeared? What do you mean?"

"They move into outlying lands. Or simply drop off the face of the planet. Oh, it's all done very privately. Very efficiently. When they come for me . . ." he said thoughtfully, as if speculating about the fate of someone else entirely, "I imagine I shall be one of the ones who just drops off. For they know they cannot silence me any other way. I am publishing a paper at the end of this week that questions the true motives of those who are running the great machine that is our government. It will not earn me any friends and will garner me enemies even more formidable than I presently have."

Senna could see that this was no longer one of his mind-twisting journeys of curious logic. She took his hand firmly and squeezed it, and said, "Nothing will happen to you. You are my teacher. You are favored by the emperor. You are protected, and your thoughts are valued. Say what you will. No ill will befall you."

"Is that a promise to me?" He seemed genuinely amused by her fervency.

"That is my conviction and belief in our system, in our society . . . and in our emperor. I believe in all three."

He couldn't help but smile. "Why?" he asked.

She was annoyed, but still couldn't help but laugh at the insouciance with which he said it. "Because I do."

"That is circular logic," he said reprovingly.

"Perhaps. But the nice thing about circular logic is that you can't break through the circle."

To her surprise, Telis Elaris then reached over and hugged her tightly. And he whispered into her ear, "Don't ever change . . ." And then he paused and added, ". . . unless it's for the better."

When Senna returned to the palace, Durla was waiting for her.

She wasn't quite certain that he was actually waiting for her specifically, but as she approached her chambers, he seemed to materialize from around a corner. "Young lady Senna," he said with a slight bow. The informal title by which Londo had referred to her had come into common usage around the palace. It seemed almost a term of endearment when spoken by the right individuals . . . one of whom Durla most certainly was not.

Once again she found herself wondering just what it was that the emperor saw in him. She could only assume that he was extremely efficient in his job. For some reason, however, that thought chilled her even more.

"Minister Durla," she replied, attending to the response as courtesy demanded.

"I hope your lessons today were appropriately stimulating to the intellect," he said.

"Yes, they were. Thank you for your consideration." She started to head toward her chambers, and Durla stepped ever so slightly to one side. It was just enough to block her without coming across as threatening. She stopped in her tracks, folded her arms and regarded him with a raised eyebrow. "Is there something else, Minister?"

"We would be most appreciative if your lessons with Telis Elaris were held within the palace from this day forward," Durla said.

"Would you?" She was not enamored of the notion, as was painfully clear in her body language and dubious expression. "And why would that be? Pray tell?"

"It is a matter of security."

"And being minister of Internal Security, that would naturally be important to you. Your concern is noted, Minister, but Telis and I find the fresh air of the outdoors to be more . . . what was the phrase you used? More 'intellectually stimulating' than the walls of the palace."

"Nor would I wish to hamper your educational growth. These are, however, dangerous times."

"Indeed. How so?"

"Agents and allies of the Alliance lurk everywhere."

Senna let out an overdramatic gasp and quickly looked around, as if she were concerned that enemies might spring out from the very walls around them.

Durla, for his part, was clearly not amused. "You can afford to take such things lightly, young lady, for your youth gives you a very limited sense of your own mortality. And since you see no enemy, you do not fear one."

"Actually, it is my understanding that something which you cannot see can be the most dangerous."

For a moment, Durla actually appeared startled. Senna couldn't quite figure out why he reacted the way he did, but then he smoothly composed himself, doing it so quickly that Senna wondered if she had perhaps imagined it all. "Quite so, and since you understand that, I take it that you will acquiesce to our request."

"You keep saying 'we' and 'our,' Durla. Is this your initiative, or the emperor's?"

"It is my recommendation. The emperor is in accord with it."

"I see. And if I ask him, he will verify it?"

"Absolutely. Although I will be hurt if you doubt my word in such an obvious manner."

Senna considered the situation. She had a feeling that Durla wasn't lying. That the emperor would indeed back up his minister of Internal Security. Then again, she was a ward of the emperor. He should care about her concerns as well. "You have also said this is a recommendation. Are you prepared to have the emperor order me to confine Telis and myself to the palace?"

To her surprise, Durla said quite soothingly, "Of course not, young lady. No one has any desire to make you feel a prisoner, or constrict your movements beyond that which you are prepared to allow. We . . . I . . . am concerned only about your safety."

"Look at it this way, Durla," she said. "I became orphaned during a time when death rained from the heavens. At a time when so many died that the corpses were piled up as far as the eye could see. And I survived all that, without your help. So I think I'm more than capable of attending to my own safety."

"As you wish, young lady. But do be careful. If something were to happen to you, I know the emperor would be most upset. And I doubt that he would be overly enthused by my presenting, as an excuse, the notion that you simply wished to continue taking the air while learning at the feet of Telis Elaris."

"Your job is not without risks, Minister Durla. Certainly you must have known that before assuming the position."

"All of life is risk, young lady Senna." He bowed and began to walk away.

And then Senna—somewhat to her surprise—stopped him as she asked, "Minister . . . have you noticed a reduction in the number of writers, artists . . . creative individuals . . . in residence on Centauri Prime?"

"No more so than usual, young lady."

"Than usual?" She found the phrasing rather odd.

"Why yes. Such types are notoriously undependable and prone to difficulties. They starve for their art and so are lost . . . or they require dangerous drugs or drink in order to achieve their 'creative vision,' and come to harm through improper dosage.

"And then, of course, there are those of a radical bent. A thoroughly pugnacious and bellicose type, given to unfortunate accidents through altercations with others who possess opposing viewpoints. A rather sordid crowd, truly," he sighed. "Oh, I suppose that handsome, loquacious types such as Elaris make them seem . . . romantic. But as a group, they are quite unstable. If you do research, I think you'll find that many of them tend to come to rather bad ends. Let us hope that Elaris is not among those."

Something in his last statement chilled Senna slightly. "What do you mean by that, Minister?"

"Why, nothing, young lady. Nothing at all. Enjoy your . . . outdoor chats." He bowed and then went on down the hall.

Senna considered his words—and then went straight to the room that was usually used for her assorted lessons. She went over the room as meticulously as she could, searching for some sign of a listening device, to see if her lessons and conversations were being monitored. But she found nothing. Finally, exhausted from looking, she flopped down in a chair and sat there, wondering what Telis would say when she told him of the exchange she had just had with Durla.

5

She only caught the flash of light from the corner of her eye.

It was several days later and Senna was seated upon the hillside, wondering when Telis Elaris would show up. She was becoming somewhat apprehensive, for Telis was never late. In fact, he was so punctual that it bordered on the annoying.

She realized that they had never finished their "game" of seeing images in the clouds. Fortunately, this day was as nicely cloudy as the other had been, and so she let her mind wander as she gazed upon the billowing fluff high overhead.

She decided that one of them had taken on the shape of a giant spider. And another, with the odd crest to it and the curious convergence of shapes, looked like the emperor's face, only scowling. Scowling at the giant spider. She found that amusing for some reason.

So absorbed was she in her game that she barely noticed the light flash coming from the direction of the city. However, notice it she did, and she sat up quickly. It was then that she heard the explosion that had accompanied the flash. She could tell from the sound of the explosion that something large had gone up, though, and naturally her first thought was that Centauri Prime was once again under attack by the Alliance.

She scanned the heavens, preparing herself for some follow-up blast, but all remained silent. Then there was a second, even louder explosion, and by that point a column of thick black smoke had begun rising from the source.

Now Senna was on her feet, shading her eyes with one hand as she tried to make out precisely where the explosion had come from. Her breath caught in her throat, and she staggered slightly. Even from where she was, she could make out that the explosion had originated in the building that housed the home and office of Telis Elaris.

She didn't even remember starting to run. She was halfway there, her legs moving like pistons, and it was only when she realized that she was cutting her feet to ribbons on assorted stones and such that she remembered she was still holding her shoes. She stopped for a few seconds, never taking her eyes off the column of smoke, almost stumbling but recovering quickly. Then she continued to run, her breath ragged in her chest, gasping for air but never slowing down.

She came to an incline, tripped, fell, and tumbled heels over head the rest of the way. The incline butted up against the street and she slid down it in a most undignified fashion. However, so many people were running around, pointing and calling to each other, that no one took any notice of her. She scrambled to her feet and staggered toward the place where the explosion had occurred.

There had been some residual fire, but fortunately most of it had been contained by the time she got there. The building was already something that had become all too common on Centauri Prime: a burned-out shell. The last of the smoke was wafting heavenward, and people were pointing and speculating in hushed tones.

Rescue workers were emerging with several bodies of persons who were obviously beyond rescue. Senna scanned their remains desperately, hoping and praying that she would not see what she most feared would be there. Her hopes and prayers went unanswered, however—the third body brought out from the ruins was clearly the charred remains of Telis Elaris. Half his face was gone, but there was enough left to recognize him.

She turned away, her hand to her mouth, trying to stifle both her urge to scream and her urge to vomit, all at the same time.

Then she heard one of the rescuers say, "We found this, Minister." She forced herself to look back, and there was Durla, taking what appeared to be some sort of heavy box from one of the rescue workers. It was scorched but otherwise undamaged, and Durla bowed slightly upon receiving it.

Something within Senna snapped.

"*Murderer!*" she howled, and she launched herself straight at Durla. Thanks to her dishevelled appearance, he clearly did not recognize her at first as she charged him, fists balled, her face a mask of pure rage. She got to within five feet of him, and then two guards were there, intercepting her and lifting her off her feet. She kicked furiously, arms outstretched, fingers clawing spasmodically, and she shouted, "You did this! You're behind this! You murdering bastard!"

It was then that Durla realized who it was shouting at him. "Young lady!" he said in obvious surprise.

"Don't call me that! Don't you *ever* call me that! You did this! You killed him!"

"Such ludicrous accusations. The girl is distraught. Take her back to the palace," said Durla unflappably as he tucked the box firmly under one arm. "We shall sort this mess out later."

"You killed him because he was a free thinker! Because he challenged! Because he made other people think! You'll pay for this, Durla! I'll make you pay!"

He shook his head sadly as Senna, still kicking and screaming, was carted away to the palace.

"Have you completely lost your senses?!"

The emperor stood over her, body trembling with indignation and perhaps even a sense of personal humiliation. Cleaned up and wearing fresh clothing, Senna sat in a chair, hands folded, looking down. Nearby, Durla stood and observed the confrontation impassively.

"You accuse my minister of murder, in front of a crowd of people!" continued Londo. "A tragic circumstance, transformed by you into a suspicion of my government! What were you thinking? Well? That was not a rhetorical question—what were you thinking?"

"I said what I was thinking," Senna said quietly. "I believe that's why you're chastising me, Majesty."

"Outrage! It was an outrage!"

Annoyingly to Senna, it was Durla who spoke up in her defense. "I beg you, Majesty, do not be harsh with the girl. She was upset, obviously distraught. Considering the circumstances, I would say it was most understandable. She did not know the truth of the matter . . ."

"The truth of the matter?" She repeated the words with no inflection. "What are you talking about . . . 'the truth of the matter'?"

Durla sighed heavily, as if he were about to release a great burden. "I would have given anything if you were not to find out this way, young la—Senna. Do you remember that box the rescue worker removed from the rubble? Well . . . the evidence found therein was—shall we say—rather damning."

"What evidence. What sort of nonsense . . ."

"The truth is," and he addressed his comments to the both of them, "that it appears Telis Elaris was, in fact, a sympathizer with the Alliance."

"What? Are you sure?" asked Londo. "Have you any real proof?"

"Positive, Majesty. The box we found contained detailed logs, correspondence . . . communications with several key member races of the Alliance who still feel that the assault on Centauri Prime should continue. Races who will not be satisfied until every last one of us, no matter how young and pretty," he said pointedly to Senna, "is wiped from existence. Nothing less than wholesale genocide will suit them."

"This is utterly preposterous," Senna said. "Telis Elaris loved his fellow Centauri. It was only because he cared for them that he tried to expand their minds, to—"

"What he cared about, Senna, was undermining and undercutting the current regime. It wasn't entirely his fault," said Durla. "I believe he himself was being manipulated by the Alliance, who found in him a convenient patsy. Be that as it may, we have also uncovered the reason for the explosion: apparently Telis Elaris was experimenting with the construction of an incendiary device. His ultimate use for it, we do not know, although we can speculate based upon his communiqués. We believe—although I emphasize, there is no proof—that he intended to assassinate you, Majesty. Blow up the palace."

"This is insane!" shouted Senna.

"Is it?" Durla asked, never coming close to losing his patience. "It was he who suggested you take your lessons out of doors, was it not? We believe he intended to detonate the bomb during one of your sessions, so that there would be no chance of you coming to harm. Apparently he felt quite affectionately toward you. In any event, while he was certainly of quite high quality as a thinker, he was a bit deficient in the category of terrorism. The device went off prematurely, and . . ." He shrugged.

Senna turned to Londo. "Majesty, surely you can't believe this. You know Telis. You know the kind of man he is . . . was. Do not let this . . . this . . ." she waggled a finger at Durla, "this *person* . . . besmirch the good name of Telis Elaris. It's bad enough that he assassinated the man. Now will he be allowed to assassinate the man's character as well?"

"Senna . . . you have become very dear to me," Londo said slowly, "but I warn you, do not overstep yourself, for it—"

"Overstep myself! Majesty, we stand in the presence of a murderer and liar! Murder and lying are not in the job description of the minister of Internal Security! Who has overstepped whose bounds?"

"We do not know that," Londo said, "and if there is proof—"

"Proof that he could easily have manufactured!"

"Interrupt me again at your own peril, Senna!"

Senna, who had risen from her chair when confronting Londo, took a step back as she realized that he meant it. She had never seen him as angry as he was at that very moment.

With a distinct effort, Londo composed himself, then said tightly, "I will inspect the evidence myself. If the findings are as Minister Durla says, well . . ." He paused, considering the matter a moment. "As a matter of internal security, I see no reason at this time to inform the populace that there may have been a traitor in their midst. Why stir matters up more than they are, or contribute more fuel to the fire of paranoia. They need peace of mind. If at the end of his life, Telis Elaris harbored traitorous alliances, that does not negate the good he accomplished through his teachings. We can always attribute the explosion to something routine—a furnace or some such. You can come up with something, I trust, Durla?"

"Yes, Majesty," Durla replied dutifully.

"Good."

"So it would seem," Durla commented to Senna, "that sometimes lying *is* part of my job description."

Senna said nothing. For some moments, in fact, no one said anything. Then Londo told her, "Since you are so concerned, Senna, about the public perception of a man who is already dead . . . do you not think you owe Minister Durla an apology for your public assault on his character, particularly considering that he is still alive to hear whatever criticism may arise from your actions?"

"If you are indeed asking me, Majesty . . . no. No, I don't believe I owe him that at all."

She looked at Londo with her chin slightly upthrust and as much moderate defiance as she dared display.

"Majesty," Durla said, coming to her rescue once more, "it is not necessary. Truly."

"Very well," Londo nodded. "Senna, you may go."

She walked out of the room, and it was only when she was a safe distance that she allowed the tears to flow.

Durla handed the box of evidence to Londo and bowed. "Return it whenever you are done, Majesty. I expect that you will find everything as I've said."

"Oh, I expect I will," Londo told him.

Durla turned to leave. He started toward the door, and then he heard quick footsteps behind him. Before he could turn, he suddenly felt one powerful hand on the back of his neck, and another grabbing him by the back of his coat. The slim minister was propelled forward and slammed face first against the wall. The impact knocked the breath out of him, and then Londo's mouth was right up against his ear, whispering to him in a sort of perversely intimate moment.

"Understand, Durla . . . if I learn that this evidence has indeed been falsified . . . that you were responsible for the death of Elaris . . . your head will wind up next to that of a fellow named Morden who was, I assure you, far better connected and far more dangerous than you. And I further assure you that I personally will attend to the task of decapitating you, with Senna there to catch your head and stick it on the pole with her own eager hands. Is that clear?"

"Majesty, I—"

"*Is. That. Clear?*"

"Yes, Majesty."

He released Durla then. The minister did not turn around. Instead he straightened his coat, smoothed some ruffled strands of his hair, and walked out of the throne room.

The moment he was gone was when the pain hit Londo.

White hot, stabbing, exploding through his brain and offering him no place to run. He staggered across the throne room, trying to locate the source, and then he realized. The keeper, the keeper on his shoulder was doing this.

He tried to reach around, to rip the monstrosity off him once and for all, but all such efforts only increased the agony, and that was when he heard a voice in his head saying, *I would not do that if I were you*.

He staggered to his throne, clutching the arms, gasping as the pain finally started to recede. But a sense of it still remained, like a great beast lurking in the high grass, ready to come at him once again if he so much as made the slightest wrong move. Even in his head, he recognized the voice of the Drakh Entire or at least the Drakh emissary who seemed to haunt the palace like an omnipresent specter of death.

"How . . . how did—"

No questions. Sit. In the throne. Hands on the armrests.

Londo did as he was instructed. He had no choice—he realized that.

You abused Durla. The voice sounded almost disappointed. *He is chosen by us. You are not to do such a thing ever again.*

"Chosen by you. Then he has a keeper, too?" growled Londo,

taking at least some measure of joy in picturing what it must have been for Durla to watch one of those abominations crawling across the floor at him.

So he was disappointed to hear in reply, *No. He does not require one. He already believes—that the Republic has become vulnerable because of its decadence, that you have lost the fire of your early years. He believes in discipline, order, and total obedience. He does not need to know of our existence, does not require a keeper. His pure enthusiasm and rightness of spirit will make him far more effective than any keeper could.*

"I'm so happy for you. Then may I ask why you need me?"

We don't.

Well . . . there it was, wasn't it. The Drakh could be accused of many things, but prevarication was not one of them.

Sounding almost regretful, the Drakh voice said to him, *We take no pleasure in this, Londo. No joy. The work you have done thus far for Centauri Prime is laudable. You have focused them, directed them, uplifted them, brought them far from their fallen state in just a few short months. Left to your own devices, you might indeed be a worthwhile emperor. But you are our device, not your own. You will attend to our wishes and remember that you can pretend to serve the people, but you truly serve us. To help you in remembering . . . you will sit silently in your throne now.*

"But—"

For just a moment, the pain welled up, like a threatening tidal wave.

Silent . . . ly.

Then Londo sat perfectly upright, staring straight ahead, looking neither left nor right.

You will remain that way . . . until we tell you otherwise. You will hear the noises, the conversations, the normal life of the palace outside . . . but you will not participate. All audiences will be refused. You will be alone for hours . . . or days . . . however long we feel it necessary in order to make our point.

You spoke of Centauri Prime being alone? You have no grasp of the concept. But you will. You will, for the greatest loneliness of all is to be alone among others. Do not move, Londo. Do not speak. Dwell on what you have done, and what will be required of you . . . and what will happen to you if you do not live up to those requirements.

Then the voice in his head ceased, but Londo—wisely—did not

move. He continued to stare resolutely ahead, lest the voices and the pain return.

I am in hell, thought Londo.

And a voice replied, *Yes. You are*.

He tried not to think after that.

It was a brisk day, the wind whipping sharply over the hills. Senna went to their place and sat upon the grass. She stared off into the distance toward the ruined building, which was already in the process of being torn down, now part of the emperor's renovation program. Considering the speed and efficiency with which the workers had been moving, a new structure would probably replace it within a week.

She had been checking through libraries, through data bases. The writings of Telis Elaris were quietly being removed, disappearing one by one.

She lay back on the grass, looked up at the clouds. She tried to conjure up images . . . and nothing suggested itself. They were just white collections of mist and vapors, and would soon go away, just as everything went away.

Tears began to roll down her face, even though she made no noise.

"Why?" she whispered.

No answers came.

The sleeper began to stir.

He did not fully realize what was happening, not on any conscious level. He simply developed the oddest feeling that everything around him was . . . incidental. That it would soon cease to have any true relevance to his life.

He went about his business, trying to ignore the faint buzzing that was becoming more pronounced in his head. When he could ignore it no longer, he went to the medical people, but their rather cursory examination found nothing. He didn't fault them for it, not really. He was having trouble explaining to them just what it was that he was feeling, so how could they know what to look for? He didn't even understand it himself.

So he pushed himself to go on with his life and not dwell on that which he did not understand. And when word trickled down that the president of the Interstellar Alliance was going to be doing a walk-through of Down Below . . . that he was, in fact, endeavoring to develop a program that would be of help to everyone there, why . . . that all sounded fine. Excellent, in fact. Down Below could use all the help it could get.

He did not realize yet that he would be assassinating President Sheridan. Assassination was the furthest thing from his mind. He was just a normal guy, trying to get on with his normal life. Thoughts of murder and mayhem were far, far away.

He didn't understand that they were going to draw quite close.

6

Vir hadn't known what to expect when he arrived back on Centauri Prime.

When he had departed, right after the inauguration, it had been under less-than-ideal circumstances. Cities had been reduced to smoldering ruins, and Londo had delivered a bizarre speech that sounded as if it was designed to fan the flames of hostility and rage against the Interstellar Alliance. *What good could possibly come from getting the Centauri people even more worked up?* Vir had wondered, mystified. They had to understand that it was a time of reconciliation. Of redemption.

Yes . . . that was what was required, Vir thought as the transport ship that carried him the final leg to his destination drew within reach of the Centauri Prime main spaceport. *Redemption*. The Centauri had much for which they had to redeem themselves.

The truth was that they had done great evil. They had attacked the Narns, they had provided aid to the most evil of evil races, the Shadows. As a race they had sinned mightily, and as a race they were being called upon to repent. Repenting for their sins, however, was not going to be easy if their ire was stirred and they were made to feel as if they—the poor, put-upon citizens of Centauri Prime—were the victims. Yes, there had been misunderstandings. Yes, there seemed to have been deliberate plots to vilify Centauri Prime in the eyes of other races. But wasn't the truth that they, the Centauri people, had left themselves open for precisely that sort of under-the-table assault?

If they had had a reputation for being peaceful, gentle, unaggressive . . . certainly no one could have manipulated them into a position where they were considered to be a threat. But the Centauri had, through their own actions and with their own blood-covered hands, made certain that everyone knew they were a dread force to be reckoned with.

Well, the reckoning had come, hadn't it. And look at what the result had been. Just look.

"Just look to your right," the pilot's voice came over the speaker system of the transport, "and you'll see the restoration of the entire north quarter of our glorious capital city. Work is continuing on the city's other sections, under the building-relief programs created and overseen by our glorious emperor. In the meantime, increased Centauri industry has bolstered our economy, supporting not only our rebuilding efforts, but also paying off—oftentimes in trade—the reparations that we have so generously agreed to pay the members of the ungrateful Interstellar Alliance."

Vir gulped. He did not like the sound of that at all. Furthermore, he had the feeling that the pilot was reading from a prepared text. He wondered just who had prepared it. He glanced around the shuttle at his fellow passengers. Everyone else in the shuttle was Centauri. He was curious to see that all of them were nodding their heads in unison over the comments about the emperor's great works . . . and unsettled to note that they were shaking their heads together and scowling when there was mention of the Alliance.

No, not good at all. He was definitely going to have to talk to Londo about it. The problem was, he had absolutely no idea what he was going to say.

He had endeavored to remain in touch with Londo, as was his mandate while he served as the Centauri ambassador to Babylon 5. He hadn't anticipated that it would become a problem. If nothing else, he had figured that the normally gregarious Londo would retain his interest in his associates back on the station. That he would be anxious to check in with Vir as often as possible, to learn who was up to what, catch up on all the latest gossip. Such had not been the case, however. Weeks, even months would go by without Vir being able to communicate with Londo at all. Instead he found more and more of his conversations being held with Durla, the minister of Internal Security. The last time that he had encountered someone that chilling it had been the notorious Mr. Morden, and there had certainly been no love lost in *that* relationship. Lives and heads lost, yes, but no love.

"I will relay your concerns to the emperor. The emperor is busy at the moment. The emperor appreciates your communiqués." These and a litany of stock phrases had tripped off Durla's lips so often that Vir knew them by hearts. And on those occasions when Vir somehow, miraculously, did get through to Londo, the emperor had always spoken with such care and judiciousness that Vir couldn't help but get the feeling that all their conversations were being monitored somehow. The thought itself should have been absurd. Londo was, after all, the most powerful person on Centauri Prime. Theoretically, there should be no one and nothing who would have the temerity and the power to oversee his interests and activities. Who did Londo have to fear?

Then Vir considered the fate of previous Centauri emperors, and filled in the answer to that: Everyone.

But Londo wasn't like other emperors. Certainly he was nothing like Cartagia, the madman. And he was nothing like the regent, who had brought their world to the brink of ruin. Londo was a good man, a decent man. That had to count for something, didn't it?

Didn't it?

Unfortunately, even in his own mind, he could not divine an answer for that.

Fortunately for everyone aboard the transport, Vir's concentration wasn't necessary for the transport to land safely. So his thoughts were able to ramble about all manner of concerns while the craft settled safely onto its landing spot in the main spaceport.

"Ambassador Vir!"

Vir's first impulse was still to look over his shoulder, to see if someone else was being hailed. Hearing the designation "ambassador" in front of his name was still something of a jolt to him, and he always felt slightly guilty—as if he were an imposter. Or perhaps a mistake had simply been made and another Vir was being summoned . . .

In this instance, however, he managed to fight the impulse and look instead toward whomever it was that was endeavoring to get his attention.

There was a rather tall individual standing there. He was somewhat pale in complexion, with sunken eyes and a voice that seemed to originate from somewhere around his ankles. When he walked it was with a slight hunch, as if he perpetually had to lean forward to hear what you had to say. His medium-high hair was quite light, as pale in its way as his skin tone. Standing next to him was a young boy who couldn't have been more than thirteen. Curiously, although the tall man was dressed in the sort of finery that Vir had come to associate with the imperial court, the boy was sporting some sort of uniform, such as Vir had never seen before. It was mostly black, which gave Vir eerie flashbacks to the Psi Corps, but it was broken up by a bloodred sash draped across his chest.

"Ambassador Vir," said the tall man. "I am Castig Lione, chancellor of Development, attached to Minister Durla's office. It is an honor to meet you. Throk, take the gentleman's bags."

"Oh, that's quite all right," Vir started to say, but he spoke too slowly. The teen, Throk, was already at his side and was gripping firmly the bags that Vir held in either hand. Vir took one look into the boy's eyes, and promptly released the bags. The boy wielded them easily . . . actually, with a great deal more ease than Vir had carried them. Vir told himself that it was just because he was tired from the trip. "I . . . wasn't expecting anyone to pick me up, actually. I just figured I'd make my way to the palace on my own. I didn't mean to put anyone out."

Lione smiled. When he did so, however, it looked as if he were in some sort of vague pain. Just as quickly as it appeared, the smile vanished. "You are everything that I have heard. Humble and self-effacing, as if you still do not appreciate your importance."

"Well . . . once upon a time, you have to understand . . . being ambassador to Babylon 5 not only wasn't especially important . . . it was actually sort of a . . . well . . ." He lowered his voice as if he was concerned about offending Londo, who was nowhere in sight. ". . . a joke. A position that no one took particularly seriously."

"Times change," said Lione.

"Yes, they certainly do. And who is this young man? Throk, I believe you said his name was?" Vir smiled broadly at him and was greeted with an unflinching, sullen face, and eyes that somehow gave him a free-floating sense of anxiety. "Is there some significance to the uniform?"

"Throk is one of the first members of the Centauri youth group. We call them the Prime Candidates. And indeed, they are excellent candidates to be the next generation of leaders of our world."

"Oh, a play on words! That's very cute," said Vir.

Throk gave him a look that, Vir realized, could have brought on a new ice age if there were a way to harness it. "We are not cute," he said succinctly.

"Throk . . ." chided Lione warningly.

"Sir," amended Throk stiffly. "We are not cute, sir."

"I . . . stand corrected," said Vir, who was already feeling more and more creepy about the entire business.

"Chapters of the Prime Candidates are opening across Centauri

Prime. The young are the hope of the future, Ambassador, as is always the case. So it was felt that one of the best things that could be
done for the morale and spirit of our citizenry was for them to see the
energies and enthusiasm of our youth harnessed in a positive manner."

"And what do the Prime Candidates do, exactly?" Vir asked
Throk.

Throk did not hesitate. "Whatever Chancellor Lione tells us to."

"Oh."

"They do public works, public services. Clean-up campaigns, running public information offices . . . that sort of thing," Lione explained.

"That all sounds wonderful. And this was the emperor's idea?"

"Minister Durla's, actually, but the emperor embraced it immediately. I was then brought in by Minister Durla to oversee the program . . . and also explore other means of lifting morale throughout
Centauri Prime."

They climbed into a waiting transport that immediately hurtled
in the direction of the palace.

"You know . . . I have a thought on that."

"On what, Ambassador?"

"On boosting morale. There's this remarkable Earth game I was
introduced to on Babylon 5 by Capt—by President Sheridan. If we
could organize teams to play it, that might do wonders."

"Indeed." Castig Lione once again made that slightly winced
smile. Throk sat in the seat just ahead of them and stared resolutely
forward. "What might that be?"

"It's called 'baseball.' "

"Indeed," Lione said once more. "How is it played?"

"Well," said Vir, warming to the topic, "you have nine men on
each side. And one man, he stands in the middle of the field, on an
elevated pile of dirt, and he has a ball, about this big." He shaped the
imaginary spheroid in his hands. "And there's a man from the other
team, and he stands a distance away holding a stick."

"A stick."

"Well, a large stick. And the man on the dirt throws the ball at
the man with the stick."

"Endeavoring to injure or kill him?" Castig Lione's interest
seemed piqued.

"Oh, no. No, he tries to throw it past him. And the man with the stick tries to hit it. If he misses it, he gets two more attempts to try and hit it. If he hits it, he runs to a base—"

"A military base?"

"No, it's a square, about so big. He tries to run to the base before one of the other men on the field gets the ball there ahead of him."

"And . . . if he accomplishes this . . . what happens?" Lione didn't seem to be quite as intrigued as he had been when he had thought the object was to concuss the man with the stick.

"If he doesn't make it, he's out."

"Of the game?"

"Oh, no, no he can try later when it's his turn again. But if he does make it to the base, then he has a chance to try and get to another base."

"That seems rather pointless. Why doesn't he just stay on the one he's on?"

"Because if he gets to a second base, then he gets to try for . . ."

"A third base?" Lione's interest was definitely flagging. "Is there a point to all this somewhere?"

"Oh, yes! After he gets to the third base, he gets to try to go home."

"Home? You mean he leaves the game?"

"No, it's called home base. If he gets to home base, then his team scores a run. And they do this back and forth, getting runs or outs, until there's three outs from each side, and that's called an 'inning.' And the game goes until nine innings, unless it's tied in which case it can go on forever, or it rains or everyone just gets sick of it."

Castig Lione stared at Vir, then asked, "And this is a popular game on Earth?"

"Humans love it," said Vir.

And Throk said dourly, "No wonder the Minbari tried to wipe them out."

7

"Vir! *Viiiiir!*"

Londo's greeting of him was big and boisterous and not at all what Vir had expected. Then again, there was a large party going on, and in that sort of environment Londo was most definitely in his element.

It was all quite exciting for Vir. Certainly he had attended enough parties, particularly in Londo's presence. The Londo of old was something of a magnet for such festivities. Many were the revelries that he was able to recall on Babylon 5, although admittedly his memory of some of them was recalled through a bit of a haze. A pleasant haze, but a haze nonetheless.

But this . . . this was a party in the court!

For all that Vir had been through—for all of the secret plots, and his own hideous involvement in such dire schemes as assassinations—he had never truly left behind the relatively innocent individual that he once had been. And that individual was the fool of the Cotto clan, the embarrassment, the one who was never going to amount to anything. When he had been shunted away to Babylon 5, to serve as aide to the equally despised Londo Mollari, it had simply been the latest insult in a life laden with insults.

To be part of the court, to rub elbows with the movers and shakers of Centauri rank and society . . . inwardly he still felt a sort of disbelief over how everything had turned out. This was not how it was supposed to go for Vir Cotto. He was supposed to eke out an existence, and try not to get into anyone's way. That had been the entirety of his aspirations.

So to be arriving in court, to be able to hold his head high . . . he still felt as if he had to pinch himself to make certain that he wasn't dreaming it all. That was how he felt, even though he knew that the dream had its dark, nightmarish side. Yes, he knew that all too well.

The grand reception hall was alive with activity. There was song and dance and merriment. A scantily clad dancing girl bumped up against Vir and smiled at him . . . at *him* . . . in a most sultry manner before pirouetting off, thin veils trailing from her hands. Waiters bearing an assortment of gourmet tidbits converged on him from all sides, almost stumbling over one another to serve him. People were dressed in the most glorious finery, chatting and laughing and acting as if they had not a care in the world.

"Vir!" Londo shouted once more and began to make his way through the crowd. When one is the emperor, such an action is far less taxing than it would be for others. The crowd magically melted before him to make way, closing itself behind him as he passed. It gave him the appearance of being a great ship moving through the ocean. *The ship of state*, Vir told himself.

Londo was holding a drink. He passed one nobleman and, without hesitation, plucked the drink from the man's hand and bore it toward Vir. It took a moment for it to register on the nobleman, but when he realized who it was who had absconded with his drink, he simply gestured toward one of the wandering waiters and signaled that another would be required.

"Vir! I must tell you a riddle!" Londo said as he thrust the glass into Vir's hand.

Several things were tumbling about in Vir's head: to thank Londo for the drink; to tell him he didn't need it; to tell Londo that he, Londo, was looking quite well; to tell him that he was pleased that he had been invited to this get-together. All of this occurred to him, but was promptly washed away by the unexpected declaration. "A . . . riddle?"

"Yes! Yes, it is quite clever. Senna told it to me. Clever girl, our young lady."

"Yes, you've told me about her. Tragic thing, the loss of her teach—"

"Do you want to hear this riddle or not?" Londo demanded.

"Oh . . . absolutely, yes." Vir bobbed his head.

Londo draped an arm around Vir's shoulders, bringing his face closer. The smell of alcohol was even more pungent than usual. "What is greater than the Great Maker . . . more frightening than a Shadow ship . . . the poor have it . . . the rich need it . . . and if you eat it, you die."

Vir silently mouthed the elements of the riddle, then shook his head. "I give up."

"You give up!" Londo sounded almost outraged. "You give up?

That is your problem, Vir. That has always been your problem. You give up, far too quickly. You have to give things thought, Vir. Even if you do not succeed, you have to at least *try!*"

"All . . . all right. Let me think. Greater than the Great Ma—"

His thought process was promptly interrupted when a voice from at his elbow said, "Ambassador. What a pleasure it is to see you."

Vir turned and saw Durla standing there.

He had seen the man before in passing, but not since Durla had been promoted to the ministry. Durla had never really registered on Vir, back when he was captain of the guards. But now that he was seeing him, really seeing him for the first time, he sensed that this was a man to watch out for.

"And I, you, Minister," Vir replied easily.

"How nice that you were able to get away from Babylon 5 to attend this little celebration. I'm sure you've been very busy there."

Vir watched Londo's gaze flicker from Durla to Vir and back. He seemed curiously content to watch the two of them converse. It was as if Londo had something very specific he wanted to see accomplished, but Vir could not for the life of him imagine what that might be. The last thing that Vir was interested in doing was getting into some sort of verbal sparring match with Durla just because it might suit Londo's purposes, whatever those might be. Nevertheless, there was something in Durla's tone and attitude that Vir couldn't help but consider off-putting. It wasn't in the words so much, but in the condescending voice attached to it.

"Oh, yes . . . yes, I've been very busy," Vir said.

"I'm sure. Although," Durla continued, "the true future of the Centauri Republic would lay, I think, with what is developing on Centauri Prime, rather than on a hunk of metal light-years away. A place that is the base of operations for an Alliance that is dedicated to wiping the Centauri off the face of creation, eh?"

"Minister," Vir said carefully, "with all respect, if the Interstellar Alliance were 'dedicated' to it, I doubt we'd be all standing here right now, in an intact palace, enjoying this quite wonderful wine. Excuse me!" he called to a passing waiter, indicating with a gesture that he could use a refill. Vir normally wasn't a drinker, but in recent years he had driven his tolerance level up, just through practice. A lengthy association with Londo Mollari tended to do that.

As the waiter scurried off to fulfill Vir's request, he added, "Keep in mind, Minister, that I'm posted on Babylon 5. I've known the president of the Alliance for a great many years. I wouldn't presume to comment on what I've heard goes on here, so you might want to consider carefully your own sentiments when speaking about the Alliance."

"And what have you heard 'goes on' here?" Durla asked with one eyebrow slightly raised in curiosity.

Vir looked down and saw that the next drink was in his hand, as if it had materialized there by magic. He downed half of it in one gulp. He had a feeling that this evening, he was going to need it. "Oh, crazy rumors. People disappearing. Our more moderate politicians losing face, losing power . . . losing lives. And all of them being replaced by associates of yours."

"You overestimate me, Mr. Ambassador," Durla said, sounding quite sincerely modest. "Granted, I tend to recommend to the emperor people whom I know to be trustworthy. But since Internal Security is within my purview, naturally it would make sense to bring in those who I know will be loyal to the Republic."

"Don't you mean, to you?"

"I say what I mean, Ambassador," Durla replied, unperturbed. "In point of fact, it is the emperor who is the living incarnation of the spirit of the Centauri Republic. If I am to be concerned about loyalties to anyone in particular, it should be to him."

"How very gracious of you, Minister," Londo finally spoke up. "These are, after all, dangerous times. It is difficult to know whom we can trust."

"Absolutely true," Durla said. He clapped Vir on the shoulder. "I believe that I may have given you the wrong impression, Ambassador. May my tongue snap off if I say something that gives you a moment's concern."

"Now that's something I'd pay to see," Vir said.

Apparently missing the sarcasm, Durla continued, "Ultimately, we all want the same thing. A restoration of Centauri Republic to the arena of interstellar greatness we once enjoyed."

"We do?"

"Of course, Ambassador!" Durla said, as if he were stating a given. "At this point in time, to many, we are nothing but a joke. A beaten, fallen foe. Entire systems are allied against us and would keep us down. Once . . . once they quivered in fear at the very mention of our name. Now . . . they quiver with laughter."

"Terrible," intoned Londo, as if he'd had the conversation a thousand times before. Vir couldn't help but notice that Londo was putting away liquor at somewhere around triple the rate that Vir was maintaining. Indeed, faster than anyone in the place, it seemed. "A terrible thing."

"And even now, as we rebuild, as we break our backs to settle the 'reparations' while we try to restore our own pride ... they watch over us. They treat us as we once treated the Narns. Now what would you call that?"

"Poetic justice?" ventured Vir.

As if Vir had not spoken—indeed, Durla probably hadn't even heard him—Durla answered his own question. "Insults! Insult piled upon insult! The potential for greatness still lives within Centauri Prime, still burns like a fever within the bodies of our people."

"Aren't fevers generally considered a bad thing?" Vir asked. "You know ... sometimes you die from them ..."

"And sometimes they bring greater clarity of vision," said Durla.

"I usually just get headaches."

"We walked among the stars," Durla said forcefully. "When you have had the stars, how are you supposed to content yourself with the dirt beneath your feet? Do you know what I want for my people, Ambassador? Do you want to know the truth? I want my people to reclaim their rightful place in the galaxy. I want to see the Centauri stretch forth their hand again and command the stars. I want a rebirth of glory. I want us to be what we used to be. Does that seem too much to ask, Ambassador?"

It was Londo who replied, swirling a drink around in his glass and staring down at it. "No," he said softly. "No ... it does not seem too much to ask at all."

Durla was about to continue, but someone called his name from over on the other side of the room. Apparently some sort of friendly dispute was going on, and Durla was being asked to come and settle it. He bowed quickly and graciously to Vir and Londo, and headed off.

Several more officials came toward Londo, clamoring for his attention, but Londo waved them away. Instead he placed a hand on the small of Vir's back and said, "Come, walk with me, Vir. Catch me up on all the latest developments."

"Well, here's a late development: I do not like him, Londo. This Durla. Not one bit." Vir was speaking in a whisper, albeit an angry one.

"Durla? What is wrong with Durla?" Londo sounded almost shocked.

"Look, don't take this wrong, but . . . in some ways, he reminds me of you. That is, the way you used to be."

"He doesn't remind me of me at all."

"Are you kidding? All those things he was saying about what he wants us to be? Doesn't that sound like something you might have said once?"

"No. I never would have said any such thing."

Vir rolled his eyes in annoyance as Londo guided him down one of the large corridors. "Where are we going?" he asked.

"On a tour. Much work has been done on the palace since you were last here." He glanced at Vir. His vision appeared a bit bleary. "So let me understand this: you say that Durla reminds you of me, and on that basis you don't like him. I suppose I should be insulted, no?"

"When I first met you, back then you . . . well, you were somewhat intimidating, Londo. And you had these visions for what the Centauri should be. And you . . ."

"Fulfilled them," Londo said softly.

"Yes. And millions died because of it."

"Such harsh words. Do you judge me, Vir? You dare judge the emperor?" There was challenge in the words, but in the tone there was only interest.

"I know you, Londo. Sometimes I think I know you better than anyone alive . . . or at least, anyone who's left alive. He shares your dream, Londo. And look what became of it. Look at all the death, destruction, and tragedy that arose from it."

"The road to one's destiny is never a smooth one, Vir. There are always bumps along the way . . ."

"Bumps! Londo, we slaughtered the Narns! We spread a reign of terror! And that sin came back to revisit us a hundredfold! Those actions came solely because of the kind of thinking that Durla is standing there spouting! When are we going to learn, Londo? What's it going to take! The annihilation of every Centauri in the galaxy?"

"Why are you asking me?" inquired Londo. "Do you know who you should ask? Rem Lanas."

"I'm sorry . . . what?" Vir felt as if the conversation had abruptly veered off at another angle completely. "Rem Lanas? Who is—"

"He is on Babylon 5, as I recall. Has been for some time. Very wise individual. Do you know why you are here, Vir?"

Vir was having trouble following the thread of whatever it was they were supposed to be talking about. "Well, I . . . well, no, Londo, to be honest. I'm pleased that this party is being held, just because it's nice to see our people celebrating something—anything—even if it's just a group pat on the back to enjoy the reconstruction plans. But I'm not sure why you asked me specifically to come."

"What are you insinuating, Vir?"

"Insinuating? I . . ." He sighed. "Londo . . . perhaps, well . . . you may have had a little too much to drink. Because to be honest, you're not talking very sensibl—"

"Could you possibly be implying," continued Londo, "that I couldn't speak to you via standard communications means if I desired to? That I'm worried about being unable to find a secure channel? That everything I say could be monitored by others? You're not saying that, are you, Vir?"

Mr. Garibaldi had once used an expression that Vir had found most curious: he had spoken of "the dime dropping," as a means of indicating that someone had just realized something. It wasn't a term Vir completely understood, particularly because he had no idea what a dime was, or where it might drop that would inspire in any way a moment of clarity.

However, at that moment, as Vir listened—really listened—to what Londo was saying, he suddenly got a vague inkling as to what a dime dropping might mean to him personally.

"No," Vir said very carefully. "I didn't intend to imply that at all." But he said it with such a careful tone of voice that he hoped to make it clear to Londo that he had grasped the subtext.

The mists of emptiness that had clouded Londo's eyes up until that moment seemed to part, ever so briefly. He nodded wordlessly. Then he opened his mouth to speak once again . . .

. . . and he staggered.

"Londo?"

Londo passed his face in front of his hands as if trying to brush away cobwebs, and when he lowered his hand there was an expression that seemed a combination of anger and resignation. "Building up your tolerance to alcohol, I see," he muttered.

"Somewhat, yes," Vir said.

"I wasn't talking to you."

"But—"

Londo suddenly switched his mood, sounding rather jovial again. "We have a superb gallery that is a tribute to previous emperors. We took existing statues and paintings, gathered them in one place—come, Vir! You should see it!"

"*Uhm* . . . all right . . ."

Chatting with what seemed excessive cheer, Londo guided Vir to the end of the corridor, hung a sharp right, then a left, and led him into a very sizeable room. Just as Londo had boasted, the walls were lined with a most impressive array of paintings and sculptures, the latter ensconced on carefully crafted shelves inset into the walls.

The first painting that naturally caught Vir's eye was Cartagia. Londo saw where Vir was looking, and echoed Vir's thoughts aloud: "Why is he here, eh?"

Vir nodded. "He was insane, Londo. An ugly part of our history. He shouldn't be here with the others."

"He has to be, Vir, *because* he is a part of history. If we do not recall that which we have done wrong, how can we be guided toward that which is right?"

"Apparently not everyone can agree on what is right and wrong," Vir said ruefully, glancing over his shoulder as if worried that Durla was going to be standing right behind him.

"You wouldn't be referring to Durla, would you? Calm yourself, Vir. His is not the only opinion out there."

"One wouldn't know it to look at the people in that room. They—"

"Vir . . . it doesn't matter. Look at these paintings. Are they not lovely?"

Vir was beginning to lose all patience with his emperor. "Yes, they're very lovely, but that's not the point—"

"Emperor Turhan . . ." Londo indicated one painting. "A great man."

"A great man," sniffed Vir. "With his dying words, he urged us to attack the Narn. You should know, you were the one he whispered them . . . to . . ." Vir's voice trailed off as he saw the expression on Londo's face. Once more, a dime dropped as he realized the awful secret Londo was hinting at . . . that Turhan's last words were *not* words of war. "Londo . . ."

"He died wanting peace with the Narn . . . and said that we and Refa were damned. A wise man, that." He said it without any hint of anger. If anything, he sounded amused.

But Vir was horrified. He took a step back, the blood draining from his face. "Londo ... Great Maker, Londo ... how could ... how could you—"

Londo shrugged.

"That's it? That's all the answer I get? A shrug? Londo, how ... how could you?"

"I have heard that question a great many times in my life, Vir, and interestingly, the answer is always the same: Easily."

Vir had absolutely no idea what to say. He had never before been rendered utterly speechless by Londo. Londo, for his part, seemed utterly unperturbed by Vir's clear discomfiture. Instead he simply said, "We do what we must, Vir. We always do. All of us. Take Emperor Kran. Do you remember him, Vir? Do you recall what happened?"

Vir's head was still spinning, as he tried to pull together all the fragments of what Londo had been saying. "Emperor Kran ... vaguely, yes. But that was before I was born, it—"

Londo had stopped in front of a bust of Kran. It was easily the smallest one in the room, as if its inclusion had almost been an afterthought. "Such a short-lived reign he had ... barely a footnote in our illustrious history. Ruler during a period of great transition. At the time, the Centauri houses were more fractured than ever before. The previous emperor, Turis, had been quite weak-willed, and with his passing, all the houses had commenced fighting for power. It threatened to be a bloodbath. Poor Kran ... do you recall what happened to him?"

"Yes, I think so. But—"

"Sometimes it is possible to agree on what is right and wrong. And we would not want the wrong things to happen again. Not to anyone. Not to *anyone*, Vir. Do you hear me?" Londo's voice was rising with unexpected vehemence. "Do you hear me, Vir? Are you attending to the words coming out of my mouth?"

"Yes, yes, of course." Vir felt more lost than ever. "Every word."

"Good. I am glad we had this talk. It will be best for all of us. Come ... the party is progressing without us. We wouldn't want them to think that fun can be had without us in the room, eh?

"Do you know what, Vir? And I want you to remember this: Everything around here, all that we have rebuilt, all the power at my command ... it makes me think of what I truly have. Not only that, but what we will all, within less than a week's time, all have."

"And what would that be?"

"Ah," grinned Londo. "That's all part of the great riddle of life, isn't it."

And with that utterly cryptic remark, he headed out of the room, leaving a completely perplexed Vir behind, to scratch his head and wonder what in the world had just occurred there.

When Vir entered his quarters for the evening, he was astounded to find the nubile dancing girl he'd been ogling earlier. She was wearing considerably less than she had been before. To be specific, she was clad in his bedsheet, which was wrapped around her on the bed. Vir stood there a moment, and then realized that since his mouth was moving, it would probably be at least good form to have syllables emerging in conjunction with the movement. "Uh . . . uh . . . uh . . . hello . . ."

"Hello," she purred.

"I'm . . . sorry to disturb you. I thought these were my assigned quarters. I'll just be out of your way . . ." Then Vir saw his suitcase over in the corner, and realized that he was exactly where he was supposed to be. So, apparently, was she.

"Would you care to join me?"

"Why? Are you coming apart?" Vir then forced laughter at his rather feeble attempt at humor. He saw no change in the small smile on the woman's face, and so he composed himself. "Uh . . . look . . . perhaps there's been some mistake . . ."

"You are Vir Cotto?" She repositioned herself, sweeping the blanket around her. Vir suddenly felt rather sweaty. He also felt some stray movement in the area of his chest and willed himself to calm down.

"Yes. But . . . may I ask how . . . that is to say . . ."

"Minister Durla felt that he might have offended you . . . and out of respect to your long history with the emperor, he asked me to make sure that there would be no hard feelings."

At the mention of Durla's name, even the most preliminary stirrings of interest promptly evaporated. "Durla. I see. Well . . ." Vir cleared his throat forcibly. "Here's a thought. I'll turn around and avert my eyes, and you can go get dressed and tell him everything's fine, and I appreciate the thought. All right?"

Disappointment flickered across her face. "Are you sure?"

"Miss . . . believe me when I tell you, decisions aren't always my strongest thing. I kind of go back and forth. But about this, yes, I'm absolutely sure." He turned his back to her and waited. He heard the rustling of the sheets as she slid out of bed, the whisper of cloth against her body as she dressed.

Moments later her hand trailed across his back as she cooed, "Good night then, Ambassador."

"Good night," Vir said in a strangled voice.

He waited long moments after the door hissed closed before he dared to trust himself to turn around. Then he let out a sigh of relief when he saw that she was, indeed, gone.

Durla. Durla had sent her. The very thought was horrifying. Furthermore, when he'd turned his back to her, he'd watched the shadow she cast quite carefully, to make sure she didn't come at him with a knife while his back was turned. That, rather than generosity, would be much more in character with Durla's way of doing things.

"Now I remember why I don't spend a lot of time on Centauri Prime. I hate it here."

He made sure his door was locked and changed quickly for bed. But sleep did not come. Instead he lay on his back, staring up at the ceiling, thinking about what Londo had said. It seemed so random, so confusing, as if Londo was unable to hold a coherent thought in his head.

Who was Rem Lanas? And all that conversation about Emperor Kran? And . . .

That riddle. About what was greater than the Great Maker? What did that riddle have anything to do with anything? The truth was, it seemed completely unrelated to anything that had gone on.

What was greater than the Great Maker? The rest of the riddle made no sense, couldn't progress any further, because the truth was that, quite simply, nothing was greater than the Great Maker. Oh, certainly it was impossible to understand why he had allowed the Republic to slip into such disarray, why he had stood silently by and allowed the bombings and . . .

Suddenly Vir sat up, his eyes wide, and he felt a momentary sense of glee, almost childlike in its exuberance.

"Nothing," he said out loud. "The answer is nothing."

It made perfect sense. Nothing was greater than the Great Maker. Nothing was more frightening than the Shadow ships . . . to that, Vir would personally attest. The poor have nothing. The rich need nothing. And if you eat nothing . . . then you die.

A good riddle. A thought provoker.

But then Vir thought of something else Londo had said. Something about . . .

What had Londo's exact words been?

"Everything around here, all that we have rebuilt, all the power at my command . . . it makes me think of what I truly have. Not only that, but what we will all, within less than a week's time, all have." And he had referred to it as being part of the great riddle of life.

Nothing. Londo was telling him that he felt he had nothing. As if he wanted to make sure Vir was aware that he was truly unhappy with his situation. But why? Why not just come out and say so? And why was he so unhappy anyway, if he was being given the opportunity to rebuild Centauri Prime in his own image. Where was the tragedy, the sadness in that?

And . . . they would all have nothing? Within a week's time?

It made no sense.

Or perhaps it did, and Vir was simply unwilling or unable to put it all together.

The next morning he went straight to the throne room, but guards blocked the door. "I need to see the emperor," he said.

The guards simply stared at him as if he hadn't spoken.

"It's urgent."

"I'm afraid that the emperor is seeing no one today." The voice came from behind. It was Durla, strolling calmly down the corridor and looking so at home that it seemed to Vir as if Durla thought he owned the place.

"And why is that?"

Durla shrugged. "I do not question my emperor's orders, Ambassador. I simply obey them. I would suggest that you do likewise."

"How do I know that those are his orders?" Vir demanded. "How do I know he's even still alive?"

Durla appeared startled at the very suggestion. "I am shocked that you would insinuate some sort of plot against the emperor, Ambassador. I assure you he's in his throne room. He simply desires seclusion."

"Look," Vir said hotly. "Unless I—"

The door to the throne room suddenly opened.

Vir turned and peered through and, sure enough, there was Londo on his throne. He sat there, resolutely, staring straight ahead, not so much as an inch of his body twitching or giving any indication that he was alive. And then, ever so slightly, Londo turned his head and looked in Vir's direction. He nodded once as if to say, *It's all right. Go.* Then he went back to staring straight ahead, not speaking, not even giving any indication that he was aware Vir was still in the doorway.

Vir stepped back and the doors closed. He turned to Durla, who simply smiled and said, "Have a safe journey back to Babylon 5. Do visit us again . . . very soon." And with that he headed off down the corridor.

The sleeper approached wakefulness. One of the dark ones was nearing. He sensed its approach and prepared to come to full consciousness. He had remained hidden in the darkness, waiting for his chance, preparing for the opportunity to serve the dark ones.

It was a confusing time for him. He felt as if his mind were splitting in two, and yet merging for the first time. As if he were about to encounter a long-lost twin from whom he had been separated moments after being spit from his mother's womb.

He found himself staring at shadows for long periods of time. There was quite an abundance of them in Down Below. Each of them seemed to cloak its own mysterious secrets. Once, like most people, the sleeper had feared shadows. But now he found himself embracing them, feeling the coolness of them.

Then the shadows began to call him . . . one in particular. He felt himself drawn to it, to one particular corner. There was no one else around. Step by unsteady step he drew closer and closer to it, sensing that for the first time, his life was going to make some degree of sense. Indeed, of late he had been filled with a curious emptiness.

He remembered his parents, his mother holding him close, his father schooling him in his first lessons. He remembered them . . . but only as if from a distance, as if his mind embraced them, but they were absent from his heart.

He remembered the first woman he had made love to, the press of her flesh against his, the warmth of her kiss. He remembered her . . . but he could not actually feel her. He knew that he had been intertwined with her, but could not feel the sensation of it.

It was as if the entirety of his life had been some sort of video, observed but not actually experienced firsthand.

He wondered if this was a commonplace feeling. If other people felt the same way about their memories.

Meantime, deep within him, something not quite biological, not quite technical, stirred and moved in response to the summons from the shadowy area.

He moved toward the corner, and there was something there . . . something grey, with a hand outstretched, summoning him . . .

. . . no . . . not him . . . it . . .

8

Zack Allan, the security head of Babylon 5, was staring at Vir, one brow arched, his piercing eyes filled with open curiosity. "Rem Lanas? You want to find out about a Rem Lanas?"

Vir, sitting in Zack's office, kept his hands neatly folded in his lap. "If it wouldn't be too much trouble."

"Is he one of yours? I mean a Centauri?"

"That's right. Normally, we could find one of our own people, of course, but thanks to the bombings, our records are a mess. We think he's here, but we're not sure."

"Important in some way?"

Vir shifted uncomfortably in his seat. "Is there any reason you're asking me so many questions, Mr. Allan? Not that," he added quickly, "I mind answering them. I don't. I wouldn't mind answering your questions all day. I really didn't have anything else blocked out on my schedule. So if you want to keep—"

Zack put up a hand to still the torrent of words spilling from Vir. "I just wanted to know," Zack said slowly, "if he presents any sort of a security risk and if I should be worried."

"A security risk! Oh . . . oh, no. That's funny." Vir quickly laughed, a sort of high-pitched blurt. "That's really funny. A Centauri, presenting a security risk. No," he said, suddenly serious. "No, none of our people present any sort of a risk, security or otherwise. We, that is, I, wouldn't want anyone to think that the Centauri in any way are threatening. Because, you know, as soon as that happens come the ships, and the booming, and the shooting, and, well . . . it's a mess. We don't want that. No one wants that. I know I don't, you don't . . ."

"Rem Lanas."

"I'm sure he doesn't, either."

"I mean," Zack said patiently, "who is he? Why do you need to find him?"

"Well . . ." Vir *harrumphed* to buy himself a few seconds, and then said, "Money."

"Money? What about it?"

"Rem Lanas has come into a sizeable amount of it. His father died. And Lanas has come into a sizeable inheritance, so his parents want to get in touch with him, let him know . . ."

" 'Parents.' You just said his father was dead."

"Yes, that's . . . right. That is, his adoptive parents. His father gave him up for adoption when he was quite young, and when his father was dying, he felt so guilty that he left everything to his son. It's a tragic story. Very unexpected death. His father was an opera singer, you see, and he was performing an outdoor concert, and his mouth was wide open as he was trying to jump an octave, and suddenly this low-flying bird—"

"Okay, okay, okay," said Zack quickly, clearly not wanting to hear the climax of the story. "Let me see if we've got any record of a Rem Lanas coming through here."

As Zack checked through the computers, Vir's mind was racing. Lying simply was not his strong suit. He felt tremendously uncomfortable and very exposed whenever he was trying to do it. One would have thought that, working with Londo for as long as he had, he would have acquired a knack for it. The one thing he had going for him was that he tended to babble to the point where people would accept whatever he was saying, just to shut him up. With one lie, he was ineffective. With an avalanche of lies, he could squeak by.

The thing was, he wasn't sure who Rem Lanas was, or what significance he held. But out of nowhere, Londo had made mention of him.

Vir remembered that day on Centauri Prime, that day when Londo had made his address to the Centauri people, an address that had reeked of anger and had seemed more an urging for revenge than reconciliation. When Sheridan, Delenn, and G'Kar had expressed their reservations about such a curious direction for his speech, Vir had loyally assured them that Londo must have had his reasons. He had believed it at the time, and he believed it still. Londo always had reasons for what he did. Some of them were truly horrific, but they were reasons nonetheless.

So when Londo had spoken of this Rem Lanas fellow, Vir—after fighting through his initial confusion—had resolved that somehow, for some reason, Londo was trying to tell him something. For that reason, he had gone straight to Zack's office as soon as he had returned to the station. He wasn't sure why he was there, or what he was trying to find out, or what he would do with the knowledge once he did find it, but he couldn't think that far down the line. He had to operate one step at a time.

"Got him," Zack said.

Zack's declaration brought Vir out of his reverie. "You do? Where?"

"I don't mean that we actually have him in custody . . . why? Should we?"

Vir laughed nervously. "Of course not. Why would you?"

"According to this," continued Zack, looking over the records, "he arrived on the station about six months ago." He paused, studied the computer screen for a few more moments, and then said, "This could be a problem."

"What? What's a problem?"

"Well," said Zack, scratching his chin thoughtfully, "there's no record of him leasing any rooms here. No job employment record. If I had to guess, he's probably in Down Below."

"Down Below? Are you sure?"

"No, I'm not sure. For instance, if he'd somehow managed to sneak off the station without our knowing it, he'd be gone. Or he might have gotten a room or job using faked ID."

"But that doesn't make a lot of sense. If he had fake ID, why would he use it for one thing, but not the other?" Vir said.

Zack grinned. "Very good, Mr. Cotto. You might have a future in the exciting field of security."

"Really? You think so? Or you are kidding?"

"I'm kidding."

"Oh." Vir felt slightly crestfallen.

"But you're right. There's no reason for him to come in under his real name and then fake his presence elsewhere. Which brings me back to my original guess: he's Down Below. Residences down there are pretty much catch-as-catch-can; set up a tent and you're a resident. Run money for one of the shady types down there, and you're employed. Do you want me to send some people down to find him?"

"No," Vir said quickly. "I'll handle it. I'm, well . . . I'm a friend of the family. I promised I'd do it. It's kind of . . . an honor thing."

"Oh. An honor thing."

"That's right. Well, thank you for all your help. If you could forward a copy of his photograph and records to my quarters, I'd be most appreciative." Vir stood, pumped Zack's hand with such ferocity that he threatened to snap it off at the wrist, and then left Zack's office as fast as he could.

When he got to his door, he stood there, slightly out of breath, composing his thoughts. His hearts were racing and he didn't even fully grasp why that would be the case. All he knew was that he was beginning to sense that something was happening . . . something that Londo actually had the answers to. But Londo would not tell him more than he already had, would not give him anything more than dribs and drabs . . .

Would not? Or . . . could not?

Was it possible that Londo had simply told him as much as he could, somehow? Even that made no sense, though. There had been no one except Londo and himself there in the portrait gallery. Was Londo that concerned that he was being watched, listened to wherever he went in the palace? But they could have gone outside, then, or found a place—some place, *any* place—that could be shielded from prying eyes and ears. Londo would certainly have been clever enough to come up with somewhere that was secure.

But . . . what if there was no place left that was secure?

The notion was utterly horrifying to Vir. Could that be possible? Could it be that someone was capable of monitoring Londo, no matter where he went? Perhaps they had managed to implant some sort of tracking or listening device upon him. But . . . why would he stand still for something like that? Why would he submit to it? He was the emperor. The emperor of the Centauri Republic! Much of the Republic might be in ruins, but it still was what it was. One had to respect the office, if not the man holding it.

Then again, I assassinated Londo's predecessor, so who am I to talk . . .

If that were the case . . . if Londo was somehow wearing some sort of bugging device, or if—at the very least—there was someone whose presence was so pervasive that even Londo was wary of it, then that was a situation that had to be addressed. But who could be responsible for such a state of affairs?

Durla. That had to be the answer.

Perhaps, Vir reasoned, Durla was blackmailing him somehow. Perhaps he had gotten his hands on some sort of dire truth about Londo, and was trading upon silence in exchange for power. And while he was at it, he was keeping Londo on a tight leash . . .

It made Vir wonder—what could Durla possibly know that would cause Londo to submit to that . . . that slimy little man's will, rather than allow it to be made public? After all, Londo's greatest and most awful actions weren't secrets, they were part of the résumé that had obtained him the rank of emperor in the first place. What could Londo possibly have done that would be considered so repellant?

No matter what it was, the whole business made Vir extremely edgy. It made him wonder just how paranoid he himself was becoming, and how paranoid he should be. Durla definitely knew Vir's background, and Vir had the uneasy feeling that he, too, might be targeted somehow. It depended, of course, on just how seriously Durla perceived him as a threat, and whether Vir stood in the way—intentionally or not—of whatever it was that Durla saw as his goal.

Vir's mind was spinning, and as he finally opened the door to enter his quarters, he jumped nearly a foot in the air when a voice said, "Hi there."

Vir sagged against the wall, clutching his major heart. "Mr. Garibaldi," he managed to gasp. "What are you doing here? How did you get in here?"

"When you've had a job like security chief," Michael Garibaldi said, rising from the chair in which he had apparently made himself quite comfortable, "you pick up a few things. And you hang on to them, even when you move upstairs to become the head of security for the president of the Alliance. Speaking of which . . . he'd like to see you."

"He would?"

"Yes. What? Does that make you nervous?"

"Nervous?" laughed Vir. "Why would you say that?"

"Well, when you're nervous about something, you tend to flap your hands about a bit . . . kind of like you're doing right now."

"What? Oh, this. No, no . . . I'm just having some minor circulation problems, so I'm trying to get the blood flowing." He flailed his hands for a moment, then said, "Well, that seems to have done it," and folded his arms tightly across his chest. "What does he want to see me about?"

"Beats me. You know how it goes . . . 'ours is not to question why, ours is but to' . . . well, you know."

"Yes, of course I do. I do? I mean . . . actually, I don't. Ours is but to . . . what?"

"Do or die."

"Ah. What a wonderful saying," Vir said with a marked lack of enthusiasm.

"It's from a poem, actually. 'The Charge of the Light Brigade.' "

"Oh. It's about a brigade that charges at faster than light speeds?"

Garibaldi let out a sigh, then smiled gamely and gestured toward the door. "I'll explain on the way," he said.

They stepped out and headed down the hallway. Vir's mind was in even more turmoil. Garibaldi, as always, wasn't giving any indication as to what was on his mind. What did he know? How *much* did he know? For that matter, how much did Vir himself know? He felt as if he had no grounding at all, as if he were about to float away.

Garibaldi was chatting away about something of absolutely no consequence. Vir continued to smile and nod and give every indication he was listening, which he really wasn't. He rubbed the corner of his eye . . . and saw . . . something.

It was just there, just for a moment, but when Vir turned his gaze to look head on, it was gone. He blinked, rubbed his eye again, and tried to spot whatever it was, without truly knowing what it was he was endeavoring to see.

"Vir, are you all right?" asked Garibaldi, actually sounding a touch concerned.

Vir tried to recreate for himself the mental impression that had been left upon him. He thought he had spotted someone, someone cloaked, watching him with what appeared to be a wry smile. But now he was gone, and Vir was wondering whether or not he was completely losing it from the stress.

Yes, that was it—stress. More stress than he had ever really known. And the killing aspect of it was that he still had no clear idea of just what it was he was stressed over.

With more honesty than was probably wise for him at that particular point in time, Vir answered, "No, Mr. Garibaldi. No, I'm not all right. And you know what? You know what the absolute worst part of it is?" Garibaldi shook his head. "The worst part," continued Vir, "is that if I *were* all right . . . the feeling would be so unfamiliar to me, that I'd probably be totally terrified of it and wouldn't know what to do. Do you know what I'm saying?"

"Yeah. Yeah, I think I do. Basically, you're afraid to let your guard down."

But Vir shook his head. "No. That's not quite it at all. It's not that I'm afraid to do so. It's that I've forgotten how."

"Vir," Garibaldi said slowly, "considering the things that have gone on here ... and the things that continue to go on back on Centauri Prime ... maybe that's a blessing in disguise."

"Then it's a very cunning disguise," said Vir.

John Sheridan rose from behind his desk when Vir entered. Dressed in his customary dark suit, he stroked his neatly trimmed, slightly greying beard and looked at Vir pensively. Vir tried to get a read off Sheridan's face that might indicate exactly what the problem was, but Sheridan was far too old a hand to let the slightest hint slip through. Sheridan had been president for nearly a year, and in the four years that Vir had known him, he had never seen the man tip his hand until he was ready. "Vir, it's good to see you," he said, extending his hand. "Your trip to and from Centauri Prime went without incident, I trust?"

"Oh yes. The best kind of space travel. The uneventful kind."

He shook Sheridan's hand firmly. It was just one of the many Human traditions to which he'd had to become accustomed. He recalled very clearly when he'd first arrived on Babylon 5—he had been so nervous that his hands had been incredibly clammy.

Vir had never forgotten the expression on then-Captain Sinclair's face, or the way he had fought to maintain a polite demeanor while subtly trying to wipe his drenched hand on his trouser leg. As for Londo, well, Londo had just been too stunned to say or do anything other than to get Vir the hell out of there.

He'd come a long way in the succeeding years. Yet, in many ways, he felt just as disconcerted as ever.

"That's good. That's good." Sheridan rapped his knuckles briskly on the desk. "Well ... I'm sure you're quite busy ..."

"Actually, no. I just got back, so my schedule is wide open."

Vir was just trying to be helpful, but he could tell from Sheridan's expression that that wasn't what he had wanted to hear. He realized belatedly that it was simply a conversational gambit, a means of jumping briskly to the point. "But if anyone's busy, it's you, Mr. President," Vir added quickly, "and I appreciate your taking the time to discuss ... well, whatever it is we have to discuss. So ... why don't we get right to it, then."

"Yes, I ... suppose we should." He paused for a moment. "This is in regard to the tour of Down Below that's scheduled for tomorrow."

"The tour," Vir echoed, his face a perfect blank.

"Yes. There's a movement among various members of the Al-

liance to attend to the conditions in Down Below. They feel it represents, well . . . something they're not comfortable with. Some of the
races don't like to be reminded that their cultures have any 'have-
nots,' and Down Below is most definitely a haven for the unfortunate."

"So they want to get rid of a haven?"

"Not exactly. There's a sort of reclamation project in the works.
Various races are pooling their resources, trying to convince many of
the expatriots who have fled to Down Below to return to their Homeworlds. Plus, there are corporate sponsors who are interested in becoming involved in Down Below. Cleaning it up."

"It's hard to believe that would be possible."

"I know. Taking the dark underbelly of Babylon 5 and making it
over into something approachable—I swear, some sponsors actually
believe they can transform Down Below into a place so friendly that
people would take their families down there, on holiday. It's a pipe
dream, I think, but . . ." He shrugged. Vir mirrored the gesture. "In
any event, representatives from the various sponsors and member
races are gathering for this tour. It's been fairly well publicized, actually. If you ask me, it's more an exercise in politics than anything
else. A chance to stage a media event in order for the representatives
to look good to the folks back home. Oldest political maneuvering in
the book. And, as you know, an invitation went out to you, asking you
to be a part of the tour. Since you are the Centauri representative to
Babylon 5, it only seemed right."

"Yes, of course. And don't think I didn't appreciate it," said Vir.

In point of fact, he didn't remember receiving the invitation.
Vir's appointment as ambassador was still relatively recent. He didn't
even have an assistant—one had not been assigned him. His personal
finances were extremely tight, particularly after the bombings had
left his family's holdings in disarray, and he still hadn't had any sort
of concrete budget established by the home office. He had hoped to
discuss that problem with Londo, but somehow the opportunity had
never presented itself.

As a result, Vir often felt a bit overwhelmed. Fortunately he had
a great many organizational skills of his own, what with having been
Londo's aide for all those years. But while it was one thing simply to
be the aide to the ambassador, to juggle both positions was proving
something of a strain.

Still, he saw absolutely no reason to admit as much to Sheridan.

So instead he nodded and smiled and maintained the fiction that he was perfectly clear on just what it was that Sheridan was getting at.

"The problem is . . . I find myself in a bit of an uncomfortable situation," Sheridan admitted. "The simple fact is that several members of the Alliance looked over the list of invited attendees, saw that your name was on it, and became rather . . . incensed."

"Incensed?"

"Understand, Vir, it's nothing personal," Sheridan said quickly. "I know you to be a fine, upstanding, and highly moral individual. But the others, they don't know you, and just assume you to be a . . ."

"Typical Centauri?" He saw Sheridan's discomfiture and sighed sadly. "It's all right, you can say it. I know my people's conduct hasn't won us a large number of allies. We've raped what we've sown; isn't that how you Humans would put it?"

"Actually, we'd say 'reaped,' but considering what was done to some worlds by the Centauri . . ." Then he shook it off. "No. No reason for rehashing the past. The bottom line, Vir, is that several key members' races have stated that they don't want you—that is to say, any representative of Centauri Prime—along on the tour. There's still a good deal of anger and bruised feelings, not only over the Republic's past actions, but in response to the current attitude that's being displayed on Centauri Prime—toward the Alliance. Everything from Londo's speech to the publication of *Verity*, the new Centauri official newspaper."

"Oh yes. *Verity*." Now that was indeed something with which Vir was quite familiar. Since the restoration had begun, the various independent publications available on Centauri Prime had dwindled very nearly to nonexistence. But then, out of nowhere, *Verity* had appeared, billing itself as the "Voice of the Centauri People."

It purported to be an utterly independent publication, but the rumor was that it was simply the mouthpiece of certain government factions. Now that Vir had been back to Centauri Prime, he would have bet that Minister Durla's hand was somewhere deep into *Verity*'s pockets, controlling everything that went on with the publication. There was no way to prove it, though, and there was certainly no reason to raise the issue with Sheridan. It wasn't as if he could do anything, or should even if he could.

Verity took every opportunity to besmirch the name, honor, and intentions of the Interstellar Alliance. The publication advocated a return to Centauri greatness . . . although Vir couldn't help but notice that precisely how they might return to greatness was always left

rather vague. It was as if the publication was content to stir nationalistic fires among the readership without actually giving them a tangible goal. Or at least, not just yet.

"So you're saying that you don't want me to attend," Vir said.

"No. No, I'm not saying that at all. The Alliance has to understand that the best way to work toward a future is to do so with as
many allies as possible. And that includes the Centauri. I'm letting
you know about the hostility, though, because it's very likely that
there will be some who will do everything they can to make you feel
uncomfortable. Rest assured, though, that I will do everything within
my power . . ."

"That . . . won't be necessary," said Vir quietly. "I have no desire
to put you in a difficult position."

"Vir—" Sheridan had to laugh. "—I'm president of the Interstellar Alliance. Being in difficult positions comes with the job description."

"Yes, I know that. Nevertheless, that doesn't mean that I have to
make the job any more difficult than it already is, right? The simple
truth, Mr. President, is that I don't want to be somewhere that I'm
not especially wanted. Trust me on this: I've had a lot of experience
with not being wanted in various places. So I've got a fairly thick skin
when it comes to this kind of thing."

"Vir—"

Vir got to his feet. "I very much appreciate the opportunity to
have this talk, Mr. President. I'm glad we did. I'm glad I know where
I . . . where we, that is to say, the Centauri Republic . . . stand."

"Vir, didn't you hear what I said?" Sheridan said, in obvious exasperation. "I'm not about to let the Alliance push me around. I was
just giving you a sort of 'heads up' over a potentially difficult situation, but that doesn't mean . . ."

"Actually, Mr. President . . . it does. It does mean . . . precisely
what you think it does. I have to go now."

Vir headed for the door. Sheridan came around his desk, looking
rather concerned. "Vir . . ." he started to say.

Vir turned to face him, squared his shoulders and said, "I think
. . . I think it'd be better if you called me 'Ambassador Cotto' for the
time being." And with that, he walked out of Sheridan's office.

9

Everything seemed so clear to Durla, although rarely more so than when he was sleeping.

When he was awake, he knew what it was that he wanted for Centauri Prime. But there was so much to deal with, so many details to attend to. People clamoring for his attention, this chancellor wanting something, that minister requiring five minutes of his time. It was always five minutes, at least in theory. Naturally, once he was in any given meeting, five minutes became fifteen, or twenty, or half an hour, and the next thing he knew his entire schedule was simply shot. It was just so easy to get distracted by everything.

But when he was asleep, why, there was when he saw the future—his future—with glorious clarity.

He saw himself standing hundreds of feet tall in the air, a giant holographic projection that could be seen for miles. That, indeed, could be seen all over the world. He saw himself addressing the people, leading them, rallying them, and they were shouting his name over and over, praising him, begging him to let them share in his glorious and great vision.

He spoke to them of the magnificence that was Centauri Prime's destiny, of all that the great republic was going to accomplish under his leadership. Once more they shouted his name, and over and over again. It was quite exhilarating, really.

He had always aspired to greatness, ever since he had been told that it was something he would never be able to accomplish.

His father was a military man, and very demanding. He had produced two sons, within a year of each other, and it had taken very little time in their development to realize who was the favored son. It wasn't Durla. No, it was his older brother, Solla.

It had been difficult for Durla to hate Solla. In addition to being a great scholar and a brilliant soldier, Solla had also possessed a kind heart. As fearsome as he could be in times of combat, he was equally compassionate when dealing with his younger brother. Only a year separated them, true, but it might as well have been a chasm. Durla had had to work for everything that he achieved, whereas for Solla it seemed to come easily. He made it all appear effortless. He rarely seemed to study, and yet he scored higher grades than Durla. Durla never saw him practicing, and yet Solla's blade was easily the deadliest in the city.

Everyone knew that Solla was going far.

That was why Durla had to kill him.

The final straw had been Solla's woman. She had been incredibly beautiful, amazingly exotic, the daughter of a highborn noble. And young Durla, just turning his twentieth year, had seen her during one of their infrequent trips to the emperor's court. Unfortunately for Durla, the woman had seen Solla, and become instantly smitten with him. Solla was likewise taken with her, and who could blame him? Luminous eyes, a long, red, plaited braid that hung alluringly off the side of her head, a body so firm and sculpted that when she walked the sinew of her muscle played gloriously just beneath her bronzed skin. Every time Durla saw her, his body ached for her.

As it turned out, he wasn't alone. There was another Centauri as well, who served in the imperial troops alongside Durla and Solla. His name was Riva, and his passion for the woman—Mariel—was so great that he and Solla came to blows over her. A vicious battle it had been, and Solla had won because, well, Solla always won. Riva, however, had loudly vowed vengeance, declaring that his conflict with Solla was not over by a longshot.

This was all the opening that Durla had needed. Smitten with the woman, resentful over his brother's greatness and the way that his parents had always treated Solla with the respect and idolization Durla had felt he was entitled to, Durla had required no further incentive. He had poisoned Solla . . . and himself.

That had been the trickiest aspect of it. He had ingested the same poison that he had placed in Solla's food. It was the most effective means of avoiding suspicion. What he'd had to do was be certain to eat enough to show genuine signs of illness, but too little to prove fatal to him. He had succeeded, and no sooner had Solla breathed his last, the venomous poison having consumed his body, than Riva had been accused of perpetrating the deed. Riva's fellow squad mates had gone to arrest him. Unfortunately—or fortunately, depending upon one's point of view—Riva hadn't surrendered quietly. Ultimately, he didn't surrender at all, but instead resisted arrest, which was always a foolish notion when those who are trying to arrest you, *a*, outnumber you and, *b*, are already incensed with you because they believe—however mistakenly—that you are responsible for the death of their friend.

As a result, by the end of the arrest, pieces of Riva wound up littering the immediate area.

This had all been tremendously beneficial for Durla, as was to be expected. His grief-stricken parents had lavished their attention on him, partly out of guilt, but mostly because he was their only remaining son and they knew that he was their only chance for vicarious success.

As for the girl . . .

Durla had gone to her with his medals on his breast and his heart on his sleeve. He had gone to her and, while acting the tragedy-struck younger brother, also made it clear to her that he adored her, and hopefully no longer from afar.

She had looked at him with a mixture of amusement and pity. "Pathetic boy," she had said archly, although it was a curious choice of words since she was, in fact, several years younger than he. "My house has greater plans for me than being tied to you. Your brother was going places: Places of strength. Places of power. But you . . . you will only see such places from a distance. At least, that is what my father says, and he is usually quite intuitive when it comes to such things. He thought highly of Solla as husband potential . . . Riva slightly less so, but viable. You, though? You will always be the younger brother of the noble Solla, who was cut down in his prime. You, I am afraid, don't matter very much at all."

Then she had laughed and walked away, with a sway of slender hips under a stunningly sheer fabric. "Mariel!" he called after her. "Mariel, wait! Wait, I love you! If you only had any idea of what I did to be with you—"

She didn't, of course. That was likely fortunate, for if she had known, Durla would have wound up in prison . . . if his father and mother hadn't killed him first. Instead, Mariel was shortly thereafter linked with the House Mollari. Her hand in marriage had been given . . .

To him.

To Londo Mollari.

Durla had been present at their bonding. He had no idea why he had subjected himself to it . . . no. No, he did have an idea. It was more like a fantasy, actually. He fantasized that Mariel would suddenly come to her senses at the last moment. That she would throw over Mollari for him. That she would run from Mollari, realizing the hideous mistake that she was about to make, and call to Durla to rescue her.

And then . . . then there would be a glorious battle. He would fight his way out, Mariel at his side singing his praises. He would battle through the crowd, and then he and Mariel would run and keep running, leaving it all behind to start a new life.

It was a very nice fantasy. Unfortunately it had no relation whatsoever to reality. The bonding ceremony had proceeded without interruption, and Mariel hadn't so much as glanced in Durla's direction.

He stood in the back of the room, trembling with suppressed rage as the sight, the very thought, of Mollari sent him into barely contained spasms of fury. Mollari was an appalling specimen of Centauri manhood. He was too old for Mariel, he was too ugly for Mariel. Mollari was a respected house, true, but Londo wasn't an especially promising member of that house. A third-level bottom feeder at best, that was Durla's assessment of him. Everything about Londo had grated on Durla. The way he wore his hair, the scowl lines in his forehead, his deep, pronounced northern province accent, his tendency to declaim as if, even in casual conversation, he was speaking to people from a balcony. A thoroughly deplorable and unlikeable individual, that was Londo Mollari.

And yet it would be his lips upon Mariel's. It would be his hands caressing her, his tentacles that—

It was all that Durla could do to remain there and see the ceremony through to its end. But he did, and when the crowds of wellwishers surrounded Londo and Mariel as they prepared to depart, Durla had made certain to hang far back. He kept waiting for Mariel, at the very least, to look around and see if she could spot him. She did not. Instead she never took her eyes from Londo. She seemed happy to be married to him, content with her lot in life.

Inside, Durla was screaming.

That had been many years earlier, of course. His interest in Mariel had been a blistering hot obsession forged in the fires of youthful interest, and nothing more. That was what he told himself. He was over her; she was part of his past . . . indeed, truth to tell, she had never really been a part of his life at all. Merely a fantasy.

And yet, he had never married. Never even seriously pursued a romantic relationship.

Instead he had focused all his energies upon his career. If he could not please himself, at least he could work on pleasing his parents, in general, and his father, in particular. In that regard, he attained a measure of success.

To his father, it was Solla who remained the true jewel in the family crown. Even in death, Solla was thought of more highly. However Durla managed to work his way through the ranks by dint of sheer determination and hard work, and that sort of dedication had to count for something.

In the meantime, he had kept tabs on Londo Mollari. It hadn't been difficult. People generally spoke of him in very derisive tones, making no secret of their opinions. Mollari would talk longingly of times past and how he wanted the Centauri Republic to be what it once was. But anyone could speak of such things; it took a man of action and vision to actually bring them to fruition. Mollari was neither.

If he had kept his mouth shut, it wouldn't have been such a problem, but Mollari was renowned for getting himself liquored up and shouting at the top of his lungs about what the Republic could be and should be. When he had received the assignment of ambassador to Babylon 5, the word around the court was that, at last, Mollari would be sent someplace where even his bellowing tones would not be heard.

Durla had loved it. He wanted nothing but to see Mollari spiral into hopeless disgrace.

And who knew? Perhaps he would become so bored and fed up with his lot in life that he would do the honorable thing, throw himself on his sword and put an end to it all. Once that happened, Mariel would be available to him once again. And if Mollari waited to dispose of himself, giving Durla enough time to work himself up to a position of sufficient importance, why . . . perhaps Mariel might see him in a very different light.

Some nights as he lay on his spartan, military cot, Durla would envision the shade of Mollari, screaming from the afterlife in helpless frustration as Durla bedded his widow in far greater fashion, and with greater potency, than Londo ever could have achieved.

There might well have been people in the court who were more surprised than Durla, when word of Londo Mollari's growing power base began to trickle back to the Homeworld. But no one could have been more horrified than he. The last thing he needed—or desired—was for Londo Mollari to make a success of himself, to turn his career around. Unfortunately, to Durla's horror, that was precisely what happened.

His horror turned to delight when Mollari unceremoniously tossed Mariel aside, divorcing her along with one of his other wives, Daggair. He had chosen to keep as his wife a diminutive, brittle shrew named Timov, and that decision had mystified a number of people who were familiar with all three wives, and who would have wagered their life's fortunes that—if Mollari were to keep only one wife—it would be the stunningly beautiful Mariel. Ultimately, that had left the way clear for Durla once more, but his luck still had not improved.

His calls to Mariel went unanswered. Gifts he sent her remained unacknowledged. The silence was an obvious response: he had not sufficiently acquitted himself in the grand scheme of things to have placed himself on Mariel's horizon.

And with Mollari maneuvering himself, positioning himself to be the next emperor, Durla became certain he had to build his own power base within the government. Such a power base would have to consist of friends and allies who were his and his alone. But Durla, as yet only the captain of the guards, had no power of his own, no means of bringing in his people. Once Mollari became emperor, naturally he would bring in his own flunkies, and Durla would be frozen out.

As much as it galled him to do so, Durla had embarked upon the only strategy he could devise: he decided he would be the *perfect* captain of the guards. He would get as close to Londo as possible, with an eye toward obtaining a position of power and, once he had done that, building from there. He figured the entire process would take a number of years, and hoped that nothing would dramatically change Mariel's marital status in the meantime.

To Durla's astonishment, however, his timetable was thrown completely out of whack when Londo—defying all predictions of the court pundits—promoted him to the key position of minister of Internal Security. Mollari had proven himself a bizarre study in contradictions. For Durla had had the distinct and unshakeable impression that the emperor really couldn't stand him. That somehow Mollari had sensed, on a very basic level, that Durla despised him, hungered for power, and wouldn't rest until he himself was wearing the white.

But for reasons that surpassed understanding—call it stupidity, call it a death wish, call it whatever one desired—Mollari had not only entrusted Durla with formidable responsibility, but offered no resistance whatever to Durla's placing loyal associates in key positions of power.

Durla didn't know why Mollari was doing it. He had theories. One he found the most plausible was that Mollari was, for some reason, experiencing massive guilt over the war he had engineered, and so was setting himself up to fail. It not only made the most sense, it was just about the only one that made any sense at all.

On this particular evening, he had been dwelling on the curious chain of events that had brought him to his present state when he had fallen asleep. Probably because everything was so fresh on his mind, faces flittered past him as his consciousness hovered in the grey area between sleep and wakefulness. His parents, his brother, other soldiers, Mollari, and looming above them all, Mariel, with her perfect teeth and her eyes sparkling . . .

"Durla," she whispered to him.

She was holding out her hand, and the dream was most curious, for it didn't seem as insubstantial as dreams normally are. "Durla." She called him once more, and this time she beckoned to him. A miasma of color was swirling about her.

Durla saw himself through his mind's eye, stepping toward her. He took her hand. *No*, he mused, *this is definitely not like other dreams*. Usually dreams simply provide a feast for the visual memory. But when he took her hand, it felt firm and warm and alive.

"Come," she said, and she tugged on his hand slightly, but just to test the situation Durla resisted. Instead of moving, he pulled her toward him, gripped her shoulders, and kissed her roughly. She didn't resist; her body seemed to melt against his. Warmth flooded over him, and then she was no longer in his arms, but instead a few feet away, gesturing coquettishly for him to follow. "Time enough for that later, my love," she said teasingly.

He followed her then, unreality swirling around them. Clouds of red and purple seemed to pulse with an energy all their own, and Durla realized they were in hyperspace, moving effortlessly through that light-speed bridge. They didn't appear to need a space vessel; they were above such petty needs, beyond them, outside them.

"Where are we going?" he asked.

"You'll see," she replied.

Hyperspace dissolved around them, and a world materialized far below Durla's feet. Then there was a sudden flash of light, and Durla found Mariel and himself standing on the planet's surface. The sky hung in an orangy haze, and the dirt beneath their feet was kicking up in clouds of dust.

"Where are we?" Durla asked. "What is this place?"

"A fringe world. It's designated K0643," Mariel said. She squeezed his hand affectionately and added, "Walk with me."

He did so. And as they walked, he realized he had never known such happiness, such bliss. He was afraid to speak anymore for fear of shattering the moment and sending himself spiraling back to wakefulness.

"The Centauri Republic must expand," she said.

"I know. We must show the allied worlds that we are to be feared, to be—"

But Mariel shook her head. She didn't seem the least annoyed with him; indeed, her evident fondness for him only appeared to be growing. "You speak of conquest. That is not your immediate concern."

"It's not?"

"No, my love."

He thought he was going to cry out with joy, and was barely able to contain his euphoria. *My love! She called me "My love!"*

"You must look for that which no one else knows about. There are other worlds, worlds in which the Alliance has no interest. Remote worlds such as this one. You must mount archaeological investigations. You must dig. You must locate. While you do this, the Interstellar Alliance will laugh at you. They will sneer and say, 'Look at the once-great Centauri Republic, rooting around on barren worlds and scraping about in the dirt like the basest of creatures.' Let them say these things. Let them lull themselves into a false sense of security.

"It will not last, and they will discover the error of their ways . . . but by then, it will be too late. Look outside Centauri Prime, Durla. There, and only there, will you find your true greatness."

"And you? If I do these things, I will have you?"

She laughed, and nodded, but then added warningly, "Do not seek me out. As tempted as you may be, do not do so. If you chase me, I will find you contemptible. I must come to you. You must know that by now. I must be drawn to you, and only then will you truly be able to call me your own."

"And this planet offers the way?"

"This, and others like it. You have the resources. Organize the diggers. Organize the crews. Assign the manpower. You can do it, Durla. I believe in you. And you can believe in me."

She gripped both of his hands, kissed him gently on the knuckles, and then released him. They did not drop to his sides but remained there, in midair, and he looked at them as if they were appendages belonging to someone else. She backed away, gliding, almost floating. He tried to move toward her, but she easily kept the same distance between them, even as her arms stretched out toward him in mute pleading.

Durla twisted in his bed, his arms flailing about in the real world as he tried to touch Mariel in the dream sphere.

And then he stopped thrashing, as a small, spidery creature descended from his right temple and scuttled across the floor. The last few feet to its destination, it did not even bother to walk, but instead vaulted the distance. The dreamweaver landed on Shiv'kala's abdomen and nestled there securely.

"Well done," Shiv'kala said softly.

He will not take action due to this one vision, warned the dreamweaver, a special offshoot breed of the keeper.

"Yes. I know. It will take several instances of this 'recurring dream' for him to truly embrace it. But once he does . . ."

He did not need to finish the sentence.

He heard footfalls. Durla had cried out once or twice during the session, and apparently night guards were coming by to ascertain whether or not he was all right.

The guards opened the door and peered in, but Durla had calmed. He was sound asleep, his chest rising and falling steadily. They performed a scan of the room that was so subtle Durla didn't even stir. The scan accomplished nothing.

And so they moved off, never seeing the Drakh as he stood quietly in the shadows and planned.

The sleeper was completely awake. Within him resided the will and the means to accomplish that which he had been designed to accomplish.

The procession was moving toward him, and the sleeper moved himself into position . . . and waited . . .

Soon . . . soon the reason for his existence would be carried out. Soon, very soon . . . Sheridan would be dead. It was only a matter of moments.

10

Vir sat in his quarters, staring at the wall and wondering whether there was any point in his continuing to remain at Babylon 5. He had spent a sleepless night pondering the question and was no closer to an answer now than he'd been before.

As an ambassador, he felt his talents were questionable at best. And even if he were the greatest, most skilled diplomat in the history of the galaxy . . . what good would it do if no one was interested in speaking with him?

He felt it more and more, every time he would walk around the station. The eyes upon him that seemed to regard him with barely concealed contempt. Or scorn. Or anger.

Once upon a time, Babylon 5 had seemed a very intimidating place to him. Secrets lurked behind every corner, and he had always felt as if he were watching helplessly while Londo descended into darkness. At the time that it was happening, he would have thought it insane if someone suggested to him that he would become nostalgic for those days.

But indeed, that was exactly the case. As complex as his life was, as terrifying as that slow downward spiral into war and even murder had been . . . those were, in fact, the good old days. At least people had liked him then. He had had friends.

Garibaldi had certainly liked him well enough, because obviously he had never considered Vir any sort of threat to B5 security. Now, however, the Centauri were considered a perpetual problem, a race not to be trusted, not to be left to their own devices. A race who would leave you with a dagger quivering in your back if you let down your guard. And Garibaldi, whose responsibilities included anticipating and neutralizing any potential security problems for the entirety of the Interstellar Alliance, had come to regard Vir with suspicion at all times.

Sheridan . . .

He had considered Sheridan a friend. A bit distant, what with all his responsibilities as captain of Babylon 5, but a friend nonetheless. Someone to whom he could unburden himself. But the truth now was that Sheridan didn't dare be friendly with him. It might cause too many negative ramifications for him with the rest of the Alliance. Not that Sheridan would admit to such a thing; he was too much the individualist to let public sentiment sway him from following a particular path. Vir, though, couldn't find it within himself to risk putting Sheridan into that position. The stakes were too high, the Alliance too important in the long run, to risk upsetting member races just because Vir felt lonely.

Lennier . . . of all of them, he missed Lennier the most. When they had both been mere attachés serving their respective diplomatic leaders/mentors, they had met regularly to unburden themselves to one another. Of all of them, Lennier had probably best understood what it was that Vir was going through at any given time.

But Lennier had joined the Rangers, for reasons Vir had to admit eluded him completely. Lennier was deeply religious, thoughtful, a pacifist. What business did he have traipsing about the galaxy as a man-at-arms? When Vir had mused out loud to Londo about that, Londo had looked thoughtful for a time. He seemed to be running through his mind everything he knew about Lennier, reaching some conclusions. Then he had said to Vir, "There is an old Earth organization—very much romanticized—whose history might provide you with some answers, if what I suspect is correct. Read up on the French Foreign Legion."

Vir had done so, but had come away from it understanding no more than he had when he'd begun. Soldiers who joined a demanding, even cruel organization in order to forget their past? A past usually haunted by beautiful but unattainable women who'd broken their hearts . . . at least according to the "romanticized" literature Londo had recommended. Vir had absolutely no idea how that could possibly apply to Lennier, and had said so. Londo had simply shrugged and said, "What do I know of such things?" and dropped the subject.

Londo.

He missed Londo. He missed the way things had been. Even when they were bad . . . at least Vir had had an idea of what was going on. Now here he was, in a position that supposedly offered him more power and authority, and yet feeling more confused and helpless than ever before. There he had been, speaking to Londo of the mysterious Rem Lanas and Emperor Kran, and he had no idea whatsoever what any of it had to do with anything.

Rem Lanas, a homeless Centauri who hid in Down Below. No criminal record, no nothing. The thought of roaming around Down Below under any circumstance wasn't an attractive one to Vir, and he had delayed the prospect for as long as possible, while trying to determine if there was any particular reason he should seek out this individual. Londo had seemed of the opinion that he should, but really, who knew what was going through Londo's head anymore? He seemed so erratic, so inwardly torn. Not for the first time, Vir found himself wondering if Londo hadn't genuinely had some sort of mental collapse. It wasn't a pleasant thought, but it certainly seemed to be a valid explanation.

And Emperor Kran? What was the point in discussing rulers long gone?

"Emperor Kran," Vir said out loud.

Why had Londo been speaking of him? What was it that Londo had said, again?

Sometimes it is possible to agree on what is right and wrong. And we would not want the wrong things to happen again. Not to anyone. Not to anyone, Vir. Do you hear me?

Just what had happened to Emperor Kran? Vir realized that he couldn't recall all the details. He'd been killed, that much he remembered. Assassinated. Then again, so had a number of Centauri emperors, so on that basis alone he hadn't really stood out.

Vir moved to his computer terminal and started checking records, pulling up history files. The difference between Kran and the others who had been assassinated, as Vir started to remember, was that unlike others—such as Cartagia—Kran hadn't really been that bad. He'd had a good heart, good ideas, and a determination to try and bring the feuding houses of the Republic together. His interest hadn't been self-aggrandizement or personal enrichment, but the betterment of all Centauri Prime.

After skimming some of the highlights of Kran's life, Vir started reading over the details of Kran's death.

It had been so stupid. A waste, a tragic waste. Kran had grown impatient with the noble houses of Centauri Prime, because he felt they had lost touch with the common people. The houses, after all, basically consisted of people of rank, of status, of title. A relatively small percentage of the planet's population had held a staggeringly large percentage of the money and access to the world's resources.

Kran felt that the best way to remind the houses of where their obligations lay was to bring them down to the common folk and "reintroduce" them.

Centauri Prime was like any other world: it had its seedier side. There were places where the poor went when they had nowhere else to go. Where people in need scraped together meager livings with whatever they could get their hands upon. And, as was always the case, those above knew where those below resided. But those above simply found a way to turn off that part of their mind that would have caused them to feel pity or empathy for those with nothing. "They got themselves into it," was the most frequently heard comment, or "Let someone else handle it," or similar sentiments.

Kran wasn't about to stand for it. His intention was to realign the thinking of the houses' heads in the same way that one trains an offending pet not to relieve himself inside the house. In the case of the pet, you are to shove the creature's nose into his own waste product. It was Kran's notion to do the same—metaphorically speaking—with the houses' heads.

He amassed a "Great Expedition," as it was dubbed. He brought together all the houses' heads for a guided tour through the seamier side of Centauri Prime. His intention was twofold: to remind the household heads that there were those in desperate need of help, and to provide, by his physical presence, a symbol of hope to all those who were too indigent to share in the planet's wealth.

His long-term goal had been to build a sort of global sense of patriotism. He sought to cause all of Centauri Prime to pull together as one, the great and the small, with the ultimate aim being a return to the greatness that had once marked the Republic. "One cannot build a palace on a foundation of mud," he had written. "The mud must be treated, crafted into a foundation upon which greatness can be created."

He had sought unity. He sought—ironically enough—an alliance. Vir couldn't help but smile to himself in a sort of sad way. In some ways, Kran reminded him of Sheridan in that regard.

So there Kran had been, planning for magnificence, thinking about ways of elevating the whole of Centauri society. According to the history text Vir was reading, the procession of the Great Expedition had wended its way into the dark quarters of Centauri Prime, and had been quite a sight to see. All the richest Centauri, dressed in their finery, looking and probably feeling completely out of place as they gazed—many of them for the first time—upon the faces of need and want, of hunger and frustration. Their ignorance of the conditions of the poorer Centauri had led them to apathy, and Londo had once told Vir that ignorance and apathy were a lethal combination. Ignorance can be cured by education, apathy attended to by finding something, somehow that can stir the blood and move the soul to take action. But ignorance and apathy, entwined inseparably around each other, form a wall that is nearly insurmountable.

Kran had taken it upon himself to crack through that wall and, by all accounts, the initial moments of the Great Expedition began to do just that. The heads of the households were transfixed, unable to turn away from the sight of such need. It was said that some of them were even moved to tears.

That was when it had all fallen apart.

The man's name was Tuk Maroth. He had been born poor, raised poor, and had viewed the nobility and the greatness of the Centauri upper echelon only from a distance his entire life. He sat in the gutter, watched the approaching procession through eyes filled with hate and envy. He told people later that all he could see was the sun glinting off the gilt and trimming of the greatcoats of the nobility. And the emperor . . . . "He seemed to shine, to glow," Maroth had said, "as if powered by all the souls of those who had died with nothing, so that he might have everything." Apparently the thing that had sent Maroth completely over the edge was the shining imperial crest which hung around Kran's neck.

Maroth later claimed it had been a purely spontaneous act, and that he had no idea what came over him. This was widely thought to be some sort of appeal for leniency, as if a temporary madness that drove him to regicide was somehow more acceptable.

Kran never even saw the shot coming. One moment he was smiling, waving, nodding. There was a great deal of noise from the crowd; he probably didn't hear the shot. But the next thing he knew, he was looking down in astonishment at the vast stain of red that was spreading across his chest. His legs sagged and his dumbfounded guards, who had not been expecting any such assault during such a well-meaning and philanthropic mission, caught him. Maroth turned and fled, disappearing into the back alleys of the district. Kran was rushed directly to the hospital, but it was far too late. He was dead by the time he got there. Indeed, there were some who said that he was dead before the guards even caught him.

The incident touched off waves of recriminations, including one particularly massive riot in which the nobles sent the military to storm the poorest quarters of the city, demanding the assassin, demanding justice, and generally taking the opportunity to vilify the poor in their own minds by condemning them all for the actions of one. By doing that, they basically absolved themselves from any sense of responsibility for helping the needy. An entire section of the city went up in flames before Maroth was turned in, by his grief-stricken mother as it turned out. The poor woman subsequently took her own life by stabbing herself, cutting out the womb that had once housed the child who had grown up to commit such a heinous act.

However it was the power brokers of Centauri who got to write the history. The power brokers who had stormed the poor and later sought to excuse their actions. So when history referred to Kran in later years, it portrayed him as a fool who had misplaced his priorities. The poor, it was decided, had brought their lack of fortune upon themselves, deserved whatever happened to them; and any ruler who felt any sympathy for them likewise had coming to him whatever tragedy should occur.

Vir set aside the reading material and shook his head in dismay. Poor Londo. Obviously what he'd been telling Vir was that he, Londo, was doomed to fail. That history was going to judge him a fool.

Or worse, Londo was concerned that he was going to die at the hands of some demented assassin. Or . . .

Or . . .

"*I'm an idiot!*" Vir shouted as he leaped to his feet so violently that he slammed his knee on the underside of the table.

He didn't take time to note the pain. His mind raced, trying to figure out what to do. Then quickly he went to his closet and found old clothes. It wasn't difficult. Vir had lost a considerable amount of weight in the past months, but he had kept the clothes that no longer fit him properly because he wasn't the type to waste anything. To say nothing of the fact that, should he wind up gaining the weight back, as had happened to him from time to time, he wanted to have something he could fit into.

He hauled out one of his old suits, a mismatched shirt, vest, and pants and threw them on. The unfortunate combination and the fact that they hung loosely on him combined for a generally satisfactory air of shabbiness.

He returned to his terminal and hastily printed out a photo. Then he hauled out his cloak. He rarely wore it; it had been a going-away gift from his mother, which he had never quite understood. It was a hooded, all-weather garment, which made no sense as a gift for going to Babylon 5—how much weather variation was there going to be on a space station? It wasn't as if there were days he needed to bundle up because it looked cloudy with a chance of rain.

But he drew it about himself now as if a major thunderhead were rolling in, and drew the hood up over his head to conceal his features. Thus outfitted, he made his way to Down Below, and prayed he would be in time.

Perhaps the prospect of descending to Down Below had been anathema to Vir, but he knew he had no choice. Again he weighed all the options, and this seemed unfortunately to be the only viable one.

It was the smell that hit him first. The atmospheric filters in Down Below weren't as efficient as they were in other sections of the station. To some degree, that was understandable. The designers of Babylon 5 had never intended that anyone would actually live in the service corridors and excess storage area that constituted Down Below, and consequently they had not provided for the same amount of ventilation and the number of ducts there were throughout the rest of the place. Add to that the severe lack of proper sanitation facilities, and it combined to make Down Below someplace one avoided if one could at all help it.

At least no one was staring at Vir here. In that respect, as ironic as it sounded, it almost made Down Below preferable to up above. Every so often, someone would glance in Vir's direction, but only in terms of assessing whether or not he appeared to present some sort of danger. On those occasions, if Vir caught their glance, he would peer out from beneath his hood and flash a sickly little smile that practically cried out that he was no threat whatsoever. The mute questioner would then go on about whatever unseemly business he needed to attend to.

In his hand, Vir clutched the picture he had printed out. It was the last known image of Rem Lanas. Vir had stared at it for so long that he felt as if every curve of the man's face was permanently emblazoned in his mind.

He scanned the throng that was perpetually milling about, trying to spot some sign of his quarry. It didn't seem a particularly promising means of accomplishing what he needed to do, but he could see no other way. He tried not to draw any attention to himself, and that wasn't especially difficult. No one seemed to care about him . . . or, indeed, about anything.

He looked sadly at the assortment of makeshift tents and homes that had been erected hodgepodge throughout Down Below. He saw several people, a family by the look of it, grouped around an open flame and cooking something that seemed to have once been some sort of vermin. The very sight of it was enough to cause Vir's stomach to buck. In a way, it helped put his life in perspective for him. Here he had been so miserable over his personal situation, not liking the way that representatives from the Alliance had been looking at him. *Looking* at him. That should be his biggest problem. At least he had clothes, food, and shelter. At least he had all the amenities and wanted for nothing save companionship. But companionship was a very small thing compared to everything that these poor, needy people required.

He spent several hours wandering around, even becoming so bold as to start asking random people if they had seen Rem Lanas, holding up a picture to jog their memory. Most times he simply got blank stares. It might have been that they didn't know, although it was just as likely that they didn't care. First of all, Rem Lanas wasn't their problem. And second, this odd Centauri who was asking around was obviously an outsider, despite his ill-fitting clothes, possibly even operating undercover for some organization. Why should they cooperate with him? When had anyone cooperated with them, after all.

It was a rationale that Vir could easily understand, although he would probably have been even more forgiving if lives had not been potentially on the line.

Presuming, of course, that he was right, and hadn't simply conjured the entire thing out of some crack-brained misinterpretation of purposefully cryptic remarks made by Londo.

That was when he heard noises.

The sound came from a distance away. It was an assortment of voices, several of them trying to talk at once, but there was one louder than the others. Whereas the others were speaking with high emotion, the most commanding one came across as firm and reasonable. It was a voice that Vir knew almost as well as his own or Londo's. It was Sheridan's voice.

The tour was coming through. The "reclamation" project of which Sheridan had spoken.

Vir looked around, trying to see if there was any sign of Rem

Lanas. There was nothing. Perhaps he had missed him, or perhaps Lanas had come in behind him, circled around somehow.

As he stood there, the residents of Down Below began to look around at one another in confusion, unable to figure out just what the commotion was all about. Clearly some of them thought they were being rousted, as had happened before during periodic security sweeps. However, there wasn't any sound of scuffling or of weapons being fired in warning. Everything certainly seemed peaceful enough.

There were side passages that extended off in a variety of directions. Maybe Lanas was lurking down one of those, Vir reasoned. It was still a long shot, though, and he was begining to feel that he was handling this situation completely wrong. That, despite his assorted concerns, he should have gone to security. He should have trusted this business to anyone except himself.

He started to turn in one direction . . .

. . . and a flash of light caught his eye.

He was momentarily confused. He wasn't sure where it had come from or what had caused it. All he knew was that the flash drew his attention to another corridor—one he hadn't noticed before. Then he gasped in astonishment, unable to believe his luck.

It was Rem Lanas. He was around Vir's height, but thinner, with long arms and narrow shoulders. Vir was dumbfounded. Despite his memorization of Rem's features, he glanced at the printout nevertheless. Lanas looked a bit more dishevelled than he appeared in the picture, but it most definitely was him.

He was standing in a narrow alleyway, just around the corner from the main corridor, his hand resting against the corner of the wall. He was clearly listening for something. Listening, and glancing around the corner every so often, as if to try and determine just how quickly Sheridan and the others were approaching.

And now Vir could see Sheridan and the others, far down the corridor. Lanas was positioned in such a way that he could walk only a few steps and easily intersect the group's path. Sheridan and the others were ringed by guards, with Zack at the forefront. Vir could see Zack scanning the crowd, scrutinizing anyone who came within range, glancing at their hands . . .

Their hands. Of course. To see if they were holding weapons.

Vir did likewise, staring at Lanas across the way. Lanas' hands were empty. He didn't seem to have a weapon on him. Nonetheless, there was something about him that practically screamed "threat." As quickly, as unobtrusively as he could, Vir began to move toward him. Drawing within range presented no immediate difficulty; Lanas was paying no attention to him whatsoever. His concerns seemed entirely focused elsewhere.

Let me get there, Vir was intoning to himself. *Let me get there.* The problem was, he had nothing concrete upon which to base his actions. But somehow he felt driven nonetheless, as if he were caught up in forces that were compelling him to behave in a certain manner. It wasn't the first time he had felt that way, certainly. But all the other times that feeling had come over him, it had always been Londo who had been piloting the ship, so to speak. This time it was up to Vir . . . presuming the "it" was what he thought it was. There was still always the possibility that he had totally misinterpreted everything, that this was all the result of his fevered imagination working overtime.

He drew closer, closer, and Rem still wasn't noticing him. Now Vir could clearly make out the look in Rem's eyes, and it was a look that he found frightening. It was as if Lanas wasn't even present in his own head. His eyes were wide but empty, as if his body were simply being worn like a cloak. His body was stock still, frozen, but poised, like a great animal preparing to pounce, or perhaps a trap waiting to spring shut.

And his throat . . .

Vir's gaze was immediately drawn to Rem's throat, because—insanely—it seemed to be moving all on its own. It was pulsing gently, rhythmically. Vir had no idea what could possibly be causing such a thing.

Sheridan was still a distance away, getting closer with every passing moment . . . but then again, so was Vir as he drew nearer to Rem.

It was when Vir was only a few feet away that Rem Lanas noticed him.

Vir had no idea if he had made some movement, done something that might have drawn Lanas' attention to him. Maybe some sort of sixth sense that warned him of danger had come into play. Whatever it was, Lanas' head snapped around and his wide, eerily vacant eyes focused on Vir. His throat seemed to pulse more violently.

Vir froze in his tracks. He had no idea what to do. And then, his mind racing desperately for some sort of strategy, he did the only thing he could think of. He threw back his hood, a grin splitting his face, and he cried out joyously, "Rem! Rem Lanas! I *thought* that was you! It's me! Cotto! Vir Cotto! How are you!"

Lanas tilted his head slightly. He seemed to be having to make an effort to focus on Vir.

"Don't tell me you don't remember me!" Vir continued. "After all those crazy times we had together!" As he'd spoken, he'd drawn to within a couple of feet of Rem.

But Sheridan and the others were also drawing closer. Rem snapped his head back in the direction of Sheridan's path, started to move toward him. Vir stepped around to intercept, and Lanas really, truly focused on Vir for the first time. Something terrifying entered those eyes, something dark and fearsome, and Vir could almost hear voices screaming in his head.

And the throat was no longer pulsing. It was . . . undulating.

There was something in it. Something moved up the throat, and Lanas began making a hacking, coughing noise in his larynx, his lips trembling as if he were about to vomit.

Acting completely on instinct, Vir lunged. Rem took a step back, tried to dodge around him, but his movements were slow and awkward, and Vir collided with him. They went down in a tumble of arms and legs, and Vir found himself positioned just behind Rem, Rem's head pinned against the crook of his knee. Automatically, Vir reached around and grabbed Rem's lower jaw, shoving it up while bracing Rem's head against his own leg. Essentially, he had him in an utterly awkward but nevertheless effective headlock.

Rem struggled violently, the gagging continuing. No words were spoken, no one shouted for help. A group of people had assembled at the far end of the alley, but their backs were to Vir and Lanas. Instead they were watching Sheridan's approach. One or two glanced in the direction of the struggling Centauri, but clearly decided it was some sort of personal issue that did not merit their involvement.

"Stop it! Stop it!" hissed Vir. Vir wasn't one of the more physically aggressive types around. He couldn't remember the last time he'd been in a fight, and he had absolutely no combat technique, no confidence in his ability to handle himself in a battle. But he was being prompted by pure desperation, and from that was born the strength and determination he needed.

Then he saw something starting to protrude from between Rem's lips.

It was all Vir could do not to cry out in terror. The thing was thin and black, like some sort of tentacle, and it was shoving its way through Rem's mouth, trying to get free. The pulsating in Rem's throat had ceased. Clearly this was the thing that was trying to get out of him. Vir was sweating profusely, trying not to panic as another tentacle managed to slide through, despite his best efforts. He yanked up as hard as he could, and Rem's own teeth crunched through the tentacles, severing them. They fell to the ground, writhing about on their own for a moment before ceasing. But Rem's head began to shake furiously, the thing inside now either in agony or just wildly determined to get out. Vir redoubled his efforts, but his fingers, thick with perspiration, began to slip.

Then Vir realized that Sheridan was still talking, but his voice was moving beyond them. He had passed by, and the entourage was following him. That realization, that momentary victory, caused him to relax his guard for just a second.

It was enough. Lanas suddenly shoved backward, catching Vir on the side of the head. Vir fell back, his head ringing, and from his vantage point on the ground he saw Rem's mouth open wide. Some sort of creature leapt out of it.

It was small and black as its tentacles had been, covered with a thick layer of fur. It had four more functioning legs in addition to the two that had been truncated, and the force of its ejection from Rem's mouth caused it to smack against the far wall of the alley. It spun about a moment, orienting itself. It was no bigger than the palm of Vir's hand.

It screamed in fury, though the sound wasn't audible. Vir heard it in his head.

Vir, momentarily stunned by what he was seeing, lay helpless on the floor, and then he gasped as the thing scuttled at incredible speed across the way, straight toward his face. He had a brief glimpse of something sharp sticking out of the thing's back and he realized that it was some sort of stinger. There was no time for him to get out of the way, no time to do anything except let out a truncated cry of fear.

And then the black boot came down.

It smashed to the floor of the alley mere inches from Vir's face, crushing the creature under it effortlessly. Vir gasped in astonishment as the booted foot twisted back and forth in place for a moment, grinding the thing thoroughly into the ground. When it stepped back, there was nothing more than a black and red pulped mess.

11

Vir looked up.

And he saw the individual that he had only thought he'd seen earlier. The man was dressed in grey robes, and although Vir couldn't see his hooded face completely, what he did see looked quite young. He couldn't have been more than thirty.

Rem lay on the ground, staring upward. The cloaked man stepped forward, crouched down over him and seemed to study him for a moment. Then he passed a hand over Rem's face, and Rem closed his eyes. His chest began to rise and fall in a natural sleeping rhythm.

"He'll be all right," said the cloaked man. When he spoke, it was in a very soft voice, so soft that Vir had to strain to listen. "He'll sleep it off for a time, and when he comes to, he'll have no idea why he's here. He'll be of no harm to anyone."

"What happened?" asked Vir, hauling himself to his feet. "Who are you?" Then he noticed the man was holding a staff. The ends of the staff appeared to be glowing softly. In barely contained astonishment, Vir said, "Are you a . . . a technomage?" The notion was both fascinating and frightening. Vir had had dealings with the science-based sorcerers nearly four years earlier, and he had found it one of the most daunting experiences of his life. When the techno-mages had finally left on their journey beyond the Rim, purportedly never to be seen again, Vir had breathed a sigh of relief. Yet now, apparently, he owed his life to one.

"Yes . . . but a cloistered one. My kind don't get out much. My name is Kane."

"It is? Really?"

"No. Not really," admitted the initiate. "It's a chosen name. I'm not about to tell you my real name, of course. Names have power, and I'm not going to give you power over me of any sort. Rather a foolish notion, really."

"That's a good philosophy," said Vir. "Thank you for squishing that . . . that . . ."

"Sleeper. Leftover biotech from the Shadows. Resided in your friend here," and he tapped Rem's body with the toe of his boot, "wiped his memory, and waited until it was ready to fulfill its mission."

"To assassinate Sheridan."

Kane nodded. "Yes. All Lanas had to do was get close enough, and the creature would have done the rest. It has quite a good jumping range. And once it landed on Sheridan, it would have stung him, and he would have been dead before they could get him to Medlab."

"Just like Kran."

"What?"

"Nothing. But why now? And why Lanas?"

"It wasn't just now. There were times before. There will probably be other times, although death may take different forms. As for why Lanas," and beneath his robes, Kane shrugged. "Luck of the draw. Purely random chance. They had to pick someone. They picked him."

"They who?"

"That," smiled Kane, "would be telling. You don't need to know . . . yet."

"But—"

"Tell me," Kane drew closer to him, studying him thoughtfully, "why you chose to handle this matter on your own, why you did not summon security."

"I . . . I didn't have enough to go on. Not for sure. I had guesses, hunches, that was all. Besides, the most upsetting thing was the thought of letting it get around that the Centauri were involved in an assassination attempt. Even if it turned out to be false, there would be inquiries, and interrogations, and word would leak to the other members of the Alliance. I didn't want that. Centauri doesn't need it. Things are bad enough as it is."

"So you risked your own life, limb, and neck in order to try and head it off and protect the Centauri reputation."

"I . . . guess so, yes," Vir agreed. Then, worried, he added, "You're not going to tell anyone, are you?"

"Why would I do that?"

"I . . . I don't know. I don't know a lot of things," Vir admitted. "Starting with—"

But Kane held up a hand to quiet him. "No. Do not start. Because if you do, there will be many answers that I cannot give you. Not yet. But I will tell you this much, Vir ... your actions have been quite impressive. I was observing you to see what you would do, and you do not disappoint. It very much seems as if the darkness has not reached you."

"That's good to know, that—" Vir paused, and then said, "The, uh ... the darkness?"

Kane took a step toward him, and there was hardness in his eyes. "It stretches its coils from Centauri Prime to here. It lurks hereabouts, but it thrives on your Homeworld. Knowledge is power, Vir. I seek knowledge on behalf of the techno-mages, and they in turn seek knowledge from your world, for it is there that the dark power will continue to grow. You will have to make some rather severe choices soon. Very, very soon."

"I ... have no idea what you're talking about."

"Good," said Kane, apparently satisfied. "I was going for cryptic."

"You succeeded."

"That's a relief. I am somewhat new at this, after all. Now I have to work on mysterious. Ah ... your associate is stirring sooner than expected."

Vir turned and glanced at Rem Lanas. Sure enough, he was sitting up, holding a hand against his head as if he had a seriously splitting headache. "What ... happened?" he inquired.

"I'll tell you in a moment," Vir said, and looked back to Kane.

He was gone. There was no sign that he had ever been there, other than a crushed, red and pulped creature on the floor.

"He's got the mysterious part down pretty well, too," said Vir.

12

Londo had known it was a test. There was absolutely no doubt in his mind at all.

"Sheridan is to die, you know," the Drakh had said.

The comment had snapped Londo from his reverie. There, in his throne room—the place that was the symbol of his power and, for him, the further symbol of the sham that he was—he was startled as the now-familiar voice spoke from the shadows. What was truly chilling was that Londo had realized he was, in fact, *aware* that Shiv'kala was watching him. At least, he'd been aware on some sort of subconscious level. And it hadn't even disturbed him.

The notion that he could actually get used to this half life he was living—even take it for granted—terrified Londo more than anything that had come before.

It had taken a few moments for the comment to sink in. "What?" Londo had said.

The Drakh had laid it all out for him. Told him the plan, told him about Rem Lanas. Told him about the creature that lived within Lanas. He had been picked at random, taken off the streets. It was the randomness that they had felt would be the greatest strength. Someone with no established grudge toward Sheridan, no particular hostility toward the Interstellar Alliance. Lanas was just a nobody. A nobody who wasn't particularly strong willed, not particularly intelligent. All he was, in the final analysis, was useful.

When the Drakh had finally stopped speaking, Londo squinted in the darkness at him. Shiv'kala just stood there, unmoving, unblinking, that same, frightening little smile in place. "And you have told me this . . . why?"

"He was your friend. I wished to let you know of his impending fate . . . so that if you desired to say your goodbyes . . . you would have the opportunity."

A test. No . . . not just a test.

A trap.

Londo had known it, had been positive of it. The Drakh could just as easily have said, "Sheridan is to die soon. Drop him a nice note," and been done with it. No, he had told Londo everything there was to know because he wanted Londo to have that knowledge . . . in order to see what he would do with it.

Londo had not slept. For two days, he did not sleep. He had gone back and forth in his head, envisioning Sheridan as his great enemy, as the leader of an Alliance that had mercilessly assaulted his beloved Centauri Prime. Someone who had turned his back on them. And Delenn, his wife . . . she had a way of looking at Londo in the most insultingly pitying way.

But try as he might, he had not been able to erase from his memory all the times when Sheridan had been of service to him. Those years on Babylon 5 had been the best years of his life. He had not realized it at the time; it had merely seemed a period of slow, steady descent into darkness. But the fact was, Sheridan and Delenn had indeed been there for him on a number of occasions. Not only that, but he was positive that in their own way, they had been pulling for him, hoping that everything would turn out all right for him. The fact that everything had developed so abysmally—that he had become the single most powerful, and weakest, man in the Centauri Republic—was certainly not their doing, not at all. He had brought his fate solidly upon himself.

He had tried to sleep, but had managed only moments of rest, at most, before he would drift back to consciousness. During that time, he had felt the keeper shifting in mild confusion. Obviously the creature itself needed to rest as well, and had synchronized itself with Londo's own sleep period. So when Londo became mentally distressed, the keeper likewise experienced discomfort. The thought gave Londo some degree of satisfaction.

Finally he had not been able to take it anymore. But he had known that he would have to be crafty. He could not simply mount an obvious rescue mission, or inform Sheridan. Such an effort would probably be prevented by the keeper. In the event that the keeper could not stop him, certainly it would inform the Drakh, who might in turn change their plan . . . and let their displeasure with Londo be known in a most direct and unpleasant manner. Londo desired to save Sheridan, but not at the price of his own skin. Londo was not that generous.

So he had summoned Vir. The timing had been perfect, for the celebration in the palace had actually been Durla's idea. Durla had sponsored it, naturally, as a means of gathering all his allies and supporters and showing them his elevated position in the court. Since the idea had originated with Durla—Durla, the puppet of the Drakh who probably didn't even know who truly pulled the strings—the Drakh in turn would not question it or suspect some sort of duplicity on Londo's part. An invitation to Vir would be the most natural thing in the world.

So he had brought his old associate, his old friend—possibly his only friend in the galaxy, really—to visit. The invitation had attracted no attention whatsoever, as Londo had hoped.

Then had come the next step: Londo had started drinking almost as soon as the festivities had begun. The problem was, he had needed to walk a fine line. The challenge was to consume enough alcohol to render the keeper insensate, as he had found he was capable of doing. By accomplishing that, he would be able to speak to Vir more or less freely, without the keeper—and by extension, the Drakh—becoming aware of what he was doing. The problem was, if he imbibed too much, he would become so incoherently drunk that he wouldn't be of any use to Vir, to Sheridan, or even to himself.

So Vir had come, as invited, and Londo had taken him aside, fighting to remain on his feet while the liquor swirled around his brain, leaving a pleasant fog hanging over him. But Londo had proceeded with caution nevertheless, and it had been most fortunate that he had. For as he had begun to bring Vir current with the situation, as he had begun to unfold the plan in small bits . . . he had felt the keeper stirring to wakefulness. He had sent the creature into inebriated insensibility, but it had fought itself back to moderate sobriety with a speed that was both alarming and annoying. Apparently it was starting to build up some degree of tolerance to alcohol. Londo would have to reassess the amount of liquor it was going to require from now on to render the keeper unawares.

Londo dealt with the setback as best he could. He had tried to cue Vir to the danger presented to Sheridan by seeking historical precedent. Londo could sense that the keeper was suspicious of the conversation. It sensed that something was going on, but it wasn't entirely certain just what that might be. No pain was inflicted, no forcible commands were relayed into Londo's skull. But the creature had been most wary indeed, and so Londo had needed to be wary as well.

It had been tremendously frustrating for him. Part of him had simply wanted to drop the carefully chosen phrases, the historical allusions, and simply tell Vir what was going on. But he knew there would be immediate action of some sort taken by the keeper. Who knew the full powers of the monstrosity perched upon his shoulders? He knew it inflicted pain, and that it monitored his actions, but he had no reason to believe he had seen the outer limit of its capabilities. Perhaps it could blow out his brain stem with but the merest mental effort. Maybe it could send him into seizures, or stop his hearts, or . . . anything.

He wanted to do something to prevent Sheridan meeting a gruesome death at the scaly hands of the Drakh, but the simple fact was that he wasn't especially inclined to sacrifice himself to that endeavor. He still valued his own skin above Sheridan's.

After Vir had left, Londo had monitored the news broadcasts carefully. The keeper had thought nothing of Londo's watching the news. He was, after all, the emperor. It was only appropriate that he should be keeping himself abreast of current events. And when the news had carried the item about Sheridan's leading a highly publicized tour of officials into Down Below at Babylon 5, Londo's spirit had soared. It had been everything he could do to prevent himself from shouting out with joy.

Then his enthusiasm had dissipated. He could almost feel a dark cloud radiating from the keeper, and it was at that moment—even as he saw news footage of the obviously unharmed Sheridan leading the tour—that he had it confirmed for him that, yes indeed, this had been a test. A test that he had failed, because he knew that they knew. He wasn't quite sure how he was aware of it. Maybe the telepathic bond was becoming two-way. But he did, in fact, know, and now all that remained was waiting for the retaliation to descend upon him.

"Was it worth it?"

Londo was sitting in the private library that had traditionally been the province of the emperor. The Centauri set great store by it. The emperor was considered to be something akin to a living repository of Centauri history, and it was intended that he carry within his head all the great deeds of his predecessors, and the many magnificent accomplishments of the Republic. Because that duty was so respected and sacred, the highest priority was given to providing the emperor with a secluded and well-guarded place where he could indulge his historical interests to his hearts' content. Indeed, there might not have been a more secure room in the entire palace. There were many books there, and many assorted relics from the illustrious past.

So it was that when Shiv'kala's voice emerged from the darkness and asked "Was it worth it?" Londo jumped, so violently startled that he nearly knocked over the reading table. He got to his feet, trying to maintain some degree of dignity in the face of such a clumsy response. The light was quite dim in the library; he couldn't see Shiv'kala at all. "Are you here?" he asked, wondering for a moment if perhaps Shiv'kala was only speaking in his mind but was, in fact, elsewhere entirely.

"Yes. I am here." Upon hearing the voice again, Londo could indeed tell that Shiv'kala was physically in the room. But his voice seemed to be floating from everywhere. "And you are here. How nice."

"Nice," Londo said tersely, "is not the word I would have used. What do you want?"

" 'Want' is not the word I would have used," countered Shiv'kala. "I do not 'want' to do what I must. What *we* must."

"I don't know what you're talking about."

"Do you not?"

Londo started to feel something, and braced himself. It was the beginning of . . . the pain. Except it was different somehow. They'd hit him with pain in the past, but he sensed that this was not going to be like the other times. Rather than hitting him suddenly and violently, this time around the pain was starting from a much lower baseline. It gave him cause to think that perhaps he was developing a tolerance for the psychic and physical torment they were inflicting upon him. For that matter . . . perhaps it was totally unrelated to the Drakh at all.

"Are you doing that?" demanded Londo, putting a hand to his temple.

"You have done it, Londo," replied Shiv'kala. There was that familiar resignation in his tone. "You . . . and you alone."

"I do not know—" The ache was increasing now, reaching the previous levels and growing greater. Londo was finding it hard to breathe, and it seemed as if his hearts were pumping only with effort.

"Oh, you know," and any trace of sympathy or sadness was suddenly gone from the Drakh's voice. There was only hardness, and cruelty. "You have made a fool of me, Londo."

"I? I . . ." And suddenly Londo staggered. He tripped over the chair in which he'd been sitting and crashed to the floor, because he had been wrong. What he was feeling this time was far worse than anything he had ever endured before at the hands of the Drakh. Perhaps it was worse than anything he had felt in his entire life. He realized belatedly that the agony had started off slowly to put him off guard, to make him think that perhaps it wouldn't be so bad. He had been wrong.

His body began to spasm as the pain rolled over him in waves. He tried to distance himself mentally, tried to shut down his mind, but there was no possibility because the pain was everywhere, in every crevice and fold of his brain, in every sensory neuron of his body. He opened his mouth to try and scream, but he couldn't even do that because his throat was paralyzed. All he was able to muster was inarticulate gurgling noises.

"I told the Drakh Entire," continued Shiv'kala, as if Londo were not writhing like a skewered beast, "that you could be trusted. That you knew your place. They requested a test. I provided it. You failed it. That, Londo, is unacceptable."

Londo completely lost control. Every bit of waste fluid in his body evacuated, something that hadn't happened since he was two years of age. The sensation was humiliating, the stench was repugnant, and then both of those spiraled away as the agony continued to build. His soul, blackened and battered as it already was, cried out for release. He remembered how he had wanted to die all those months ago, how he had been ready to end it, but he realized that he had been a fool, because he had never wanted to die the way that he did now. At that moment, he would have given anything for the release of death. He would kill his friends and loved ones, he would annihilate a hundred, a thousand innocent Centauri. He would do anything at all just for a cessation of the agony that was hammering through him.

And then it got worse.

He felt himself being torn apart, he felt every single organ in his body liquefying, and he knew, he just knew, that his brain was dissolving and flooding out his ears, he could practically feel it, and the pain was frying his eyes and his teeth were spiking through his gums, his tongue had swollen and was blocking his windpipe, there was burning in every joint that made the slightest movement pure agony, and so he tried to stay still, but the pain prodded him to move and then there was more anguish and it just kept building until it reached the point where he forgot what it was like not to hurt.

And then it stopped.

Just like that, all at once, and he couldn't move because he was lying there numb and foul-smelling, and he felt as if he would never be able to present himself with dignity ever again, he would never feel safe again, he never wanted another soul to look upon him because he was hideous and disgusting and had been reduced to a quivering, gibbering wreck of a man. The very thought was revolting to him, and yet he couldn't help it; he was so relieved that the pain had abated, for however short a time, that he cried copious tears, his body shuddering convulsively.

"Do you know how long you endured that?" Shiv'kala asked quietly. Londo tried to shake his head, but if he had been able to answer, he would have said it had been hours. Perhaps days. "Nine seconds," Shiv'kala continued, apparently knowing that Londo was not going to be in any sort of shape to reply. "You felt that way for precisely nine seconds. Would you like to endure that for twenty or thirty seconds? Or even better . . . twenty or thirty minutes? Or hours, or days?"

"No . . . no . . ." Londo's voice was barely recognizable as his own. It sounded more like the guttural grunt of a dying creature.

"I did not think so. I doubt that you would survive it. Even if you did, I likewise doubt you'd like what you became as a consequence."

Londo didn't reply. None seemed necessary, and he doubted he could have strung a coherent sentence together anyway.

Apparently not caring about Londo's newly discovered reticence, Shiv'kala said, "That was your punishment, Londo. Punishment, however, will not be enough. You must do penance. Do you understand? Do you hear what I am saying?"

He managed to nod.

"Good." Shiv'kala had moved from the shadows and was now standing directly in front of Londo. He tilted his head and regarded the emperor with curiosity. "Tell me, Londo . . . would you kill Sheridan yourself . . . if the alternative was more punishment?"

For all the world, Londo wanted to shake his head. He wanted to spit at the Drakh, he wanted to cry out defiance. He wanted to stumble to his feet and fasten his hands around the scaly throat of that grey-skinned monstrosity. At that point, he didn't care anymore if hidden bombs blew his people to bits. He didn't care if he died in attempting to strangle Shiv'kala. All he desired at that moment was the opportunity to try and, even more, the will.

Instead he simply nodded. For he knew it to be true; at that moment, he would do anything. Kill Sheridan, kill Delenn, kill Vir, kill Timov . . . anything, anyone, whatever it took, if it meant not getting another taste of that agonizing "punishment." Even though his body wasn't presently being subjected to pain, the memory was still fresh within him. He needed no reminder of what he had just been through; if nothing else, the stench floating from him made it very difficult to forget.

"Well . . . you do not have to kill Sheridan," Shiv'kala told him. "For the moment, we shall let him live. You see . . . there is a relatively recent development that has come to our attention. Sheridan is going to become a father, you see."

Londo was slowly managing to draw breath into his chest, steadying his racing hearts. So it took a few moments for Shiv'kala's comment to fully register on him. He was still lying on the floor, but he managed to raise his head ever so slightly. "Fa . . . father?" he asked.

"That is correct," said Shiv'kala. "Your penance, actually, will be quite simple."

Shiv'kala was moving then, and Londo could not take his gaze from him. He was heading toward the relics . . . toward a shelf with several urns of varying purposes. He studied them thoughtfully, and then reached up and took one from the shelf. It was silver, with a burnished gold inlay.

Londo knew the one he was taking. It had a very specific purpose in Centauri tradition, and he had no idea why Shiv'kala could possibly be interested in it.

And then a slow, horrible thought began to dawn on him. He brushed it aside just as quickly, though, convinced that he could not possibly be correct. It was unthinkable, beyond the pale, even for the Drakh. They could not, they would not . . . and certainly they could not think to make him a party to . . .

Then the Drakh opened the folds of his garment.

"No," whispered Londo. "No . . . please . . ." From the floor, he still could not move, but he began to beg, all thought of dignity long gone. "No . . ."

Shiv'kala did not even acknowledge that he had spoken. His chest was undulating in a most hideous fashion, as if it were alive with sentient cancer sores. He placed the vase on a nearby table and then unscrewed the base. He set it aside . . . and then put his hand to his chest.

"You wouldn't . . ." Londo pleaded. Even though he knew that it was hopeless, he continued to implore Shiv'kala to reconsider.

Once again, the Drakh made no response. Instead, ever so delicately, he pulled a creature from within a fold in his body. The crea-

ture was similar to the keeper, but smaller. Its eye was closed. As
alien a being as it was, Londo could nevertheless tell that it was sleeping, perhaps even hibernating.

Shiv'kala held the thing proudly in his palm for a moment. He
ran a finger along the ridges of its body in a manner that appeared
almost paternal. It was all Londo could do not to vomit. Then he
placed the creature on the base and screwed it back onto the urn.
Londo, at that point, couldn't even get a word out. He just shook his
head helplessly.

"When Sheridan and Delenn go to Minbar . . . you will go there
as well. You will deliver," and he touched the vase with a long finger,
"this gift. You will order the bottom sealed to discourage inspection
by Sheridan. The keeper within will be able to escape when the time
is right."

"A . . . child?" Londo couldn't believe it. "A helpless child?"

"The son of Sheridan and Delenn . . . yes, it will be a son . . . but
it will not always be a helpless child. When he is grown . . . he will be
of use to us. The keeper will see to his destiny. And you . . . will see
to the keeper."

"No." Londo, to his own astonishment, was managing to shake
his head. "No . . . an innocent child . . ."

"If you shirk your penance, Londo," Shiv'kala said calmly, as if
he had been expecting Londo to protest, "you should consider the
consequences for all the innocent children on Centauri Prime. But
before any of them . . . Senna will bear the brunt of our . . ." His lips
twisted in that foul semblance of a smile. ". . . displeasure."

"Not . . . her . . ." Londo said.

"Emperor, you do not seem to realize how little say you have in
the matter. Now . . . will you cooperate?"

Hating himself, hating life, hating a universe that would do this
to him, Londo could only nod.

Then his vision began to lose focus as one more wave of pain
washed over him. He shut his eyes tightly, letting it pass, shuddering
at the sensation. When he opened his eyes again, Shiv'kala was gone.
Gone, having left Londo alone with his humiliation and pain and
weakness. Londo, who would forever know that not only did he have
a breaking point, but it had been reachable through means that
seemed almost effortless. It made him wonder just how much more
the Drakh could do to him. As horrifying a notion as the thought suggested, was it possible that—until now—the Drakh had actually been
going *easy* on him?

He wondered how much worse they could make it for him.

He wondered why threats to Senna struck so closely to him.

He wondered if he would ever know a time when he was actually, genuinely happy to be alive ... even if the feeling lasted for only a few moments.

And then, as the brutalizing that his body had endured finally caught up with him, he wondered no more as he lapsed into merciful unconsciousness.

13

The lady Mariel was busy writing a suicide note when the knock at the door interrupted her.

Her task was not one that she had undertaken lightly, or spontaneously. Indeed, she had been laboring over it for some time. She had worked over the word choice, selected one, and then discarded it, wanting everything to read properly. It hadn't been an easy business, this writing notion. She would choose a word, then pace the length of her villa—which was hideously small, a gift from her father when she reached her age of ascension and, at this point, the only piece of property remaining to her, sufficiently secluded off in the forest so that it had been spared the bombings of Centauri Prime—only to return to her work and cross out the word. "How do writers do it?" she asked at one point, although there was no one there to answer.

No one there.

Once upon a time, there had always been someone there. But not anymore. Thanks to Londo . . . they were gone. All the suitors. All gone. Fortunes, gone. Life, gone.

She wasn't entirely certain that she was actually going to go through with the suicide. Granted, she was depressed, but the more overwhelming concern for her was that she was bored. She lived this pointless existence, filling days, killing time, and accomplishing nothing. Society was closed to her, doors slammed shut . . . again, thanks to Londo Mollari.

When his holographic image had loomed over all of Centauri Prime, she had stood there at the window of her villa and screamed imprecations for the entire time that the figure had stood upon the horizon. Right after that, she had started the suicide note, deciding that a world where Londo Mollari was emperor was one in which she simply did not want to exist anymore.

But since the suicide note was going to be her last act of record, she wanted it to be just right. And since she was not a writer by nature or by craft, well . . . it was taking a while. Still, she was quite close to finishing a useable draft, and then—that would be that. The only thing remaining would be selecting the means, and she was sure that she would probably go with poison.

Certainly she knew enough about different types, and what would be both effective and painless. Her mother had taught her well in that regard, possessing rather extensive knowledge on that topic. Her father had also been well aware of her mother's erudition along those lines. It had served nicely to keep him in line, and he was quite candid in stating that his wife's mastery of terminal ingestion was the secret to the length and relative calm of their marriage.

When the knock came at the door, Mariel put down her work and called, "Yes?" while making no attempt to hide the irritation in her voice over being interrupted.

"A thousand pardons, milady," came the reply from the other side of the door. The speaker sounded rather youthful. "But your presence is requested at the Development office."

"The what?" Having been forcibly removed from the life of politics and the court, Mariel paid very little attention these days to the government or the way in which it was set up.

"The Office of Development, overseen by Chancellor Lione."

It wasn't a name that meant anything to Mariel. She began to wonder if this was some sort of elaborate prank. Or worse, a ploy to get her to open the door so that some sort of assassination attempt might be carried out. After all, Londo was emperor now. If he carried within him a need for revenge against her, certainly he would have the resources to dispatch someone to attend to it.

Then again, she was preparing to kill herself anyway. If someone was going to show up and do the job for her, certainly it wasn't that much different. Still, protocol had to be observed.

"Just a moment," she said. She was wearing the sheerest of nightgowns. She had little need to get dressed these days, since she was on her own and no one came to visit her. Even the fellow who delivered food to her once a week simply left the supplies outside the door. Indeed, that had been one of the considerations that had sent her thoughts toward suicide. It wasn't just the humiliation and the ennui, it was also a matter of practicality. Soon what meager savings she had would run out. The delivery fellow had intimated that an "arrangement" might be able to be worked out, and he had suggested it with an unmistakeably lascivious grin. The thought of falling so far that she was actually considering the "arrangement" had been what had finally propelled Mariel's thoughts down the road of embarking upon final festivities. It had also resulted in the supplies being left outside the door.

For the sake of propriety, she tossed on a robe over her gown—a sheer robe nonetheless—and answered the door.

There was a very serious-faced young man standing there. She noted his discipline; his gaze did not so much as flicker over the lines of her body. If her beauty had an effect on him, he did not let it show. "Lady Mariel?" It was intended as an interrogative, although there was very little question in his tone.

"Yes."

"I am Throk of the Prime Candidates. Chancellor Castig Lione wishes to see you."

"Does he now?" She arched one curved brow. "And he has sent you to fetch me?"

"Yes, milady."

"And if I do not choose to go?" She said it with a slightly toying tone. She had not played with a young male in some time. Pleasantly, she found that it still amused her. "Will you take me by force? Will you sling me over your shoulder as I struggle and plead for mercy?"

"No, milady."

"Then what will you do?"

"I will wait until you choose to go."

"Then that is what you will have to do." With that, she closed the door.

It was getting late in the evening. She prepared herself a meager and carefully rationed dinner, ate it slowly and sparingly, worked on her suicide note, read a bit, then went to bed. When she awoke the following morning, she glanced out her front window and was dumbfounded to see Throk standing exactly where he had been the previous afternoon. As near as she could tell, he hadn't moved from the spot. He was covered with morning dew, and a passing bird had seen fit to relieve itself on his shoulder.

She opened the door and stared at him. "My, my. You're quite determined, aren't you."

"No, milady. I simply have my orders. Returning without you would not be following my orders. I was told to treat you with all courtesy. That, in fact, to treat you with discourtesy would result in my answering directly to Minister Durla."

"Who?"

"Minister Durla. The minister of internal security."

"Oh." She frowned. The name was vaguely familiar, but she couldn't place it. No matter. It probably was not important. "And so you have chosen to wait."

"One choice is no choice, milady."

"A good point. Come in."

"I will wait here, milady, if that is acceptable."

The edges of her mouth crinkled. "And if it is not acceptable?"

"I will still wait here. I was informed you could be quite seductive and was explicitly told not to enter your domicile for fear of being distracted from my mission."

"Ooo. 'Quite seductive.' I like the sound of that." She laughed lightly then. This was the most amusement she'd had in ages. "Very well, Throk. Remain there. I will attire myself in something more suitable and then go with you to speak with this chancellor of yours. Oh . . . and Throk . . ."

"Yes, milady."

"A pity you didn't come in. I was going to let you watch me change." She winked one eye lazily as she noted a telltale movement under Throk's shirt while the youth fought to keep an impassive face. She slid shut the door, then leaned against it and laughed some more, her shoulders trembling in silent mirth. She'd forgotten what it was like to entertain herself in that manner.

The day was getting off to quite a start.

The Office of Development was more than just an office. It was an entirely new building, tall and gleaming, part of the renovations that had been going on across Centauri Prime. Most impressive, she had to admit. Castig Lione's office was on the top floor, which, for some reason, didn't surprise Mariel in the slightest.

Lione rose from behind his desk as Throk ushered her in. "Milady Mariel," he said, the picture of graciousness. "Young Throk left to fetch you yesterday. We were beginning to lose hope."

"Your noble officer was delayed in rendering assistance to me. He is to be commended," Mariel said smoothly. Just to see Throk's expression, she cupped him under the chin and tickled him behind the ear. Nonetheless, he remained impressively impassive.

"Well done, Throk," Lione said. "You may leave us, now."

"Yes, sir," Throk said in a voice that sounded faintly strangled. He bowed quickly to Mariel and got out of there as quickly as he could.

"My congratulations, milady," said Lione, as he gestured for her to take a seat, which she promptly did. "You have managed the formidable feat of causing Throk to be disconcerted. I thought no one was capable of that."

"I am not no one," Mariel said.

"True. Quite true." He seemed to contemplate her for a moment, and suddenly said, "I have been remiss. Something to drink?"

"No, thank you."

He nodded, then pulled a bottle from his desk drawer, poured himself a glass, and downed it. "You are doubtlessly wondering why I desired to see you."

"No."

"You're not?"

She gave a small shrug of her shapely shoulders. "The world and the events that transpire within it are altogether too insane for my tastes. I prefer to simply allow them to unfold, rather than try to anticipate anything."

"Well said," he chuckled. "Best not to give things too much thought. That way lies madness."

"Speaking of madness, how is the emperor?"

The well-delivered jibe prompted an appreciative chuckle from Lione. "I, of course, would never dare to make such an obviously disrespectful comment," he said. "But I suppose that having been married to the emperor at one time accords certain . . . privileges. Are you sure you want nothing to drink?"

"Quite sure. What I would like," and she rearranged her skirts delicately around her shapely legs, "is to know why I have been summoned here. I do have a good many things to attend to . . ."

"Do you. Do you really." Something in his voice had changed ever so slightly. A slight coldness crept into it, perhaps even a hint of contempt. Lione glanced at his computer screen, apparently checking a file that was displayed upon it. "Once upon a time, milady, your activities were quite easily tracked. They consisted of a series of public appearances, parties, social engagements at high-profile establishments, and so on. However, I have no clue as to what you might be up to this fine afternoon. No sign of any activities at all. Or perhaps you're simply trying to keep a lower profile these days."

Her lips thinned as her smile dissipated, to be replaced by a hardened look of barely restrained impatience. "Are you endeavoring to make a point, Chancellor? If so, what are you trying to say?"

"I would assume, milady, that I am not saying anything you do not already know. As closely as we can determine, you have fallen on extremely hard times. You are nearly out of money." Apparently warming to his topic, he leaned forward, interlacing his fingers. "Furthermore, it was bad enough when you were simply divorced by Londo Mollari. But now your former mate has risen to the exalted rank of emperor. That makes you an imperial discard. The men who once flocked to you so eagerly now desire to keep their distance. They do not desire to tempt fate, in the event that the emperor might either form a new attachment to you, or else seek you out for some rather distressing punishment. Your beauty may well be without match, Milady Mariel . . . but there remain quite a few women out there to choose from, many of them well-connected. And few of them present anything resembling the potential difficulties that would face anyone seeking your . . . favors."

"Did you bring me here to insult me?" Mariel asked. She could feel her irritation mounting quite rapidly. She had not been certain why Lione had wanted to see her, but never would she have been able to guess that it was because he wanted to torment her.

"Not at all." He seemed stricken that she could think such a thing. "Milady, I have nothing but the utmost respect for you. I have brought you here at the suggestion and recommendation of Minister Durla, but also because I genuinely believe that you will fit in nicely with our plans here at the Office of Development. Although what we have in mind is, well . . ." And he smiled. "Not precisely within the official purview of this office, if you understand my drift."

"I would like to say that I do, but I would be lying."

He stood then. She remained where she was as he sauntered around the room. Since he had only half risen from his chair earlier upon her arrival, she had not realized quite how tall he was. "There is a great deal of resentment toward the Interstellar Alliance, at present," he said.

"At present?" She chuckled lightly. "There has been for some time, and that situation will continue, I'd wager."

"Yes, as would we. And since the IA promises to be something of a presence in the galaxy for some time to come, we have a certain . . . obligation, shall we say . . . to protect Centauri interests in that regard."

"Protect them how? They have already dropped enough bombs upon us to wipe out a less hardy race. It's a bit late for protection now, is it not?"

He looked out his window, seemingly pleased with the view. "It is never too late, milady. I am overseeing the creation of a . . . a department, if you will. A quiet section of the government that is not of the government . . . if you see my meaning."

"I am . . . beginning to," she said after a moment of consideration. "You're speaking of a bureau within the Centauri government charged with spying upon the Alliance."

"Please, milady," protested Lione. " 'Spying' is such an *ugly* word."

"Really. What word would you prefer?"

" 'Espionage.' Far more elegant, don't you think?"

"You speak of things that could potentially involve great risk," said Mariel thoughtfully. "I do not embark on such undertakings lightly. What would you have me do?"

"Only that which you are more than capable of accomplishing, milady," said Lione. He had been circling the room, but now he stopped next to her. In what might be seen as a somewhat bold move, he rested a hand on her shoulder. "Your beauty, if I may say so, is exceptional."

"You may say so," Mariel told him. "And you are implying that a beautiful woman may accomplish a great many things, particularly when it comes to eliciting information from easily manipulated men."

"Quite."

"But beauty, my dear chancellor, is very much in the eye of he who beholds it," she reminded him. "The most beautiful Centauri woman on the face of this planet may be considered quite hideous by a Drazi, for example."

"True enough," admitted Lione. "But you are overlooking two things. First, there are many cross-species standards for beauty that you already surpass. To Human eyes, you are exceptionally attractive. Also, your features would not be found displeasing by a Minbari. And my understanding is that the Narn . . . well, the Narn find pale skin rather exotic, so I'm told."

"You're told correctly," Mariel said, remembering the attentions paid her by G'Kar. Certainly part of their relationship had been spurred by the fact that G'Kar drew great pleasure from cuckolding his old opponent, Londo, but certainly the Narn was attracted to her as a female, as well. "And the second thing that I am overlooking?"

"Charisma, milady. You have a great deal of charisma, and I am certain that it would serve you in good stead, even with those races who would consider a Centauri female to be less than aesthetic."

"Why, Chancellor. You certainly know how to flatter a woman."

"But I do not do so idly, I assure you. I feel you could be a most valuable operative for us, Milady Mariel. And I speak not only in terms of espionage. There may be the occasional requirement for sabotage or . . ."

"Murder?" she finished the sentence. "Oh, but let me guess: 'murder' is a distasteful word as well."

"Since you bring it up . . . I personally have always preferred the term 'relocation.' "

"Relocation?"

"Yes. To the next life."

"Ah." She smiled. Clearly the chancellor was not without a sense of humor, however morbid it might be.

He came full circle around his desk and seated himself once more. "Doubtless you are wondering how this will benefit you directly."

"It did cross my mind. Unless you were intending that I should become involved out of the goodness of my hearts."

"I have no doubt that there is much in your hearts, milady, but how much could be honestly described as 'goodness,' I would not care to find out. In answer to your question: Titles and lands, I regret, presently would be out of my reach to provide you. This aspect of my office must maintain a low profile, and to elevate you in such a manner would be too conspicuous. It might draw questions.

"However, we can easily provide you with attractive remuneration, drawn from certain discretionary funds we have at our disposal. Furthermore, I believe you will find that certain doors to society will slowly begin creaking open for you once again. Your attracting some attention can only be beneficial to the cause. Just . . . not too much attention, if you—"

"Understand your meaning? Yes, Chancellor, it's quite clear."

"Your missions would come from this office, and you would answer directly to me."

"And if I were to find myself in any sort of difficulty derived from my espionage activities? If the truth behind one of my 'missions' were to come out, and I found myself facing charges of being a spy? What then?"

"Then," sighed Lione, "I am afraid that you would very likely find yourself in rather disastrous straits. Might I suggest that you not be found out?"

"So you are saying I would be considered . . . disposable." She smiled humorlessly. "It would not be the first time. Since Londo already disposed of Daggair and myself, I have some experience in being considered easily dispensed with."

"Do you think that the lady Daggair would be interested in becoming involved, as well? Or, for that matter, the lady Timov? Granted, she is still the emperor's wife, but our understanding is that there is no love lost between the two of them. She might be willing to accommodate us."

Mariel gave the question some serious consideration. Then, slowly she shook her head. "I would not, if I were you, Chancellor. Daggair very much enjoys playing at being the manipulator. Politics and gamesmanship are something of a hobby to her. But she remains a dabbler, nothing more, with overmuch confidence in her abilities. I doubt she truly would have the stomach for the stakes that you're describing.

"As for Timov . . . you underestimate her, I think. She is superb at developing rationalizations for disliking Londo, but in my opinion, rationalizations are all they are. She was quite young when she married Londo, and she was quite starry-eyed when she did so, although it was an arranged marriage. I believe that some of that stardust remains, although it is very much tucked away in the corners of her eyes where she thinks it will not be noticed. I would not count on her being willing to betray Londo. Furthermore she is far too outspoken, and certainly does not suffer fools gladly. There is no subtlety to her, which would make her a less-than-attractive candidate.

"There are, however, others," she added thoughtfully. "Other individuals who might very well be of the caliber that you are looking for. In my time, I have had the opportunity to make the acquaintance of many 'dubious' individuals. I can provide you with a list of names, if you are so inclined."

"You see? Your usefulness to us begins already." Then he tilted his head slightly. "You seem thoughtful, milady. Is all well?"

"I am just . . . thinking about the other wives. Londo's, that is. Sometimes I look back on that part of my life as if it was someone else's entirely." She laughed softly. "Do you know what Londo used to refer to us as? 'Pestilence, famine, and death.'"

Lione shook his head politely. "I am afraid I do not understand the reference."

"Oh, it relates to Earth. Londo is quite the aficionado with Earth legend. One of their religions apparently states that, when their judgment day arrives, it will be heralded by four horsemen. And three of them would be pestilence, famine, and death."

"Earth customs seem to hold endless fascination, not only for Londo, but for his former protégé, Vir, as well." Clearly struck by a thought, he added, "Who would the fourth horseman in this mythical quartet be?"

She frowned, trying to recall, and then her face brightened. "Oh yes. War."

"War." Castig Lione chuckled. "Considering where Londo led us to, that is quite appropriate, don't you think?"

"I try not to think, Chancellor," Mariel said. "Oftentimes it gets in the way of living my life."

"So we have an understanding then, milady?"

"Yes. Yes, I believe we do." She extended a hand in a rather elegant fashion and Castig Lione took it suavely and kissed her knuckles. "I can trust to your gentlemanly nature, I assume, to make my 'remuneration' a fair one, so that we need not discuss such annoying matters as exact sums at this time?"

"I am quite certain, milady, that you will not be disappointed."

"And I thank you for thinking of me in this matter."

"Well, milady . . . as I mentioned earlier . . . to be honest, it was Durla who suggested your name to me in connection with our endeavors."

"Durla . . ." Her face blanked a moment, and then she recalled once more. "Oh, yes. That minister person. Do be so kind as to pass my thanks along to him, then. And by all means, Chancellor . . . do not feel circumscribed by the business nature of our relationship."

"Milady?"

Mariel, clearly not feeling any need to expound beyond that, simply withdrew her hand from his, then walked out of the room, stopping only to toss a small-but-knowing smile over her shoulder.

It seemed to Castig Lione that Durla was taking extreme pains to sound casual when he inquired, "Oh . . . and did you have the opportunity to meet with the Lady Mariel?"

Durla had regular weekly meetings with Lione to discuss an assortment of projects. Indeed, Durla had meetings with all of the chancellors who answered to him. Lione was accustomed to them. In his case, he would sit there and speak at length about plans of the Development Office, both short- and long-term, and Durla would appear to be listening and nodding, although whether he was truly attending to anything that Lione was saying, Lione never really knew for sure.

This time, however, Durla seemed quite attentive. His forced attempts to appear nonchalant came across as just that: forced. Lione wasn't entirely certain why that would be, although he did have his suspicions.

"Yes. Yes, I did."

"And how did it go?"

"It went quite well. She is an extraordinary individual, the lady Mariel is. A great deal of charm and personal charisma. Your assorted suggestions for our bureau of espionage have been superb up until now, Minister, but the inclusion of Mariel may well be one of your most perspicacious selections yet."

"Good."

The minister said nothing for a time, and Lione couldn't quite tell whether he was expecting Lione to continue speaking or whether Durla was simply lost in thought. To play it safe, Lione said, "I have been giving some thought to naming the division of the bureau, sir."

"Naming?" Durla momentarily seemed puzzled.

"Yes, Minister. Certainly we should have a means of refering to the division that is to oversee the gathering of information and other . . . activities . . . in regard to the Alliance. However, calling it the Espionage Division would seem a bit obvious."

"Yes. Yes, absolutely, I agree." Durla pursed his lips, considered it, and then said, "Designate it as the Division of Public Works."

"Public works. Very well, Minister. May I ask how you—"

"Did she say anything about me?"

The question had come out all in a rush from Durla, and it caught Lione momentarily off guard. "She, Minister? Do you mean the lady Mariel?"

"Yes, yes. You did tell her that it was upon my recommendation that she was being brought into the Division of Public Works."

"No, sir, because at the time, we were not calling it the—"

"Do not fence with me, Lione," said Durla, in a voice that seemed to suggest Castig Lione was suddenly in danger. By this point, Durla's attitude had more or less confirmed Lione's evaluation of the situation, but Lione was not about to say what was on his mind. He had a feeling that doing so could prove to have rather nasty consequences. "Did you mention me to her. I simply wish to know."

"Why do you wish to know, sir?" asked Lione.

"Because," Durla said steadily, "if I should happen to encounter her at a formal function, I wish to know if she knows that I know of her involvement so that I do not say something out of turn."

Lione slowly nodded, running Durla's last sentence through his mind a couple of times to make certain that he had followed it correctly. "I . . . understand, Minister. In point of fact, yes, I did mention your name to her. Twice, I believe, although I would not swear to it."

Durla suddenly seemed rather interested in tapping the surface of his desk with his finger. "Indeed. And . . . what did she say? In regard to me, I mean. She did indicate that she knew who I was."

It might have been Lione's imagination, but it seemed as if Durla was puffing out his chest slightly as he said that, as if completely absorbed in his self-image. "Yes, sir. In fact . . . now that I think of it . . . she did ask me to thank you for recommending her."

"She did!" Durla slapped his hand on the desk as if he'd suddenly had an off-the-cuff recollection of where he had left his wallet. "And why did you not say this earlier, Lione? If you are to be overseeing an intelligence-gathering division, it might behoove you to be more efficient in transmitting important information to me, without my having to drag it out of you. Do you not agree?"

"Wholeheartedly, Minister. I shall endeavor to do better in the future."

"Did she say anything else? You said she knew who I was. Of course she did," he answered his own question. "She must know. Everyone does."

"She definitely had an awareness, Minister. When I mentioned your name, she said . . . now what was it? Ah. She said, 'Oh, yes . . . that minister person.' "

The temperature in the room dropped substantially.

" 'That . . . minister person?' Are you quite certain that is what she said?"

"Word for word, sir."

Durla's face hardened, and it was at that moment that Lione knew precisely what to do. He leaned forward in his chair, his tall frame almost bending in half as he gestured in a conspiratorial way that Durla should lean forward. Clearly confused, Durla did so, and when Lione spoke, it was in the whispered tone of someone sharing a very great secret. "She is a very subtle individual, sir."

"Subtle."

"Sublimely so, yes. However, sir, she is still merely a woman . . . and I have always been a fairly astute judge of the breed, sir."

"I don't quite follow you, Chancellor."

"I believe, sir, that she may have more . . . consideration for you than she lets on. Oh, but . . . perhaps I'm speaking too boldly here—"

"No, no," Durla said quickly. "I need to know whatever might be on your mind, Chancellor. By all means, be bold."

"Well, Minister," the Chancellor said, warming to the topic, "although her words seemed dismissive, there was something about her tone of voice that indicated otherwise. Almost as if she was trying mightily to give the appearance of having only the slightest notion of who you were. But let us be realistic, Minister . . . who on Centauri Prime does *not* know Minister Durla of Internal Security? The idea that she would not be instantly familiar with your name is simply absurd. A far more reasonable supposition is that she was being—"

"Subtle?"

"Yes. Precisely. I could see it in her eyes, sir. It was quite evident . . . if one knows what to look for."

"Well . . . that is excellent. Most excellent," Durla said, looking remarkably cheered. Lione sat straight up again and Durla continued, "I have no doubt that she will be a valuable addition to the Division of Public Works. Good work, Lione. Good work all around."

They chatted for a few more minutes about assorted business matters: The current membership of the Prime Candidates, and how it could be increased. An archaeological project that Durla, for some reason, was in the process of commencing on some outlying world. But Lione wasn't listening. Instead his mind was racing in regard to the situation that had presented itself to him in such stark and clear relief. There was no doubt, as far as Lione was concerned. Clearly Durla was besotted with the woman. When it came to matters involving the lady Mariel, Durla obviously could not be counted on to think straight.

That was a useful piece of information to have. Lione had no idea quite yet how, or if, he would turn it to his advantage. But he had no doubt that, sooner or later, it would come into use. A useful little hole card . . . and one that would be his to play when it suited his needs.

PART 2

2265–2267

Nighttime

14

Senna was becoming increasingly worried about the emperor.

Naturally she had something personal at stake. In her nearly two years at the palace, she had become rather used to the comforts. Her continued residence there was contingent upon not only Londo's good graces, but his continued health.

But it was more than just that. She had a feeling about him, a sense that in some way, he was truly aspiring to greatness. He wanted so much for his people. He loved Centauri Prime with a passion that she felt was unmatched by anyone else in the palace.

That, of course, was no great measure, because Senna did not particularly like anyone else in the palace. Durla seemed to be omnipresent, watching her with those cold and deadly eyes, like a great animal waiting to spring upon unwary prey. Durla's preferred right-hand man, Castig Lione, was not much better. Then there was Kuto, Durla's newly chosen Minister of Information, although as near as Senna could tell, Kuto's major activities involved the suppression of genuine information . . . or, at least, the free flow of ideas. From her vantage point in the social strata, Senna could watch clearly the slow disappearance of any persons who expressed opinions contrary to the directives the government foisted upon the people.

The people. Great Maker help the people.

A number of times during the many months she had resided in the palace, Senna had made forays into the city. She had made certain to leave behind her richly stitched and elaborate dresses, and instead had favored simple, relatively unattractive garments. She had moved among places that Londo would most likely—and most unhappily—have disapproved of. And the things she heard were most disturbing to her.

There was constant talk of anger toward the Alliance, indicating emotional wounds that had never been healed. She remembered the child who was hobbling about with one leg gone at the knee, his lower leg having been crushed by falling debris and amputated; his parents hadn't had the money to pay for prosthetics to replace it. She recalled the woman who said she never slept anymore, that every small sound during the night awakened her as she believed that more bombs were about to be dropped upon her. From the woman's haunted visage, Senna could tell that the woman wasn't exaggerating her plight. Senna's hearts went out to her, and she wished once more that there was something she could do.

Although their stories of horror and mental anguish were all different, their current sentiments seemed to be consistent. The resentment toward the Alliance still burned hotly, and even as Centauri Prime was being rebuilt, it appeared to Senna that it was being rebuilt for a reason. And that reason was the launching of some sort of attack against the Alliance. The specifics of it didn't seem clear to anyone. It was more a free-floating sense of anger, which permeated the social structure of Centauri Prime, from the top through to the very bottom.

The truth was that Senna had no more love for the Alliance than anyone else. But some aspects of her education, including her all-too-short time with Telis Elaris—whom she continued to think of at least once a day, and always with a sense of grief and loss—had led her to conclude that the path upon which the Centauri Republic seemed determined to tread could not be the correct one. Indeed, it could very well lead to an even greater disaster. Centauri Prime had been pounded into the ground but, ultimately, most of the Republic's citizens were at least still alive. They were being permitted to rebuild, and even the economy was showing signs—slow signs, but signs nonetheless—of beginning to recover.

If the Republic, once it was rebuilt, resumed its old ways and came into conflict once more with the Interstellar Alliance, things might go far worse for them the next time. How apt, how poetically just would it be, if the illegal mass drivers—the ultimate in ground punishment, gathering in space debris and raining it down in concentrated form—were used against Centauri Prime, just as the Centauri had wrongfully used them against the Narn? By the time the Alliance got through with them, there might not be a single Centauri left alive. Rather than recapture the glory of republics past, the Centauri might find themselves extinct. Within a generation everything that the Centauri Republic had ever accomplished, for good or ill, would be dust and forgotten.

Senna did not want to let that happen, but she didn't have the faintest idea how to go about preventing it. One female could not possibly prevent the Centauri Republic from committing mass suicide, which seemed the likeliest outcome if Centauri Prime continued on its present course.

The only hope she could possibly discern lay with the emperor. He, however, seemed to be slipping farther and farther away with each passing day.

Oh, there were the occasional good days. On those occasions, Londo would laugh or joke with her, tweak her cheek in an affectionate manner that could not possibly be considered anything other than paternal. Sometimes he would regale her with tales of the Republic in the past, or share with her some examples of his impressively extensive collection of slightly ribald jokes. In short, there was any number of times when the emperor was someone she genuinely wanted to be with.

The rest of the time, however . . . well, when he would look at her, it was as if he was staring at her from the bottom of a very deep pit. His were the eyes of a man who somehow, in some manner that she could not begin to comprehend, had seen his own future. And it was apparently not something that was going to be pretty or desirable.

Now, as she approached the emperor's study, Senna hoped that perhaps she would encounter Londo during one of his more convivial moods. Because if he were in that sort of state, then she might actually be able to share with him her concerns over the future of the Republic. Certainly there was no one else in the palace with whom she could speak on any sort of open basis. Everyone else had the misfortune of being male, or the sort of political in-fighter who wouldn't hesitate to use anything that Senna said against her. She had no desire to provide any potential enemy with that sort of ammunition. But the emperor . . .

The emperor, for some reason, she was not afraid of. If anything, she was afraid *for* him.

She peered in through the study, and saw him slumped at his desk. For the briefest of moments, she thought he was dead. That was until she heard the snoring, however; at which point she knew that Londo was still among the living . . . although barely so, it seemed.

And then she thought morbidly, *A shame he's not dead. He'd stay well preserved for some time if he were.* As soon as the notion went through her head, she chided herself for it. What a horrible thing to think, particularly when it was obvious that the emperor was hurting emotionally.

She studied him thoughtfully and wished that there was some way that she could reach directly into his mind. Sense his thoughts, ease the pain. Do something, *anything* possible to help this basically good man, or at the very least have some idea of what it was that was eating away at him.

Then she noticed that he had been working on something.

His hand was resting on it. She dared not touch him in order to move his hand and see better, but then—as if he were unconsciously urging her to look—he moved his arm. In his slumber, it slid off the desk and hung limply at his side.

She looked more closely and saw that it was a book. A book that he was apparently writing by hand. How very, very quaint. Most people, it seemed to her, preferred data crystals and such. She could only guess why he might want to work in what some would consider an archaic fashion. Perhaps he felt it added a sort of personal touch. Or maybe he was inspired by the numerous books of history, many of them handwritten by past emperors, which were said to line the walls of the private library. By continuing in that tradition, he was making himself a sort of living link to the past.

From a purely pragmatic point of view, by confining his writings to one book that he carried with him, it also meant that his thoughts and musings would be kept in his possession at all times. The moment anything was put onto a computer, even as a private file, there was always the danger that someone, somewhere would be able to carve their way into the system and access it.

She toyed with the notion of picking up the book, examining it. Certainly there was nothing to stop her from doing so, with the sole exception of her conscience. Obviously this was a work in progress, and it was unlikely that Londo would want anyone perusing it before he felt it was ready.

Even so . . .

Well . . . if she didn't actually turn the pages, that wouldn't be so invasive, would it? After all, she was simply looking down at the open ones. Why . . . who could fault her for that? It wasn't as if she had been seeking it out. Besides, certainly Londo meant for it to be read sooner or later. What point was there in writing a history if no one was going to see it. And it was a history, she was quite sure of that. Because she had just kind of, sort of, well . . . just happened to lift the title page ever so slightly and spotted the word, carefully delineated in Londo's own script. Then, ever so delicately, she laid the book flat again so that she could see just what Londo was writing about at that particular moment. The book appeared already to be half full. Apparently Londo had been quite busy.

She started to read, although she wasn't touching the book at that point. But when she saw just what it was that she was reading, her eyes went wide with surprise.

Minbar! The emperor had been on Minbar! She remembered when he had disappeared from Centauri Prime, some five months before. His departure had been unannounced and rather unexpected. Durla had tried to act as if he had been expecting it, but even he had seemed a bit caught off guard.

Londo had been gone for three weeks, and there had been a bit of confusion and nervousness bandied about, although Durla had done an excellent job of staying atop all the problems that had cropped up. And then, after a time, the emperor had returned. Senna realized that it was from that point on that she had really noticed the change in him. He seemed . . . smaller than he had before. Diminished somehow. It was nothing she could truly put her finger on, but she was certain that she wasn't imagining it. Something very bad had happened, and she now knew that whatever it was that had happened to so dispirit the emperor, it must have occurred on Minbar.

Despite her better judgment, Senna set aside all pretense to the contrary and started reading what Londo had written. She still didn't pick up the book, as if not touching it would somehow negate any invasion of privacy or breaking of trust. Instead she leaned with her knuckles on the table and read in earnest.

Apparently Londo had gone to Minbar to meet with Delenn and Sheridan. Delenn was with child, and at the point in the narrative where the page began, Londo was recording an encounter with the president of the Interstellar Alliance and his "lovely wife," as Londo put it.

Senna continued to read:

It was clear to me that they were to be somewhat guarded in my presence. I could see it in Sheridan's eyes, feel it even when he wasn't looking at me. He was suspicious and unsure. I suppose I could not blame them, truly. They were not expecting me simply to show up on Minbar. Now that I was here, they had no clue as to what to anticipate. It had to be especially perplexing for Sheridan, since he believed himself a superb strategist, and my appearance on Minbar did not fit any proscribed pattern he could anticipate.

As for me . . . I had my own difficulties to deal with, my own "secrets" to attend to. So not only was I a bit more boisterous than I normally would have been, left to my own devices, but certainly more effervescent than the moment called for. No doubt that increased the level of their suspicions.

We were seated in the dining room which, I must admit, was not particularly lavish. These days it seems to me that the palace on Centauri Prime is more of a prison than a home. Nonetheless, at least it is a decorative prison. The food, as far as I was concerned, was mostly inedible; even the most elaborate Minbari delicacies are, at best, bland. But I smiled through it as we chatted—once more—about how surprised Sheridan and Delenn were to see me. Surprised . . . and even a bit disconcerted. When I commented on it, they promptly denied it, of course. They wished to be polite. Considering the purpose of my being there, it seemed almost quaint that such was their concern.

Our conversation broadened to surprising people in general. "Another of the benefits of being emperor . . ." and then I added, almost as an afterthought, "or president in your case . . . is not so much the people who are pleased to see you in office. It's the people who are furious that you're even alive, let alone holding a position of power. Knowing that every day you succeed, they die a little inside . . . makes the endeavor eminently satisfying."

Sheridan cast an uncomfortable glance at Delenn and then forced a polite smile. "I hadn't really thought of it in those terms," he said.

I thought of the looks I get from my ministers, and the scheming eyes that watch my back as I pass, thinking of how delightful my spine would look with a dagger protruding from it. "Oh, you will. You will," I assured him.

There was an uncomfortable silence—one of many in the evening—and then Delenn said, "If you don't mind my saying so, Emperor Mollari—"

I waved a scolding finger. "Londo, please."

"You told *me* to call you Emperor Mollari," said Sheridan.

Indicating Delenn's ensemble, I replied, "You don't look as good in that outfit as she does." This actually prompted the first genuine smile of the evening. "Go on, Delenn."

"I was just going to say that your attitude toward us is . . . ." She paused, searching for the right words. ". . . quite improved over the last time. When we were all on Centauri Prime, you said some . . . un-kind things."

I waved dismissively. "Playing to the audience, Delenn, nothing more. I need to get my people fired up in order to begin the long and difficult process of rebuilding. There's politics," and then I looked significantly at them, "and there's friendship. And when I learned that you were with child, and that you were finally coming here to stay . . . how could I not come and convey my personal best wishes."

When she read that, Senna's hearts leapt. So grim Londo had been as of late, so sullen. Was it possible that he indeed presented one face to his people and advisors, and another to those he truly considered his friends? For some reason, it made Senna want to know the real Londo even more. The one who genuinely cared about reconciliation. Already she could see that it made sense, although she wasn't entirely sure that she agreed with the tactic. She under-stood it, though. Saying whatever was necessary to get the people stirred up. Yes. Yes, it did make sense. After the battering, the bomb-ings . . . their spirit was at a low ebb. First and foremost, he had to get them to *care* about something, to manufacture some sort of passion and energy. And if it was directed at first in a negative manner, well . . . at least it was there. Once it was present, he could then steer it whichever way he wanted it to go.

She looked back at the book and continued to read . . .

Delenn and Sheridan looked at each other, and I could tell what was going through their minds. They were hoping that what I said was the truth . . . but they were not certain.

I suppose I could not blame them. I have been living so many lies for so long, even I am not certain what the truth is anymore.

Senna's face fell when she read that. It certainly wasn't the senti-ment she was hoping he'd express. "Living so many lies?" What did that mean?

As Sheridan and Delenn tried to make up their minds, my own thoughts began to race as to possibilities under which we might . . . chat in an open manner. I had, after all, certain con-siderations that needed to be attended to. "I would raise a toast to you, but there doesn't seem to be anything at hand. Do you

have a little Brivari, Mr. President? Some of that excellent Earth
whiskey tucked away in a box somewhere?"

"No," said Sheridan. "Since alcohol is dangerous for Minbari, I decided to leave all that stuff at Babylon 5."

Immediately I remembered, and could have kicked myself
for the oversight. Lennier had told me that alcohol engendered
murderous rages in Minbari. Foolishness. Foolishness of me to
forget that. For now there was no way I would be able to . . . relax sufficiently, to be able to truly open up. With flickering hope,
I asked, "Surely there must be a little . . ."

"Not a drop," Sheridan said firmly. "I'm surprised that you
didn't bring your own supplies."

I glanced at my shoulder and felt a slight twinge of warning.
"My associates do not allow me such pleasures anymore. I suppose they feel I am dangerous enough sober. No reason to make
things worse."

We continued to eat in silence once more, and then I felt a
slight qualm in my mind, through that damnable connection. But
this time it was not a warning that came from within, but from
without. I glanced up and immediately saw the problem. Delenn
was looking at me, her eyes narrowed, as if she was perceiving
that which she could not . . . indeed, must not . . . be allowed to
see. And yet I was

Senna stopped reading, thoroughly confused. What could Londo
possibly be talking about? What was Delenn "perceiving" that she
should not? The only thing Senna could guess was that Delenn was
intuiting something about Londo's state of mind. He wanted to retain his privacy, keep his purposes and thoughts obscure. After all, he
had spoken of "living lies," a comment that bothered Senna greatly.
Obviously, Londo was worried about letting anyone get too close to
him emotionally.

Although the comment about "that damnable connection" still
mystified her.

   And yet I was almost tempted to do nothing. Perhaps . . .
perhaps if she perceived, if she knew and understood . . . then
they would be able to take the proper action, know the precau-
tions that they should employ.

   That was when a little voice in my head urged me to stop
stalling. It wasn't words that I heard so much, but a sense that I

should get on with it . . . lest there be dire consequences for all concerned. And I knew that I had no choice. No choice at all.

His conscience. He was wrestling with his conscience over some sort of decision, probably having to do with whether he could trust Sheridan and Delenn. Senna felt herself utterly caught up in the drama of the moment.

"So, Delenn," I said quickly. That startled her from her concentration and she muttered an apology. "You haven't asked me about my gift."

"What gift?" Delenn responded. She still seemed a bit befuddled by her long gaze into the dark places of my life, and she turned to Sheridan.

Sheridan, ever the diplomat—and, of course, eager to distance himself from the great Centauri Republic and its even greater emperor—said, "We really can't . . ."

"Oh, it's not for you," I quickly assured them. Then I clapped my hands, and one of my retainers entered with the urn. It was draped with a white cloth, so naturally it drew some degree of curiosity, particularly from Delenn. At least there are some aspects of females that cross all races, and inquisitiveness appears to be a universal womanly trait. Sheridan just looked suspicious. Of course, he had long practice at it.

The retainer set the vase down and left, and I removed the cloth with just a bit of a flourish. I have to admit, it was a rather impressive looking bit of pottery . . . at least, from the outside.

Sheridan picked it up, and it was everything I could do to repress a shudder. Instead, sounding remarkably sanguine about it, if I do say so myself, I said, "It is a Centauri tradition to give this to the heir to the throne when he or she comes of age. It is very old."

"It's beautiful," Delenn said. "But we cannot possibly accept."

Naturally, I would have been more than happy to oblige them. Instead I had to say, "I insist."

"Won't they miss it back home?" asked Sheridan.

They were asking so many questions, so many damned questions. It was an annoying trait. They never accepted anything at face value, never took the word of others. They had to keep asking and probing until they themselves were satisfied.

"The tradition is not well known outside the palace," I said. "Besides, I have no heirs and, when I am gone, I suspect the Centaurum will do all it can to eliminate the position of emperor. If I am going to be obsolete, and that is going to be obsolete, then I may as well make sure it goes someplace where it will be appreciated."

Lies intermingled with truth. I was becoming quite facile with it. Truthfully, I did not think there was any chance whatsoever that the position of emperor would be eliminated. There are far too many people who crave the ultimate power of that office. The very people who would be in a position to do away with the office of emperor would be the very same people most eager to don the white themselves. Little good may it do them.

And besides . . . I knew of the prophecy. I knew I was ordained to be followed by an emperor . . . by at least one . . .

This revelation stunned Senna for a moment. A prophecy? She had read assorted books of Centauri prophecy. Certainly there were women who were quite legitimate seers, and their forecasts were well known. But she didn't recall any published prophecy that specifically mentioned Londo. Or that cited when or if the position of emperor would be done away with. Was it some sort of private reading that had been done just for him?

She hoped that his next words would spell out what the prophecy was, or where he had divined it from. Instead, as she read on in eager anticipation, she felt a flicker of disappointment . . .

At that moment, a Minbari entered and whispered something into Delenn's ear. I suspect that he was of the same "caste" as Lennier, for he had that same, quiet manner as the star-crossed Ranger. Delenn nodded and rose. "Something has just come up," she said. "If you will excuse me."

For a moment I thought that perhaps somehow, through some miracle, she had figured it out. That she actually knew. But then she walked out of the room without so much as a backward glance, and that was how I knew she remained blissfully oblivious.

Sheridan then faced me, and I hoped that he was going to continue to try and dissuade me from presenting him with the gift. Instead he picked that horrendous moment to allow me to be magnanimous. "Well, if I can't talk you out of this," he said, ". . . well, thank you. When should I . . . ?"

The words I was about to speak felt as if I was allowing poison to drip from my mouth. "When your child, male or female, turns sixteen years, then you hand it over."

"I notice the bottom part is sealed."

Great Maker, nothing slipped past the man. I kept my expression bland, though, as I fabricated on the spot, "Yes. I'm told that it contains water taken from the river that flowed past the first palace, two thousand years ago."

He actually looked intrigued as he gently set the vase down.

We chatted for a bit more, but with every passing moment I became less and less enthused, more and more anxious to simply get out of there. I felt as if the walls were closing in. My breath was heavy in my chest. I tried to tell myself that it was simply the different atmosphere on Minbar, but I could not ignore the fact that I was likely suffering from some sort of attack of anxiety. Suddenly I knew that if I did not get out of the dining room, if I did not get away from the urn, I would go mad right there, right on that very spot. They would mark the floor as a historical site, the place where the great Emperor Londo Mollari lost his mind and collapsed from the strain of a tormented conscience.

I began to make my excuses to Sheridan, talking about how I was needed back on Centauri Prime. How they could not function without me. I tried to make it sound like a great trial and task. I laughed about it, shared with him how daunting such awesome responsibility could be. And all during that time, I wanted to do nothing more than flee the room. But I tend to think that, had I done so, such an action might well have piqued his curiosity and sent him off in directions that it would be best not to go.

Mercifully, Delenn returned before too long. She seemed distracted, saddened. Her smile was a forced thing, her luminous spirit momentarily diminished, but she did her best to try and bring herself back up to her normal levels of cheerful and thoughtful social interaction. Then I was in the midst of saying my good-byes as we walked down the corridor toward the exit.

"Are you sure you can't stay a little longer?" asked Sheridan.

I was not entirely certain how serious he was. I think, in a perversely ironic way, he actually meant it because he was moved by my magnanimous "gift."

"No, the affairs of state weigh on me just as they do on you,"

I said. "Besides, I'm sure you would like to settle in and get down to creating the greatest empire in history, yes?"

It was a good exit line. Nice, noncommittal, even a tacit acknowledgement of the inevitable greatness of the Interstellar Alliance. I could depart their lives with a smile and the knowledge that, at the last, I was the same charming and amusing Londo as in the earliest days of Babylon 5, rather than this dark and forbidding presence that I have become.

I wanted to turn away, to say nothing more . . . but I could not help myself. There was so much more that needed to be said, that should have been said and never would be. I felt a gentle stirring, a mild warning, a rebuke in advance that seemed to say, *Keep your distance. You have done your duty, your penance, now leave. Simply . . . leave.*

That, more than anything, spurred my next words as I said to them with terrible earnestness, "One thing I want you to know, to understand and to hold in your thoughts in the years to come . . . I want you to know that you are my friends, and you will always be my friends, no matter what may happen. And I want you to know that this day . . . this day in your company means more to me than you will ever know."

Then I sensed their presence. Durla's guards, two of his closer and more dedicated followers, hovering there. Obviously Durla had a sense of how long I should be spending with Sheridan and Delenn, a mental approximation that I can only assume was provided for him by means he does not truly understand himself. He had imparted those time limits to the guards, and they were coming in search of me, their presence a gentle but firm reminder of just who was watching whom.

The word *Go* filtered through my brain, and I did not even have to bother to look in the direction of my watchers to know that they were there. "It appears I must go now."

"I know," said Sheridan. Of course, the fact was that he did *not* know. He thought he did, thought he comprehended, but he understood nothing. Not really. The odds are that he never would.

And his lack of comprehension was underscored by the last words he would ever speak to me on the surface of Minbar. Because if we were to face each other again, I knew it was likely going to be across the interstellar plain of battle, perhaps snarling at one another via view screens. Or else we might, just might, meet as keeper and prisoner, should Sheridan's fates turn against him and he wind up a prisoner on Centauri Prime. Of course, in my own situation, the concepts of prisoner and keeper are extremely fluid, and I constantly find myself occupying both positions at the same time. I am he who holds the fate of millions, and I am he whose fate is held by other keepers.

And I know that the situation will never be reversed. I will never face Sheridan with myself as a prisoner, for were it to come to that, I will be dead before such an encounter took place. They will certainly attend to that.

So Sheridan spoke his last, unknowingly sardonic words to me then as we stood for the last time as peaceful equals: "You're always welcome to come back, Londo."

"More than welcome," echoed Delenn.

They were good people, I knew that. They deserved better than what was coming to them, better than what I had done to them. Then again . . . so did I. Except my living hell was of my own making, whereas their future living hell . . . was also of my making. Is there any more blackened and stained soul in existence than mine?

I could hardly get out any words. I managed to say, "Thank you . . . good-bye . . ." And then I was gone, my guards walking on either side of me, escorting me back to my ship. I thought I overheard Sheridan and Delenn discussing Lennier just before I was out of earshot, and I wished I could have heard more. He was a good lad, Lennier. I spent some time with him. In retrospect, he may be the only individual who ever spent extended time in my presence without becoming tainted in some manner. A good and pure soul is his. I envy him that.

Through the glass of my cruiser, I watched Minbar receding, and then, naturally, I heard an all-too-expected voice. The voice that said *You*

"You! You! What are you doing?"

Senna jumped back, completely startled, her hand jumping and knocking the book off the table. Londo had awoken, and he was looking up at her with pain-filled and bloodshot eyes that were seething with anger.

"What are you doing! How much did you read? *What did you read!?"*

Senna's mouth opened, but no words emerged. Londo was on his feet, and he had risen with such fury that he knocked aside the writing table, sending it crashing to the floor. He sounded more than just angry.

He sounded terrified.

"I . . . I . . ." Senna finally managed to get out.

Londo grabbed up the book, slammed it shut. "This was private! You had no right . . . *no right!*"

"I . . . I thought—"

"You didn't think! Not for a minute! What did you read here! Tell me! I will know if you are lying, tell me!"

She remembered how just a short time before, she had been thinking how she had never been afraid of Londo. That sentiment was gone. She had never been more terrified, not just of Londo, but of anyone, as she was at that moment. "About . . . you and Sheridan and Delenn. You gave them the urn."

"And then?" He grabbed her by either shoulder, shook her, and there was such tumult in his eyes . . . she remembered being a very small child, looking to the skies as her father, Refa, held her tightly, and there were storm fronts rolling in. And those darksome clouds had been the single most frightening thing she had ever seen . . . until this moment, when she looked into the eyes of Londo Mollari.

"And then?!"

"And then you left, never to come back, and I'm leaving too, all right, all right?!" Senna cried. And she tore away from him, sobbing and choking so hard that she couldn't even catch her breath. She thought she was going to be ill. She ran then, ran as fast and as hard as she could, ran from the room and almost crashed into Durla. His eyes widened as he took in Senna's agitated state, and the condition of both the furniture and the emperor.

"It's your fault, it's *all your fault!*" she howled in his face.

"Young lady . . ." Durla began, but he got no further as her hand flew, almost on its own accord, to smack against his face and leave a huge flaming red area the size of her palm on his cheek. Durla staggered from the pain of the impact, but Senna didn't stay around to see the results of her action. Instead she ran down the hallway, her arms pumping, her breasts heaving.

In her room, she tore away the fine dress she was wearing. The cloth, the beautiful, gilt-edged, shimmering cloth made a most satisfying ripping sound as she shredded it. Naked, she yanked together some assorted articles of clothing, tossed them on in a hodge-podge manner, and threw a cloak around her shoulders.

She heard a crack of thunder from outside. The skies were opening up and rain was starting to hammer down. She didn't care. She couldn't stay in the palace a second longer, not when she knew what she knew. And as she ran out into the rain, she realized that the most frustrating thing was that she knew what she knew . . . was nothing. And it was the nothing that she feared more than anything.

15

When Senna had not returned after a week, Londo summoned Lione. To Londo's utter lack of surprise, Durla showed up with him. "I had some matters to discuss with you, Majesty," Durla said, "and since Chancellor Lione stated that you desired to—"

Londo was gazing out the window at the city. Without even bothering to turn around, he said to Lione, "I have a little task for your Prime Candidates, Chancellor."

"They, and I, are at your service, Majesty," Lione said, bowing slightly.

"Senna is out there somewhere. I want her found, and I want you to alert me as to where she is. I will handle matters from there."

Lione and Durla exchanged glances, and then Durla cleared his throat and took a step forward. "Majesty," he said politely, "are you sure that would be for the best?"

"She is one young woman, Durla. If I cannot save one young woman," and he gestured out at the city, "how can I save all of them?"

"That's not quite what is at issue, Majesty. I was simply thinking that perhaps this is a matter that should not be pursued."

"Indeed." Londo's voice was carefully neutral, his back still to them.

"Obviously, Majesty, the young woman is ... how shall I put this? ... an ingrate, Majesty. After all you have done for her, after all the time she has resided here ... and this is how she treats your hospitality?"

Londo was silent for a time.

"Majesty?" Durla said carefully.

At that point, Londo turned to face them. His eyebrows were knitted in apparent surprise. "Chancellor ... you are still here?"

"You have not dismissed me, Majesty," Lione said in confusion.

"I did not think it necessary. I have given you your orders ... or," and his voice took on a cutting edge, "were you operating under the assumption that I was coming to you as supplicant, putting in a request that you could attend to or disregard, at your discretion?"

"No, Majesty, it's just that . . ."

"I have told you what to do. Your only response should be to bow, say, 'Immediately, Majesty,' turn and leave. Apparently you did not comprehend that. So . . . we shall try it again. I will give the order. You will respond as expected. And if you do not do so . . . I will have you executed within the hour." He smiled and spread his hands as if greeting an old friend. "That sounds fair, yes?"

Lione paled, and he visibly gulped. Durla looked in confusion from Londo back to Lione.

"I have a little task for your Prime Candidates, Chancellor," said Londo, without waiting for Lione to reply. "Senna is out there somewhere. I want her found, and I want you to alert me as to where she is. I will handle matters from there."

"Y-yes, Majesty."

Londo fixed him with a deathly glare. "You were supposed to say, 'Immediately, Majesty.' " Lione's back stiffened so abruptly that there was an audible crack. Then Londo smiled wanly and said, "Close enough. Go to, eh?"

Chancellor Lione almost sprinted from the room, and Londo turned his gaze upon Durla. Londo's eyes seemed almost hooded, as if a veil had been drawn over them. "Now . . . what business have you, Durla?"

"Majesty, perhaps the Senna matter should be examined in more de—"

"What. Business. Have. You."

It was quite evident to Londo that Durla was wrestling with the notion of continuing the discussion . . . but then he very wisely reconsidered. Instead, he said, "You have inquired about the archaeological dig on K0643."

"Yes. I have."

Londo felt a slight stirring on his shoulder. And he knew why.

Several months previously, he had been examining various budget items, and he had come across Durla's fringe world project. The reasons behind it completely eluded him. At that point, he had dictated a computer memo to himself to speak with Durla about it. Before he could follow through, however, the shadows had moved ever so slightly and Shiv'kala had emerged from them. Londo had not known he was there, and by that point had given up trying to figure out whether the Drakh was simply omnipresent, or whether the keeper summoned him and somehow he managed to materialize on an as-needed basis.

"That is a worthy project," Shiv'kala had told him. "I do not suggest you challenge it."

"May I ask why?"

"Yes."

There was a pause, and then Londo had said, "Very well: why?"

And Shiv'kala, naturally, had made no response, unless one counted melting back into the shadows as a response. Londo, feeling haggard and weary by that point, had simply signed off on the item, reasoning that any project that got the people of Centauri Prime interested and involved was worthwhile.

But now . . . now things felt different. It wasn't that they necessarily *were* different. However, they *felt* that way. For ever since he had left that urn with Sheridan and Delenn, forever damning not only their unborn child, but himself, it was as if he had hit rock bottom.

After the explosive conflict with Senna, though, something within him had simply . . . snapped. It was like a mental bone had broken, and now it was beginning to reform, tougher and harder than ever. It was most unexpected to Londo, who had been so accustomed to despair that he had almost forgotten what a glimmer of hope could look like.

He still knew better than to go head-to-head with Shiv'kala, for that was certainly a lost cause. But he was beginning to reacquire a bit of his fighting spirit. Major acts of defiance, particularly face-to-face, might well be beyond his capabilities. But smaller such actions or inconveniences . . . what was the phrase? Nibbling to death by cats? Yes . . . that was it. What a marvelous turn of phrase those Humans had.

"Majesty," Durla was saying, "what do you wish to know about the project?"

"I do not understand the reason for it," Londo said. He felt the tingle of alertness on the part of the keeper, but he ignored it. "I wish you to explain it to me."

"It is all in the original proposal, Majesty, which you appro—"

"The report is not here, Durla. You are here. I am here. We can speak to one another, yes?"

"Well . . . yes, of course, Majesty, but I . . ."

"So? Explain."

Ohhhh, the keeper was not happy with the direction of the conversation. In a way, the keeper's reaction was of morbid fascination to Londo, for Londo was curious as to whether or not Durla knew of the Drakh's existence. His actions, his attitudes, had led Londo to wonder about it, but he could not be sure. So by pushing Durla, gently but firmly, Londo was taking a stab at answering the question for himself. If Shiv'kala or one of his associates made themselves known right then and there, that would certainly settle the question, wouldn't it.

"Well . . . unemployment is obviously a serious problem for us, Majesty. A number of key businesses were destroyed during the bombing." Durla shifted uncomfortably from one foot to the other. "So my office felt that reclamation and exploratory projects might be of benefit in terms of building a sense of accomplishment and pride. The salaries paid to the excavators in the case of K0643 are minimal, but they have room and board, in addition to—"

"This world," Londo said, tapping some research he had done, "is reputed to be haunted, yes?"

Durla laughed scornfully at that. "Haunted, Majesty?"

"A place of lost souls. A world of darkness, tainted by evil. Have you heard these things?"

"Yes, Majesty," Durla said, his lips thinned nearly to a sneer. "I have also heard tales of Rokbala, the evil soul-stealing monster who hides under beds and swipes the souls of naughty children. My older brother told me of him when I was three. It kept me awake at night at the time. Now, however, I sleep quite soundly."

Londo nodded slightly in acknowledgement of the apparent childishness of the concern, but then continued. "Nevertheless . . . we certainly have projects that could employ willing members of our race in a fulfilling manner right here on Centauri Prime. K0643 is on the Rim, of all places."

"Majesty," said Durla slowly, "we must look for that which no one else knows about. There are other worlds, worlds that the Alliance is not interested in. Remote worlds such as this one. We must mount archaeological investigations. We must dig. We must locate. While we do this, the Interstellar Alliance will laugh at us. They will sneer and say, 'Look at the once-great Centauri Republic, rooting around on barren worlds and scraping about in the dirt like the basest of creatures.' " Durla's voice hardened. "Let them say these things. Let them lull themselves into a false sense of security. It will not last, and they will see the error of their ways . . . but by then, it will be too late. We must look outside Centauri Prime, Majesty. There, and only there, will we find our true greatness."

Slowly, Londo nodded. "That is a very impassioned speech, Minister."

"Thank you, Majesty. I believe passionately in the things that I do."

"Oh, I'm sure you do," Londo told him. "But I would be most curious to know . . . from where you got the idea."

"From where? Majesty . . ." And he shrugged. "It just came to me."

"Just . . . came to you."

"Yes, Majesty."

He felt an even more pronounced stirring on his shoulder that told him all he desired to know. "Very well, Durla. Since you have such passion for your work . . . who am I to gainsay you, eh?"

"Thank you, Majesty. And now, if you wouldn't mind, there are some other—"

But Londo put a hand to his temple and sighed heavily. "In point of fact . . . I am a bit fatigued. Let us discuss other matters later, if that is acceptable to you, Durla."

"I am but here to serve your wishes and the best interests of Centauri Prime," he said graciously, and walked out rather quickly. Londo had the sneaking suspicion that he had been quite anxious to get out of the room.

He sat back and waited.

It didn't take much time at all. He sensed Shiv'kala's presence, and he turned to face the Drakh. Shiv'kala stared at him for a long moment, and then said quite softly, "What are you playing at, Centauri?"

Londo smiled, and said two words:

"Quack. Quack."

Shiv'kala tilted his head slightly, looking at Londo—for once—with utter lack of comprehension. Then, to Londo's delight, he simply glided back and away into the shadows without another word.

"Quack quack," Londo said once more, this time with relish.

16

It had not been one of Senna's better weeks.

Although sections of the capital city had been rebuilt, there were entire areas that still were in desperate need of renovation and recovery. But the money had been slow in coming, for there were only so many directions that the government could go. By startling coincidence—or perhaps not so startling, in truth—it was the areas of the city inhabited by the poorer inhabitants of Centauri Prime that were getting the least attention.

And there were fewer sections, it seemed, that were getting less attention than the area known as Ghehana.

Ghehana had a reputation that long preceded it, as a place where one could live if one was in extreme financial difficulty. And if one was willing to do whatever it took in order to survive, then one could easily find a home there.

Even during the time that she was on her own, Senna had heard horror stories about Ghehana. It was where no decent person truly wished to go, and yet it was where an amazing number of people seemed to wind up. Senna had never thought that she herself would ever seek refuge there.

But it had been to Ghehana that she had fled. She had tried to remain in the central parts of the city, but those were for the well-to-do or, at the very least, for those who had money to spend and places to live. She had not wanted to be reduced to begging in the streets, but as it turned out, she hadn't had the opportunity. Soldiers attached to the Office of Development had been instructed to make sure that no one was loitering around, because it was felt that seeing homeless or out-of-work people would only reduce the morale of those who really counted on Centauri Prime.

This was a city, a world, a race that was on the upswing. Prospects were bright. Employment was up. Destiny was manifest. Everyone knew that—sooner or later—there would be a reckoning between the great Centauri Republic and the supremely arrogant races who comprised the Alliance. Piddling, backward, nowhere species who once wouldn't have been worth the Republic's time to conquer. Oh, yes . . . the score would be evened, there was no doubt of that. To that end, however, work, dedication, progress, and a patriotic heart were the orders of the day.

Homeless beggars, on the other hand, were just too depressing for words. And so, every effort was made to shunt them elsewhere. Where they went did not matter, so long as they went there.

On one or two occasions, as soldiers sent Senna scuttling out of a doorway in which she had taken refuge, or away from a street corner that she was standing on for too long, a soldier would look at her with curiosity, as if he vaguely remembered her from somewhere. But Senna would quickly hustle along, and withdraw from their sight as quickly as possible.

So it was that she found herself in Ghehana.

The area frightened her. Even after two years, there were still piles of rubble in places where buildings had been. Worse, there were people actually living within the piles, having carved out spaces for themselves. The streets, rarely cleaned, were thick with dirt and grime. Isolated fires flickered in areas where people gathered to warm themselves.

Senna had managed to get a small amount of money to tide herself over by selling a few of the fineries that had belonged to her at the palace, objects that she had grabbed up at the last moment. She had used the money sparingly, managed to buy food with it, but she was running extremely low on funds, and the growling of her stomach made her realize that she was once again going to have to spend some of them.

She was also tired of sleeping outside, hunkering down in doorways, lying in alleys. Her clothes were filthy, she desperately needed a bath, and she had so much dirt under her fingernails that she was convinced they would never come clean, even if she had the opportunity to cleanse them.

She leaned against the corner of a building, trying to decide just what in the world she was going to do, and then she heard someone clear their throat quite loudly. She turned and saw a Centauri male, slender, about medium height, short cut hair, with a generally disreputable look about him. He was grinning widely at her and she could see the glimmer of a gold tooth on the right side of his mouth.

"How much?" he asked.

She stared at him. "What?"

"How much for your time?" He coughed once. There was an ugly rattling sound in his chest.

She still didn't comprehend . . . but then she got it. "Oh. No. No, I'm not . . . I don't do that."

"Oh, I think you do. Or would." He seemed to be looking right through her, dissecting her with his eyes. His gaze made her feel filthy down to her soul. She drew her tattered cloak around her, but then he stepped closer and roughly drew it aside. "If you were cleaned up a bit, you'd actually be quite pretty," he allowed. "You're young. How experienced are you? How many have you done at one time? Three? Four?"

"Get away from me!" she said hotly, pushing him. He staggered slightly, and then suddenly took a step forward and pushed her back. The movement caught Senna off balance and she fell, hitting the ground hard. Passersby, on their hurried way to this or that activity, most likely illegal, didn't so much as slow down.

"Don't stand around out here, my dear, unless you intend to do something with what you've got," the man said to her.

And then someone was standing behind him, and the someone said in a calm, measured and controlled voice, "I believe the young lady said she wished you to get away from her. You had best do as she says and move along."

Senna gaped in astonishment as she saw who the newcomer was. Her assailant, however, did not bother to turn around. "Oh really. And who died and left you in charge?"

"Cartagia. And, after him, the regent."

Something about the voice prompted the man to turn slowly and see just who it was that was addressing him. He looked into a very familiar face, and his spine stiffened and his legs began to tremble slightly.

Londo Mollari, dressed in rather ordinary garb that was attracting no attention from anyone, continued, "And if you wish to be the next to die, I can certainly oblige you." He snapped his fingers and there were two men on either side of him. Although they were likewise clad in unmemorable clothing, from their look and bearing it was clear that they were guards. In synch, they opened their coats slightly to reveal gun butts tucked just inside. Furthermore, each of them had fairly vicious blades dangling from their belts.

The man who had been harassing Senna immediately backed up,

and now his legs were shaking so violently that he could hardly stand. "Muh . . . muh . . . muh . . ."

" 'Majesty,' I believe, is the word you are seeking," Londo said drily. "I believe it would be best for you if you went on about your business now, yes?"

"Yes. Yes . . . absolutely," said the man, and he bolted from there so quickly that he practically left a vapor trail behind him.

Londo watched him go with a vague look of satisfaction on his face, and then he turned to Senna.

Senna, for her part, couldn't quite believe it. Londo extended a hand to her and it was only then that she remembered she was still on the ground. "Well," he asked. "Are you going to let me help you up? Or are you, perhaps, going to bounce a rock off my head?"

She took the hand and stood, dusting herself off. "How . . . how did you know where I was?"

He shrugged as if it were a trivial matter. "An emperor has ways, my dear. Come," and he gestured in front of her. "Let us walk for a bit."

"Majesty," one of the guards said in a low voice, looking around with clear suspicion. "Perhaps it would be wise not to remain. From a security point of view . . ."

"Is the most powerful individual on this planet to be the most helpless, as well?" Londo asked. "Any other Centauri, from greatest to least, can move about with confidence. Is that to exclude me? These are my people. I will deal with them as such. Come, Senna." And he began to walk.

She hesitated, and Londo turned to her, indicating once more that she should follow. This time she did as he specified, falling into step beside him. As they walked, various passersby recognized him and reacted with assorted degrees of amazement. Some bowed. Others looked confused. One or two exhibited airs of scorn. Londo serenely ignored them all, acting as one of them but apart from them.

"I . . . did not expect to see you again, Majesty," Senna told him. "After the . . . after . . ."

"After you invaded my privacy?"

"I . . . did not mean to—"

He wagged a finger at her. "Do not say that. Do not think you can fool me. I've had experience with enough wives to know how the female mind works. You did precisely what you set out to do."

"But I thought you were writing a history book. One that would be publicly available anyway. It didn't occur to me that you were writing so private, so personal . . ."

"It is a history nonetheless. However, it is one that I assume will be published posthumously. Once I am gone," and he shrugged, "what do I care of what people know of my innermost feelings and concerns."

"If people knew those, though, Majesty, they . . ." Her voice trailed off.

He looked at her with interest. "They what?"

"They would feel better about the future of Centauri Prime," she said. "Perhaps even about themselves. I . . . Majesty, lately I don't feel as if I even know you. And I have been living in the palace for some time, so if I don't know you . . . who does?"

"Timov," Londo said ruefully. "If anyone knows me, it is she. She is my first wife. My shortest wife. My loudest wife. Not my most dangerous . . . that would be Mariel. But Timov, she was . . ."

"Is she dead?"

"No. She has sworn to outlast me. She would not give me the satisfaction of having her precede me to the presence of the Great Maker." He waved it off. "It is pointless to speak of her. Why did you run off?"

"Because you frightened me, Majesty."

He took her by the elbow and turned her to face him. "I was angry with you. I shouted at you. That was the extent of what you faced . . . and that frightened you? My child, if you accomplish only one thing in the time that you spend with me, it has to be to raise your tolerance level in terms of what does and does not frighten you. There are terrifying things in this galaxy, Senna. Things so monstrous, so evil, so dark, that it takes tremendous courage simply to look them in the eye . . . eyes," he quickly amended, although she wasn't sure why. "If you are to make your way in life, you must not be so easily daunted by something as relatively trivial as an old man shouting at you."

"You are not old, Majesty."

"Aging, then, if that preserves your delicate concerns. An aging man shouting at you." He paused and then said, looking as if a great deal hinged on her answer, "How far . . . did you get in the narrative? Where did you start, for that matter?"

"At the beginning and end of your dinner and time with President Sheridan and Delenn."

"And no farther?"

She shook her head, looking so earnest that no reasonable person could possibly doubt her. "No, Majesty. No farther. Why? Is there something there I should not read?"

"You should not read any of it," he told her flatly, but it seemed to her as if his body was sagging in visible relief. "It is . . . first draft, if nothing else. It is not ready to be read by someone else. What I write in those pages are my initial thoughts, but as I prepare the history for publication, I will craft it into something that is more . . . appropriate to an emperor, and less politically charged, if you understand my meaning."

"I . . . I think so, Majesty. It's just that . . ."

"What?"

"Nothing."

"No," he said firmly. "You are not to do that with me, Senna. Not ever. You do not start a thought out loud, and then seek to pluck it back as if it was never released. Finish the thought."

"I . . . just did not want to hurt your feelings, Emperor."

Londo made a dismissive noise. "My feelings, Senna, are beyond your ability to hurt, I assure you. So . . ." And he waited for her to continue.

"Well, it is just that . . . when you grabbed the book from me, you not only seemed angry . . . but you were also . . . well . . . afraid. At least, that was how it looked to me. Afraid that I had read something that I should not have read."

"It was simply the timing," he said easily. "I had been having—shall we say 'unpleasant'—dreams, and then I awoke, confused and disoriented, and found you there. Was there fear in my eyes? Perhaps. All manner of notions were tumbling around in my head. But you should not read too much into what you saw at that moment."

The way he said it and explained it, it almost all sounded reasonable. She wanted to believe it. She wanted to be able to return to the palace because, truth to tell, she had become comfortable there. She had come to think of it as her home. Yes, there were people there she found distasteful, even somewhat frightful. But that would certainly be the case wherever she resided, wouldn't it? And she also felt that Londo . . . needed her somehow. Not on any sort of romantic level, no. She didn't think for a moment that that was entering into the picture, and she was quite certain that he would never even try to take advantage of her in that way, because of her youth and out of respect to her late father. She was certain Londo would think such a thing utterly inappropriate.

"Was there anything else in there," Londo said slowly, "that caused you any confusion or concern? Now is the time to speak of these things, Senna."

"Well," she admitted, "the things that you wrote in that book . . . they made it sound as if you have some great secret that you keep hidden within you. There was such curious phrasing, and it seemed as if you felt you were being watched all the time."

He nodded. "A fair comment. And understandable, since you did not read earlier parts of the narrative. The secrets are—"

He was cut off as a man bumped into them at that moment. He wore grey, enveloping robes with a hood drawn up, and he seemed quite intent on hurrying on his way. His hurried movement actually brought him into contact with Londo for a moment. The guards immediately stepped forward, alert, and Senna didn't blame them, since such an incident could easily cover a knife thrust. But the hooded man moved right on past, and Londo seemed barely to have noticed him. For one moment, though, the man glanced in Senna's direction and smiled. She couldn't help but notice that he was quite handsome, and then he vanished into the crowd . . . a crowd that was slowly becoming more dense as word of the emperor's presence began to spread throughout Ghehana. The guards relaxed their defensive posture only slightly, and still kept a wary eye on the crowd.

"The secrets," continued Londo, "involve that which you must already know. Sooner or later, it is the destiny of the Centauri Republic to try and reclaim its place in the power structure of the galaxy. When, and if, I encounter Sheridan again, we will be enemies. There was a time . . . I have not felt like that since . . ."

His voice had trailed off. "Since when, Majesty?"

"I had coordinated a military assault against the Narn," Londo told her. "The details are not important; suffice to say that it was the first strike by the Centauri Republic in our endeavor to obliterate the Narn. When the assault was already in progress, before word of it had become public . . . the Narn ambassador to Babylon 5, a fellow known as G'Kar, bought me a drink, shook my hand in friendship, and spoke of a bright future. He did not know—though I did—what was about to happen. It was not a pleasant feeling for me. It still is not. Sometimes, Senna, you look upon an enemy and wonder what it would have been like in another life, if you and he were friends.

"Well, I genuinely was friends with them. I look back upon those days as if I am watching someone else's life, rather than my own. I did not realize . . . how very fortunate I was at the time. All I felt was the discontent. Discontent that rose within me until it pushed out every other attribute I had. In those days, when I spoke in anger of what Centauri Prime had once been, I breathed fire. Here is the interesting thing, Senna: when you breathe fire, you are usually left with ashes in your mouth."

"But then . . . then why go down that same path again? If it brought you nothing but unhappiness . . ."

"Because the people need it, Senna. The people need something to believe in. That might not have been the case even as recently as a generation ago, when the memories of what it was like to be feared throughout the galaxy had grown faded and dim. But the current generation of Centauri know what it was like to be world beaters. They have tasted blood, Senna. They have tasted meat. They cannot be expected to go back to grazing on plants. Besides . . . this time it will be different."

"How? How will it be different?"

"Because," he said with conviction, "those who were running Centauri Prime were power mad or insane or both. They lost sight of what was truly the important thing: the people. The people must always come first, Senna. Always, without exception, yes?"

"Yes, absolutely."

"I will not ever forget that. My goal is simply to obtain for the Centauri people the respect that they so richly deserve. But we will not mindlessly destroy, we will not endeavor to lay waste to all that we encounter. Before, we overreached ourselves, became greedy and overconfident, and we paid a price for that . . . a terrible price," he said, glancing at a fallen building. "But having paid that price, having learned from our mistakes, we will proceed down a path that will bring glory to the Centauri Republic without taking us to ruination."

"That . . . does not sound all that unreasonable," Senna said slowly. "You . . . might have put it that way to President Sheridan . . ."

"No," was the firm reply. "He cannot be trusted, Senna. For the time being, we cannot afford to trust any except each other. We must proceed with caution. Who knows, after all, how Sheridan might misinterpret or inaccurately repeat anything that I say to him. So I speak of friendship and stick with generalities. That is the way such encounters must be handled, at least for now. Do you understand?"

"I . . . think I do, yes. I just wish that you didn't have to be, well . . . so lonely."

"Lonely?" A smile played on his lips. "Is that how I come across to you?"

"Yes. In the journal, and even in person sometimes, yes. Very lonely."

"Believe me, Senna . . . there are many times I feel as if I am never alone."

"I know exactly what you're talking about."

"You do?" He raised an inquisitive eyebrow. " 'Exactly' how?"

"The guards all the time, and Durla, and Lione, and Kuto, and all the others . . . they hover around you . . ."

"You are a very perceptive girl," he said, letting out what seemed to Senna to be another sigh of relief.

"But that's not the same as having companionship. It's just not the same at all."

"I suppose you are right."

"I am . . . at least I could be . . . company for you, Majesty. As . . . you see fit, that is."

"Senna . . . what you can do for me is return to the palace and live safely and happily there. To be honest, that is all that I require of you. Will you do this for me?"

"If . . . it will make you happy, Majesty. Sometimes I think few enough things do. So if my presence would help in that regard . . ."

"It would," Londo said confidently.

"Very well. Although I just want you to know . . . I could have survived out here, on my own, if it was necessary. I just want us both to know that."

"I understand fully," Londo said. "I appreciate you clarifying that for me."

One of the guards stepped in close and said with some urgency, "Majesty, I *really* think it is time for us to go."

Senna looked around and saw that it was becoming more and more crowded with each passing moment. People seemed to be assembling from everywhere. Within a short time it would become impossible to move.

Londo surveyed the situation a moment, and then said softly to the guard, "Step back, please." The guard did so, a puzzled and concerned look on his face, and then Londo turned to face the crowd. He said nothing, absolutely nothing. Instead he stretched his arms out in front of himself, held them level for a moment . . . and then spread them wide, making his desires known simply by a gesture.

To Senna's utter astonishment, the crowd parted for him, creating a clear avenue down which he could proceed.

That was precisely what he then did, walking down the avenue, nodding to people, and as he did he worked the lines that were on either side of him. He would nod to this person, touch another's hand, speak a few words of encouragement to yet another. It was one of the most amazing things Senna had ever seen. Just like that, with no apparent effort, Londo had created an impromptu parade, with himself, Senna, and the guards as the entirety of the procession.

And as they moved through Ghehana, someone called out Londo's name. "Mollari." And then someone else followed suit, and another and still another, until they were chanting it over and over.

"Mollari. Mollari. Mollari . . ."

Londo basked in their adulation, smiling and nodding, and Senna realized that there had been a great deal of truth to what Londo had said. The people needed something to believe in, something to elevate them above themselves. And for the time being, that "something" was going to be Londo Mollari himself. Londo the Emperor, Londo the Rebuilder, Londo the Lover of the People, who was going to bring prosperity to Centauri Prime and rebuild the Republic into something that every Centauri could be proud of.

But he still seemed lonely.

And that was something that Senna decided she was going to do something about.

The Centauri worker wished that he were anywhere else but here.

He had wandered off from the main dig site, feeling tired and thirsty and fairly fed up with the company of his fellows. All of them seemed hideously happy to have some kind of employment, however marginal, and they were laboring under some sort of bizarre delusion that somehow the needs and interests of the great Centauri Republic were going to be served by working at a useless archaeological dig on some damned backwater planet, using antiquated tools and having no clear idea of what it was that they were actually looking for.

"Idiots," he said, not for the first time. It was at that point that he decided he had had it. He took his dirt cruncher, aimed it just below his feet, and fired it straight down. By all rights, by all instructions, there shouldn't be anything there in particular. He was determined to take out his ire by burning the cruncher out completely, operating it at high speed for longer than it was meant to operate.

The cruncher pounded about ten feet straight down, and then something came back up.

The worker never really had the opportunity to figure out what it might be. All he knew was that one moment he was happily pushing his cruncher to the maximum, and the next some sort of black energy was enveloping him and he heard a scream, which he thought was his own except he realized it was inside his head, and not quite like anything he had ever heard before.

Then he heard nothing else, ever again, as his body was blasted apart in a shower of gelatinous body parts that spattered over a radius of about fifty feet. Since he was spread so wide and far, no one who subsequently stumbled upon any part of his remains truly understood what it was they were looking at.

When he didn't show up for sign-out that evening, he was marked down as absent without leave, and his pay was docked accordingly. Meantime, eighty feet below, something went back to standby mode, and waited for a less abusive summons.

17

Vir tossed about in his bed as the giant sucker-woman approached him.

There was a look of pure evil in her eyes, and her arms were outstretched, and she was waggling her fingers, and at the ends of those fingers—Great Maker protect him—there were the suckers. Each one smacking its "lips" together, hungering for him, ready to attach themselves to him and try to suck the life clean out of him. Somewhere from all around him, he heard Londo's voice shouting, "Run, Vir! Run! Don't let her get to you!" Vir, however, was rooted to the spot, his legs refusing to obey his commands. He wanted to run away, but he simply couldn't.

She drew closer, closer still. Her bald pate gleamed with a pulsing black light, and she laughed with a sound that had once filtered from the forest as primitive beings had squatted around their fires and glimpsed fearfully into the darkness. When her lips drew back in a hideous simulated rictus of a smile, he could see her fangs dripping with blood, and the suckers were nearer, still nearer, and there was no escape . . .

That was when Vir finally managed to get a scream out, and the scream was so powerful that it roused him from his dream, forcing him to sit up, gasping, looking around, trying to figure out what in the world had just happened.

As he did so, he realized that there was the insistent buzzing of the door chime. His bleary eyes focused on a clock near his bed. It was the middle of the night. Who in the world was showing up at this insane time.

"Go away!" moaned Vir, flopping back onto his bed.

There was no reply from outside other than the renewed pushing of the door chime.

A warning trilled in the back of Vir's brain. What if it were an assassin, hoping to catch him confused, disoriented, and particularly vulnerable. At that point, however, Vir simply didn't care. The notion of someone blowing his head off, at that moment in time, seemed preferable to trying to go back to sleep, where sucker-fingered women might be lurking about in the recesses of his consciousness, waiting to prey upon him as soon as he relaxed his guard.

"Lights dim," he snapped irritably, and the lights in his quarters obediently came to half. Even that modest lighting was enough to make him feel as if his eyes were being seared from their sockets. He rose from his bed, snagged his robe, put his right arm in the left sleeve, twirled in place as he sought in futility to catch up with the trailing sleeve, snagged it, realized his error and then yanked the robe off and put it on correctly. The buzzing continued throughout all of it, to the point where Vir didn't even bother to find his slippers, but instead padded barefoot across the room as he shouted, "I'm coming, I'm coming! Hold on already!"

He got to the door, disengaged the locking mechanism, wondered if he was going to be staring down the muzzle of a vicious weapon when it slid open and decided that he definitely didn't care at this point.

The door opened wide, and he let out a short, high-pitched shriek.

"Is this a bad time?" asked Mariel.

Vir couldn't quite believe it. *What is she doing here?*

She was waiting for his response, and he sought to find his voice. "Uh ... no. No is ... fine. I wasn't doing anything. Well ... I was sleeping ... but, you know, that really doesn't require too much effort. In fact, it's a bit of a waste of time. There's so many other better things I could be doing. You know, I think I'm just going to give up sleep altogether. There's far more efficient ways to go about living your life, you know, than wasting time sleeping. I mean, I've been getting nine, ten, twelve hours sleep, but I think I could do with a lot less. Like ... one. One would be good. Or ... three, which is what I had tonight," he said, double-checking the clock to make sure he had that right. "Yes, three is good. Three is plenty. I can't believe how well I'm functioning on just—"

"Ambassador ... may I come in?"

Again, as was often the case, Vir had to fight the impulse to glance behind himself. "Yes. Yes, by all means. Come in. Come in."

She did so, glancing around the suite as she did. "My, my. I like what you've done with the place, Vir. Back in Londo's day, it tended to look a bit like a museum. A Londo Mollari museum, considering he had portraits of himself all over. How long has it been, Vir?"

Not long enough. "Quite . . . some time, Lady Mariel," Vir told her. "Four, five, six years. Time flies when you're having fun. Or when you're having . . . well . . . whatever it is that I have."

"I remember quite clearly the last time I was in this room."

"Really? When was that?" Vir was hoping that his sense of feeling flustered would depart soon.

"When Londo had a small orgy with myself and Daggair. Both of us, at the same time. Would have been three had Timov been willing . . ."

That was definitely more than Vir wanted to know. He stepped quickly away, wishing that he could cover his hands with his ears, but that would hardly seem professional. He also dismissed the notion of shouting "la la" at the top of his lungs. "I was . . . not expecting to see you here, Milady . . ."

"Mariel, please. We have no need for formalities," she said softly. "You are, after all, an ambassador. I am simply the former wife of a sitting emperor. I see no differences between us."

Eyeing her uncomfortably, Vir said, "I . . . see a couple." He cleared his throat loudly. "Can I get you something? Something to drink or . . . something?"

"That would be quite nice. Are you sure this is not a bad time?"

"Oh, don't be silly!" he said as he poured her wine from his private stock; the stuff that he only consumed when he was extremely nervous. He tended to go through a bottle a day. "You just caught me a bit off guard, that's all. I wasn't expecting you."

"I wasn't expecting to be here myself," Mariel said as she picked up the wine and sipped it daintily. "I was to connect on a shuttle through here, but the connecting flight met with a bit of an accident."

"No one hurt, I hope," he said.

"Not hurt. Just dead. I'm told the fireball was quite spectacular, although naturally it didn't last all that long, since it was in space at the time."

Vir felt his tongue drying up. He tossed back an entire glass of the wine in one shot and started pouring himself another.

"Anyway . . . since I am here on Babylon 5 until a new ship is dispatched, I thought I might touch base with you. See how you are getting along. I have such fond memories of you, Vir."

"You . . . you do?"

"Yes, indeed." She stared into the contents of her glass and smiled, apparently from a pleasant recollection. "Do you know what I liked about you then, Vir? Shall I tell you?"

"You don't have to."

"You made me laugh. It's not always easy for a man to get a woman to laugh, but you managed it so easily. You had a charming facade you created back then, although I could see through it rather easily, of course."

"What . . . facade would that be?"

"An air of barely controlled panic."

"Ah. Well," and he laughed uncomfortably, "you saw right through that, I guess. Clever you."

"Yes, indeed, clever me. So . . . fill me in, Vir. I have been away for quite some time." She interlaced her fingers and leaned forward. "Tell me what's been going on, on Babylon 5."

"Oh, *uhm* . . . well . . . all right." And he proceeded to rattle off as many major events as he could recall that had occurred in the past five to six years, including the Shadow War, the inauguration, and the telepath wars. Mariel took it all in, every so often interrupting with a question, but most of the time simply nodding and listening. When he was done some time later, Mariel looked almost breathless. "My," she said. "It's been rather busy. And how exciting this must have all been for you."

"I don't know if 'exciting' is the word I'd use," Vir admitted. "That almost makes it sound as if I was enjoying it. It's been more like, that my life has been moving at high speed, and I've been doing everything I can, not to be thrown off."

She laughed. She had a beautiful laugh. Vir wondered why he had never noticed that earlier.

"And you," he then said. "You must have been very busy, too, I'm sure."

She said nothing.

He stared at her as he waited for her to pick up her half of the conversation. But nothing was forthcoming. "Mariel?" he prompted.

"I'm sorry," she said coolly. "I just assumed you were having a little joke at my expense."

"What? No! No, I'd never—! What joke? What do you mean?"

"Londo tossed me away, Vir," she said. "I mean nothing to him, and he let the entire world know it." She had been standing until that time, but now she sat on the edge of one of the chairs. And Vir began to see that she was actually not remotely as cheery as she had

originally appeared. Indeed, it now looked as if she was doing everything she could to hold back tears. "You have no idea what it is like,
Vir, to be so completely diminished in society. To be tossed aside. To
have people looking at you and laughing behind your back, because
you're considered a joke."

It took no more introspection from Vir than to consider his own
life up until that point. To consider the fact that he had once been the
family joke, tossed away to Babylon 5 and made attaché to the ludicrous Londo Mollari, so that he would be out of the way and not em-
barrass anyone.

"I think I do," said Vir. "But . . . but look at you!" he added, waving his glass of wine around so vehemently that he came close to
spilling it. "How could anyone treat you as a joke! You're so . . .
so . . ."

"Beautiful," she said hollowly. "Yes, Vir, I know. And as such,
men would seek me out as a symbol of their own status. But another
symbol hangs over me in addition to my beauty. It is that of castoff.
Cast off from Londo Mollari. It stays with me, haunts me. No man
wants to be seen with me because . . ." Her voice sounded as if it
were going to break, and Vir felt his hearts going with it. Then, with
visible effort, she composed herself. "I . . . am sorry, Vir," she said
softly. "I . . . miss my old life. I miss the parties, the social whirl. I
miss the company of men who wanted to be seen with me . . ."

"There's a party tomorrow! Right here, on B5," Vir said quickly.
"A diplomatic gathering being hosted by Captain Lochley. It's not a
big deal, she has them every other month or so. Feels it's good for
morale, that kind of thing. I haven't been going lately, figuring that—
well, never mind. In any event, I could go tomorrow, with you. That
is to say, we could go. You and I."

She looked up at him. Her eyes were glistening. "That's very kind
of you, Vir. But I don't really think you'd want to be seen with
me . . ."

"Don't be ridiculous! Truthfully, I'm not sure why you'd want to
be seen with me."

"Are you serious?" she asked. "To be seen with the ambassador
of the Centauri Republic to Babylon 5? Any woman would be honored. But you may be harming your own status by squiring me . . ."

"Are you kidding? Practically everyone here hates Londo," he
laughed. Then he stopped laughing. "I . . . guess that wasn't so funny,
actually. Besides . . . who's to know?" he added quickly, as he hun-

kered down next to her. "Listen . . . when you look at a Drazi . . . can you tell one from the other?"

"Not . . . really," she admitted.

"Well, neither can I. And I'll bet you that Centauri probably look as much alike to Drazi as Drazi do to us. Drazi and all the others. The point is, they're not even going to know who you are, most likely. Not unless you wear a sign that says 'Londo Mollari's ex-wife.' "

"I had one, but I think I left it back home."

He laughed at that, and so did she, and when he laughed he patted her on the hand and she put her hand atop his, and he felt something akin to electricity upon her touch. He almost jumped from the contact.

"Are you sure about this, Vir?" she asked.

"Absolutely sure. Look, you'll go—"

"We'll go," she corrected him.

"We'll go, and it'll feel just like the old days for you. You'll have a great time."

"We'll have a great time."

"Right. We. I'm sorry, it's just that . . . well . . ." and he sighed, "I'm not all that accustomed to thinking of myself as part of a 'we.' Not for a very long time."

And then, to his shock, she tilted his chin back and kissed his uplifted lips gently. Very, very gently, no heavier than a butterfly's flutter. It was still enough to send a wave of static running along his hair.

She asked what time the party was. He told her. She told him where she was staying in Babylon 5, and where he should come to pick her up. He nodded. Then she kissed him again, not quite as lightly this time, and Vir suddenly felt as if there was too much blood in his body.

When their lips parted, with a faint smacking sound, Mariel said to him, "You are such a sweet man. I had forgotten what it was like to be with a sweet man. I'll let you get back to sleep." And with that she excused herself and left. It wasn't until Vir's aching knees informed him, some minutes later, that he was still crouching, that he thought to stand up. Then he eased himself onto the chair and sat there, stunned.

When Mariel had first shown up at his door, he had been seized by waves of panic. He remembered the horror stories Londo had told of her, remembered the chaos that had seemed to be left in the woman's wake. He remembered that Londo had almost died thanks to a present that she had given him, although she had claimed that she'd had no idea that it was remotely dangerous when she'd given it to him. He remembered the aura of darkness that had seemed to cling to her, that had made her almost frightening to look at.

All that had been washed away by the utter vulnerability she had projected upon arriving in his quarters. He had felt all his hesitations, all his concerns melting away, one by one, until he had been left with only one raw, stunned thought:

*She's one of the ones Londo got **rid** of? He must have been out of his **mind!***

The ambassadorial reception turned out to be one of the turning points of Vir's entire career . . . if not his life.

It was almost as if he were attending it while having an out-of-body experience. Normally, if Vir attended such functions—as he had once or twice in his career—he remained firmly planted, back against a wall, nodding to some people, making small chitchat with others, and frequently holding Londo's drinks when Londo ran out of hands to hold them with—which was often. In short, when Vir had been there, his entire contribution to the evening was that he had . . . been there.

Lately it had been something of a horror show for him. He had spent many years making what he felt were friends among the population of Babylon 5. But he had spent the past year and a half watching them disappear, one by one. Londo, Lennier, Delenn, Ivanova, Sheridan, Garibaldi, even G'Kar—he who had made Vir more uncomfortable on one occasion, dripping blood from his hand in an elevator, than Vir had ever been in his life before or since. All of them were gone.

Oh, Captain Lochley was there, and she was polite enough, but she tended to keep him at an emotional distance, as she apparently did with everyone. And Zack was there, but Vir always felt as if Zack was regarding him with suspicion, waiting for Vir to pull a weapon or something. That might have been Vir's imagination, but nevertheless, that was how he felt.

As for the rest of the members of the Alliance, well . . . they had very little patience for him indeed. It wasn't personal; they hated and feared all Centauri. Somehow, that didn't make it any better. It was little wonder that Vir had stopped attending the gatherings altogether.

This night, though . . . this night was very, very different.

This night, Mariel was there in full force.

When Vir went to pick her up, he was stunned to see how small her room was. It was barely large enough for someone to turn around in, and it certainly wasn't located in one of the more upscale sections of the station. Nevertheless, Mariel managed to look radiant. She was attired in a remarkably simple, unadorned dress, but its lack of decoration was part of its strength, for there was nothing to distract from her pure beauty.

And beauty she possessed in abundance, for all that she seemed to devalue it. When the door to her room opened, she was simply standing there, in the middle of the room as if she were on display, her hands folded daintily in front of her. Vir busily tried to remind his body that breathing was an autonomic reflex, and his lungs really shouldn't be forgetting how to expand and contract. His lungs didn't seem to be listening, and breath remained in short supply for some moments.

When he finally did start breathing regularly again, Mariel asked, in a voice barely above a whisper, "Do I . . . please you, Vir? You would not be ashamed to be seen with me?"

Vir literally couldn't find words to reply. When he did speak, the result was an almost incoherent string of syllables, rather than useful phrases. Fortunately enough, the utterances managed to convey the fact that he was not the least bit ashamed.

She took a step closer to him and said softly, "I think . . . when you first met me . . . I was very likely a bit arrogant."

"No! No, not at all."

"If I was, you would certainly be too polite to say so. So in the event that I was . . . I apologize to you now. I hope you will forgive me." She kissed him once more, and this time Vir's head fell off.

At least, that was what it felt like. He stood there stupidly for a moment, then felt around for his head, reattached it to his shoulders, and somewhere during that activity, Mariel said, "Shall we go?"

They went.

Vir couldn't believe the evening. It was like a dream . . . except, of course, for the absence of women with suckers on their long fingers.

For the entirety of the dream, Mariel was a delight. If the ambassadorial gathering was a vast ice field, as far as relations with the Centauri went, Mariel was a spring thaw, she was the warming sun, she was . . .

"All that *and* a bag of chips," Zack Allan commented, and he nudged Vir in some sort of comradely fashion that caught Vir flat-footed.

"Excuse me?" Vir said.

"Your date," Zack said, pointing toward Mariel who was, at that moment, gaily capturing the interest of half a dozen ambassadors at once. There was a roar of laughter at some comment she made, and most of the ambassadors were smiling widely, except for one who was frowning furiously. But that wasn't of major concern, since that was how his race showed that they were happy. Fortunately the Divloda ambassador, who tended to display extreme pleasure by urinating uncontrollably, had not been able to make the gathering, to the dismay of no one at all. "She's all that and a bag of chips."

"Is that good?" asked Vir.

"What do *you* think?"

They watched Mariel working the room. The female ambassadors, Vir noted, regarded her with cool disdain bordering on outright distrust. But the male ambassadors from any race came flocking to her. Mariel was lucky that she didn't slip on the drool that was rapidly collecting on the floor.

And Vir laughed. He had forgotten what the sound of his laughter was like. "I think that's very good."

Zack chucked him on the shoulder. "You lucky dog. Where did you find her, anyway?"

"She's Londo's . . ." Vir caught himself. ". . . old . . . friend."

"And now she's your new friend. Well, don't you let her get away, Vir."

"I'll certainly try not to."

Zack Allan wasn't alone in his comments. Other ambassadors, one by one and even in pairs came over to Vir during the evening, and asked him about Mariel. The problem was, Vir wasn't the world's greatest liar. He had little talent for it. As long as he had been working with Londo, that hadn't been a problem, for Londo had been more than capable of attending to that function. Now that he was on his own, however, Vir had no fallback.

So this time, rather than rattling off a long, implausible story, he operated on the notion that less was more, and proceeded to be extremely vague. He met all inquiries with raised eyebrows, smiles, and occasional winks.

"Tell us truly, Vir," one ambassador said, "is she of the nobility?" Vir shrugged, looked mysterious, and rolled his eyes as if to indicate that a higher guess should be forthcoming. "A duchess? A . . . a princess?" Vir then gave a slow, lazy wink, and the ambassadors nudged one another and smiled knowingly, as if they had managed to wrangle some dark secret from Vir.

Every so often, Mariel would return to Vir as if he were home base, taking him by the arm, drawing the conversations back over to him. It all began to make sense to Vir. People tended to judge one by the company one keeps. All these years, Vir had kept company with Londo Mollari, and that had worked against him terribly, in the long run. Londo was a man who held much darkness within him, and he cast a long shadow. Vir had been swallowed up in that shadow. The murkiness had clung to him long after Londo's departure. But that was now in the process of changing, as the light of Mariel broke up those shadows and left Vir standing in the light.

By the wee hours, Vir felt as if he was flying. It was at that point that Mariel came up to him once more, as she had several times before, and entwined her arm through his. "Now is the time to leave," she said softly.

Vir had a drink in his hand, and several more working their way through his system. "But the party's still going on!" he protested.

"Yes. And it is never good to be among the last to leave. By departing earlier, you see, it gives them time to speak of you with one another in glowing terms after you have gone."

"*Ooooohhh,*" Vir said, not really understanding.

"Not only that, but it makes it seem as if you have things of greater importance to do. That also makes you desirable."

"Oh. That's clever. I like that. That's very clever. I only wish it were true."

And Mariel took his face in her hands and looked him squarely in the eyes, and there was great significance in her voice. "It *is* true. You do have more important things to do."

Then Vir understood. He very quickly said his good-byes, and to his amazement, not only did the ambassadors seem regretful that they were leaving, but several of them made noises about wanting to see Vir again. They must get together, have lunch, have dinner, their aides would be in touch, have a good evening, have a wonderful evening, we must do this again soon. All the niceties, the traditional little pleasantries that were the standard coin of the realm of social interaction, but coin that had long been missing from Vir's personal treasury.

When they left and stepped into the transport tube, Vir—still just the least bit uncertain—said softly to Mariel, "Should I . . . escort you back to your room?"

She smiled at him with a smile that could melt steel. "I'd rather you escorted me to yours."

Feeling more bold than he ever had in his entire life, Vir took her by the shoulders and kissed her. It was rather clumsy and he succeeded mainly in clonking his upper teeth against hers. "Oh! I'm sorry! I'm . . . I'm . . . suh . . . sorry!" he stammered.

"It's all right," she assured him, and she returned the kiss with such expertise that Vir felt as if his entire body was aflame.

When their lips parted, Vir whispered to her, "You are all that . . . and a . . . a . . . a box of popcorn."

She frowned. "Is that good?"

"I think that's very good," he said.

And later that night, as their bodies intertwined, Vir whispered to her, "Don't leave . . ."

"If you want me to stay, I will," she told him.

"Yes . . . yes, please stay."

And she did.

18

The months passed quickly.

Vir could not remember being happier. It wasn't as if Mariel was with him all the time; far from it. She came and went, heading off visiting friends or associates. But Babylon 5 apparently had become her home base, and every so often Vir would be delighted to learn that she was returning. During their time together, he was deliriously happy. And when they weren't together, Vir nevertheless still felt like a new man. He walked with more spring in his step, new confidence in his attitude.

Not only that, but when others on Babylon 5 looked his way, he would greet them boldly or snap off a salute. He would walk right up to people, address them by name, ask them how they were doing. In short, he started behaving as if he had every right to be there. And others began responding to him differently, as well, treating him with the respect he should be due. When Mariel wasn't with him, they invariably asked how she was. When she was with him, they would look at Vir with open envy.

He loved every moment of it. He finally felt as if he, Vir Cotto, was coming into his own—when his world came crashing down on him.

Mariel had just departed Babylon 5 again when Vir strode into his quarters—using that same snappy stride despite the fact that it was quite late. As he had in the past, he stood for a moment in the center of his quarters, already regretting her absence. She had a certain scent to her, a perfume that clung to her. He'd never asked her the name of the scent. It hadn't mattered. It was a beautiful scent. Everything about her was beautiful, wonderful . . .

He picked up a picture of her that now permanently adorned his shelf, and smiled at it.

The picture began to speak.

"Greetings, Chancellor. It continues to go well."

Vir let out a yelp and dropped the picture. It crashed to the floor, and he stared down at it in utter confusion.

The photograph began moving, the equivalent of a video screen image. And with Mariel's voice it was saying, "Tomorrow, as per your instruction, I'll be departing for the Nimue Homeworld. The undersecretary of Defense has offered me a standing invitation—he extended it last month during an early morning brunch, and I'm taking him up on it. I believe he will share with me some interesting insights into the Nimue Department of War." Then she paused, smiled, and nodded, as if listening to a conversation that Vir couldn't hear. "No, Chancellor, I doubt that he knows he's going to share them with me. But I can be . . . persuasive . . . as you well know."

Vir remembered the brunch. He had been there. And now that he thought about it, the Nimue undersecretary had been lavishing a great deal of attention upon Mariel. But he had thought nothing of that; so many people clearly found themselves drawn to her, yet at the end of the day, he was the one she went home with . . .

But . . . what was of far greater consequence was that the picture was inexplicably still talking. How could that possibly be? It had to be some sort of trick. For Mariel hadn't gone to Nimue . . . she had returned to Centauri Prime, to visit relatives. That's what she'd told him, that's what—

"No, Chancellor, I doubt Vir suspects. He remains a fool. A useful fool. He has, however, been an aid to the cause, albeit an unwitting one."

"Stop it!" Vir shouted at the picture, which gave no indication at all that it heard him. "Stop doing this! *Stop it!*"

And suddenly, the picture did stop talking. The image of Mariel was restored to normal. Vir stared down at it, his chest heaving, and he didn't even realize at first how hard he was breathing.

"The truth hurts," a voice said.

Vir whirled. Then he stared in amazement, before that amazement turned to anger. "Of course. Kane. I should have known."

The techno-mage initiate bowed slightly, as if he were on a stage. He kept his staff clenched tightly in his hand. He was standing just inside the door, which was closed behind him. "The very same," Kane acknowledged.

Vir hadn't seen him since the incident with Rem Lanas. In looking back upon it, Vir had almost felt as if the entire thing had been some sort of strange dream. Kane had appeared at a crucial moment in his life, only to slip away again, as if he had never been there. Though Vir had been certain that he would hear from the initiate soon thereafter, when he hadn't, he'd begun to wonder if he hadn't been suffering from some sort of delusion.

The delusion was back now. This time, however, Vir didn't feel the slightest bit of intimidation. He pointed a trembling finger angrily at the fallen photo. "That . . . was a cruel joke to play. Why . . ."

"It was no joke, Vir," Kane replied. "It was an actual recording. We've been observing her ever since she set foot on the station. Once it was clear that she was going to remain here . . ."

"We?" demanded Vir. "There are more of you?"

"No," Kane said quickly, although he looked subtly chagrined. "I meant to say 'I.' "

"I don't care what you meant to say!" Vir told him, abandoning any attempt to hide his anger. "Making up that thing about Mariel, changing her image to—"

"Vir, *listen* to me. I didn't make up anything. That really happened. Even an initiate has ways."

"Then have a way out!"

He stepped toward Kane as if to grab him, but Kane extended his staff and shoved one end under Vir's chin. "I wouldn't," Kane said dangerously, "if I were you."

It brought Vir to a halt, and enabled his senses to come swimming back to him. "I just want you out," Vir said stubbornly. "And I want you to stop making things up about Mariel. That trick you just did . . . it's a trick. That's all."

"You do not understand," Kane told him, slowly lowering his staff. "The way of the techno-mage is the way of truth. All of our 'magic' is based in, and adheres purely to, reality. We don't deviate from that path . . . ever. For any of us to use our powers to misinform, that would be a violation of our most sacred beliefs."

"And to buy into the words you're putting into Mariel's mouth would be a violation of *my* most sacred beliefs," Vir countered sharply.

"You should not blame yourself, Vir Cotto. Mariel is far more than she seems. Even she is unaware of her full capabilities . . . and you can feel some relief that that is the case. For if she did . . ." He actually shuddered slightly.

Vir once again indicated the door. "There's nothing you can say to convince me that Mariel is anything but—"

"Perhaps her own words could have a bit more impact," Kane said.

Before Vir could protest, the image of Mariel started speaking to the unknown "chancellor" once again.

"Poor Vir . . . I almost feel sorry for him, in a way," Mariel purred. "The other ambassadors have no love of the Centauri, certainly . . . and as a result, they draw particular entertainment from a Centauri female who speaks in rather withering tones of her 'paramour.' Of course, the amusement I share with the ambassadors makes them that much more pliant when they are speaking with me, so who is the greatest fool in the end, yes?"

"This is evil," said Vir. "I have witnessed evil, I've seen it in action, and this is one of the most evil things I've ever seen anyone do, Kane." His voice rose along with his fury. "You are to shut that down, right now, or I'll—"

"He only goes as high as three, did you know that? And usually not even that," continued Mariel.

Vir, who had been looking at Kane, whipped his head back to the picture frame. Every drop of blood drained from his face.

"What does she mean by that?" Kane inquired, seeming genuinely interested. "I confess, I don't quite understand the reference. It—"

"Shut up," Vir demanded hollowly.

Mariel laughed in the picture. "I know, Chancellor, I know. It is all I can do to feign interest. Perhaps I should start bringing something to read while Vir entertains himse—"

"*Shut up!*" Vir bellowed, but this time it wasn't at Kane. Instead he grabbed up the picture and threw it with all his strength at the wall. The frame shattered, and Vir stood there leaning against a table, trying to keep himself upright even as he felt the strength draining out of his legs. Kane started to speak, but Vir raised a finger and said, "Be quiet. I need to check something."

Moments later he had Zack Allan on the Babcom screen. The security chief didn't appear the least bit tired, but because of the lateness of the hour, Vir felt obliged to say, "I hope I didn't wake you."

"Me? Nah. I only sleep on duty," Zack said with his customary deadpan expression. He tilted his head slightly and asked, "Vir, are you okay? You look . . ."

"I need you to check something for me. Mariel . . . when she de-

parted the station several hours ago, do you have a record of where
she was bound?"

"I couldn't say for absolute sure, because she could easily make
connections. But we'd have checked her outbound ticket. That's
SOP."

"Where was it for? Hers, I mean?"

"Is there a problem?"

"I'm not sure. Can you just check please."

"Because if there is, I—"

"Would you just check please?"

Clearly taken aback by the fervency in Vir's voice, Zack nodded
and said, "Hold on." The words "Please Stand By" appeared on the
screen and then, an eternity later, Zack reappeared. "Nimue. She
was heading for Nimue. Does that tell you what you need to know?"

"Yes. Yes, it does. Thank . . . you."

"Is Mariel all right?" asked Zack. "I hope there's nothing wrong,
and if there is, then let me know how I can help. Because she's . . ."

"Yes, I know. She's all that and a box of cookies. Thank you, Mr.
Allan," and Vir shut down the connection before Zack could say any-
thing else well-meaning—something that would cut like a knife to
Vir's soul.

There was an uncomfortable silence for a time, except that to
Vir, it didn't seem uncomfortable at all. He sat and stewed in it,
thinking about the world in which he lived. Thinking about the
fantasy life he substituted for real life. Thinking that, until Mariel
had come along, the last time he had really felt good about anything
had been when he was looking at Morden's severed head atop
a pike.

He had known. Deep down, he had really known that Mariel had
been up to something. That she was using him, that she was up to no
good. But he hadn't wanted to believe it, displaying what appeared to
be an infinite capacity for self-delusion. The proof was that he hadn't
spoken to Londo of it. Not a word had he breathed to his former
mentor, about his association with Mariel, because he had known
without question what the response was going to be. He would have
told Vir that he was completely out of his mind. That he had no business associating with someone like Mariel, that she would be using
him, and so on and so forth. That knowledge should have been Vir's
barometer, indicating what he was truly involved with. But once
again, he had ignored all the warning signs with single-minded determination.

"For what it is worth," Kane said softly, looking genuinely contrite, "I am sorry."

"It isn't worth a damned thing," Vir said.

"Then perhaps this will be worth something: Mariel is not the problem. She's merely the pawn of others. Even those who appear to guide Mariel are themselves guided. There is a great darkness residing on Centauri Prime."

"A great darkness." Vir echoed the words without putting much inflection to them. "Is that a fact?"

"Yes. It is."

"And is that supposed to make me feel better, somehow? Less used? Less foolish?"

"No." Kane approached him and came uncomfortably close. Vir's instinct was to take a step back, but filled with a newfound stubbornness, he held his ground. Kane didn't appear to notice. "What it is supposed to do is fill you with a deep burning rage. It's supposed to make you realize that there is more at stake than your ego, or your hurt feelings. It's supposed to make you realize that you, Vir Cotto, have a destiny. And you must—you *must*—rise to the level of the man that you can be, in order to fulfill it."

"I see. And is it your job to help bring me to that destiny? To help me rise up and become all that I am capable of becoming?" asked Vir sarcastically.

"Well . . . no," admitted Kane. "In point of fact, I should be keeping out of it entirely. My job is simply to relay information to others, but otherwise stay completely out of the line of fire. Unfortunately, I find that I can't. I can't simply stand by and allow the Drakh to—"

"The who?"

"The Drakh," Kane said with an air of portentousness. "Servants of the Shadows."

"The Shadows are gone."

"But the servants remain," insisted Kane. "And their darksome influence is all throughout Centauri Prime. Ultimately, it is their hand behind Mariel's involvement. They also control Londo Mollari."

"And you know this for a certainty."

"For a time, I only suspected. So I took steps to make sure. It took some time, I admit. I stayed outside the palace and waited for

Londo to emerge, since I didn't want to chance setting foot into the palace itself."

"Afraid?" Vir said challengingly.

Kane did not hesitate. "Absolutely," he said.

That, more than anything, Vir found absolutely chilling. If an initiate of the techno-mages was afraid, then Vir should by rights be bordering on total panic. He gulped and tried to appear undaunted.

"My patience was eventually rewarded as Londo finally emerged, dressed in fairly informal garb, and headed into a section of Centauri Prime which I believe is called Ghehana."

"Ghehana? Why would he go there?"

"He was seeking a young woman who had been residing at the palace, apparently. While Londo was there, I came into close enough contact with him that I was able to place a recording device upon him. As I feared, the Drakh detected it before long. It may have put them even more on their guard, but at least I was able to confirm for myself their presence."

Before Vir could say anything further, Kane stretched out his hand and a holographic image appeared on it. "It recorded everything within the room," Kane said, "for a few moments, until it was discovered. I thought you might want to see."

There appeared a small image of Londo, flickering ever so gently in Kane's hand. And he was talking to . . .

Vir gasped. Not since the last time he had seen Morden had he felt that he was looking upon the face of pure evil. The creature he saw Londo speaking to . . . even without all the warnings that Kane had voiced, Vir would nonetheless have trembled just to see it.

The Drakh was speaking to Londo about something . . . Vir caught the word "dig" and a designation . . . K0643, although he had no idea what that referred to . . . and then the Drakh appeared to react to something. He stretched out a hand and the picture fritzed out of existence.

"He was a bit more perceptive than I anticipated," Kane admitted with a touch of regret. "After going to all that effort, all I managed to get was that small bit. Still . . . at least it should be enough to convince you."

"To convince me of what?"

"That," Kane said cryptically, "you shall have to determine for yourself."

"No, no, *no*," Vir snapped, biting off each word. "Don't start going enigmatic on me. I'm having a rough enough night as it is. What are you expecting me to do with this . . . this information you've tossed in my lap? For that matter, how do I know that this, above all else, isn't some sort of trick?"

"If your interest has been piqued, then I suggest you get together with Londo, and get him quite intoxicated, if that is possible. Once he is sufficiently inebriated, say to him the word, 'Shiv'kala.' Watch him carefully to see his reaction. But only say it to him when he is truly drunk, because I suspect that if you speak the word while he is sober, then you will surely die before much time has passed.

"As for what I'm expecting you to do, Vir, I'm only asking whatever it is that you are personally capable of. No more, and no less, than that."

He bowed slightly and headed for the door.

"Wait a minute!" Vir called, but the door slid shut behind the initiate. He headed after him—the door opened mere seconds after Kane had passed through it . . . and Vir wasn't, for some reason, even remotely surprised to find that Kane was gone.

At that moment, Vir wasn't sure who it was he hated more: Kane, Mariel, the Drakh, or himself.

He turned back into his quarters and sat down on the bed. Thought of the press of her warm flesh against his. Had there been any of it that she had truly enjoyed? Had it all been a sham? Did she ever feel the slightest twinge of regret over the true motives behind what she was doing? What would he say to her when she returned? She'd show up, expecting that things were going to be exactly as she had left them, unaware that anything had changed. If he said anything to her, she'd likely deny it. Perhaps she would deny it because none of it was true. Perhaps . . .

No. No, it was true. Because as far as Vir was concerned, it all made so much more sense than the notion that a woman like that could become besotted with a man like him.

Vir had absolutely no idea what to do. He desperately felt as if he needed someone to talk to about the matter, but he couldn't think of anyone. Everyone he might vaguely have trusted was gone.

He didn't fall asleep that night, which wasn't surprising. He dressed the next morning as if in a fog. Stepping out into the corridor, he encountered two ambassadors who solicitously asked after Mariel and looked at him in a way that he would have once seen as genuine smiles, but now saw only as smirks. He turned right around and headed back to his quarters.

He sat on the couch, trembling with fury and indignation, and then he began to cry. It was unmanly, it was undignified, but he was alone and he didn't care. He grabbed a pillow and sobbed into it, felt as if his soul was emptying out into that pillow. He would expend all his strength into expelling all his misery and loneliness—and just when he thought he had no more strength to continue, a new fit of weeping would seize him and he would collapse all over again. When he had finally gotten all of the misery and self-pity out of his system, he found that most of the day was already gone.

What was left within him was a cold, burning desire for revenge. Revenge against the shadowy forces that had twisted and turned his life back on itself for years and years now. He had stood helpless before the advent of the Shadow ships that swarmed across the skies of Centauri Prime. He had watched Londo's slow descent into a darkness from which he could never return, and he had been unable to prevent it. He had experienced his own personal hell as he had found the blood of an emperor on his hands.

Once more he thought of Mariel, and the merest passing thought of her was enough to enrage him. Ordinarily, he would have been quick to let such feelings go. Life, he had always felt, was too short to let it be caught up in fantasies of vengeance. Not this time, though. This time the hurt had been too personal, the cut too deep. This time someone, or something, was going to suffer consequences for what they had done to him.

Perhaps what drove Vir the most was that, for the first time in his life, he didn't care about himself. At least that much of the self-pity remained with him, but it had been forged into something else. It wasn't as if he was despondent. Instead, he was taking that lack of concern for his own well-being, and crafting it into an attitude that he sensed would serve him in the months—perhaps years—ahead. He was not particularly anxious to die, but the notion of life wasn't holding any exceptional allure for him either. Vengeance was beginning to ascend over concerns for his personal safety.

He picked himself up and turned his attention to the computer terminal, checked the schedules and saw that there was a transport bound for Centauri Prime the very next morning. He told himself that the serendipity of the timing provided yet another sign that he was embarking upon the right course.

He lay upon his bed that evening, quite convinced that he would never be able to so much as close his eyes. To his subsequent surprise, he fell immediately asleep.

The next morning he headed straight over to the departures area, walking as if he had blinders on, looking neither right nor left, barely acknowledging anyone he passed, even if they greeted him. He purchased a one-way ticket to Centauri Prime, wondered whether he would ever again set foot on Babylon 5, and came to the realization that he didn't care.

As Vir departed B5, he didn't notice Kane watching him go, nor did he see two other similarly robed figures who were standing beside Kane, one male, one female.

"You play a dangerous game," said the female, "as does Vir. He has no true idea of what he faces."

"Neither do we," replied Kane.

"But we, at least, have an inkling. He has nothing except what small pieces of information you have been dropping upon him."

"That will have to do."

"I mislike it," the woman said firmly.

The man standing next to her chuckled. "You mislike everything, Gwynn. At least Kane is stirring things up."

"Perhaps. Let us simply hope," said the woman known as Gwynn, "that we do not get caught up cooking in the stew being stirred."

Usually for Vir, the time spent in space travel seemed positively endless. He didn't particularly like such journeys, and usually spent them on the edge of his seat, waiting for something to go wrong, waiting for the bulkhead to buckle or the oxygen to leak or the engines to go dead or some other catastrophe to hit. For Vir was always all-too-aware of the fact that a very unforgiving vacuum surrounded them, and only the relatively thin ship's hull stood between him and a violent death. On this voyage, however, he gave it no thought at all. His thoughts were focused entirely upon Centauri Prime and what he would do once he arrived there.

Unfortunately, he didn't really know. He wasn't sure how he would approach Londo, or what he would do about the Drakh, or what he *could* do. These and any number of other considerations tumbled about in his mind.

No one was there to meet him when he arrived at the Centauri Prime spaceport, which was fine. He hadn't told anyone he was coming. He wanted his arrival at the palace to come as a total surprise. Somehow he sensed that the only thing he really had going for him was surprise. He wanted to make his movements and actions as unpredictable as possible.

The bottom line was, the only person he trusted anymore was himself. As much as he wanted to trust Londo, he had seen far too much for him to be able to place any real confidence in the emperor.

Nor did he trust the techno-mage initiate. His first encounter with techno-mages, on Babylon 5, during their great migration, had led him to think of them as tricksters. The terrifying illusion they had cast, of a monstrous creature threatening to rend Vir limb from limb, still occasionally haunted his dreams.

Techno-mages, as a group, had their own motivations, their own agendas. There was still the very distinct possibility that Kane had fabricated this entire thing. That there was no such thing as a "Drakh." What he had shown Vir had been so short, so conveniently minimal, that it was impossible for Vir to know for certain just how forthcoming Kane was being. He might have fabricated the entire thing from whole cloth, as a means of undercutting Vir's support for Centauri Prime—and that for reasons Vir could only guess. Which might have meant that the business with Mariel was also fabrication . . .

But no. No, Vir was positive that wasn't the case. The farther he was away from Babylon 5, the longer he was away from that arena that they had shared, the more clear it became to him.

Vir arrived at the palace and was greeted with polite surprise by Londo's personal guard. He was escorted to a waiting room, there to wait until there was a hole in the emperor's schedule that would allow him to meet with Vir. "Had we only been expecting you, we would have accommodated you with far greater efficiency," Vir was told. He shrugged. It made little difference to him.

And as he sat in the waiting room, he couldn't wipe the vision of Mariel from his mind. But he was determined that that was exactly what he had to do. He pictured her face, lathered with contempt, and mentally he started to disassemble it, feature by feature. Plucked out the eyes, removed the nose, the teeth, the tongue, all of it, until there was only a blank space where a woman had occupied so much of his attention.

And when she was gone—or at least, when he believed her to be gone—he knew one thing for certain. He knew that if he never, ever, saw a wife of Londo Mollari again, it would be too soon.

The door to the waiting room slid open and Vir automatically started to stand. He rose halfway and froze in position.

It wasn't Londo standing there in the doorway. Instead it was a diminutive Centauri woman, her face round, her eyes cool and scornful, her lips frozen in a perpetual pucker of disapproval, her demeanor glacial.

"You've lost weight, Vir. You look emaciated. You should eat something," said Timov, daughter of Algul, wife of Londo Mollari.

At that moment, Vir seriously considered gnawing his leg off at the knee just so he could escape.

Rumors had begun to filter through the dig.

There had been the reputation, of course. Everyone knew the stories. But no one had taken it seriously, not really seriously. There had been discussions of it in the evening hours, but in the early days of the dig, the chats had been like the laughter of children camping out.

But months had passed, and there was a sense that they were getting close to something. Nobody knew what that something was, but there was a general and unmistakeable air of foreboding, even among people who were of such a sober-minded nature that they would never have bought into a concept as quaint as a place being "haunted."

Then, there was the question of the disappearing diggers.

When one had vanished, no one had thought anything of it. But over the long months, several more had disappeared. At first this had been chalked off to simple desertion, but several of the men who had disappeared had been workers who had absolutely no reason to depart. In fact one of them, a fellow named Nol, just before he had gone missing, was talking about how the dig was the best thing that had ever happened to him. It had gotten him away from a wife he could not stand, children whom he didn't comprehend, and a life that had done nothing but go sour for him. So when Nol had disappeared, that really got eyebrows lifted and tongues wagging.

In short, no one knew what was going on. There was some brief discussion of a mass desertion, but representatives of the Ministry of Internal Security had caught wind of it and come in short order to calm the agitation of the workers. Still, to play it safe, workers had started traveling in groups of three or more at all times, never wandering off on their own, never searching around in areas that were considered off limits.

They also started spending more time in town. Ironically, there had been no town there before. But, in a case of form following function, a small trading community had arisen primarily to accommodate the workers. The odd traveler passed through from time to time, but for the most part it was a tight-knit, normal community. Or at least, as normal as could be expected with the aforementioned air of foreboding hanging over it.

Meantime, the digging drew closer and closer to that which had been hidden and forgotten for millennia . . .

19

Two years before Vir Cotto found himself in Timov's presence, Londo Mollari had looked at the expression on the face of his aide, Dunseny, who had just bustled into the throne room, and had known instantly.

"She's here, isn't she," was all Londo had said.

Dunseny managed to nod, but that was about all. This was an individual who had served Londo's assorted needs for years, and he had never seemed daunted by anything that Londo had thrown at him, or any duty that had been required of him. But now he wore a look of total befuddlement, bordering on intimidation, and *that* signaled to Londo the arrival of the diminutive terror known as Timov.

Londo sighed heavily. He'd had a feeling that the time would come. He just hadn't known when.

It was somewhat like death in that regard. Although maybe not; he actually had a fairly clear idea of what that felt like, and of when his own mortality would finally catch up with him. This led him to realize that Timov was even more fearsome and unpredictable than death. *She probably would be rather taken with that notion*, he mused.

"Send her in," was all Londo said. The aide nodded gratefully. Londo could easily understand why. Obviously the last thing the poor bastard wanted to do was go back and tell Timov that the emperor had no time for her.

Moments later, Timov bustled in, looking around the throne room with a vague air of disdain, as if she were trying to determine the best way to redecorate.

Then she looked straight at Londo. "The curtains in here are ghastly. You need more light."

"No surprises," Londo murmured.

"What?"

" 'What' indeed—that is the question before us, Timov. As in, 'What are you doing here?' "

"Is that all I get from you, Londo? A coarse interrogation? Waves of hostility? I am your wife, after all."

"Yes. You are my wife. But I," and Londo rose from his throne, "am your emperor. And you will show proper respect to me, as befits a woman in the presence of the supreme ruler of the Centauri Republic."

"Oh, please," Timov responded disdainfully.

But then Londo stepped down from the throne and slowly advanced on her. "Down to one knee, woman. If you had taken this long to respond to a direct command from Emperor Cartagia, he would have had your head on a plate in an instant. You will genuflect in my presence, speak only when I permit you to speak, and obey my orders, or by the Great Maker . . . I will have you taken out and executed immediately, and your head placed on a pike as a warning to other disobedient wives everywhere! *Do you understand me?*"

Timov didn't budge. His face was only a few inches away from hers. And then she took out a handkerchief from her sleeve and dabbed at the right corner of his mouth.

"What are you doing?" asked Londo.

"You have a bit of spittle right there. Hold still."

Londo couldn't quite believe it. He felt as if he were trapped in some bizarre dream. "Have you lost your mind? Didn't you hear one word I said?"

"Yes. And if you're about to order soldiers to come in here and take me away so that my head can adorn your exterior fixtures, then you needn't look like a crazed animal while you're doing it. As wife of the emperor, *I* at least am aware that I have an image to protect. You should start considering yours. There." She tucked the handkerchief away, then serenely folded her hands in front of her. "All right. I'm ready," she said, her chin pointed upward. "Summon the soldiers. Take me away because I'm not subservient enough. I know it's what you've always wanted."

He stared at her for a time, gaping in open incredulity. And then, slowly shaking his head, he walked back to his throne.

"I am curious, though," Timov continued, as if the conversation was meant to continue. "Will the means of execution be the actual beheading? Or will I be killed in some other fashion, my decapitation to occur subsequently. It will make a difference in terms of the last outfit I wear. For example, there's liable to be much more blood in a beheading, so I'll probably want to wear something arterial red to get a better blend. But if something more bloodless is chosen, such as the administering of poison, then I'll probably want to wear one of my blue dresses—probably the one with a bit more scoop at the neck. I know, it's somewhat more daring than my usual ensemble, but since it will be my last public appearance, why shouldn't I leave tongues wagging? Of course, the one with the gold brocade could—"

"Oh, shut up." Londo sighed.

She was actually quiet for a moment, and then, sounding rather solicitous, she said, "You seem fatigued, Londo. Shall I get the guards for you?"

"Great Maker . . . I do not believe it. It cannot be possible."

She folded her arms. "What cannot be possible?"

"That I've actually missed you," he said with slow disbelief.

"Yes. I know you have."

"I never would have thought it could come to this."

"Would you like to know why you miss me?" she asked.

"Could I stop you from telling me?"

As if he hadn't spoken, Timov slowly circled the perimeter of the throne room as she said coolly, "Because you are surrounded by people who treat you as emperor. But you have not been an emperor for most of your life. You are much more accustomed to being treated as simple Londo Mollari. That is your natural state of being, and I believe you long, to some degree, for a return to those days. That is why you are so lonely . . ."

He looked at her askance. "Who said I was lonely?"

"No one," she said with a small shrug. "I simply surmised that—"

"Noooo." He waggled a finger at her. "It is all coming clear now. You've been speaking to Senna, yes?"

"Senna." Timov made a great production of frowning. "I don't seem to recall anyone by that name . . ."

"Don't try lying to me, Timov. I have far too much experience with it, so I can spot it when even the most expert of liars is engaging in the practice. And you are not at all expert, because you are much too accustomed to saying exactly what is on your mind, always, without exception. I think that if you tried to lie, your jaw would snap off."

"I will take that as a compliment." She sighed. "Yes. Senna contacted me."

"Eh. I knew it."

"She is worried about you, Londo. Heaven knows too few people around here are. They care about you only in regard to how they can use your power to further their ends, or how you can best serve their needs."

"And you know this how?"

"Because I know the mentality, Londo. I know the situations that draw certain types of players to certain sorts of games."

"And what is your game, Timov?" he asked, waving a finger at her. "Am I supposed to believe that you are here motivated purely out of concern for me? I will accept that about as readily as the claim that you never heard of Senna."

"I make no bones about it, Londo. I'm tired of having you hold me at arm's length. There is status, power, money that are owed me as the wife of an emperor. You've made no effort to contact me and bring me here, no effort to make me a part of your court, as is my due."

"You have wanted for nothing."

"That is true. The titles and lands of House Mollari are quite nice, and my lot in life is certainly of a higher caliber than poor Daggair or Mariel . . ."

" 'Poor' Daggair or Mariel?" He snorted. "Are you going to tell me that you actually have some degree of pity for them?"

"No, I wouldn't insult your intelligence by claiming that. But their situation was somewhat dire, last I heard."

"And have you done anything to improve that situation for them, using the resources you have at your disposal?"

"Of course not," sniffed Timov. "I do for them exactly what they would have done for me."

"As always, Timov, you can be counted on."

"You meant that sarcastically, I know, but the truth is that you know you always can count on me. I'll wager that even as we speak you're surrounded by backstabbers, yes-men . . . all manner of bottom feeders. You need someone who will be honest with you, tell you precisely what she thinks—"

"What 'she' thinks," Londo echoed mirthlessly.

"—and will never betray you. You said it yourself, Londo. With me, you always know where you stand."

"Except my situation is quite different now, Timov. I am emperor now. The stakes have been raised."

"Not for me. For the Durals, the Liones, the others of this court, there is a certain advantage to trying to get you out of the way, for they can then attempt to seize power themselves. Whatever power I have, on the other hand, derives solely from you. If you are gone, so am I. So I would have far more at stake."

"So you are not simply in this for the money. That is not all you care about?"

Slowly Timov walked to the window and looked out across Centauri Prime. Londo couldn't help but notice that she ran her white-gloved hand across the windowsill and looked at the fingers. Obviously she didn't like what she saw, because she shook her head in mild reproof. Londo made a mental note to speak to the cleaning staff.

"If all I cared about was money, Londo," she said after due consideration, "I would not have provided the blood donation that saved your life when you were comatose on Babylon 5, some years ago. All I had to do was allow you to die, and I would have inherited—along with the other two wives—the entirety of your estate."

"I thought you were never going to tell me about that."

"I wasn't. But I felt that—" She stopped suddenly, turned and looked at him. "Wait. How did . . . you knew? You *knew*?"

"Of course I knew. Do you think I am stupid?"

"But . . . but how?"

"One of Franklin's medtechs let slip that I had undergone a transfusion. I know I have a rare blood type, and I know that you have the same, from back when we had our premarital medical exams. So I asked the medtech if you were the donor. He admitted that you were, but begged me to keep the information to myself."

"So that was the reason that you chose me as the wife to keep." There was a small settee with a thin cushion along the window, and she sat in that now, shaking her head in amazement.

"He begged me to keep the knowledge to myself, because he didn't want Franklin knowing that he had—what is the Earth saying?—spilled the peas. So why are you telling me now, after all this time?"

"Because," she said, looking slightly put out that her dramatic revelation had been preempted, "I want you to know you can trust me."

"If you mean that I can trust you not to betray me . . . no, of course I do not believe that. Then again," he added as he saw that she looked slightly crestfallen, "I cannot afford to trust *anyone* that far. That is a simple and sad fact of my life."

"I will stay here for a time, Londo," Timov declared. "I can certainly keep myself occupied during the days and nights here. If nothing else, Senna could use a positive female role model in this place."

"And you think you can locate one for her?" Londo queried.

Timov's lips thinned in her best "we-are-not-amused" expression, which was the one she most often wore and had thoroughly perfected. "If you are truly lonely, as Senna suspects . . . then you will have me to turn to. As for me, I will be able to avail myself of the rights to which I am entitled as your wife."

"Unless, of course, I divorce you as well," Londo said quietly.

She studied him carefully. "Is that what you intend to do?"

"I do not know. I will be considering all options."

"Fine. You do that," she said primly. "In the meantime, kindly assign someone to aid me in transporting my things to my room. I assume that somewhere in this decorated mausoleum you can manage to locate some sort of accommodations. I know better than to assume that I will be sleeping with you." She shuddered. "I still remember that ghastly display you put on with Daggair and Mariel. Shameless."

"Ah, yes," he said nostalgically. "What did you call it? Oh yes. My 'sexual olympics.' "

She made a loud *tsk tsk* noise.

"This is an absurd situation, Timov, you know that. To have you here, floating about the palace, expressing your disapproval of me? Undercutting me in front of—"

"I did not say that, Londo. Kindly do not put words in my mouth, or attribute to me actions that I do not intend to engage in. While in the presence of others, your courtiers and other rabble, I would never think of saying anything the least bit demeaning or, in any way, challenging your authority."

He stared at her, feeling as if he'd just been hit in the head with a brick. "Are you serious?"

"Of course I'm serious. Respect for the man is one thing; respect for the office is something else again. Private is private, Londo, and public is public. It would be nothing less than hypocritical of me to embrace the privileges of being the wife of the emperor while tearing down that same emperor in the eyes of his subordinates. I am here to help you rule, Londo. To rule wisely and well. But you cannot rule without the respect of others, and a woman who diminishes her ruler husband while others are within earshot, by extension, diminishes all of Centauri Prime. Because while you are emperor, you *are* Centauri Prime, heaven help us."

"I see."

For a long moment he said nothing, and then he reached over and tapped a small button on a stand nearby his throne. It sounded a chime that immediately brought Dunseny running. The aide glanced with clear apprehension at Timov.

"Kindly bring my wife, and her belongings, to the Empress Suite at once."

"Yes, Majesty," said the aide, his head bobbing obediently. Then he paused and inquired, "Where . . . would that be, Majesty?"

"Wherever my wife says it is," Londo replied.

"Thank you, Londo," Timov said. "I will withdraw now, to bathe and wash off the dust of travel." And then, to Londo's complete astonishment, Timov bowed in a perfect curtsy, bobbing her head, bending her knee in such elegant fashion that it seemed as if she'd been doing it all her life. As she did so, she extended one hand and let it hang there for a moment.

Londo, surprising himself to a degree, stepped down from the throne, took her hand and gently kissed her knuckles. Timov looked up at him, then, and there was actually a sparkle of merriment in her eyes. "If we do this right, Londo," she said in a low voice, "we might actually have some fun." With that, she rose, turned her back, and strode from the throne room.

He sat there for a moment in silence, and then, very softly, he began to count out loud. "Three . . . two . . . one . . ."

"Why are you counting?" came the voice of Shiv'kala.

"A private joke," Londo said to him, not even bothering to turn in his direction. "You will allow me my occasional indulgences in such things, I hope. I have so few these days."

"The woman."

"What of her?" asked Londo.

"She is . . . unexpected."

"Women often are."

"Her presence could be . . . troublesome. Have her leave."

"For no reason at all?" Londo demanded.

"You are emperor. You do not need a reason."

At this, Londo stood, stepped down from the throne and walked straight toward the shadowy edges of the room from which Shiv'kala always seemed to materialize—it was as if he stepped sideways out of space. "Even an emperor does not like to do things for no reason," Londo told him. "Emperors who do so tend to lose things, such as their popularity. That is often followed by the loss of life, or at very least certain bodily appendages to which I have become quite accustomed, thank you very much. I can handle Timov."

"We are not convinced." Shiv'kala paused a moment, then

stepped ever so slightly into the light. His customary expression of amusement, mixed with disdain, was firmly in place. "You like the woman, don't you. Through your bluster . . . and her abrasiveness . . . you still like her."

"It is not about 'like.' "

"What then?"

"You," Londo said, stabbing a finger at the Drakh, "have no idea how it felt. That woman, and her fellow wives, pushed at me and yammered at me to advance through the ranks of society. They wanted me to obtain power so that they, in turn, would know comfort and privilege. It never stopped. And Timov was the loudest in proclaiming that I would never amount to anything. When the post to Babylon 5 came available, I knew it was considered a joke. I seized it anyway, because it meant that I would be as far away from them as possible. Now I have reached the pinnacle of Centauri status. I admit it: it will amuse me to have her nearby, so that she can see firsthand just what I—the *nothing*—have amounted to. That I am the pride and puissance of the Centauri Republic. That I am the living history of the imperial line of Centauri Prime. That I am—"

"Our servant."

The words, harsh but true, hung there. Londo had nothing to say in response.

"Let her remain, if it pleases you," Shiv'kala said quietly. "But do not let her get too close to you."

"That will not happen," Londo said confidently. "She has no desire to get close to me. She wants to enjoy the power and prestige, but I know her. She will become bored with it soon. And she will tire of watching people treat me with respect. She will find that she cannot hold her tongue; it will be too galling for her. She will leave of her own accord, and in that way I will be spared a needless conflict."

"Very well. But know this, Londo . . . if it does not develop as you say . . . the consequences will be on your head." And with that, Shiv-'kala had faded back into the shadows.

"The consequences will be on my head." Londo had replied, making an amused noise deep in his throat. "Aren't they all?"

"You've lost weight, Vir. You look emaciated. You should eat something," said Timov, daughter of Algul, wife of Londo Mollari.

Vir was immediately on his feet, putting his hand on his stomach. "I've . . . gotten many compliments, actually."

"Well, let's have a look at you," Timov said. She walked up to him, gripped him by the shoulders, and turned him this way and that as if inspecting a side of beef. He started to say something, but she shushed him as she continued her examination. Finally she turned him around to face her and said brusquely, "I suppose it's healthier for you . . . still . . . you're not quite as huggable as you once were."

"I'm not as . . . what?"

And Vir was dumbfounded as Timov threw her arms around him and squeezed him tightly. "It's good to see you, Vir," she said. She stepped back and looked up at him with an amused sparkle in her eye. "You poor, horribly abused, put-upon fellow. I never thought you'd last out the year when I first saw you. And yet here you are, the ambassador to Babylon 5." She looked closely at his face. "You do look a good deal more wan, though. Far more worry lines. And your eyes . . ." She held his chin, staring into them, not unkindly. "They've seen terrible things these past years, haven't they. Things you'd much rather have closed them to."

"Well . . . yes . . . but if I had, I would have kept bumping into furniture."

She laughed at that, and then gestured that he should sit. He did, and she did likewise.

"Not to sound presumptuous, Lady Tim . . . Empress Timov—"

"Timov, please. We're old friends."

"Are we? I mean . . . yes, of course." Vir felt as if his entire world was spinning off its axis. He needed time to cope with the shifting ground beneath him. "Timov . . . what are you doing here? How long have you been here?"

"The better part of two years, actually," Timov told him. "I very much doubt that Londo thought I would be here this long. Truthfully, I wasn't expecting it either. Things have just . . . worked out."

"Worked out . . . how? Are you and he . . ." Vir wasn't quite sure how to proceed with the sentence.

"The secret of our marriage's success has always been our lack of communication," said Timov. "I wouldn't say that we communicate all that much more now. But when we do, there is a . . . relaxed manner about it. We have been through much in the past years, Vir . . . particularly him. It has changed him. Made him more than he was . . . and less. I think he is trying to strike a balance now."

"And you're providing that?"

"After a fashion, in a small way," she allowed. "There is still much that needs to be done, much that needs attending to—"

At that moment, the door opened. Durla stepped in quickly . . .

and came to a dead halt when he saw Timov and Vir. He forced a smile, and it was rather obvious that it was an effort to push it onto his face. "Ambassador Vir," he said with so much cheerfulness that he sounded as if he were medicated. "I heard that you had arrived. Shame on you for not advising us ahead of time. Highness," and he bowed to Timov, "I can attend to the ambassador's needs from this point. I'm certain you have other matters of far greater importance that need attending to . . ."

"Greater importance than chatting with an old friend?" she said, scoffing. "Not at the moment, no. Of course, to some degree I owe that to you, Minister. The Minister here," she said, turning to Vir, "has gone to great effort to try and minimize my calendar of activities. Is that not so, Minister?"

"With all respect, Highness, I have no idea to what you could possibly be referring."

"I'm sure you don't," Timov said flatly, in that particular tone that still caused Vir's bladder to feel slightly weakened. "Now if you don't mind, Minister, Vir and I were in the midst of a conversation. I'm certain you wouldn't want to disturb us, would you?"

"Certainly not," said Durla, as he bowed deeply and exited backing up.

All business, Timov turned back to Vir and said, "That man has got to go. He oozes bile. I have no idea why Londo keeps him around, but he is a frightening little person. He has arrayed an entire support group of key appointees, all of whom are loyal to him rather than Londo. I will do whatever it takes to find a way to rid the palace of him and his ilk. That, at the moment, is my major concern. Well, that and Londo . . ."

"He's my concern as well."

"Is there some specific thing that has prompted you to come here?" she asked.

Something in Vir's head prevented him from being utterly forthcoming. He wasn't sure precisely what it was, but he knew he just wasn't comfortable with telling Timov about Kane. Perhaps she might think he was being used, or that he was foolish for becoming involved with techno-mages, even initiate techno-mages.

"I've . . . been hearing things," he said carefully.

"What sort of things?" She leaned forward intently, and it was quite clear that she wasn't going to settle for vague generalities.

But thanks to his lack of talent for dissembling, he knew that if he tried to make something up, he would fail miserably in the endeavor. So he cast his mind back to his conversations with Kane, and something came to him. "K0643," he said.

She looked at him oddly. "What would that be?"

"It . . . has to do with digging," he told her.

"Digging?" Timov looked rather confused.

Small wonder. Vir was somewhat befuddled about the matter himself. "Yes. I've just been hearing . . . well . . . odd things in connection with it. I was hoping to see what Londo knew about it . . ."

"Let us see what I can find out first," Timov said thoughtfully. "I will make certain that Londo knows you're here. He'll probably want to see you this evening. In the meantime, I'll make a few inquiries into this . . . K0643, you said?" He nodded. She rose and said, "Come. I'll show you to your guest quarters."

"Thank you. And . . . if I may say so, Timov . . . I'm really pleased over the way this has been working out. After my recent experiences . . ."

"Experiences?" She looked at him curiously. "What sort of experiences?"

"Oh, well . . . it's nothing you really need to worry about. It was my problem . . . well . . . not anymore . . ."

"Vir," she said with an air of impatience, "just tell me what you mean."

"Well . . . it's just that, when I saw you, I was . . . I'm a little ashamed to say it . . ."

"You needn't concern yourself, Vir. Just speak your mind."

"Well . . . I took one look at you and thought, 'Oh, Great Maker, not another of Londo's wives. Not after my involvement with Mariel.' But I realize now that I was completely—"

She took him by the arm and sat him down so forcefully the bench shuddered under him. She sat opposite him and said, very slowly, "What . . . 'involvement' . . . with Mariel?"

He told her everything, and as he did, Timov grew paler and paler. The only thing he left out was the exact details of what Mariel had been saying to the unseen "chancellor." But he gave enough generalities to put across his sense of personal violation. When he was finished, she whispered, "You . . . incredibly lucky man . . ."

"*Lucky?*" He couldn't quite believe what he'd just heard. "Timov, with all respect, how could anything about that experience possibly be considered lucky?"

"Because," she replied, "you're still alive."

That which had been hidden for millennia was only days away from discovery.

The casualties were rising.

And in the darkness, the Drakh stood ready. They spoke among themselves, communed. How many casualties would there be? How many workers would be sacrificed to the defenses that belonged to something that had been hidden for so long that it had been forgotten by all save the most loyal.

The answer came back: fifty percent. Perhaps sixty percent of the workers would be lost in that first burst of energy. The Shadows, of course, could have started the homing device with no casualties at all. For the Drakh, however, it was trial and error. And the Drakh had no desire to sacrifice any of their own. So naturally it made sense to use their pawns. They were a trivial concern.

All that mattered was the Hidden Base. The base that could only be reached through K0643. The Hidden Base, known to the Drakh as Xha'-dam. Xha'dam, the place that would enable them to bring the power of the Shadows to the galaxy once more. And if they did their job properly, why . . . perhaps the Shadows would see the greatness of their work and would return. Return to praise the Drakh, and raise them up above all that lived, or at least, all that remained living.

The Drakh Entire was becoming impatient. To be so close . . . so close . . . and yet have to proceed with caution. It was maddening.

But they maintained their patience, for time was on their side. It was not, however, on the side of the rest of the galaxy . . .

20

Kuto swayed into Durla's office with his customary wide gait. Durla stared at Kuto and wondered if it was possible for the man to get any fatter. As it was, Kuto's girth was so impressive that it was difficult for him to ease himself into a chair and, once he was there, disengaging himself from it became equally problematic.

For all that, Kuto had a rather avuncular manner that made him quite pleasant to spend time with, and a boisterously loud attitude that was well suited to someone who was designated the minister of Information.

"A moment of your time, Minister," he boomed to Durla, sliding into a seat before Durla could possibly have the opportunity to tell him to come back later. The chair creaked protestingly under his bulk, but Durla was used to that. "I assure you, it won't take long."

"What is it, Kuto?" asked Durla, putting aside his work.

"Well . . . there has been a good deal of interest being expressed lately in relation to K0643. Since I oversee information, people tend to come to me about such matters, and I address their queries, particularly when public statements might become necessary. Plus, when the inquiries come from high places . . ."

Durla put up his hands in the hope of getting Kuto to focus. The minister of Information had a habit of going off on annoying tangents. "Could you be just a bit more linear, Kuto. What inquiries? What high places? And why should a public statement be necessary? K0643 is simply one of the assorted job works being overseen by this ministry. I don't see how the public need concern itself overmuch."

"Well, I would have thought that to be so, Minister," said Kuto, scratching his copious chins. "The interest has been happening by degrees, however. First . . . we've been getting quite a few inquiries from families of workers who went to the site . . . those who disappeared and haven't been heard from again."

"If workers get tired or bored or simply depart their posts, we can hardly be held responsible," Durla said impatiently. "A certain degree of attrition was anticipated."

"Attrition is one thing, Minister. But outright disappearances?"

"If some are viewing this as an opportunity to begin a new life elsewhere, we cannot be held accountable for that, either. Is there anything else?"

"I'm afraid so. You see, the emperor's wife has also been making inquiries . . ."

"Timov?" Durla let out a long, frustrated sigh. "Why?"

"I couldn't say. But she's been checking about, and has garnered some information—"

"Why was anything told to her at all!" Durla demanded.

"Because what she sought was not classified information," Kuto said reasonably. "Should anything have been kept from her?"

"No. No, I suppose not." Durla leaned back in his chair, rubbing the bridge of his nose, feeling suddenly very, very tired.

Thinking of the project made him think of Mariel. After all, it had been she who had come to him in the dream and urged him on. There had to be an answer to it all, of that he was quite certain.

He had deliberately distanced himself, however, from Mariel's activities, and particularly those activities that were coordinated through the office of Chancellor Lione. He suspected that Lione was beginning to intuit something about Durla's feelings for her, and those feelings might be misinterpreted. If there was one thing that Durla did not want to allow, it was anything that might be seen as weakness.

Still . . .

"Kuto," Durla said, leaning forward in a manner meant to suggest that great secrets were about to be imparted. Kuto tried to respond, but leaning forward wasn't his forte. So he stayed where he was. "I am a bit . . . concerned about several individuals. Several people have attained important positions in a variety of . . . projects. Since I have you here, I thought perhaps I might entrust you with their names, and that you might check into their current whereabouts for me. However . . . it might be best if you did this without letting anyone know that the request came from me. And I would also prefer if you did not speak to Chancellor Lione about the matter."

"Chancellor Lione?" Kuto raised an eyebrow. "Is there a reason to doubt—"

"No. Not at all. But . . . this is my preference. I can trust you to honor it?"

"Of course."

Durla rattled off a half dozen names, the vast majority of whom he was picking at random off the top of his head. One of the names mentioned, however, was that of Mariel. Kuto didn't appear to react to her name any more than he did the others whom Durla mentioned. "And once I've found out what you wish to know?"

"Then relay the results to me."

Kuto nodded. "And what about Timov?"

"She is becoming rather tiresome, that one," Durla admitted. "Still, as long as the emperor expresses no wish for her to leave, we must honor his desires in the matter. Mustn't we?"

"And if his desires change?"

"Why then," Durla said quietly, "so does her . . . location."

Kuto nodded, smiled, left Durla's office . . . and went straight to Castig Lione to inform the chancellor that, yes indeed, his hunch had been right, and Durla had inquired about Lady Mariel.

Wheels within wheels. And moving like a wraith, through the minds of each and every player, flowed Shiv'kala, smiling from the darkness of their innermost ambitions, and secure in the knowledge that the Drakh would ultimately benefit from all . . .

21

When Vir came to, he felt a throbbing at the base of his skull, and when he tried to rub it he discovered that his hands were chained to the wall of the cell that he was occupying.

He pulled at the manacles and had absolutely no success in budging them. As the reality of his situation started to dawn on him, he pulled with greater and greater aggressiveness, but his only response was the loud rattling of the chains. By rapid degrees, his panic level began to elevate, and he pulled with even more ferocity, still to no avail.

Then he shouted, but that was an even bigger mistake, because he only succeeded in making his head hurt mightily. It was at that point that he managed to come to the realization that he was experiencing a thumping great hangover.

That, in turn, led him to remember the previous night, which had been one of great festivity and merriment. He was utterly perplexed as to how something that seemed to be going so right could possibly have ended up so wrong . . .

Some fourteen hours earlier Vir had puttered around in his quarters and wondered when, or even if, Londo was going to take the time to see him. Indeed, he was wondering a great many things, up to and including whether or not his presence on Centauri Prime was one great big mistake.

Then he reviewed, once again, the reasons he had come. The claims of a great darkness that had fallen upon Centauri Prime, that some sort of strange race had gained a hold over Londo. And above all of that, he recalled the sense of personal humiliation over the entire business with Mariel. All of that served to steel his resolve, and made him more determined than ever to see through what he had committed to do.

The door to his quarters chimed, and he went to open it. Timov

was standing there, and there was an unmistakeable look of concern
on her face. "I have some information for you regarding K0643," she
said without preamble. "It's a planet."

In quick, broad strokes she laid out what she had learned of the
world. Of how it was a pet archaeological dig that had been initiated
by Minister Durla. Of how some spoke of it as being haunted, as unlikely and improbable as such a thing might be. Of how people were
vanishing from the site. "I'm wondering if there isn't some sort of
cover-up attached to it," Timov said suspiciously.

"But what would they be covering up? Is there any concrete example of wrongdoing?"

"No, but I—"

"Well!" boomed a familiarly loud voice. "Well, well, *well*! And
what is this, eh? Is my former aide-de-camp dallying with the wife of
the emperor, eh?"

Vir was astounded at the change that had come over Londo.
What he was seeing here was the Londo of old. A man in good spirits, in good cheer, a man who appreciated the presence and even the
companionship of others. He didn't simply walk into the room, he
practically exploded into it, with huge strides that ate the distance between himself and Vir in no time. He embraced him as he would an
old friend, and Timov as well, which astounded Vir all the more.

It was at that point that Vir became convinced Kane was completely wrong. This wasn't a man who was being controlled by fearsome beings, whose life was beholden to creatures lurking in darkness. No, it was simply impossible. Londo was no good at concealing
things from Vir; Vir knew far too much.

But . . .

Londo *had* known about that attempt on Sheridan's life. He had
found that information somewhere, and from his attitude and actions
the last time they'd been together, it had very much seemed as if
Londo was acting like a man who knew he was under constant observation. Could that have been the case, at the time, but he was no
longer under such scrutiny? Or was it that he had simply become so
accustomed to it that he acted as if it meant nothing anymore?

Vir decided he didn't dare relax his guard. He did, however, return the embrace.

"You must come to my private dining room this evening . . . this
very hour!" Londo declared. "We shall discuss old times . . . we will
laugh as of old . . . we will make sport and make merry, eh? We shall

celebrate your return home, Vir, for whatever the reason is that you have chosen to bless us with your presence. What is the reason, eh?"

"Just lonely, Londo," Vir said quickly. "Just anxious to feel the ground of Centauri Prime under my feet again. And I wanted to breathe the fine air of our Homeworld instead of the recycled atmosphere of Babylon 5. You must know the feeling."

"Ohhh, I know it very well. Very well, indeed. And Timov, you are looking fit this evening." He kissed her suavely on the knuckles. "You will bring the illustrious Vir to the private dining room, and join us, eh? We will make an evening of it. It will be like the old times for the three of us."

"The three of us didn't have any old times together," Vir said reasonably, "unless you count your coming into your quarters while I was trying to stop Daggair and Timov from killing each other."

"Ah, well Daggair will not be with us this evening, so you can rest assured that this night will go quite smoothly, Vir. Timov, I can trust you to make sure that Vir does not get himself lost in this vast abyss that is our home."

"You may count on me, Londo."

"You know, Timov . . . these days, I believe I am finding that to be the case more and more. Well!" And he clapped his hands and rubbed them together briskly. "I have a few more stops to make during my early evening circle of good cheer. I will see you in . . . shall we say . . . an hour?"

"Sounds great!" Vir said cheerfully. It was the first time in ages that he was actually looking forward to spending time with Londo.

"Excellent! Excellent!" Londo then draped his hands behind his back and walked out of the room.

"My! He certainly is . . . boisterous," Vir observed.

"That was how he used to be all the time, when we were first married," Timov said. "And you know, the thing that I consider most upsetting, is that in those days, his outspokenness and boisterousness were remarkably annoying to me. More . . . they were an embarrassment. But now I look upon it, and it's taken me this long to realize . . . that he can be a rather charming individual."

"I've always thought so," Vir said diplomatically. Indeed, the apparent change in Londo's attitude was enough to lend a certain amount of hope to Vir's expectations for his stay on Centauri Prime. Nevertheless, the words of Kane stayed with him, and he had brought along several rather potent bottles of wine just for the occasion.

When he joined Londo that evening, Timov was already there,

and after a brief pause, while his thoughts appeared to be elsewhere, Londo seemed delighted when Vir produced his alcoholic donation. Before long he was completely involved with the evening's private festivities.

What impressed Vir the most was the easy camaraderie that had grown between Londo and Timov. He couldn't get over it. When he had seen the two of them together on B5, there had been nothing but hostility between them. It was as if they were born unable to stand the sight of one another. But here there was laughter, merriment, an open appreciation of each other's presence.

And as Londo had become more and more inebriated, his attitude seemed to go beyond that of a man who was becoming drunk. He seemed liberated, deliriously so. His laughter rang out so loudly that occasionally guards stuck their heads in to make certain that nothing was amiss.

"Vir, where have you been all this time!" Londo cried out, clapping Vir on the back and then sliding off a chair. "I had forgotten what it was like to have you as a drinking companion!"

"That's probably because I don't really drink very much," Vir replied.

This just caused an even bigger reaction of hilarity from Londo, who poured himself another drink, decided that the glass was too time-consuming, and took a swing directly from the bottle. Timov hadn't had nearly as much to drink as Londo, but she was quite nicely toasted herself. Vir was amazed to see that, in that condition, the woman was positively giggly, more like a teenage girl than the stern and severe woman she normally tended to be.

"To Centauri Prime!" Londo called out, raising the glass, which was still full. He took another swig from the bottle, then threw the glass. It shattered against the wall, spreading thick purple liquid across it. Londo stared, bleary-eyed and said, "I suppose that should have been empty, yes?"

"It should have been empty, yes!" Timov said, laughing. She hauled herself to her feet. "Londo . . . I'm going to call it a night."

Londo looked out at the dark sky. "That certainly would have been my guess," he agreed.

"Good night, my dear," she said, and then she kissed him. It was quite an overt gesture for Timov, and Londo was clearly surprised by it. Their lips parted, and then she touched Londo's cheek and said softly, "Perhaps I will see you later." With that, she walked out.

"What do you think she meant by that, eh?" asked Londo, taking another swig of liquor.

"I . . . think maybe she meant that she would see you later."

"You know, I think she did." Londo looked wistfully in the direction that she had departed.

It was at that point that Vir took a deep breath, and then he said, "So . . . tell me about Shiv'kala."

At first, Londo said nothing at all. It was as if his alcohol-saturated brain needed extra time to process the comment. Then, slowly, he turned his gaze on Vir. His eyes were so hazed over that it was impossible for Vir to get a feeling for what was going on behind them. "What . . . did you say?" he asked.

"I said . . . tell me about Shiv'kala."

Londo waggled a finger and Vir drew closer. With a sodden grin on his face, Londo said, "I would not . . . say that name again . . . if I were you . . ."

"But . . . is there a reason you can't tell me about Shiv'kala?"

That was all Vir remembered.

In his cell, Vir realized that that was the point when Londo had whipped the bottle of wine around and knocked Vir cold. That was where the dull ache at the base of his skull had come from. Knowing it, however, didn't make the knowledge any better, nor did it improve on his situation.

"Help!" he called experimentally, but no one responded. He shouted once more for aid, but it was no more forthcoming the second time than it had been the first.

The evening had gone terribly, terribly wrong . . . to put it mildly.

Londo had never in his life sobered up so quickly, so completely. The moment that name had escaped Vir's lips, every bit of inebriation had dissolved.

Part of it was that the keeper, which was enjoying the same blissful alcoholic haze as its charge, had been snapped to full attentiveness when the Drakh's name was mentioned. Part of it was Londo's immediate realization that something had to be done, and done instantly. Unfortunately, he had no idea what that something might be, and so he had reverted to the simplest and most straightforward means of handling a problem, especially when it involved hearing something that one did not want to hear. He silenced the source.

In this instance, silencing the source entailed nothing more involved than knocking him cold. That he had managed with no effort.

He stood over Vir's prostrate form, and naturally, as he had already suspected would occur, Shiv'kala emerged from his state of perpetual hiding. Never had the Drakh seemed more grave than he was at that moment. "This one must die," Shiv'kala said.

"No," Londo said.

"Pleading will not help."

"That was not a plea. That was a statement."

Shiv'kala looked at him with pure danger in his face. "Do not defy me."

Without a word, Londo crossed the room to a sword hanging on the wall—ornamental but nonetheless lethal. He pulled it from its sheath and turned to face the Drakh. He held the sword firmly in his right hand. His intent for its use was clear.

"I defy you," said Londo. "I will kill you if I have to."

"You are insane," the Drakh told him. "You know what I can do to you. The pain . . ."

"Yes. The pain. But you siphon it through the keeper, and the keeper is not functioning . . . up to its best levels at the moment. Nor am I. But a drunk lunatic with a sword can still do a great deal of damage."

To demonstrate, he took two lurching, staggering steps toward the Drakh. He was having trouble standing, and his hand-eye coordination was almost nonexistent. But that didn't make the blade any less deadly as it whipped through the air.

"Now then," Londo said. "You can try to stop me . . . with the pain . . . but the question is . . . will I still be able to cut you in half . . . before you stop me completely?"

"If you kill me," Shiv'kala said quietly, "I will simply be replaced by another of the Drakh Entire. And my replacement will not be nearly so generous as I have been."

"Perhaps. But you will still be dead. Unless, of course, your own life means nothing to you, in which case your death will be . . . besides the point." He took another several steps, slicing the sword back and forth like a scythe whacking through wheat.

It was clear that he was not bluffing.

Shiv'kala did not back down, did not panic, did not even come close to doing so. Instead he said coolly, "Very well. Simply have him locked up for now. We shall settle his situation later. I give you my word that I will not call for his death . . . if you do not attempt mine."

Londo considered this, as well as his alcoholic haze would allow him. Then he tossed the sword aside, lurched to the door, and summoned the guards. They saw the emperor's condition, saw the unmoving Vir upon the floor. What they did not see was the Drakh who, to Londo's utter lack of surprise, had vanished.

"Lock him up," Londo said.

"On what charge is he being arrested, Majesty?" asked one of the guards.

Londo stared at him through bleary eyes. "For asking too many questions. Pray that you don't wind up his cell mate." Then he staggered out into the hallway, his thoughts racing.

He had been deluding himself into thinking things could go back to the way they had been. That he might actually be able to find happiness and camaraderie with loved ones. He had been fooling himself. By having people close to him, he was simply putting them in danger from the Drakh. At least Senna had a sort of dispensation, her presence in the palace was a trade-off for having to endure Durla as minister. Say what one would about the Drakh: At least they had kept their word when a bargain was made.

But Vir . . . poor, stupid Vir, deluded Vir, Vir who had somehow stumbled across the name of Shiv'kala and, in uttering it, had drawn a huge target on his back. What was going to happen to him now? Londo had to get him out of the horrific situation that he had hurled himself blindly into.

Friends, lovers. They were liabilities to him, he understood that now. Luxuries he simply could not afford. For as long as they were around, he would continue to fool himself into thinking that he could have something vaguely approaching a normal life.

He entered his quarters and stopped dead.

Timov was in his bed.

Draped across the top of the bed, she was dressed in an alluring nightgown, with an inviting smile playing across her face. Not even on their honeymoon, the requisite consummation of their arranged marriage, had she looked so happy to see him.

"Hello, Londo," she said. "I thought you'd never get here."

"You can't be serious," he told her.

"Don't worry," she assured him. "I know you've been drinking a bit, and won't necessarily be at your best . . ."

"But . . . now? Now? After all these years? Certainly you can't be—"

"Londo," she said with a gentleness of which he would have

thought her incapable. " 'All these years' is exactly the problem. So many possibilities have been sacrificed to vituperation, and to the two of us working out anger over our being forced together by our families. It's taken a lot for me to realize that it needn't be that way. What I need to find out is if you've come to that realization, too."

He had. He wanted to take her in his arms, to love her, to make up for all that wasted time. But even as he wanted it, he knew that it was impossible. Those who were close to Londo, those whom he loved, had a nasty habit of dying. The further that Timov was from him, the better, for her sake.

And besides, he had the monstrosity sitting on his shoulder. What if, in the act of love, she managed to detect it? At the very least, thanks to the keeper's presence, there would be no privacy. Everything that he and she felt and shared would become part of the awareness of the Drakh Entire. The notion was ghastly, horrific. Something as personal, as private and intimate as that, belonging to the gestalt mind of those creatures? It would be as if she were being raped without even knowing it. And he, Londo, would be the instrument through which it had occurred.

He cleared his throat and tried to give his best impression of someone seized with anticipation of an event that was eagerly awaited and long in coming. Timov actually—Great Maker help him—giggled in a faintly girlish manner. "Why, Londo. You seem positively nervous. I haven't seen you this nervous since our wedding night."

"I was not nervous on our wedding night," he said archly, stalling for time as his mind raced.

"Oh, of course not. That's why you were trembling the entire night."

"You left the windows open and there was a stiff draft."

"And is anything . . . stiff . . . this evening?" she asked.

Londo gulped. He hardly recognized the woman. She had never been an enthusiastic bedmate, even in the earliest days, and he had just written that off to a fundamental lack of interest on her part. He was beginning to perceive, however, that it wasn't lack of interest in the act, so much as it was in him.

For just a moment, he considered it. Then he felt the keeper stirring on his shoulder, as if its own interest was piqued, and immediately he dismissed the idea from his mind. However, dismissing Timov was not quite as easy.

And it had to be done with finality. There was no choice; he simply could not risk a recurrence of this night, ever.

He tugged uncomfortably at his shirt and said, "If you wouldn't mind . . . I could use a few minutes to slip into something . . ."

"Less confining?"

"Exactly, yes." He nodded. He backed out of the room, never taking his eyes off her. He allowed his breath to steady, his pulse to slow so that his heart wasn't hammering against his chest.

And then he summoned Durla. Quickly, straightforwardly, he outlined for Durla exactly what he wanted done. The minister's eyes widened as Londo explained it. Of course, this was something that was solidly within Durla's comfort zone; indeed, he would probably enjoy it, for Londo knew all too well that there was no love lost between Durla and Timov. The unjustness of it rankled at Londo; of the three of them this night, the only one who would actually have a pleasant evening was Durla, who was certainly the least entitled. Truly, the Great Maker had a perverse sense of humor some nights.

Timov was beginning to wonder if Londo would ever return. It was one of those situations where one starts to ponder how long one would stay before realizing that the person being waited for was not going to show up.

Then there was a sound at the door, and she looked up. Londo was standing there, smiling at her, dressed indeed in far more loose-fitting attire. He looked younger, more handsome, more vital than she could recall seeing him. Or perhaps it wasn't really him; perhaps it was her, or the way she was seeing him. It was as if years of resentment had been scraped away from her, like an encrustment from the hull of a ship.

She said nothing then. There didn't seem to be any requirement for words. He came to her then, lay with her, and kissed her more passionately than she could ever recall. She was stunned at the vehemence of it. In her imaginings, it was as if he was kissing her in a way that was to make up for all of the sourness of the past . . .

. . . or . . .

. . . or to last him for the entirety of their future, as if this was it, the last time they would be together.

Immediately she brushed the notion aside as ridiculous, paranoid, a residue of the antipathy they had felt for one another all these years. This was their time, and nothing was going to spoil the mo—

The doors of the bedroom burst inward. Londo immediately sat up, his head snapping around, and Timov saw that there were several soldiers standing in the door. In between them was Durla.

"Unless you truly desire to see the city from the vantage point of your head upon a pike," growled Londo, "you had best have some incredibly good explanation for your presence here."

Durla took two steps forward and said in a firm, unyielding voice, "Highness . . . I regret to inform you that we have uncovered evidence indicating that the lady Timov was plotting against the crown."

"That's preposterous!" Timov said immediately. "You can't be serious."

"Do you think, milady, I would put forward this charge if I were not positive?" asked Durla, reeking with disdain. "I am more than aware of the gravity of the charge and the stakes involved. So rest assured that I would not say this unless I knew it for a fact. She has allies, Highness. Allies who would like nothing better than to see you removed from office, your head upon that same pike that you alluded to just now. She is to search out your weaknesses, and when she has compiled them, she and her allies will strike."

"Londo, throw him out!" Timov said, rage building. "Don't listen to these calumnies! They . . . he . . ."

Londo was looking at her in a way that she couldn't even begin to decipher. It seemed to be a mixture of anger and horror and infinite loss.

"I should have known," he said quietly.

The immensity of the meaning implicit in those words stunned her at first. "You . . . you can't actually be saying that you believe these mendacities! You—"

"Why else!" he demanded. "Why else would you embark on this seduction? What was it to be, eh? Poison, perhaps? Or a simple dagger between the ribs? Or did you just want me to lower my guard sufficiently so that I would tell you something you could use against me."

"Londo!" She didn't know whether to laugh or cry. In absence of anything else, rage began to consume her. "You would actually think that of me? Of me?"

"Get out of here," he whispered.

"Londo . . .?"

"Get out of here!" he fairly exploded. "Take her away! Lock her up! Now!"

"Are you out of your mind!" she shrieked as she got to her feet, and then the guards were upon her, dragging her out.

Londo watched her being pulled away. He felt as if his hearts were being ripped out along with her. Her voice echoed up and down the hallway, her protests, her voicing of her hurt, but there was nothing he could do. Nothing he dared do. He was still shuddering inwardly at the vomitous feeling he'd had of the Drakh watching his final, amorous moments with her in a sort of clinical manner, as if he were not a man but a laboratory specimen being put through his paces.

Durla approached Londo. He had never seemed quite so tentative before. He said in a low voice, "Sufficient, Majesty?"

Londo couldn't even stand to look at him. "Get out," he said in a voice that sounded as if it were being issued from somewhere beyond the grave.

For once in his life, Durla was wise enough to leave a room without endeavoring to have the last word.

22

The next morning, Timov was brought before him. It ached Londo just to look at her, but he kept his face impassive . . . as dead-pan as Timov's own was. Guards stood on either side of Timov, watching her warily. Londo thought their caution was rather amusing in its way, as if they were concerned that somehow this small woman would overwhelm them.

He sat on his throne, with Durla standing nearby, watching with narrowed eyes.

"Timov, daughter of Algul," Londo intoned, "evidence has been uncovered that indicates treasonous activities on your part against my government."

"Yes. I'm sure it has," she said crisply.

"If you are tried . . . you will be condemned."

This comment clearly startled Durla. He turned and looked at Londo and said, " *'If'* she is tried, Majesty? But surely—"

"It is our decision," Londo continued, as if Durla had not spoken, "that such a trial is not in keeping with the more forgiving and tolerant tone of this administration. As we always have, we seek to heal rifts and build for a greater Centauri Republic. The Republic will not be served by the condemnation and execution of the wife of the emperor. If forced to take that road . . . we will walk it, of course. But we are offering you the opportunity to depart, now and forever. You will maintain your title and station, but you will never come within one hundred miles of this place. And if you persist in seditious activities, this case will be reopened and reexamined. That is the of-fer I am making to you, my lady." He paused, and then added, "I sug-gest you take it."

She regarded him for a long moment. "What was it, Londo? Was it that I reminded you too much of the man you had been . . . and could be? Or was it that I reminded you too much of the man you are. For you to believe some trumped-up charges—"

"Your decision, my lady?" he said coldly.

"Well, let me think," she replied, her voice dripping with sarcasm. "Either I can choose certain death . . . or I can choose the option of keeping away from a place that I never want to set foot in again, and refraining from activities that I never embarked upon in the first place. What a difficult choice. The latter, I should think."

"Very well. Your belongings have already been packed for you. Personnel will be provided for you to escort you to wherever you wish to go."

"I wish I could escort you to where I wish you would go," Timov shot back. "Or was that a seditious thing to say."

"No. Simply rude. Good-bye, Timov." For a moment his voice caught and then, sounding husky and forced, he said, "Enjoy . . . your life."

Not sounding the least bit conflicted, Timov shot back, "Good-bye, Londo. Rot in hell."

When she was gone, Durla turned to Londo and began, "Majesty . . . that may not have been wise. Leniency could be viewed as weakness, in some quarters."

"Durla," Londo said very softly, "if you say one more word—just one—I will demonstrate my strength of moral character by breaking your neck with my bare hands. Yes?"

Durla, wisely, said nothing.

Londo walked away from him then and out into the corridor . . . only to discover Senna running toward him, looking quite distressed. He could surmise the reason. He tried to walk past her, but she would have none of it, instead saying, "Majesty! Timov, she—I—I thought everything was going so . . ." She threw up her hands in frustration. "I don't understand!"

"With any luck, Senna," Londo said, "you never will." And he headed off down the corridor.

Vir looked up forlornly as the door to the cell opened, and he gaped in astonishment when he saw Londo standing there.

"What am I doing here, Londo?" he demanded.

Londo glanced at the manacles and then called to the guards. "Unlock him. Release him."

"Release . . . you mean it's over? I can go? I . . ."

One of the guards walked in with the key and undid his manacles.

They popped open and Vir rubbed his wrists, looking in utter confusion at Londo.

"It was a misunderstanding," Londo said.

"*A what?* Londo, you knocked me cold with a bottle of wine! Just because I said a name!"

"A name," Londo replied, "that, if you are very, very wise, you will never say to anyone, anywhere, ever again."

"Londo, listen to me—"

"No, Vir. I am the emperor now. I don't have to listen. That is one of the conveniences. You will listen. I will speak. And then you will leave." He took a deep breath, glanced at his shoulder, and then said, "We have different roads to walk down, Vir, you and I. And we must watch each other from a distance. Do you understand? A distance. The thing is . . . we cannot be hurt. Not really. Death holds no terror for either of us."

"It . . . it doesn't?"

"No. For we are protected, we two. Both of us. Protected by visions, protected by prophecy. You know of what I speak."

Vir, in fact, did. He knew of Londo's prophetic dream wherein he had seen himself, an old man, dying at the hands of G'Kar.

And Vir had been present when Lady Morella had made a prediction that both of them would be emperor, with one succeeding upon the death of the other. But she had not been specific as to who would be first to wear the white. Obviously it had been Londo. That meant that Vir would succeed to the throne upon Londo's passing, which meant that—until Vir actually ascended—he was safe from harm. At least, from fatal harm.

"We can tempt our fates," continued Londo, "but ultimately, they should be on our sides. Each of us, in our way and to a degree . . . is invincible. However, it is a funny thing about the fates. It's not wise to push them too far, because they have a tendency to push back. So . . . I suggest we pursue our destinies at a comfortable distance from each other, lest our mutual fates become crossed, and the result is to the liking of neither of us. So . . . swear to me that you will not speak of these matters again. That you will return to Babylon 5, and keep your head out of the line of fire. Can you swear that to me, Vir?"

Vir gave it a long moment's thought.

"No. I'm sorry, Londo . . . I can't," he said finally. "I will never stop hoping that you retreat from the road that you're walking. I will never stop searching for a means to turn you away from it. And I will

never stop being your friend . . . even if, eventually, I find that I have .
become your enemy."

At which point Vir firmly expected that the manacles would be
reattached to his hands, and that he would be tossed back into his
cell, to be forgotten by all.

Instead, Londo smiled. Then he patted Vir on the shoulder and
said, "Close enough." He gestured for the guards to follow him, and
moments later, Vir was alone in the cell, the door wide open.

"Londo?" Vir called cautiously.

At that point, Vir was just paranoid enough to believe that—if
he chose to walk through the door—he might be shot under the
guise of being an escaping prisoner. But when he stuck his head
out—fully prepared for it to be blown off—he saw no one in the corridor.

He walked cautiously down the hallway, then saw a door standing open at the end. He emerged into sunlight, possibly the sunniest
day that he could recall in all his life on Centauri Prime.

Sunny . . . but there was a chill, as well. Although he couldn't
quite be sure whether the chill was in the air, or in him.

As soon as he had taken several steps away, the door slammed
shut behind him. Vir turned and saw that he was outside the palace.
There was no way back in. That was all right with him; there really
wasn't any place in there for him anymore. At least, not for the time
being.

Durla felt as if he was having a reasonably good day. It wasn't going exactly the way that he had hoped . . . but all in all, it wasn't bad.
He settled in behind his desk, prepared for the rest of the day to be
fairly productive.

At that point, Kuto showed up, all joviality and pleasantry, and
brought Durla the information he had requested. Calmly and methodically, he went over each name as Durla nodded, and listened to
each one, and acted as if he cared about any of them aside from the
one he was waiting for.

Then Kuto got to Mariel and her activities—where she had been,
what she had been up to, and, most significantly, whom she had been
up to it with.

Durla managed to contain his reaction, instead simply nodding
and taking in that bit of information with the same equanimity with
which he had attended to the other names. He actually managed to

wait until after Kuto had left and was a significant distance from his office before he let out an agonized and strangled scream.

At that point, he didn't know whom he wanted to kill more: Vir Cotto, for whom he had had no assassination plans up until that point, or Londo Mollari, for whom he had a very detailed assassination plan all worked out. Either one, however, would give him extreme satisfaction.

In his private quarters, Londo Mollari watched the slowly receding figure of Timov, walking proudly away down the main walk, head held high, dignity intact. He thought, for some reason, that he heard a distant scream, and decided that it was simply his soul giving voice to its feelings.

Vir walked the perimeter of the palace, heading toward the main street. As he did so, he saw, not far away, Timov. She and a small entourage of guards were heading in the other direction. For just a moment, he was certain she clearly spotted him out of the corner of her eye, as she cast a half glance in his direction. Then, thrusting her chin out slightly, she pointedly turned away from him and walked off in another direction.

"Hello. Are you busy?"

The voice startled him. It came from his immediate right. He turned and saw, standing at the mouth of an alleyway, a cloaked figure who he was already coming to know quite well. On either side of the figure, however, stood two more cloaked individuals whom he didn't know at all, one male, one female.

"Actually, Merlin, I'm not busy at all. Who are your associates?"

"These?" He nodded to the female and male in turn and said, "Gwynn . . . Finian . . . this is Vir. Vir here is going to help us save the galaxy . . . provided he's not doing anything important at the moment."

"No," Vir said, glancing in the direction of the palace, which now seemed very far off. "I won't be doing anything especially important for . . . oh, I'd guess at least a decade or so."

Gwynn looked him up and down with open skepticism. "Are you sure he's going to be of use to us?"

"Oh, absolutely," Vir responded, as if she had addressed him. "You see . . . I'm invincible."

"You're very fortunate," said Finian.

And Vir thought that, far off in one of the upper palace windows, he could see the small, distant and vague outline of Londo Mollari, looking out at the city and then turning away.

"More fortunate than some," said Vir. "Far more fortunate . . . than some."

ARMIES OF
LIGHT AND DARK

**EXCERPTED FROM *THE CHRONICLES OF
LONDO MOLLARI—DIPLOMAT, EMPEROR,
MARTYR, AND SELF-DESCRIBED FOOL.*
PUBLISHED POSTHUMOUSLY. EDITED BY
EMPEROR COTTO.**

EARTH EDITION, TRANSLATION © 2280

**Excerpt dated (approximate Earth date)
December 14, 2267.**

My "masters" are pleased with me this day.

In retrospect, it is rather difficult to believe. Today, I stood in opposition to the Drakh who calls himself Shiv'kala. He ordered me to kill Vir Cotto, my former aide and, according to the predictions of Lady Morella, the future emperor of the Centauri Republic. Quite probably one of the few individuals in the galaxy whose continued existence gives me any fragment of joy whatsoever. Shiv'kala wanted Vir dead because Vir spoke his name, indicating that Vir has obtained knowledge he should not possess.

Such a coward, Shiv'kala. Such a damnable coward. But then, that is the way of creatures that live in shadow, as anyone who has ever lifted a rock can attest, having watched the bugs beneath scurry away. As for Shiv'kala, he lives within the shadow of a shadow, and so is even more likely to fear the light.

Not that he would admit it, of course. Those who are the most afraid are also the quickest to speak with the air of confidence. They believe that, as a result, observers will not detect their fear.

Just once—just once—I would give anything to see the fear I know he carries within him appear on that monstrous, craggy, blue-grey face of his.

I do not know where or how Vir learned the name Nor do I have any idea what prompted him to sit here, in the great palace of Centauri Prime, and ask me about Shiv'kala Obviously Vir has some sort of hidden allies, although I could not say whether they hug the shadows as assiduously as do my own associates They sent him in, asked him to speak the name, and in doing so, used him It was a rather reckless thing, and I can only hope that Vir will take the time to castigate them severely for placing him in such an untenable position

So when Shiv'kala ordered Vir's death, I stood up to him Yes, I did I waved a sword around and spouted threats. I had no idea if I could carry off those threats, mind you, but I made them sound most sincere And Shiv'kala—somewhat to my surprise, I admit—did not press the matter Truthfully, I don't know what I would have done Would I really have attacked Shiv'kala? Tried to butcher him, knowing that his death would only have unfortunate consequences for me, and potentially lethal repercussions for my beloved Centauri Prime? After all, the Drakh still have their fusion bombs in place, ready to wipe millions of my people out of existence with the simplest press of a button.

The Drakh possess the ultimate trump card.

But they will not be quick to use it, I think. It is my belief that Shiv-'kala views me as some sort of experiment or project. He seems interested in seeing whether he can break me in some way Break my spirit, break my soul—presuming I still have such a thing. If I do, it is very likely so blasted and blackened by now as to be unrecognizable

I am not entirely certain why that would be of such importance to him. It could be that if I am completely broken, I can be of greater use to the Drakh. On the other hand, for all I know, he has a side bet with his fellow Drakh as to whether I can be broken. These Drakh enjoy playing their little games, and I am simply a pawn to be moved around from square to square.

Not even a king. Just a pawn.

Vir came to this place to help me, as did Timov. It is truly amazing how one's perceptions can turn around. When I was young, I thought so much of the position of emperor. I thought so little of Timov. When I first journeyed to Babylon 5, I met Vir and thought very little of him.

Oh, and I thought very little of myself, which was why I was so quick to drown my sorrows in drink.

It is amazing how much things change. Now I consider Vir to be the last, best hope that my beloved Centauri Prime has for a future. And I consider Timov, whom I held in such disdain, to be one of the noblest women it has ever been my honor to know. As for myself . . .

Well . . . I still think very little of myself. It's interesting how many things change, while many other things remain exactly, depressingly, the same.

The Drakh have some sort of new plan brewing. I can always tell when something is going on. Shiv'kala, the Drakh who is my primary keeper, has a way of comporting himself when there is some particular scheme afoot. I have no idea, however, what it might be.

It is my understanding that many captors and their keepers develop a love/hate relationship with one another. I suppose that Shiv'kala and I have that, to some degree. I love to hate him. It was Shiv'kala, after all, who insisted on putting that bastard, Durla, into place as my minister of internal security. Durla, in turn, has placed his own people in other key places, and I am slowly becoming isolated from any potential allies. I am both the most and least powerful individual in all of Centauri Prime.

The only person left in this entire palace who brings any joy to me is Senna, the young girl who is the daughter of the late Lord Refa. I took her under my wing, educated her, and made her my personal project. My sentiment was simplicity itself: I felt that if I could save this one girl, then perhaps I would have that much better a chance of saving all of Centauri Prime.

Yet the girl is a liability, even though she does not know it. She is yet another pawn in this great game of power and revenge that Shiv'kala and the Drakh have continued to play. By keeping her close at hand, the Drakh continue to remind me of the control that they have over me. Apparently, having a small one-eyed creature called a keeper permanently affixed to my shoulder is insufficient to do the job.

I think of what might have been. I think of all the possibilities that lay before me in my youth. I always promised myself that I would make no compromises, if power were ever given to me. Yet I have lived my life making nothing but compromises. No . . . it has actually been worse than that. At least when one compromises, one gets something in return for making a concession. I have been given nothing, nothing at all My power is an illusion, my efforts to safeguard Centauri Prime a waste of time

Bah

I am doing it again. So often, I find it easy to slip into self-pity Wallowing is my most comfortable state of being, be it either in an alcoholic stupor or a psychologically induced state of despair Instead of being designated emperor, I should be called "head wallower" out of a sheer sense of accuracy

There is still much to do There are still things that I can accomplish. Shiv'kala wanted to dispose of Vir, and I threatened him in such a way that he actually backed down. It was the closest thing to a triumph that I have had in quite some time It gave me a small measure of hope That is most dangerous, of course Once hope sets in, who knows what could happen next? Hope might lead to a belief that all will work out for the best.

Perhaps it will Perhaps it will at that.

If only I knew what the Drakh were planning. If only I knew whether Vir might be able to stop it.

Such a thing would seem beyond credibility Vir has his better attributes, certainly I could not have asked for a more loyal friend and follower And the prediction by the Lady Morella, that Vir will follow me as emperor, gives me—oddly enough—a sense of comfort. Of all the individuals I know, he probably has the best chance of doing a good job.

But if the Drakh have some sort of revenge-driven plan in the offing, it will require a true hero to prevent it. For all that I respect Vir, for all that he has grown up under my "tutelage," a hero most definitely he is not.

And I, of course, cannot even warn anyone If there were to be a strike against the Interstellar Alliance, it would be impossible for me to alert President Sheridan or any of his people The only possible means of doing so would be to use Vir as a go-between, and Shiv'kala has seen to it that Vir has been exiled from Centauri Prime.

I shall have to find a way around that.

My keeper stirs—the alcoholic stupor into which I've placed him is starting to wear off As always, I must secure this journal and make certain that the dangerous game I am playing is not detected. In a way, this historical record is a small bit of rebellion, which helps to keep my soul and spirit alive.

But a small bit of rebellion is all that it is. Truth to tell, I am no more a hero than Vir. That is quite a shame, for Centauri Prime could very much use one at this point in our history. Let us hope that a hero steps forward.

And let us hope I do not have to act as the instrument of death when and if he does.

1

Vir stood before the giant, crackling energy gate. The ground around him was littered with bodies. On the other side of the gate loomed something so dark, so evil, that he was paralyzed with fear, and then he remembered a time—days, even hours ago—when he had been convinced that he could never, would never, be afraid of anything ever again. He would have laughed at his arrogance were he not too terrified to laugh, and his thoughts spun back to that period a short time before . . .

It seemed to Vir a lifetime ago that he had stood before the techno-mages and trembled. In fact, it had not even been the techno-mages themselves. Instead he had quivered as shadows in a darkened corridor had loomed around him in a most threatening manner.

Vir had been going to speak with the techno-mages on Londo's behalf. The mission had seemed fraught with peril at the time. Londo had required him to inform the techno-mages that he, Londo, wished to meet with them.

That was it. That was all. Tell them that Londo wanted to set up a meeting. Beginning, middle, end of the assignment. But oooohh, how his knees had knocked, and oooohh, how the breath had caught within his chest, all because of an assignment that had involved nothing except acting as Londo Mollari's messenger boy.

He reflected upon that incident, and found the man he was at that time to be rather amusing, even buffoonish. What a charming, amusing individual he had been. He had always acted out of concern for everyone's needs.

That person was dead.

His death had not been abrupt. Instead it had been an agonizingly slow process, as he died by degrees. The final deathblow had been when he had slain the Emperor Cartagia . . .

No. No, on second thought, that wasn't it at all. No, the deathblow to the man that Vir Cotto had once been had come on the day when he had waggled his fingers cheerfully at the severed head of Mr. Morden, as it adorned a pike outside the imperial residence. Oh, certainly, he had once commented how much he looked forward to such an event, but he hadn't really meant it. The truth was that it hadn't been all that long ago that seeing a bodiless head would have been enough to make him physically ill.

Yet there he had stood, *reveling* in the death of an enemy. Granted, Morden had been the incarnation of evil, but even so . . . it had been a truly hideous punishment. And the Vir of old would never have taken such personal joy and satisfaction in witnessing its aftermath.

But that was the Vir of old.

Vir had been struck by fear over many things in his life. Those huge Shadow ships, or the techno-mages, or the sight of Londo sliding toward darkness while he, Vir, could do nothing to stave off the inevitable.

However, the single most frightening thing he had ever had to contend with was pondering the future. If a few short years had turned him into the current incarnation of Vir Cotto, what in the name of the Great Maker would he be like years further down the line?

Casting aside these thoughts, the Vir-of-the-moment, however, was determined not to dwell on such things. Instead he tossed restlessly in a small vessel belonging to the very beings from whom he had cowered in fear, only a few years before.

On some level, he knew that he should be afraid of even entering a vessel belonging to techno-mages. However, in the past week alone, Vir had discovered that the new, deliriously joyful love of his life, Mariel, had actually been stringing him along. She had been playing him for a fool, using him simply to position herself so that she would have greater access to assorted diplomats and ambassadors on Babylon 5. He could only guess why, although he suspected that espionage very likely had something to do with it. Then he had learned that Londo was involved with beings that were servants of the long-gone Shadows, creatures called the Drakh. One of them was named Shiv-'kala, and the mere mention of the name had been enough to get Vir thrown into a Centauri Prime dungeon. If Londo had not interceded and freed him, Vir would already be dead.

He wondered just what it had cost Londo to purchase Vir's freedom. What had he promised to do in exchange? What further piece of Londo's soul—presuming there was any of it left—had been traded away so that Vir could continue on the twisted path of his own destiny?

He couldn't remember the last time he had slept soundly. Once he had entered the techno-mage vessel, however, the female named Gwynn had led him to a seat and told him in no uncertain terms to go to sleep.

"Sleep," he had said bitterly, the stink of the dungeon still heavy in his nostrils. "You can't be serious. Sleep, my dear woman, is absolutely the last thing that I'll be capable of. Thanks anyway."

Whereupon Gwynn had touched two fingers to his temple, and suddenly the room was swimming. Vir's eyelids had been unable to sustain him, and in an instant, he had passed out. It was not, however, anything remotely resembling a peaceful dream state. Images of Mariel, Londo, Timov, Durla, all tumbled one over the other, fighting for dominance in his mind. There was Londo, white-haired and tired, many years hence, with a glass of some sort of liquor clutched in his hand. He appeared to be waiting for someone.

And then someone was approaching him. It was Vir, and he had his hands out, and they were around Londo's throat, strangling him. Suddenly Vir's hands were transformed into Narn hands, and Vir was cast outside of the moment, watching as G'Kar stood over Londo with murder in his eyes . . . no. In his eye.

Durla was there as well, and he was dancing . . . yes. He was dancing with Mariel, while Chancellor Lione plucked away an aimless tune that Vir could not identify. Curiously, both Mariel and Durla were covered with blood.

There was a full-length mirror standing nearby. Vir stared into it, and he saw himself clad in the imperial white. He turned back and there was Londo, with no G'Kar in sight. He looked as he had when Vir had first met him. He looked so young. Only nine, ten years had passed since that day, but Great Maker, what a decade it had been. Londo, who had seemed so burdened with his crushed expectations of what the Centauri Republic should be, nevertheless seemed relatively carefree compared to what he would eventually become. He raised a glass to Vir and tilted it back.

Blood poured from the glass and splattered all over Londo's face. Then he placed the glass down and reached toward Vir with a blood-covered hand. Vir stepped back, back, then bumped against a wall. There was nowhere for him to go, nowhere for him to retreat. Mariel and Durla waltzed past, onto a balcony, and then went over the railing and vanished from sight. Vir opened his mouth to cry out, but his voice was not his own. Instead it was the cry of millions of souls issuing from his single throat. Outside the balcony off which Mariel and Durla had just plunged, he could see Centauri Prime . . . and it was burning. Great tongues of flame were licking a sky thick with inky black smoke.

Vir startled himself awake. He realized, in a distant way, that he should probably have cried out when he woke up. He did not, however. It was as if nothing could scare him anymore.

"—foolishness," he heard a voice saying. It was the female, the one called Gwynn. "Foolishness, Kane. That's the only word for it. This isn't what we're supposed to be doing."

"It is an adventure, Gwynn. If we were not interested in adventure, we would be better off using our abilities in some truly appropriate manner . . . like standing on street corners and pulling rabbits from hats while people throw money." That was Kane's voice. Vir knew it all too well. Although Kane had saved his life, Vir had already come to hate him. For it was Kane who persisted in telling Vir the truth of things, and these truths inevitably served to make Vir's life all the more difficult. There was something to be said for the bliss of self-delusion.

"Finian, tell him we should turn away from this course," Gwynn demanded.

"I don't know that we should," replied Finian, the third of the techno-mage trio. "A situation needs to be investigated. We're on the scene. We should investigate."

"You always agree with Kane! There's no point in talking to you."

"If you know that for a certainty, why did you bother asking me in the first place?" Finian replied reasonably.

"Because I'm as great a fool as you, that's why."

"Then it's fortunate that you're with us. Who else would want to be seen in the company of such a fool?"

Gwynn made an impatient noise and turned away from them. Her gaze went to Vir and she blinked in surprise. "Oh. You're awake. He's awake, gentlemen."

"I thought you said he'd be asleep for at least another hour," Kane said as he moved to stand next to Gwynn.

"So I thought."

"Sleep," said Vir, "is overrated." He looked at the three of them, struck by the similarities and yet also by the differences.

They all had their hoods back, and Vir could see that they all wore their hair, or lack of same, in an identical manner. In all three instances, what little hair they had was trimmed so close that it might well have been done with a razor. Starting at a point just above their foreheads, the hairstyle angled back in two strips like a "V," with a third band starting at the same point and running straight back.

Gwynn was the tallest of the three, and certainly carried herself with the most imperiousness. She seemed the type who not only did not suffer fools gladly, but also gladly made fools suffer. Vir found himself hoping that he didn't fall into her personal definition of a fool. Kane's jaw was pointed, as if perpetually outthrust in challenge, his skin dark and his eyes deep set and unreadable. Finian, by contrast, was the shortest of the three, with a round face and remarkably pale blue eyes that seemed sad . . . or amused . . . or perhaps amused by the sadness of it all.

"So, Vir," Kane said briskly, rubbing his hands together as if he were anticipating the start of a truly engaging game of chess. "Are you ready to help save the galaxy?" Gwynn rolled her eyes and shook her head. Kane pretended not to notice.

"You mentioned that before," said Vir, "without going into any detail. I don't suppose you'd, ah . . . care to tell me now, would you. Just how, specifically, we're going to be doing the rescuing of the galaxy."

"We are heading to the Centauri dig on K0643," Kane told him. "And there—"

"There what?" Gwynn interrupted him. "I think it best we get that settled here and now, Kane. When we discover the true nature of the dig—or, I should say, when we confirm our suspicions—what is it your intention that we do? You say 'save the galaxy' in a way that could only be considered blithely overconfident. You *are* aware that you're exceeding the parameters of our assignment, are you not?"

"As are you," Finian pointed out.

"Be quiet, Finian. I'm simply here to make sure that he," and she stabbed a finger at Kane, "doesn't get into any trouble."

"Oh, of *course* not."

Gwynn looked up, startled. It was Vir who had spoken, and he was making no effort to stop the sarcasm dripping from his voice. "No, Kane never gets into trouble. Just me. I'm at the forefront of every one of his efforts." He rose from his seat and, as he spoke, shook his head, as if he were having trouble believing what he had been through. "There was an assassination attempt on Sheridan, and Kane could have stopped it with no trouble. Instead he let me almost get killed before he stepped in. Then Kane wanted to convince me that there is a 'great darkness' on Centauri Prime and set me up so that I got myself thrown in prison."

"And yet, here you are," Kane pointed out.

"No thanks to you."

"Actually, I seem to recall—"

"All right, all right, yes, on at least one occasion, it was thanks to you," Vir allowed. "And maybe there were more occasions that I didn't know about. The point is this: I don't mind throwing myself into danger at this point."

"You don't?" Finian raised one nonexistent eyebrow. "I wouldn't have fancied you the heroic type, myself."

"No, I'm just tired, and I'm fed up," said Vir. "Sometimes I think a hero is just a coward who's too tired to care anymore."

"There's something to be said for that," admitted Gwynn.

"As I was saying, if I'm going to throw myself into danger, this time you're going to be right beside me, Kane. You, too, you two. I know that Kane is only a cloister techno-mage. That he's been kind of . . . of stashed away all this time, off in your hiding place. That he hasn't really spent much time in the outside world, so he's not as proficient . . . no offense . . ."

"None taken," Kane said calmly.

". . . he's not as proficient," continued Vir.

Kane cleared his throat loudly. "You didn't have to repeat it," he informed him.

"Oh. Sorry. Anyway, he's not . . . well . . . you know, it's what I said. That way . . . in the whole techno-magic and -mage thing. But with you two along, we—"

"Actually, I am only a cloister as well," said Gwynn.

"You—?" He couldn't quite believe it.

He turned and looked at Finian, who nodded sheepishly. "Guilty as charged."

"Oh, *perfect*," said Vir. "We're going into a dangerous situation, and none of you is an upper-echelon techno-mage." He rubbed the bridge of his nose. "Perfect. All right, then, remind me: Why are we going to K0643?"

"Because the Drakh are interested in something that's there, which is probably Shadow-related. Oh, and because diggers have been dying, trying to get to it."

"Oh, well, of course. Naturally. If there's someplace where evil is hovering and people are dying, that's certainly the *first* place I'd want to be."

"Then you're in luck," said Kane.

"I was kidding."

"So was I."

Vir shook his head and—not for the first time in his life—the words "Why me?" echoed within it. As always, no answer was forthcoming, although he fancied that he could hear Fate laughing deliriously and rolling on the floor somewhere, amused by his predicament.

Laughing. Yes, he could hear the fates laughing at him. He stood before the energy gate, his thoughts pulled momentarily from the past to the present, and not only could he hear laughing, but also he could detect an eerie howling. It was the voices, the voices that were crying out their contempt for his ambitions, as if to say, "Pathetic little creature . . . thinking that you—you of all people—could save the galaxy? What makes you more worthy of living than all those around you, who died in witnessing the power before you?"

"Nothing. Nothing makes me more worthy," said Vir, and he knew it to be true.

The howling increased, and Vir felt himself being lifted off his feet, dragged toward his death. He was surprised to discover that his death was, in fact, something he wasn't looking forward to . . .

2

Vir hadn't been entirely sure what he was expecting to find when he arrived at the dig site, but whatever he *did* fancy he'd see, it didn't match up with what they actually found down there.

Empty buildings. Lots of them.

The entire dig had a ramshackle feel about it, as Vir and the techno-mages made their way through the narrow streets. Actually, "streets" might have been too generous a word. There were assorted pathways that ran helter-skelter through the settlement, but nothing had actually been paved. At some points the paths became so narrow that, if Vir and the others had encountered someone coming in the opposite direction, there would have been a considerable problem in dealing with it. However, that situation never actually presented itself.

There were others around. They heard them more than they saw them, and voices floated to them, carried upon the breeze. It was a very stiff breeze, almost a steady chill that Vir could feel slicing through right to his bones. Occasionally there were people congregating at street corners and in makeshift pubs. Vir caught scattered words here and there, and the words were quite disturbing. They were words such as "disappeared," "dead," "quit," "afraid."

"Dead." That one was said quite a bit.

There was only one other word that Vir heard with any greater frequency, and that word was "haunted."

Haunted.

Once upon a time, Vir would have laughed derisively at such a word. But his time on Babylon 5 had served as a serious education into the realm of the supernatural . . . or, at least, it had given him an introduction to the notion that there was more in heaven and earth than was dreamt of in his philosophy. He had lived in a place where people who captured souls and nightmare beings from unknown realms of space had been all too real.

For the men he passed in the settlement town of K0643, it seemed, the line between truth and fiction, between the easily understood and the incomprehensible, had become blurred. For Vir himself, the line had long ago been completely erased. Anything was capable of happening to him. He felt that this was the only possible mind-set for him to maintain, since anything—more or less—generally did have the habit of happening to him.

"I know you."

The voice startled him. He turned and saw a fairly unremarkable, but nonetheless instantly identifiable Centauri who had just emerged from one of the pubs.

Months earlier, a Centauri citizen had been used as a helpless pawn in an assassination attempt on John Sheridan, the president of the Interstellar Alliance. He had been unaware of the part that had been assigned him, and it had only been intervention on Vir's part that had prevented the citizen from carrying out the murderous design that had been thrust upon him. The individual's name had been Rem Lanas, and it was Lanas who was now standing in front of Vir, with clear astonishment on his face.

Before Vir could say another word, Lanas grabbed him by the front of his heavy coat. Vir thought for a moment that it was an attack, but then he realized that Lanas was, in fact, imploring him. "Please," he said, "Don't take me back to Babylon 5. You . . . you said we could keep it between us. Don't tell anyone I'm here. I'll . . . I'll leave if you want, I'll—"

"Calm down! For pity's sake, calm down!" said Vir, gripping him firmly by the shoulders. "Will you take it easy? I have no more intention of turning you over to the authorities now than I did then. What are you doing here?"

"Working," Lanas responded, appearing surprised that Vir would even have to ask. "Why? What else would anyone be doing here? For that matter . . . what are *you* doing here?"

"Well . . . we're here to check into some . . . things. We've heard that this place was, well . . . haunted. And we felt that it would be in the best interests of the Republic to look into it, as ridiculous as the whole haunting thing might sound." He forced a laugh to underscore the alleged absurdity of the notion.

Lanas was looking at him oddly. "Who is 'we'? Is that the imperial 'we'?"

"What? Oh! No, no, 'we' as in myself and my—" He turned and gestured toward the techno-mages.

They weren't there. There was only empty air behind him.

Vir stared dumbly at his open and gesturing hand for a moment, and then said, "—myself and my . . . fingers. Yes, that's right," and he waggled them to display them properly. "That is to say, my fingers and I. I have names for each of them. Would you like to hear—?"

"No. No, that's . . . quite all right," said Lanas carefully, clearly not wanting to offend the man, quite possibly a lunatic, who was standing in front of him.

Suddenly switching his tone of voice, Vir inquired, "There seem to be fewer people here than I imagined there would be. Why is that?"

Lanas seemed to give great thought to what he was about to say. Ultimately, he glanced around, as if concerned that someone might be eavesdropping, and then he said, "Not here."

"Not here? You mean there are people not here?"

"No, I mean we shouldn't talk here. Come."

Turning, he started quickly down the makeshift road. Vir followed, pausing only a moment to glance over his shoulder and confirm for himself that there was no sign of those who had been accompanying him.

Within a few minutes, Vir was sitting in the small quarters that had been assigned to Lanas. To say it was unadorned was to understate the matter. A few sticks of furniture in a one-room domicile in a large, prefabricated building—that was the entirety of Lanas' living quarters. "I'm sorry I've nothing to offer you to drink. I wasn't expecting company. Not that I would have been able to provide anything even had I known you were going to be here. Minister Durla keeps us on a fairly restricted regimen around here."

"Does he."

"Yes. He doesn't want us spending his time and his money drinking. He believes that eating, working, and sleeping should constitute the entirety of our existence here."

"And you put up with that?" Vir was appalled. "But there's more to life than that! There's . . ."

"Oh. And he keeps prostitutes supplied in abundance."

"Ah." Vir bobbed his head in comprehension. "He, uhm . . . he does?"

"Yes. He believes they provide a necessary release." He shrugged. "Apparently they fit into the budget more easily than liquor. Less expensive, too."

"That's very frugal of him," Vir said.

"They actually have an incentive bonus program, where they—"

Vir quickly put up his hands and forced a grin. "That's . . . that's quite all right. I get the idea. I don't really need to know more than you've told me. In fact, I wouldn't have been upset to know less." He cleared his throat, and then said, "So, you were going to tell me about . . ."

"Yes." Lanas nodded. Despite the fact that it was just the two of them in the room, he still lowered his voice. "Between the mysterious disappearances, and the people who have quit, the workforce has dropped by seventy percent. The advantage is, those of us remaining are being given sizable raises just to keep us here. The disadvantage, of course, is that we might not see our loved ones ever again. That would probably be more disturbing to me if I actually had loved ones." He shrugged. "I know it sounds insane. But somehow you just wind up adjusting to the idea that people disappear around here."

"Yes, I can guess that you would," Vir said, thinking about the abrupt disappearance of the techno-mages. "And do you have any idea what might be causing it? Any cluc?"

"None at all. All I know is this: We've a primary excavation area in which we've managed to get deep beneath the surface of this misbegotten world. A number of men have disappeared along the way, some mysteriously, some running away. We have no idea what we're searching for, or what's going on here. But I will tell you what made an impression on me. Minister Durla came here once to inspect the facilities. I saw him several times during his stay here, and every time I did, there was something in his eyes."

"You mean, like an eyelash?"

"No," Lanas shook his head in exasperation. "I mean a look, a . . . sensation. As if he was pleased over the existence of this dig, for some reason that none of us could fathom. I certainly know I couldn't."

"And he's given you no clue as to what you're looking for."

"No. The only thing I know is that he increased the shifts. We're working around the clock now. Day and night. Right now the Odd Squad is on."

"The . . . what?"

"That's what we call them. The Odd Squad. A group of particularly aggressive diggers that sort of ended up working with one another. Word is that they're all former criminals or some such. Used to hard labor. They thrive on it. Enjoy doing it better and faster than anyone else because they somehow prove something to themselves."

He stopped and shrugged. "Ah, but I shouldn't be second-guessing other people's motives. When you get right down to it, who ever knows why anyone does anything, right?"

"Oh, I can, uhm . . . definitely agree with you on that one," Vir said.

"In any event, if anyone gets down to the bottom of whatever it is that we're digging around for, it's going to be the Odd Squad. They claim they can smell danger and then run screaming toward it. One of them . . . Ciril, I think his name is . . . says he's looking forward to meeting Death so that he can punch Death in his privates and then assail him with a string of off-color remarks. I'm not sure why anyone would want to anger Death; but then again, it's not my fantasy. In any event, at the behest of the Odd Squad—men possessed if ever I saw them—lights were rigged to provide illumination. That was something I oversaw, actually. Electronics is my field of expertise . . . although considering the circumstances we keep meeting under, I wouldn't be surprised if you thought I wasn't much good at anything. Whenever the—"

Suddenly, a severe rumble rippled up from below them. Vir was utterly disconcerted. The sound was so deep, so all-encompassing, that for a moment he thought a fleet of Shadow vessels was soaring through the sky, their sheer weight causing vibrations as they passed. Lanas, for his part, didn't seem especially put out. "And we're getting those more often, too," he said as the trembling subsided.

"Quakes? Why? Is this area built on a fault line?"

"Not to the best of our knowledge, no. But it keeps happening just the same. No one knows what causes it."

We do.

Vir looked up, confused and surprised when he heard that. "You do?" he asked.

"No, I just said we didn't." Lanas looked utterly confused. "Was I somehow unclear?"

We know. Get out of there, Vir. Matters are moving faster than we anticipated.

There was no longer any need for hesitation on Vir's part, for naturally he knew just who was most likely to be projecting commentary directly into his skull. In an instant, he was on his feet, and through clenched teeth he said to Lanas, "I have to go. Thank you for your hospitality."

"But I wasn't being particularly hospitable . . ."

"You didn't try to threaten me, terrorize me, or toss me into prison. These days, that's enough for me to consider myself ahead of the game. It's been charming. Have to go. Bye."

Rem Lanas stared in confusion as Vir bolted out the door so fast that it barely had time to slide open for him. Then he just shook his head and murmured, "I've heard that Babylon 5 does strange things to a man. But until I met Vir Cotto, I never realized just how strange."

When Vir stepped out of the building, he looked to his right, then to his left. At that point he was tapped on the shoulder with enough force that it caused him to jump slightly, startled. Then he glared at the three techno-mages who were standing exactly where Vir had been looking, moments before. "How do you do that?" he demanded in exasperation.

"A magician never reveals his tricks," Kane informed him.

"Yes, but you're not a magician. You're a cloister."

"True," Kane admitted.

"Have no fear, Kane," Finian said brightly. "I suspect once we are finished with this business, we will no longer be looked upon as cloisters."

"I'm so happy for the both of you," Gwynn responded sarcastically. She turned to Vir and said, "Vir, you're an ambassador. You're a high-ranking official for the Centauri. You *must* tell them to cease the excavation immediately."

"Excellent idea," said Vir. He paused. "And what reason should I give?"

"That if they continue on this course, they will enable beings of great evil to obtain power that should not be theirs. This they will, in turn, utilize for wholesale death and destruction."

"They may not buy that," Vir said.

"Vir," Kane said urgently, "time is not our friend."

"Then why don't *you* stop this excavation! Conjure up some ghosts to scare the people away; they think the place is haunted as it is. Or just . . . just magic everyone back to Centauri Prime, to buy some time. I don't know, something, *anything*."

"Our mandate is clear—we can only observe," Gwynn said. As urgent as her plea had been, clearly she was the most aggressive stickler for protocol of all of them. "We act on behalf of each other, for mutual protection, but that is all we are supposed to do, unless we are otherwise instructed . . ."

"As I was instructed to take steps to save Sheridan's life, for example," said Kane.

"Okay, okay, fine," said Vir with a growing lack of patience. "So if that's the case, then why don't you manage to go get some new instructions, okay? Just wave your . . . your magic wand, or whatever, to find out whether you can do something about the current situation. You know, the one involving all sorts of evil that could be unleashed on the galaxy while we're standing here discussing the fine points of Techno-maging 101."

Kane did not seem amused. "My associates and I are endeavoring to inform the techno-mages of the present situation, but in the meantime—"

"Endeavoring?" Vir looked at them questioningly. "What do you mean, 'endeavoring'? Is there some problem?"

The cloisters looked at each other with a combination of annoyance and uncertainty. "Our initial attempts to contact them have . . . fallen short," Kane admitted.

"Fallen short? How? How fallen short? How short, I mean?"

"We've been unable to reach them," Gwynn said flatly. "There is something about this place that interferes with our communications spells."

"Forget the spells! Pick up a phone! Use some standard means of communication!"

"The techno-mages cannot be contacted through any 'standard means.' "

"Oh, right, right," Vir said sourly. "That's a sign of just how advanced they are; you can't reach them at all."

"We'll keep trying," said Kane. "In the meantime, you do what you can."

"Fine, fine, whatever," Vir told them. "I'll find out who's in charge and use whatever authority I can to get things shut down, at least for a while. But I'm warning you right now, whoever's running the dig probably isn't going to take me all that seriously. Most people don't."

Kane stepped forward and put his hands firmly on Vir's arms. "We do. We take you most seriously, Vir. We have every confidence in you. If you can't get this done, then no one can."

"No one can tell me what to do," Renegar said.

Renegar was the most jowly Centauri that Vir had ever seen. He was large and beefy, his hair cut unfashionably and defiantly short.

He had thick lips, small eyes, and arms so powerful that they looked capable of snapping Vir in half with little to no difficulty. And when Renegar spoke, it was with a deep raspy voice that seemed to originate from his knees.

He was, quite simply, not someone with whom Vir wanted any difficulties.

Renegar sat behind his desk in his office, both of which seemed too small for him. There was a good deal of clutter about. Vir would never have known, to look at him, that this fellow was in charge of anything of any importance, let alone an excavation mandated by someone as highly positioned as Durla, the minister of internal security.

"I'm not telling you what to do," Vir assured him quickly.

"That's a relief," said Renegar. He did not, however, sound relieved. He just sounded as annoyed as he had been when Vir had first come knocking on his door.

"But certainly," Vir continued gamely, "you must know that there's something wrong on this world. You've had people disappearing from this project in alarming numbers."

"Centauri are soft." There was clear disgust in his voice. "That's always been our problem. Whenever any sort of difficulty is involved, we fold up. Call it quits. In some ways, you have to admire the Narn. Say what you want about them, but we conquered them and they still never quit. Took them years and years, but they fought for their freedom and obtained it. We wouldn't fight for freedom. Someone conquered us, we'd roll over and die, and that would be that."

"I'm so pleased we're having the opportunity to discuss this," Vir said, "but it's not exactly what I wanted to focus on right now, if that's okay. People aren't just leaving because they're tired or bored or they've had enough. There is a great evil here, and your men are in terrible danger. Terrible, terrible danger."

"And you know this . . . how?" inquired Renegar.

"Sources."

"What sort of sources?"

Vir endeavored to remember just where Renegar was on the social scale. He drew himself up haughtily, or at least as close to haughtily as he could get, and informed Renegar, "The sort of sources who choose not to be identified at this time."

"So you can't tell me."

"That is correct."

"And this great danger facing us . . . you can't tell me about that, either."

"I'm afraid not."

"But I'm just supposed to halt work on this project, on your say-so. Tell me, Ambassador Cotto, do you know Minister Durla?"

"I've . . . had some dealings with him, yes," said Vir somewhat wryly.

"Minister Durla, he's not vague at all. He tells me exactly what he wants done, and exactly when he wants it done by. Because of that, I tend to listen to him. Have you taken this matter up with him?"

"No."

"What do you think would happen if you did?"

Dissembling was not one of Vir's skills, learned or otherwise. "I doubt that he would be particularly amenable to listening to me."

"So why should I be more so?"

"Because," Vir said with unexpected vehemence, "you're here and he's not. Because he," and he pointed in the general direction of Centauri Prime, many light-years away, "is not going to care about the lives of the people here. And I thought that perhaps, since you are directly in charge of them, you just might care. Look, while we're talking here, going back and forth and around and around, the risk is growing with each passing minute. We're running out of time. In fact, we may already be out of time. Don't you understand? People aren't just disappearing. They're dying."

For just a moment, Renegar seemed slightly uncertain. Then his face, and hearts, hardened once more. "I have no proof of that."

"You have my word and the evidence of your own eyes: your populace is dropping. What else do you need?"

And at that moment, lending support to Vir's long-held notion that the Great Maker had a fairly perverse sense of humor, there was a sound of an explosion. It came from the direction of the excavation, but it was far more than just an explosion. It was as if the entire planet had been struck by a massive object, and nearly shattered by the impact. The office shook so violently that Vir didn't have the slightest chance of retaining his footing. One moment he was standing, the next he was on his back. Renegar fared no better: his chair tilted backward and spilled him to the ground.

Oddly enough, there was some benefit to that happenstance, for a huge chunk of the ceiling came free and crashed down right where Renegar had been. It might not have been of sufficient weight or impact to kill him, but it certainly would have been enough to give him a concussion—or worse.

Renegar, moving with surprising grace for one so large, tumbled out of his chair and scrambled to his feet. He looked at Vir with confusion, and Vir was pleased to see that—for the first time since they'd made each other's acquaintance—Renegar didn't seem smug or self-satisfied. Apparently Vir's predictions of imminent disaster carried a bit more weight when disaster suddenly presented itself.

All of Vir's instincts told him that now was the time to get the hell out of there. To head back to the landing point where the techno-mages had surreptitiously landed their vessel, and get as far away from this world as humanly, or inhumanly, possible. Vir knew, however, that he had reached a point in his life where his instincts were going to be of no use whatsoever. The impulses for self-preservation, for acting with caution, those were going to have to be tossed aside. At this point, not only did Centauri Prime need more than that, but Vir needed more than that, as well. For there was no way, absolutely no way, that he could bring himself to follow his instinct and return to Babylon 5, hide in his quarters, pull the blanket over his head and ignore the darkness that had fallen upon his world and threatened his people. That was the trouble with knowing what lurks within the shadows, he realized. One can't figure out where to look anymore. If you gaze into the shadows, you blanch at whatever may be in there looking back at you, and you jump as the shadows move. If you look into the light, not only are you blinded by its intensity, but also it serves to remind you that you should be doing everything you can to expunge the darkness. Light does not allow for excuses.

"What's . . . happening?" Renegar gasped out. The tremors were continuing, becoming more pronounced with each moment.

And Vir began to detect a scent in the air. The smell of energy having been released, perhaps, or the aroma of ozone as if a massive lightning strike had occurred not far away. His back against the wall, Vir pushed with his feet and shoved his body to standing. He was surprised that, when he spoke, his voice was steady.

"What's happening?" Vir called over the rumbling, keeping himself standing upon unsteady feet. "I'll tell you what's happening. Exactly what I warned you would happen. Get out of here, if you know what's good for you. Get off this planet. And you haul yourself back to Centauri Prime"—his voice became louder, more strident—"and you tell Minister Durla that this entire business was a disaster. And you remember that Vir Cotto was the one who tried to warn you. Remember who your friends are, Renegar. It might save your life someday. Now go! *Go!*"

Renegar's head bobbled so loosely that for a moment Vir flashed back to Morden on the pike. Then, without another word, Renegar stumbled from the office. Vir followed him, but whereas Renegar headed in the direction of the spaceport, staggering as the ground bucked beneath him, Vir headed in the other direction.

He had to see for himself. He had to know, firsthand, just what it was he was up against. So while his senses screamed at him to run the other way, he forced himself to head toward danger. It wasn't difficult to figure out which way to go. There was a glow not far distant, and he could see discharges of energy flitting through the air, like static electricity.

And there was a structure.

He couldn't quite make it out. It was, after all, in the heart of an excavation. But he could make out the upper reaches of it, and it seemed curved and . . .

. . . and it was rising.

Vir froze in his tracks, but not from the sight of the structure. Instead it was from the Centauri he saw lying on the ground nearby. To be exact, all he saw was the man's upper half; the lower part of his body so horribly charred that it was almost unrecognizable as anything that had once been living. The man was basically dead, but he hadn't fully come to terms with that fact yet. Through one good eye he saw Vir and he reached out in mute supplication.

Vir realized that this was the very first test of his new bravery and resolve. For there was a large rock right nearby, and all hope was gone for this poor bastard. If Vir had any compassion within him, he would pick up the rock and use it to crush the head of the agonized Centauri.

He reached for the small boulder, gripping it firmly, and stood over the prostrate form of the dying man. He raised his arms high over his head, looked down into the terrified expression of the fatally crippled Centauri.

"I'm sorry," whispered Vir, as the rock slipped from his suddenly nerveless fingers. It thumped to the ground next to head of the Centauri, who had no idea what Vir had been about to do, or indeed not too much of an idea about anything at that point.

Vir stumbled back and away as the ground continued to tremble. He stepped over a small outcropping of rock that had blocked his view moments before . . . and there were more Centauri in various states of dismemberment. There were also more, far more, who were simply charred corpses. Vir shut his ears to the agonized cries all around him and kept moving, trying to convince himself that the immediate danger was past. That whatever had happened to these unfortunate souls had occurred at the instant that the energy had been released.

What had released that energy, however, or what had set it off, he could not even begin to guess.

Then there was more rumbling beneath Vir's feet, but he suddenly realized that its point of origin was, in fact, overhead. Something was dropping from the sky, something huge. At that moment there was so much smoke and fog, released from the energy discharge, that he couldn't quite make out anything beyond large, nebulous shapes. They were drawing closer, however, with each passing moment. *Drakh ships,* said a voice in his head, and he had no idea how he had known it. But once the thought was there, he knew it to be true.

Vir looked around, hoping that one of the cloister techno-mages would suddenly pop into existence, stepping from the corner of his eye into full view. They weren't forthcoming, however, and a panicked thought went through his mind. *What if they're gone? What if they were too near the site and somehow they were killed when the . . . the whatever-it-was . . . was released?*

He tried to tell himself that such a happenstance was impossible. That these were techno-mages, after all. Then he reminded himself that they were, in fact, cloisters. That they weren't necessarily possessed of all the learning and knowledge of a techno-mage. A genuine techno-mage, after all, need not fear anything . . .

If they're not afraid of anything, why did they run away? Why did they leave known space?

For Vir, who was seeking so many answers to try and make sense of the universe around him, this was the most easily answered question of all.

Because they're smarter than you are.

Though he knew full well the stupidity of his actions, Vir kept moving. It was almost as if he had been seized by a compulsion to prove something to himself. He had, after all, failed that first test. He'd left a fellow Centauri to go through the last dregs of a tortured death. But there were others like him; what was he supposed to do, bash in all their heads? Since when had he become the lord high executioner of Centauri Prime?

This, though . . . this he could do. This was something he had to do. Just keep one foot moving in front of another, keep going, see what's ahead, and ignore what's above. He kept issuing orders to himself. *Just keep going. One doesn't have to be exceptionally brave to keep moving.* At least, that's what he told himself.

There were more vessels coming in from overhead, and in his mind he actually swore he could hear something that sounded like . . . singing. Many voices joined as one, and he couldn't understand the words on any sort of intellectual level. On a gut level, even a spiritual level, the voices and words chilled him to his soul. They seemed to be coming from everywhere and nowhere, all at once, and somehow he knew that they were originating from those rapidly approaching vessels.

There were large arrays of rubble ahead of him, and he realized that they were the remains of buildings that had been at the edge of the dig. He clambered over them, trying not to think about people who might be buried beneath, knowing that there was nothing that he could do for them other than prolong their agony. He had never felt more helpless.

Once again he felt as if he was simply a pawn in some greater game that he could not even begin to imagine. A slow anger began to build in him. Under ordinary circumstances, it was the kind of feeling he would have tried to bury entirely, for to acknowledge such feelings or—even worse—act upon them could lead to disaster. He had acted on behalf of others before, particularly during the crisis with the Narn, but he had done so in secret, praying that he wouldn't be caught, and the risks that his actions had entailed were in the abstract. *If* he had gotten caught aiding the Narn, *then* there would be unfortunate consequences. This danger, however, was in the here and now, and it might very well have been that the greater immediacy further inflamed Vir's emotions.

He wanted to be angry, because emotional fatigue could only carry one so far. He wanted to be angry enough to see the day through, to put a stop to whatever this . . . fearsome, loathsome influence over Centauri Prime was. It was anger that carried him over the rubble, though he fell several times and thoroughly banged himself up. It was anger that drove him to ignore the fact that the technomages appeared to have vanished. It was anger that made him look up and curse at the dark vessels, which he did not recognize, as they skimmed lower over the planet's surface. It was anger that ultimately brought him to the edge of the excavation.

It was a violent surging of stark-staring fear that bolted him to the spot.

"A jumpgate," he whispered.

Which was true as far as it went. It was a jumpgate unlike any Vir had seen before. The thing was massive, having now risen out of the ground, apparently after being buried deep beneath it. The structure itself was so dark that it seemed to absorb the light from overhead. Rather than the smooth, even edges of a standard jumpgate, this was jagged and irregular, as if the architect had embraced chaos over symmetry and elegance of form.

Energy crackled around the gargantuan structure. There appeared to be three of the black ships, although they were so huge that Vir had no idea of what the crew complement might be. They hung above the jumpgate, just hovering there, as if they were communing with it somehow.

Then the power of the jumpgate flared, greater than before. And Vir fancied that, somewhere in the back of his mind, he could hear something cry out, and the cry was in turn answered. Never in his life had he heard—and not heard—anything quite as eerie. The energy in the gate grew greater still, and the ships began to tremble in sympathy with it. It was as if, in some bizarrely perverse manner, they were making love to one another, energy building upon energy until a release would be achieved.

What a time to think of sex, Vir's mind scolded him. In a sick sort of way, he might actually have found it mildly amusing.

That was the moment when Vir was yanked off his feet.

The gate let out a roar then, like a great pouncing beast, and Vir wondered if he were about to witness another unleashing of the gate's power and energy. He considered two things, rather belatedly. First, if that was genuinely what was going to happen, then Vir had put himself squarely on the firing line, and might well be incinerated within seconds. And second, he remembered the predictions of Lady Morella, which stated that Vir would rule after Londo. Londo himself had said that the predictions as much as made Vir invulnerable. Vir, however, wasn't feeling especially invulnerable at the moment.

He began to tumble toward the gate, rock and debris being pulled all around him. There was a twisted girder sticking up from the ground, and it seemed fairly well embedded. In any event, Vir certainly wasn't in a position to be fussy. He threw his arms around the girder, held on for dear life as the newly opened gate continued to roar with animal fury. Beyond the coruscating energies that the gate was unleashing, Vir thought he could see . . . hyperspace? Or something else? Yes, yes, definitely something else. He had gone through jumpgates enough times, and knew what to expect. This was like nothing he had ever seen.

The incredible draw of the gate started to lift Vir's feet clear off the ground, yanking him horizontal. His legs thrashed about, seeking purchase, and he managed to snag the toe of one boot around the girder. With all his strength he pulled himself to a vertical position, wrapping his legs around his anchor.

There were more ships than just the three he had seen before, more and more descending every moment. Five, six, ten . . . he lost count. They entered the giant, crackling energy gate, and with each passing, he once again heard that uncanny, frightening cry in his head, as if something within the gate was welcoming home the ships that were passing through it.

The ground around him was littered with bodies. On the other side of the gate was something so dark, so evil . . . Great Maker, how could he have thought, for even a moment, that he was too tired to be afraid?

He knew that the definition of a brave man was one who did what needed to be done, despite his fears. But he had no definition for a man who was not only paralyzed with fear, but also in fact had no idea what to do at all. The only term he could come up with was "out of one's league."

In his fevered imagination, he thought he could hear the voices deep within the gate actually speaking to him. They were laughing, laughter mixed in with the words, and they were crying out their contempt for his ambitions as if to say, *"Pathetic little creature . . . thinking that you—you of all people—could save the galaxy? What makes you more worthy of living than all those around you, who died in witnessing the power before you?"*

"Nothing. Nothing makes me more worthy," said Vir, and he knew it to be true.

And with that admission, the planet seemed to give up on him. The gate suddenly appeared to increase its efforts, determined that Vir would no longer defy it. The bits and pieces of body parts that lay strewn about the area were sucked in. The girder was torn loose from its moorings, and the jolt dislodged Vir's grip . . . not that holding onto the no-longer-anchored girder would have done him a bit of good. Vir tumbled over and over, limbs flailing, and the roaring of the gate reached out to him in triumph.

When suddenly there was another, smaller hole, directly in front of him.

He realized at the last moment that it was a small ship, and the exterior hatch was irised open, hanging squarely in his path. Tumbling end-over-end as he was, he was unable to see anything clearly, although he thought he caught just the briefest glimpse of Finian, standing just inside the hatch. Then he was in the ship, his forward momentum carrying him to the far bulkhead, and he slammed against it.

For a long moment he couldn't move. He lay there in a tangle of arms and legs, twisted like a contortionist. And sure enough, there was Finian, except he wasn't taking the time to determine how Vir was holding up. Instead he was dashing toward the front of the ship, shouting, "Kane! He's in! We've got him! Let's go!"

Kane said something Vir couldn't make out, and he heard both Finian and Gwynn exclaim in shock, *"What?!"* Suddenly the ship lurched once more. As tossed around as Vir was, he knew with utter certainty which way they were going: toward the gate.

It was obvious that Gwynn and Finian were also aware of that, as Vir stumbled into the front section of the ship. They were standing on either side of Kane, who was calmly manning the controls. At least, that's what Vir thought he was doing, but he couldn't be quite sure because the controls were unlike anything that Vir had ever seen. Everything was utterly smooth, with simple, glistening, black panels. He couldn't see any separation between anything. He wouldn't have had a clue as to what to touch where, but Kane was operating with apparent sure-handedness.

"This is an information-gathering mission, Kane!" Gwynn said for what sounded like the hundredth time. "We're not supposed to be heroes!"

"Or martyrs," added Finian. His customary defense of Kane seemed to have been abandoned.

"I've no wish to be either one . . . but I'm doing what I must," said Kane.

Gwynn drew back her fist, looking ready to do something rather unmagical with it, such as caving in Kane's head. If that, however, was what she was going to do, she waited too long. Because then the gate was right there, right in front of them, and there was simply no way to avoid it.

The ship spiraled through, elongating, and then collapsing back on itself, as Vir heard the voices laughing at him . . .

* * *

A deathly silence fell over the dig site of K0643, broken only by the occasional howling of a less active wind, and the distant sobbing of one legless Centauri who was watching the blood seep out of himself. Miraculously, he had not been hauled away by the force of the gate, having been wedged against an outcropping and unexpectedly held there by the natural formation of the rock.

His name was Ciril, and he had looked forward to being able to defy Death, punch him in the guts.

His enthusiasm for that meeting waned, along with his life. And when his crying finally stopped, only the wind was left.

3

Vir knew perfectly well what a trip through hyperspace was supposed to be like, and this wasn't it.

There were great similarities in the look and the feel. But even to Vir, who wasn't exactly a battle-hardened veteran space jockey, it felt different. As opposed to a journey through hyperspace in which one guided oneself via the use of carefully mapped pathways, this voyage felt as if the ship was somehow being propelled in a specific direction. If they had been in a planetary atmosphere, he would have said that they had a strong tailwind.

"Where are we going?" Vir said.

Gwynn didn't even bother to look at him, but Finian cast a glance and muttered, "Not just where. Why?"

"Because we're supposed to," Kane said. He sounded rather detached from the entire matter, even though he was nominally guiding the ship.

"We're supposed to?" Gwynn looked to Finian in obvious hope of some sort of explanation, but his helpless shrug indicated that he was as in the dark as she. "Are you saying you've been given some sort of . . . of separate instructions?"

Not for the first time, Vir was struck by the difference between these cloisters and the techno-mages he and Londo had encountered in the past. His current companions didn't maintain the constant air of superiority, the portentousness that usually accompanied a techno-mage's every word.

Of the three of them, Vir suspected Gwynn was the closest to having the requisite arrogance down pat. But her inexperience was allowing her obvious frustration to bubble over, most likely due to the unusual circumstances into which they had been thrust.

"Well?" she prompted when she decided Kane hadn't replied quickly enough.

Kane turned and looked at her then, and there was something in his eyes. His voice sounded as if it were coming from another time and place, perhaps even another dimension, as he said, "I have seen it."

At that moment, Vir was reminded of what Kane had once said to him, after one particularly nebulous comment: "I was going for cryptic."

"You succeeded," Vir had said to him. Now, after all this time had passed, he couldn't help but feel that Kane had succeeded once more. For once again, Vir had no idea what he was talking about.

Of significance, however, were the reactions he prompted from Gwynn and Finian. The comment obviously had meaning to them. It truncated all discussion, brought the entire disagreement to a screaming halt. Instead, all Gwynn asked—sounding not unimpressed—was "Are you certain?"

"Yes."

"Very well." It struck Vir as a bit amusing; Gwynn was acting as if she was giving permission for something in which she had no actual say. Or perhaps . . . perhaps she was just saying to Kane that she understood a bit more what had led him to propel them into the jumpgate, rather than attempting to get safely away.

Finian likewise was nodding. Vir just wished that he could be as sanguine. He wanted to ask just precisely *what* it was that Kane had seen, but he had the distinct impression that any such inquiries wouldn't be welcomed.

Suddenly, the ship lurched, and for a moment Vir was certain that they had been struck by some sort of blast attack. But Kane said with confidence, "We're coming out of the funnel."

"Funnel? What funnel? I never heard of a funnel," said Vir.

"You wouldn't have. It's theoretical," Kane told him.

"Ah. Of course." Vir didn't have a clue to what Kane was talking about.

Finian, however, saw fit to take pity on him. "It's Shadow tech," he explained. "Think of it as a sort of wormhole within hyperspace. A subsystem or subroutine, if you will. One beginning point, one end point, no detours. When you use a funnel, it renders you undetectable to any other ships that might be traveling through hyperspace at the time. Limited utility, but handy if you want to build a fast path to somewhere."

"And where would the somewhere be? At this moment, I mean?" said Vir.

"I don't know," Kane admitted. "It will take a few minutes to determine—"

His voice trailed off. He was looking ahead through the main viewing port, and Finian and Gwynn were doing likewise. Vir turned to see just what it was that had grabbed everyone's full attention. He had no idea what he was supposed to see, but—considering the reactions of the mages—what he did see certainly wasn't at all what he would have expected.

"Nothing," he said. "I . . . don't see anything."

And indeed he did not. They had dropped into normal space, but there was absolutely nothing ahead of them. A good deal of nothing, in fact.

"Nothing is what you're supposed to see," Gwynn informed him.

"Ah. Good. Then I'm right on top of things, I guess."

"Take us in slowly, Kane," Gwynn continued, as if Vir hadn't spoken, and indeed for all Vir knew, she hadn't even heard him. "We're a relatively small ship, and it's not as if they're expecting us. With any luck, we can escape detection entirely."

"And without any luck?" Vir asked.

The look they shot his way was all the response he required. Unfortunately, he still didn't know what was going on. Clearly there was some sort of imminent threat, some immediate danger . . . but he wasn't seeing it at all. Furthermore, the dark vessels that had preceded them had vanished entirely. Where could they have gone? And what was this threat? Nothing seemed to be presenting—

Then, after a moment, he looked again . . . and he saw it. Or rather, he didn't see it.

The stars were there . . . but they weren't.

The area of space ahead of them was—there was no other way to express it—interrupted. It was broken by a patch miles across, where the stars didn't appear to be shining. There was, indeed, nothing ahead of them, but it was a nothing that was most definitely something. It didn't have any sort of geometric shape to it. It was so large, so irregular, that even though he could detect the outline with his unaided eyes, he still couldn't get any sort of mental image as to what it actually looked like. But at least he knew it looked like something. Or nothing.

His head was starting to hurt.

"You see it now," Finian said with faint approval. Vir might have been imagining it, but he felt as if Finian was actually rooting for him in a way.

"What is it? Or maybe that should be, What *isn't* it?"

"It's a null field," Finian replied. "Think of it as almost a sort of portable black hole . . . except you can go in and out. It absorbs all light and all manner of sensory or energy probes. It can utterly convince instrumentation that it's not there. And people who encounter it won't bother to see with their own eyes, because they've become so heavily dependent on technology . . ."

"So says the techno-mage," Vir commented.

There was silence for a moment, then Finian said with a small smile, "Touché."

"So do we go in?" Gwynn asked Kane. Vir was mildly surprised; until that point everything from Gwynn's attitude had given him the impression that she felt she should be in charge. Yet now she seemed to be deferring, however nominally, to Kane.

Kane simply nodded.

Vir wished at that point that he had a weapon.

"Here."

As if reading Vir's mind, Kane reached into the folds of his cloak and extracted something solid and round, about the size of Vir's fist. Vir turned it over and over, trying to discern some hidden meaning. Nothing immediately presented itself.

"It's a rock," Vir said.

"That is correct."

"Is there any particular reason you've given me this?"

"I thought you might need a weapon. I suspect you did, as well."

"Yes, but I . . ." He stared at it in confusion. "A rock? Why a rock?"

"Nature's weapon. Really, the only weapon that nature intended humankind to have," said Kane. "You will do well with it."

"Thanks. And here I didn't get you anything," muttered Vir, shoving the rock into his coat pocket and reminding himself, not for the first time, that hooking up with the techno-mages might not have been the brightest idea he'd ever had.

There was silence as they approached the null field. The techno-mages didn't appear to be especially concerned, but Vir was reasonably certain that it was simply a facade they had adopted. They simply had no intention of coming across as apprehensive when an outside observer such as Vir was present.

"Time to null field . . . eleven seconds," Kane announced. Vir glanced around the control board and saw no sign of a chronometer.

Yet somehow he didn't doubt the accuracy of Kane's time estimate. "Ten . . . nine . . . eight . . ."

Vir steadied himself and, for a moment, thought about requesting that they turn the damned ship right around and head back to the excavation world. They had discovered something hidden by the Shadows; something that would likely have serious consequences once the technology therein was employed. Rather than risking their necks, perhaps the intelligent thing to do was get out safely and alert . . .

Who?

Alert Londo? But Londo had evicted him from Centauri Prime. It was possible that, after a period of time, tempers would cool and relationships could be normalized, but that time certainly wasn't when Vir was still dusting off dirt left over from his stay in a Centauri dungeon.

Tell Sheridan? The Alliance? This Shadow technology had been unearthed as a result of a Centauri dig. Vir knew exactly what the perceptions would be: that he, Vir, was acting as an informant against his people. And that the Centauri themselves—particularly the government—had, in fact, allied themselves with fearsome creatures who had served even more fearsome masters. The problem was that all of that might very well be true. But Centauri Prime certainly didn't need that information getting out, causing even further deterioration of their relationships with every other sentient race in the Alliance.

No, the Shadow influence, whatever it was, had to be expunged quietly, from the inside. If the Alliance even suspected that the Centauri were in league with servants of the Shadows, they might show up to bomb Centauri Prime once more, and this time they might not cease their efforts until the Centauri Homeworld was nothing but uninhabited rock.

Centauri Prime had to be kept clear of this situation. Vir could take no chance that this . . . this whatever-it-was might be linked to the Centauri Republic. The consequences might be fatal and he, Vir, would be responsible.

But neither could he simply turn away and ignore what he was now a party to. If this *was* Shadow technology, about to be employed against other races, how could anyone of conscience stand by and do nothing? And, he realized with a shudder, there was no guarantee that this technology wasn't going to be used against Centauri Prime itself.

He muttered something and Gwynn glanced at him, even as Kane continued the countdown. "What did you say?" she asked.

"Something my mother used to say," Vir told her. "An old saying: 'One choice is no choice.' "

She nodded. "A good saying."

"Three . . . two . . . one . . ."

Space seemed to elongate around them, as if they were pushing through a gigantic wall of clear gelatin or squishy water. Vir prayed that the null field simply provided limited invisibility, rather than some genuine offensive means of beating back intruders.

Then, just like that, they were through.

This time, even the techno-mages gasped. It wasn't a sound Vir liked. The concept of startled techno-mages wasn't one he happily embraced. On the other hand, he certainly couldn't blame them.

The structure that hovered within the confines of the null field was massive beyond Vir's imagination. It would have dwarfed Babylon 5. For that matter, in terms of sheer mass, it might very well have dwarfed entire planets.

The Shadow Base—for that was what Vir had come to think of it as—reminded him of nothing so much as a gigantic coral reef. It seemed to stretch almost into infinity, with numerous entrances pockmarking its craggy exterior.

"Xha'dam," breathed Finian.

Vir looked at him in polite confusion. "What?"

"Xha'dam," he repeated. "It's nearly legendary . . . mythic. Reportedly a Shadow base to end all bases. So huge that—"

"They named it?"

Finian rolled his eyes and looked away.

There was some sort of activity at the far end of Xha'dam, and Vir tried to figure out what it was. The Drakh ships had reappeared, and had converged there. To Vir's confusion there seemed to be some sort of planet there as well. But something didn't . . .

Then he realized. "Great Maker," he breathed. "That's . . . not a planet."

"It's a Death Cloud," said Kane.

"A what?"

"A Death Cloud. Theoretically, it envelops a world and rains destruction down upon it."

"Like a . . . a mass driver or something?"

"A Death Cloud is similar to a mass driver," Finian said, "in the way that an adult with heavy artillery is similar to an infant with a toy hammer."

The comparison was horrific. Londo had been present when mass drivers had been used on the Narn homeworld, and the description he had given had been so ghastly that Vir had wondered about the minds of the people who had come up with such a weapon. Now, upon witnessing something that was infinitely worse, Vir thought of the Shadow creatures, and knew that they were more than mere alien beings. The Shadows were incarnations of all the darkest and worst impulses that the mind of sentient beings had to offer.

"You said 'theoretically,' " said Vir. "You mean it was never actually used . . . ?"

"Our understanding is that it was close to completion when the Shadow War actually ended," said Finian. "Naturally, our information was hardly comprehensive. We're techno-mages, not omniscient. We didn't know the where of it, for example, or how close to completion it actually was."

"From the look of it, the answer is 'Very,' " observed Gwynn.

"That's why we took such an interest in the Centauri excavation," Finian said. "We thought that the Drakh might be seeking out lost Shadow technology, and suspected that this might be part of it."

"The Drakh. Their servants."

"Yes. But even in our wildest suspicions, we never thought . . ."

"I did," said Kane in that same oddly distant tone.

Yes, of course. He had "seen" it. Vir still felt, rather wisely, that pursuing an inquiry along those lines would likely be folly. "So what do we do? How do we stop it . . . ?"

And then they heard it.

Even though sound didn't travel in space, they still heard it. Whether there was some sort of atmosphere attached to Xha'dam, whether the null field was capable of transmitting it, Vir didn't know, nor would he ever know. What he *did* know, however, was that there was a massive rumbling that seemed to envelop everything around them.

It was as if they were trapped within a massive hurricane. They weren't being spun about, but the pounding all around them made Vir feel as if his teeth were going to be jarred loose from his mouth. No . . . it was worse. It was as if his skull was going to be jostled out of his head.

The Death Cloud was moving.

"In answer to your question, Mr. Cotto," Gwynn said grimly, "we don't stop it."

"That thing wasn't near completion," Finian said, unable to keep the sound of horrified realization from coloring his voice. "It was complete. All they had to do was turn it on. If the Shadows had unleashed it during the war . . ."

"We'd have been ready for it!" Vir said with rising alarm. "And we would have had the Vorlons backing us up! Better that it should have been used then. We'd have had a better chance against it! Now, we've none!"

"Vir . . ."

"I'm sorry, Kane." Vir pulled himself together. He took a deep breath, reminded himself that this was absolutely the wrong time to come unraveled. The simple fact was that Gwynn was right. There was no way to stop it. Already the Death Cloud was moving off, out of the null field, surrounded by several Drakh ships that acted as an escort. "They're going to test it," Vir said suddenly.

"What?" said Gwynn.

But Finian nodded. "Yes. Yes, I bet Vir's right. Whatever they're planning to use that thing for, they're not just going to take it right into battle. They're going to run a test on it first. Kane, have we got the area tracked yet?"

Kane nodded, looking over star charts that he cued up on a nearby screen. "We're near the Daltron system. There's one inhabited world there . . . the seventh planet out, with a population of three billion. Minimal space flight capacity."

"We've got to get word to them," said Vir.

Gwynn was shaking her head. "Never get there in time. And if the Drakh intercept our message, they'll know we're here. We'll lose the element of surprise."

"We can't simply not warn them! We have to tell them to—!"

"Tell them to what?" said Gwynn coolly. "Abandon their planet? A world isn't a cruise ship, Mr. Cotto, where everyone can just jump into lifepods when things go badly. Besides, you heard him: minimal space flight. They have no defenses, and they can't get away. Even if we manage to alert EarthForce or the Alliance, we're too far out here. Too remote. No one will get here in time."

Vir didn't know which he found more upsetting: the reality of the situation or Gwynn's icy, dispassionate assessment. *"Don't you care?"* he finally exploded.

"Care? About things I can't prevent? No, Mr. Cotto, I don't.

What I care about are those things that I *can* prevent. Such as the chance that another planet destroyer might be built."

"Another . . ."

"Yes. Like that one." And she pointed.

Vir felt his gorge rising. For there, still at the far end of Xha'dam, he could see the skeletons being erected already for a second and third Death Cloud. With the finished model as an indelible mental template, he immediately knew the constructs in progress for what they were.

"They learn fast, the Drakh," said Finian humorlessly.

"Possibly some construct 'bots, or similar machines that they've put into place," Kane guessed. "There may be some Drakh remaining behind, though, overseeing it." He paused, and then said, "I'm taking us in."

It took a moment for Vir to register what he was saying, and then he comprehended. They were heading into Xha'dam, for a very obvious purpose: to destroy it.

"I'm picking up several key energy sources," Kane continued.

"I thought our sensory devices weren't working."

"Outside the null field, Vir, that was correct. But now that we're inside the null field, we're not hampered anymore. I'm bringing us into the closest entry port . . . or at least what looks like one. That should still keep us a fairly safe distance from whatever Drakh might be here. With any luck, we can get in and out without any problems."

"But what about safeguards?" Vir asked. "Certainly the Shadows would have built in—"

"Not necessarily, Mr. Cotto," Gwynn responded. "The null field would certainly have served as a means of avoiding discovery. And in the unlikely event that someone did stumble across it, certainly the Shadow vessels themselves would have been more than capable of dispatching any intruders. It is indeed more likely that they saw no need to integrate any sort of traps into the base's design."

"And if they have?" Vir couldn't help but ask.

"Fortunately, we have a plan to deal with any traps that may be lying in wait for us," Finian told him.

"Oh? Really?" Vir felt somewhat encouraged at that news. "What's the plan?"

"We send you in first."

Vir stared at Finian and saw a slight twinkle of amusement in his eyes. It was, however, only slight, and then deftly covered up. Vir only wished that he could find it remotely comical.

"I am concerned," Kane said abruptly. "Going on the assumption that we survive this . . . in the unlikely event that any Drakh are on Xha'dam, it would not be wise for them to see Mr. Cotto's face. What one Drakh knows, he can relay to others with the speed of thought. But they need not know the face of their opponent. Vir . . . I shall have to conceal your features. Are you prepared?"

Vir paused for a moment, then nodded yes. And then, a bit nervously, he added, "Will it hurt?"

"Unlikely."

Kane pulled a black mask with string ties from within the folds of his garment and handed it to Vir. Vir looked at it, somewhat crestfallen. "Is that the best you've got?"

"Would you prefer a bag over your head?" Kane inquired.

"Is this a vote?" Finian asked. "Because if we get to choose what he should wear . . ."

"Never mind." Vir sighed as he pulled the mask on and decided that, yes, definitely, he was not enthused with what passed for humor among techno-mages.

The fact that the entry into Xha'dam went as smoothly as it did should have been enough to still some of Vir Cotto's fears. It did nothing of the kind. Instead all it did was heighten Vir's concern that disaster was imminent. As he reasoned it, each passing moment increased the likelihood that they would be discovered, and the fact that they hadn't been found out only brought them seconds closer to the inevitability of being spotted.

However, the techno-mages moved as though with full confidence that they would not be detected. And Vir had to admire Kane's sure hand at the controls. He guided the small vessel down an assortment of progressively smaller passages, before finally determining that they had gone as far as they could go. Despite Finian's earlier jest that Vir was going to serve as a walking decoy, the trio of cloisters offered Vir the opportunity to remain aboard the ship.

Vir shook his head vigorously. "I'm going to see this through," he said firmly. "Besides, if the Drakh show up and come after whoever's in this ship, well . . . I'd rather take my chances with you than without you."

"Very well" was all Kane said.

The exit door irised open, and Vir almost choked on the air. As absurd as it sounded, as ridiculous as the notion seemed, even in his own head . . . the air smelled of evil. He knew it was absurd. Atmosphere couldn't possess abstract concepts of morality as part of its chemistry. Of course, Vir could ascribe to the stale air just about any virtue he desired. In point of fact, though, there was no way that the air itself could be evil.

And yet it was.

It wasn't that it smelled particularly foul. But even as it filled his lungs, he felt as if darkness were filling not only his body, but his very soul. He wanted to suck down oxygen. He wanted to vomit up whatever it was that was getting into his circulatory system. He wanted to seize control of the ship somehow, and send it hurtling out of this abysmal place of shadow, as quickly as he possibly could.

Instead he forced himself to follow the three cloister mages and hoped that he wasn't making the worst, and last, mistake of his life.

The walls weren't dissimilar to those of a series of caverns. As Vir walked, he would rest his palm against them now and again, and whenever he did so he would quickly yank his hand away. The walls felt incredibly cold. No, it was more than that. It was as if coming in contact with the walls allowed them to suck the heat out of Vir. Yet, if he didn't touch them at all, they had no immediate effect.

Kane, Gwynn, and Finian moved forward purposefully, so much so that Vir felt hard-pressed to keep up. The passages formed a virtual labyrinth, and yet they found their way through with ease. Vir felt tremendously envious of them. Part of him wondered whether he hadn't missed his calling. Perhaps he should have become a techno-mage himself. Rather than fighting off panic at the very thought of the science-based magic users, he would be one of them and instill trembling fear in . . . well, in people like himself.

For just one moment, he allowed himself to become preoccupied with this rather pleasant reverie. As he did so, he turned a corner . . . and discovered that the techno-mages were gone.

"Oh, not again," he moaned softly.

This time, however, he was quite certain that they hadn't simply vanished to avoid being noticed. Instead it was probably something far more pedestrian, namely that he'd made a wrong turn and become separated from them. But all was not necessarily lost, for he had a general idea of where they were going.

The concept was that they were going to head for a major power source and, presumably, blow it to hell and gone somehow. With any luck, that explosion would in turn take out the entire Shadow Base . . . while, ideally, giving them enough time to get the hell off the base before it went.

And locating the power source didn't seem as if it was going to be that much of a chore. He could hear rather distinctly a steady, distant thrumming sound, a slow pulse that beat so regularly that he felt as if he were somehow inside a living body. He made his way toward the source, at first tentatively, then becoming more and more self-assured. It appeared that the techno-mages had been correct. He didn't set off any alarms, nor did he run into any unexpected traps. Obviously, the Shadows had been overly confident.

He thought that, right up until the moment that he turned a corner and ran into a Drakh who was heading in the opposite direction.

Vir remembered being a child, wandering about in the woods once during a camping expedition and suddenly finding himself face-to-face with a wild animal. It hadn't been an especially fierce one, but nevertheless, young Vir knew that they were on the animal's home territory, and that carried with it an advantage. But his father had seemed to materialize at the side of his petrified son, and had said with confidence, "Don't worry. He's just as startled to see you as you are to see him."

That was certainly the case now. The Drakh was caught completely flat-footed. Any notion that Vir had that he might have tripped some sort of alarm disappeared when he saw the expression on the alien's face. Clearly the creature had had no idea Vir was going to be there; he had simply been going on about his business and found himself face-to-face with an intruder.

Vir, however, had a momentary advantage. After all, he at least had known that he might run into trouble, whereas the Drakh had been wholly unprepared. Vir drove himself forward off one leg, summoning all his strength and bravery and swinging from the hip as his father had taught him, back when young boys were routinely beating him up. His right fist connected squarely with the Drakh's head, and Vir felt a shock of pain that ran the length of his arm up into his shoulder.

The Drakh rocked slightly back on his heels, but otherwise didn't seem to feel the blow.

Realizing that he was in trouble, Vir took a step back as the Drakh advanced, and the grey-toned creature let out a horrifying shriek of anger that rooted Vir to the spot. Then suddenly the Drakh froze in place, his eyes going wide in astonishment. He was looking at a spot directly over Vir's shoulder.

Had he been thinking fast, Vir might have chosen that moment to press for an advantage. Instead he turned and looked to see what the Drakh was staring at. Instantly, he felt his blood turning to ice water in his veins.

It was a Shadow.

Vir had never actually seen one, except in the outermost periphery of his darkest nightmares, and yet he knew the Shadow warrior for what it was the moment it scuttled forward from the darkness. He could hear a scream in his head like a thousand souls being thrown into damnation, and there was a scrabbling sound as its pointed feet moved across the rocky surface of the floor.

A mixture of amazement and joy appeared on the Drakh's face, as he clearly waited for the Shadow to issue some sort of order. And suddenly the Drakh's head snapped around, as two hands touched either side of his temples. His eyes went wide in confusion when the Shadow warrior failed to leap to his defense.

Then the Shadow disappeared. It didn't fade into the darkness from which it had sprung; instead it simply vanished. The Drakh didn't comprehend what had just happened, but neither was he capable of staying conscious long enough to find out. Instead he simply sagged to the ground, and as he did so, Vir saw Gwynn standing behind him. Her long, tapering fingers released their hold on the Drakh's forehead, letting the Shadow servant collapse with a most satisfying *thud*.

"I . . . I got separated," Vir stammered out.

"Obviously," she said, with the air of one who did not suffer fools gladly. Feeling very much the fool, Vir could understand her impatience. "Come."

He followed her, staying so close on her heels that he nearly stepped on her a couple of times.

The tunnels seemed to be widening out around them, and the sounds ahead of them were getting louder. Vir squinted against an increasingly bright light, and as he did so, he commented, "Kane said that he 'saw' that we had to be here. What did he mean?"

Gwynn said nothing.

"Did he have some sort of . . . of psychic vision? Is that it? Some sort of look at the future?"

"Do not," she warned him, "inquire too closely into the affairs of wizards. You may not like the answers."

"Don't inquire?!" It was all he could do not to stammer. "In case you haven't noticed, I'm up to my *neck* in the affairs of wizards! So you'll forgive me if I make an inquiry or two!"

"Very well," she said archly. "You are forgiven."

Vir rolled his eyes and wondered why he had even bothered.

They approached an archway that loomed high ahead of them, and went through it. The sound clearly emanated from the other side, so loud that Vir couldn't have missed it even if he were deaf. Considering the volume that was engulfing him, he began to worry that he might indeed wind up without hearing, at that.

The place was huge, as Vir had suspected it would be. But it was like no power core that he had ever seen. There were towering columns all around him, except there was no sense of symmetry. Structures appeared to come together, then split apart from one another. It reminded him of nothing so much as a gigantic spider web made entirely of stone . . . except it wasn't exactly stone. It was some sort of porous, black material, which glowed from within with a blue fire.

He didn't have a clue as to where to look first. Gwynn, meantime, called out, "Kane! Finian!" Her two associates stepped out from behind different parts of the power room. "Vir ran into a Drakh. They're apparently not all at the other end of the base, as we had hoped."

"Then we must attend to this quickly," said Kane.

"Okay, so what do we do?" Vir asked. "Can you just, I don't know . . . wave your hands or say some magic words and blow this place up?"

"I'm afraid not," said Finian. "We cannot use our tech for destruction. Only for creation."

Vir's eyes widened. "You're not serious." But the other nodded in affirmation. "Okay, fine, how about this!" he sputtered. "How about you use your power to create a big chunk of empty space where this base used to be!"

"You must do it, Vir."

"Me!" He gaped at Kane. Then, realizing it was pointless to argue, he waved his hands about and said, "Okay, okay, fine. What do I do?"

"Blow it up."

"How?"

"Quickly." And then he pointed over Vir's shoulder, and Vir— against his better judgment—looked where Kane was indicating.

More of the Drakh were coming. There appeared to be at least a dozen of them, perhaps more, and they were pouring in through the entrance that Vir and Gwynn had just used, nineteen yards away.

"This could be a problem," murmured Finian.

That seemed, to Vir, to be something of an understatement. He backed up, watching what seemed like a wave of dark grey advancing on them quickly.

And suddenly Vir and the techno-mages ran in one direction.

And then another. And then another, and still another.

Vir had no idea which way to look first, but neither did the Drakh. Suddenly the entire power room was cluttered with Virs and techno-mages, and no one could possibly have known which way to look or which was which.

"Hurry! Hurry!" whispered Kane, and he shoved Vir in the back, to start him running. Then the techno-mages moved off in a variety of directions, and suddenly Vir was alone in a crowd.

The Drakh made no sound, yet seemed to move in unison as they literally threw themselves into the chaos. They carried what appeared to be small weapons in their hands, though Vir couldn't make out precisely what they were. They looked vaguely like PPGs, but there was something different about them.

Suddenly there was a rush of air and something small and presumably lethal hurtled past Vir's face, missing by the narrowest of margins. It made a metallic noise just beyond him and Vir's head snapped around to see what it was and where it had landed. It appeared to be a spike, about as long as one of his fingers, narrow and sharp and extremely deadly. It was embedded in a rocklike "web strand," and was still quivering from the impact.

Vir had to credit the illusions provided by the techno-mages, however. If the genuine Vir had been the only one reacting with obvious horror, he would easily have stood out. Instead every single one of the mirages dashing madly about had the exact same look of fear and trepidation. Several of them were even "hit" by the spikes and reacted as if they had been mortally wounded. The way they doubled over, staggered about and such, it was impossible to determine whether one of the lethal missiles had actually embedded itself in a corporeal body or had passed harmlessly through an illusion. Any technology capable of creating such instantly adjusting holograms was beyond Vir's ability even to contemplate.

Not that he had the time for pondering. Instead he had to concentrate on one thing and one thing only: coming through this madness with his head still firmly attached to his neck.

He wove his way through the bizarre structure, trying to find some sort of vulnerable point. Not that he had any idea what he was

going to do once he located it. It was most unlikely that he would encounter a large sign that read "Press here to destroy Shadow Base."

He darted left, right, right again . . . and suddenly found himself
in what appeared to be another area entirely. There was still the
humming of tremendous power around him, but there was something
else, as well. Control panels still looked like control panels, no matter what technology was crafting them, and that was exactly what he
had found. Even more important, he saw a holographic image floating nearby that he recognized instantly: it was one of the Death
Clouds that was still under construction. With horror, Vir noted that
the device was already much further along—it actually seemed to be
nearing completion.

Small robotic drones were moving around it in a smoothly coordinated display of activity. They were not, however, acting entirely on
their own. A Drakh was overseeing the entire operation, making sure
that each of the 'bots attended to its assigned task as smoothly and
efficiently as possible.

Vir knew this because the Drakh was sitting right there in front
of him, doing his job. He turned and saw Vir, and for a moment, they
simply stared at each other.

Then the Drakh let out an angry screech, and from the folds of
his garment he yanked out what appeared to be one of the spike-
firing weapons.

Vir's reaction was entirely automatic. Given time to reflect on it
later, he wouldn't even remember pulling the rock from his pocket.
All he knew was that one moment the stone was in his pocket and the
next it was in his hand, and just as the Drakh brought up his weapon
to fire, Vir let fly with all his strength. The rock crashed squarely into
the Drakh's head, and the Drakh let out a shout of fury even as he
toppled backward. Fumbling his weapon as he fell, his finger spasmodically tightened on the trigger. As a result, the spike embedded
itself squarely in the Drakh's chest. The Shadow servant let out a last
strangled protest, and then collapsed altogether.

Vir didn't even take the time to be horrified—the silence around
him told him the techno-mages must have drawn the Drakh off in another direction. He just stepped over the fallen one and went quickly
to the controls. He looked them over for a moment, trying to determine what was what. The robots that had been assembling the Death
Cloud had ground to a halt, twirling calmly in space and obviously
waiting for further instructions.

"There."

Vir jumped involuntarily at the sound of Kane's voice coming from practically in his ear. He saw Kane standing right at his shoulder, studying the controls. There was no hint of confusion on Kane's face—it seemed to Vir as if Kane understood everything. He pointed at several panels in sequence. "That one . . . then that one . . . then rest your hand on that and tell it to do what you want it to do. It will respond."

"Are you sure? I'm not a Drakh . . ."

"You do not have to be. The Shadows designed this equipment to be as simple to operate as possible. Even the most ignorant person, with a modest bit of training, can handle it."

"Oh. Good." Vir didn't exactly feel flattered by that piece of information, but this wasn't the time to take offense. He touched the panels in the order Kane had indicated, then placed his hand where he was supposed to. At first nothing seemed to be happening, even though Vir was concentrating so hard that he thought the top of his head was going to blow off.

"Just remember who is in charge," Kane counseled him.

Vir nodded, then realized he had been having trouble simply focusing thoughts, perhaps out of sheer nervousness. "Move away," he said firmly and, sure enough, the robots began to clear themselves from the Death Cloud.

The robots were not, however, Vir's major concern. He had given that command more or less as a test, in preparation for something more extensive and, ideally, more final. He took a deep breath, which rasped unsteadily in his chest, and then he ordered, "Move into position."

For a moment nothing happened, and then the Death Cloud slid gracefully forward and around the end of Xha'dam, positioning itself so smoothly that one would have thought Vir had been doing it all his life.

He steadied his nerves, focusing on the far end of the Shadow Base, and then in a quiet voice of command, said, "Fire."

No response.

Vir immediatcly assumed that the Death Cloud must not have been far enough along to have been given any sort of detonation capacity. Really . . . how could it be? When they had first spotted it, it had been little more than a skeleton. Even with all the advantages the Shadow tech provided, it simply wasn't conceivable that any sort of weapon of mass destruction could be brought into working order in that short a—

Then the Death Cloud shuddered slightly, as its weaponry dis-
charged—directly into the far end of the Shadow Base. Even as far
away as they were from the source of the destruction, Vir still felt the
base trembling around him from the impact.

More hits, more firing upon the base, as the Death Cloud—operating in some sort of automatic program now—started to progress
down the base's length. Then, on the holographically reproduced image, Vir saw more explosions, this time from within Xha'dam itself.
The vibrations became more pronounced, even though the source of
the devastation was still miles off.

"Now would be a good time to leave," Kane said, with such calm
that one would have thought the base's destruction could have no immediate impact upon him.

Vir's head was bobbing. "Yes . . . yes, I think you're right."

He turned to head for the door, and suddenly Kane was shoving
him to one side. Vir tumbled to the floor, wondering just what in the
world was going on, unable to comprehend why in the world Kane
would have suddenly attacked him. Then he heard a slight whisper of
a noise, a *pfwwt* of air, followed by another, and he half sat up and
twisted around to look behind him.

Kane was standing there, looking down in what almost seemed to
be amusement. Three spikes were imbedded in his chest. The cen-
termost one happened to be the one that he had intercepted when he
had pushed Vir out of the way. The second and third were still quivering, having just been shot into him. Vir, to his horror, saw the
Drakh lying on the ground, his fingers still twitching around his
weapon, apparently not as dead as they had assumed him to be.

It all happened so quickly that Kane had no time to react or prepare a spell to freeze them in place. He tried to use his staff for support, but instead sank to his knees, and the Drakh focused on Vir. Vir
desperately threw himself to one side as the Drakh squeezed off two
quick shots. Both of the needle darts flew past him, but he tripped,
hit the ground, and found himself lying there, eye-to-eye with the
fallen Drakh. The creature swung the weapon around and Vir found
himself staring right down the barrel.

"I can't die," he whispered. "Londo said so. I'm invincible."

Not giving a damn about fate, Centauri predictions, or Londo
Mollari, the Drakh squeezed the trigger. His weapon made an oddly
vacant sound—one that had a uniform quality across a variety of cultures. It was the sound of a weapon empty of ammunition.

The Drakh uttered a word that Vir could only surmise to be a curse in the Drakh's native tongue, and then the creature began to haul himself up. Suddenly the entire room shook violently, and the Drakh flopped over onto his back. This time he didn't get up. The creature emitted a sound that could only be a death rattle, and his head slumped to one side.

Kane was still on his knees, looking somewhat perplexed as he stared at the metal projectiles sticking in his chest. Vir hauled him to his feet, shouting, "Come on! Hurry! Back to the ship!"

"I do not think . . . that is going to happen," Kane said softly.

"Oh no you don't!" Vir yelled at him. "I am *not* about to go back to your techno-pals and tell them that I left you behind! And they're going to tell me that if I'd dragged you along with me, maybe they could have saved you, and the next thing I know, someone's going to be wearing my head for a hat! No thank you!"

Kane tried to say something else, but Vir wasn't listening to him. Instead, with a strength he never would have dreamt he had, Vir yanked Kane to his feet and started hauling him, draping one of Kane's arms around his own shoulder to provide support. They stumbled out of the control room and down the corridor, and Vir didn't even want to think about what was going to happen if they ran into a Drakh because they had absolutely no defense at all.

Kane sagged, and Vir thought desperately to himself—to himself, and to whatever deity might be willing to listen—*Please. Please let us get back to the ship without any problems. Please.*

They rounded a corner, and there was a Drakh standing there. Vir froze, almost losing his grip on Kane. He saw, out of the corner of his eye, that Kane actually had a grim smile on his face, and for a moment he was certain that the techno-mage had completely lost his mind.

That was when Vir realized that the Drakh wasn't moving. He wasn't looking at Vir and Kane; they simply happened to be standing directly in the path of his blank gaze. Then the Drakh sagged to the ground to reveal Gwynn right behind him. "The Drakh and I were having a chat," she said.

Her dark eyes widened as she realized Kane's condition. For a moment her veneer of unflappability slipped, and then she composed herself. She moved forward quickly and brought Kane's other arm around her own shoulder. The two of them helped Kane toward the ship without a word. The shaking around them grew more violent, and Finian joined them on a dead run. He cast a glance at Kane's condition, but made no comment.

They half ran, half stumbled into the ship as the door irised shut behind them. "Where are the rest of the Drakh!" Vir called out.

"In case you haven't noticed, Mr. Cotto, this place is about to blow up," said Gwynn.

"I know. I caused it."

"Well done," said Finian, who had seated himself at the controls. But there wasn't a great deal of congratulations in his voice, for his attention was split between getting the ship into motion and glancing worriedly over at Kane. Kane, for his part, seemed to be staring at the spikes in his chest as if he were studying someone else's body.

"Get those out of him! Can't you help him? Wave a magic wand or something!" Vir shouted with increasing agitation. The frightening calm that had settled upon the cloisters was to him the most disconcerting thing.

Gwynn glanced at Vir for a moment, looking as if she wanted to explain something of great consequence. Then obviously she changed her mind, and instead crouched next to Kane, studying the spikes. Then she looked up at Kane, who simply shook his head. There was sadness on his face, as if he felt more sorry for her than for himself.

Vir started forward, and suddenly the ship shifted wildly. Finian was hardly handling the vessel with the same calm assurance that Kane had displayed. His jaw was set in grim determination and he shouted, "Hold on!"

Vir, who by this time was lying in a crumpled heap on the far side of the ship, considered the advice to be a classic case of too little, too late.

On the monitor display, he could see the rapidly receding Shadow Base, and then suddenly it vanished entirely. For a moment he had no idea why, and then he remembered: the null field. They had emerged from it, and the base had securely vanished back into its invisibility.

Just as the display showed where they had come from, it also provided a view of where they were going. The jumpgate appeared just ahead of them and, sensing the approach of a ship, flared to life.

A moment before the mage ship leaped into the gate, they saw the null field suddenly split apart. Gigantic chunks of Xha'dam spiraled away in all directions. There were pieces of the planet destroyer as well, ripped to shreds by the force of the explosions that the device itself had instigated. A fireball, feeding on itself and the continued detonation of Xha'dam, grew wider and faster, and for just a moment, Vir was certain that the thing was going to engulf them.

That was when space again seemed to stretch all around them, and an instant later they had leaped into the gate and were propelled at speeds that would have once been considered beyond all imagination.

Vir picked himself up off the floor and went quickly over to Gwynn and Kane. Kane's face looked absolutely ashen, his eyes were misting over. "Do something!" Vir urged once again.

Gwynn's detached demeanor cracked. "Don't you think I would if I could!" she said angrily. "If I could help him . . . if any of this could have been avoided . . ."

Something about the way she said that brought realization to Vir. "What he saw . . . what he said he saw . . . it was this, wasn't it."

"Some of this," Kane said softly. "Not all. But 'twas enough. 'Twould serve."

"Do all of you—"

"See the future? Have visions of what is to come? Some. A few of the full techno-mages, full adepts . . . but a cloister?" Gwynn shook her head and regarded Kane with something approaching reverence. "Never. He is most blessed."

Vir gestured helplessly. "You call this blessed? Great Maker, at least pull those out of him!"

"It would be . . . too late," whispered Kane. "And it would simply cause . . . a bloody mess. Vir . . . there are things you should know. Must know. Things that . . . only you can stop."

He leaned in closer to Kane. "What are they?"

Kane's eyes momentarily refocused. "Don't worry. You already know them."

"What? I . . . I don't understand."

And he had to strain to hear Kane say, "Good. I was . . . going for cryptic." The faint smile remained on his face even as his head slumped to one side, and then he was gone.

Vir let out a sigh. "You succeeded," he said, as he reached over and closed Kane's eyes.

4

They emerged from the jumpgate, spiraling at high speed into the surface of the planet designated K0643. Finian barely yanked the nose of the ship up in time to prevent it from slamming into the ground, and the ship suddenly went straight up like a surface-to-air missile. He called out, "Something's wrong!"

"Oh, now what?" said Vir, not sure how much more he could take. He kept trying to tear his gaze away from the fallen Kane. He saw that Gwynn was still crouched next to him, and she was gently caressing the curve of his jaw with the side of her hand.

"It's not us! It's the gate!"

Vir immediately saw what he was talking about. Energy was crackling all around it, but far more violently than before. The thing was trembling wildly, and fissures were appearing all through it. It began to splinter, to shudder under some sort of pressure that Vir could not even guess at, and then the arch began to crumble in upon itself. Within moments, gigantic chunks of it were tumbling to the ground. Then with a roar, the gate collapsed completely.

"Good riddance," muttered Finian.

"But what caused it to happen?" demanded Vir.

"Not what. Who," Finian said suddenly, getting the ship's trajectory under control. "Look." Apparently in order to illustrate his explanation, he keyed the monitor to zoom in on a lone individual standing on the uppermost outcropping of some rocks. It was wearing immediately recognizable long robes, a hood drawn over its head, and a telltale staff gripped solidly in its right hand. Its left hand was placed on its hip in a casual manner, as if this being was impatiently waiting for a late-arriving bus.

"Is that who I think it is?" Gwynn asked.

"I suspect so."

"Who? Who is it?" Vir wanted to know.

They did not reply. For some depressing reason, that didn't surprise him at all.

Finian guided the vessel toward a convenient landing point at the outer edge of the excavation. Vir could see on the monitor screen that the cloaked figure was making its way down to meet them. Despite the rockiness of the terrain, the newcomer moved with self-assurance. Vir was certain, beyond any question, that it was a techno-mage.

In truth, Vir was still having trouble believing any of this had happened. After the business with Elric back on Babylon 5, he had been pleasantly certain that he would never see a techno-mage again. The thought didn't bother him a bit. Now he was ass-deep in them. He started to wonder grimly if perhaps he should just ask where the techno-mage recruitment office might be so that he could sign up and be done with it.

As soon as the ship's landing procedures had cycled through, Finian and Gwynn positioned themselves at the door. Gwynn laid Kane down gently and respectfully on the floor, and removed her own outer cloak to cover the fallen cloister with it. They stood before the door of the ship, waiting. Then it opened, and the hooded figure stepped through.

He pushed back his hood and Vir saw a very curious-looking individual. He was completely bald, with a strong jaw and piercing gaze. There was a bleak twinkle in his eye, as if he knew the entire universe was based on some cosmic joke, with death as the great punch line.

"Galen," said Finian in acknowledgment, and he bowed. Gwynn followed suit.

Galen took the entirety of the situation in with a glance, including the presence of Vir and the corpse of Kane. "Pity," he said. "He had potential. So," he continued, as if that was to be the end of the mourning period, "would you care to tell me what the hell you three . . . I'm sorry, you two . . . thought you were doing."

"I did it, too," said Vir tentatively.

"Yes, but you don't count. Don't worry, though. You will eventually."

"Oh. Thank you. I guess."

In quick, broad strokes, Gwynn outlined for him what had happened. The one whom they addressed as Galen might have been carved from marble for all the expression or reaction he displayed. Every so often he would glance at Kane's covered body as Gwynn continued her narrative. Most of it, of course, Vir already knew, but then Gwynn got to a point in her recitation that was news to Vir.

"As we were departing," she said, "I managed to capture a Drakh and ask him a few questions in a manner he could not ignore. They had intended to use the Death Clouds . . ."

"Those massive planet killers," said Galen, just for his personal confirmation.

"Yes. Those were going to be the centerpiece of their new fleet. The Drakh have been rebuilding their vessels, preparing themselves, but the Death Clouds were intended to tilt the balance utterly in their favor."

"And to what end did they intend to employ them?"

"The Drakh blame John Sheridan and his wife, Delenn, for the departure of the Shadows," Gwynn told him.

Galen nodded slowly. "That's probably because Sheridan and Delenn told them to go away. In the end, you have to credit the Shadows with at least having the good taste to leave a party when asked to depart." The words sounded flip, but Vir could tell there was very much an edge to them. Galen's hatred for the Shadows was palpable, and Vir could only guess what sort of personal suffering Galen had known at their hands . . . or claws . . . or whatever. "Do you think the Drakh would be willing to follow suit? Leave if we ask them to?"

"I doubt it," said Gwynn.

"So do I. Proceed, then. They blame Sheridan and Delenn . . ."

"And because of that, it is their intention to punish the species that gave birth to them. Their plan is to use the Death Cloud on Earth. By this point, they will already have tested it on Daltron 7. If it operates as I suspect it will, there will be nothing left there. Not a being, not a bird, not a bug . . . nothing. That is the fate they have planned for Earth."

Upon hearing this, Vir's spine froze, as did several of his major bodily organs. But Galen's deadpan expression never wavered. Gwynn might just as easily have told him that the Drakh intended to orbit Earth, spew harsh language, and leave.

"And what about Minbar?" he inquired.

"A plague. They intend to annihilate the seat of the Interstellar Alliance with a plague."

For the first time, true darkness of worry passed over Galen's face. It was as if he was confident that the Death Cloud could be handled, but germ warfare presented an insurmountable problem. "They have created a plague?"

"No. They don't know how to build or grow the virus. The Drakh aren't that advanced. They are superb scavengers, and can manage machinery and construction adroitly enough. But replicating Shadow-created viruses is beyond them. However, they managed to salvage enough of the virus from Z'ha'dum to accomplish their aim."

"How much?"

"Enough to wipe out an entire world."

To Vir's astonishment, Galen actually let out a sigh of relief. "We're most fortunate then."

He couldn't believe it. "Fortunate! They're planning to wipe out all of Minbar, and you call that fortunate!"

"Well . . . not if you're Minbari, certainly," said Finian. Gwynn made an angry face at him that indicated it would be best if he kept his mouth shut.

"Enough virus for only one world means that the situation is containable," said Galen. "Be grateful it's not enough for a hundred worlds."

"And are you going to just let it happen?"

"I will do what I can. *All* that I can."

"That may not be enough!"

"And what will you do, Vir Cotto?" Galen demanded abruptly. "Will Centauri Prime reveal its duplicity in this matter? Inform the Alliance of its involvement with the locating of the gate that led the Drakh to the weapons they craved? Leave itself open to charges of being accomplice to attempted mass murder? Will *you* do all that can be done, Vir Cotto . . . or will you simply do all that you can do?"

Vir looked away then. Galen was simply saying things that had already occurred to Vir, but he was loath to admit it. With billions of lives on the line, Vir's main concern still remained avoiding any threat to Centauri Prime and its largely innocent people.

"I will take that as my answer," Galen said icily. "Be aware, Ambassador . . . whatever hostility you may feel for the Shadows, their servants and their . . . technology . . . pales beside my own."

"I doubt that," Vir told him.

Galen smiled slightly. "Doubt is always to be preferred in all things. Very well, Vir Cotto. I will wave my magic wand, and poof! Centauri Prime will have no association with this business. I've already dispatched the unfortunate artifact your excavation uncovered. I've covered your tracks for you."

Surprised, Vir pointed at the fallen rubble that had once been the Shadow gate. "You did that?"

"Of course I did."

"I thought techno-mages couldn't use their abilities to destroy. That's what they told me," and he indicated Gwynn and Finian.

"That is true . . . for them," said Galen. "Then again, there are always . . . possibilities."

"And is saving the Earth and Minbar among those possibilities?" The thought that the Homeworlds of Delenn or Sheridan, or both, might be annihilated was horrifying to Vir, and the knowledge of Centauri Prime's culpability was almost too much to bear. At least, however, that would remain his burden and his alone, with any luck.

Some luck.

"It is . . . a possibility. A distinct one. And you, Vir Cotto . . . take solace in the awareness that, without your involvement, it could have been far, far worse. So much so that it would not have mattered whether Centauri Prime's involvement became general knowledge or not. For truly, there would have been no worlds in the Alliance left to care."

Without another word, Galen turned away from him and started to walk off. Vir looked around, still unsure as to what was to happen next. Finian rested a hand on Vir's shoulder then, and said, "Leave it in Galen's hands. He will attend to it, if any can. None are more dedicated to eliminating Shadow technology than he. As for you, Vir . . ." and his lips thinned. "Nice disguise."

Vir realized that he was still wearing the mask that he'd been handed earlier. Feeling sheepish, he pulled it off his face. Galen shook his head with an imperious air, and then said, "Go home, Vir Cotto."

"Home." Vir shook his head. "You don't understand. I have no home. Centauri Prime will have no dealings with me, and Babylon 5 . . . if I never see the place again . . ."

"Then it would be a waste of possibilities," Gwynn said.

"What sort of possibilities?"

"For starters," Finian said, "there is still work to do. You may feel you are no longer welcome on Centauri Prime, and you are likely right. However, you remain Ambassador to Babylon 5. They are not likely to replace you; they consider the position a waste, and so will not bother to fritter away manpower. And the ambassador of Babylon 5 can still get things done. You have contacts from the past . . . and from the present, have you not?"

Vir thought about Rem Lanas, and about Renegar, both of whom had certainly gained a degree of respect for Vir as a result of this debacle. He had warned them of what was to come. They would remember that. They would know to attend to what he said. They would know to trust him, as much as anyone trusted anyone these days.

And there had been other allies, free-minded and free-thinking Centauri—many of them rather young—who had provided aid when Vir had sought to surreptitiously help the Narn during the war.

Moments earlier, he had felt so alone, and yet he was starting to realize that such was not the case. It was just that he had tied so much of his belief in his power and influence to Londo. And when Londo had turned him away, why, that seemed to be that. But it wasn't necessarily the case, as long as Vir didn't allow it to be. Granted, his self-esteem and image among others in the Alliance had been dealt a vicious blow by his duplicitous lover, Mariel . . . but she could be overcome, as well. Perhaps even used in a manner that would be to his advantage.

There were indeed possibilities, if he was willing to see them.

"Yes," Vir said slowly, his mind racing. "Yes, I have . . . contacts."

"We will be in touch, then."

Vir nodded, the words not fully registering at first. Then they did. He turned and said, "And when you're in touch, what will you . . ."

They were gone. Finian. Gwynn. The one called Galen. And the ship.

The ship that had been his ride.

"What am I supposed to do? *Walk* back to Babylon 5?" Vir demanded. But there was no one there to reply. Then, physically and mentally, he shrugged. The bottom line was that techno-mages, even cloister techno-mages, still bothered the hell out of him. He would find other means of getting back to Babylon 5 . . . and then, why, then the work would truly begin. The work that would lead him to . . .

What? What would it lead him to?

He had told Londo Mollari that he would remain his friend . . . even if he became his enemy. He had the disturbing feeling that his continued activities would lead him to that point sooner than he wanted, and he would find out whether the sentiment he had expressed was, in fact, true.

And he had a further disturbing feeling that he wasn't going to like what he found.

EXCERPTED FROM
THE CHRONICLES OF LONDO MOLLARI.
Excerpt dated (approximate Earth date)
January 9, 2268.

I believe the expression my former friend, Mr. Garibaldi, once used was "It has been some kind of party." That, I can assure you, it very much has been.

The festivities have been progressing in a nonstop fashion. Naturally I cannot participate in them. In fact, officially I must scorn and condemn them, and such public rejection has prompted some reactions of outright hostility from my beloved people. After all, they expect uniform support from their emperor. How dare I imply that their rejoicing over the misfortune of others might somehow be inappropriate, or in bad taste or—dare I say it—shortsighted.

People have very little patience with that which they do not wish to hear.

Then again, considering the number of individuals who endeavored to sway me from the course that brought me to this cursed throne, I am certainly the last person who has any right to make such observations, eh?

As of this writing, it has been one Earth week, or perhaps two, since the unleashing of the Drakh plague upon the hapless Earth. I am not certain precisely how long it has been, since I have spent much of the time in an alcoholic haze. As always, this is partly motivated by the presence of my little friend and his intolerance for liquor. But it also represents my nominal participation in the fever of celebration that has gripped Centauri Prime and has plunged it into an orgy of rejoicing. Such actions are always risky, for they have an unfortunate habit of attracting the notice of Fate and her damnable sisters, Poetic Justice and Irony.

For years now, Centauri Prime has grown more and more isolationist. We have spun a cocoon around ourselves, posted large metaphorical signs that have instructed others to keep away from us. If the Interstellar Alliance has desired to have no congress with us, we have had equally as much antipathy for them. As is always the case when a people draw inward, we have examined ourselves spiritually, as well as politically. We have sought answers, tried to determine just how and why such an unfortunate and vile fate as being bombed to the edge of oblivion had been visited upon us. There were some who said rather loudly, and quite frequently, that our willingness to consort with "lesser" races had brought the wrath of the Great Maker upon us. We had allowed ourselves to become weak, our purpose to become diluted. The fact that no one could quite agree on just what that purpose might be did not seem to deter the philosophy. The Alliance had assaulted us because it was the Great Maker's will. What an odd combination of paranoia and spiritual resignation that was.

But there was another side to that reasoning. A side that said that, if we were willing to rededicate ourselves to the worship of the Great Maker, the rebuilding of Centauri Prime, and an understanding that the only friend of Centauri could be other Centauri, why . . . then it was possible that the Great Maker might smile upon us once more. In doing so, he might very well lead us to renewed greatness. Most importantly, he would smite our enemies with his wrath and with his mighty hand.

It was partly to that end that Minister Durla installed his former teacher of religion, one Vallko by name, into the newly created position of minister of spirituality. It was a ludicrous concept for a post, I thought, and I was quite sure that there would be an outcry.

I was correct. I am always correct. It is a curse I live under. Well . . . one of many.

Unfortunately, the outcry was one of uniform approval, and many were certain that a new and definitively positive step had been taken toward improving the lot of the poor, beleaguered residents of Centauri Prime. Minister Durla was perfectly willing to support Vallko's tenure by making attendance at spiritual meetings mandatory for the citizenry. But it was not necessary. Vallko's services are invariably packed, the temples creaking at the doors, or at least I am told that it is so. I have not attended any.

Minister Durla scolds me for this. Let him. My response to him is that,

if the Great Maker is everywhere, why is he any more at Minister Vallko's temple than in the throne room? Indeed, he has more reason to
be in the throne room, for that is where the true power of Centauri
Prime resides, and it is there that the Great Maker can and should have
the most influence.

It may be, however, that I say this with less forcefulness than I would
like, probably because we both know it to be nonsense The power lies
elsewhere. Durla, of course, thinks that it lies with him, and I'm certain
he thinks I am foolish enough to believe that it resides in my hands. It
is, in fact, Durla who is the fool, but I am disinclined to inform him of
his . . . misapprehension.

Still, Durla does what Durla will. He never misses one of Vallko's
services, of course. He likely reasons that it is wise to be seen there, and
in that he is quite possibly correct. By being perceived as a regular con-
stituent of Vallko's, he allies himself—by extension—with the Supreme
Being. It is a very crafty, very wise maneuver, and one that I can appreciate since it was the sort of thing I would once have done.

After all, it was hardly long ago that I endeavored to make it appear
as if I was receiving a blessing from the techno-mages. I did so to boost
myself up the ladder of power. It is difficult for me to believe that I now
look back upon those occasions as times of innocence.

The news of the misfortune that befell Earth came during one of Vallko's spiritual gatherings. By all accounts, the place went mad with joy.
It took long moments for Vallko to calm the assemblage, and his next
words were extremely canny and well chosen. What he said was this:

"It is not fit, or meet, or responsible for Centauri to rejoice in the mis-
fortunes of others. Throughout our history, we have dealt with other
races with compassion, always with compassion. Granted, there have
been races that did not see that compassion for what it was, and re-
belled. The Narn, naturally, come to mind. In dealing with them, however—in dealing with any who operated in a manner contrary to the
interests of the great Centauri Republic—we did exactly what we had
to do. No more and no less.

"And we never, under any circumstances, took joy in the destruction
of lives or the annihilation of others. Pride, yes, we took pride, and that
is natural and to be expected, for the Great Maker wishes us to take
pride in our accomplishments. When we perform an act of greatness,
we are doing so in his name and are honoring him.

"But simply taking pleasure in the pain and suffering of others . . .
that, my good friends, is not appropriate.

"Instead . . . we shall pray. And the prayer should continue for days, as many days as we of Centauri Prime wish to pursue it. For you see, when they assaulted us, the Alliance transgressed against the chosen people of the Great Maker. They angered the Great Maker. Now they have paid the price. We cannot and must not, of course, ask the Great Maker to relent in his anger against them, for who are we to question his will? He does what he must, as do we all. So instead, my good, dear friends . . . we will pray that the Great Maker gives guidance to the poor souls of Earth. That he makes them, and their allies, realize the error of their ways. For if they do, then the Great Maker will spare them the suffering that they will otherwise have to endure. In fact, he will be happy to spare them, for ultimately the Great Maker is a being of kindness . . . as are we, for were we not made in his image?

"Pray then, my friends. Pray in a loud and sustained manner. Raise your voices and make a joyful noise unto the Great Maker so that he will hear you and know that you are sincere."

It was brilliant, the way he handled it, truly. As repulsive as I find those who manipulate the words and spirit of the Great Maker for their own ends, I must admit that people like Vallko have a style and ingenuity that I can only envy.

Centauri Prime wanted to rejoice over the misfortune of the Humans. But the Humans still have many friends and staunch allies, none of whom would take kindly to the good people of Centauri Prime throwing a very loud, very raucous, and very premature celebration over the demise of everyone who had the misfortune to be stuck on the planet Earth when the Drakh virus was unleashed.

So instead Vallko found a way for the Centauri to vent their sentiments without bringing the ill feelings—and possibly the wrath—of other races down upon us. The celebration would commence at Vallko's direction, and it would be as boisterous as could be. However, for all intents and purposes it was being done, not out of a sense of celebration, but instead in the hopes that the Great Maker would provide succor to our former tormentors.

Very crafty. Very devious. Very, very effective.

There is, after all, a fine line that separates tragedy from debauchery. I should know. I have certainly crossed, and even erased, that line any number of times.

Even now, I hear the "mourning" going on outside. The entire city is lit up and has been that way for days on end. I have no idea where the energy that my people display is coming from.

Part of me wishes to wade into the revelry and tell them the truth.

Oh, yes. Yes, I know the truth, for Shiv'kala has told me. That it was our workers, our excavators, who uncovered the gate that, in turn, led the Drakh to the planet destroyer. Without that weapon at their disposal, they never would have made their attack upon the Earth. We, the proud Centauri, are responsible for the attempted destruction of the Humans. It was a retaliation, commenced because of the Drakh need for revenge—the Drakh wished to strike back at the Humans because of the outcome of the Shadow War. Yet the Shadows brought the darkness to Centauri Prime, a darkness that continues to this day, long after the last of the Shadows has gone. If anything, we should be kissing the Humans' feet and striving to find a way to help them in their search for a cure.

Instead we hypocritically rejoice while pretending to be praying for their betterment and survival.

Why Shiv'kala speaks to me of such things, I do not know. Perhaps he revels in my helplessness, wishing to drive home to me just how ineffective I am at such times. Perhaps he is simply a sadist. Perhaps it is another test.

I tire of the tests.

I tire of a great many things. Yet my fate, if I am to believe the dream that has me dying at the hands of G'Kar, is at least another ten years away. I cannot go through that much time fatigued. I must find something to do.

Senna still represents an interesting project. And Vir . . .

Vir . . . I must find a way to bring him back. Of that, I am quite certain. Granted, his last time here was a disaster, but I think he knows enough to keep his mouth shut and make no mention of Shiv'kala again. But how would I convince my captors that Vir should be allowed to return?

And Timov. What of her?

I have wondered from time to time in the past weeks whether I would hear from her again. A part of me hoped that she would somehow see through the charade. That she would realize the trumped-up charges were for her own good, and that I was desperate to get her off this world for her own safety.

How foolish that sounds, as I write it here. How infinite is one's capacity for self-delusion. Timov has no reason to assume that my little endeavor was anything other than what it appeared on the surface. I am never going to see her again.

Well . . . it is probably for the best.

Yes. Yes, it is.

Two of my wives, if I never see them again, that will be more than satisfactory. But Timov, I will miss. She, I should think, will likely not miss me, and for this I will not blame her.

The celebrations—my pardon, the "prayers"—continue loudly and raucously outside. There appears to be no end to them. I shall not participate. I must remain aloof, above it all. I suppose, of course, that I could go to some insulated room, shut myself off from the boisterous sounds. But I cannot bring myself to do that. You see . . . I still like the Human race, despite all that has happened. I believe that they will rise above this. In fact, I think they will surpass us. I see where the Centauri Republic is, and where the Humans are, and I see them as a star that is only just now beginning to truly burn. Our star, on the other hand . . . is fading. Not that any of my people believe it, of course. Why should they? I do not want to believe it myself. I have a sense of it, though, perhaps because I see myself as the incarnation of the Centauri spirit . . . and I can feel my own star, deep within me, beginning its own steady burnout.

And still the celebration continues.

Would that I could walk among them and tell them that they are very likely extinct, that they simply do not yet know it. I cannot say this to them, however, for they will not wish to hear it and, truth to tell, I do not wish to believe it. I hold out hope for my people, all the same, although I hold out even more hope for the Humans.

5

Londo had discovered, over the years, that one gets into certain habits, particularly when one is emperor. So it came as something of a shock to him when his habitual pattern was rudely disrupted one morning when he discovered the abrupt absence of Dunseny.

Dunseny had had the great honor of being Londo's personal servant, valet, and majordomo. He had been a retainer at the house of Mollari since the days of old, and had been with the family for as long as Londo could remember. He had first joined House Mollari when, of all things, Londo's father had won him in a rather fortunate hand of cards. They had not expected much of Dunseny, arriving in their service in such an odd and backhanded manner, but Londo's father had been pleasantly surprised. Dunseny, in fairly short order, had proven himself to be efficient, attentive, and completely trustworthy.

Londo had been quite young when Dunseny first came aboard, and at the time Dunseny had seemed quite ancient to him. He was tall, soft-spoken, with piercing eyes that seemed to take in everything so that he could attend to whatever was needed as quickly and efficiently as possible. His hair, cut to a respectable medium height, had been grayish white for as long as Londo could remember. He always wore a suit of black, buttoned all the way to the collar, with no other adornment. The emperor suspected that, were he able to step back in time, he would see that the Dunseny of those bygone years had actually been considerably younger than he recalled. Nevertheless, the illusion to Londo was that Dunseny had never aged. That, indeed, he bordered on the immortal. He had come into this world old, and would remain that way . . . well . . . forever.

For the first years of his reign, Londo had been content to let Dunseny remain at House Mollari, but every so often he had found himself requiring Dunseny's services as valet. He had come to realize that he trusted no one but the faithful retainer to attend to such things. Londo's requests, and thereafter demands, became so regular that Dunseny began—politely, but firmly—to complain. He pointed out that, despite appearances to the contrary, he was not getting any younger, and the running about between House Mollari and the royal palace was wearing on him somewhat.

"Finally! A problem presented to me that is easily solved!" Londo slapped his hands together briskly as if he were about to deal out a deck of cards. Then he declared, "I shall bring you on as my full-time personal valet. You and your family will be given superb quarters here in the palace, and no strenuous commute will ever bother you again, yes? This is satisfactory? Or do you need to discuss it with your wife and children?"

"My wife passed away of the Lung Blight that swept our city three years ago, Highness," said Dunseny calmly. "And my only son was killed during the assault on Centauri Prime by the Alliance."

"Oh," Londo said faintly. He felt terrible, although for the life of him he couldn't quite figure out why. Perhaps it was because, in all this time, he had never even thought to ask Dunseny something as simple and polite as "How is your family?" Certainly, he had assumed, Dunseny would have told him. Instead he had carried on in his duties at the family house, and for Londo as needed.

Londo cleared his throat and straightened his coat, although it hardly needed straightening. "That is . . . a pity. You certainly have my regrets, Dunseny."

"That means a good deal, Highness," Dunseny said with a carefully detached expression. It was impossible for Londo to tell whether Dunseny was being sarcastic. He decided to give the old man the benefit of the doubt.

"So it is settled, then?" asked Londo.

Dunseny bowed slightly. "How can I refuse he who wears the white?"

And so Dunseny had come into Londo's full-time service, while Londo hired certain others, hand-picked by the reliable Dunseny himself, to run the family estate. When Londo awoke each morning, Dunseny was there to awaken him. He was there to lay out Londo's clothes, to prepare his bath, to handle his manicure, to oversee the tasting of the royal food—not that Dunseny handled *that* himself; that questionable honor went to another, a perpetually nervous individual named Frit.

As time passed, Dunseny's responsibilities expanded until he was keeping the royal calendar and attending to the coming and goings of those who wished to see Londo at any given time of the day. Soon it became well known that, in order to see Londo, one had to go through Dunseny first. It wasn't as if Dunseny endeavored to limit access to Londo. Far from it. He simply organized the time of all petitioners, deciding who would take priority and determining what it was that Londo would find most important and worthy of being dealt with first. Invariably, Dunseny's judgment was right on target.

It even caused a miniscandal when, on one or two occasions, Londo had actually turned to the old valet and asked him what he thought of a particular situation that had come before the throne. It would likely have engendered an even greater reaction had Dunseny not offered advice or observations that were accurate, just, and proper. It was difficult for anyone to become upset with him, and indeed Dunseny's popularity within some circles only served to benefit the emperor.

So it was little wonder that Londo let out a most unemperor-like scream one morning when he was awakened by a gentle touch on his shoulder, but opened his eyes to see someone other than his faithful retainer.

It was a young man, around seventeen or eighteen years of age. He wore black clothing, broken by a red sash, and his eyes glittered, unblinking, like some animal peering out appraisingly at him from the jungle.

"Who are you!" Londo shouted. He half sat up in bed, a bit chagrined at the yelp he had emitted, but still determined to muster some of the dignity his high office afforded him. "What are you doing here?"

"I am Throk," said the teen. "I serve Minister Lione as one of—"

"Of the Prime Candidates, yes, yes." Londo gave an impatient wave. He was more than aware of who and what the Prime Candidates were. They were a youth group, in operation for five years now, answering to Chancellor Castig Lione and serving Centauri Prime in a variety of ways, a number of which served to make Londo quite a bit nervous.

Then he rewound something through his head. His eyebrows knit in puzzlement. "Minister Lione? I thought he was Chancellor Lione. This is the same Lione, yes? Chancellor of development?"

"The same," said Throk.

"Since when did he become a minister?"

"Minister Durla oversaw his appointment. Were you not consulted, Your Highness?"

"No, Your Highness was not consulted."

"Is there a problem with the appointment, Your Highness?"

The question immediately set off an alarm in Londo's head.

He did not know what Throk was doing there. He did not know where Dunseny was. He felt as if he was being pelted with information and being challenged to keep up. But the one thing he *did* know for certain was that he most definitely did not want to say precisely what was on his mind in the presence of this individual. This "Throk," this Prime Candidate, might as well have had Durla's head on his left shoulder and Lione's head on the right.

"The only problem I have with it is one of protocol," Londo said coolly. "At the very least, I should be informed of such matters in an orderly fashion, so I am not left open to the possibility of committing some minor gaffe. How would it be if I addressed Minister Lione as Chancellor? Certainly that could make for a potentially embarrassing situation, yes?"

"Yes. Absolutely, Your Highness." Throk's face remained utterly inscrutable. Londo reminded himself never to play cards with this young man. Then he further reminded himself that he had absolutely no idea what the young man was doing in his private chambers.

"Where is Dunseny?" Londo asked.

The slightest flickering of puzzlement danced across Throk's face. Londo couldn't tell whether what he saw, however briefly, in the teen's expression was a momentary loss of control, or else a carefully permitted "slip" so as to somehow ingratiate himself with the emperor. "I thought you knew, Your Highness."

"Of course I know," Londo said. "I simply have this odd quirk. I enjoy having people tell me about matters with which I am already familiar. Again: Where is Dunseny?"

"Dunseny informed Minister Durla that he wished to retire. That he was feeling his age and desired to slow down. Minister Durla consulted with Minister Lione and it was felt that—from a security point of view, if nothing else—appointing a Prime Candidate as your new valet would be the best fit. I had the honor of being selected. Shall I draw your bath for you, Your Highness?"

"I do not care," Londo said, "whether you draw a bath or draw a breath. Dunseny said nothing to me of retiring."

Throk shrugged slightly. "Perhaps he was concerned that he would be letting you down, and could not bring himself to face you, Your Highness."

"Perhaps." Londo, however, did not bother to speculate out loud on the other, more likely, "perhaps." Specifically, that "perhaps"

Dunseny had been forced out for some reason. If that were the case, then Londo had every intention of doing something about it.

He rose from the bed and said in a firm, commanding voice, "You may leave me, Throk."

"Sir, if I have failed to satisfy you in some way as your valet . . ."

"You have neither failed nor succeeded, for you have not been given the opportunity. There will be no decision in the matter until I have spoken with Dunseny."

"But, Highness, Minister Lione was quite specific in his orders that—"

"Ahhhh," said Londo as he belted his robe tightly around him. "What a fast-rising individual Lione is. Who would have thought that, in such a brief time, he would have ascended from chancellor to the ministry . . . and now, who would have thought it possible! Castig Lione is now the emperor!"

Throk looked puzzled once more, and this time it was clearly genuine. "No, Highness, you are the emperor," he said slowly, as if worried that Londo might have forgotten that.

"You don't say!" said Londo, voice dripping with sarcasm. "For a moment I thought there was some confusion on the matter, what with your giving his orders priority over mine. Or perhaps *you* were simply confused over the matter, Throk? Could that be it?"

Throk opened his mouth a moment, and then closed it. He nodded.

"I thought it was. Now you will leave, unless you feel that further challenging of my wishes would be of benefit to your long-term health. For I assure you, Throk, I have executed men younger, handsomer, and far better connected than you. Admittedly, I have not killed a teenager in some time. But one teenager more or less . . ." and he shrugged his shoulders to indicate just how unimportant such a demise would be in the grand scheme of things.

Throk needed no further hints. He departed the room.

Londo, dressed in a hood and cloak that concealed his familiar visage, rapped firmly on the door of Dunseny's home. It was a small, unassuming domicile, which had been deeded over to Dunseny many years earlier by Londo's father, out of recognition for his faithful service. There was a pause, and Londo knocked again. This time he heard the shuffling of feet, the slow approach by a measured tread that he recognized with as much confidence as he would recognize his own voice.

The door opened and Dunseny peered out. He looked slightly bewildered at first, but then his face cleared as recognition dawned. He bowed slightly. "Highness," he said. "In what capacity might I serve you this—"

Londo made an impatient wave. "Do not stand on ceremony with me, Dunseny. We have known each other too long. To you, I am simply Londo, as will always be the case."

"Very well, Londo."

There was a pause, while the two men stood staring at each other, and then Londo said, "So? You leave me standing on the doorstep without being invited in? Is this how you treat your emperor?"

His gaze flickered over Londo. "Not wearing the white. Incognito?"

"In a manner of speaking. I will not ask again to be allowed into your home . . . a home my family has provided you with."

"Yes, I know. Your generosity has always been unstinting."

Still he did not move aside.

"Dunseny," Londo said in a level tone, "what is transpiring here? I learn, thirdhand, that you desire to leave my service? Why? And why do we stand in this manner, as if I am an unwanted salesman?"

"Because," Dunseny replied, "I have nothing to hide."

Londo blinked in confusion. He had no idea what in the world Dunseny could possibly be talking about.

And then, suddenly, like a lightning flash, it came to him.

Someone, somewhere, was watching. Or else Dunseny had reason to believe that might be the case. By remaining outside, keeping themselves in plain view—with, perhaps, portable listening devices or even a passable lip reader in the vicinity—no one could possibly accuse Dunseny of anything.

Dunseny clearly saw the understanding that flashed across Londo's face, for he nodded ever so subtly. Londo tried to glance around without turning his head, but he didn't spot anyone immediately. There were passersby in the street, none of whom seemed to be paying particular attention, unaware that the emperor—the personification of Centauri Prime—was standing among them. Yet spies might be anywhere around them. For that matter, there were other residences nearby, a number of them several stories high. Someone could be watching from any of those.

Londo was certainly accustomed to the sensation of not being alone. With the keeper, the foul, one-eyed creature, forever bonded to him, Londo would never know solitude again. Still, this sensation of paranoia was an uncomfortable one.

"It is my desire," Londo said slowly, "that you return to my employ as my valet."

Dunseny spoke slowly and deliberately, as if the words had been meticulously rehearsed. He was an old man, yes, but he had never seemed old until that moment. "As I told Minister Durla . . . I have served for many, many years, and I feel I need rest."

"Are you ill? Is there some infirmity?"

"As I told Minister Durla . . . I have served for many, many years, and I feel I need rest."

He had repeated it with such word-for-word precision that no doubt was left in Londo's mind as to the truth of things. Whether it had been done to rob him of Dunseny's advice, or simply to further isolate him, or to bring in one of the Prime Candidates to monitor his actions . . . none of the reasons mattered. His voice low and tight, he said, "Were you threatened? Did he threaten you?"

"As I told—"

"Minister Durla, yes, yes, I know! You have made that abundantly clear!"

"Londo . . ." And for the first time, there was a true hint of tragedy in his voice, "I am an old man. I have done my service. Do not ask of me more than I can give."

"If you were threatened, I can . . ."

"Protect me? If I were threatened . . . and I do not claim that I was, I speak merely hypothetically . . . are you saying that you could protect me, Londo, if I had been threatened?"

His eyes seemed to drill deep into Londo's soul, and they both knew the answer even though Londo did not dare say it. Dunseny smiled sadly, and spoke words that shredded Londo with their simple truth: "I am not convinced you can even protect yourself."

There it was. And the hell of it was, he was right.

"I wish you all the luck in the world with your reign, Londo Mollari. You will have no stauncher supporter than I. But if it is all the same to you, I think it would be best if I supported you . . . from a distance."

The response was little more than a husky whisper. "Of course. It will be as you desire."

Dunseny nodded in what was clearly gratitude. Londo stepped back and allowed the door to quietly shut.

In the final analysis, he had indeed been little more than a salesman, trying to sell one old man on the notion that he was someone upon whom the old man could depend. As it turned out, he was not a particularly effective salesman at that.

When the door to the emperor's inner chamber slid open, Senna was naturally expecting to see the emperor within. So she blinked in surprise when she saw one of those disturbing members of the Prime Candidates standing in front of her. For his part, he studied her as if she were some sort of microscopic bacterium.

No. No, there was more to it than that. He seemed to be appraising her, and even more than that—he appeared to like what he was seeing. Not surprising: her blue gown was richly embroidered with gold brocade, and displayed her shapely figure quite well. Her high cheekbones and level gaze gave her an almost regal bearing. She found that she wanted to leap out of her skin, considering it so unclean that she had no desire to sport it any longer, and run shrieking down the corridor.

Fighting to retain what protocol would consider the correct and proper approach, Senna asked, "What are you doing here? This is the emperor's private residence."

"I am Throk, his new valet."

"Where is Dunseny?" she demanded.

"Elsewhere."

She arched a most unamused eyebrow. "I can see that you are going to be a fountain of information."

"You are Senna, are you not?" he said after a moment. "Daughter of Lord Refa. The emperor plucked you off the streets and gave you a home here in the palace four or five years ago. Educated you, clothed you, fed you. He refers to you as 'young lady' as if it were a title. You are, for all intents and purposes, the daughter he never had."

Sarcastically, Senna patted her hands together in appreciation. "Quite a litany, Throk. And most unfair. You know much of me; I know nothing of you."

"I am Throk, of the Prime Candidates. Beyond that, there is nothing of much relevance."

Senna did not seem particularly inclined to accept that, however. "Oh, I don't know about that," she said, stepping closer to him. "How you came to be the emperor's personal valet, after Dunseny tended to him so well for so long, is certainly relevant."

"You have a very regal bearing," he told her.

It was not a comment that she expected. It flustered her momentarily, and that angered her in turn, because the last thing she wanted was to be at a loss for words in his presence. "Thank you," she said with clear resentment.

"You are welcome."

She turned, yet felt as if his stare was boring straight into the back of her head. There was something truly frightening in that gaze, she decided, something that threatened to draw her in. There was—and she thought she might have been imagining it—an incredible determination to serve his masters. And she sensed that he would be perfectly willing to go over, or through, anyone who stood in the way of his accomplishing that task.

Something told her that the best way to handle Throk was to go on the offensive. Turning back, she looked straight into his eyes. Rather than stand there and be overwhelmed by that steady, unwavering gaze, she took the initiative. "How many of you are there?" she asked.

"Just me," he said.

"I mean, how many of the Prime Candidates are there?"

"Ah. I am sorry. That information is restricted."

"Why?"

"Because Minister Lione has restricted it."

"And why," she inquired, pushing steadily onward, "has Minister Lione restricted it?"

"Because he has," came Throk's answer. Disturbingly, it seemed a perfectly lucid answer to him, even though Senna recognized it for the simplistic circular logic that it was. It was because it was because it was because it was. Such a maddening mind-set could leave them there all day, going in circles.

"I do not understand," she said, making one last effort, "the need for restriction. Has he given you any reason, beyond that he simply desires to?"

"There is strength in numbers and strength in the element of surprise," he replied, startling her slightly that he was saying anything more on the subject. "To conceal the number of your troops gains you an advantage over those who would oppose you."

"But Throk," she pointed out, sounding almost hurt that such a notion would be entertained, "do you consider me an enemy?"

The fact that no answer was immediately forthcoming chilled her. For an instant he seemed like a beast of prey trying to decide whether to devour her.

"I consider you Senna. That is all."

"The lady Senna," she corrected him.

At this, Throk looked only momentarily surprised. "I was unaware that the emperor had conferred a formal title upon you."

"Neither the emperor nor I feel compelled to discuss all matters with everyone."

"The emperor should not keep such secrets."

"I do not consider it appropriate for you, Throk, to decide what counsel the emperor should and should not keep. Furthermore," and her eyes narrowed, "considering that I cannot even get a straight answer out of you regarding the population of your little club, I do not see that you have much right to complain about such matters as secrecy."

He inclined his head slightly, and there was a mirthless smile there. "The lady Senna is quite correct."

It was then that a familiar voice came from behind. "Well, well . . . getting acquainted, are we?"

Senna stiffened when she heard the tone in Londo's voice. There was a hint of joviality, but she instantly knew it to be false. She had been residing for too long in the palace to think otherwise. She turned to find the emperor walking toward them, and his stride was very slow and very measured. There was none of the bounce in his step that she saw when he was in a good mood. "Yes, Highness. Apparently we are," she said. "Throk here says that he is your new valet."

There was a long pause from Londo and then, his voice sounding measurably forced, he said, "That is certainly my understanding, yes."

"And Dunseny is . . . ?"

Londo permitted the question to hang there for a long moment, and then all he said was, "Not."

Senna thought she caught, from the corner of her eye, a brief smile of satisfaction from Throk.

"I have been taking a bit of a stroll around the palace, Throk," Londo said. He walked up to the young man, arms folded, and continued, "I have not done so in quite a while, you know. I have tended to stick to several small areas in which I feel . . . more comfortable. But now I am taking a good look around, and you know what I am seeing? A goodly number of Prime Candidate uniforms with—and this is the most startling part—Prime Candidates inside them. Some of them even assuming positions of moderate authority, yes." He nodded to Senna. "You have noticed this too, have you, Senna?"

Truthfully, Senna had not. Lately she had not been paying all that much attention to what went on around her. Senna was old enough that she had outgrown teachers. But the participation that women had in Centauri society was sufficiently limited that she hadn't really been allowed that much else to occupy her time. A girl her age was usually primarily interested in finding a husband and seeking social status, but such things were of no interest to Senna.

So she had busied herself in continuing her studies, even though various scholars no longer sought to fill her head with knowledge. Instead she filled it herself, devouring every written word that she could get her hands on. Senna knew, in her hearts, that she was residing in a time of living history, so she felt compelled to familiarize herself as much as possible with all history that had gone before. She sought to delve into schools of thought, philosophies, all manner of things.

Now she realized that this had occupied so much of her time that, over the past months, she had barely been aware of the world around her.

She was also quickly realizing how unaccountably stupid such an attitude was. What good did it do her to learn of things past if she was remiss in applying her knowledge to things present. Still, one of the first rules of surviving in the present was never to let on what you did and didn't know, if you could help it. If knowledge was power, concealment of knowledge—or of the lack thereof—was more power.

"Yes, Highness. I did notice the . . . proliferation of the Prime Candidates," she lied boldly.

"And what do you make of that, eh?"

"That it remains difficult to find good help."

She wasn't quite certain what prompted such a snide retort, but it appeared to delight the emperor, who laughed raucously and declared, "Well said, Senna! Well said!" It did not, unsurprisingly, seem to amuse Throk in the slightest. Still, he was quite adept at keeping his feelings hidden. The only indication he gave that he had heard the comment at all was a slight thinning of his lips.

"She is quite the wit, our young lady, is she not, Throk?"

"If you say so, Your Highness," Throk said delicately.

"How nice." Just as quickly as it had appeared, the humor vanished from Londo's tone, and he said with a dour harshness, "It is comforting to know that, in some instances, that which I say still carries weight. You may wait for me inside, Throk. I have some private business I wish to discuss with the lady Senna."

"Highness, I . . ." Throk reflexively began to protest.

But Londo did not tolerate it for so much as a microsecond. "It would seem to me, Throk," he said curtly, "that you do not have much future as an aide or valet if you cannot obey as simple an order as waiting in another room. Is it too taxing an ordeal for your Prime Candidate mind?"

Throk opened his mouth to reply, and then clearly decided that not only was a reply unnecessary, but it also bordered on the unwise. So he simply turned and entered the chambers.

The moment the doors slid shut, Senna turned to Londo and demanded, "Highness, are you actually going to let them get away with this?"

"Get away with what?" inquired Londo with a surprisingly placid look. "People come and go. Dunseny chose to leave."

"I don't believe that. Neither do you."

He laughed softly. "Did you know that, not all that long ago in the grand scheme of things, the people of Centauri Prime did not believe that our world was round?"

"Yes. I knew that."

"Did not believing that make the world flat?"

"No," she admitted, "but that is not the point . . ."

"Actually, Senna . . . it is." He placed a hand on her shoulder. "There are battles that can and should be fought, and there are battles that should not be. In the case of the former, let nothing stop you. In the case of the latter, let nothing start you."

"Are you saying—"

"I am saying that the world can be a greater classroom than anything in all the schooling you have received over the past few years. However, you have to pick and choose where the classrooms are, who the teachers are, and what lessons are worth learning. You understand, yes?"

"I . . . think so. You're saying . . ."

But he raised a finger and put it to her lips. "Ah ah ah," he remonstrated her. "In the classroom of life, this is a silent quiz, not an oral examination. Any thoughts you might have, keep them to yourself. Learn by doing, not by speaking." Apparently having said everything he wanted to say, Londo nodded in satisfaction, seemingly to himself, then turned to head into his private chambers.

And when the words came to her, they came out all in a rush.

Though she would have done anything she could to stop them, she
blurted out, "What are you afraid of?" She swore she could actually
see the words departing her lips. She snatched for them, trying to re-
trieve them, but naturally that did no good. Londo turned again and
fixed her with that steady, occasionally unblinking stare he often displayed.

To her astonishment, he replied, "The dark."

The simplicity of the answer caught her off guard, and then she
said, "Well, Highness . . . that's not all that surprising. To some degree, everyone is afraid of the dark."

"True. Very true." He waggled a finger at her and told her, "But
I am one of the few . . . who knows exactly *why* everyone is afraid of
the dark. The others do not. If they claim they do, they are either remarkable fools . . . or remarkably knowledgeable. It will be for you to
distinguish between the two."

"Me?" She was obviously confused. "What about you?"

"I?" He snorted. "I can barely distinguish between my various
imperial vestments. How fortunate I am . . . to have Throk here to
make certain I do not commit some sort of social faux pas."

"Yes. You have Throk," she said, unable to keep the bitterness
out of her voice.

"He is an available young man, Senna, with interesting prospects.
You could do worse, you know."

She couldn't quite believe what she was hearing. "Throk? You
cannot be serious, Highness."

"Have you given thought to it, Senna? It is through a husband,
after all, that women gain power in our society . . . attaching themselves to a powerful mate. It would be expected of you by this age. It
would not be thought of as at all odd, were you to begin walking the
corridors of power while appearing eager and interested in all that
goes on around you."

"I'm not interested in gaining power, Your Highness."

"How intriguing," he said slowly, with a smile. "Aside from the
kitchen staff, you may be the only person in this entire palace who is
not interested in that." He gave it a moment's more consideration.
"And I would not wager against the kitchen staff, now that I think
about it."

"I wish Timov was still here," Senna said.

"As do I."

She looked at him askance. "They say that she was plotting
against you. Was it true?"

"I do not know," he said, although she suspected from the quick flicker of regret in his eyes that he was not being entirely candid. "It is something of a shame, I suppose. To not be able to know who around you can be trusted."

"You can trust me, Highness."

"Yes," he said, but he sounded noncommittal. "There are many others, though. Throk, Durla, the other ministers. All with their own agendas, whispering among themselves, planning, discussing. Conversations to which I am not privy. It would be of great use . . . to know what they were saying. A pity such things are not possible. Well, good evening to you then, young lady."

"Good evening to you, Highness."

She watched him enter his private chambers, the door sliding noiselessly shut behind him . . . and she couldn't help but think that, somehow, he seemed a bit . . . smaller . . . somehow.

It was not until later that evening, when Senna had gone to bed, that Londo's words came back to her and the true meaning became clear. She sat up abruptly and was about to run directly to the emperor, despite the lateness of the hour, to see whether she had properly understood his meaning. Then she realized that to do so would be to undercut what it was he was asking, presuming she fully understood what it was he was asking. So instead she contented herself to lie back down, knowing that it would be a sleepless night as her hearts pounded anxiously in her chest.

Londo lay upon his bed, staring up at the ceiling into the darkness. As always, the darkness looked back at him. "You are there," he said abruptly.

There was a stirring from the wall nearby, and one of the shadows separated from the rest. The Drakh called Shiv'kala slowly approached, and then stopped several feet away. "We are always here," he said.

"I suspected as much. So . . . how much influence did you have in this, eh?"

"Influence?"

Londo propped himself on one elbow. "If Dunseny had not gone quietly, would you have seen to it that he met with an accident? Is that it?"

Shiv'kala laughed. It was the single most chilling sound that he was capable of making. When Londo heard it, part of him wanted to crawl all the way back to infancy and hide in his mother's womb, and even there he would likely find no shelter.

"The Drakh," Shiv'kala said, when his mirth had sufficiently passed, "care nothing about your hired help, Londo."

"You did not position Throk to be your spy, then."

"Do not be foolish. A keeper resides upon you. What further need have we for a spy?"

"I do not know," Londo admitted. "I do not know why you do much of what you do. And if I try to shine light upon you, in my search for answers, your very nature absorbs it."

"Your paranoia is flattering, but unnecessary . . ."

"In this instance," Londo added.

Shiv'kala paused only a moment, and then said, "Yes. In this instance. Minister Durla does not need our urging to keep an ever-closer eye on you."

"Durla. Your favorite. Your cat's-paw. If he knew . . ."

"If he knew . . . it would be no different."

"Then why not tell him?" asked Londo, with a hint of challenge in his voice.

"If you wish."

Londo was startled at that. "You will tell him? Tell him of the darkness that covers this world? Tell him that he is minister only because you put him into place? That he does not truly serve Centauri Prime, but rather the whims of the Drakh—servants for the most dangerous and evil beings the galaxy had ever known? That you even invade his dreams, sending him your bidding and allowing him to think that they are his notions?"

"Absolutely," Shiv'kala confirmed. Then his voice dropped from its normal, gravelly tone to just above a whisper. "And then . . . I will tell him of you. Of all that you have done . . . and will do. Of how he, Durla, has at least some semblance of free will . . . whereas you, monitored by the keeper, have none. That you are both the most powerful and the most impotent man on all of Centauri Prime. All this will I tell him. And every time he looks at you, you will know . . . that he knows. He will know you for the wretched thing that you are. Is that . . . what you desire?"

Londo said nothing. Indeed, what was there to say?

"Do you see," Shiv'kala told him, "how I protect you from yourself, Londo? Someday . . . you will thank me."

"Someday . . . I will kill you," replied Londo.

"It is good to want things," Shiv'kala said.

The door hissed open and Londo sat up, blinking in the light that was flooding in from the hallway. Throk was standing there, silhouetted in the brightness. "I thought I heard you talking, Highness. Is there an intruder?"

Londo half twisted to look behind himself. The area where Shiv-'kala had been standing was completely illuminated by the corridor lighting, and there was no sign that the Drakh had ever been there at all.

"I am . . . simply talking to myself," said Londo.

"It sounded as if you were having an argument, Highness."

"I was. I suppose"—he sighed—"that is because I do not like myself all that much." He hesitated, and then said, "Were you standing outside that door this entire time, Throk?"

"Yes, Highness."

"And you did that . . . why?"

"In case I was needed, Highness."

And after he dismissed the Prime Candidate for the remainder of the night, he tried to determine who filled him with a greater sense of foreboding. Shiv'kala . . . or Throk.

EXCERPTED FROM
THE CHRONICLES OF LONDO MOLLARI.
Excerpt dated (approximate Earth date) June 17, 2268.

Would that I could keep this journal on a regular basis. But I only feel safe making notations such as this one when my "associate" has lapsed into an alcoholic haze. Since I must consume the alcohol needed to accomplish this, it becomes that much more difficult for me to focus on what I am writing. I hope that future generations will be able to translate my handwriting. And I hope the reader will understand, sometimes I have to cover several months at a sitting, to the best that my occasionally strained memory will allow.

Senna.

I am so proud of her. It did not take her long at all to understand that which I could only hint at. Nor did she ever come back to me, after that veiled conversation, and outright say "You want me to spy on them! You want me to garner information where I can, through whatever means are necessary, and convey it to you! After all, I am 'only' a young girl, presumably looking for a man to whom I could attach myself. And men tend to speak liberally to those females whom they would like to impress."

No, she never questioned, but I knew. The way she looked at me at breakfast the next morning, there actually was a glimmer of excitement in her eyes. An excitement that bespoke an almost conspiratorial air, as if there was some great secret the two of us shared that neither of us dared speak. I could not guide her, of course. Clever girl, though . . . she figured it out all by herself.

Even more clever, she waited—took no immediate action. After all, it would have seemed curious if, after treating Throk so coldly, she had abruptly changed her attitude toward him. Throk may have been many things, but foolish he most definitely was not.

Instead she began slowly. It wasn't difficult; Senna and I habitually dined together several times in the course of any week, and naturally Throk was always there. One evening, when Throk deftly refilled a glass of wine for me, Senna said—as if Throk was not there—"He's very attentive, isn't he."

The remark came out of nowhere. I had a spoonful of food lifted to my lips, but did not consume it. " 'He?' " I said. Then I saw her gaze flicker significantly to Throk, and naturally I understood. "Ah. You mean Throk."

Throk visibly perked up at that. He quickly covered it—I will credit him that. He was really somewhat masterful at internalizing anything that might betray his thoughts to an observer.

"Yet you would think," Senna continued smoothly, "that he would notice I, myself, have no wine at all."

"You do not customarily ask for it, Lady Senna," Throk said.

"A lady need not ask," she told him primly. "A lady is asked by others."

He nodded in acknowledgment of the point and held up the bottle. "Lady, would you care for—"

"I thought you would never ask," she said, and laughed very liltingly.

And I thought to myself, Great Maker, she was born for this. Then I remembered who her father was—the late Lord Refa—and I realized that, yes indeed, she truly was born for it. Considering her family tree, it was impressive that I had not yet wound up with a dagger between my ribs.

Then again, the day was young.

Having received her wine, wise girl, brilliant girl . . . she paid Throk no more mind. This no doubt convinced the young man that her comment had merely been a passing observation, a slight jest at his expense.

The next time we ate together, she actually engaged him in conversation. I was surprised—or perhaps not all that surprised, I suppose—that Throk was a bit more outspoken with Senna than he was with me. After all, any inquiry I made as to his background simply got me a respectfully terse reply. But for Senna, he proceeded to put forward what seemed to be his entire lineage. He boasted of his parents, both of them names that I instantly recognized.

Throk was of the House Milifa. Milifa was a member of Durla's circle of acquaintances, a group who had come to refer to themselves as the

New Guard. I knew them, and their type, all too well. They had opposed Emperor Cartagia . . . but always from hiding. Whenever anyone had spoken of actually overthrowing Cartagia, or trying to do something about his insane rule that was destroying all of Centauri Prime, the House Milifa—along with any number of others—were the first to be the last. They were eager for a change, but even more eager to allow someone else to do what was needed to implement it.

Yes, I knew the type all too well. They only acted when they felt there was no risk of harm to themselves. Which meant that if Throk of the House Milifa was being put into position, and others of his ilk were coming in, then they considered the path to be a fairly obstacle-free one.

Since I was on that path, I was obviously not considered much of an obstacle.

Great Maker help me, they may very well be right.

I could, of course, endeavor to change their thinking, make them work harder to achieve their goals. But for the moment, I am content to let matters unfold as I watch. Let them bluster about, those who speak of how Centauri Prime must return to its destiny of greatness. In their hearts, they are bullies, who will only strike against their enemies once they are convinced that they can crush them completely, without any fear of retaliation.

Now that I think of it, this might be considered a fairly accurate description of me. Perhaps there is less difference between the new guard and the old guard than any of us would care to admit.

So Senna began paying more attention to Throk, and Throk was clearly rather pleased. Not only was Senna an attractive and vivacious individual, but Throk attained a bit more status with his fellow Prime Candidates when he appeared with the "young lady" on his arm. Senna was masterful, managing to keep him at arm's length while all the time making him think that he was worming his way into her affections.

And then periodically she would find ways to convey to me whatever it was she had learned. She would do it in the most casual of ways, saying, "Oh, you will never guess the latest gossip," and tell me in a lighthearted manner all sorts of information that was of varying degrees of use to me. Most of it was of little utility of course. Senna, being young and inexperienced, wasn't really capable of distinguishing what might be truly important. She could not cull the most pertinent information; it simply spilled out, and was left to me to sort it out.

This kept up for several months, and I took it all in. I began to feel like a spider in the middle of a web, watching insects flutter about and trying to determine what might be the tastiest morsel.

Recently, for example, she told me something that may be of tremendous use. Something that might very well enable me to manipulate Durla without his realizing it, and might actually enable me to bring Vir back here with a degree of impunity.

I have come to realize just how important Vir is to all of this. I remain surrounded, watched from all sides. With the addition of Throk to my retinue, and Shiv'kala hovering in the shadows, and the keeper attached to me at all times, I am the single most watched individual on all Centauri Prime . . . possibly in all the universe. Even for dear Senna, there is only so much that she can do. I need someone from outside, someone who can move about, someone who can provide a lifeline to the outside world.

A lifeline.

Interesting choice of words, since oftentimes I feel as if I am drowning in silence.

No matter. Vir shall come back, be free to come and go as need be . . . with Durla's blessing, more's the irony, if I manage this correctly.

In a way . . . a very small way . . . I regret pulling Senna into this morass of subtle espionage. For all her lineage and her teaching, she is still young and naive. But these are fearsome times in which we live, and perhaps I am doing her a favor after all. The sooner she learns to manipulate and deceive, the better chance she'll have of surviving. In fact, if she becomes truly skilled at such things, I might marry her myself. Marry her and then, of course, divorce her. That way she will fit in nicely with my other ex-wives.

6

Vir customarily came to the Zen garden on Babylon 5 for thoughtful contemplation. He did not normally stop by for the purpose of having a coronary. Yet, as it so happened, that was nearly what occurred.

It used to be that various individuals gave him a wide berth whenever they saw him. He was, after all, Centauri, and that was not a race that had a particularly positive profile with most others. It was, Vir supposed, understandable. After all, when one bombards another race's world into rubble, there's bound to be some fallout.

But Galen had been right; Centauri Prime had not replaced him as ambassador. Whether they were throwing him a bone or further punishing him, he could not say. The thing was, Vir had almost become accustomed to his status as an outcast. He had grown used to the fact that, although he was supposed to be the Centauri ambassador, he was in fact unwelcome at almost any diplomatic gathering. But then Mariel had entered his life, and things had turned around. Charming, vivacious, Mariel had gathered men to her with greater ease than a sun draws space debris into its orbit. And for a time, Vir had basked in her reflected light. Suddenly it had seemed to him that people looked at him differently, with a new sort of respect. When he passed people in the hall, they smiled, waved, clapped him on the back, and chuckled. Yes, they always chuckled, or laughed, and Vir took this as a sign of pleasure and happiness to see him.

They still chuckled and laughed. But now it galled him, for now he knew the truth. Now he knew that Mariel had been making a laughingstock of him, behind his back. When people looked at him, they saw only a fool.

Mariel had been around a good deal less lately, which suited Vir just fine. He knew that simply throwing her out, severing the relationship, would attract not only her attention but the attention of whomever it was she was reporting to . . . an unknown "chancellor," he had learned, although he didn't know which one.

The thing was, he had been so besotted with her that if he suddenly dispensed with the relationship, she would know something was up. He didn't want to take any chances, so he had settled for arranging to be elsewhere whenever she was around. Naturally, since she simply regarded him as a means to an end, she didn't really care that they kept missing each other. She did keep leaving video messages, clucking about how much she hated that lately they were little more than two ships passing in the night. *She's quite the little actress,* thought Vir.

Still, after months of playing the dodging game, Vir had tired of it. On this particular day, she was scheduled to return from wherever it was she had gone off to, and Vir had no desire to depart Babylon 5, to find somewhere where he could kill time. He was sick of killing time.

It was more than that, though. A cold, burning anger was being fueled within him every time another person on Babylon 5 smiled at him and asked how Mariel was. Even people back on Centauri Prime were interested in her. Senna, of all people, had sent him a message just the other day. It had been a chatty, gossipy message, which was odd considering that he couldn't remember the last time she had contacted him. It hadn't even been sent from within the palace; he could tell by the return frequency. It was from some independent, public communications outfit that anyone could walk in and use.

"I heard from a friend of a friend that you and Mariel are together," she had said. "How interesting. This friend of a friend told me that Minister Durla rather fancies Mariel himself. So you are quite the lucky fellow, actually getting the better of Minister Durla, because you know, no one ever does."

So even on Centauri Prime, where he was persona non grata, they knew of the damnable association. Little did they suspect that Vir's supposed romantic coup had actually cost him terribly. Whatever small bit of standing he might have had remaining to him had been damaged, probably beyond repair.

This knowledge made him want to get back at Mariel somehow. His upbringing told him that, given the circumstances, disposing of her wouldn't be out of line. Any number of dandy little poisons would suit the occasion perfectly. But he couldn't bring himself to pursue that avenue. It simply wasn't his style.

Then again, risking life and limb to destroy a mysterious Shadow base wasn't exactly his style either. Nor was assassinating an emperor, as he had inadvertently done with Cartagia. His style was changing so rapidly that he was having trouble keeping up with it. It was as if another Vir were running on ahead, leaving the original one to gesture helplessly and beg not to be left behind.

He wondered what he was becoming, and further wondered if it was anyone, or anything, he was going to like.

The Vir Cotto who had first come to Babylon 5 had been, in so many ways, a child.

"And all children grow up," he said tonelessly as he sat in the Zen garden, staring down at the sand beneath his feet.

"All children save one," came a voice, so close at his shoulder that he yelped. He jumped from the bench and turned to see who had entered so silently that Vir hadn't even heard him.

"Galen!"

The techno-mage inclined his head slightly in acknowledgment. "The same."

"What are you doing here?"

"Speaking to you. Your time is drawing near, Vir Cotto. And when it comes, you must be prepared for it."

"Prepared for it? Prepared for *what*?" Vir shook his head with obvious incredulity. "Since techno-mages started advising me, I've had a woman come into my life, embolden me, love me—or pretend she loves me—just to put herself into a position to spy on others. What could I possibly do to prepare myself for that?"

"She used you. Everyone uses everyone, Vir Cotto. When you grow up, you will understand that, and be the greatest user of all."

"*There's* something to look forward to," Vir said dourly. Then he frowned. "Who doesn't grow up? You said—"

"Peter Pan. A Human boy who refused to grow up, and resided instead in a place called Never-never land ... which you got to by going to the second star on the right, and straight on until morning."

"I don't have time for stories," Vir said impatiently. "You must want something. What is it?"

Galen rose and began to walk. Automatically, Vir got up and fell into step beside him. "You must return," Galen told him.

Vir didn't even have to guess at what he was referring to. "To Centauri Prime."

"Yes. There are forces bringing the world forward to a destiny it truly desires. For every action, however, there is an equal and opposite reaction. That is an immutable rule of the universe. You are to be the opposite reaction."

"Well, here's another immutable rule: I can't return there," Vir said flatly. "I have contacts there, yes, and I've been getting messages to them, and they to me. But you need someone who can walk about freely, who can move in high circles. I'm not that person."

"Yes. You are," said Galen. His eyes sparked with a flint-like precision. "You need to figure out how you can be."

"You figure it out. You have all the answers, after all."

"No," Galen said softly. "No techno-mage has all the answers."

"Really."

"Really." Then his lips thinned in what might have been a smile, although Vir couldn't be sure. "We do, however, have all the questions."

Vir rolled his eyes and shook his head. "I don't know what you expect of me," he said finally. "You're acting as if I have some real influence. At this point, the only influence I have is through Mariel."

"Is she not enamored of you? Would she not aid you?"

Vir laughed bitterly at that. "Mariel aids herself. She wouldn't . . . she . . . sh . . ."

His voice trailed off. An idea was beginning to trickle through him.

"Vir Cotto . . .?" inquired Galen.

"Quiet!" If anyone had told Vir some years back that he would be telling a techno-mage to silence himself, Vir would have thought they were out of their mind. What was even more astounding was that the techno-mage did, in fact, shut up. He cocked his head with slight curiosity, but otherwise seemed more than content to let Vir's train of thought head down the track.

Vir was walking slowly, but his mind was leaps and bounds away. A flood of notions rolled over him. He turned quickly, half expecting to find that Galen had disappeared in the same way that his associates did. But Galen was still standing there, cradling his staff, watching Vir with what seemed to be cold amusement.

"Can you make her love me?"

Galen blinked in a vaguely owlish fashion. "Love."

"Yes."

"You."

"Yes."

The techno-mage said nothing at first. He didn't even move. He was so immobile that he might have had some sort of paralysis spell cast upon him, for all Vir knew.

"You want to control her," he said at last.

Vir nodded.

"You want me . . . to make her so enamored of you that she will do whatever you ask, whenever and wherever you ask, rather than take the slightest risk of upsetting you."

"Exactly," said Vir with grim eagerness.

"And you desire this . . . why?"

"You want me to be able to return to Centauri Prime. I've come to realize that she's the key to it. Londo knew it . . . Londo always knows," Vir said, shaking his head in grudging admiration. "And he got Senna to get word to me, probably because everything he says and does is carefully monitored. That's why she sent it from outside the palace. You would think that that alone would have tipped me off."

"You are a fool, Vir Cotto," Galen said softly.

"Maybe. But I'm a fool that you need." Vir was not about to let himself be intimidated, even by a techno-mage.

"You ask me to make this woman love you. I can do this thing. It is within my power. I can make her love you with such intensity that she will shatter every bone in her body rather than fail you."

"I think we can, you know . . . avoid anything that will call for self-mutilation."

"Indeed." Galen was thoughtful for a moment. "And will you admit to yourself why you have asked me to do this?"

"I already told you."

"No. No." Galen shook his head. He walked toward Vir then, and Vir was sure it was his imagination, but it seemed to him as if Galen was getting taller, wider, more impressive with every step. "That is what you have told me. The truth of it is, though, that you wish to punish her, and you see me as the instrument of that punishment. You do not wish simply to use her. You wish to humiliate her for your own personal satisfaction. It is unworthy of you, Vir Cotto."

"You're wrong," Vir said tightly. "And I don't understand you. You people, you techno-mages . . . you always talk in vague, prophetic, mystical, oblique ways. You don't stand there and psychoanalyze people right down to exactly why you think they do things."

"I save obliqueness for matters of galactic import," retorted Galen. "When I speak of foolish actions and foolish individuals, I tend not to talk in subtext. What is the matter, Vir Cotto? Was I too on-point for you?"

"You were wrong, that's all."

"So you say. And so you will keep saying, probably to your grave." Galen sighed softly. "Very well, since it is the end we desire, I shall provide you with the means that you desire. But when you do return to Centauri Prime . . . it will be with this."

He held out his hand barely an inch from Vir's face, and there was a flash of light that made Vir jump back. At that, he saw Galen's face register grim satisfaction. Then Vir frowned as he saw a triangular, black device in Galen's palm. He couldn't be sure, but the way the light played across it, it seemed to be shimmering. "What is that?" he asked.

"Shadow technology," Galen told him. "Defies detection by any and all sensory devices you would care to name. Once you have returned to Centauri Prime, as you walk around the palace, or anywhere on the planet, this will supply readings that will inform me of Shadow technology on your Homeworld. The detection range is, unfortunately, limited—Shadows hide themselves quite well. So you will have to be on top of the Shadow tech for this device to work."

"And how will I tell you what I find?"

"You will not. The device will. Wear it anywhere on your person, and it will do the rest. And this," his hand flashed again, this time revealing a cylinder inside a small case no larger than Vir's thumbnail, "will enable me to contact you during the hunt. Insert it into your ear before you arrive on Centauri Prime. It will be undetectable. You won't be able to communicate with me, but I will be able to tell you where to explore if there are any readings that elicit further inspection."

Vir took the cylinder, tucked it into his pocket, then turned the triangle over in his hands. "You're looking for hard evidence that there are Drakh on Centauri Prime."

"We know they are there, Vir Cotto. What we do not know is how pervasive their presence is."

"Why can't you look for yourselves?"

"We have our reasons."

"How did I know you were going to say that," Vir said sourly. "So tell me . . . if there are Drakh . . . and they find me with this thing on me . . . what will they do?"

"Almost certainly, they will kill you."

Vir sighed heavily. "How did I know you were going to say that, too?"

"If they do kill you, Vir Cotto . . . you can take solace in one thing."

"Oh, really? What would that be?"

Galen smiled mirthlessly. "Mariel will mourn for you quite spectacularly."

And with that, he turned and left, his long coat sweeping across the floor and yet, oddly, stirring up none of the gravel that lay about.

Vir had consumed half a bottle of liquor when she arrived.

The damning thing about looking at Mariel was that, every time he did so, he desperately wanted to put aside all that he knew about her. He wanted to believe once again that, when she looked at him, he was all that mattered in her mind and hearts. That he wasn't simply some tool, a buffoon she was manipulating as adroitly as she manipulated everyone. He couldn't do so, however, and he fancied that—despite all her skill in covering what was going through that scheming mind of hers—he could now see the duplicity in her eyes.

"Vir!" she said quite cheerily as she placed her bags in the quarters that they had been sharing for nearly a year. "Vir, you're here!"

"Vir, Vir, Vir is here," he echoed, sounding more drunk than he had realized. Some of the words were slurred.

"It has been ages, darling," she said, and she reached down, took his chin in her hands and kissed him lightly.

Vir wondered when Galen was going to put the spell on her.

Then he looked into her eyes, really looked . . . and she was looking back at him in a most curious manner. It seemed to him, as paradoxical as it sounded, that her eyes were misting over and clearing at the same time. As if . . . as if she was seeing him for the first time . . . but seeing him only under very specific circumstances.

Great Maker, Vir thought, *he already got to her—*

And then she lay down on the bed beside him, began to do things to him. Extraordinary things, and he felt as if he was having an out-of-body experience. Sensations pounded through him that he had only experienced in the vaguest of ways, in the most nebulous of dreams, and never did he think that there was anything like that in real life. Mariel was everywhere, and he twisted and turned, actually trying to get away from her, but it was impossible. There was no holding her back, no holding himself back. His entire body pounded as if there were too much blood in his limbs.

"I love you," she whispered in his ear, over and over again. "My dear, my sweet . . ."

He tried to push her away, but he couldn't muster any strength. He felt as if his mind was overloading, and finally desperation gave him power. He shoved Mariel off before it could go any further, and rolled off the bed. Scrambling backward to the nearest chair, he hauled himself onto it and looked at her, still curled up on the bed, now half naked. Her luminous eyes were full of love, and she started to move toward him once more.

"That's enough," he said. "Just . . . stay right there. Okay?"

She looked up at him, stricken. "Are you sure?"

"Yes: I'm sure." He stood and tried to pull his disheveled clothes together into some semblance of orderliness. It was everything he could do to focus on what was right and proper, given the situation. And part of his mind sneered at him and said, *Right and proper? You asked a techno-mage to brainwash the woman into loving you, justifying a petty revenge by claiming that it will end up benefiting Centauri Prime. You might as well take advantage of what she's offering you. You deserve it, and she'll delight in it.* But as quickly as that suggestion echoed through his mind, he blocked it out.

Was she truly brainwashed? She didn't have a vacant, thought-expunged expression. That had been a concern . . . that she would become vapid, mindless. He could see, though, that it wasn't the case. All the canniness, all the intelligence, all the craftiness that he had come to see and understand was still part of her—all of that was still intact. That came as something of a relief, because otherwise she would be useless to him . . .

. . . useless . . . to him . . .

He pushed that thought from his mind, as well, for he didn't like what it said about him.

Yes, the intelligence was there, but the overwhelming emotion that radiated from her was pure adoration. He hadn't planned for what had happened earlier. Some part of him had found it hard to believe that the techno-mage could actually do as he said he would. When Mariel first went for him, a part of him still thought it might be some sort of prank. But the intensity of her fervor had swiftly disabused him of that notion.

He felt dirty.

He kept telling himself that he shouldn't. That, of the two of them, Mariel was by far the one with far filthier hands. This was a woman who had used sex and raw emotion as weapons, mere tools in her arsenal. She wasn't deserving of the slightest dreg of pity for having those tools turned back against her. Indeed, she had gotten off lightly, for she didn't know that that was what had happened to her.

Then again, it might be that it was her very lack of understanding that made the whole business so repellant to Vir.

He had had no intention of bedding her, no matter how tempting the prospect seemed. He had instead planned to keep her at arm's length, make her feel some of the agony, the unrequited emotion he had experienced. Certainly the notion had seemed most attractive when he'd first conceived it. Yet now he was repulsed by its very essence. He had to seek out Galen, get him to remove the spell. Restore her to normal so that she could . . .

So that she could tear him down again. Lampoon him, spread rumors about him, and make him even more ineffective than he already was.

He stared at her. It was exactly as Galen had said; clearly the woman was ready to destroy herself lest she disappoint him. A far cry, certainly, from what the conniving bitch had been mere hours before. His hearts hardened against her, and if he didn't like the way he felt at the moment . . .

Well . . . he would feel differently tomorrow.

"Do you not want to enjoy me, Vir, my love?" she whispered. "Shall I not show you how much I love you?"

The answer to both questions was yes, but with a determination and strength of will he did not even know he possessed, he managed not to answer truthfully. Instead he said, "I'm sure it would be a really okay experience . . ."

"Just okay?" Her disappointment was palpable. "Let me show you. Let me erase whatever doubts you might have and provide you with boundless—"

"What I want you to do . . . is not touch me for a while."

"Not . . . touch you?"

"That's right."

She looked stricken. "Not caress you? Not feel your firm flesh beneath my fingers? Not take your wiggling—"

"None of that," Vir told her. "There's, uhm . . . there's a lot of things I have to take care of for a while. I need to focus, and I can't be distracted by, uhm . . . romantic liaisons. So I need you to keep your distance."

"My distance? My . . ."

He shot her a look and she seemed to wilt. Very quietly, she said,

"All right, Vir. If that is what will make you happy, then it will make me happy. I live for your happiness." She paused, and then said, "Shall I stay away from you at the party tomorrow?"

"Party?"

"The reception. For the Delgashi ambassador . . ."

"Ohhhh, right. Right." He hadn't paid attention to the social calendar, since he had been planning, until fairly recently, to be gone from Babylon 5 for a while. "No, you should not stay away from me at the party. In fact . . ." He started warming to the topic. This was the reason, he remembered, that he had Galen perform his little miracle. ". . . in fact, you'll show up on my arm . . . and be openly adoring . . . and when you work the room and talk to other ambassadors, you're going to tell them how great I am. How intelligent, how . . . how . . ." His mind raced, and then he said, ". . . how . . . everything I am. All my positive attributes."

"All of them? That could take a very long time, my love. We might be at the party much later than you had previously anticipated."

"That'll be fine," Vir replied, settling into the chair. "With any luck, we'll have all night and into the next morning. I can trust you to do this, Mariel? Because it's very important."

Mariel looked as if the breath had been knocked out of her. Her reaction was so extreme that Vir wondered for a moment if she were being seized by some sort of fit. When she managed to pull some air back into her lungs, she said, "I will be worthy of it, Vir. Worthy of it . . . and you."

"That would be fine."

"Would you like me to . . . ?" She raised herself from the bed and motioned significantly for him.

"No. No, that's quite all right," he said quickly, backing up and nearly toppling the chair as a result. "Just stay right where you are."

"Very well, my love." She arranged the blanket delicately around herself and sat there, perfectly still. Her eyes still large, she regarded him with open curiosity. "Would you not be more comfortable over here, my love?" She patted the bed next to her.

"No. Nooooo, no. No, I'm fine right here," Vir replied. "Comfy cozy."

"All right, Vir." She lay back down, but that adoring stare remained fixed upon him, and he watched until the lateness of the hour got the better of her. Her eyes closed slowly, but inexorably, in slumber. Vir was left alone in the room, and told himself that he had achieved some measure of revenge this night. That he had managed to take back some of that which had been taken from him.

By morning, the pain in his lower back also had something to say about it from a night spent upright in the chair. Mariel, however, was still asleep, and he watched the steady rising and falling of her breasts with a sense of wonder.

"What have I done?" he whispered, and for a moment he half hoped that Galen would magically appear, to answer the question. But instead there was simply her slow inhaling and exhaling, and the sound of his hearts pounding against his rib cage.

The reception could not have gone better, even in Vir's wildest dreams.

Mariel was her usual, animated self. No living soul could have detected any change in her demeanor and deportment . . . right up until she slapped the Drazi ambassador's aide.

Vir didn't see it happen, because his back was to the incident. He was standing at the bar, pouring another healthy draught. He was amazed, not for the first time, at how his alcoholic intake had jumped ever since he had taken over Londo's position as ambassador. Only a few years ago one drink alone would have been enough to reduce Vir to near incoherence. Two would have knocked him cold and left him with a roaring hangover the next morning. Now it seemed he had to drink several times his old levels just to feel any sort of pleasant numbness.

Behind him, he heard a fairly constant stream of chatter, which was customary for such gatherings. And then, with the suddenness of a blast from a PPG, he heard the unmistakable sound of palm across flesh. He turned, partly out of sheer curiosity and partly out of boredom, for no one had been going out of his way to strike up a conversation with him. He'd even been considering just calling it an early evening. He almost dropped his glass when he realized that the origin of the strike had been none other than Mariel. She was facing the aide to the Drazi ambassador, and her cheeks were brightly flushed with anger. The aide was gaping at her with undisguised astonishment.

"How dare you!" Mariel said, and she was making no effort to keep her voice down. There wouldn't have been much point, really. The sound of the slap had been more than enough to capture the immediate attention of everyone in the room. "How dare you speak so insultingly!"

"But you . . . he . . . Drazi not understand!" babbled the hapless aide, and Vir immediately knew what the problem was. This was unquestionably one of the many individuals to whom Mariel had spoken so disparagingly of Vir in times very recently past. Yet now she must have been singing his praises, as ordered, and the sudden change in her attitude had caught the Drazi—and no doubt whoever else was nearby him—completely off guard.

Immediately, trying to head off any kind of major confrontation, Captain Elizabeth Lochley stepped subtly but firmly between Mariel and the Drazi. "Is there a problem here?" the B5 station commander asked. Then, without waiting for an answer, she turned to Mariel, and added, "I don't take kindly to physical assaults upon diplomats. Well, on anyone, actually, but diplomats in particular," she amended. "Diplomatic incidents and little things like wars tend to develop from such unfortunate encounters. Care to tell me what provoked this?"

"He did," Mariel said immediately. "With his snide comments about Vir."

"You yourself said—" the confused Drazi started to protest.

"I myself? What does it matter what stupid things I may have said in the past?" she asked rhetorically. "What matters is the here and the now. And the simple fact is that Vir Cotto is the best man . . . the best ambassador . . . the best lover . . ."

Vir colored slightly at that, then noticed the newly respectful stares coming from everyone within earshot—which at that point was pretty much everyone. This eased his discomfort quite quickly. He even squared his shoulders and nodded in acknowledgment of his newly announced status.

". . . the best everything," Mariel continued. "I will not stand by and see him insulted. He is my love, he is my life." She went to him then and ran her fingers under his chin in a teasing, loving fashion. Vir smiled and bobbed his head affectionately while, at the same time, trying not to feel chilled to the bone. *She deserved it, she had it coming, just keep telling yourself that.* He couldn't tell whether his conscience was buying it or not.

Lochley led the Drazi away, and for the rest of the evening the various diplomats and ambassadors seemed to be reevaluating Vir. It was a delicate game. After all, they didn't know that *he* knew the damage Mariel had done to him. So naturally they tried not to let on, endeavoring to get a feel for Vir without letting him realize that they were doing so. Vir, of course, could tell immediately, and was doing all that he could not to let on that he knew. It was a bizarre sort of shadow dance, and Vir couldn't help but wonder how in the world he had been led onto the dance floor.

It finally reached a point where Vir couldn't stand it anymore. Rather than listen to Mariel extol his many virtues one more time, Vir excused himself and bolted into the corridor. He simply needed some distance, some time . . . and some firm conviction that what he had done was going to pay off in the long run.

His theory was quite simple: if Mariel could be so convincing with the members of assorted races, how much more likely would she be in handling members of her own species? Which meant that if he could get Mariel to start talking to the right people on Centauri Prime, he would be making his triumphant return in no time. The problem was still that he was going to have to figure out who the "right people" were. Londo was definitely not among them. He had, after all, been married to her. She'd been responsible for nearly killing him . . . "accidentally" utilizing a booby trap that she had purchased on Babylon 5. He had divorced her, for heaven's sake. So Vir was quite sure that Londo would be immune to her charms. And Londo had spent a good deal of his life—usually when he was fairly inebriated—regaling people with horror stories of what his wives had been like.

The thing was, Vir was quite certain that the great court . . . even the Centaurum itself . . . was being taken over by new, young, aggressive individuals. They brought with them a large degree of arrogance and self-certainty. Women were not held in tremendous regard within the Centauri power structure, and there was only a handful of exceptions. So no one was likely to consider Mariel a threat. It was that very lack of consideration that Vir could turn into an advantage.

Still . . . when he considered what she had become . . . what he had turned her into . . .

"Second thoughts?"

The question originated right at Vir's elbow, and he was so startled that he was positive his primary heart had stopped.

Galen was standing there, looking at him grimly . . . and even a bit sadly.

Vir automatically looked right and left, as if he were in the midst of a clandestine meeting. No one appeared to be coming, and Vir had a nasty suspicion that Galen had only shown up because there was no one around to see them together. At that moment, however, he didn't much care.

"How did you do it?" Vir asked immediately, without preamble.

"Do it?" Galen raised a mocking, nearly invisible eyebrow. "You mean stir her dedication?"

"Yes."

"I spoke to her."

"You spoke to her." Vir wasn't following. "What did you say?"

"Fourteen words. It takes fourteen words to cause someone to fall in love."

Vir wasn't quite sure he was hearing properly. "That's . . . that's it? Fourteen words? I thought . . . I figured there was some sort of device or something . . . gimmicks . . . techno-mageish things that reordered her mind or . . . fourteen words? Only fourteen?"

"As with all things in life," Galen told him, "it is quality, not quantity, that matters."

"If you . . . that is to say, if I . . ." Vir wasn't quite sure how to say it, and Galen didn't seem inclined to make it easier for him. "If at some point in the future, I change my mind . . . that is to say, she's not needed to be this way anymore . . ."

"Your resolve weakening already?"

"No," Vir said immediately. "No problems with that. Still sure, thanks."

"I am so pleased." He didn't sound it. "The answer is no. What's done cannot be undone. People say things, words they regret, and then announce, 'I take it back.' Words cannot be taken back, ever. Ever. That is why they should be carefully considered. Children have a rhyme: 'Sticks and stones shatter bones, but names can never hurt you.' They are children. What know they of the truth of things?

"You will always be her greatest priority, Vir. She will be able to function perfectly well in all capacities . . . but your well-being and interests will remain her paramount importance."

There was something in his voice, a tone, which was unmistakable. "You disapprove," Vir said after a moment. "You did what I asked you to . . . but you disapprove."

"I think . . . I liked you better when you stammered more. You had more charm." Galen gave that same chilling smile. "What you have done . . . what I did . . . was nothing less than robbing the woman of free will."

"And what she did to me? What was that?" demanded Vir.

"Ahhhh . . ." The exhale came from him in a manner that sounded almost like relief. "And there it is, finally as I said. You operate out of your injured vanity. That was your motivator."

"You didn't answer my question," said Vir, raising his voice

slightly, but still keeping it at a respectful level. The last thing he
wanted to do was get Galen angry with him, and speaking in a disrespectful tone might do exactly that. "When she had her free will, she
used it to injure me, manipulate me. Is what I did to her . . . what I
had you do to her . . . as bad as that?"

"No."

"You see? That's exactly the poin—"

"It's worse," he said, as if Vir hadn't spoken.

Vir had no answer to that, but merely scowled.

"Would you like to know the single greatest tragedy here?"

"Could I stop you from telling me if I wanted to?" Vir replied.

As if Vir hadn't spoken, Galen said, "Even I cannot create love
from nothing. There had to be feelings, emotions already present. An
ember that I could fan to full flame. Despite what you may have
thought, Vir Cotto . . . the woman did feel something for you. Something deep and true. Given time, the feeling might actually have been
genuine. But you will never know."

"I don't want to know. Love isn't high on my priority list right
now," Vir told him with a bit more harshness than he would have
liked . . . and more fervency than he truly believed. "In fact, considering the road ahead of me, I doubt I'd want it, or know what to do
with it if I had it."

"Then perhaps I was wrong. Perhaps there are twin tragedies this
day."

Once again, Vir said nothing.

"Good luck, Vir Cotto. You will need it," Galen said. He turned
and walked off, rounding the corner of the hallway.

"Wait!" said Vir, heading after him. "I still want to know what—"

But when he followed Galen around the corridor edge, he discovered—to his utter lack of shock—that Galen was gone. By that
point, he was becoming quite accustomed to the abrupt comings and
goings of techno-mages . . . which wasn't to say that he was especially
thrilled by them.

7

"Come meet us in the Zocalo." That had been the entirety of Mariel's message.

Vir wondered just who the "us" might be, even as he hurried to the Zocalo in response to Mariel's summons.

It had been a very strange month for Vir. Mariel had ceased her sojourns from Babylon 5. Instead she had remained primarily on the station, continuing to be her entertaining self. And all during that time, she had continued to talk up the virtues of Vir Cotto to whomever would listen. Fortunately she was able to do so in such a charming manner that she didn't make a nuisance of herself. Vir had total strangers winking at him, nudging him in the ribs. Zack Allan was back to telling him how Mariel was "all that and a bag of chips," an expression that continued to make no sense to Vir, no matter how many times he heard it.

Even Captain Lochley seemed to be regarding him differently. She said nothing to him at first, merely appeared to be evaluating him whenever he happened to be passing by. Finally Vir had gone up to her and said, "Is there a problem, Captain?"

"Problem? No."

"Then why do you keep acting as if you're ... I don't know ... sizing me up or something?" he had asked.

She had smiled slightly. "I apologize. I wasn't aware I was being that obvious."

"Obvious about what?"

"About wondering how such a mild, unassuming individual can ... how did she put it ..." In a fair approximation of Mariel's voice, she intoned, " '... can reduce a grown woman to tears of ecstasy with one well-placed, gentle caress.' " Then she batted her eyelashes at him.

That was more than enough incentive for Vir to stay away from Captain Lochley.

It was an exercise in the surreal for Vir, considering that, although they continued to share quarters in order to keep up the appearance of the relationship, Vir never touched her. Mariel had seemed hurt at first, but finally she had complacently settled into the life, satisfied that the distance was what Vir truly wanted. And if it was what Vir wanted, that was more than enough for her.

In the night, as he lay upon the spare mattress he had obtained and tossed on the floor, he would hear her whispering to him, calling to him, like a siren of old, trying to tempt him. Galen's words kept coming back to him, and Vir felt as if he was doing penance for his deeds by depriving himself, while his body was screaming to him to indulge himself. *No one would ever know. She says you do it anyway. She wants it. You want it. What matter how it came to this pass. Seize the day, spineless one!* His inner dark side was quite vocal on the subject, while his conscience seemed disgustingly mute. This provided no end of irritation to Vir, who couldn't remember the last time he had had a solid night's sleep.

It had been a very long month.

"Come meet us in the Zocalo." Who could it be?

He hurried into the Zocalo, Babylon 5's most popular gathering place, and glanced around. A number of aliens waved at him and he waved back in an unenthusiastic but determined fashion, even as he continued to scan the room. He spotted Mariel in short order, and there was a Centauri seated across from her at a table. Vir couldn't see who it was, because he was facing away from Vir. But then Mariel pointed and the man at the table turned.

Vir's breath caught in his throat.

"Minister Durla," he said, trying to sound casual but unable to mask his complete surprise. "What an honor. I was unaware that such an . . . an esteemed person was coming to Babylon 5."

"These are dangerous times, Cotto," Durla told him. "I find it best if I do not advertise my comings and goings. The Centauri have too many enemies. We are hated by all."

As if on cue, a half dozen individuals, of varying races, walked past Vir and every single one of them greeted him warmly, or winked at him, and one of them playfully nudged him in the shoulder. There was something about the appearance of boundless virility that simply commanded respect. Vir wondered why that was, and realized he couldn't even begin to hazard a guess. It may have been the single most depressing realization he'd had all year.

"Vir is beloved by all," Mariel said promptly, apparently feeling the need to underscore that which assorted passersby had already made quite obvious.

"Yes. So it appears," Durla said, and although there was a smile etched on his face, there was no warmth in his smile, and a positive chill emanated from his eyes. "I was speaking to Mariel of this, and other matters. The lady Mariel used to be quite the social creature. However, apparently that is no longer the case. She says she is more than content these days to remain full-time on Babylon 5 . . . because of you, it seems, Cotto."

"The minister apparently came all this way to discuss my social calendar, Vir. Isn't that amusing?"

"I have pressing business not far from here," Durla corrected her archly. "I simply thought I would stop by and visit with our ambassador. And what better way to begin that visit than to discuss how our ambassador is doing in his post with the woman he calls . . . lover."

That was all Vir needed. Those few comments told Vir everything that he needed to know.

Once upon a time, Vir had been one of the most "obvious" of individuals, seeing nothing beneath the surface, accepting everything that was said to him. But during his time with Londo, and then on his own, he had learned that people rarely said what was on their mind. Indeed, oftentimes they said anything but. Unlike Galen the technomage, the rest of the world tended to converse almost solely in subtext, and Vir had become quite fluent in the language.

He immediately assembled a series of inferences, all of which seemed quite solid. He knew that Mariel had worked in some sort of spy or information-gathering capacity. To accomplish that end, she had made a habit of traveling to assorted points of interest, and had culled assorted useful tidbits from those with whom she flirted . . . or whatever it was she was doing with them. But since Vir had become the focus of her life, she had been relatively station-bound. Since she reported to someone on Centauri Prime, that someone must have wondered why her patterns had altered so drastically.

Vir was quite certain Mariel would have taken no time to inform her contact of just exactly why she was staying put. She would, naturally, be waxing eloquent about the wondrous creature of light that was Vir Cotto. This would inspire an even greater degree of curiosity.

Had she been reporting directly to Durla? Vir didn't think so; in the recording Kane had provided him, as evidence of her duplicity, she had been addressing someone as "chancellor." Durla was a minister at the time of that message, so she had been speaking to an underling. Why, then, had Durla come, instead of the underling?

Coincidence? Never ascribe to coincidence that which could be attributed to a plan.

Besides, Vir already knew the answer. Senna had told him. Durla had an interest in Mariel, and that was an interest Vir could readily exploit for all that it was worth.

The man was taken with her. The minister Durla had some sort of preoccupation with Mariel.

That was all Vir needed to know.

"Yes, yes, that's right," Vir said quickly. He slid into the seat next to Mariel and draped an arm around her. She seemed thrilled by the contact. She started to put her hands in places she shouldn't, and Vir discreetly but firmly placed them somewhere less inflammatory. "Lovers. My lover. Her and me. What can I say?"

"What indeed," Durla said coldly. In an obvious, and somewhat failed, attempt to lighten the moment, Durla continued, "I was just telling the lady Mariel that she is sorely missed back on Centauri Prime. For far too long has the court been deprived of her sparkling presence . . ."

"Tragic. Absolutely tragic," said Vir. He turned to Mariel and, taking a leap of faith, said, "Mariel, perhaps you should return to Centauri Prime. I know you've been out of the social whirl back home for quite some time." That was, in fact, an understatement. Mariel had been something of an outcast ever since Londo had divorced her. Although her presence on Babylon 5 had naturally precluded her being back on Centauri Prime, certainly she had been considered a pariah.

Fortunately for Vir, Mariel responded exactly as he expected. "What need have I for Centauri Prime when I have you."

"Nevertheless," Vir said, "Centauri Prime is home. To feel its soil beneath your feet, to breathe the good air of the Homeworld . . ."

"I couldn't *think* of going without you."

Perfect. It couldn't have been any more perfect if he had scripted it himself. He turned to Durla and said, with an air of tribulation in his voice, "What can I say? She wouldn't think of going without me. But I fear I'm somewhat . . . how shall I put it . . . I'm less than desirable to certain individuals on Centauri Prime, including—tragically—the emperor. So I reside here, in exile." He sighed so heavily he thought his lungs would implode.

"A true tragedy," Durla agreed. Vir waited. He knew the rest of the sentiment would be forthcoming, and he was absolutely right. "We should do something about that."

"But what can we do?" Vir said with total resignation.

"Yes, what can we do?" Mariel echoed.

"I am . . . not without influence," Durla said slowly. "It may well be that the ambassador's abrupt departure from our Homeworld may actually turn out to be nothing more than a tragic misunderstanding. Allow me to have a talk with the emperor. You are, after all, still our ambassador. You should be representing the greatness of our republic to others. But if you are kept in ignorance of that republic . . . if you can only come so close and no closer . . . your effectiveness is tremendously limited."

"That's exactly what I was thinking!" Vir said with a tone of wonderment. "You and I, we're thinking on the same level, Minister! Who would have thought?"

"Who indeed," Durla responded dourly, but he quickly brightened. "And of course, the lady Mariel would accompany you, I assume."

"Oh, naturally. Naturally," Vir said quickly. "That goes without saying . . . although, you know, it never actually hurts to say it."

"Yes. There are things that should always be said. For example . . ."

There was a long pause on Durla's part, and the break in the conversation caught Vir's attention. "For example?" he prompted.

"Well . . . we should always discuss our successes. And our failures as well. That way we can be candid with each other. We can all know where we stand."

"Candor is a good thing," Vir agreed. "I mean, after all, we're all on the same side, right? We all want what's best for Centauri Prime."

"Absolutely," said Durla. "For example, I had an archaeological dig that I was overseeing. Something that was providing jobs for many grateful Centauri. But the project seems to have fallen apart. It is, in short, a failure. Even a tragic failure, it seems." He lowered his voice and shook his head. "Lives were lost. A sad, sad thing. You . . . wouldn't know anything about that, would you . . . Ambassador?"

Immediately, Vir's mind was screaming. What did Durla know about Vir's presence on K0643? Had Renegar or Rem Lanas told Durla that Vir had been there? Did he associate Vir with the destruction of the Shadow base? Did he even know about the base?

Vir's impulse was to start talking, and keep on talking. That was what he had a tendency to do whenever he was nervous. But it had never been clearer to him than it was at that moment that he was going to have to change his method of operation. Clamping his teeth shut with a visible effort, Vir considered the situation, and decided that the absolute last thing he could do was give in to his primary impulse.

"What is there to know, Minister?" he asked.

"Perhaps nothing. Perhaps a great deal."

"Well," said Vir, steepling his fingers and fixing a calm, level gaze on Durla. "At such time when you have decided which it is, you can let me know and we can talk further on the matter. Isn't that right, Mariel?" he inquired.

He got the exact answer he expected. "Whatever you say, Vir," she said, smiling that high voltage smile at him. She turned back to Durla. "Is he not brilliant?" she asked.

"Brilliant," Durla agreed flatly. He rose from the table. "It has been a pleasure speaking with you, Ambassador. And I look forward to seeing you on Homeworld again as soon as possible."

"And I you, Minister." Feeling uncustomarily bold, Vir inquired, "That project of yours . . . I would hope that there are others to replace it, considering that apparently it has fallen through?"

"Oh, yes. Yes, there are always other options," Durla said. "I am always coming up with new concepts, new ideas."

"How fascinating." Vir leaned forward, all ears. "I've always wondered . . . where do great thinkers such as you get your ideas?"

Durla actually laughed softly at that, as if the question—or perhaps the answer—was very amusing. He leaned forward, resting his knuckles on the table, and said, "Dreams, Ambassador. I get them from my dreams."

"What a productive use of your slumber. Here, all I ever get is a good night's sleep," said Vir.

Durla's already thin smile became even more so. It was as if his lips were vanishing from his face entirely. "How very fortunate for you. Good day to you, Ambassador . . . my lady Mariel." He took her hand and kissed her knuckles suavely, then turned and walked away.

Vir watched him go, never taking his eyes from him. Mariel, for her part, seemed to have forgotten the minister immediately. Instead, she was taken with the notion of returning to Centauri Prime. "Will it not be wonderful, Vir? You and I, in the thick of society. There I will be, with you on my arm, so proud. The proudest woman there. Everyone will look at us, and I can only imagine what they will say."

As it happened, Vir could imagine, as well. Londo would be chuckling over Vir's foolishness, just as Timov had displayed astonishment that Vir would take up with the potentially lethal woman. Durla would be watching for some crack in the relationship that would allow him to move in. Perhaps he wouldn't even wait. Obviously he had had designs upon Mariel for some time, and was only now feeling confident enough in his position of power to make a move. That very confidence might prove to be extremely problematic for Vir. And then there would be everyone else, who would likely wonder what the slightly buffoonish Vir Cotto was doing arm in arm with the emperor's cast-off wife. They might not necessarily hold Mariel in the same esteem that the diplomats on Babylon 5 did. Once they returned to Centauri, any number of possibilities presented themselves . . . none of them particularly pleasant.

She took his hand, then, and whispered, "Did I please you, Vir? Did I handle him in a way that satisfied you?"

He felt a twinge of guilt, and he thought of the things Galen had said to him. It made him feel small. Once again, he felt as if, after everything he had been through, he was little more than a plaything of the techno-mages. Only months before, he had felt like a galactic hero, fearlessly battling Drakhs . . . well, battling Drakhs, at least . . . and single-handedly destroying secret bases . . . well, single-handedly with help. Yet now he looked into Mariel's eyes, and felt smaller than the smallest of Centauri.

That night, after settling into bed, he dreamed. It was a very short, but very stark dream. Mariel was simply standing there, looking at him, making no motion toward him. The top of her head was gone. From the headband up, there was nothing, as if a huge section of her brain had simply been removed. And there were tears rolling down her face. No audible sobs accompanied; there was just the wetness. He reached toward her to wipe away the tears, but he could get no closer to her. A distance behind her, Galen was there, shaking his head, but otherwise mute.

Vir startled himself awake. Across the room from him, Mariel was sleeping soundly. But something prompted him to draw close to her, and when he did so he could see that there were dried tears upon her face.

He sat back and pondered the notion that it took only fourteen words to get someone to fall in love with you.

Only fourteen words. It seemed like so few.

He leaned forward and whispered to Mariel, "I'm sorry."

Only two words. It seemed like more than enough.

But it was not. And he knew it. And there wasn't a damned thing that he could do about it except fall back into a fitful sleep, while trying to convince himself that what he had done was right. Unfortunately, there were not enough words in all the Centauri language to do that.

It was so simple.

Durla puts forward an air of utter confidence, but it is only an air. He has come too far, too quickly, you see. His position as minister was a gift to him from the Drakh, who perceived him as a useful tool for their assorted plans. As a result, he was thrust into his position with no experience in the ins and outs of court intrigue. He has learned quickly and well . . . but he is still learning.

I, on the other hand, could teach seminars.

Getting him to visit Babylon 5 was simplicity itself

Secrets are the currency in which we all trade. Senna's little investigations, her chats and probes, had told me what I needed. The New Guard, namely Durla and his ilk, still had not quite grasped the notion that keeping certain things to themselves could only benefit them. But they were still relatively young and foolish, and so when they learned things about each other, they had a habit of speaking of it to one another. The more one speaks of things, the more likely those things are to reach certain ears.

Ears such as mine.

It had been during one of my routine meetings with Durla, to discuss upcoming public projects. He was, at that point, seeking approval for a new structure that was to be overseen by newly minted Minister of Development Lione, in conjunction with Kuto, the minister of information. The design for the structure was simple and elegant. It would be the tallest building in the area. It would loom like a great tower over the city, gleaming pure and white, and it would have no windows. To me, it sounded most claustrophobic, but Durla insisted that it was for the security and protection of those who worked within. "Spies are everywhere," he said to me with great significance.

This building was intended to house assorted offices and bureaus dedicated to the rebuilding of Centauri Prime, and to the service of the public. It was felt that, by making it so plainly visible, it would be a source of inspiration to all of Centauri Prime. It even had a name, a name which the perpetually avuncular Kuto had come up with during one of their brainstorming sessions. He dubbed it the Tower of Power, and it was a name that—Great Maker preserve them—stuck. Ghastly name, that, but they seemed pleased with it, and it was their eye-sore, after all, so I suppose they were entitled to call the beastly structure anything they wished.

So there was Durla, in the throne room, and he was pointing out to me the beginning of the Tower of Power's construction. "It will point the way, Highness," he told me with confidence.

"To where?"

"To the stars. To our destiny. To the legacies that we will leave."

"I see. Of course," and I sighed heavily, "what good are the stars when one has no one to share them with, eh?"

It was a comment calculatedly conceived to snag Durla's attention, and it succeeded perfectly. He looked at me with curiosity. Normally I contributed very little to our "conferences." He spoke. I listened, and nodded, and gave approval to whatever it was he wished to do. We didn't chat or make small talk. So for me to say something vaguely approaching normal discourse was most unusual.

"How do you mean, Highness?" he responded curiously.

I sighed even more heavily. "We speak of legacies, Durla, but what do we mean, really? Is our legacy the achievements we strive for? The changes we make on Centauri Prime?"

"Absolutely," he nodded.

But I shook my head. "What you and I do here, someone else can undo when we are gone. We delude ourselves into thinking that we do something of permanence, but there is no certainly in that. No," and I waggled a finger, "the only true legacy for which we can strive is family. Loved ones. People to whom we will mean more than programs or building plans or imperial mandates."

"I . . . never thought of it quite that way, Highness," said Durla, but he didn't appear quite certain of what it was I was saying.

"I have no loved ones, Durla. My one wife will forever hate me . . ."

"But Highness, you asked me . . ."

"I know, Durla, I know. Do not be concerned; I am not attempting to blame you for the end of that relationship." I shook my head. "There were good reasons for doing what I did, and having you do what you did. I do not regret them. But she is gone now. I have no children. Daggair, one of my former wives, is skulking about, who knows where. And as for Mariel . . ."

He looked at me askance. I could see that I had finally caught his attention. Thank you, Senna. "What of her, Highness?"

"I understand she resides with my former aide. Amazing, is it not?" I shook my head. "He does not understand her as I do."

"What is there to understand, Highness?"

I waved dismissively. "Oh, you do not care about these things . . ."

"The female mind is always of interest to me, Highness," he said with as close to a smile as that wretched man was capable of achieving.

"Well," I said, rubbing my palms as if I was warming to a topic of great interest, "Mariel adores men of power. She is drawn to them. She sees Vir as such, I suppose, perhaps because of his connection to me. I am something of her nemesis, you see, and she will do anything to try to get back at me. That is the way such women are; they are obsessed with indulging their petty vengeance. Why," and I laughed at what I was about to say as if the very notion were absurd, "I would wager that if she could find a means of coming here to the court, to achieve some sort of success, then flaunt that success in front of me, why . . . she would be in heaven. Her heart would be filled to overflowing with joy . . . to say nothing of devotion to whatever man could put her into that position. Ach! But we speak of foolishness! I waste your time, Durla, when I am sure you have far more important matters of state to attend to."

"I . . . always have time to discuss whatever you deem worthy of discussing, Highness." He sounded properly obsequious in tone. Once upon a time, he had always had that tone. Of late, he had spoken with arrogance far more in keeping with his elevated level of self-importance. But in this particular instance, some of the old Durla was peeking through.

From that point, I gave it no more than ten days before he would travel to Babylon 5, to meet with Mariel. The thing was, I had no real idea of what would happen from that point on. The truth was, Durla was not Mariel's type. I knew that for a certainty. Powerful he may be, and Mariel is indeed drawn to powerful men, that much was true. But Durla was a puppet. He did not know it, of course.

But Mariel would have known. She had an infallible sense of what true power was, and her instincts would inform her that Durla was but a surrogate for some other person, or persons, who wielded the true power. Consequently, she would not be interested in Durla, possibly without even fully realizing just why she had no inclination toward him.

I knew that I was leaving a good deal up to Vir. I was giving him an opportunity, but that was all that I could give him. I was unsure of just what sort of true attachment Mariel might have to Vir, but I could only assume that it was artificial. Nor did I think that Mariel was likely to transfer her "affections" to Durla, unless she was absolutely positive that somehow it would bring her power.

So it would be up to Vir to realize that this was his means of returning to Centauri Prime. Durla would show up with a mission to find the means of bringing Mariel back, and Vir would have to find a means of not only causing that to happen, but of making certain he was part of the equation.

In a way, I suppose it was something of a test. Truthfully, I had no idea if he was up to it or not. But I had begun to believe, to some degree, in fate. If he were destined to return to Centauri Prime, then he would find a way. If it was not meant to be, why then, he would not.

So Durla went to Babylon 5, and Durla returned . . .

And today, Vir is returning to Centauri Prime, with Mariel on his elbow. They have already arrived at the palace and, by all accounts, she is utterly devoted to him. I have to admit: I am impressed. It appears Vir has outdone himself. It could be, of course, that Mariel is simply pretending, although why she would engage in such shenanigans is a matter of curiosity.

I could, I suppose, take some pride in his actions. Oddly, I am not sure whether I should or not. Any man who can wind up with Mariel professing undying devotion is a man that, perhaps, should be feared. I hope I have not done myself a disservice. It would be somewhat ironic if I wound up going to extra effort, just to bring a nemesis into my very backyard. After all, I had always thought that nemesis to be G'Kar. I wouldn't be expecting my greatest enemy to be wearing the face of a friend.

Then again, fate has a habit of making its own choices.

8

At first Gwynn couldn't be quite sure that she had come to the right place.

She made her way through the streets of Ghehana, one of the seamiest sections in all of Centauri Prime, and certainly the worst part of the capital city. She did so adroitly, masking her presence with practiced ease. It wasn't that she was invisible, but anyone who happened to glance in her direction simply didn't notice her; their gaze would have slid off her without registering any sort of actual presence.

It would not, however, serve in all circumstances. As confident as she was in her ability, the shadows stretched all around her in this particular section of town, and she found herself checking to see whether the shadows moved. This was not paranoia on her part. The Drakh seemed to move in and out of darkness with as much facility as their departed masters. She had the very disturbing feeling that the Drakh would have no problems discerning her being there at all.

She paused outside one building that had the correct address—she was supposed to find Galen here. She placed her hands against the front door and closed her eyes, reaching out. Yes. Yes, Galen was definitely within. She sensed mage energy that could only be originating with him.

The door, however, was locked. This provided an impediment for her for as long as it took her to say, "Open." The door immediately attended to her and opened. What was interesting to note was that the door was not an automatic one, and only three people present on Centauri Prime would have been capable of getting it open simply by telling it to do so. Gwynn was one, the other was inside, and for all she knew, the third might be, as well.

As it turned out, he was. Finian was standing right there when the door opened up, and he bowed to her with a sweep of his cloak. As annoying as his attitude could be sometimes, she had to admit that she was pleased to see him. The months after the passing of Kane had been hard on Finian, for they had been friends for many years, and Finian had not taken Kane's death well at all. He had been so despondent over it, in fact, that there had been some talk about his place within their society. Finally, it had been Galen who had spoken on his behalf, which struck Gwynn as curious. Galen had spent almost no time with Finian, had barely said ten words to him, as far as Gwynn knew. Yet he had spoken so passionately on Finian's behalf that the others had given the young mage adequate time to come around.

Apparently he had, although Gwynn thought she could still see traces of mourning in his eyes.

"Where is he?"

"No patience for niceties, Gwynn?"

"Good evening, Finian. Where is he?"

"Upstairs."

Gwynn followed Finian up a narrow flight of stairs, which creaked under her feet. A smell of moisture wafted through the air; something was leaking somewhere. She could also hear vermin scuttling around within the walls. This wasn't exactly where she would want to establish her summer home.

At the top of the stairs, she had to duck slightly under a low overhang and step over a puddle, and then they emerged into a small room where Galen was seated. Hovering in front of him was a holographic display that was constantly shifting, and it only took Gwynn a moment to realize that it was some sort of point-of-view device. In Galen's hand there was a small, black object, which was glowing softly in the dimness. She recognized it immediately as a recorder. It was taking in all the images from the display.

"Is he in?" she asked.

Galen nodded. "Nothing untoward so far, however. Still, the evening is young."

"Unless he's caught. Then the day is over," Finian pointed out.

"He knew the risks," Gwynn said.

Finian's eyes narrowed. "And if he does, what of that? Are we then not to be concerned? Tell me, Gwynn, just how cold are you, anyway?"

Gwynn's temper flared and she did her best to pull it under control. "Now listen to me, Finian . . ."

"A better idea," Galen's sharp voice cut in, "is if you both be quiet." He was studying the holograph. "Vir . . . nothing so far. Keep as you are, though. If I see something that requires further investigation, I will instruct you. Do you understand?"

The holographic image moved up and down once. Vir must have nodded.

There was silence for a moment, and then Gwynn said softly, "He's quite brave, actually."

"He does what needs to be done," said Galen. "No more, no less."

"As do we all. Which reminds me, Galen . . . how transpire things with the *Excalibur*? Does the captain there . . . what is his name again?"

"Gideon."

"Does he know that you are here when you are not there?"

"No. Nor, I should think, would he care. Given the situation on Earth, he has more pressing matters to concern himself over than my whereabouts."

There was silence for a time, as the holographic view continued to change. Then it stopped. Vir had come to a halt. Galen leaned forward and said intently, "Vir Cotto. Can you hear me? Is everything all right?"

No response.

"Vir," Galen prompted again, this time with just a touch more urgency. "Vir, are you . . ."

Suddenly the image moved again, swiftly side to side. It was as if Vir had jerked his entire body. Then the image started moving again, indicating that Vir was once more underway.

It was the first time that Galen had allowed any of the tension he must have been feeling to show. He sat back and let out an unsteady sigh, then pulled himself together and went back to watching the holographic representation with all the emotion of a statue.

Then, so softly that she could barely hear herself, Gwynn said, "Do you think anyone suspects what Vir is doing? What he is up to?"

"If they do," Galen replied slowly, "then he is very likely dead."

"Does he know that?" asked Finian.

Galen looked at him levelly. "Let us hope not."

And suddenly, Galen sat upright, as if galvanized into action.

"Vir!" he said sharply. "Don't go in that room! There's something there . . . some terrible danger!"

But the holographic image started to shift again. Vir wasn't doing as Galen instructed; instead he was heading into the very room Galen had just told him not to enter.

"He can't hear me," Galen said.

"They know. They must know," said Finian. "And there's nothing we can do to save him."

Even before Gwynn arrived at her destination, Vir found himself back at court. It was bustling and active, exactly as he remembered it. There was a gathering being held in the Great Hall, and it seemed to Vir that Durla and his associates certainly enjoyed partying.

It was somewhat disconcerting for Vir to realize that virtually every familiar face was missing. Lords Teela and Surkel, Minister Dachow, High Minister Sulassa . . . even old Morkel was gone, and Morkel had been there forever. Morkel had managed to survive even Cartagia, and that was a formidable challenge in and of itself. Now they were gone, every one of them, replaced by individuals who obviously knew one another, and all of whom were quite friendly with Durla.

Durla, for his part, seemed extremely interested in determining that Vir and Mariel were having a good time. He brought person after person, minister, chancellor, assorted Prime Candidates, all before Vir and Mariel in a steady parade of faces and names so dizzying that Vir knew he'd never be able to keep them all straight.

Mariel, for her part, remained her charming self. Whatever stigma had been attached to her being a cast-off of the emperor seemed to have dissolved, mostly because it was clear that Durla was making every effort to make certain that Mariel and Vir were part of the in crowd. It seemed to Vir that Durla was determined to let Mariel see just how respected and powerful he, Durla, was.

Vir was finding it hard to quibble with the treatment they had received thus far. When they had received the summons from Centauri Prime, stating that the emperor was willing to set aside his "differences" and welcome Vir back with open arms, Vir had been of two minds. He had been pleased, since it meant being able to return to the planet that had given him birth, and there was certainly that sentimental attraction for him. It also meant that he would be able to accomplish that which he had promised Galen he would accomplish. He would be able to see for himself just how pervasive, if at all, the Shadow influence was on Centauri Prime. He knew there was *something* present, certainly. After all, Londo's disagreement with him had come from his mention of a name, a single name—Shiv'kala. Obviously that was a name associated with something dark and fearsome that Londo did not wish to have spread about. That alone was enough to support the notion that something frightening stalked Centauri Prime.

Londo had still not made an appearance, and Vir was beginning to wonder if he was going to do so at all. After all, despite Vir's suspicion that Londo was the guiding hand orchestrating his return, he had no real proof. If there was one thing Vir had learned, it was that he could not possibly know Londo's mind for sure. In many ways, Londo had long ago become a stranger to him. Every so often Vir saw flashes of the man he had once known, but only flashes. It was as if that man was a beacon of light, enveloped by darkness and only able to peer out for the briefest of moments before being enveloped by the shroud once again.

"You are Vir Cotto?"

He turned and saw an individual whom he had witnessed in action on vid, but not seen in person. "Minister Vallko. Yes, I'm . . . that is to say, right. I'm Vir Cotto."

The minister of spirituality looked him up and down for a long moment. He was a head shorter than Vir, and yet Vir couldn't help but feel as if the minister towered over him. "A pleasure," he said at last.

"To meet you, too. I've seen some of your meetings. Your prayer meetings, I mean. You're very persuasive. Very powerful speaker."

Vallko bowed slightly, but he did so without breaking gaze with Vir. "I am but the instrument of the Great Maker. What humble gifts I possess come from him."

Something that Galen had said to him months before returned to him. He had liked Vir better when Vir stammered. Since that time, Vir had come to a realization: others would very probably like him better that way, as well. In recent years, Vir had found that his thought patterns had become clearer, more laser-sharp. If he so desired, he could put forward a very polished and confident face. But that might very well put people on their guard, and it was probably going to be better for Vir if people thought that he was a bit of a bumbler. Better to be underestimated than overestimated.

So when he addressed Vallko, he played up the hesitancy in his speech. "That's very, uh . . . humble," Vir said. "Self-effacing and, well . . . everything else."

"Thank you," Vallko said again, and Vir could see assessment filtering through Vallko's eyes, which were cold and appraising. "It helps that we are all of one mind. We all care about what is best for Centauri Prime."

"Absolutely," Vir said, his head bobbing furiously.

"What do you think is best?"

Vir's head stopped bobbing. He noticed that one or two other ministers appeared to have slowed in their glide around the party and were giving an ear toward the conversation. "Me?"

"Yes. You."

Vir sensed the trap being laid for him. He laughed, and then smiled wanly. "What I think is best is whatever the Great Maker thinks is, you know, best. And me, I don't . . . you know, I think that there are others much more, you know . . . that is to say, qualified . . . to decide such things. So I'm more than happy to listen to their advice. Like you. People like you. What is in the interests of the Great Maker, do you think? Does he, you know . . . talk to you directly, by the way? Like, a huge voice from all over . . . or does he, I don't know . . . write to you. Drop you a line. How does that work, I'd really like to know." He stared at Vallko with open curiosity, obviously anticipating some deeply intriguing response.

Vallko laughed softly as if he'd just been told something quite amusing. "I am not blessed enough to converse directly with the Great Maker. I divine my knowledge from those to whom he has spoken. The greatest, wisest of us. And there are . . . feelings," he admitted, apparently grudgingly. "I have feelings of what the Great Maker would like for his people, feelings that I convey to the followers."

"And you have a lot of followers," Vir said admiringly.

"They are the followers of the Great Maker. I am merely his vessel."

"Well, that's . . . that's nice," said Vir, apparently at a loss for words. He just stood there, seeming to have nothing more to offer to the conversation.

Vallko looked him up and down once more, and then made a small *hmmf* noise that certainly sounded to Vir as if he was being dismissed. Then Vallko inclined his head slightly and walked off, the other assorted courtiers following suit, leaving Vir to his own devices.

He saw Senna over in a corner, surrounded by assorted Prime Candidates. He remembered Throk from one of his previous trips to Centauri Prime. The lad had grown by at least half a foot, and he seemed even more forbidding than when Vir had first met him. He also seemed to be paying a good deal of attention to Senna, who was playing and being charming to several of the Candidates. She cast a very quick glance in Vir's direction, and he had a feeling that she would have given anything to break away, but that didn't seem possible. She gave an almost imperceptible shrug and then looked back to Throk, who was babbling on about something that Vir couldn't begin to discern. Throk's attention was taken from Senna at only one point: when Mariel walked by. She didn't appear to notice him, but he reacted to her passing with a sort of goggle-eyed stare before pulling himself back into the moment and returning his attentions to Senna.

"You will never have a better time."

The voice was in his head and Vir jumped slightly. He had forgotten that he had inserted the listening device into his ear, but there came Galen's voice, loud and clear. Galen, of course, was correct. No sign of the emperor, none of the guests was paying him any particular mind. If he felt like strolling around the palace, now was when he should do so.

"Okay," murmured Vir, before remembering that it wasn't a two-way audio link. He checked to make sure that the small triangular recording device was still in place, just under his coat, and then—trying to look as casual as possible—strolled out of the great hall.

He strode up and down the palace corridors in a rather aimless fashion, trying his best to look as casual as possible. He hummed a tune to the best of his recollection, although he suspected that he was botching most of the notes. He walked into this room and that room, as if he were giving himself an extended guided tour. He heard Galen's voice in his head from time to time.

"Vir . . . nothing so far. Keep as you are, though. If I see something that requires further investigation, I will instruct you. Do you understand?"

Vir, to indicate compliance, bowed at the hip, to mimic the shaking of a head. Then he kept moving.

He had gotten to sections of the palace that he had never before been in. At one point he heard footsteps, moving with swift, sure strides. Guards. No one had specifically told him that he wasn't supposed to be there . . . but then again, no one had specifically told him it would be okay.

He glanced around nervously, then saw a large statue to his right. It was Cartagia, of all people. The sight of the emperor whom he had assassinated caused his hearts to skip a beat. The statue was a remarkably powerful, lifelike rendition, superbly carved. The demented smirk was so perfectly rendered that he was certain it had been carved in life. But it had been defaced, someone having scribbled words across the chest. At least, Vir thought it was words, but he didn't recognize them. It said "Sic Semper Tyrannis."

The footsteps were drawing closer. Vir backpedaled and took refuge behind the statue, trying to will himself to be even thinner than he already was. His mind was already racing, trying to determine a cover story. If he was found, he could always say that he had been inspecting the back of the statue for any further damage.

Around the corner they came: two members of the Prime Candidates. Vir could see them clearly from where he was positioned.

Their faces were remarkably slack. The look on them was almost supernatural, as if their minds were elsewhere. Then, right as Vir watched . . . a change passed over their expressions. Their tread slowed, and they looked at one another as if seeing each other for the first time. They glanced around, apparently a little puzzled as to why they were where they were. One shrugged, as did the other, and they continued on their way. They were so caught in their personal moment of befuddlement that neither of them afforded the slightest glance in Vir's direction. He had no idea what to make of what he had just seen.

He started down the corridor once again. He wasn't sure why it should be so, but he felt himself feeling colder. It was purely in his imagination, though—he was sure of that. But he wasn't entirely certain why . . .

Certain why . . .

Why . . .

The next thing he knew, there was a voice in his ear saying, "Vir Cotto. Can you hear me? Is everything all right?"

At first, Vir said nothing. It was as if he had to remind his body to respond to the commands from his brain. Something had completely blanked him out.

"Vir," and Galen's voice was sounding more concerned than before. *It's nice to know he cares*, Vir thought mirthlessly. "Vir, are you . . ."

He still wasn't moving, however, and it was with tremendous effort that he pushed himself forward. His feet felt tremendously heavy, but each step took him farther and farther, and soon he was walking with—if not confidence—at least some degree of surety.

He wasn't sure if it was his imagination again, but it seemed to him as if there was less and less light. What in the world was going on, anyway? It was as if he'd entered a floating black hole.

There was a room off to the left. He glanced in. Nothing. Another room to the right, and still nothing. Every step, though, it was becoming harder and harder to focus. He realized belatedly that the two young Prime Candidates had come from a cross-corridor, and had not actually been in this particular section of the palace at all.

Every nerve in Vir's mind was telling him that he would be well advised to get out of there. But he was concerned that he might not have such an ideal opportunity again. He had to keep moving, had to hope that he was going to be able to pull this together—whatever "this" turned out to be. He suddenly wished that he had a weapon on him, which would have been an interesting experience for him considering that he'd never used one before.

He suddenly realized that he wasn't hearing Galen in his ear anymore. Perhaps the techno-mage simply had nothing to say.

Then he saw the door.

His eye had almost gone right past it, which was curious in and of itself. Given that this was the palace there was nothing extraordinary about it. It was a large double door, decorated with elaborate carvings around the edges. It seemed to have a slight reddish tint to it, although Vir couldn't be certain whether that came from the door itself or was just some sort of trick of the light.

He studied it for a long moment, waiting to see if there was any response from Galen.

Nothing.

The chances were, then, that it was perfectly safe. Either that or Galen wanted him to go in and see what was what.

Once upon a time, Vir would have hesitated. Indeed, he might very well have headed in the opposite direction entirely. But he had been through too much at this point in his life to be afraid of something as benign as a door. Besides . . . he was invincible.

Still . . . even invincibility didn't mean that one couldn't exercise a reasonable amount of caution.

He placed one ear against the door to see if he could hear anything.

It felt like ice.

He pulled his head away, momentarily concerned that the door was so cold that his ear was going to stick to it. It pulled away from the door easily enough, but the sensation had been extremely disconcerting.

"What's going on here?" he wondered out loud. The door was antique, with an elaborate handle on it. It didn't slide open and close automatically like most of the doors in the newer sections of the palace. In a way, Vir felt as if he was stepping back into another time.

He gripped the handle firmly.

In his entire life, Vir had never been as close to death as he was at that moment.

Galen did not panic. Never came close. But he immediately turned to Gwynn and Finian, and said, "We have to get word to him. Have to stop him."

"If we go in, the Drakh will know we're there," Gwynn said flatly. "They were able to detect us within the Shadow base, and that was in unfamiliar territory. They've had several years to lace the palace with detection devices. They'll know the moment we're there."

"We have to do something! Look!" Finian said, pointing at the holographic representation still floating before them.

There was the shimmering outline of the door. And on the other side of it was a distinctive outline—that of a Drakh. There was something else beyond the Drakh, something else in the room that was great and dark and pulsing, and Gwynn couldn't make out at all what it was. But she knew one thing for sure: within seconds, Vir was going to see it, and it would be the last thing he ever saw. For the Drakh, from his body posture, was clearly poised and ready to leap upon Vir the moment the doomed Centauri set foot within. It figured that the Drakh wouldn't simply lock the door in order to prevent intruders from entering. Anyone who was curious enough to intrude into that area was someone the Drakh wanted disposed of.

"There's no time. They have wards against us," Galen said.

"What?" Galen's words were stunning to Gwynn. "They've actually erected wards?"

But Galen wasn't talking to her. Instead he was leaning forward intensely, as if trying to get through to Vir with sheer force of will. He saw Vir's hand entering the holo image, reaching for the handle to open the door. "Vir!" he shouted. "Vir . . . back away from it! Do not go in there! Hear me, Vir! *Vir!*"

"Vir!"

Vir froze in place at the unexpected voice that seemed to explode within his head. He turned and blinked in surprise, like an owl in the full glare of daylight. "Londo?"

The emperor of the great Centauri Republic stood at the far end of the corridor, and it was impossible for Vir to tell what was going through his mind. Was he about to erupt in fury over Vir's presence in this part of the palace? Would he lecture him over his involvement with Mariel? Would he demand to know why Vir had dared set foot back on Centauri Prime when it had been made quite clear to him that the best thing for him to do was stay off the Homeworld for good?

Londo approached him slowly, swaying slightly. Vir tried to determine whether he was drunk, but he didn't think so. Then he realized what it was: Londo was out of breath. It was as if he'd been running from some other point in the palace to get to Vir before . . .

. . . before what?

Vir wanted to glance back at the door, but something stopped him from doing so. He wasn't quite sure why, but he didn't want Londo to realize that he had almost entered there. Or perhaps . . . perhaps Londo already did know. It was so hard to say for sure. Nothing seemed certain anymore.

Londo slowly strode toward him, and Vir braced himself, uncertain of what was about to happen. And then Londo covered the remaining distance between them with quick, urgent steps, and he threw his arms around Vir in a hug so forceful that Vir thought it was going to break his ribs. "It is good to see you," he whispered. "It is very, very good." He separated from him then and gripped Vir firmly by the shoulders. "You," he said decisively, "should always be at my side. That is the way it was meant to be with us, yes?"

"Well, now, I don't know anymore, Londo," Vir said slowly.

"You do not know? Why?"

Londo had a firm arm around Vir's shoulder, and he was starting down the hallway, away from the door. Vir had absolutely no choice but to fall into step next to him. "Well," Vir said reasonably, "the last time we saw each other, you told me that we had separate paths to walk, and we should walk them from a distance. And right before that you knocked me cold because I said . . ." He felt Londo's fingers suddenly clamp onto his shoulders with such force that, with a bit more strength, his arm might find itself dangling from the socket. ". . . because I said something you said I should never say again."

The grip eased, ever so slightly, on his shoulder. "That is correct," said Londo. "But that was last year, Vir. Things change."

"What things have changed, Londo?"

"Have you not noticed? You've had time to mingle here, I take it. Meet and greet all of the various ministers and political heads of

Centauri Prime. Certainly you must have some observations to make regarding them, yes?"

"Well . . ." Vir paused. "Putting aside the fact that I don't know any of them . . ."

"Ah . . . that is not a fact that I would put aside so quickly, Vir. There are no familiar faces anymore, Vir. And those faces that are there . . . they seem to look right through me, as if I were not there. Do you know what, Vir? When enough people look at you as if you are not there . . . do you know what happens next?"

"You . . . stop being there?"

"That," sighed Londo, "is unfortunately absolutely correct. I am not looking to you to be here all the time, Vir." He stopped walking and turned to face Vir, and this time when he took him by the shoulders, it was almost in an avuncular manner. "But your last visit was so unfortunate, so tempestuous . . . I just want you to feel that you can come and go here as you please. That you will not be a stranger here."

"If that's the case, why didn't you simply invite me back here? Why all the subterfuge?"

"Subterfuge?" Londo raised an eyebrow. "I'm not certain exactly what you mean."

There was a hint of warning in his voice, and Vir immediately realized that he had erred. He wasn't sure why or how. It was just the two of them. There was no one else around, as near as Vir could see. Londo didn't even have a retinue of guards following him. So it wasn't as if they had to watch everything they said. Then again . . . how could Vir know for sure? There might be spy devices planted anywhere and everywhere. Why not? After all, he was carrying a device on him that—at that moment—was feeding information directly to Galen.

So if he went into detail as to the little bits of information that Londo had been feeding him, he might very well betray all Londo's efforts, to someone who was listening in on their every word.

The slightest flicker from Vir's gaze to Londo was enough to let the emperor know that he understood. Out loud, however, Vir said mildly, "I suppose 'subterfuge' isn't the right word. I suppose what I'm asking is, why didn't you just come right out and say so."

Londo nodded ever so slightly in mute approval. Without saying a word, they had said everything. The rest was simply for the benefit of whomever else might be listening.

"It is not simply for me to say," Londo answered him. "There are many considerations that must be made these days. For all the power that I wield, there are others whose feelings must be considered."

"Others such as Durla," Vir said hollowly.

Londo inclined his head slightly. "Durla is minister of security. You, Vir, seemed on quite friendly terms with Timov. We know what happened with her."

"But that's—"

Londo didn't let him finish. "And let us not forget that you are stationed on Babylon 5."

Vir wasn't following. "So?"

"So you spend a good deal of time associating with members of the Alliance. They are rather pervasive on Babylon 5, after all. I think—and this is purely my speculation, mind you—I think Durla does not entirely know where your loyalties lie."

"My loyalties?" Vir actually laughed bitterly at that. "Londo, the people on Babylon 5 regard me with suspicion because I'm Centauri. If it weren't for Mariel charming all of them, none of them would even be speaking to me. As it is, even with their speaking to me, I know they still don't trust me. Perhaps I should tell Durla that . . ."

"Oh yesss. Yes, you do that," Londo said with heavy sarcasm in his voice. "You go right to Durla and tell him that the Centauri ambassador to Babylon 5 garners no respect and is not trusted. That is certain to elevate your stature here at court."

He knew Londo was right about that, but wasn't entirely sure where to take it from there. "So . . . so what do you suggest?"

"You are here, Vir. For now . . . that is enough. Durla seems inclined to tolerate your presence here, and that should be enough to keep the situation stable for the time being. From what I understand, Mariel is working the same magic here that she was able to perform on Babylon 5. We have a new court, you see. The stigma attached to her, as a discard of the great Londo Mollari, seems far less problematic for all the new faces presently inhabiting the court. We should not be surprised over that, Vir."

"We shouldn't."

"No. Because, you see, the Centauri have no sense of history. There was a Human who once said 'Those who do not listen to history are doomed to repeat it.' You know," and he chuckled softly, "for a backward race, those Humans certainly know what they're about."

"Did a Human say those words scribbled on Cartagia's statue?"

They had passed the statue only moments before, and Londo

cast a glance behind him, even though the statue was out of sight. His eyebrows knit a moment in confusion, and then he remembered and smiled, showing his pointed canines. "Ahhhh yes. Yes, they did. I wrote them."

"You?" Vir couldn't help letting his surprise be in evidence. "You did?"

"Yes. I wrote them in honor of you . . . our answer to Earth's Abraham Lincoln. Oh, wipe off that innocent look upon you, Vir. Did you think I wouldn't find out? Helping to save the Narns. Do you think me entirely without my own resources, Vir?" He made a scolding, clucking noise with his tongue. "You must think me the greatest fool on Centauri Prime."

"Oh, no, Londo!" Vir protested. "I don't!"

"It's all right, it's all right," Londo told him. "In all likelihood, it's an accurate enough assessment. The point is, Cartagia died at your hand. And part of you . . ." His voice softened. "Part of you died that day, too. Yes?"

"Yes," Vir said softly.

"Well . . . when Abraham Lincoln died, his assassin called out, 'Sic semper tyrannis.' It is an old Earth tongue called Latin. It means 'So is it always with tyrants.' Anyone who is a tyrant can look forward to similar unhappy endings. Words for us both to live by. For me . . . and for you . . . when you are, eventually, emperor."

"The prophecy," Vir sighed. "Sometimes I wonder whether to believe it. Sometimes I wonder whether to believe in anything."

"I stopped wondering about that a long time ago."

"And what was the answer you came up with?"

"Believe in nothing," Londo told him. "But accept everything."

Vir laughed bitterly at that. "And if you do that . . . what? You'll live longer?"

"Oh, Great Maker, I hope not," sighed Londo. "But it will make the time you are here that much more tolerable."

Minister Castig Lione threaded his way through the courtiers and got to Mariel's side. She was deep in pleasant conversation with several others when he placed a hand on her arm and said, "Lady Mariel . . . if I might have a minute of your time?"

"For you, Minister?" She smiled that dazzling smile that could bring most mere mortals to their knees. "Two minutes."

She draped an arm through his elbow and together they moved off from the crowd. Castig Lione guided her, gently but firmly, to his office in another wing. Because of his great height he had to bend somewhat to do so, but he managed to accomplish the task and still look less than foolish. The moment his office door was sealed behind them, he turned to face her with a grim expression on his face. "Would you mind telling me," he said briskly, "what you are playing at, milady?"

"Playing at?" She looked genuinely puzzled. "I do not understand, Minister."

"You, Lady Mariel," and he stabbed a finger at her, "are supposed to be working for this office. You are supposed to be reporting to me. Instead," he said with arch sarcasm, "you appear to be spending most of your time under Ambassador Cotto."

She didn't come close to losing her composure. "Are you implying I am not doing my job, Minister?"

"No, I am not implying it. I am coming right out and saying it. The amount of valuable information you have been turning in regarding the Alliance has dwindled. Need I remind you, milady, that this office is serving to keep your account at a healthy level. You would do well to remember that, unless you believe that Ambassador Cotto's personal fortune will be enough to sustain you."

"Vir is not a rich man, Minister, and furthermore I resent—"

"I resent this game you are playing, Lady Mariel," Lione told her flatly. "Cotto was simply supposed to be a cover, a means to an end. Yet you seem to have lost sight of that and become genuinely enamored of him. That is not tolerable."

"A woman's heart cannot be regulated by memos and mandates, Minister. It's high time you remembered that."

"And it is high time you remembered, milady, that Vir Cotto is—"

"Is not up for discussion, Minister. That aspect of my life is personal."

"A personal life is a luxury you cannot afford to have, milady," Lione shot back.

"As long as I am associated with you."

"Correct."

"Very well," she said with a small shrug. "Then I will resign, effective immediately."

"It is not that simple, milady," Lione said.

"It is for me."

"No. Not for anyone." His voice became low and—most frighteningly—friendly. "You are a spy, Lady Mariel. There are those who would not be pleased to know that their confidences have been leaked to this office. I assure you that I can make certain, with no hint of connection to this office, that some of those individuals find out just what you have been up to."

Mariel glared at him, her jaw steely and twitching. "You would not dare."

"Yes. I would. Tell me, milady . . . how long do you think you would survive then, eh? You and your beloved Vir Cotto. I would not care to take those odds."

She was silent for a long moment. "What do you want?" she finally asked.

"What you do in your own time is of little interest to me, milady. But I want more of your time devoted to me. I want it to be as it was. If it is not," and he smiled, "then it will not be anything. And neither will you. Is that clear . . . Lady Mariel?"

"Perfectly." Her grimness of expression was a marked contrast to Lione's.

"Good. Enjoy the rest of the party, then. And I shall look forward to hearing from you . . . on other matters."

It was the laughter that followed her out that most angered Mariel, and she resolved to make certain that Lione paid for his arrogance at the earliest opportunity.

9

It was early the following morning, and few were stirring within the palace, when Vir quietly made his way out. The one thing that had made the evening slightly bearable was the fact that, when Vir had gotten to the quarters assigned to Mariel and him, Mariel was already asleep.

There was something different about her, he noticed. Usually she appeared utterly relaxed, sleeping the slumber of those who are content with their lives and all the decisions therein. But there was something about her this night that seemed . . . taut. Something was on her mind, and Vir wished that there were a way of climbing into her head and seeing what was in there.

Perhaps Galen could—

No. He pushed that notion straight out of his head, even as he worked his way down to Ghehana.

Despite the ungodliness of the hour, the streets and sidewalks of the seamier side of Centauri Prime were bustling with a variety of individuals with whom Vir would be very happy to have no association whatsoever. Some of them glanced his way, but Vir took care not to make eye contact with anyone. It was a childish notion, he knew, the thought that as long as he didn't actually look at someone, they couldn't harm him. The very idea was enough to make him laugh over the absurdity of it. Except he didn't feel like laughing.

He knew exactly where he was supposed to go, the address having been whispered in his ear. Shortly after Londo had walked with him back to another section of the palace, Galen's whispering had started up within his ear once more. He thought it might be his imagination, but Galen sounded ever so slightly rattled, and even a bit relieved. This actually wasn't a pleasant impression to have. If something had occurred that was enough to disconcert a techno-mage, Vir was rather daunted to think that he might very well have been in the middle of it.

He tried to ignore the steady smell of the area around him. There had been rain earlier, and there were still thick globs of dirt and mud on the streets, which Vir had to do his best to step around. He realized that, if he was going to make any sort of habit of coming down to Ghehana, he was going to need special shoes . . . or, at the very least, shoes he didn't particularly care about.

Someone broke off from the darkness as Vir approached his goal, and for a moment he assumed it to be one of the techno-mages. But instead, it was a surly individual, who eyed Vir balefully. He said in a low, wine-soaked voice, "Give me money."

Vir stopped in his path. "I . . . don't have any money," he said cautiously.

The next thing he knew, there was an object in the man's hand, and he was advancing on Vir. "Find some," he rasped.

Vir's instinct was to run. And then, for no reason that he could readily discern, he suddenly realized that he wasn't afraid. All he felt at that moment was annoyed. The thought of everything that he had been through, all the emotional turmoil that he'd sustained, steeled him. He stopped backing up and instead stood his ground. "Get out of here," he said sharply.

The somewhat drunk and belligerent Centauri who had been advancing on Vir paused, looking confused. Vir realized that he must have looked like fairly easy pickings, and the would-be assailant couldn't understand the abrupt change in Vir's attitude. "What?" he said, sounding rather stupid.

"I said get out of here. I have better things to do than waste time with you."

There was the unmistakable sound of metal sliding from a container, and a sharp blade emerged from the handle in the man's hand. He said nothing more, but came straight at Vir.

Vir backpedaled, but not from fear. Instead, he crouched and scooped up a large handful of dirt and mud. He threw it with a strong sidearm toss, and the thick sludge landed in his attacker's face. The man coughed, blinded, and waved his hands around as if he were capable of gripping handholds floating in the air. Vir, meantime, did not hesitate. He stepped quickly forward and swung his right fist as hard as he could. His knuckles collided with the man's chin and Vir immediately realized that bone striking bone was an extraordinarily stupid idea. His fist seized up and convulsed in pain, and he let out an agonized yelp. His attacker, however, wasn't in a position to hear it, for he went down, apparently unconscious before he even hit the ground. The knife that he had been wielding clattered to the cracked pavement.

A full thirty seconds passed, Vir rooted to the spot. Then he began to tremble as he just stared at the man lying senseless a few feet away. The anxiety of the moment caught up with him, and it was frightening, but it was also exhilarating.

"Nothing like fighting for your life to make you appreciative of it, eh?"

He turned and found Finian standing nearby. The knife was in Finian's hand. He was looking at it, apparently studying his reflection in the blade, which was long and straight. "Nice weapon. Do you want it?"

Vir automatically started to say no . . . except he heard the word "Yes" come out of his mouth.

"Ah. Vir Cotto, hero. Play the role . . . to the hilt," he said dramatically, and he handed the weapon over to Vir, handle first. Vir moaned softly at the pun, but nevertheless retracted the blade and slipped the knife into the inside pocket of his coat. "Come," Finian continued. "This way." With a small smile, he added, "I am pleased that you are here. I feel so much safer now."

Vir let the remark pass. Instead, he followed Finian toward a building, briefly affording a glance at his erstwhile attacker. Odd. His assailant had seemed so big before, somehow. Now he appeared pathetic. And Vir . . . Vir felt tall.

He followed Finian into the nearby structure, and up the narrow steps to a landing where Galen was waiting for him. Galen was simply standing there, holding securely onto his staff and watching Vir with glittering eyes. Gwynn was nearby, her gaze flickering from Vir to Galen and back again.

"You are alive," Galen said. He seemed mildly surprised. For obvious reasons, this did not elevate Vir's spirits. He turned and entered a room.

"Shouldn't I be?" asked Vir, following. He wasn't entirely sure he wanted the answer.

"It was a near thing," Galen told him. "Look."

The holographic image that had been generated via Vir's recording device hung in the air in front of them. His eyes went wide when he saw the creature skulking on the other side of the door that he had been about to open, and another shadowy shape beyond. He could feel all of the resolve and confidence that he had accrued from his encounter outside, and all of it was leaking away from him as he stared, transfixed, at that . . . that . . .

"Shiv'kala." The name suddenly came to him. He looked to Galen for confirmation.

But it was Gwynn who answered. "Quite possible," she said, "although we cannot know for sure. That, however, is not the most disturbing image you will see."

"That isn't?" The notion that there could be worse than that was almost too much for Vir to take. When he thought of how close he had been to mindlessly wandering into the middle of that . . . that Drakh nest . . .

He felt anger bubbling within him, but he wasn't entirely sure where to aim that anger. At first he wanted to direct it at the technomages for thrusting him into the midst of the danger. Then he wanted to unleash it instead at Londo, who had helped to foster an atmosphere in which these . . . these creatures could skulk about. "What could be more disturbing than that?" Vir demanded.

"Do not ask questions, Vir . . . to which you do not really want the answer," Galen replied, but his hand was already moving. It passed through the holographic image, which now was replaced by another, more familiar image than the creature lurking behind the door. There was Londo, bright, smiling, or at least forcing himself to smile. Coming toward him with arms outstretched and cheer etched on his face and . . .

And something else.

Vir leaned forward, not quite sure what it was that he was looking at. "What . . . *is* that?" he whispered.

There was some sort of fleshlike curve on Londo's shoulder. The view of it, however, wasn't as clear as the rest of Londo's image in the picture. Londo drew closer, and now it came into clearer relief. It was like some sort of . . . tumor or . . . something. Vir shook his head in confusion.

"That . . . lump? Is it . . . is it some sort of illness? Why didn't I notice that before?"

"It is a kind of illness, yes. A sickness of the soul, implanted by the Drakh," said Gwynn, speaking with an intense grimness.

"It is called a keeper," Galen told him.

"A keeper? It's . . . *called* something? What do you mean? That thing's not alive, is—"

And then the keeper was looking at him. Its fleshy exterior

stirred, as if from a sleep, and its single, malevolent eye opened and looked straight at him.

Vir let out a shriek of terror. To his own ear it was a pathetic sound, weak and womanish, but he couldn't help it. It was reflex. He backpedaled, his legs going weak, and Finian caught him before he fell. A few minutes earlier, he had brazenly faced off against an armed opponent, and patted himself on the back for his stalwart action. Yet now he was screeching and running from something that wasn't even there.

Except it wasn't simply the image of what he was seeing. It was seeing it perched on the shoulder of someone whom he had once trusted.

And two words went through his head: *Poor Londo*.

"Wh-what does it do? Does it control his actions? Read his mind?"

"In a manner of speaking. It does not superimpose its will upon him . . . but punishes him in a way that can make refusal to cooperate very . . . uncomfortable," Gwynn told him. Her voice seemed to be dripping with disgust; the creature clearly appalled her no less than it did Vir, though she was handling it with a bit more equanimity. But only a bit, which Vir derived some cold comfort from. "Nor does it read his mind . . . but it reports his actions to the Drakh. It is merged with Londo, bonded. It will be with him until he dies."

It happened so quickly that it took Vir completely without warning. Staring into the single eye of that monstrosity, thinking about what it must be like for Londo to have that thing permanently attached to his body—never being alone, never a moment's peace—a wave of nausea swept over him that would not be denied. He felt his gorge rising and stumbled over to a corner of the room. There he heaved until no contents remained within his stomach . . . including, he suspected, a few pieces of the lining. He gasped, revolted at the smell on the floor near his shoes, and then he stepped back. He couldn't bring himself to look directly into the eyes of the technomages, so ashamed did he feel. When he did glance up, Gwynn was looking away; Finian appeared sympathetic, and Galen's face was a mask of unreadability.

It was as if clearing the food from his stomach helped him to focus his thoughts, oddly—and disgustingly—enough. He took a slow, shaky breath and didn't even bother to apologize for his loss of control. After all, what was there to say about that? Instead he said, "That . . . thing . . . the keeper . . . can it be affected by alcohol?"

"Affected?" said Gwynn, looking slightly confused. Vir had a feeling she hadn't expected anything approaching a coherent sentence out of him at that moment, much less a fully formed thought.

"Affected. Impeded. If Londo drinks enough . . ."

"Yesss . . ." It was Galen who spoke. "Yes. The keeper would be susceptible to it. The emperor would be able to operate with a relative amount of privacy."

"And it would probably take less to get the creature drunk than it would Londo," Vir mused thoughtfully.

It was all becoming clear to Vir. With the mental picture of that frightening, single eye seared into his brain, it was as if he was suddenly seeing the past with true clarity. Things Londo had said, attitudes, passing comments . . . they all made sense now. And . . .

And Timov . . . well, that was obvious, too, now, wasn't it. She *had* to be gotten rid of, forced to leave. Vir's belief that they were becoming closer hadn't been his imagination after all. That had been what prompted her precipitous departure. Londo must have engineered it, doing so not because he truly wanted her to depart, but because he was concerned over her getting too close. What sort of true intimacy could anyone develop with a sentient pustule seated upon one's shoulder, observing every moment of intimacy?

All of Londo's actions were comprehensible . . . and pitiable . . . and . . .

Great Maker, what had Londo gotten himself into?

"Could they have implanted the creature against his will?" Vir asked hollowly.

Galen shook his head. "No. He may have had trepidation about it . . . but ultimately, the bonding can only occur when the recipient is willing to allow it to happen."

What hold could they possibly have had upon him? How could they have forced him to endure such an invasion of his body, of his mind? Could it be that he actually welcomed it? Vir found that inconceivable. Londo had too much pride. To permit a creature whose perpetual presence would remind him that he was nothing but a puppet of shadow-dwelling monsters—there was no way that Londo would have welcomed such a thing.

And if they did force it upon him in some way, how horrific must that have been for him? To stand there, helplessly, while that . . . that thing was bonded to him, for life . . .

Vir had no idea what to feel. Suspicion, fear, horror, pity, all warred for dominance in him.

"I have to talk to him," Vir said. "I have to let him know that I know. I have to—"

"Are you that eager to be a dead man?" Galen asked bluntly.

"No, of course not, but—"

"Acknowledge the keeper, you doom yourself. It is your choice."

"Galen is correct," Finian said. He did not look unsympathetic to Vir's plight, but it was clear that he was firmly in Galen's court on this. "Look what happened to you with the passing mention of Shiv-'kala, one of the Drakh. If you let Londo know that you are aware of the keeper's presence, the Drakh will likely not let you draw your next breath."

"It was one of your kind who told me to mention Shiv'kala in the first place. And you almost sent me wandering straight into a death trap in the palace," Vir said hotly. "How nice to know that you've suddenly started worrying about my welfare. Why? Because you think you're going to need me for something else, as well?"

"We did not intend for you to wander into a death trap," Galen said. "We lost contact with you. Undoubtedly due to interference by the Shadow tech. I regret the inconvenience."

"Inconvenience! If I'd walked into that room, I would have been dead!"

"And we would have been inconvenienced," Galen replied levelly.

"Ha. Ha. Ha," Vir said, making no effort to hide his lack of amusement at Galen's retort. Then he turned back to the holograph which had shifted angle. Londo had draped an arm around Vir's shoulder as they walked. And there, from this new perspective, Vir saw the keeper even closer than before. There it had been, mere inches from his face, peering at him with that unblinking, unnatural eye, and he had not known. He could feel it now, boring into his brain . . .

"Shut it off," Vir said.

"It will be instructive to observe the—"

"Shut it off!"

Galen stared mildly at Vir for a moment, then waved his hand slightly and the image disappeared.

No one said anything for quite some time. Finally, it was Gwynn who stepped forward, and said to Vir, "You begin to understand what we are up against."

"What we've seen here," Finian pointed out, "is only that which a cursory examination of the palace was able to uncover. There is likely much, much more. The Drakh infestation goes straight to the heart and soul of Centauri Prime."

"A heart that is clotted. A soul that is blackened," said Vir. He was shaking his head, scarcely able to accept what his own eyes had seen and what he knew now to be absolutely true. "Do I tell Londo? Go on a drinking binge, put the keeper out, find a way to tell him I know?"

"Absolutely not," Gwynn said forcefully, and there was shaking of heads from the other two techno-mages, indicating their agreement. "The situation is not only as bad as we feared, but worse. We had been holding out hope that, with you serving as a positive influence upon him, Londo could be won over to our cause and help to eradicate the Drakh. We know now that cannot possibly be the case."

"Absolutely correct," Finian confirmed. "Londo cannot be trusted. It's that simple."

"It's more complicated than that," Vir shot back. "Despite everything that's gone on—in fact, now that I know the truth, it's more like, *because* of everything that's gone on—Londo is my friend. He—"

"He cannot be trusted," Galen said, indicating that the subject did not warrant discussing.

"It's not just a matter of trust. We need to help him."

"You wish to help him? Kill him."

The cold-bloodedness of Galen's suggestion was horrifying to Vir. "Kill him. Just like that," he echoed with incredulity.

"Just like that, yes."

"I, personally, don't expect you to do that, Vir," Gwynn said with a glance to Galen, "but, in many ways, you would be doing him a great favor."

"Forget it. He's my friend."

"He's their ally. That is all that matters."

"Not to me, Galen. Not to me," he said with fiery strength in his voice and growing contempt for the techno-mages. "You know what? You know what? In a lot of ways, you're no different than the Drakh. Hell, no different than the Shadows. You use people for your own ends, and you don't give a damn who gets hurt as long as your goals are accomplished."

"We are more like our enemies than we care to admit," Galen said, which surprised Vir somewhat. He hadn't expected any sort of confirmation of a sentiment spoken mostly in anger. "Nevertheless, there are . . . differences."

"Such as?"

"We have more charm, and we're better dancers," Finian offered.

Everyone stared at him.

"I thought the moment might benefit from a bit of humor," he said.

"Would that something humorous had actually been said." Gwynn sniffed.

"Fine, then," Finian said, obviously annoyed that his moment of levity had been so soundly rebuffed. "So what do you suggest we do?"

"The information must come from someone trustworthy," Galen said thoughtfully, stroking his chin. "There are those who will not trust anything associated with a techno-mage. There is one reasonable course of action. I shall tell Gideon. He, in turn, will convey what we have learned to the Alliance, where—"

"Where they can bomb us into nonexistence?" said an alarmed Vir. "They'll learn of something Shadow-related existing on Centauri Prime, assume the worst—"

"Probably a safe assumption," Gwynn said.

Vir pointedly ignored the comment, and continued, "—and the bombs will start dropping again. And this time they won't back off until they've flattened us."

"Sheridan, then," suggested Finian. "Gideon trusts Sheridan. If he—"

"Not Sheridan. Not Gideon. Not nobody," Vir said with an air of finality. "This is an internal problem on Centauri Prime. So we'll handle it internally. That's all."

"There is far more at stake here than that," Gwynn made clear to him. "We're not talking about some low-level politician lining his pockets with graft. We are speaking of an entire race using Centauri Prime as its stronghold, with a biologic weapon perched on the shoulder of your world's emperor . . ."

"That's right. My world. *My* world," Vir said in no uncertain terms. "And I will attend to my problems on my world, and we will keep them that way. I don't want others catching wind of this. If they do, it'll be a bloodbath, and I will not be a part of that."

Gwynn appeared ready to square off and go head to head with him, possibly on matters of priorities, or possibly just to have the opportunity to beat the crap out of him. But the slightest touch of Galen's hand on her shoulder stilled her. Vir wondered whether Galen was simply quite persuasive, or whether there had been some ensorcellment employed. Galen looked him up and down, and finally asked, "What, then, will you be a part of, Vir Cotto?"

"I won't turn against Centauri Prime."

"You have to do something. You cannot simply walk away from what you have seen here."

"I'll keep an eye on things. Keep myself apprised. Learn what there is to learn, make certain that things don't go too far . . . or if they do, then I can . . . I can . . ."

"Then you can what?" said Galen.

"Then I can make them go back to the way they were."

Galen shook his head. He did not look particularly convinced, and Vir couldn't entirely blame him. He didn't sound especially convincing. But he spoke with a conviction that he was not entirely certain he felt. "Look, the fact is, you need me."

"Do we?" There was cold amusement reflected in Galen's eyes.

"You said it yourself. You need me to put something together. I can do that, but it will have to be done slowly. It's obvious now that I can come and go as needed."

"Coming and going may be insufficient."

"Then what would be sufficient, Galen?" demanded Vir in exasperation. Before the techno-mage could say anything, he suddenly put up a hand. "No. Never mind. I know what to do."

"What?"

"It's enough that I know. Let's leave it at that."

"Let's not," Galen said firmly.

Their gazes met, and Vir knew that Galen wasn't about to let this go. It was obvious that the techno-mage was not happy at all with the notion of simply keeping covered up the darkness that had infested Centauri Prime. He was obviously still leaning toward making public the firsthand proof they had acquired. But Galen knew that, in doing so, he was effectively dooming all of Centauri Prime. The Alliance would not see the Drakh influence as a cancer that could be surgically removed; they would simply sweep in and kill the patient, and then pat themselves on the back for a job well done.

It was Gwynn, however, who spoke, as if she had read his mind. "You desire to know how we are different from the Drakh, Vir? The Drakh would put your race on the firing line and care nothing for their actions. The death or survival of the Centauri carries no weight with them, one way or the other, except in terms of how it serves their interests. We do not wish to be the bearers of information that will cause the demise of the Centauri, unless we have to. Provide us with reasons not to, and we will be able to cooperate with you. But you must give us something—or we can give you nothing."

So he told them what he had in mind.

To a great degree, he was making up his strategies as he went. He was fully cognizant of the fact that they would take time, and he made that clear to them, as well. The technomages listened patiently, thoughtfully, and when he was done, they looked at one another. To Vir, it seemed as if they were communing. He had no idea whether that was within their power to do, and at that moment he didn't care overmuch. All that mattered was making sure that Centauri Prime survived for as long as possible. Every day that passed meant another day that the Drakh could spread their influence . . . but it also meant another day that his people were alive, and where there was life, there was hope.

"Very well, Vir," Galen said after a time. "I still do not approve—"

"I don't need your approval," Vir interrupted. "Just your silence."

"For now."

Vir inclined his head slightly in acknowledgment. "For now, yes."

"Good luck to you, then," Finian said. "There's a good deal riding on your ability to accomplish these things, Vir."

"Are you vaguely under the impression that I'm unaware of that?" Vir said, sounding more snappish than he would have liked, but understandably so given the circumstances, he thought. "Now if you'll excuse me—"

He turned, and suddenly Galen said, "Oh, and Vir . . . one other thing . . ."

Vir whirled toward him, his patience as frayed as rotting leather. "What, Galen? What 'one other thing' are you going to toss at me now? That I should be careful because I'm risking not only my life, but also those of others? That I shouldn't trust you to keep your silence? That out there, the people of Centauri Prime are blissfully sleeping, unaware of the fact that we are conspiring to try and prevent them from certain annihilation, and that I'm probably never going to sleep again? That my best, and possibly only, friend in the world, has a one-eyed parasite on his shoulder and is suffering every hour of every day, and that the only way he'll ever know peace is in the grave, and I can't do a damned thing about it, so I shouldn't let it worry me? Is that what you are going to say?"

Very mildly, Galen replied, "No, I was going to say you might want to remove the microphone from your ear. It won't stay in there forever, and you shouldn't have to answer questions if it falls out at an inopportune time."

"Oh. Uhm . . ."

But there didn't seem to be a lot he could say in response to that.

He tapped the device out of his ear into his palm, placed it on a table, and walked out without a look back.

"That man," Finian said, "is the last, best hope for peace in the galaxy."

"I think I'm the one who's going to have trouble sleeping tonight," Gwynn said dourly.

I wish there were some way I could have prevented it.

Alas, poor Vir. It was inevitable, I suppose. Here he was, the poor fellow, making another return visit to Centauri Prime, in the company of Mariel. And he leaves without her. In a way, it is the most beneficial thing that could have happened to him. What is most remarkable is the brave face that he is putting on it. But I do not believe it. Vir is the type to give his heart fully, and not wisely, and he could not have committed a more grievous error than giving it to Mariel.

But to lose her to . . . that . . . person? Feh. Whatever difficulties I may have with Mariel, no matter how poisonous I consider her, it grieves me to see Vir hurt . . . . even as I am led to believe that this is probably the best thing that might have happened to him.

10

Durla leaned forward in his chair, clearly not certain that he had heard Vir properly. "Do I . . . what?" he asked.

"Want her," Vir said flatly. He was speaking with a remarkable air of boredom and disdain that Durla would never have thought possible from the ambassador. It was possible that he had underestimated him. But before he made any adjustments in his view of Vir, he had to fully understand what it was that Vir was asking. "Do you want Mariel?" Vir repeated.

"Ambassador," Durla said in a slow, measured tone, "putting aside for a moment my personal wants and desires . . . the lady Mariel is a free woman. She cannot be bartered."

"Women," Vir said, "do as they're told. Of course," he added ruefully, "they have an annoying way of letting us know what they want so we can tell them to do it, eh?"

Minister Durla had trouble believing this was the same person he had met with on Babylon 5, in the Zocalo, a little less than a year ago. Vir seemed so . . . so blasé. So world-weary. Durla had also believed that, when they had first met, Vir had felt some degree of trepidation toward him. Now, however, the ambassador was speaking as if they were old friends. Durla wasn't entirely certain what was prompting this degree of familiarity, and although he also was not sure that he appreciated it, he wasn't entirely sure that he disliked it, either. He had thought he'd had Vir Cotto fairly well pegged as a harmless buffoon. If he was wrong about that, then it might be entirely possible that Cotto actually posed a threat. On the other hand, he might also prove useful. It was far too soon to make a judgment.

"Certainly," Vir continued, "you must have noticed that the lady Mariel is paying an annoying amount of attention to you."

"She seemed . . . quite friendly, yes," said Durla. "But I wasn't attributing it to anything save general sociality."

The truth, of course, ran far deeper than that.

Durla had known Mariel since they were both young, and he was in love with her, had been for as long as he could remember. She had always aroused a hunger within him as no other woman had, before or since. In order to attract her attention and interest, he had raised her from obscurity—a condition prompted when Londo Mollari had dismissed her—and assigned her to work under Chancellor, and later Minister, Lione. She owed everything about her current return to status to Durla, and he had silently—and foolishly, it seemed—waited for her to notice and appreciate him.

Instead she had hooked up with Vir, so that Durla barely made any impression on her. It had been enough to drive him to paroxysms of fury.

When he had finally managed to calm down—a process that had required several months—he had decided that he had had enough of subterfuge. Under the guise of desiring the return of Vir Cotto and a reinstatement of his relationship with the emperor, all out of his concern for Londo's well-being, of course, Durla had arranged for Vir and Mariel to be his occasional guests. During that time, he had done everything that he could to attract her notice, to impress her with his power and privilege. That was, after all, what she ultimately sought.

However, it had seemed to him that his efforts had remained utterly in vain. Oh, she was polite enough, charming enough . . . but she spoke incessantly of Vir and of how wondrous an individual he was, to the point where Durla was wondering why he had even bothered. He had reached a point where he had resigned himself to never having Mariel, because he couldn't begin to understand how the woman's mind worked.

And now, all of a sudden, Vir had simply wandered into his office, dropped down into a chair opposite Durla's desk, and began chatting. From nowhere, his "offer" in regard to Mariel had been broached. Durla wanted to think it some sort of absurd joke. After everything he had done, after the scheming and involved placement of individuals . . . it couldn't be that simple, could it?

"It's more than being sociable, I assure you," said Vir. For a moment he looked uncomfortable and fidgeted slightly in his chair. He lowered his voice slightly, and asked, "Can I trust your discretion, Minister?"

"Of course! Absolutely," Durla said.

"Because I have my pride, the same as any man. And this, well . . . this situation . . . is not one that I am exceedingly pleased over."

"It never leaves this room," Durla assured him.

Vir leaned forward, his fingers interlaced, and in a low voice—as if concerned that they were being overheard—he said, "The fact is, the woman doesn't stop talking about you. Whenever we are alone, and even in the company of others back on Babylon 5, she speaks of nothing *but* you."

"When she is with me, she speaks only of you."

Vir waved dismissively. "A cover, nothing more. She is a subtle creature, the lady Mariel, and it wouldn't be in character for her to speak so effusively of you when you're near her. But she hasn't been covering as well lately as she had been. You must have noticed."

Durla thought about it, and realized that Vir was right. She had been looking at Durla differently. Her hand, lighting upon his shoulder, had remained a bit longer than would have been normal. She had definitely been more flirtatious.

He had been afraid to hope, though . . . hadn't dared allow himself . . .

"But what she says to me in private, well . . ." Vir shook his head. "She's made her sentiments quite clear. The simple fact is that she wants you, Durla. She's dying to be with you. And, to be blunt, I'm getting tired of listening to it. Listening to her pining away. And as for our sex life, well," and he snorted ruefully. "How do you think I felt when she cried out, 'Oh yes, yes, Durla, yes!' at exactly the time you wouldn't want to hear another man's name mentioned. I mean, honestly!"

"How . . . how embarrassing that must have been for you. And to admit it now . . . But . . ." He shook his head. "I don't understand. If she desires to be with me, why doesn't she just . . . I mean, she is not your chattel, your property . . ."

Vir looked even more uncomfortable than before. "Well, to be honest . . . in a way, she is."

His eyes narrowed. "What do you mean?"

"I mean," Vir said with a great sigh, as if unspooling a deep secret, "that the Lady Mariel is not . . . how shall I put it . . . not with me completely of her own free will."

At first Durla had no idea at all what Vir could possibly mean. But then he did. In a hoarse whisper, he said, "You're . . . blackmailing her?"

Vir looked taken aback. "Blackmail? You accuse me of blackmailing my own paramour for the purpose of getting her to be with me?"

"My apologies, Ambassador, I didn't mean—"

"Don't apologize. That's pretty much it."

Durla had no idea what to say. On the one hand, he found it repulsive. On the other hand, he almost admired Cotto for the sheer audacity—to say nothing of the almost jovial way in which he admitted to it. "What are you, uhm . . . how do . . . that is to say . . ."

"What am I blackmailing her with?" He shrugged. "It really wouldn't be honorable of me to say, now, would it."

"Perhaps. But then again, it isn't exactly honorable of you to have blackmailed her in the first place."

"A good point," admitted Vir. "But then again, a man who lusts after a female will do just about anything. Besides . . . she served a very specific purpose. She made me look good."

"Look good?" Then he understood almost immediately. "To others on Babylon 5."

"Exactly. You know, Durla, you've seen her. A man with a woman like that on his arm, fawning over him . . . it can't help but raise him in the estimation of other men. But let's be honest, okay?" He leaned forward. "Look at me. Seriously, look at me. Do I look like the kind of man that a woman like Mariel would be drawn to? I have my moments, certainly, but let's face it: I'm not her type. You see, though, why I wouldn't want this information to leave the room."

"Of course, of course. For others to think that she stayed with you simply out of fear that you would expose her via some . . . extortionist threat. Still . . . you are essentially saying you want to be free of her, for all intents and purposes. To 'give her' to me, as you put it." He leaned back in his chair, his fingers interlaced. "Why? If there is one thing that I have learned, Ambassador, it is that people rarely act out of the goodness of their hearts. Generally speaking, they want something. What do you want?"

Vir let out a long, unsteady breath. Some element of his polished demeanor seemed to be slipping, and it might well be that his genuine emotions were beginning to slip through. Without looking at Durla, he said, "Believe it or not, Minister—I was once a decent man. A man who never would have dreamt of forcing a woman to be with him. I . . . used to be someone else. Someone I liked better." His gaze flickered back to Durla. "I have been viewing some of Minister Vallko's prayer meetings lately. Got them via vid delay on Babylon 5. Even went to one in person this morning. And he was talking about what Centauri Prime should be, and what we should be. Of what we should be living up to, and how we should be aspiring to what we once were."

"The minister is a very inspirational speaker," agreed Durla. His chest swelled slightly with pride. "I chose him, you know. As our spiritual minister."

"Did you. I'm not surprised." He let out his breath in a slow, steady stream. "In any event . . . I was thinking about what he said . . . about being what we once were. And I found I was getting . . . nostalgic, I guess is the right word. Nostalgic for the kind of man who would never have done what I was doing. I suppose that sounds ridiculous."

"No. Not at all."

"Of course, there's the question of whether you are interested in her?" His eyebrows arched in curiosity. "Are you?"

It was everything that Durla could do, all the control he could muster, not to shout *Yes! Yes! For as long as I can remember! For as long as I have felt passion for any woman, I have wanted her!* Instead he was the picture of calm as he said, "She is not . . . unattractive. Indeed, some might even term her vivacious. I admit, I have not been particularly aggressive in the pursuit of women as of late. There have been so many things on my mind. It is difficult to attend to affairs of the heart when one is weighed down by affairs of the state."

"Oh, absolutely . . . absolutely. Still . . . we have a problem here. Perception is everything, as I'm sure you know. I am trying to do the right thing, but I do not need people to believe that I was tossed aside by the lady Mariel in favor of you. I don't have to tell you how that will make me look." Durla nodded, and Vir continued, "Nor do I desire that people know the circumstances under which Mariel stayed with me. You, on the other hand, don't want people thinking that you are getting a woman who was tossed aside by not only the emperor, but by the ambassador of Babylon 5. That, likewise, would not reflect well on you."

"All valid points."

Vir leaned forward intently. "How much do you like her? Really like her, I mean?"

Durla looked at him askance. "What," he said slowly, "are you suggesting?"

Vir smiled. "Are you a gambling man?" he asked.

"Under the right circumstances," said Durla. "Tell me what you have in mind."

Ever since the bombing, there had been a systematic eradication of anything remotely related to Humans, Earth, or the Interstellar

Alliance in general. For a while Humans and their assorted absurd influences had been stylistically quite popular on Centauri Prime, but ever since Earth had become the mortal enemy, Vallko had been calling for an aggressive return to the Centauri roots. Naturally, the Centauri had been happy to accommodate him in all things.

Or nearly all things. With one notable exception that proved particularly convenient in Vir's current plan.

Poker.

The insidiously addictive card game had worked its way so thoroughly into Centauri culture that, no matter what Vallko might demand in terms of isolationist activities, no one—especially the upper classes, with whom it was so popular—was inclined to give up what had become a preferred pastime. So a rumor was begun that poker had actually been invented by an early Centauri ambassador, who had in turn introduced it to Humans, and so the game continued in its popularity.

This particular evening, a fairly brisk game was underway. Londo knew that it was happening, and as he sat in the throne room, he thought of how—once upon a time—he would have joined them. Now, of course, he was emperor. It would be considered unseemly, inappropriate. What would people think?

"I am the emperor," he said out loud with a sudden start of realization. "Who cares what people think?"

He rose from his throne and headed for the door. Throk was immediately at his elbow, saying, "Highness, I thought you said you were staying in for the evening . . ."

"As I do every evening. I tire of repetition. Life is too short, Throk. We go."

"Where do we go, Highness?"

Londo turned to him, and said, "In my day, I was quite the poker player. I understand there is a game going on right now. Take me to it."

"Highness, I don't know that—"

"I don't believe I asked for your opinion on the matter, Throk," Londo told him flatly. "Now . . . will you do as I instruct, or must I attend to this on my own . . . and find a way to make my displeasure clear to you at a later date?"

Moments later, an uneasy Throk was leading Londo down a long corridor. From the far end of the hall they actually heard laughter. It seemed to Londo he could not recall the last time he had heard anything approaching genuine merriment in the palace. Instead the place seemed to be suffocating in intrigue, backroom politics, and deals that usually did not bode well for the good people of Centauri Prime.

The laughter approached a truly high-decibel level, and he could make out people speaking in a scoffing tone, apparently not believing something that one of them was saying. Londo could make out a few words here and there: "He's not serious." "A bold move." "You would not dare."

And then there was a sudden silence.

At first Londo thought that the abrupt cessation of noise might be due to his arrival on the scene, but as he entered he saw that all attention was focused away from the door and instead on two players at the table. His blood froze when he saw who they were.

One of them was Vir. The other was Durla. Each was peering at the other over fans of cards that they were clutching in their respective hands. Also seated around the table were Kuto, Castig Lione, and Munphis, the newly appointed minister of education and one of the most singularly stupid men that Londo had ever met. Their cards were down; clearly they were not part of this confrontation.

Londo wasn't sure whether he was happy or distressed that Vir was among them. The more acceptance that Vir had among the ministers, the easier it would be for him to come and go, and therefore the more likely it would be that Londo could have him around to chat with whenever he desired. On the other hand, the last thing he wanted was for Vir to become like those power-grubbing predators.

"Did I come at a bad time?" inquired Londo.

They looked at him then, and started automatically to rise. "No, no, don't get up," he said, gesturing for them to remain where they were. "I was thinking of joining you . . . but matters seem a bit intense at the moment. I assume there are some elevated stakes before us?"

"You could say that," Vir commented.

Kuto stirred his bulk around on his chair to face the emperor, and said, "The ambassador has wagered his paramour."

"What?" The words didn't entirely make sense to Londo at first, but then he understood. He looked at Vir incredulously. "You are . . . not serious."

Vir nodded.

As much antipathy as Londo felt for Mariel, something about this made his stomach turn.

"Vir, she is a free woman. You cannot 'wager' her . . ."

"Actually, I can. She will respect a debt of honor, should it come to that," Vir told him.

"But how can you use her as you would a ... a marker!" demanded Londo.

"Because I was out of money," Vir said reasonably. "And besides ..." Vir gestured for him to come over and, when he did so, held up his cards. Londo looked at them. Four kings.

"Oh. That's how," said Londo.

"The ambassador is seeking to cause me to rethink the wager," Durla said thoughtfully. "And the emperor is aiding him in this. Hmm. Whether to take the bet or not. A considerable amount of money and a woman on the line. The woman has no true monetary value, for her own resources are limited, but there is a certain ... nostalgia value to her. What to do, what to do." He looked at his own hand, and then said, "Very well. The bet is called."

Vir placed his cards down triumphantly, a smile splitting his face. Durla blinked in obvious surprise. "That," he said, "I was not expecting."

"Thank you," said Vir, reaching for the chips that represented his winnings.

But without taking a breath, Durla continued, "Just as, I am sure, you were not expecting ... this." And, one by one, he placed four aces upon the table.

There was a stunned hush around the table. Londo looked from one to the other, waiting for some sort of word, some type of reaction. And then Vir laughed. He laughed long and loud, and then reached over and gripped Durla's hand firmly. "Well played!" he said. "Very well played! I will inform Mariel at once."

"You are an honorable man, Vir Cotto," Durla said formally, "and a most formidable opponent. I have nothing but the greatest respect for you."

Vir bowed graciously, and stepped back from the table.

"*Viiir*. A moment of your time," Londo said, falling into step beside him, and they walked out of the room together. Londo opened his mouth to speak, then became aware of the footsteps behind them. Without even looking back, he said, "Throk, some privacy if you would not mind."

Throk, by this point in their relationship, knew better than to argue, and he faded back from the scene.

"Vir," Londo said briskly, "what do you think you have done? Might not Mariel have something to say in this matter?"

"Not really," said Vir coolly. "She won't mind. To be honest, I think she was getting bored with Babylon 5, and nostalgic for the halls of home. What's the matter, Highness? Don't want to have to deal with her hanging about the palace? Worried?"

"No, I am not worried . . ."

"You should be," Vir's voice suddenly grew harsh. "She tried to kill you, Londo. We both know that. Oh, she claimed it was an accident. She said she had no idea that the statue was rigged. But it's not true." All the words came out in a rush. "She knew before she set foot on Babylon 5 that you were planning to divorce two of your wives, and she wasn't going to take any chances. She'd had past dealings with Stoner, and arranged with him to bring the artifact to Babylon 5 for 'resale.' When Stoner sold it to a merchant, he slipped the merchant a note that a certain elegant Centauri woman would come by and express interest in it . . . and that she would simply point rather than pick it up, since the touch of any Centauri would trigger it. So if you have any sympathy for her, Londo, I wouldn't if I were you."

Londo was stunned by the outpouring of information. "How do you know all this?"

"She told me."

"And she told you . . . why?"

"Because I asked her. Recently, in fact. Oh, but don't worry, Londo . . . she's no threat to you anymore. She has . . . other considerations."

"Vir, putting aside what you have told me—and I admit, it is a good deal to put aside—I was not concerned about Mariel so much as I was about you."

"Me? Why? I would think you'd be happy I'm quit of her."

"Because," Londo gestured helplessly, "she seemed to make you happy. I thought she had, perhaps, changed. Yet now I see," and his gaze searched Vir's face for some sign of the naive young Centauri he had once known, "that she has not changed half as much as you."

"I grew up, Londo. That's all," Vir told him. "It happens to all of us. Well . . . all of us except Peter Pan."

"What?" Londo blinked in confusion. "Who?"

Vir waved him off. "It doesn't matter. Londo, look . . . with all respect to you and your position and everything . . . just stay out of it, okay? This simply isn't your concern."

And with that he picked up the pace and hurried off to his quarters, leaving an extremely perplexed emperor in his wake.

* * *

Mariel had almost finished gathering her things when there came a chime at the door. "Yes?" she called as the door slid open, and then she blinked in surprise. "Well. To what do I owe the honor?"

Londo entered, his hands draped behind his back, and he said, "Hello, Mariel. You are looking well."

"Greetings, Highness. Should I bow?" She made a formal curtsy.

"Oh, I think there is little need for such formalities between us, my dear." He approached her slowly and carefully, as if she were an explosive. "So tell me, Mariel . . . what is your game this time, eh?"

"My game?"

"You have switched allegiances, I hear. From Vir to Durla. Decided that he represents your best hope at getting up in the world?"

"In case you had not heard, Londo," she said evenly, "I was not present at the game where I was bartered away. No one asked me my opinion. But Vir has made it quite clear to me that his honor is on the line. I have been given no choice in the matter. Besides—" she shrugged "—Durla is a pretty enough man. He seems to fancy me. He is well positioned within the government. Vir had charm and humor, but that will only go so far. This is a fairly practical happenstance for me. And I have long ago lost any illusions as to what my purpose in life is."

"And what would that purpose be?"

"Why, Londo . . . to make men happy, of course. Did I not do that for you?" She smiled sweetly and traced the line of his chin with one slim finger. "There are some things in which I have always excelled."

"Including manipulation of events when they suit your fancy. Answer me truthfully, Mariel, if such a concept is not entirely foreign to you: Did you arrange that card game somehow? Did you mastermind this entire business?"

"Why on Earth would I need to 'mastermind' anything, Londo?" she demanded, a bit of the carefully held sweetness slipping away. "If I decided I preferred Durla to Vir, what was to stop me from simply approaching Durla . . . especially if, as you likely suspect, I care nothing for Vir save how he suits my purposes. Why would I feel the need to resort to some sort of convoluted business with a card game?"

"I do not know," Londo said thoughtfully. "But if I find out . . ."

"If you find out, then what, Londo? All parties are satisfied with the outcome of what transpired this evening around that table. The only one who seems to have difficulties with it is you, and you are not involved."

He took a step toward her, and in a flat voice said, "It occurred on Centauri Prime. I, the emperor, *am* Centauri Prime. That makes me involved. Something in this business is not right."

"Something on this planet is not right, Londo. Perhaps you'd better serve the interests of Centauri Prime if you concentrated on that, rather than the outcome of a hand of poker."

The door opened once more and a member of the Prime Candidates was standing there. "Lady Mariel," he said with a sweeping bow, "I was sent by Minister Durla . . ."

"Yes, of course. That bag, and that one there," she pointed to several packed suitcases. "I have arranged for my belongings from Babylon 5 to be sent to me as soon as possible." She turned to Londo and looked at him with wide, innocent eyes. "Is there anything else, Highness? Or am I dismissed?"

His jaw shifted several times as if he were cracking walnuts with his teeth. "Go," he said finally.

"By your leave," she said with another elaborate curtsy, and she headed off down the hall, leaving Londo scowling furiously and wondering what in the world had just happened.

She had haunted his dreams.

The dream image of Mariel had come to him, years ago, and told him to begin the dig upon K0643. And in later months, the dreams of Mariel had made repeat visits, and told him to do other things. She had been his dream guide, the means by which his mind had worked and planned and plotted the destiny that Centauri Prime was to follow. At first when she had come to him in his dreams, he had not remembered it upon waking. But in later weeks and months, the fragments had coalesced. The connection, the bond between them—spiritually, only, of course—had become more firm, more intertwined, with every bit of guidance that his subconscious mind had given him. He had even taken to sleeping with a recording device next to him, so that if he happened to wake up during one of his dream sessions, he would be able to grab the device and make a record of whatever thought had occurred to him. That way nothing would ever be lost.

And in many of those dreams, she had promised that, sooner or later, she would be his. All it would take was patience and dedication, and she would eventually come to him of her own volition.

Now it had happened.

He could scarcely believe it.

She stood there in his room, clad in a gown so sheer that—at certain angles of light—it was practically invisible. "Hello, Minister," she said.

He entered the room on legs that suddenly felt leaden. "Greetings, Lady," he replied, and he realized that his voice sounded rather hoarse. He cleared it forcefully. "I think you should know that . . . if you desire no part of this . . ."

She came slowly toward him. To Durla, it seemed as if she were gliding across to him on ice, so minimal were her movements, so gracefully did she walk. She faced him and draped her arms around his shoulders. "I am," she said softly, "exactly where I wish to be . . . with exactly who I wish to be."

"This is . . . so abrupt," he said.

But she shook her head. "To you, perhaps. But for me, it has been long in coming. I have admired you from afar, Durla . . . Certainly you must have realized that when you came to Babylon 5."

"You spoke mostly of Vir."

She laughed, her voice chiming like a hundred tiny bells. "That was to make you jealous, my dear Durla. Certainly a man of the world such as yourself must have seen through it. A man who has accomplished all that you have accomplished, done all the things that you have done. Why you," and she began to undo the top of his shirt, "are the single greatest leader on this planet. Everyone knows that."

"Everyone does, eh?" His pride was swelling, and that wasn't the only thing.

"Of course! Who is it who conceives of, and oversees, all the reconstruction projects? Who is the power behind the emperor, developing programs, picking the key people for the right positions? Who has a true vision of what this world should be? Who stirs the people's hearts and souls? Did you not conceive of the Tower of Power? Did you not handpick Vallko to uplift the spirits of all Centauri Prime? And who knows what other grand plans you have!"

"They are grand, yes." He paused. "Do you want me to tell you about them? Are you interested?"

"I am interested only in that they are reflections of your greatness," Mariel said, and her warm breath was in his ear. He thought his legs were going to give way, and it was all he could do to remain standing. "But we need not hear of such matters now. We have other things to do . . . things of much greater interest," and she took his face in her hands, "and you have been waiting for them . . . for quite some time. Haven't you."

He nodded. His throat was seized up; he couldn't get a word out.

"Well, you don't have to wait any longer," she said, and she kissed him slowly, languorously.

Their lips parted, and he whispered, "You knew . . . somehow you knew, all this time, didn't you."

"Of course I knew."

"About the dreams . . . how you've been in them . . ."

Her gaze flickered for just the briefest of moments, and he took it to be confirmation of all his beliefs. Then he was entirely caught up in the moment, as she said quickly, "Yes, all about the dreams. All about all of it. And this is where we are meant to be now, Durla . . . our time and our place."

She was undoing something at her shoulders, and the gown slid from her. And then he was upon her, like a ravening creature, unleashing something that had been pent up all this time . . .

And as they came together, she took herself out of her mind. Vir's image filled her mind, filled her body, and she thought of how it had all come to this.

I have been bad, she thought, *and led a bad life, and have done terrible things and used people, and this is my punishment. Because Vir told me Durla is the key to it all. That Durla will have information that we need. That I must be by Durla's side, always, for that is the only way I can get information to Vir as he needs it. Being with Durla is what will make Vir happy, and I must make Vir happy. If I do not make him happy, I will die.*

So I must leave him to be with Durla, to be where my beloved Vir most needs me. But whenever Durla's arms are around me, whenever he loves me, it will be my Vir that I am feeling and thinking of. And someday, someday, my Vir will come for me, and we will be together forever and ever, through death and beyond. And this . . . this means nothing in the meantime. Nothing at all. I will smile and gasp and whisper small names and say all the things that are meaningless unless I say them to Vir, but they will keep Durla, and I will be able to learn from him what I need.

I will be the spy that Castig Lione calls me, and I will cooperate, and be everything Durla wants me to be so that I can be what Vir needs me to be. Vir, I love you, I love you so much, come for me soon, Vir, I will wait . . . wait forever and ever . . .

And when Durla saw the tears running down her face, she told him that they were merely tears of joy, and he believed her because it felt so good to believe . . .

Vir stood on the balcony that overlooked the wonders of Centauri Prime. He thought about what was going to be needed to keep the people safe, and the sacrifices that had to be made.

He thought of how Durla adored him now, for he had given Durla that which the minister most desired while, at the same time, maintaining both their dignities. For that, Durla would be eternally grateful.

He knew Durla's type all too well. Creatures who operated with a sense of manifest destiny, and a certainty that fate was going to play things their way and ultimately give them everything that they wanted, if they simply persevered. He might have some initial trepidation, but Vir knew that Durla would not question Mariel's willing defection too much, for the last thing he would want to do under the circumstance is look too closely at what had been handed him.

It all had to be handled internally. All the darkness, all the lies, all of the frightening presence lurking just out of sight—it was up to Vir to have to deal with it. Vir and whomever else he could gain as an ally, willing or otherwise. Because if the Alliance or Sheridan or any of them caught wind of anything that was going on, then Centauri Prime would end in flames. Vir was certain of that much. He could not see that again, could not go through that horror one more time. He would do whatever was necessary to stave off such a horrible happenstance.

Because it was going to get worse.

He had made some initial inquiries. He had gone to men such as Rem Lanas and Renegar, men who had barely survived the horror of K0643. They knew that Vir had tried to warn them, and had come to realize that when Vir Cotto spoke of warnings, then those warnings were ignored at one's extreme peril. And they were hearing things, distant things, stories from friends of friends of friends. Stories of parts of Centauri Prime being harnessed for very, very secretive work, but they weren't bringing in just any Centauri worker, oh no. No, apparently the ministry wasn't happy with the outcome of K0643, and because scapegoats were needed, the workers were targeted. It must have been that the workers, in their ham-handed way, had mismanaged and mishandled that dig.

So now there was new work being done, work of a secret nature, and it appeared that the workforce was being culled entirely from the Prime Candidates. The youth of Centauri Prime, the hope of the future, being employed for some sort of dark and fearsome business that Vir could not even begin to guess at.

He needed to know more, but Lanas and Renegar were nervous, at least to start out. He knew that they would come around, that they could and would provide him with more. They, and others like them who were becoming aware that something was terribly wrong on their beloved Homeworld—although just how wrong, Vir was not prepared to tell them. Not yet. Vir needed someone inside, and quickly.

There had been only one likely person.

He had told himself it was the only thing to do. And when the morality of it got to him, he thought of wicked women and of how the punishments they received were certainly due to their wickedness. And of how those who administered those punishments were pure of motive, without any stain upon their souls.

He thought of all that, and then felt a cold wind cut through him, unseasonably chilly. He drew his robe tight and gazed up into the cloudless night sky, and he clung to that rationalization until he could sustain it no longer. Finally, he spoke the truth that he and only he knew.

"I am damned," he said to the emptiness around him, and there was no one within earshot to tell him otherwise.

EXCERPTED FROM
THE CHRONICLES OF LONDO MOLLARI.
Excerpt dated (approximate Earth date) May 5, 2270.

The idiots. The blind idiots.

Did they truly think that they could continue along this path without someone noticing? Did they believe that Sheridan and his associates would continue to be blissfully unaware of what is happening here?

I knew perfectly well that there were scans being done from orbit, every so often. We have had no privacy here on Centauri Prime. They watch over us as if we are children, making certain we do not scamper about in a woodpile with a lit flame. They worry that we will hurt ourselves . . . hurt ourselves by developing weaponry or militarization that will be used against them, thereby forcing them to try and annihilate us.

Apparently Durla and his brilliant associates had the beginnings of a war machine being created on the continent of Xonos, the former stronghold of the Xon—the other race on Centauri Prime, which we wiped out many years ago. There was machinery being created there, which Durla claimed was to be used for agriculture. Agriculture! As if Sheridan was going to believe that. And the next thing I knew, I was left attempting to smooth over the ruffled feathers of the Alliance, assuring them that no, no, we Centauri are a peaceful people who harbor no hostility toward anyone.

Sheridan did not buy it for an Earth second, I'm sure. He said he wanted the Xonosian buildup dismantled. That there was concern the devices being developed there could be used for war. Durla is having fits. Vallko is getting the people stirred up and angry over this new Alliance oppression. Kuto is endeavoring to put a positive face on all of it, but is not coming close to succeeding—and I suspect that lack of success is by design.

And today

Today I almost killed Throk.

He has shown increased designs upon Senna, and although she has been polite and receptive—even teasingly flirtatious—she has tended to keep him at arm's length. I have noticed that for some months now, and if I had noticed it, then certainly Throk did as well. He was becoming increasingly frustrated that their relationship was going just so far, and no further.

Last week, he approached me about arranging a marriage with her. When he walked into my throne room, I assumed that he was approaching me simply in his capacity as my aide. Imagine my surprise when he said, "Highness . . . I wish to discuss the prospect of marriage."

I stared at him in confusion for a moment, and then said, "Throk, I admit that I have gotten used to you as my valet, but I hardly see the need to formalize our association in that way."

Ah, Throk. No sense of humor. "No, Highness. Between myself and your ward, Senna."

Now I admit my inclination was to think of Senna as little more than a child, and about Throk the same way. I realized, though, upon his inquiry, that not only is she of marriageable age, but that Throk would very likely be only the first of many . . . presuming that I did not agree to the match.

Throk spoke very properly, very formally. "I desire to arrange a match with Senna. I come from the respectable house of Milifa, my father is—"

"I know who your house is, Throk," I said impatiently. "I know your lineage. You wish to be husband to Senna? You are aware of what that entails? You are prepared for the responsibility?"

"Yes, Highness. I think she will make a superb first wife."

"Indeed." Why did I not consider that a ringing endorsement? "And how does Senna feel about the concept?"

He looked extremely puzzled. "Does that matter?"

"Not always," I admitted. "But it does to me, in this case." I turned to one of the guards and requested that he bring Senna to me. Within minutes she entered, quite the grown woman. I felt bad for her; she had spent most of her time in recent months socializing with the Prime Candidates who were inhabiting virtually every corner of the palace these days. There were almost no women in the palace aside from serving women. I could have done better on her behalf, in finding her females to associate with. But I suppose it was a bit late to start worrying about such considerations.

"Senna," I said, "Throk here has asked that I arrange a marriage."

Her eyes sparking with slightly evil amusement, Senna said, "I hope you two will be very happy together, Highness."

I turned to Throk and said, "She has learned her lessons well."

Throk did not seem amused. Then again, he never did, so it wasn't as if that was anything new.

"Senna," I said, feeling that dragging things out would not help matters. "Do you wish to marry Throk?"

Her gaze flickered from him to me, and then, not unkindly but firmly nevertheless, she said, "Since you are asking me, Highness . . . I have nothing but respect and friendly feelings for Throk. But I do not wish to marry him, no. There is no insult intended. I do not wish to marry anyone."

"Well, there it is then, Throk," I said, turning to him.

He looked as if he had been utterly blindsided. "That . . . is it? There is to be no discussion?"

"She has said no. There does not seem to be a good deal of latitude in that decision. No is no, and I suspect—since it is Senna we are discussing here—that no amount of chat will convert no to yes. Senna, however, clearly hopes that you will be able to remain friends. I naturally hope that you will be willing to honor her request."

"But a woman does not have a say in the matter!" Throk insisted, somewhat stridently.

"Under many circumstances, yes," I agreed. "But these are not many circumstances. These are circumstances that I am controlling, and I will value Senna's wishes over yours. That is all."

As it turned out, it was not all. Later that day, when I was passing Senna's room, I heard arguing. I recognized both raised voices; Senna and her frustrated suitor were obviously having a bit of a difference of opinion. My first inclination was to allow Senna to handle the matter. She was, after all, an independent young woman who knew her own mind and was more than capable of handling someone like Throk.

But then there was the angry retort of skin striking skin. Senna's voice cried out, and I heard a body hit the floor. I stepped toward the door, but it did not open. Angrily, I turned to my guards and pointed mutely to the door. Without a moment's hesitation, they stepped forward and forced the door open. I strode in ahead of them, a breech of protocol but I doubt that they could have stopped me.

Senna was on the floor, as I suspected she would be. Throk stood over her, his hands balled into fists, and he was shouting, "You have shamed me in front of the emperor! You have—" That was when he noticed me. Immediately he straightened up and started to say, "Highness, this is not what—"

I did not feel like hearing his explanations, or even the sound of his voice. I did not care how much influence certain "others" had over Throk's service to me. With two quick steps, I was right in front of him. It might not have been fair, but at that moment I saw all the frustration, all the arrogance, all the difficulties and scrabbling for power from all those around me, all personified and condensed into this one individual.

I drew back a fist and swung. It was, I am pleased to say, an impressive blow, particularly considering how out-of-practice I was. Throk's head snapped around and he went down without a sound. It was, I confess, a bit disconcerting, that silence. He glowered up at me, and he did not even put his hand to his chin to rub the area where I had struck him. Apparently he did not want to give me the satisfaction of seeing him in pain.

"I believe," I said tersely, "that your time in my service is ended, Throk."

"Minister Durla assigned me to—"

"Minister Durla works for me," I thundered. "I decide what will be! Not him! Not you! Me! Minister Durla will find something else to assign you to, and I can only suggest, for your continued health, that it be something that will not bring you into contact with Senna. Now get out of my sight!"

He got to his feet, not slowly, but not with any overt hurry either. He looked at me for a time, and I notched up my glower. He looked down at that point, which I took some small measure of pride in noting. And then, without another word, he walked out.

"Are you all right, young lady?" I asked.

"I . . . did not need to be rescued, Highness," she replied. "I could have handled him myself." Then she smiled ruefully and put a hand to the part of her face that was still flared red from the impact. "But I appreciate not having had to."

"Do not think upon it any longer. He is out of your life, for good. I shall see to that."

Tomorrow I will be speaking with Lord Durla, making sure that Throk is given an assignment that will keep him far away from her. I hope she does not end up losing her association with the other Prime Candidates. I could wish for a better set of friends for her, but at least it's peo-

ple roughly her own age with whom she's having social intercourse
There is something to be said for that.

If only I could handle this business with the Alliance as easily as I dispatched Throk. A quick punch to the face and that was all that was required. The realm of politics is, unfortunately, slightly more complicated.

At least, I think it is.

Perhaps I should try punching Sheridan in the nose someday and
see if anything positive comes from it.

11

"Mr. Garibaldi will see you now."

The secretary was so remarkably gorgeous that Lou Welch had a hard time removing his gaze from her. "Breathtaking," he muttered.

"Pardon?"

"This office," Lou said quickly, gesturing around them. "It's really impressive." He rose from his seat and continued, "Me and Michael, we go way back. God, his living quarters were smaller than this outer office. He's come a long way."

"Yes. He has." The face remained lovely, but the smile was thinning in a slightly unattractive fashion. "And if you go on in, I'm sure he'll be happy to tell you just how far."

"Hmm? Oh! Yes, right," Lou said, and he headed into the inner office.

Garibaldi rose from behind his desk, hand extended, a broad smile on his face. Welch couldn't help but admire the trim shape Garibaldi had kept himself in. He'd been concerned that the years spent running the major conglomerate of Edgars/Garibaldi Enterprises might have softened Garibaldi up, but he knew at once that his concerns had been misplaced. Garibaldi looked as whipcord sharp as ever when he stepped forward, and said, "Lou! Lou, it's great to—"

His eyes narrowed. "What's wrong," Lou said, puzzled.

"You have hair," Garibaldi said.

"Oh. That." Slightly self-conscious, but simultaneously preening, Welch ran his fingers through his thick shock of black hair. "I had a thing done."

"A thing. Uh-huh," said Garibaldi.

"Kind of went in the opposite direction from you, huh, Chief? Put the 'baldy' in Garibaldi, did ja?"

"My secret weapon," Garibaldi deadpanned, in reference to his own hairless pate. "I bounce light off it into the eyes of my enemy, blinding them. Plus, if I'm marooned on a desert island, I can reflect the sun off it to summon passing airships. You get stuck on a desert island, Lou, all you get to do is pick sand mites out of your follicles. Sit down, sit down. Can I get you something to drink? Club soda or something?"

"No, no, I'm fine, thanks," Welch said.

Garibaldi walked back around his desk and dropped down into his seat. "So," he said, steepling his fingers, "why don't you tell me what you've been up to."

"Well, now, Chief . . . you're the one who tracked me down, invited me to come here to Mars for a chat," Welch said slowly. "Why don't you tell me what I've been up to?"

"First off, you don't have to call me Chief," Garibaldi said. "We're not on B5 anymore. 'Michael' will be fine. Even 'Mike.' "

"Okay, Chief."

Garibaldi rolled his eyes, and then he refocused himself. "Okay," he said gamely. "Basically, you received a promotion to personal guard for President Clark . . . but then you resigned from EarthForce back during the . . . unpleasantness. Since then you've been serving as a private security consultant for a number of small firms. In addition, you've gotten yourself quite a reputation as a tracker. People call you 'The Ghost.' You have a knack for not being seen when you don't want to."

"I blend in well," said Welch. "It's the hair."

"I'm sure it is," said Garibaldi. "You don't know it, but you've actually worked for Edgars/Garibaldi a couple of times. Some of our smaller holdings."

"I didn't know that."

"Actually, you probably did."

"Well, yeah, I did," Welch admitted. He leaned forward, curious. "So what's up, Chief? You didn't bring me here just to catch up on what I've been doing."

"Take a look at this," Garibaldi said. He cued up an image on the computer screen behind him, and some aerial views of what appeared to be a construction site of some sort appeared. "What do you see?"

Welch frowned as he studied it. While he did so, Garibaldi's intercom beeped at him. He tapped it, and said, "Yeah?"

His secretary's crisp voice came over. "Your eleven o'clock appointment called. He's running a little late, but he'll be here as soon as he can. He apologizes profusely for any inconvenience."

"Not a problem. Let my wife know that we'll probably have to push lunch back half an hour, will ya?"

"Yes, sir."

"Your wife." Welch shook his head in wonderment. "Still hard to believe those words are coming off your mouth. Funny . . . I thought for a while you had a thing for that Psi Corps woman . . . what was her name?"

"Talia," Garibaldi said, tonelessly.

"Yeah. Do you ever hear from her? Whatever happened with her, anyway?"

Garibaldi appeared to consider for a time before replying. "She had a change of mind. So . . ." and he gestured toward the images on the screen.

Welch immediately knew that he had unwittingly stepped in some sort of delicate territory, and promptly decided that it wouldn't be a good idea to press the matter. Instead he said, "Well . . . seems to be some sort of munitions factory. Where is it?"

"Xonos. A sparsely populated continent on Centauri Prime. Shots were taken by an Alliance probe, about a week ago. Centauri claim that it's actually tools being developed for agriculture. Stuff to clear land."

"You could clear land with it," Welch said slowly. "Of course, if anyone were living on the land, they'd be cleared, too." He drummed his fingers on the table.

"What are you thinking, Lou?" Garibaldi asked.

"I'm thinking that it looks like a munitions factory. That if they wanted it to look like a tool development site, they could have done so. I'm thinking that it looks exactly like what they want it to look like. Did they know that they're being watched?"

"Oh, yeah."

"Okay. So I'm thinking decoy."

Garibaldi nodded. "Exactly. They erect a site that our probes can't help but spot so that we can all argue about it, and distract us from what they're really up to."

"And that would be . . ."

"We don't know," admitted Garibaldi. "And *that* is what President Sheridan would like us to find out."

"Us?"

"He wants this small, Lou, at least for the time being. The Interstellar Alliance is busy haggling with Centauri Prime over this site. Let 'em. If this is all there is to it, then we don't have to get anyone worried. If, on the other hand, there's more to it, then the president wants to be the first to know about it and—with any luck—shut it down before things get out of hand."

"Sounds to me like he's out to treat the Centauri with kid gloves. Any particular reason?"

"I don't know that I'd characterize it as kid gloves. I know he'd like to avoid an all-out war. And I think, in a way—for old time's sake—he'd like to see Londo manage to turn things around for Centauri Prime."

"You mean turn things around so that, instead of feeling beaten and suppressed, they feel ready to launch a war again?"

"Not that much around," Garibaldi said. "At any rate, he wants to dispatch a team to Centauri Prime that would be equal parts diplomatic and equal parts—"

"Snoops."

"Exactly. What the president wants is a small group of people who know Londo from the old days, and hopefully can appeal to sentiment to make sure that this doesn't spiral out of hand. At the same time, he wants some folks who are cynical and suspicious enough to be able to take a hard look at things, find out what's going on, and do what needs to be done. He wants me in on it. And I'm figuring that having you to cover my back and check around wouldn't be a bad thing at all. So . . . are you up for it, Ghost?"

"The job pay or am I doing this out of the goodness of my heart?"

"Goodness of your heart."

"Then I'm in."

Garibaldi laughed. "Lou, I was kidding. Of course the job pays. You're being hired."

"Terrific. Then I'm even more in than I was before. Sounds exciting, Chief. The two of us against Centauri Prime. They don't stand a chance."

"Well, now, I figured maybe we'd even the odds just a bit. It's going to be three of us."

The intercom beeped at them again. "Your eleven o'clock is here, sir."

"Should I wait outside?" asked Welch.

"No, no, not at all. Actually, this is the third member of our little group. Send him in," he said to the intercom.

"This third guy someone who'll fit in on Centauri Prime?"

"Oh, yeah," said Garibaldi. "He'll blend perfectly. Hardly anyone'll even notice him. He can walk around on Centauri Prime and not get a second look."

The door slid open, and Welch turned and rose from his seat. Then he blinked in surprise. The newcomer took several brisk steps, stopped, and then half bowed with his fists to his chest. "Greetings, Mr. Garibaldi. And Mr. Welch, is it not?"

Welch was so surprised that he didn't even bother to hide his incredulity. He turned to Garibaldi, and said, "*He's* going to fit right in on Centauri Prime? *Him?*"

"Trust me," said Citizen G'Kar of Narn, with an amused glimmer in one eye. "You won't even know I'm there."

12

It was rare that Londo actually allowed himself to display genuine emotion in front of Durla, but this was one of those very rare times. He rose from the throne even as he gaped in astonishment. "Are you sure? Positive?"

Durla nodded firmly. "There is no question, Highness. Positive identification was made when they came through customs."

"That he sent Mr. Garibaldi does not surprise me," Londo said slowly, beginning to pace the throne room. "And Welch, I vaguely remember him. He is obviously there as backup for Garibaldi. But G'Kar? *Here?*"

"He was a most impressive individual," Durla said. "I was there when he broke free of his restraints in defiance of Cartagia. It was . . . the most remarkable thing I have ever seen."

"It may well be the most remarkable thing that ever was," replied Londo. "I am not entirely sure whether Sheridan is brilliant, or a fool, or both."

"What shall we do, Highness?"

Londo looked bemused. "You are asking me what to do? Minister, I am stunned. Shocked and appalled. Customarily, you tell me how things will be, and that is that. To what do I owe this honor?"

"You diminish your contribution, Highness," said Durla.

"I know precisely what my contribution is, Durla. Do not seek to fool me. It ill becomes you. Or has Mariel schooled you better in the ways of deceit?"

Durla stiffened when Londo said that. "I do not see the need to insult the lady Mariel, Highness."

"Believe me," Londo said firmly, "no one could insult the lady Mariel." He waved it off dismissively. "Very well. Simply put, they will be extended every courtesy. They are here to speak. Let them speak. Obviously, Sheridan has hand-picked this particular group of individuals because he hopes to play upon old loyalties."

"And . . . has he succeeded?" asked Durla.

Londo snorted derisively. "My loyalty, Durla, first, last, and always, remains to Centauri Prime. As you well know."

Durla bowed and said, "As you say, Highness."

"Yes," Londo said faintly, and with less conviction than he would have liked, "as I say."

As they approached the front steps of the palace, G'Kar slowed a bit. Garibaldi noticed it and hung back, causing the guards who were escorting them to stop. He put a hand on G'Kar's arm, and said, "Is everything all right?"

"Just . . . some unpleasant memories," G'Kar said slowly. "Odd. I had thought that they would not pose a problem. Interesting how there are always new things to learn about oneself, isn't it."

"Very interesting," Garibaldi agreed. But from the look on his face, he wasn't sure what they were talking about. "Do you want to wait out here for—"

But G'Kar shook his head firmly. "I will be fine. Do not worry about it. After all I have been through, I think I can handle a bit of unpleasant nostalgia and a flight of stairs." He took a deep breath and, moments later, they were entering the palace.

Several ministers were waiting there to greet them. None of them were familiar faces to G'Kar . . . save for one. He stared at him for a moment, and then said, "Have we met, sir?"

"Not really, no. I am Minister Durla," answered the Centauri. He introduced the others who were with him, and the one who caught G'Kar's attention the most squarely was the one known as Vallko, minister of spirituality. "The emperor is most anxious to meet with you," Durla told them. "Right this way."

They followed their escort down a long hallway, and G'Kar couldn't help but notice the guards who watched them warily. No . . . him. They were watching him. G'Kar was beginning to wonder if his presence there wasn't meant to serve primarily as decoy. Everyone would be so busy watching him, that they wouldn't pay nearly as much attention to Garibaldi and Welch.

The silence was broken only by the sounds of their footsteps until Vallko finally said, "My understanding is that you are something of a religious figure on your Homeworld."

"So I have been designated," G'Kar admitted. "It is not a status that suits me, truth to tell. Fortunately enough, I have managed to convince my people to accept me in a manner that is more appropriate."

"And that would be?"

"As an advisor. A proponent of restraint and . . . dare I say it . . . wisdom. But I do not wish to be considered a god, or even a leader. I am more than content to let others lead, and I will simply stand on the sidelines and applaud or do what I may to guide their efforts."

"Restraint." It was the minister introduced as Lione who now spoke, as if G'Kar had said nothing beyond that word. "What an odd word to hear from a Narn. You are generally considered a rather warlike race, with restraint being a term that has little-to-no meaning for you."

"Yes, I have heard that, too. Then again, I have also heard that the Centauri are a vomitous pack of lying, rapacious bastards." There were audible gasps of anger from the ministers, and Garibaldi fired G'Kar a look that the Narn ignored. He was speaking so pleasantly that it was hard to believe that he was attempting to give offense. "Now, of course, whenever such calumnies are uttered, I step right in and say 'No, no! One must not believe what one hears!' Oh, certainly, the Centauri imprisoned me several times, and gouged out my eye, and covered my back with so many whip scars that to this day I still cannot sleep properly. But is that any reason to condemn an entire race? Of course not! Broad and unfair characterizations are anathema to civilized society, don't you agree, Minister?"

The towering Lione looked as if he were ready to assault G'Kar with his bare hands, but Durla merely smiled in what seemed polite amusement. "Wholeheartedly, Mr. Ambassador."

"Please, please . . . ambassador no longer. 'Citizen' G'Kar will suffice."

"Citizen G'Kar it is. This way, please."

They walked down another hallway, and G'Kar noticed that Lou Welch seemed to be frowning at something. He tried to see what had caught Welch's curiosity, and it quickly became evident: it was the black-suited young people who seemed to be all over the palace. Black, with some sort of red sash over them like a badge of honor. "Who are they?" G'Kar abruptly asked, indicating one of the passing young men, who fired him a glance.

"The Prime Candidates. Our youth group," said Minister Lione.

"Ah. Hitler Youth," Lou Welch said.

Lione looked at him in confusion. "What?"

"Nothing," Welch said promptly, apparently happy to let the

matter drop. Lione shook his head in a manner that indicated he found all Humans to be extremely puzzling.

They were ushered into the throne room, which was empty. *Londo always did prefer to make an entrance,* thought G'Kar, and his instinct was quite correct. Moments later Londo walked in with such enthusiasm that he seemed like a white-clad tornado. "Mr. Garibaldi!" he called out as if Garibaldi were on the opposite side of the city. "Citizen G'Kar! Mr. Walsh!"

"Welch," Lou corrected him.

"Ach. Who cares? You're here, whatever your name is. Sit, sit." He gestured toward the Centauri who had accompanied them. "You may all leave us."

G'Kar was pleased to see that the ministers looked decidedly disconcerted. "Highness," Durla said slowly, "if you are going to discuss matters pertaining to Centauri Prime, should we not be here to represent the people's interests?"

"I am the people," Londo replied. "One of the many burdens that I happily bear. When old friends chat it is merely a get-together, Durla. Bring in ministers, and suddenly it becomes a council. There is no need for that at this time. But rest assured, if I feel that someone is needed to escalate matters to the breaking point and beyond, I will send for all of you instantly. Now you may go."

"But Highness," Durla began.

Something in Londo's demeanor shifted quite subtly. "Do not confuse my use of the word 'may' with the notion that you actually have a choice in the matter."

Durla mustered his dignity, then gestured to the other ministers. They followed him out and the doors shut behind them, leaving only a handful of security guards behind.

The fact that the guards were there, though, was enough to convince G'Kar immediately that Londo wasn't going to say anything that he wasn't comfortable with having repeated to Durla. It was his suspicion, based not only upon Londo's passing comments, but also his abundant knowledge of just how Centauri politics worked, that Londo was under careful watch at all times.

"So—" Londo rubbed his hands together "—how long will you be here, eh? If you wish, I can provide a tour of Centauri Prime. You can see all that we have accomplished."

"That . . . is actually what we've come to talk about," Garibaldi said, shifting in his chair. He leaned forward, resting his arms on his knees. "As you know, we were sent by the president . . ."

"Yes, yes, Sheridan informed us of your visit. I cannot tell you the rejoicing there was, knowing that the Alliance is so concerned about our welfare, that they feel the need to check on us constantly. It is very uplifting to the spirit, yes, to know that we are so beloved."

Garibaldi ignored the sarcasm. "The factory on Xonos . . ."

G'Kar watched Londo very carefully. Mollari certainly had the ability to keep his cards close to his vest, but G'Kar fancied that, by this point, he could tell when Londo was out-and-out lying. Londo, however, looked at Garibaldi with what could only be considered wide-eyed innocence. "The agricultural site, you mean. I had this discussion with President Sheridan. We have, as your people say, beaten our swords into plowshares, Mr. Garibaldi. Would you now take issue with how we plow?"

"There's just concern that things may not be the way that they're being presented to us."

"In other words, you think we are lying."

"Not in other words," G'Kar spoke up. "Those are exactly the right words."

Londo, to G'Kar's surprise, laughed slightly at that. "Now I see why he is here," he said, indicating G'Kar. "He says all the things that will anger me, leaving you free to be as charming as possible. Or at least, as charming as is possible for you."

"Look, don't get the wrong idea . . ."

Londo rose from his seat. "I cannot do more than be open with you, Mr. Garibaldi. I can do nothing more than hide nothing. You are free to look wherever you wish upon Centauri Prime, at whatever you wish to examine. Inspect the facility on Xonos . . . I shall arrange transportation for you there tomorrow."

"Why not tonight?" Garibaldi said quickly.

"Tonight if you wish," Londo shrugged. "I had thought you would be tired, and desire some time to recover from your trip. But if tonight is what you desire," and he turned to his guards to arrange it.

"No, no, that's all right," said Garibaldi. "Tomorrow would be fine. No need to put anyone out. You're right, we could use some time to rest up."

"Very well," Londo said, equally agreeably. "Your guest chambers are already arranged, and tomorrow . . . tomorrow we shall take a trip to Xonos. Now, if you'll excuse me . . . affairs of state that must be attended to, and all that."

"Thank you, Your Highness," Garibaldi said formally.

" 'Your Highness?' " Londo looked both surprised and amused.

"Please, please, Mr. Garibaldi. We go too far back, you and I. You, and your associates, can feel free to address me as," and he paused dramatically, " 'Your Majesty.' "

"Why are we waiting until tomorrow?" Welch asked.

Garibaldi was busy unpacking the few articles of clothing he had brought with him. Welch, who had brought even less than Garibaldi, already had his gear stowed in the adjacent room. "Because there's not going to be anything there," Garibaldi told him flatly. "Whenever people are eager to have you inspect something—their apartment, their ship, their planet, whatever—doesn't matter. It means they've already got whatever it is you're looking for safely tucked away where they think you'll never find it."

"So you're saying his being willing to be forthcoming is just proof that he's covering something up."

"More or less," said Garibaldi. "There's one of two options here, Lou. Either the Centauri really are up to nothing . . . or they're up to something, but it's not here."

"Which begs the question of, if they are up to something . . . where is it happening."

"Yup. Any thoughts?"

Welch gave the matter some consideration, pacing the room while scratching behind his ear as if trying to tickle his brain into operation. Finally he said, "You believe in gut hunches, Chief?"

"You've known me this long, you have to ask me that?"

Welch chuckled at that and then grew serious again. "Those kids. Those Prime Candidates. They were all over the place, did ja notice?"

"Yeah, I noticed. It was kind of spooky. No matter which corner we turned, there were more of them. It was like running into clones of the same person."

"I think they might be the key to this. Or at least they might be worth exploring."

"What do you have in mind?"

Welch stepped out onto the narrow balcony and gestured for Garibaldi to join him. He did so, and Welch pointed. "See 'em?"

Garibaldi looked where Welch was indicating. There was a small cluster of the Prime Candidates heading in the direction of the city. They were moving in synchronous step, with such perfect regimentation that they might well have been the same person, simply replicated.

"So I was watching them from my balcony a little bit ago. There were more of them, heading in exactly the same direction, and some coming back, also from the same place."

"You want to follow them."

"Exactly, Chief. See where they lead. See what comes up."

"All right," Garibaldi said. "When did you have in mind?"

Welch abruptly coughed, very loudly and hoarsely. Then, with a greatly exaggerated croaking, he said, "I think I feel a cold coming on. It should be pretty nasty by tomorrow."

"I'll send your regrets along," Garibaldi said.

G'Kar heard the soft footfalls behind him and did not even have to turn to see who it was. "Hello, Your Majesty," he said.

Londo came up behind him, his hands draped behind his back, and he was clearly puzzled. "Londo. You, G'Kar, of all people, know that 'Londo' will more than suffice. I was told you were down here. Is there any particular reason? Were the accommodations I provided for you so wretched that you think a dungeon would be preferable?"

For that was indeed where they were; in the subterranean dungeons far beneath the palace. G'Kar was standing at the doorway of one particularly odious chamber, with a stench so foul that Londo had to fight to repress his gag reflex. He heard the faint scuttling of tiny claws across the floor and wondered what sort of vermin were running about within.

"Oh, no, the room you've arranged for me is more than satisfactory," said G'Kar. "I am simply reminiscing about this . . . my home away from home."

At first Londo had no idea what G'Kar was talking about, then abruptly he understood. "Of course. This was where Cartagia put you. This is the very cell."

G'Kar nodded. He actually patted the door frame as if he was happy to see it. "You would probably say that your Great Maker moves in mysterious ways, Londo. I would tend to agree. Cartagia put me in here with the hope of breaking an enemy of Centauri Prime. Instead he is long gone, and I have survived and have become far more formidable than even Cartagia could have imagined. I learned a great deal while I was down here. It helped to forge me into what I am today."

"And . . . what are you today?"

"Do you mean . . . am I your enemy?" G'Kar said.

"Yes."

"Ah, that is the nice thing about matters being the way they are between us, Londo." He turned to face the emperor. "We do not have to mince words, you and I. No, Londo. No, I am not your enemy."

"If you were, would you tell me?"

"A reasonable question. No. Very likely not."

"I see," sighed Londo. "You are disgustingly candid, G'Kar. It is a trait I once found charming. Now it is merely annoying. And tell me . . . if you were my friend, would you tell me that?"

"Of course I would," said G'Kar.

There was silence.

"You," Londo said, "are the single most irritating individual I have ever met."

"You see?" G'Kar replied. "What could be more proof of friendship than that? Who but a friend could be anywhere near as irritating as I am?"

At that, Londo laughed low in his throat. "Would you care for a drink, G'Kar? For old time's sake? For the memory of whatever it was we once were . . . or might be again?"

"That," G'Kar said briskly, "sounds like an excellent idea."

G'Kar turned away from his one-time prison and followed Londo up to his private quarters. Halfway there, a most surprising face greeted G'Kar. "Lady Mariel!" he said as he saw her approaching from the other end of the hallway. "A pleasure to see you!"

"Likewise, G'Kar," she said softly. "I had heard that you had once again graced us with your presence."

"Are you," and his questing glance went from Londo to Mariel and back, "in favor once more in the court?"

"In a manner of speaking," she said with that customary dazzling smile. "Not in the emperor's favor, particularly . . . but in favor nonetheless."

"Does she not remain as charming as ever?" said Londo jovially. Then he laughed, as if he were about to say something preposterous. "You know, we three should get together more often. We always have so much fun when we do."

"The last time we did, as I recall, you almost died," G'Kar reminded him.

"Yes, yes, I know. That is what provides the fun, yes? That sense that anything can happen. You know," and he lowered his voice conspiratorially, "I actually thought . . . you will laugh . . . I actually thought that you, G'Kar, and you, Mariel . . . were having an affair."

"No!" said Mariel, shocked. "Londo, how could you?" G'Kar's face bore a similar look of incredulity.

"Oh, the imagination plays remarkable tricks, my dear," Londo told her. "At one point during my party, I saw G'Kar toss a grape to you. The passing of fruit is a quaint Narn custom that is part of the Narn courting ritual. The fruit symbolizes sexuality, or some such thing. Yes, G'Kar? Yes? No? Am I recalling correctly?"

"I've heard something about that old tradition, yes," G'Kar said dismissively, "but sometimes, Londo, a grape is just a grape."

"Yes. So I hear," Londo said. "In any event, what is past is past. Mariel . . . would you care to join us?"

"Oh, I don't think so, Highness," Mariel said. "I had best be to bed. There are others who require my attention."

"To bed, then. G'Kar . . ." and he gestured for the Narn to follow him. "I hope you were not offended by my little speculation," he said as they continued down the hall, the Lady Mariel heading off in the opposite direction.

"Not at all, Londo."

And then, in a low voice, Londo said, sounding no less friendly, "I know the two of you were together, G'Kar. Please do not insult my intelligence by implying that I am unaware of that which is so obvious. I would hate to become enemies again, particularly over a woman who means so little to me. We understand each other, yes? Good! So . . . did you know that, as emperor, I have the best wine collection in all of Centauri Prime?"

"Somehow," said G'Kar, "I'm not the least bit surprised."

13

Lou knew that the journey to Xonos would guarantee that Garibaldi, G'Kar, and Londo—plus whatever assorted guards and such were going to be accompanying them—would be gone until the late evening. That had been what he was hoping for, because the cloak wasn't at its most effective during broad daylight. Early evening was fine, and nighttime . . . well, nighttime, forget it. There was simply no chance of spotting him, no matter how hard you looked. Somehow the cloak seemed to stretch and shape the shadows to conceal him, so it took minimal effort for him to keep his presence concealed.

"Cloak" was probably a misnomer. He had never really known what he should call it. A "web," perhaps. A "screen" might also be accurate enough. But somehow, "invisibility cloak" gave it a certain panache.

The "Ghost." He'd heard that name mentioned, and it always amused him tremendously. If they only knew. If any of them only knew.

He'd kept to himself during the day, naturally. After all, if he was claiming that he was ill, the last thing he'd want to do is gallivant around the palace in what was obviously the pink of health. So he spent the day reading, keeping the door closed, allowing meals to be brought to him—during which he covered himself up in the bed and made assorted disgusting noises so that the servants would be inclined to leave the food and depart as quickly as they could.

When he saw the sun sinking on the horizon, however, that was when he made his move.

He removed the delicately woven cloak from the hidden bottom of his suitcase and unfolded it carefully on the bed. He'd never forget the day that he had stumbled upon it, exploring that fallen ship on Cygnus 4. He'd been working a security gig at a power plant there, employed by an eccentric owner who was convinced that hordes of crazed Martians—little antennaed green ones, not the real thing—were trying to take over his factory. While he'd been there, planetary sensors had detected a ship entering the atmosphere, a ship that had spiraled down and disappeared from the sensors as quickly as it had appeared. Welch, along with a team, had been dispatched to inspect it and make sure that no crazed Martians with their killer death rays were emerging to conquer the relatively unappealing Cygnus 4.

What Welch had found was a ship unlike any he'd ever seen. It looked slightly like one of those bizarre spiked ships that had shown up on ISN several years before, but it had significant differences, as well. It was as if it shared the same technological base, but had gone off in another direction.

He had discovered a creature therein, a creature unlike any race he'd seen before, even on Babylon 5. Grey-skinned, and chilling to the bone. The thing had been killed upon impact, and Welch couldn't have been happier. He had the feeling this wasn't something he wanted to face while it was breathing.

And upon further inspection—while telling the rest of his people to stay back in case there was some sort of danger—he had discovered the cloak.

He hadn't known what it was at first. He had, however, managed to scare the hell out of himself, for he had seen the fine, silvery, woven fabric and had attempted to pick it up. In doing so, he let out an alarmed yelp as his forearm abruptly vanished. Convinced that he had permanently maimed himself, Welch had fallen back, only to find his arm rematerializing instantly. He stared stupidly at his arm, turning the hand back and forth as if to assure himself that it was, in fact, there. Then he reached for the fabric once again, a bit more confidently this time. He'd wrapped it around his hand, and that disappeared as well, but this time he wasn't the least bit alarmed.

He had never seen anything like it, and he was reasonably certain that it had no parallel in current science. The closest comparison he could make was that it was like a changeling net, except what it did was transform anyone over whom it fell, so that they effectively blended seamlessly into the background. Through experimentation, Welch had discovered its limitations, including the fact that it remained deactivated as long as it was folded in upon itself. Unfolded, however, it began working instantly—a tremendous inconvenience that time he had unthinkingly tossed it into his bedroom and then taken half a day to find the damned thing again.

None of the others in his security team had seen the cloak, and he hadn't been about to volunteer knowledge of its existence. Instead, he had carefully hidden it, and used it judiciously on subsequent jobs. He had, as Garibaldi made note, acquired quite a reputation, although people didn't truly realize just what it was he was getting a reputation for.

So there on Centauri Prime, Welch draped the cloak around himself, head to toe. He looked down and could see the rest of his body perfectly. That was one of the aspects of the cloak that it had taken him a little while to understand: Once he was completely under it, he was visible to himself. But if any part of him was uncovered, then he himself couldn't see the parts that were hidden. It made a strange kind of sense to him. The only thing he could figure out was that the cloak somehow managed to bend light around it, convincing onlookers that they were seeing things around it. But if light was completely bent away from whoever was wearing it, then that meant light wouldn't be reaching the wearer's eyes, and he would be effectively blinded. So obviously the thing was crafted to make sure that didn't happen. How, he couldn't even begin to guess.

He did know that if he brought it to an EarthGov lab or something, they could probably figure it out. But he sure as hell would never see it again, and he wasn't about to let such a valuable acquisition slip through his fingers.

He emerged from his room, glanced right and left, then started down the corridor. Two guards were approaching. Just to play it safe and make sure that the cloak was functioning, he made a grotesque face and tossed an obscene gesture at them. They didn't acknowledge his presence or give him so much as a glance.

Perfect.

Lou headed toward the main entrance of the palace, and while on his way he heard youthful voices. Unless he very much missed his guess, that was a group of the Prime Candidates, on their way out. He congratulated himself on his timing, which apparently could not have been more perfect.

Sure enough, there were half a dozen of them heading out. Welch couldn't help but notice that they didn't seem to interact like normal teenage boys. There was no banter, no bravado, no strut or cock-of-the-walk attitude. Instead they spoke in straightforward, businesslike terms. They kept their voices low, obviously wanting to keep Prime Candidate business to themselves. This was definitely not a group that Welch would comfortably have fit in with, even when he had been a teenager.

They headed away from the palace, going in the same direction as the other groups that Welch had observed the previous day. Lou fell into step behind them. As always, he kept his strides modest, and was careful not to swing his arms or in some other way move in a remotely jaunty fashion that might possibly dislodge the cloak. The last thing he wanted to do was suddenly materialize. Needless to say, that would likely have attracted attention.

They headed into town, and Welch caught sight of a massive tower that looked to be about in the center of the city. He'd heard someone make passing reference to it when they had first landed on Centauri Prime. The "Tower of Power," they'd called it. It was supposed to be symbolic. As far as Lou was concerned, it was symbolic of how much of an eyesore people could construct in their city if they were really, really dedicated.

They kept on moving, Lou right behind them. The farther they got into the city, the more nervous Lou felt. He was invisible, yes, but he wasn't intangible. There were quite a few folks on the streets, and people could still bump into him if he wasn't careful. Since no one was making any effort to stay out of his way, it was everything that Lou could do to stay one step ahead of Centauri passersby. He also almost managed to get himself killed when he forgot that a passing vehicle couldn't see him and wasn't about to stop for him. Only fast reflexes and a bit of luck enabled him to get out of the way in time.

During that near-accident, Welch momentarily lost sight of the Prime Candidates. For a moment he thought he'd completely blown it, but then he saw them turn a corner, and he sprinted after them. Luck was with him, for that section of the sidewalk happened to be clear of pedestrians for the moment. Otherwise, he would never have managed to keep up with them; either that, or he would have had to act as a sort of invisible football lineman, knocking people out of the way so he could get to where he was going.

One of the things he noticed was how people seemed to look at the Prime Candidates. He considered them to be a fairly creepy bunch of young men, but it seemed to him that Centauri chests swelled with pride when the Candidates walked past. Welch couldn't believe it. The truth was so obvious and clear to him: here were the youth of Centauri Prime, being brainwashed into good little soldiers who did whatever they were told with no thought, no conscience. Welch believed as much in the chain of command as any military man, former or no. But he also knew that swearing to obey orders, at least in EarthForce, didn't mean tossing aside morals and doing whatever was asked of you, no matter how repellant. Although he hadn't seen much of the Prime Candidates in action, he could see it in their eyes, in their demeanor. These kids didn't care about anything except their organization and the people who ran it.

He saw them head into a fairly nondescript building that was set off by itself. There wasn't anything on it to identify it as a gathering place. Yet, not only did the group of Prime Candidates that he had been following enter, but several others came out. It was enough to make Lou very, very curious as to just what might be inside the building. Might be nothing. Might be something useful. No real way to tell unless he went in and looked around . . .

He had no desire to simply walk in, though. An invisible entrance might be noticed. So he took up a post just outside the door and waited. He had all the time in the world. He leaned against the wall, started to whistle softly, and then caught himself and shut up. He did so just in time; a man walking by was looking around in mild confusion. He shrugged it off and continued on his way.

Then the door slid open. Two of the Prime Candidates emerged, deep in conversation about something called Morbis. The name meant nothing to Welch, but he tucked it away into his brain, for subsequent reference. The moment they were clear, the door started to shut again, but Lou bolted for it. The door paused a moment automatically, its detection device registering Lou's presence even though he was invisible. But there wasn't an alarm setup for the door; it simply had a detector to inform it when to open and close. The brief stutter-stop-and-start of the door didn't attract much notice from the Prime Candidates because it was so brief. One of them obviously thought he had noticed something out of the corner of his eye, for he hesitated and glanced back at the door. But it slid closed without any problem, so he chalked it up to a momentary glitch before heading off on his own business.

The place didn't seem particularly imposing or impressive to Lou. Nevertheless, he wasn't about to dismiss it. The furnishings were very stark and utilitarian, but what there was, was meticulously maintained. Everything was scrubbed down and shining. He heard small groups of the Prime Candidates speaking in different rooms, but their conduct within those rooms was no different than outside. It was all very business-like. Obviously the Prime Candidates never felt the need to let down their hair . . . no pun intended.

Welch moved very carefully. He didn't want to bump into any of them within the narrow confines of the halls. That would be extremely bad. Even so, moving with caution, he was able to get a feel for the downstairs section of the place. Mostly it was a series of small meeting rooms. Several of them were empty, and the rest of them had small groups of Candidates, talking in a way that indicated they were being debriefed, or something else official. He saw their reflections gleaming in the polished surfaces and wondered how many man-hours it had taken them to hone everything to that kind of shine.

There was a flight of stairs to his right. Welch placed a tentative foot on the first step, wanting to make sure it didn't make any noise. It seemed to be sturdy enough, and he put more pressure on it until he was standing on it with his full weight. The step didn't emit so much as a squeak. Slowly he made his way up the stairs, moving with increasing confidence, to say nothing of a sense of urgency. After all, if someone came trotting down the steps, they might bang right into him.

He got to the upper floor, and this one seemed a bit different from the downstairs. Here there appeared to be genuine offices, rather than chat rooms. He could only assume that it was where the "upper management" of the Prime Candidates came to work. That, however, might provide him with more information.

A Prime Candidate walked out of one of the offices. He had a look of concentration on his face, and he seemed to exude authority. As he walked past Welch, another of the Prime Candidates came trotting up the stairs, and called to him, "Throk! A moment of your time, please. We need to discuss the troop dispatches to Morbis. Also, construction seems to be slowing down on Nefua."

The one called Throk made an impatient noise and followed the other Prime Candidate downstairs. This left the office open and unoccupied, and Welch wasn't about to squander the opportunity. He sidled in to see whatever there was to discover.

At first glance, there didn't appear to be much. The office was as spartan in its contents as any of the others had been. Just a desk with a computer terminal, and a couple of chairs. Not so much as a picture on the walls or on the desk. But then Welch noticed that the computer had been left on, and he placed himself in front of the screen so he could study what was on it.

What he saw caused him to go completely slack-jawed. It was a good thing no one was able to see him, because if they were, they would think that he looked like an imbecile.

Throk had been in the middle of juggling Prime Candidate assignments, but it was the location of the assignments that startled Welch. Lou was horrified to see, from manpower estimates, that there were in excess of two thousand members of the Prime Candidates, and it appeared from what he was seeing that a sizable number of them were *not* on Centauri Prime at the moment. These names that he'd heard since arriving—Morbis, Nefua—they were outlying colony worlds. Border worlds, worlds that wouldn't automatically be associated with the Centauri or, indeed, with any major power. And those weren't the only worlds involved, either; there were at least half a dozen more listed.

They were being used as mobilization sites.

Welch realized that he and Garibaldi had gotten it exactly right. Xonos has been a red herring. The real action was happening at planets that were light-years from Centauri Prime. They were developing weaponry. They were assembling troops, undergoing training, all in the darkest secret. It was easy enough to keep the secret, though, because the initial talent pool at least was being drawn from the ranks of the Prime Candidates. Young recruits who didn't attract much attention, and who could be relied upon for complete, unswerving discretion and dedication.

Essentially, the Centauri were moving from one colony world to the next, leapfrogging as they managed to organize forced labor on each one. There were no cries of conquest to the Alliance, because the Centauri were basically conquering themselves. Those colonists who had thought they had managed to build a new life for themselves by staking claims on outlying worlds were discovering that they had been deluding themselves. The Prime Candidates, along with handpicked individuals from the ministry, were coming in and strongarming them into aiding in a military buildup. Faced with the prospect of having support for their colonies yanked altogether, the colonists had no choice whatsoever but to comply. Thus was the Centauri government managing to build up its military muscle, all while flying below the radar of the Alliance.

It was possible that Londo knew nothing about this. Ministers Durla and Lione seemed to be running the Prime Candidates almost single-handedly. And Welch had the feeling that Londo had very little to do with day-to-day affairs of state.

Still, it didn't matter how much Londo knew or didn't know. Something had to be done about this, because Centauri Prime had had limits placed upon its militarization by the Alliance, and this was simply an attempt by the Centauri to engage in a buildup without detection. It appeared everything that had been whispered about the Centauri was absolutely true. They couldn't be trusted, even to the smallest degree.

Fortunately, as near as Welch could tell, the buildup still was in its preliminary stages. They had managed to catch it early enough that something could still be done about it. Once the Alliance was informed, they could shut it down before . . .

The shadows in the room . . . seemed longer than they had before.

Lou was certain he had to be imagining it. But there was something else; he felt a chill running down his spine, seizing it. He tried to turn his attention to the computer; however, he was unable to.

Something was happening, something was wrong, definitely wrong, but he had no idea what it could possibly be.

The chill seemed as if it were permeating his entire body, as if frost were developing on him and seeping right into his pores. He looked down at himself, but there was no change. Everything was fine.

Still, it was enough to convince him that it was time to get the hell out of there. He had a data crystal in his pocket, not by happenstance. He had hoped that he might stumble onto something useful, and he had come prepared. He shoved the crystal into the proper receptacle and downloaded as much information as possible. Then he pulled out the crystal, pocketed it, and turned to head for the door.

Throk was standing there, occupying the entirety of the door. He was going to have to wait until Throk got out of the way, because obviously he couldn't push him aside while he was invisible . . .

Except . . .

Except Throk was looking at him. Right at him.

Very cautiously, Lou moved to the left of the desk. Throk's eyes followed him. Lou looked down at the polished surface of the desk and saw his reflection staring back at him.

"You," Throk said, "should not have come here."

He had no idea what had happened, no clue how the mechanics of the cloak had failed him. But obviously they had. Still, Lou felt no real alarm. He was too old a hand at this, and wasn't one to panic easily. The thing to remember was, these were kids, playing at being officials. Whereas he was an adult and, as a representative of the Interstellar Alliance, he had just caught them at a breech of the agreement that restricted their military buildup. They were busted, and that was all there was to it.

From a psychological point of view, Lou Welch had the upper hand.

"All right, son," he said, dropping any endeavor to hide himself, since it obviously wasn't working. "Why not stand away from that door right now. We don't want any sort of trouble—"

"You," Throk said again, his voice sounding dull and empty, and even a bit resigned, "should not have come here." Even as he spoke, he reached into his belt and pulled on a pair of thin, flexible black gloves.

Then he came toward Welch. He approached with an economy of movement, as if he were in no hurry. Welch started to move right, but the room wasn't that big, and Throk easily continued to block his exit by sidestepping slightly.

"I'm warning you, kid. I'll break you in half. So don't try anything stupid." The one thing Lou had going for him was that Throk had made no attempt to call for help. Obviously he felt that he could handle this on his own. That, Welch knew, would prove to be his undoing.

Throk was within range now, and Welch went for him. Although he had received plenty of training as a member of EarthForce, Lou Welch was a barroom brawler from way back. He had the instincts and moves of a slug-out artist, and he used them now. He feinted with his left, then swung a quick right. It was a good swing, a fast snap from the hip.

Throk brushed it aside as if it were a punch thrown by a child. It barely grazed Throk's upper chest, and did no damage.

Lou swung again. Throk stepped slightly back so that the punch missed entirely, throwing Lou off balance, and before Welch could recover, Throk came in fast. The move didn't seem like anything, but it was so quick that it was like lightning, and Throk's punch shot in hard.

Lou tried to put up a defense, but Throk punched through it as if it were tissue paper. One punch doubled Lou over, and the second smashed in his face. Lou went down, blood fountaining from his shattered nose, and he felt an immediate swelling.

He tried to say something, tried to speak with bravado and say "Nice shot, kid," but he couldn't talk. He had the hideous feeling that the kid had just broken his jaw, but that the pain hadn't fully registered on him.

And then Throk grabbed him by his new hair, pulling him to his feet as if he weighed nothing, and Welch couldn't believe the kid's upper torso strength. The true significance hadn't fully dawned on him; he was still too busy being surprised by the power in his opponent. Throk got a firm grip on him, one hand holding him by the scruff of his neck, the other on the back of his belt, and he slammed Lou Welch into the wall, causing a crack in it. The impact was so violent that Lou literally saw stars.

For a moment he thought he saw Babylon 5 float across those stars in orbit, and then he felt nauseated, and decided that he was going to have to have that checked out later. Then he remembered that he was in the middle of a fight, except it didn't seem like much of a fight, but more of a slaughter.

Fight back! Do something! Let this little punk know who's in charge! Lou twisted free with an unexpected burst of strength, then turned and hit Throk as hard as he could in the gut. His fist connected with a stomach that felt as solid as rock. He thought that he might have broken a knuckle.

Then the room started to swirl. The exit suddenly seemed closer, and Lou tried to will himself over to it. At first his body didn't respond and then he was moving, a step toward it and then to . . .

. . . and then he was in the air. For one delirious moment he thought he was flying, and then he realized that Throk had lifted him clear of the floor and was holding him over his head. Then the floor was coming up to meet him with horrifying speed, and he crashed into it and lay there, the breath knocked out of him, unable to move. Everything hurt.

Throk's knee was jammed into the back of his spine and he felt hands on either side of his head.

Guess you showed him who was in charge was the last thought that flittered through Lou Welch's mind before Throk ruthlessly, but efficiently, snapped his head around and broke his neck.

Throk didn't move his hands until he felt Lou Welch's pulse cease. He found it interesting, from a clinical point of view, how the pulse kept going for some seconds after Welch had effectively died. He wondered if Welch was, in fact, already dead before the cessation of the pulse, or whether that was just some last, lingering reflex. In the end, it didn't make that much difference, he decided, as long as the result was the same.

He released his grip and stood, shaking out his hands. Then he turned and saw the grey figure in the corner of the room. The figure that seemed to be part of the shadows, and then separate from them. Throk stood paralyzed. While he was killing Lou Welch, his heart had barely sped up. He had simply acted in the defense of Centauri Prime, and had done so in as brisk and efficient a manner as he could. He had been so detached from it that he might well have been watching someone else perform the action.

What he was seeing now, though, struck at him. He felt an odd combination of fear . . . and . . .

. . . honor.

"Who are you?" Throk demanded in a loud voice, except that when he spoke it actually came out as barely above a whisper.

"Shiv'kala," said the grey creature. He reached down and lifted some sort of odd shroud from Welch's corpse. Speaking as much to himself as to Throk, he murmured, "This belonged to us. He should not have come by it. I do not know how he did. In the end, though, it could not protect him from me. I negated its effect so that you could see him, and you did the rest . . . very well. Our confidence was not misplaced." He looked at Throk with obsidian eyes. "You will probably want to remove the data crystal in his pocket."

"What are you?" said Throk. There was now no bravado in his tone at all.

Shiv'kala stepped forward and touched one hand to Throk's temple. Throk tried to move, but was unable to do so. "I," Shiv'kala said softly, "am simply a figment of your imagination."

Throk blinked, trembled slightly for no reason that he could recall, and looked at the empty office in front of him. Then he heard footsteps pounding up the steps behind him and he turned to face several other members of the Prime Candidates. They gaped in open astonishment at the corpse on the floor and then stared mutely at Throk.

Throk offered no explanation whatsoever. None seemed necessary. Instead he simply said, "Get rid of him." As an afterthought, he added, "And remove the data crystal from his pocket."

They did as they were told, removing the data crystal, tossing it on the floor, and grinding it underfoot. Within moments, Lou Welch's body had been shoved into a bag and dragged unceremoniously down the stairs, his head thumping rhythmically on each step as he was hauled along like a sack of vegetables. The Prime Candidates who had taken on the task made sure to haul the body to a site reasonably distant from their safe house, then tossed it into an alleyway. And there they left it.

Lou lay there for a time, passersby paying the lifeless heap no mind. And then a robed figure approached him. No one cared about the robed figure because somehow their eyes seem to glide right off him if they happened to look in his direction. He knelt next to the body, undoing the top of the sack and yanking it down so that he could have a clear look at that which he already knew he was going to find. The head was swollen black-and-blue where it had struck the wall, and dried blood had coalesced all over its face.

"Poor bastard," muttered Finian. "Vir's not going to be happy about this at all."

14

"I want him dead. Whoever did this, I want him dead."

Garibaldi was trembling with barely suppressed rage. He was standing in a Centauri morgue, where he had been summoned to come and identify the body of one Lou Welch, Human. Welch's body lay unmoving on the slab, surrounded by Garibaldi, G'Kar, and Durla, their faces grim. A coroner stood nearby, impassive.

"The emperor regrets that this has come to pass," Durla began.

"The emperor regrets. He couldn't be bothered to come here, is what you're saying."

"He had other things to which he needed to attend . . ."

"So did this guy!" snapped Garibaldi, stabbing a finger at Welch. "And he's not going to get to attend to them, because one of you bastards did this to him!"

"Mr. Garibaldi, I resent that phrasing—"

Garibaldi silenced him with a gesture. "Ask me if I care," he said tersely. "Let me make this absolutely clear, Minister. Whoever did this, I want his head on a platter with some nice garnish and a few lemon wedges, and I want it now!"

"Michael, this isn't accomplishing anything," G'Kar said softly.

"You know what, G'Kar? I don't care! If I keep silent, I still won't be accomplishing anything, so I might as well accomplish nothing at the top of my lungs!"

"Mr. Garibaldi, this is regrettable," Durla said, "but the simple truth is that Centauri Prime is no more immune from crime and random acts of violence than any other world . . ."

Garibaldi circled the slab and came right up to the minister. "This wasn't anything random. He found out something, and one of your people did this."

"Found out something. What would that be?"

"About what you people are really up to."

Durla's eyes narrowed. "If you have some specific charge," he said in a measured, deliberate tone, "then I suggest you take it back to President Sheridan. If you do not, then I will thank you not to throw around unsupported allegations, since they will do nothing to alleviate the tensions between our races. To the best of my knowledge, however, we have been quite forthcoming in answering all your questions, and proving to you that your accusations of military buildup have been groundless. As unfortunate as this situation is, what it most definitely does not need is to be complicated with unrelated accusations."

Garibaldi took all this in; then he leaned forward until he was right in Durla's face. When he spoke, it was so softly that Durla had to strain to hear. "If I find out," he murmured, "that you, or someone who answers directly to you, had anything to do with this . . . then I swear to God, Minister, I will kill you myself."

"I would not advise that," said Durla calmly. "That would create an incident."

"We've already got an incident," Garibaldi said, indicating Welch. "And someone is going to pay for it." His hands were opening and closing as if he were trying to find someone whose throat he could wrap them around.

And then a voice said sharply, "I don't think threats are going to help."

"Ambassador Cotto," Durla said quickly. "Your timing could not be better."

"Or worse, depending on your point of view," said Vir. He crossed the morgue, looking around uncomfortably. "Chilly in here," he said. Then he looked down in undisguised dismay at the body on the slab. That was one thing that Garibaldi genuinely liked about Vir. It was impossible for him to hide what he was thinking. Vir's face could be read more easily than a data crystal.

At least, that's what Garibaldi once would have thought. Now, though, he thought there was an air of inscrutability to Vir that hadn't been there before. Vir had changed in the time since he'd last seen him, Garibaldi realized, and he didn't think it was for the better.

Vir turned to the coroner, who was standing a few feet away. "Do we know the cause?" he asked.

It was Garibaldi who answered. "Yeah. The cause was that he was in the wrong place at the wrong time, and found out something he shouldn't have, and was killed for it."

"That's a serious charge, Mr. Garibaldi."

"Hey!" said Garibaldi. "It's not like Lou was picked up for jay-walking! A man is dead! As crimes go, they don't get much more se-rious than that. Serious crimes require serious charges—and serious punishment."

It was G'Kar who spoke up. "At the moment, Mr. Garibaldi, the one who is being punished is you. You are not responsible for Mr. Welch's death simply because you brought him here."

"Whose side are you on?" Garibaldi said, with a sharp look to G'Kar.

"Yours and his," G'Kar said promptly. "However, he is gone, and I don't think you'll be helping anyone with histrionics. There will be an investigation, but getting angry at the men in this room will not ex-pedite it, nor will it create anything resembling the proper atmos-phere for an investigation."

"Thank you for understanding, Citizen G'Kar," Durla said.

G'Kar fired him a look that froze the words of thanks in his throat. "I don't want, or need, your appreciation, Minister. What I want is your cooperation . . . and yours, Mr. Ambassador. If you de-sire the continuation of anything remotely approaching normal rela-tions between your people and the Alliance . . ."

"Normal relations?" At that, Vir laughed bitterly. "Look, G'Kar, I hate to remind you, but at the moment 'normal' translates as 'We're watched for the slightest hint of aggressive behavior, so that people like you can be sent down to monitor us . . . and have something like this happen as a result.'" With that he indicated Welch's corpse.

G'Kar took a step toward Vir, studying him very carefully, as if dissecting him with his eye. "We are depending upon you to help us handle this matter, Ambassador. For what it is worth . . . I have al-ways had a great deal of respect for you."

More harshly than G'Kar or Garibaldi would have expected, Vir replied, "Let us be candid, Citizen. You dripped blood at my feet to symbolize dead Narn, as if it were my fault. No one in this galaxy ever made me feel smaller than you did at that moment. So you'll excuse me when I tell you that your claim to have respect for me . . . well, that isn't worth much at all."

There didn't seem anything that Garibaldi or G'Kar could say in response to that. Instead, Garibaldi looked down once more at Welch, then rested a hand on his cold shoulder, and whispered, "I'm sorry, Lou." Then he and G'Kar left without a backward glance.

"Tragic," said Durla, shaking his head sadly. "Most tragic."

"Minister . . . I'd like to be left alone with him for a time." Vir glanced at Durla, then at the coroner. "If you wouldn't mind."

"Alone? Why?" asked the coroner.

"I knew this man," Vir said. "He was a friend, after a fashion. I'd . . . like to say some prayers. They're personal. I'm sure you understand."

"Of course I do," said Durla, who looked as if he didn't, but wasn't inclined to argue. "Will you be coming by the palace during your stay? Say hello to Mariel, perhaps?"

"Perhaps," said Vir. "Thank you."

The two Centauri exited the morgue, leaving Vir alone with Welch. He stared down at the dead man, shaking his head in silence.

"How did you get here so quickly?"

It was Finian who spoke, having practically materialized at Vir's elbow. He was carrying a staff, which Vir hadn't seen him doing before. Fortunately enough, by this stage in Vir's life, it was becoming almost impossible to startle him. He merely stared at the technomage, and said, "Did the coroner see you enter?"

Finian gave him a look as if to say, *Oh, please.*

Deciding that pretty much served as an answer, Vir continued, "What do you mean, how did I get here so quickly?"

"I mean I sent a message to Babylon 5 only a short while ago, telling you what had happened. How did you manage to travel the distance so quickly?"

"I didn't get your message," Vir replied. "I . . ." Before he spoke more, he reflexively glanced around to see if anyone was listening. Then he continued, albeit in a lower voice, "I had already left Babylon 5. Mariel contacted me privately the moment she learned that G'Kar and Garibaldi were here. She felt it would be best if I was here while they were here. I think she was right, although I doubt she was expecting anything like this." He looked up at Finian. "So what happened? You wouldn't be here if you didn't have some idea."

"He had been using Shadow technology."

"Shadow technology?" Vir could scarcely comprehend it. "Where would he get that?"

"I don't know," admitted Finian. "Might have been happenstance. Most likely it was. He used a transparency web. It gave him limited invisibility. The use of it in the city drew me to him, and I arrived in time to see his body being hauled out of a building. I followed the people who were dumping him."

"What building? Can you take me to it?"

"Yes," Finian said distractedly. "It appeared to be a stronghold for those charming lads you refer to as the Prime Candidates."

Vir moaned. That was not news he had wanted to hear. The Prime Candidates—the servants of Durla, the pets of Lione. This was not going to be easy. "He found out something, didn't he."

"I expect that he did."

"I wish we could find out what it was."

Finian was silent for a moment, and then he said, "There . . . is a way."

"What? What way?"

Finian turned to him and said slowly, "The brain . . . is one of the greatest technological marvels of nature. Still, in the final analysis, it is simply a computer. And data can be downloaded from any computer . . . even one which has crashed."

"You can . . . you can extract that information from him? Even though he's gone?"

"In theory, yes. I've never done such a thing myself . . . but I know the technique. I simply . . . wish I didn't have to. Gwynn or Galen could do this with much greater equanimity than I could. But Galen has his own problems involving Captain Gideon, and Gwynn is attending to other business. So I'm afraid that I am it."

"Is it difficult?"

"A bit. I did bring a bit of help," he said, gripping the staff a bit more tightly.

"Is there anything I can do to help?"

"Yes. Keep the coroner out of here."

"Of course," Vir said matter-of-factly.

"This will take a few minutes. I don't need him in here."

"All right."

"Oh, and before you go, hand me that cutting tool, if you would."

Vir did as he was asked, then headed out to the coroner. The coroner, for his part, seemed perfectly inclined to head back into the morgue, and Vir did the first thing that occurred to him: he broke down in sobs.

"Great Maker . . . were you close with that fellow?" asked the coroner.

"I love him like a brother!" Vir cried out. He didn't even bother with the nearby chair; he simply sank down onto the floor, weeping piteously. Finding a source of tears wasn't all that difficult for him. All he had to draw upon was everything that had happened to him, and everything that he had done in the past several years, and the misery welled up effortlessly. Summoning tears was not a problem; for Vir, it was restraining them on a day-to-day basis that had been the challenge.

Consequently, Vir managed to keep the coroner occupied with finding a sedative that would calm Vir's nerves. The fellow finally located something and handed it to Vir, who popped it in his mouth gratefully and lodged it securely in his cheek so that he wouldn't swallow it. When the coroner turned away from him for a moment, Vir spat it into his hand and stashed it in his pocket.

"Are you feeling better?" the coroner asked him at last.

Vir nodded, but he still had that air of tragedy draped around him.

"I am so sorry you have to endure this," said the coroner. "You, Ambassador, are a soul in pain."

"Yes. I know," Vir said with utter sincerity.

"You need a drink. Come . . . I'll close early today, and we will go out and speak of happier things." At which point, the coroner rose and started to head into the examination room.

"No, wait!" Vir called out. "Uhm . . . stay here, just a few minutes, until the medicine kicks in!"

"You'll be fine, Ambassador. I'll just be a moment. I've already left the body out too long."

"But if you'd just . . ."

However, the coroner had already walked away. Vir felt his stomach lurching into his mouth. Finally, in a last ditch attempt to alert Finian that someone was coming, he called out as loudly as he could, *"But do you have to go back into the exam room? Do you really have to?"*

The next thing he knew, he heard an alarmed yelp from the coroner, and was certain that Finian had been spotted. He scrambled to his feet and ran into the examining room, not sure what he could possibly say or do, but determined that he had to do something.

When he got there, he found the room empty save for Welch's corpse and the coroner—who was white as a sheet. He didn't seem sickened; certainly he had seen far too much in his life for that. But his attitude was one of barely contained rage. "Who did this?" he demanded. "Who did this?"

"Did what?" said a confused Vir, and then he saw it.

The top of Lou Welch's head had been neatly removed. Sections of his brain had been meticulously and precisely removed and put into a pan nearby, and—Vir was positive that it was his imagination—just for a moment, they seemed to be pulsing as if with a life of their own.

Then whatever movement he saw, real or imagined, ceased, and he was left with his stomach wrenching itself around in fits of uncontrollable nausea. He knew he wasn't going to be able to contain himself. The best he could do was lurch to a nearby garbage can and thrust his head into it as everything that he had eaten in the past twelve hours made its violent return engagement.

The early evening air shored up Vir as he stood outside the building, leaning against the wall, his legs quivering. He had made his excuses to the coroner, which had not been a difficult accomplishment. The coroner, considering the circumstances, seemed disinclined to go anywhere, and he promised Vir a full investigation into the outrageous circumstances surrounding Lou Welch's mutilation.

"Vir."

He realized that his name had just been said several times, and it was only around the fourth or fifth time that he really, truly heard it. He turned and saw Finian standing just inside an alley, gesturing that Vir should join him. Fired by a cold fury, Vir immediately headed toward the techno-mage, joining him in the relative dimness of the alley. "How could you?" he whispered furiously, with such intensity that his voice came out gravelly.

But Finian was, at that point, totally without the casual calm that techno-mages so often affected. Indeed, he looked as shaken as Vir, and when he held up his hands they were specked with blood. "Are you remotely under the impression that was fun for me?" he demanded. "You had the luxury of becoming ill! I didn't. At least . . . not until I got out here." He leaned against the alley wall, looking shaken, and it was only then that Vir caught a whiff coming off Finian's breath. The techno-mage had been violently ill recently, as well. Nastily, Vir couldn't help but think that that was something he would have liked to see.

"There had to be some other way," Vir insisted.

"Oh, you know that, do you?" snapped Finian. "Your many years' worth of training as a techno-mage has given you that insight, has it? I'm not a ghoul, Cotto. I don't derive any sort of sick pleasure from carving up the bodies of the dead. I did what had to be done. We've all done what we've had to do. Some of us are just less sanctimonious about it than others."

"I just . . ." Vir steadied himself. "I just wish you had warned me."

"Believe me, you would not have wanted to know."

Vir knew that Finian was right about that. If, during the time that he'd been working to distract the coroner, he had been thinking about what Finian was up to in the next room over, his ghastly imaginings likely would have hampered his ability to do his part of the job. Seeing that there was no point to pursuing or discussing the matter further, Vir sighed, "All right, so . . . so did you find what we needed?"

"Throk."

"Throk." Vir didn't follow at first, but then he realized. "Throk? Of the Prime Candidates? He's the one who killed Lou Welch?"

Finian nodded. "With his bare hands."

"Great Maker," Vir whispered. "I know him. He's . . . he's just a boy . . ."

"He's a young man whom I would not care to cross," Finian said.

"But why did he kill him?"

As quickly and efficiently as he could, Finian laid it out for him. Told him of the Centauri buildup, told him of the border worlds on which it was occurring, told him of the secret agenda that was being supported by the Centaurum. Throughout the recitation, Vir simply stood there, shaking his head . . . not in denial, but in overwhelming disbelief that all this could be happening to the world of his birth.

"My guess," Finian added, "is that there was a Drakh involved in the murder, as well. I can't say for sure, because if there was, the creature didn't reveal itself while Welch was alive. But that would be the only reasonable explanation for Welch's technology having failed him when it did."

"So . . . what do we do now? We have to tell—"

"Tell who?" Finian asked quietly. "Tell what? There is no one in authority you can truly trust, and even if you do find someone . . . you have nothing you can really tell them. What would you say? 'A techno-mage extracted information from Lou Welch's brain and told me that Throk was responsible.' You have no proof, and the only verification that the Prime Candidates are likely to provide is that they'll make sure your corpse winds up next to Lou Welch's."

Vir nodded slowly. Once again, there was no point in denying anything that Finian was saying. He turned and paced for a moment, then paused.

"All right, then," he said finally. "My main job is to prevent this from getting any worse than it already is. And there's only one way to do that. But here's what I need you to do . . ."

He turned back to Finian and knew, even before he looked, that the techno-mage was gone.

"If he doesn't stop doing that, I'll kill him myself," muttered Vir.

Vir made certain to have Garibaldi and G'Kar at a safe distance from the palace when he told them. As it so happened, he had chosen the spot where Senna had, once upon a time, spent days studying with one of her teachers, gazing at clouds and wondering about the future of Centauri Prime. Vir didn't know that, of course, although the future of Centauri Prime happened to be uppermost in his mind, as well.

His more immediate concern, though, was that he needed to avoid having the outraged shouting of Garibaldi echoing up and down the corridors. Such an incident certainly would contribute very little to the cause of trying to make things right.

He needn't have worried. When Michael Garibaldi became as angry as he was at that moment, he tended to speak in a very low, whispered voice. "First," Garibaldi said, very slowly and very dangerously, "I want to know what you haven't told me."

Vir had to give Garibaldi credit. The fact was, Vir hadn't told him everything. He had said that the Prime Candidates had been responsible for Lou's death, but hadn't specified which one. He had told them about how Lou had died, but hadn't mentioned the possible involvement of the Drakh. And he had told them of the military buildup, but not how he had managed to find out about it.

"I've told you everything I can."

"Vir . . ."

"All right, fine," Vir said in exasperation. "A techno-mage sliced open your friend's brain and extracted the information that way. Happy?"

Garibaldi threw up his hands in exasperation, and turned to G'Kar. "You talk to him," he said to G'Kar, indicating Vir.

"Vir," G'Kar said carefully, "you have to understand: before we move on this information, we need to know—"

But Vir didn't let him finish the thought. "You can't move on it."

Both G'Kar and Garibaldi, who had spun back around, said, "What?"

"You can't move on it," Vir repeated. "I've told you about this as a show of good faith. You cannot—must not—do anything about it.

The only one you can tell is Sheridan, and only if he likewise promises to make no move."

"You're insane," Garibaldi said flatly. "G'Kar, tell him he's insane."

"Well," began G'Kar, "I think if you study the . . ."

"*G'Kar!*"

"You're insane," G'Kar told him.

"No, I'm not," Vir shot back. "But I'll tell you what would be insane: letting the entire Alliance know what's going on, so that they can go after Centauri Prime."

"I don't give a damn about Centauri Prime," said Garibaldi.

"Yes, you've made that quite clear. But I don't have that sort of choice in the matter."

"And we're supposed to just let this go. Is that what you're saying?"

"I'm saying that I won't let it go. I'm saying that I'm going to do something about it."

"You are," Garibaldi said skeptically. "You. Vir Cotto. You're going to do something about it."

Vir stepped in close, and there was such cold fury in his eyes that Garibaldi reflexively stepped back. "I hear the condescension in your voice, Mr. Garibaldi. I know what you're thinking. You think I'm incapable of doing anything. That I'm inept. You think you know me.

"You don't know me, Garibaldi. These days, I don't even think I know me. But I know this: this is a Centauri matter, and it shall be handled in the Centauri way."

"And what way is that?"

"*My* way," Vir said. "Believe me, Garibaldi, you want me as an ally, not as an enemy. And I'm giving you the opportunity, right now, to decide which it's going to be. Choose."

Garibaldi bristled, clearly not pleased with having ultimatums shoved in his face. But before he could say anything, G'Kar put a hand on his arm and tugged slightly, indicating with a gesture of his head that Garibaldi should follow him. Working hard to contain himself, Garibaldi did so. They put a respectable distance between themselves and Vir before speaking in low tones.

"You're expecting me to go along with this? Just go along with it?" Garibaldi said, before G'Kar could even open his mouth. "Sheridan sent us here on a fact-finding mission. You expect me to go back and tell him 'Sorry, Mr. President. We lost a man and, yeah, we found out some stuff . . . none of which we can do anything about, because

I didn't want to upset Vir Cotto.' For all we know, Vir's full of crap! For all we know, he's behind the whole thing!"

"Calm yourself, Mr. Garibaldi," G'Kar said. "You don't believe that for a moment."

Garibaldi took a deep breath. "All right . . . all right, maybe I don't. But still—"

"Lou Welch's passing was a terrible thing. I wasn't as close to the man as you, and I know you feel it your responsibility since you brought him in on this. But the truth is that, yes, we were sent here to find facts, and we have found them. Now we have to determine what to do about them."

"We tell Sheridan . . ."

"And what he, in turn, does with them will depend heavily on your recommendation. Before you give that recommendation, Mr. Garibaldi, I suggest you consider the following: The Alliance, and Earth, do not need another war at this time. Morale is at an all-time low, since no cure for the Drakh plague has yet been discovered."

"The *Excalibur* is working on it. Gideon says he's close," said Garibaldi.

"And he said the same last year. Perhaps he is. Or perhaps he is trapped in what your people call Zeno's paradox, where he perpetually draws half the distance closer to his goal, but never reaches it."

"What are you saying?"

"I'm saying that more bad news, of this significance, is not necessarily needed."

"You're suggesting we cover it up?"

"I'm suggesting that we accede to Vir's request that he be allowed to handle it. If we provide that, then you and Sheridan will have a valuable ally within the royal court. He will be a useful source of information. Plus, you have to consider the long term."

"The long term." Garibaldi shook his head. "I'm not following."

Lowering his voice even more, G'Kar said softly, "That man is going to be emperor one day. So it would behoove you to lay the groundwork now for a solid relationship. Vir Cotto is the future of Centauri Prime."

It took a few moments for Garibaldi to fully process what G'Kar was saying. "The future of Centauri Prime." He chucked a thumb at Vir, standing a short distance away, idly pulling on his fingers. "Him. That guy."

G'Kar nodded.

"And would you care to tell me, great mystic, how you happen to know that?"

Unflappable, ignoring Garibaldi's tone of voice, G'Kar said, "One evening, when Vir was rather in his cups, he told Lyta Alexander of a prophecy made by one Lady Morella . . . a Centauri seer whose veracity is well known, even on my Homeworld. Lyta and I have spent a good deal of time together in recent days, and she told me."

"So let me get this straight," Garibaldi said. Despite the flip nature of his words, he did not sound remotely amused by the notion. "You're telling me that you heard thirdhand that some Centauri fortune-teller predicted Vir would someday become emperor, and I'm supposed to let Lou Welch's killer, plus an entire secret war movement, slide, based on that. Her 'veracity is well known.' I never heard of her. How am *I* supposed to know if she's so wonderful."

"Lady Morella also predicted that Londo would become emperor, years before it happened."

Garibaldi didn't reply immediately to that. Instead he scratched the back of his neck, then looked around at Vir, who hadn't budged from the spot. "Lucky guess," he said finally.

G'Kar's gaze fixed upon Garibaldi, and when he spoke next, Garibaldi understood how this man had forged himself a place of leadership on his Homeworld. His words were quiet, direct, and filled with utter conviction.

"Michael," he said, dropping the formal surname for the first time that Garibaldi could recall, "there is something you must understand . . . and perhaps you already do, on some level. You and I, Vir, Londo, Sheridan . . . we are not like other men."

"We're not." He wasn't quite sure how to react to that.

"No. We are not. We are creatures of destiny, you and I. What we say, do, think, feel . . . shapes the destinies of billions of other beings. It is not necessarily that we are that special. But we were born at a certain time, thrust into certain circumstances . . . we were created to act, and accomplish certain things, so that others could live their own lives. It was . . . the luck of the draw. And as creatures of destiny, when that destiny is previewed in whatever small amounts it chooses to reveal itself to us . . . it would be the height of folly for us to turn our backs on it, disregard it. Indeed, we do so at our extreme peril.

"There is enough peril in the galaxy right now, Mr. Garibaldi, that I do not think it necessary to add yet more."

Garibaldi stood there for a moment, taking it in. Then, without looking at Vir, he gestured that the Centauri should join them. Vir quickly walked over to them, a look of quiet concern showing clearly on his face.

"So you want to keep this matter in-house, as it were," Garibaldi said. "Keep it quiet. Hush it up, so that the Alliance doesn't come down on you with all guns blazing, and pound you flat into nonexistence . . . just as you tried to do with the Narns."

"I could have done without that last part, but yes, that is essentially correct," Vir said dryly.

"All right," Garibaldi said. "We play it your way . . . on one condition."

"And that would be?"

"You're asking for a hell of a leap of faith here, Vir. I'm not a leap-of-faith kind of guy. I tend to look before I leap. You want me to have faith? You give me something to look at. You understand what I'm saying?"

"I . . . think so . . ." He nodded his head, but then shook it. "Actually, I'm not entirely sure, no . . ."

"Someone killed Lou Welch. That someone has to pay for it, to my satisfaction. You know who it is, don't you."

"Yes," said Vir.

"Then I want him delivered up. I don't care what you have to do, what paths you have to clear. I want it done."

"What you're asking is impossible," Vir told him.

"So is what you're asking. Me, I try to do at least one impossible thing a day. I suggest you practice the same goal, and start today. Understood?"

Vir was silent for a very long time, and then he said, "If I manage justice for Lou Welch . . . you will keep the Alliance away from Centauri Prime."

"For as long as humanly possible. You'll have the opportunity to ride herd on it. But you've got to show me you're capable of doing so. I don't care how you get it done. Just do it. Do we have a deal?"

He extended a hand. Vir, however, did not shake it. Instead he looked down a moment, and then said very softly, "Yes. I will keep you apprised."

And then he turned and walked away, leaving G'Kar and Garibaldi looking at each other in silence.

"He'll never get it done," said Garibaldi. "He'll cover for the guy. Or he'll give us more excuses why he can't be brought to us."

"I think you're wrong," G'Kar told him.

"In a way, I hope so. I'd like to see Vir succeed. I think, at heart, he's the best damned man on this planet. And in a way, I hope not . . . because I'd like the chance to find the guy who killed Lou . . . and do to him what he did to Lou Welch. Sounds like a win-win proposition to me."

He smiled, but there was nothing except pain in the smile.

15

The evening hours were stretching toward the late night as Throk approached the entrance to the Prime Candidates' safe house. There was another, main headquarters that was used for recruitment and to hold up as a symbol of all that was great and wonderful in the Prime Candidates organization, but the safe house was their true home. Indeed, he spent more time there than he did at his own residence.

Two others of the Candidates, Muaad Jib and Klezko Suprah, strode along briskly next to Throk. They were newer inductees to the organization, people whom Throk himself had brought aboard. He regarded them somewhat as protégés, and looked forward to guiding their training as members of the most glorious and farseeing group in all of Centauri Prime.

Muaad and Klezko had been a bit shaky the previous night when they'd been asked to dispose of the Human's body. But since then, Throk had had a long talk with them, and they seemed much calmer now. That was certainly a relief. They were Prime Candidates, after all. The Candidates watched out for each other, and covered each other's backs. They were working hard to adopt the same stoicism and determination that Throk so ably displayed, and he was quite sure that they were going to come along very nicely.

And then something separated itself from the shadows ahead.

Throk slowed, his eyes narrowing, and Muaad and Klezko likewise reduced their pace. For a moment, Throk had an odd feeling of déjà vu. A figure stepping forth from darkness . . . why did that seem familiar to him?

Then he saw who it was.

"Ambassador Cotto?" he said. "Is there a problem?"

Vir smiled widely and spread his hands in a manner that was both subtle and overt. The gesture looked cool, routine, and friendly; by the same token, it went to show that there was nothing of any danger in his hands. "Just wanted to talk to you for a moment, Throk. Can you spare the time?"

"Of course," said Throk. He wasn't particularly concerned about Ambassador Cotto—the man was a bumbling idiot, an amateur pretending to be a diplomat. His appointment to Babylon 5 was a waste of time, for Babylon 5 was inhabited solely by enemies of the Centauri Republic. Since the Alliance already hated the Centauri, Vir could hardly do any further damage. And he had lost his woman to Minister Durla in a card game. How utterly pathetic was that? The ministers seemed to have some regard for him since, for some reason, Durla did. But Throk knew him for what he was: an oaf. Still, even fools should be humored every now and then.

He nodded to Muaad and Klezko, who proceeded into the building. Throk then approached Vir slowly, and said, "How may I be of assistance?"

"I know you killed Lou Welch."

Throk prided himself on his unflappability. He had worked long and hard to maintain an air of such detachment, and no one, and nothing, could ever throw him off guard or off balance. But Vir's words, coming as they did from that pasty, insipid face, were the equivalent of a club to Throk's skull. And one word, one unfortunate word, slipped unbidden from between his lips.

"How . . ."

The moment the word was out of his mouth, Throk wanted to kick himself. That was the absolute last thing he wanted to say. But it wasn't for nothing that Throk was one of the foremost leaders of the Prime Candidates. Barely half a second had passed before he recovered his wits.

". . . could you think such a thing," he continued, the pause almost imperceptible.

Almost.

"Oh, come now, Throk," Vir said, as if they were long-lost friends. "How could you think I *wouldn't* know? Centauri Prime has no greater protector of its interests than the Prime Candidates, and there is no greater Prime Candidate than you. The coroner said that someone killed the Human with his bare hands. That being a figure of speech, of course. The killer wore gloves. Those uniforms of yours come with gloves, by the way . . . don't they, Throk?"

"Many people wear gloves," Throk said. "The night air is quite cool."

"Yes, yes. That's so true," Vir commiserated. "Plus, it makes it next-to-impossible to get good DNA traces off the victim."

"Ambassador, I don't know what—"

"Of course you don't, of course you don't," Vir said. He draped an arm around Throk, and Throk stiffened. "Look, Throk . . . despite appearances, I'm not an idiot. I see which way the wind is blowing. I know what the future of Centauri Prime is, and I can tell you this: it's not having the Humans hovering over us and watching our every move. It's the people like you, the Prime Candidates. You are the movers and shakers; you are the next generation of greatness. Some day," and he laughed and patted Throk on the back, "you're going to be running things. You're probably going to wind up being my boss. So I figure the best possible thing I can do is get on your good side now, right? Right?"

"Right," Throk agreed slowly, still a bit confused but trying not to show it.

"So you see what I'm saying, then."

"You are saying," Throk guessed, analyzing each word thoroughly before he released it, "that if I did have something to do with the demise of . . . what was his name?"

"Welch. Lou Welch."

"That if I was involved with Mr. Welch's demise . . . you would not care."

"It's us against them, Throk," Vir said, leaning in even closer. It was at that point that the Prime Candidate caught the whiff of liquor hanging on Vir's breath. The man was drunk. It was likely that, come morning, he wouldn't even remember the conversation. "Us against them. And me . . . I want to be us. Let them be them . . . and we're us. United we stand, divided we fall. Right? Right?"

"Right," Throk said again.

Vir nodded, staring at him a time longer, staring into his eyes so intently that Throk felt as if Vir were trying to locate some treasure inside his skull. Finally Vir released him, and said, "You, Throk . . . are going places." Then he turned and, with a slight stagger, wobbled away into the evening.

Throk watched him go, the pitiful shell of a Centauri with aspirations toward . . . something. Throk couldn't be sure what. If he truly believed that he had some place in the future of Centauri Prime, then he, Vir, was woefully kidding himself.

Shaking his head, Throk entered the safe house and strode into one of the meeting rooms. Klezko and Muaad were waiting for him, as were several others.

"What did he want?" asked Klezko.

"To make a fool of himself," Throk replied, smirking. "In that, he was quite successful." Then he frowned. "But he knew that I killed Welch. We have to find out how he knew . . . and once we have . . . we will probably have to dispose of him, as well."

Vir sighed heavily as he looked at the small cylinder in his palm. It looked like nothing. It seemed so insignificant. Yet he was holding his future, right there in his hand.

He had looked squarely into Throk's eyes when he had stated that Throk had killed Lou Welch. Vir had become quite adept at being able to see what people were thinking, spotting any hint of duplicity, just by looking in their eyes. Perhaps he had simply gotten a lot of practice by being with Londo for so long.

So when he mentioned Welch's name, he had watched Throk's eyes, his face, for some sign of innocence. Some sort of confusion as to why Vir would be saying such a thing.

Instead he had seen it plainly. Throk had been momentarily confused, but it was the confusion of guilt. He had started to say "How," and then he had paused, obviously reconstructing the sentence that would have continued "did you know?"

But Vir had known. Vir was sure. Terribly, horribly sure. He was sure that Finian had not lied to him. The techno-mages had been many things, but deceivers they most certainly were not. They seemed to have a greater love of truth than any beings he had ever encountered.

Still . . . he had to be positive, beyond even the slightest shred of doubt. Because Vir knew himself all too well, and if one fragment of uncertainty remained with him, it would haunt him forever.

And so he listened, via the device that was now in his ear. Listened carefully, and Throk—in his arrogance—wasted no time in telling him what he needed to know. "But he knew that I killed Welch."

There it was . . . the evidence right there. All Vir needed to publicly . . .

To publicly what?

Throk came from too solid, too powerful a family. The house of Milifa was tightly allied with that of Durla's . . . Mariel had confirmed that for him, even though he had already been reasonably certain of it. Plus Throk was one of the first of the Prime Candidates, and was destined for greatness. The death of one nosy Human wasn't going to stop him from fulfilling that for which he was intended.

Of course, Vir could press the matter. He could go straight to the emperor. But he had every reason to believe that Londo would never stick his neck out, not at this point in time, because there were too many people out there who were interested in severing that same neck. Particularly if he were perceived as acting in a manner that was contrary to the best interests of Centauri Prime.

Furthermore, if Vir did desire to press the matter . . .

. . . he was a dead man.

That was beyond question. If the emperor couldn't cross the powers that be, certainly Vir's prospects were nil. He would be accused of operating in opposition to the grand and glorious destiny of Centauri Prime, as personified by Throk and his associates.

So if he did seek punishment for Throk through proper channels, he would most assuredly fail, and his life would be forfeit. He would have to lock himself into his quarters on Babylon 5, and never set foot out again.

The alternative was to turn the matter over to Sheridan. But then the entire matter would become known to all. The entire Centauri Homeworld would be at risk. Who knew how many thousands, hundreds of thousands, might die in the resultant chaos?

Vir turned it over and over in his mind.

He had sought out help. He had gone to Rem Lanas, who had proven to be something of an electronics expert. He had gone to Renegar, who had been pegged to oversee the dig on K0643 because he had familiarity with demolitions. He had been in touch with them somewhat regularly since the debacle on K0643, and they had learned from that disaster: They had learned whom to trust. They had learned that some of the underpinnings upon which the movements of Centauri Prime were based were, in fact, built upon sand.

Vir had brought them along slowly, building his own foundations, brick by brick. And Lanas and Renegar had begun speaking to others. Others who had survived K0643 and were disenchanted by the Centauri brain trust that had organized what had amounted to little more than a paid death camp. And others still, freethinkers who had been driven underground or exiled.

Now, though, matters had come to a head, a bit more quickly than Vir would have liked. He was a careful, methodical thinker, and he did not desire to act precipitously. He had to act at this point, though. He had to do something. Centauri Prime was simply not ready for a war, and he was not ready to roll over and let his world be assaulted again.

Garibaldi would not be satisfied with anything less than justice.

"No choice," whispered Vir.

"You should have seen him," said Throk with amusement. "Draping his arm around me. Acting as if I were his son. He—"

Muaad's eyes suddenly narrowed. "Wait a minute," he said. "Turn around."

Throk looked puzzled. "Why?"

"Just do it."

Throk did so, and Muaad's fingers ran questingly over the back of Throk's uniform shirt. "There's something here," he said. "A small lump . . . some sort of a device."

"He put something on me?" Throk's fury was mounting immediately. "How dare he! What is it?"

"Some sort of transmitting device," said Muaad. "He was eaves-dropping on us."

Vir had known that eventually deaths would be necessary. He had wanted to minimize it.

"I am a good man," he said.

His finger quivered.

"I am a decent man."

He thought about Cartagia, crumbling, with an astounded look on his face and a heartful of poison injected by Vir.

"I am a moral man."

He thought about the Drakh he had killed when he had blown up the Shadow base.

"I am an ethical man."

His voice was becoming increasingly soft as his hand shook.

Throk had killed Welch. The others had helped remove the body, and had stayed silent. They were guilty, all guilty, of a crime that had brought Centauri Prime to the brink of war and possibly total annihilation.

"I have no choice," he said.

"I'll kill him!" said Throk. "Enough is enough! How dare he plant a voice transmitter on me! He—"

Then he remembered something else.

Vir had patted Throk on the head as well.

His hand flew up. He felt the hard round disk, hidden by his high crest of hair. He pulled at it. It was attached via adhesive.

Vir flipped open the end of the cylinder. There was a small button on it. There was water dripping onto it, and he realized belatedly that it was his own tears.

He had found and read that book. The one about how all boys grow up, except one. He, Vir, had to grow up, his childhood ending with one stroke of a button.

"To die . . . would be an awfully big adventure," he whispered. "I'm . . . I'm sorry."

He closed his eyes and pushed the button.

"Senna!" Throk cried out.

And then his head erupted in flame.

The windows of the safe house blew out, shattered glass flying everywhere. Passersby, completely unprepared, screamed and ran, momentarily convinced they were under assault yet again by the Alliance. Seconds later, the entire front wall collapsed, and the small structure tumbled down, while flames licked hungrily at it. There was more screaming, more running, and everyone was looking skyward, trying to see from where the next shot would originate.

Because all attention was directed to the heavens, no one would even have noticed if Vir had been nearby. He wasn't, however. He was several blocks away, leaning against a wall, while sobs racked his body so violently that he felt as if he would never be able to stand up again on his own. By the time rescue teams arrived to pull bits and pieces of the Prime Candidates out of the rubble, Vir was long gone.

Garibaldi stood on the balcony at the palace, watching the activity in the city some distance away. The entire area had been brightly illuminated, lights rigged to allow the rescue teams to do their job.

There was a chime at his door. "Come in," Garibaldi called, and G'Kar entered with that brisk stride of his. He went straight to the balcony and stood next to Garibaldi, who hadn't taken his eyes off the emergency scene. "Manage to find out what's going on?"

"Nothing definite," said G'Kar. Sardonically, he pointed to himself, and added, "It's not as if this is a face that is going to set Centauri tongues to wagging. You?"

"It's not as if anyone's big on Humans either," he admitted rue-fully. "The only thing I've managed to pull together is that no one seems to think it's an accident. I'm not sure if anyone is dead . . ."

"Yes. Some are dead."

G'Kar and Garibaldi turned to see that Vir was standing in the doorway. He had not bothered to ring the chime. He looked haunted.

"Who? Who died?" asked Garibaldi.

"Several of the Prime Candidates." He paused a moment, and then added almost as an afterthought, "And me."

"What?" Garibaldi shook his head, uncomprehending. "I don't underst—"

Then he realized. It all hit him with the intensity of a burst of white light.

And Vir could obviously see in Garibaldi's eyes that he under-stood. He nodded in silent affirmation.

"G'Kar," Garibaldi said. "I think that we'll be leaving tomor-row."

"We will?"

"Yes. We will."

Then G'Kar comprehended, too. "Oh," he said. "Yes. Of course we will."

Vir nodded once and started out the door. He stopped only when Garibaldi said, "Vir . . . thank you."

He turned and faced Garibaldi, and said, "Both of you can go to hell. And me, too." Then he walked out without so much as a back-ward glance.

16

"You should have let me do it."

Renegar spoke in a low voice as he sat in Vir's quarters on Babylon 5. Vir was staring at his own reflection in a bottle of liquor, and didn't seem especially inclined to respond.

"Vir," prompted Renegar. "Did you hear what I said?" The remarkably beefy Centauri seemed to take up more than his fair share of the space in the quarters. "You should have let me do it. It was my explosive charge."

"But it was my responsibility," Vir replied. They were the first words he had spoken in an hour.

It had been days since Vir had returned to Babylon 5. And one by one, the various individuals he had summoned were assembling. Soon they would be in this one room, which was not Vir's customary quarters. He had rented a separate facility on Babylon 5, under a fake name, paid for with funds pulled from a blind account. He was taking every possible step to be cautious. He was all too aware that that was how it was going to have to be for him for, quite probably, the rest of his life.

"Vir . . . look . . . you tried to warn me of things that I wasn't willing to pay attention to before," Renegar said. "I owe you for opening my eyes. I would have—"

"Renegar," Vir said slowly, "we are going to do everything we can . . . to spare lives. We are going to be as careful as possible. But I'm not an idiot. I'm not naive. I know that, sooner or later, people are going to die. Perhaps innocent people. I will do all that I can to avoid it . . . but it may very well happen."

"What are you saying?"

"I'm saying that I'm no longer going to be able to keep my hands clean."

"So you figured you'd get them dirty all at once."

Vir nodded.

"All right," Renegar said with a heavy sigh. "But if you're going to get this worked up and distraught over people dying . . . you may very well be in the wrong line of work."

"Don't think that hasn't occurred to me," said Vir.

Finally, the last of them arrived.

Vir looked around at the people gathered in the room. A dozen had been able to make the trip; that had been all that seemed judicious at the time. He had chosen them so carefully because one wrong move meant the end for all of them. If he missed a bet, if he brought a spy into their midst, he was signing their collective death warrant.

There was only one person missing . . . and, moments later, the door hissed open and he entered. Vir actually smiled when he saw him. He was the oldest individual in the room, certainly, and yet he moved with a spring in his step that evoked an old warhorse being pressed into service.

"Hello, Dunseny," he said.

The former valet of Londo Mollari bowed his head slightly. "Hello, good sir."

There were nervous, suspicious glances from several of the others in the room. Rem Lanas voiced the worries that were going through all their heads.

"This man worked for House Mollari for his entire life. Is it wise to have him here?"

"I still work for House Mollari," Dunseny promptly replied. "And the interests of House Mollari are not served by the bastards who are presently in power." He bowed slightly to Vir. "What small skills I can provide are yours, Ambassador, as you may need them."

"Gratefully accepted," Vir said.

He studied the men gathered around him. They waited for him to speak. He couldn't recall the last time people had sat in such anticipation, waiting for him to open his mouth. He wondered if G'Kar felt the same way when the Narn gathered around him and waited for him to bestow new pearls of wisdom upon them.

"All right," Vir said slowly. "There is much that needs to be done, and much we have to do. Centauri Prime is proceeding down a road that it must not be allowed to follow. And we have to do everything we can to forestall it. Even as we speak, there are installations, buildups underway on colony worlds whose very purpose has been corrupted. They have been forced into the service of an escalating war machine. We have to stop it."

"You're speaking of sabotage," one of the Centauri said.

Vir nodded. "That is exactly right, yes. All of you have had cause to suffer under the current regime. All of you are freethinkers, or have had your eyes opened by various circumstances that you could not have anticipated . . . but now that they have happened, you cannot turn away. The Centaurum is propelling our beloved Homeworld toward certain destruction, and we have to do whatever we can to head it off."

"But isn't it a delaying action?" asked Rem Lanas. "By engaging in sabotage, we're not putting a halt to anything. We're just slowing things down. Isn't it possible that, sooner or later, Centauri Prime will still be pulled into the center of a war?"

"Yes. It's possible," Vir admitted. Then, his voice strong, he continued, "It is also possible that, if we provide sufficient resistance, we will be able to get people—both those in charge and those who are disdainfully thought of as the commoners—to reconsider what they're doing. It doesn't matter how small the insect is; repeated stings will bring a body down.

"I cannot emphasize enough the danger that's involved. You are not all of the individuals involved in this effort. I did not feel it wise for any one person, outside of myself, to know everyone who is involved in our little endeavor."

"That way if any one of us is captured, he cannot turn in the entire underground at one time," Dunseny said.

Vir nodded. "Ideally, of course, if any of us is captured—Great Maker forbid—he will not turn in any of us. Death before dishonor."

There were affirming murmurs from throughout the room.

It was so easy to say, of course. So easy to believe that death would be embraced before the names of any coconspirators would be turned over.

But he had no choice now. He had gone too far. *It* had gone too far. He had no choice but to see it through.

Despite Londo's assurances to the contrary, Vir Cotto had never felt less invincible in his entire life.

"All right," Vir said. "Here's what we're going to do . . ."

Durla told them all it was an isolated event. At least, that was what he said publicly.

Privately he sang a very different tune, and promised a full investigation into the destruction of the Prime Candidates safe house, which had not proved to be so safe. Howling the most loudly was Milifa of the House Milifa, the patriarch who had lost his son in a hideous explosion that people still speak of in hushed voices, even though it happened months ago.

After all this time, Durla's investigation continued to turn up nothing concrete, only supposition. He told any and all who would listen to him that there was an underground movement brewing, a group of saboteurs who had been responsible for the killing of the handful of Prime Candidates, and who would undoubtedly make more strikes against us if given the opportunity. The problem is that relative peace causes complacency, and because there were no further assaults, Durla's theories soon lost credence.

That has all changed, however.

Today we received word that there were attacks on two of our colony worlds. And not just any attacks. The munitions plant—my pardon, the educational facility—on Morbis was blown sky high. The weapons development center—my pardon, the health facility—on Nefua is now a pile of rubble. Both blasts happened within a day or so of each other. It was a clear message to us that we are not simply dealing with happenstance or an isolated instance. This is nothing less than war . . . a war being waged from within.

Durla, however, is managing to work the situation from both sides. He cannot seem to make up his mind. Sometimes he claims that the attacks are part of an internal underground of saboteurs and protestors. Other times he states that the Alliance is behind the attacks. Occasionally he blends the two, stating that there is indeed some sort of rebellious crew of saboteurs, who are being supported and funded by the Alliance. No one appears to notice the fluidity of Durla's sentiments. Either that, or no one wishes to point it out, for fear that Durla will not react well.

It is hard to dispute Durla's success, however. Minister Vallko has been holding up Durla as an example of all that is well and good in Centauri society, and they have formed a formidable team. I worry for the direction that matters are presently taking.

And here I sit, feeling increasingly frustrated and helpless . . . but simultaneously feeling very much in control. With all that is going on, the presence of the emperor has almost gone unnoticed by those who are vying for power. They are making such noise in battling one another, that one cannot help but feel that they will end up drawing fire upon themselves. And when all that fire is burned away, then with any luck, I shall be the only one left. And would that not be the ironic, final laugh upon them all.

The one bit of good news to come from all this is that Dunseny has returned to my employ. With the passing of Throk—and good riddance to him—I was left without a valet. Apparently Durla had matters of greater importance to worry about than who should be at my side to help me on with my coat or whisper in my ear about matters that do not seem to have much in the way of great consequence for Centauri Prime. Truthfully, I do not know if I should be relieved or insulted.

I have not seen Vir recently. I should send him a message to come to Centauri Prime so that we may chat once more.

I certainly hope he is keeping himself out of trouble.

17

It had been ages since John Sheridan had set foot on Mars, and somehow he never tired of it. As he sat in the meeting room at Edgars/Garibaldi Enterprises, drumming his fingers absently on the table, it seemed to him that it almost didn't matter how many far-off worlds he had traversed. There was still something about the mystique of Mars. Perhaps it was all the old literature devoted to it, turning it into a mysterious place of strange canals, exotic multiarmed creatures, and a haven for invaders of all sorts who wanted nothing but to attack the hapless Earthlings and steal away with their women.

"President Sheridan." A voice came over the large screen, set into the wall to his right. "There is an incoming message for you."

"Put it on," he told the voice's invisible owner.

Within moments the screen flickered to life, and there was Delenn, with David by her side.

He was a remarkably handsome boy, David. A real head-turner, even at his relatively young age, if Sheridan did say so himself. Towheaded with a ready grin, and a snapping sense of intelligence and cold amusement in his eyes, both of which he got from his mother. Sheridan couldn't help but feel that David actually was more charming than his father and more intelligent than his mother. It made for a very formidable combination.

David was also, however, old enough to feel chagrin at any sort of open display of affection. Delenn, who doted on him—too much, Sheridan thought privately—had an arm draped around him, which was causing him to squirm right on-screen. He did not, however, voice protest. He knew better than that, particularly where his mother was concerned.

"I just wanted to remind you," Delenn said, "that you promised you'd be home in time for David's moving-up ceremony in school."

With a slightly plaintive voice, David said, "I already told her it doesn't matter, Father. She keeps insisting anyway."

"You promised you would be there, and I simply want him to know that a promise from his father remains a promise."

"Don't worry," laughed Sheridan. "I just have this final meeting on Mars, and then I'll be able to come home."

"You're meeting with Michael, I take it?"

"Yes. And . . ." His voice trailed off.

Immediately Delenn was obviously on the alert. "And who?" she inquired.

"Well . . . it turns out that the new Centauri prime minister is in the area. When he learned that I was here, as well, he requested a get-together. I didn't see how I could refuse him."

"A new prime minister?" She frowned. "I had not heard of this. When did the Centauri elect a new prime minister?"

"Quite recently. His name is Durla."

"Durla." She wrinkled her nose. "I know this one, John. I've read of him. Trusting any Centauri is problematic enough, but this one . . . he is a dangerous one. He is Londo, without the conscience."

"Considering I'm not sure just how much of a conscience Londo ever had, that's a rather frightening assessment," said Sheridan.

David shifted uncomfortably on the screen. "Do you need me for this anymore, Mother?"

"No, no. You can go. Tell your father you love him."

For response, David rolled his eyes and then moved quickly off-screen. Delenn reflexively took a step toward the screen, as if somehow she might be able to step through and be there with him.

"Delenn," Sheridan said thoughtfully, "a real-time connection between Mars and Minbar is not an easy thing to put together. It's complicated and it's not cheap. Did you really do this just to remind me of his moving-up ceremony?"

"It's silly," she said, but there was nothing in her demeanor that seemed to indicate that she truly thought it silly. "I have been having . . . concerns lately, John. Strange dreams . . . unlike others that I have had. I am wondering . . . whether someone is trying to tell me something."

"What sort of dreams?" asked Sheridan. He wasn't about to dismiss the concerns out of hand, even though they sounded a bit odd. After all, the Minbari often had their sensibilities informed by everything from prophecy to souls, so he wasn't about to ignore anything.

"I keep . . . seeing Centauri. I see Londo. And . . . an eye . . ."

"An eye? What sort of eye?"

"Watching me. Just an eye. Nothing more than that, and then the other night, I had a dream that it looked right through me, as if I wasn't there, and straight at David. I don't know what any of it means."

"Neither do I, but I have to admit, you're making me nervous as hell," said Sheridan.

"John . . . come back as soon as you can. I know as president of the Alliance you have responsibilities, but . . ."

"I will. As soon as I can, I promise. And Delenn . . ."

"Yes?"

"I'll keep my eye peeled."

She sighed and made no effort to hide her annoyance with him. "Sometimes I don't even know why I bother," she said, and then the screen blinked out. He realized with some frustration that he had forgotten to tell her he loved her. He hoped that she wouldn't hold it against him.

The problem was, now all he could picture was an eye staring at him.

"Thanks a lot, Delenn," he muttered.

Garibaldi was already in the conference room, chatting with Sheridan, when Prime Minister Durla arrived. Next to him walked a fairly stunning Centauri woman whom Sheridan recognized immediately.

"Lady Mariel, isn't it?" asked Sheridan. "A former wife of Londo's, correct?"

"Actually," said Durla, "the Lady Mariel is, in fact, my wife now. We married several weeks ago."

"Congratulations!"

"Thank you, Mr. President," Mariel said softly. She seemed far more reserved, far less flirtatious than the last time Sheridan had encountered her. He supposed that it was only reasonable for a newly married Centauri woman to be more restrained. Still, he couldn't help but feel that there was something more to it than that. Almost a distant melancholy, as if she had lost something, rather than gained a husband.

"And of course, I remember Mr. Garibaldi," continued Durla. "He came to visit us the year before last, as I recall. Matters were in something of a disarray at the time, I regret to say. We are getting things more solidly in hand, however."

Durla took a seat opposite Sheridan and Garibaldi. Sheridan saw that the Lady Mariel was standing, and gestured for her to take an open chair. But Mariel shook her head, gently but firmly. "I prefer to stand," she said.

"All right," Sheridan said with a shrug, and turned his attention to Durla. "So . . . Mr. Prime Minister . . . how may I be of service?"

Then he saw Durla place a small object upon the table. "May I ask what that is?" Sheridan inquired.

But before Durla could respond, it was Garibaldi who answered. "It's a recording device," he said. "I was wondering if he was going to produce it or keep it hidden."

"You knew I had it?" Durla asked, clearly surprised.

"You don't walk into the headquarters of a former chief of security without a few scans being done on you, without your knowing," said Garibaldi, sounding remarkably blasé.

"Very good. Very, very good. As you can see, though, I intend to keep this meeting open and aboveboard. Do you mind if I record it, Mr. President?"

"As long as security-related matters aren't being discussed, not at all," said Sheridan gamely.

"Very well, then. In truth, Mr. President, I only have one question, and then I will take up no more of your time."

"All right. What would that question be?"

Durla leaned forward, and there was a hawklike expression on his face. "When will you be calling off the attacks on our colonies?"

Sheridan blinked in confusion. "I'm sorry . . . what? Attacks? I'm a bit unclear as to what you're talking about . . ."

"Are you." Durla, for his part, didn't seem remotely puzzled. "Then I will clarify for you. Agents of your Interstellar Alliance have been secretly attacking various Centauri outposts. You see that we are endeavoring to build ourselves up, to make ourselves great again . . ."

"Now just hold on," snapped Sheridan, his temper flaring.

Durla steamrolled right over him. ". . . that we are attempting to purse the glory and respect that is due the Centauri Republic . . . and you snipe at us, and you endeavor to tear us down. Six months ago, there were attacks on the worlds of Morbis and Nefua. Since then, there have been more, on other worlds. Either attacks or sabotage of existing works for the purpose of slowing them down or eliminating them altogether."

"That is a complete fabrication."

"And is it a fabrication to say that certain members of your Alliance will never rest until Centauri Prime is wiped from the annals of galactic history?" Durla's voice was rising, and Sheridan felt as if the man were making a speech right from the board room.

"It most certainly is," Sheridan told him flatly.

"Is it a further fabrication to say that your Alliance has been trying to undermine the security of Centauri Prime, infiltrate it with its own people or else try to obtain influence with certain Centauri who might be amenable to disposing of the current regime?"

"This is ridiculous. Mr. Prime Minister, you requested this meeting and I agreed to it. I did not agree to having baseless accusations hurled at me."

"And when we agreed to peace, Mr. President, we did not do so with the intent of signing away the Centauri soul." He rose abruptly from the table. "I suggest you keep that in mind in your future dealings with Centauri Prime . . . lest we feel the need to deal with you in the future in a way that will make it clear just who, and what, the Centauri are."

With that, he turned and headed for the door. Mariel said nothing, barely glanced in their direction, as she silently followed Durla out of the room.

Garibaldi and Sheridan stared at each other for a moment, then Sheridan said, "You want to tell me what the hell that was all about?"

"Notice he took the recorder," said Garibaldi, and sure enough, it was gone.

"Yeah, I noticed. Are you thinking the same thing I'm thinking, Michael?"

"Grandstanding."

Sheridan nodded. "He's trying to make himself look good to the folks at home. So he records this meeting, tough-talks me, and then screens it for the Centauri so he can show them that the Alliance isn't going to have Centauri Prime to kick around anymore. Lots of huzzahs for him, boos and hisses for me . . ."

"And another step for stoking the fire of war."

Sheridan fixed a steady gaze on Garibaldi. "You really think that's what he's up to?"

"Don't you?"

"Yeah. Yeah, I do. Problem is, I can't do anything about it . . . thanks, in no small measure, to you."

"To me?" Garibaldi said in obvious surprise, apparently thinking that Sheridan was kidding.

Except that Sheridan was most definitely not kidding. "Look,

Michael . . ." and he sat down next to Garibaldi, leaning on the table. "You asked me to keep quiet the things that Vir told you. I did. You said he begged for the chance to handle it internally."

"And he's doing the job," Garibaldi pointed out. "That whole thing Durla was complaining about, the bombings and such . . . that has to be Vir's people. It has to be. And if Durla came in here to bitch about it, you know it has to be because Vir is hurting him. If it were just momentary setbacks, Durla wouldn't waste his time, even if it meant getting brownie points with his people."

"The problem with letting Vir attend to it, however, is that he *has* done a good job. Or at least apparently so."

"What do you mean?"

"I mean, Michael," said Sheridan, looking impatient, "months ago, years ago even, the Alliance governments were ready, willing, and able to do whatever was required to hold down Centauri Prime. But time has made them complacent. People have a short memory, Michael, even when war is involved. Try to tell them now that Centauri Prime might be on a road to buildup, and you're not going to get the Alliance off its collective ass to do anything about it. It's a time of peace, Michael, and people want to keep it that way. I can understand it. But it's damned frustrating. Because it means that I can't get anyone to do anything about it until Centauri Prime has engaged in a buildup so massive that it's literally going to be coming down people's throats. At that point, it may well be too late."

"Perhaps you want to call a meeting . . ."

Sheridan shook his head. "Why? I'll just learn from the Alliance members what I already know, and the Centauri can hold it up as another example of anti-Centauri warmongering. Won't that be fun."

"So you're saying we do nothing. We just stand by and let it happen."

"We watch," Sheridan said. "We wait. And we keep our fingers crossed."

"Keeping our fingers crossed," Garibaldi said with unbridled sarcasm. "Is that a military strategy now?"

"One that I'm learning to depend on more and more as time goes on," said Sheridan, holding up crossed fingers on both hands.

EXCERPTED FROM
THE CHRONICLES OF LONDO MOLLARI.
Excerpt dated (approximate Earth Date) April 18, 2273

I almost died today.

This past year . . . it has been referred to as the "Year of the Long Knives." At least, that is what they have called it in private. In public, they simply refer to it as the Time of the Great Loyalty.

Ever since his election as prime minister, Durla's reach has been everywhere. Ghehana is no more. He has sent soldiers through there, through the seamier side of Centauri Prime, with a mandate to rid it of all the undesirables. They are, after all, the most likely to plot against those who are the holders of the status quo. Who, after all, is more envious of those who have everything . . . than those who have nothing.

All the upper echelon naturally cheered this plan.

Then Durla came for the upper echelon.

Oh, not for all of them, of course. He only came for those who would not swear undying fealty to Durla, and he already knew in advance whom it was he wanted on his side. There were some who were able to purchase their loyalty, prove it that way.

But there were others—men who served before me, proud men, accomplished men—who did not like the way that Durla did business. Men who stood up to him, who spoke their mind. Who had watched Durla's people come in, month after month, until all in power answered to Durla, and who decided they could be silent no more.

Sanctimonious fools.

They were perfectly happy to be silent as long as they thought Durla was going to leave them alone. Once they realized that they were not safe, then and only then did they begin to rattle their sabres . . . at which point, Durla severed their sword arms.

He desires to do more than solidify his power, you see. He wishes to make certain that he controls the hearts, minds, the very soul of Centauri Prime. And he has systematically eliminated all those who might oppose him.

Today he came for me.

I was there in my throne room. Senna was with me. We spoke, not for the first time, of finding a husband for her. I am concerned that I might not be able to protect her forever. "I do not need protection, Highness. I am a grown woman now. I can care for myself," she said. The proud boasts of youth. How charming it is to hear it. How little she knew, as the doors burst open and Prime Minister Durla entered, swaggering and confident. He was accompanied by a small entourage of followers.

"To what do I owe this honor?" I asked calmly.

He came right to the point. "There are those who challenge your loyalty to Centauri Prime, Your Highness."

"I do not doubt it," I said. Senna looked apprehensively from Durla to me.

"It is important that the people of Centauri Prime know that their emperor is to be trusted implicitly. That their emperor is not in the grip of enemies of our Homeworld."

"I agree with that as well," I said.

"I wish to head off accusations that challenge your loyalty, Highness."

"Indeed. Very well."

Without hesitation, I turned to a guard and gestured for him to come near me. He did so, a look of confusion on his face. "Give me your dagger," I said, pointing to the ceremonial blade he wore on his hip.

The guard looked to Durla silently. Durla, clearly a bit confused, nevertheless nodded. One of my guards seeking approval for one of my orders. That alone should make clear the sort of world we live in.

So the guard handed me the dagger, and I examined the blade. "Tell me, Durla," I said softly, "do you believe in the Great Maker?"

"Of course."

"Good." Then I suddenly gripped Durla's wrist and brought his hand to the hilt of the blade. Before Durla could fully grasp what I was doing, I put the point to my own throat and closed my eyes. "Then let the Great Maker himself judge my loyalty, and guide your hand."

Then I stood there and waited.

For I knew one thing, you see.

Durla was a coward.

He loved to posture. He loved to preen. He loved to allow others to do his work for him, and maneuver behind the scenes while people suffered from his machinations. But he did not like getting his hands dirty. Ever.

He was hoping that I would cry out in protest, or fear, or lose my temper, or in some way give him something with which to maneuver. Instead I put it into the hands of the Great Maker . . . and into Durla's.

He wanted to show all the witnesses who were present that I was weak. That I would grovel before a subordinate. Instead I made a direct appeal to our Supreme Being. Durla was to be his vessel.

The Great Maker, as I suspected, had other things to worry about and did not weigh in on the subject.

Durla lowered his blade and said, in a most subdued voice, "Perhaps . . . we should speak of this later, Highness."

"I remain always at your service, Prime Minister," I replied with a deep bow, whereupon Durla and his people cleared out of my throne room.

Senna let out a long, unsteady breath of relief. "I thought . . ." she began to say.

But I waved her off. "Do not think," I told her. "It is an entirely overrated pastime."

I recently put forward the first major decree I have issued in months: I have banned any and all foreigners from this world. Any who are found here face imprisonment or worse. I have done so supposedly as a show of strength, to indicate that Centauri Prime is officially turning its back on the rest of the galaxy and stating that we wish to be left alone.

In point of fact, I do it as much for off-worlders as for ourselves. I would spare them any unpleasant fates that might befall them should they come here under the misapprehension that they are dealing with a civilized society.

It is evening now. I am alone in my study, alone with my thoughts . . . or as alone as I am ever allowed to be. The weather has been quite temperate lately, but I am beginning to sense a coldness in the air. If I were fanciful, I would say that they are the winds of war, sweeping toward us.

But I am not a fanciful person. For my reality is so ripe with madness, that to imagine flights of fancy would surely be a comedown.

The shadows grow longer, and they reach for me. I go to them quietly this night . . .

. . . but perhaps for not much longer.

OUT OF THE DARKNESS

Hiller of the planet Mipas had always been an enthusiast about Earth history. He wasn't alone in that regard; many of the residents of Mipas shared the interest. Earth history had become something of a fad. But Hiller specialized in one particular aspect of Earth activity and culture, and that was the great art of mountain climbing.

It was a practice that was virtually unknown among the Mipasians. Not that there was a lack of mountains on Mipas; far from it. There were several particularly impressive ranges, including some that rivaled those scaled by the immortal Sir Edmund Hillary, someone for whom Hiller felt a particular closeness thanks to the similarity in their names.

However, no one on Mipas had ever displayed the slightest interest in endeavoring to scale any of these peaks. All in all, Mipasians weren't an especially aggressive race—they preferred to live their lives peacefully and avoid the notice of the more aggressive and bellicose races that populated the galaxy.

Hiller, though, felt the urge to tackle the mountains.

They seemed to taunt him, their peaks shrouded in cloud and mystery. It was said that gods resided up there. Hiller didn't lend much credence to that theory, but nevertheless he simply knew that, sooner or later, he was going to have to try to find out for himself.

"Why?" his friends would ask him. "What is this need? Why this driving ambition to clamber up the side of a protruding geographic formation, at great personal risk?" Hiller would always give the exact same response. He would toss off a salute with one tentacle and declare, "Because it's there." He was rather proud of that quote, having come across it in his studies.

Now Hiller was on the verge of accomplishing his most ambitious feat. He was in the midst of essaying a climb up . . . the Big One. The Mipasians had never bothered to name their mountains. This one was dubbed the Big One for convenience' sake, simply because it was the *biggest mountain around. Many days had Hiller climbed it. Many times had he nearly fallen to his death, dangling by the tentacles before continuing his long, slow, and oozing way up the side. And finally, after many perilous days and nights, he had nearly reached his goal. He had broken through the clouds, and was using a breathing device to aid in his ascent, since the air at the mountaintop was quite thin.*

    He felt giddy. A child's wonder possessed him, as he wondered whether he would indeed witness the surprised expressions of the gods, gaping at him, when he managed to reach the peak.

    And then, as he stopped for a moment to rest, he heard something. It was a deep, sonorous sound that at first seemed to be coming from everywhere. It echoed from all the rock walls, its origin impossible to discern. Hiller looked around with frustration, then plunged a tentacle into his pack and extracted a viewer. Mist and clouds hovered all around him, but the viewer could easily punch through and give him a clear idea of what, if anything, lay in the vicinity.

    He activated the viewer and again wondered if he would find the gods waving at him. How amazing—and amusing—would that be?

    After a few moments, he began to discern shapes. They were coming from the north . . . no. No, not quite. They were coming from overhead and descending quickly, horrifyingly quickly. Two of them, no, three, perhaps four. It was impossible to be certain. What he did know, though, was that they were getting closer.

    The mountaintop began shaking in sympathetic vibrating response to the powerful engines that were propelling the objects through the sky. Pebbles, then larger rocks began to fall, and at first the full significance of that didn't register. As even bigger rocks tumbled around him, though, he suddenly realized that he was in mortal danger.

    He started scrambling back down as quickly as he could, having spotted a cave on the way up that might provide shelter. But it was too late, and he was too slow. A massive avalanche fell upon him and Hiller lost his grip. His tentacles flapped about in futility, and suddenly the mountainside where he had been clinging was gone, and he was falling, unable to stop himself or help himself in any way. Gravity had taken over, pulling him down. He hit a protruding cliff and tumbled off it, hearing things break inside him and not wanting to think about what they were. Then he landed hard on an outcropping.

    For just a scintilla of a second, he thought he actually might be able to survive. Not that he had the slightest idea how he was going to get down off the mountain, considering that he was already losing feeling below his neck. But he reminded himself that it was important to worry about one thing at a time.

However, the entire issue became academic as the gigantic pile of rocks tumbled around and upon him. He let out a last shriek of protest, frustrated that something so unfair and capricious was happening at the moment of what should have been his greatest triumph.

Fortunately, the rock slide left his head unscathed. Unfortunately it wasn't quite as generous with the rest of him. His body was crushed, the pain so massive and indescribable that his mind simply shut down, unable to cope.

And so as it happened, from his vantage point on the ledge, Hiller was able to see the cause of his death with his own eyes. They were huge ships, smaller than the gargantuan cruisers he had seen on news broadcasts, but larger than the one-to-one fighters that were so popular with the local military.

The style, however, was unmistakable.

"Centauri," he whispered. Whispering was all he could manage, and even then it would have been incomprehensible to anyone who was listening.

The Centauri ships moved off at high speed, heedless of the damage they had already left in their wake. Amazingly, the clouds seemed to part for them, as if with respect. Each ship possessed four curved fins, jutting at right angles to one another, knifing through the sky. He was able to see, far in the distance on the horizon, one of Mipas' largest cities. The ships were going right for it. The velocity with which they were moving was staggering. One moment it seemed as if they were near the mountain; the next they were practically over the metropolis.

They wasted no time at all. Their weaponry rained death down upon the city. Hiller watched helplessly, his body dying all around him, his vision becoming dark. Because of the distance involved, he saw the flashes of light that indicated that the city was being fired upon, and some seconds later, the sounds would reach him faintly, like far-off thunder.

It made no sense. Why would the Centauri attack Mipas? They had harmed no one. They were neutral. They had no enemies, nor did they desire any.

As the world faded around him, his mind cried out to the gods who had not chosen to present themselves, "Why? We have not hurt them! We never could, never would hurt them! What possible reason could they have?"

And then the words of his friends reverberated through his brain just as that organ shut down for good. His final neurons and synapses answered his own question with another—one that made ironic sense:
"Why climb a mountain . . . ?"

EXCERPTED FROM *THE CHRONICLES OF LONDO MOLLARI—DIPLOMAT, EMPEROR, MARTYR, AND SELF-DESCRIBED FOOL*.
PUBLISHED POSTHUMOUSLY.
EDITED BY EMPEROR COTTO.
EARTH EDITION, TRANSLATION © 2280
Excerpt dated (approximate Earth date)
May 14, 2274.

It is with some degree of shock and personal disappointment that I must conclude that I am losing my mind. I know this because, for the first time in . . . well . . . ever, I must admit . . . I actually felt sorry for Mariel.

Mariel, for those who have trouble keeping track of all the many players in these diaries, is my former wife. She is also the current wife of our inimitable—thank the Great Maker, for if he were capable of being imitated, I think I would have gone mad sooner—prime minister, the noble Durla. It has never surprised me that Mariel attached herself to him. She has that way about her. Mariel attaches herself to individuals of power in the way that the remora affixes itself to the stork.

For a time she was with Vir Cotto, my former attaché and current ambassador to Babylon 5. Fortunately enough for him, he lost her in a game of cards. I was shocked at the time. Now, in looking back, I can only wonder why I thought of it as anything less than Vir's good fortune.

More recently, I was walking past the rather elaborate quarters Durla keeps for himself in the palace these days. Back when he was simply Minister Durla, the minister of Internal Security, he maintained his own residence elsewhere. Since being made prime minister, he has relocated to the palace itself. This is an option open to whoever holds the

rank, but most have not chosen to avail themselves of it. Durla, however, is not like most others. He immediately took up residence in the
palace and, in doing so, sent me a very clear message, that I shall never
be rid of him. That he has, in fact, set himself a goal that is no less than
that of becoming emperor.

Not that he would admit it, of course. There are moments when he
directly challenges me, but he always does so subtly, then backs off as
rapidly as he can. For someone with such power and dominance, he
is really quite craven. It sickens me.

I wonder why it sickens me. I should be thanking what I foolishly refer to as my lucky stars, for if he had a core of genuine mettle inspiring
him, then he would be unstoppable. Durla, however, remains a bully
even to this day, and bullies are cowards. He may have gone quite far
in our society, but no matter how far one goes, one cannot avoid
bringing oneself along.

So . . . .

I was walking past Durla's quarters, and I heard what seemed like
choked sobbing emanating from within. Ironic that after all this time, I
still carry within me some vague aspect of the gallant. There were
guards on either side of me, as there so often are. My aide, Dunseny,
was also walking with me. Dunseny, the aging-and-yet-ageless retainer
of the House Mollari, used to be quite a bit taller than I was, but he had
become slightly stooped with age, as if his body felt obliged to make
some concession to the passing years. He actually noticed the sound a
heartsbeat before I did. It was the slowing of his pace that drew my attention to it.

"There seems to be a problem," I observed, hearing the sounds of
lamentation. "Do you think it requires my attention?"

"I do not know, Highness," he said, but he did so in a way that basically carried with it the word "Yes."

"We can attend to it, Highness," one of two guards who stood at
Durla's door offered.

"You?" I said skeptically. "You attend to things by shooting them. That
is not a criticism, but merely an observation, so please take no offense.
Far be it from me to offend someone who shoots things. However, I
believe I can handle this on my own."

"On your own, Highness?" the other guard asked.

"Yes. On my own. The way I used to do things before others did
them for me." Offering no further comment, I entered without knocking or ringing a chime.

Passing through the entryway, I found myself in an elaborately decorated sitting room, filled with statuary. Durla had acquired a taste for it. I felt more as if I were walking through a museum than a place where people actually dwelt. On the far side of the sitting room there was a high balcony that offered a spectacular view of the city. I had a not dissimilar view from my own throne room.

Standing on the balcony, leaning against the rail, and looking for one moment as if she intended to vault it, was Mariel. Normally her face was made up quite exquisitely, but in this instance her mascara was running copiously. The smeared makeup left trickling splotches of blue and red on her cheeks that gave her entire face the appearance of a stormy sky at daybreak.

Upon seeing me, she gasped and made a vague effort to try to clean herself up. All she did was make it worse, smearing the makeup so grotesquely that she looked like some sort of painted harridan from a stage drama. "I'm . . . I'm sorry, Highness," she said desperately, her efforts to pull herself together failing miserably. "Did we have . . . I wasn't expecting a visit from . . ."

"Calm yourself, Mariel," I said. I pulled a cloth from the inside of my gleaming white jacket and handed it to her. As an aside, I cannot tell you how much I despise the traditional white of the emperor's garb. Michael Garibaldi, my erstwhile associate on Babylon 5, once referred to it as an "ice cream suit." I do not know exactly what he meant by that, but I doubt it was flattering. I could not blame him, though; there is little about it that I find commendable.

"Calm yourself," I said again. "We had no appointment. I was simply passing by and heard someone in distress. There are so many distressed individuals out there," and I gestured toward the cityscape. "I cannot attend to all of them. But at the very least, I can help those who are within these four walls, yes?"

"That's very kind of you, Highness."

"Leave us," I said to my guards. Dunseny, ever the soul of proper behavior, good tact, and common sense, had waited in the corridor.

"Leave you, Highness?" They appeared uncertain and even suspicious.

"Yes."

"Our orders from Prime Minister Durla are that we are to remain by your side at all times," one of them said. I would record here any distinguishing characteristics he exhibited, for the sake of reference, but I cannot. My guardsmen were something of a homogenous lot. The aforementioned Mr. Garibaldi called them the "Long Jockey Brigade," I believe. I am no more conversant with the term "long jockey" than I am with "ice cream suit," but I will say this: Mr. Garibaldi certainly had a colorful way of expressing himself.

"Your adherence to orders is commendable," I said.

"Thank you, Highness."

"However, you overlook two things. Prime Minister Durla is not here. And I am. Now get out, before I command you to arrest yourselves."

The guards glanced at each other nervously for a moment, then wisely hastened into the hallway. I turned my attention back to Mariel. To my surprise, she actually seemed to be smiling slightly. Even laughing softly. " 'Arrest yourselves.' Very droll, Highness."

"With all that has passed between us, Mariel, I believe 'Londo' will suffice."

"No, Highness," she said simply. "I believe it necessary always to remember your station and mine."

A remarkable attitude. "Very well. Whatever makes you more comfortable." I took a few steps around the room, arms draped behind my back as if I were on an inspection tour. "So . . . do you wish to tell me precisely why you are so upset?"

"I see little point, Highness. It's nothing. A passing mood."

"Has Durla been abusive to you in any way?"

"Durla?" The thought seemed to amuse her even more than my passing comment had, moments earlier. "No, no. Durla, in point of fact, is not really here enough to be considered abusive. He is busy these days. Very busy." She looked down, apparently having suddenly taken great interest in her hands. "I do not begrudge him that. There is a great deal for him to do."

"Yes, yes. Destabilizing the region and sending our world spiraling toward certain destruction can be very time-consuming, I should think."

She seemed surprised by my tone. "He is your prime minister. I would think he carries out your wishes and desires. He serves Centauri Prime, and you are Centauri Prime."

"Yes, so I hear. The emperor is the living embodiment of Centauri Prime. A quaint notion. A grand custom. I think I like the sound of it more than I do the practice." I shrugged. "In any event, Durla does what Durla wishes. He no longer consults with me, or even needs me." I looked at her askance. "Or you, I should think. Is that the reason for the tears? That you miss him?"

"Miss him?" She appeared to consider that a moment, as if the thought had never before entered her head. If she was feigning contemplation, she was doing a superb job. "No," she said thoughtfully. "No, I do not think I miss him . . . as much as I miss myself."

"Yourself?"

She made to reply, but then stopped, as she appeared to reconsider her words. Finally she said, "I think of where I intended my life to be, Highness. I had plans, believe it or not. There were things I wanted to do when I was a little girl . . . not especially reasonable, all of them, but I . . ." She stopped and shook her head. "I apologize. I'm babbling."

"It is quite all right," I told her. "In all the time that we were married, Mariel, I do not think we actually spoke in this manner."

"I was trained to say all the right things," she said ruefully. "Speaking of one's disappointments and shortcomings—that wasn't deemed proper for a well-bred Centauri woman."

"Very true. Very true." And I waited.

Again, I must emphasize that I bore no love for this woman. I looked upon this interaction with a sort of detached fascination; the way one looks with curiosity at a fresh scab, impressed that such a crusted and nauseating thing could appear on one's own body. In speaking with Mariel, I was—in a way—picking at a scab. Then, since she didn't seem to be volunteering any information, I prompted, "So . . . what things did you wish to do? As a young girl, I mean?"

She half smiled. "I wanted to fly," she replied.

I made a dismissive noise. "That is no great feat. A simple ride in—"

"No, Highness," she gently interrupted. "I do not mean fly in a vessel. I wanted . . ." And the half smile blossomed into a full-blown, genuine thing of beauty. It reminded me of how it was when I first met her. I admit it. Even I was stunned by her beauty. I did not know then, of course, the darkness that the beauty hid. But who am I to condemn others for hiding darkness?

"I wanted to fly on my own," she continued. "I wanted to be able to leap high, wave my arms, and soar like a bird." She laughed in a gentle, self-mocking way. "Foolish of me, I know. I'm sure that's what you're thinking . . ."

"Why would I consider it foolish?"

"Because such a thing isn't possible."

"Mariel," I said, "I am the emperor. If you had asked anyone who knew me—or, for that matter, if you had asked me directly—what the likelihood was of such a thing coming to pass, I would have thought it to be exactly as possible as your fantasy. Who knows, Mariel? Perhaps you will indeed learn to fly."

"And you, Highness? Did you indeed dream of becoming emperor?"

"Me? No."

"What did you dream of, then?"

Unbidden, the image came to my mind. The dream that I had not had until well into my adulthood. But it's a funny thing about certain dreams: they assume such a state of importance in your mind that you start to believe, retroactively, that they were always a part of your life.

Those powerful hands, that face twisted in grim anger. The face of G'Kar, with but one eye burning its gaze into the black and shredded thing I call my soul, and his hands at my throat. This dream had shaped, defined, and haunted my life for, it seemed, as far back as I could remember.

"What did I dream of?" I echoed. "Survival."

"Truly?" She shrugged those slim shoulders. "That doesn't seem such a lofty goal."

"I had always thought," I said, "that it was the only one that mattered. I would have placed it above the needs of my loved ones, above the needs of Centauri Prime itself. Now . . ." I shrugged. "It does not seem to be such an important thing. Survival is not all that it is reputed to be."

There was a long silence then. It was very odd. This woman had been my enemy, my nemesis, yet now it seemed as though she were another person entirely. Considering what I had faced, considering those who desired to bring me down . . . the machinations of one young Centauri female didn't seem worth the slightest bit of concern.

Not so young, actually.

I found myself looking at Mariel, really looking at her for the first time in a long time. She was not decrepit by any means, but her age was beginning to show. I wasn't entirely sure why. She was older, certainly, but not that much older. She seemed . . . careworn somehow. She looked older than her years.

"Strange," she said slowly, "that we are talking this way. With all that has passed between us, Lond—Highness—"

"Londo," I told her firmly.

"Londo," she said after a moment's hesitation. "With all that we have been through . . . how odd that we would be talking here, now. Like old friends."

" 'Like,' perhaps, Mariel. But not actually old friends. For I shall never forget who I am . . . and who you are . . . and what you did to me."

I wondered if she would try to deny that she had endeavored to kill

me fifteen years earlier. If she would bleat her innocence in the matter. Instead, all she did was shrug, and without rancor in her voice say, "It was no worse than what you did to me."

"Next thing, you will tell me that you miss me."

"It is impossible to miss what you never had."

"That is very true." I looked at her with even more curiosity. "You have not told me why you were crying. That is, after all, the reason I came in here. Was it indeed because you miss 'yourself'?"

She looked down at her hands with great interest. "No. Someone else."

"Who?"

She shook her head. "It does not matter . . ."

"I wish to know, nevertheless."

She seemed to consider her answer a long time. Then she looked over at me with such melancholy, I cannot even find words for it. "I appreciate the time you've taken here, Londo . . . more than you can know. But it really, truly, does not matter. What is done is done, and I have no regrets."

"Whereas I have almost nothing but regrets. Very well, Mariel." I rose and walked toward the door. "If, in the future, you decide that there are matters you wish to discuss . . . feel free to bring them to my attention."

"Londo . . ."

"Yes?"

"My dream is childhood foolishness . . . but I hope that you get yours."

I laughed, but there was no trace of mirth in my voice. "Trust me, Mariel . . . if there is one thing in this world I am certain of, it is that, sooner or later, I will get mine. And sooner, I think, rather than later."

1

Luddig wasn't a particularly happy Drazi.

He did not like the building to which he had been sent. He did not like the office within the building. And he most certainly did not like that he was being kept waiting in the office within the building.

Luddig was a first-tier ambassador in the Drazi diplomatic corps, and he had fought long and hard to get to where he was. As he drummed his fingers impatiently on the expansive desk he was sitting beside, he couldn't help but wonder why it was that things never quite seemed to work out the way that he wanted them to.

Seated next to Luddig was his immediate aide, Vidkun. They provided quite a contrast to one another, Luddig being somewhat heavyset and jowly while Vidkun was small and slim. Not that Vidkun was a weakling by any means. He was whipcord thin and had a certain air of quiet strength about him. Luddig, on the other hand, was like a perpetually seething volcano that tended to overwhelm any who stood before him with belligerence and bombast. As diplomats went, he wasn't particularly genteel. Then again, he'd never had to be. His activities were confined mostly to his office and occasional backdoor maneuvers.

It was one of those activities that had brought him here, to Centauri Prime, to the place called the "Tower of Power." It was an impressive and elegantly simple structure that, when viewed from the ground, seemed to stretch forever to the sky.

Luddig had not come here on his own, of course. It had been set up meticulously and scrupulously in advance. No one on the Drazi Homeworld had been aware that he was coming to Centauri Prime ... well, not "officially" aware. He had brought Vidkun along primarily to have someone to complain to.

"This is how they treat Luddig of the Drazi!" Luddig said in disgust. He was one of those who chose to affect the popular Drazi habit of referring to himself in the third person. "An hour and a half we wait," he continued. "Waiting and waiting in this stupid room for this stupid minister." He cuffed Vidkun abruptly on the shoulder. Vidkun barely reacted. By this point in his career, he scarcely seemed to notice. "We had a deal!"

"Perhaps you should remind him of that, sir," Vidkun said with exaggerated politeness.

"Remind him! Of course Luddig will remind him! Drazi do not have to, should not have to, tolerate such poor attention to Drazi interests!"

"Of course not, sir."

"Stop agreeing!" Luddig said in annoyance, striking Vidkun once more on the shoulder. Since it was the exact same place, it left Vidkun a bit sore, but stoutly he said nothing. "You keep agreeing. It shows you are trying to mock Luddig!"

Vidkun tried to figure out if there was any conceivable way in which he could respond to the accusation. If he said it wasn't true, then he'd be disagreeing and thereby disproving the contention. Except he'd be calling Luddig a liar. If he agreed that was what he was doing, Luddig would shout at him that he was doing it again. Vidkun wisely chose to say nothing at all, instead inclining his head slightly in acknowledgment without actually providing any admission one way or the other.

Clearly Luddig was about to press the matter when, with miraculously good timing, Minister Castig Lione entered.

Lione was a tall man whose build and general look bordered on the cadaverous. He had such gravity about him that he could have used it to maintain a satellite in orbit, Vidkun mused. Then he noticed several of the black-clad youths known as the Prime Candidates following Lione, dropping back and away from the minister as he walked into his office. Vidkun came to the conclusion that Lione already did have satellites. They were the youth of Centauri Prime, and as near as Vidkun could tell, the best and the brightest. Their loyalty to Castig Lione was reputedly unyielding and unwavering. If Lione had told them to break every bone in their bodies, they would do so and do it willingly.

Vidkun did not, as a rule, like fanatics. If nothing else, they tended to be a bit too loud for his taste.

"Ambassador Luddig," said Lione, bowing deeply in respect. For a man of his height, bowing was no easy thing. Luddig should have appreciated the gesture. Instead he scowled even more fiercely. Vidkun rose and returned the bow, and got another quick physical rebuke from his superior. "To what," continued Lione, "do I owe this honor?"

"This honor." Luddig made an incredulous noise that conveyed contempt. "This honor. This treatment is more like."

"Treatment?" His eyebrows puckered in confusion. "Was there a problem with your arrival? My Prime Candidates were given specific instructions to provide you full protection in escorting you from the port. I cannot, of course, account for the reactions your presence might engender among our populace."

"It has nothing to do with that—"

Lione continued as if Luddig had not spoken. "In case you are unaware, all foreigners have been banned from the surface of Centauri Prime. That is how highly charged sentiments have been running. Fortunately, as a minister, I have certain . . . latitude. So I was able to arrange for your visit to our fair—"

"It has nothing to do with that!"

Lione blinked owlishly. "Then I am not quite sure what you are referring to."

"We had an arrangement!"

"Did we?"

"About Mipas!"

"Ah." Lione did an exceptional job of acting as if he had been unaware of what was getting Luddig so agitated. "You're speaking about the unfortunate, but necessary, attack on Mipas."

"Unfortunate but necessary how! Unfortunate, yes! Necessary . . . Drazi do not see that! Has Centauri Prime totally taken leave of senses? Or has Centauri Prime forgotten that Mipas is under Drazi jurisdiction!"

"Jurisdiction, yes. Curious how that happened, isn't it." Lione's calm, even lazy tone suddenly shifted. "Curious that the Drazi government paid so little attention to Mipas . . . until valuable minerals were found on it. Suddenly a world that was just beyond the outermost edge of the Drazi borders became Drazi property . . . when your government reconfigured the borders to allow for . . ." Lione actually chuckled, and it was not the most pleasant of sounds. ". . . to allow for the expanding universe theory. 'If the universe is expanding, Drazi territory must expand with it to keep up with natural law.' That was priceless, I have to admit. No one in the Alliance gainsayed you, simply because they were stunned by the sheer gall your people displayed."

"If Centauri Prime has issue with expansion of—"

Lione held up a hand, stilling the new torrent of words. "The Centaurum has no such issues. Expand territories all you wish. Reconfigure your borders and decide that you're entitled to take possession of the Vorlon Homeworld, for all we care. But Mipas, well . . ." and he shook his head sadly. "The fact is that our intelligence informed us that Mipas was acting in concert with, and providing aid to, certain insurrectionist factions here on Centauri Prime."

"Is lie!"

"Is not," Lione responded coolly. "The information we have received is quite definitive. Mipas was aiding those who would overthrow our beloved emperor and drive our prime minister out of office. Naturally, out of a sense of self-preservation, we had to take action."

Between gritted teeth, Luddig said, "We had an understanding."

"Did we?"

"Do not play games with Drazi!" Luddig warned. "Centauri Prime is as interested in mineral deposits on Mipas as Drazi! I know that! You know that! Everyone knows that! We had arrangements!"

"And how much you must have enjoyed those arrangements, Luddig," said Lione. "Under-the-table payments made to you by certain Mipas officials. And you, in turn, pass those payments along to us. A token of respect; a tithe, if you will, to purchase our goodwill. And you succeeded for quite some time, Luddig. I commend you for your industry. And I commend you for the deftness with which you managed to cut yourself in to those payments. How much did you manage to keep for yourself? Ten percent? Twenty?"

"Do you think Drazi not take risks!" Luddig said hotly. "Luddig of Drazi has his own expenses, own concerns. Certain officials turn their own blind eye to 'under-the-table payments,' as you say. Money has to cover their eyes, too. It was beneficial arrangement for all."

"Yes, yes, I daresay it was. Just as this little arrangement exists with other governments, other 'officials' such as yourselves. Others who envelop themselves in cloaks of self-righteousness, more than happy to complain publicly about the Centauri, while you have no difficulty in private backroom dealings. I can smell the corruption in all the governments of your pathetic Alliance. The odor of hypocrisy permeates even the vacuum of space, Ambassador Luddig."

Vidkun watched in fascination as Luddig became so angry that the skin flaps under his throat stood out and turned pale red. "Luddig does not have to sit here and listen to this!"

"Stand if you prefer, then," Lione said lazily. "It does not matter to me." Then once again, his attitude shifted, from torpor to quiet intensity. "Understand this, Ambassador. We stand by the results of our investigation. And since we know that the Mipasians were acting with the insurrectionists, we can only assume that the Drazi were aware of this connection and approved of it. That, Ambassador, would mean that you are—rather than our silent partners—our enemies. We do not advise that you become enemies of the Centauri Republic. That would be most unfortunate for all concerned."

Vidkun had the distinct feeling that Lione was assuming Luddig would wilt under the implied threat. To Vidkun's surprise—and, if he had to guess, to Lione's surprise as well—Luddig did not come remotely close to wilting. Instead he was on his feet, breathing so hard that it was rasping in his chest. "You threaten Drazi?" he demanded.

"I threaten no one," Lione said.

But Luddig wasn't buying it. "You are! You violate Drazi interests! You renege on deal!"

"The deal, such as it was, was entirely unofficial, Luddig," Lione pointed out. "You said so yourself. If you wish to complain about it to the Interstellar Alliance—if you wish to try to roust your fellows from their stupor and bring them into full war with us—then you will have to go public with the terms of our little arrangement. That will not go over particularly well, I assure you, because it will bring not only your own government under scrutiny, but others as well. No one is going to want that."

"Maybe Drazi do not care about scrutiny or deals," Luddig shot back. "Maybe Drazi care about Centauri thinking they can do whatever they wish, whenever they wish, to whomever they wish. Maybe Drazi believe that Alliance is willing to overlook 'deals' or treat them as stopgap measures to full war that can no longer be avoided because of Centauri stupidity and arrogance!"

Lione did not answer immediately. Instead he contemplated what Luddig had said. He leaned back in his chair, the furniture creaking under his weight, and he interlaced his fingers while studying Ludding very, very carefully.

Then he smiled.

Vidkun felt his spine seize up.

"It seems, Ambassador, that we may have underestimated the . . . vehemence with which you will be pursuing your claim. Very well."

"Very well what?" Luddig's eyes narrowed suspiciously.

"I shall take your concerns to the prime minister and we shall see
if restitution cannot somehow be arranged."

Luddig puffed out his chest with sudden confidence. "Yes! That
is attitude Drazi want to see!"

"Excuse me a moment, won't you? No, no, don't get up. I have a
small room designed for . . . private communications. Will not take
but a minute." He did not rise from his seat so much as he seemed to
uncoil.

The moment he walked out of the room, Vidkun turned to Luddig, and said, "We are dead."

"What!" Luddig scoffed at the very idea. "You saw! He spoke of
restitution! He spoke of—"

"Ambassador, with all respect, what he spoke of doesn't matter.
In these sorts of things, what is *not* said is often more important than
what is. I am telling you, we are—"

"We are Drazi! And you are coward!" Luddig said angrily, stabbing a finger at Vidkun.

"Sir, I am no coward," Vidkun said, bristling.

"Yes! Your own cowardice stops you from seeing that Centauri
do not wish to anger Drazi! You are not worthy of being aide to Luddig! A new aide will be required upon our return!"

Vidkun was about to argue the point further, protesting the accusations of cowardice, when the door opened and Lione entered
again, stooping slightly to avoid the top of the door frame. "The
prime minister wishes to see you, but his schedule simply will not allow for it today. Tomorrow, however, bright and early, he would be
more than happy to discuss the matter. In the meantime, deluxe accommodations have been arranged for you at a facility nearby. We
certainly hope that will suffice."

"For now," Luddig said noncommittally. "We reserve judgment
until we actually see accommodations."

"Very prudent," Lione said agreeably.

As they headed down to street level, Vidkun's head was spinning.
Every early warning system in his makeup was screaming at him that
they were in mortal danger. But Luddig was so overwhelmingly confident, and Lione seemed so eager to please, that he was finding it
harder and harder to believe that there was, in fact, any jeopardy. It
might be, he thought bleakly, that Luddig was correct. Perhaps he
was indeed a coward, and simply didn't have the proper mental
strength to pursue a career in the diplomatic corps.

They walked out into the street, a pleasant sun beaming down at them, and a glorious day on Centauri Prime apparently lying ahead of them. There were passersby, casting glances in their direction, but there did not appear to be any problem. There were Prime Candidates forming a protective circle around them, but Luddig—chatting animatedly with Lione—didn't pay them any mind. He was calm, cool, and confidently secure that he had a complete handle on the situation.

"Kill the Drazi!"

The shout came from someone in the crowd, and it was suddenly taken up by others. What had appeared only moments before to be a benign, loose assemblage of people suddenly firmed up into a mob.

"Kill the Drazi! Death to outworlders! Centauri Prime over all! Death to enemies of the Great Republic!" These and other sentiments suddenly seemed to come from everyone, everywhere.

And the enraged Centauri citizens were advancing, coming in from all sides.

The Prime Candidates melted away. Suddenly the protective wall of bodies was gone.

Luddig's accusation no longer registered in Vidkun's mind. He was beyond cowardice. He was terrified. The infuriated Centauri were moving toward them with one mind, and there was nowhere to go, nowhere to run. Then suddenly a strong hand was on his arm, pulling him away. The last thing he saw was Luddig going down beneath the clubs and fists of the crowd. Luddig was screaming, and it wasn't a particularly brave-sounding scream. It was high-pitched, and plaintive, and rather pathetic.

Someone held him. Vidkun let out a yelp and turned to see the face of the man who was about to kill him.

To his surprise, there was no anger in the expression of the Centauri man who had yanked him away from the crowd. The Centauri's long, black/red hair was high and swept up. His face was very angular, his chin coming almost to a point. It was his eyes that caught Vidkun the most, though. There was intensity, at least in one of them, but . . .

Then the world seemed to whirl around as someone else pulled at him, and just as quickly as he had been in the midst of danger, Vidkun was being thrust back into the Tower of Power. He staggered, looking around at his saviors: the very same Prime Candidates who had deserted them moments before, leaving them to the mercy of the mob. The red-haired Centauri was no longer in sight.

Vidkun thought he heard Luddig screaming once more, but then the scream was cut short by a sound like a melon being crushed. The expressions of the Prime Candidates never wavered. They simply stood there, like automatons.

"To my office," came a voice, the voice of Lione. Vidkun was still in shock and offered no resistance as he was escorted back upstairs. Moments later he was seated opposite Castig Lione. He couldn't help but notice that he had been seated in the chair closer to the desk: the one that Luddig had been sitting in.

Lione was shaking his head with a great air of tragedy. "How unfortunate. How very, very unfortunate," he intoned. "To think that such a thing would happen. But there are random acts of violence everywhere . . ."

"Random?"

"Yes."

"Acts of violence?" He was having trouble processing the words. He had to fight to bring his full faculties to bear upon the situation.

"Yes. Here the two of you were, walking the streets of Centauri Prime, and a lone madman attacked and killed your superior. We tried to stop it, of course."

"A . . . lone madman?" He felt a pounding in his head, as if his brain were shouting at him to pull himself together, and match what was being said with what had happened.

"Yes, of course. There's only so much protection even the most dedicated guards can offer in the face of such . . ." He shook his head. "Very likely, it was the work of the rebels and saboteurs. They were endeavoring to discredit the Centaurum, and such actions are taken to reflect poorly upon this government in the eyes of others. In any event, it is pointless to dwell upon it. My guards dispatched the madman. Justice was done, and it's important that we put the whole unfortunate business behind us."

"You ordered it!" Vidkun was trying to rally. "You ordered the assault! The mob! You!"

"Mob!" Lione sounded shocked. "I saw no mob. Nor, I would suggest, did you." Then he smiled and reached into his pocket. Vidkun automatically flinched, bracing himself for some sort of weapon to be drawn, but Lione instead simply pulled out what appeared to be a credit chip and extended it to Vidkun.

Vidkun took it, looking at it blankly. "What is this . . . ?"

"Access to a private account that Luddig set up. He thought we did not have right of entry to it. Luddig apparently thought a number

of things that were in error." He shrugged. "It was where he was siphoning payments from the various worlds . . ."

"Worlds?"

"You don't seriously think that Mipas was unique, do you?" The
very notion appeared laughable to him. "No, no . . . Luddig had a
number of 'clients.' There are quite a few worlds out there in which
the Drazi maintain interests. Interests that stem from tradition . . .
and from profit.

"Everyone is interested in protecting his or her interests, Vidkun.
Luddig, unfortunately, is no longer capable of protecting his. You
are. His interests . . . have become your interests. And very likely his
position . . . presuming you are canny enough, judicious enough,
and . . ." He cleared his throat and indicated the credit chip with a
nod. ". . . generous enough to make things happen. If, that is, you are
interested in doing so."

He stopped talking for a moment, and it seemed to Vidkun as if
he was waiting for Vidkun to say something. But the Drazi did not
speak. Something warned him that it would be wiser not to.

Lione's lips thinned into a death's-head smile.

"You could, of course, take a more aggressive stance," he acknowledged. "Try to rally the Alliance against us. Endeavor to prove
your case. Anger a good number of people; upset a number of agree-
ments that are understood amidst more people than you would truly
believe possible. You could do all that. I have to admit I would not
advise it. But it is a way you might go."

Vidkun found the nerve to speak. "And if I indicate that is what
I am going to do . . . then I, too, would suffer an accident."

Slowly Lione shook his head. "That would be a foolish position
for me to take. You could agree to anything I say . . . then once you
are off-world, safely beyond concerns for your own life and limb, you
might say and do anything you wish. Threats are extremely unreli-
able. What I am endeavoring to point out is that cooperation is far
more to your advantage. It will benefit you. It will serve your needs.
You do have needs, I assume. You are still quite young. There are
things you want to accomplish, goals you wish to achieve. A quiet understanding will get a great deal that rabble-rousing and accusations
will not."

"And in the meantime, you will attack more worlds, as you did
Mipas . . ."

"Mipas was a threat. If you believe nothing else I tell you, believe
that. We acted in self-defense, nothing more. You seem a reasonable

person. How can any reasonable person condemn us for that? That is indeed the entire point of the barter system which Luddig so deftly oversaw. The moneys paid are an act of good faith. We do not ask for it; it is offered freely. Even if we were not paid, we would still not attack. Assorted worlds have these arrangements with us at their behest, not ours. They misunderstand the Centauri mind-set. We are not out to destroy others, no. No, not at all. Our intention is simply to make certain that no one ever attacks us again. We are not bullies. We just desire to show that we are strong. You do see the difference, do you not?"

"Yes. Yes, I do," Vidkun said slowly.

"That is good to know, considering that Luddig apparently did not see the difference. We do not take well to threats. But cooperation . . . that is different. And there are many who are most anxious to cooperate with Centauri Prime." He sat forward and, in doing so, almost seemed capable of bending from the hip and leaning over the entire desk. "I am hoping . . . that you are one of those. For your sake. For ours. For the sake of the continued interests of the Drazi Homeworld. To all of that, Vidkun . . . I'm sorry . . . *acting Ambassador Vidkun* . . . you hold the key."

Vidkun nodded slowly in acknowledgment.

"The prime minister would still like to meet with you tomorrow," Lione told him. "Are you amenable to that?"

Once more Vidkun nodded. He thought about Luddig, beaten to death by the crowd. And he thought about the contempt with which Luddig had addressed him, the way that Luddig had made him feel.

"I believe I am," Vidkun said. "And I believe . . . I should inform my government of the tragic circumstance that led to Luddig's passing. It is . . . commendable how quickly you were able to dispose of his assailant."

Lione inclined his head in acknowledgment of the compliment. "We of Centauri Prime are only concerned with doing what is right."

2

Twenty years . . .

Delenn was very likely as aware of the passage of time as any other person alive. Always in the back of her mind lurked the knowledge that her beloved husband, her soul mate, John Sheridan, the man who had virtually reconfigured the way of the galaxy, had only twenty years to live. That had been the price of survival on Z'ha'dum. If she could go back in time, if she could prevent any one moment, it would be that one. An impressive priority, considering some of the horrific things she had witnessed in her time, some of the disasters that had occurred to those whom she loved.

Twenty years to live . . .

The enigmatic being named Lorien had brought John Sheridan back from the dead through means Delenn had never fully understood. What she *had* understood, though, was that the "fix" was only temporary. That after a mere two decades, Sheridan would simply shut off, like a light.

Twenty years to live . . .

That's what she'd been told . . .

. . . fourteen years earlier.

Once upon a time, she had been able to put such considerations out of her mind, sometimes for days on end. Lately, though, not a day—sometimes, it seemed, not an hour—passed without her dwelling on it.

Despite her closeness with her husband, though, despite the deep bond they shared, she was able to keep her concerns from him. Occasionally he would notice that she seemed preoccupied, and would remark upon it. She would easily deflect his comments by saying that she was thinking about David, their son. At twelve years of age, he was growing into something that was an impressive combination of mother and father. Remarkably, David seemed to possess elements of both their personalities. He was fully capable of being a young hellion, tearing about their home on Minbar with a definitely Human enthusiasm and abandon, much to the chagrin of his mother, the amusement of his father, and the utter frustration of his teachers.

On the other hand, when faced with studies, David consistently rose to the occasion with such facility that his teachers wondered just how much he could accomplish if he applied himself fully.

Outwardly he appeared Human. The color of his hair had shifted over time. He had gone from being towheaded to dark-haired, and he tended to wear it long. This annoyed his father, whose old military instincts kicked in. Every so often, he would extol the virtues of a short haircut, but David seemed to pay such critiques no mind. Curiously, his eyebrows retained their light color, but the dark eyes beneath remained evocative of his mother.

He did, however, possess his father's charisma. That much was unmistakable. Nor was his charisma limited to its effects on Humans; Minbari women—grown women—would do double takes when he passed, looking him up and down appreciatively while he winked at them or came up with some bon mot that always prompted gentle laughter or looks of amusement.

This tendency was something that drove his mother to distraction ... particularly when David's father would watch such exhibitions and grin approvingly. Only when he noticed Delenn's silently annoyed gaze did John Sheridan quickly try to cover his paternally proud smile.

Six years to live ...

That thought would come to her at times such as now, when Sheridan was openly agitated about something. She desperately wished that he would set aside his burden as president of the Alliance. She had pointed out on any number of occasions that "president" was an elected office, for a particular term, and that it might not be a bad idea if Sheridan considered pushing more strongly for an open election, to find a replacement. Sheridan did consider it, but every time he tried to follow through, the other member races saw it as some sort of desire on his part for a vote of confidence. Naturally they gave him that vote with gusto and enthusiasm, and inevitably some other disaster would occur that would keep John Sheridan firmly in office.

It was as if the Fates themselves were conspiring against them, making sure that they would never know a time of peace.

Six more years to live ...

At night in their bed she would whisper to him, *"Let's run away,"* and some nights he would actually seem to reflect on it. In the dead of night, he would speak of laying down his burden, of spending his remaining years in peace. And then the dawn would come, and the John Sheridan of the nighttime would disappear, replaced by John Sheridan, man of responsibility. Consequently, it pained her when so much as an hour, even a minute of his day caused him aggravation. But she had no control over it. All she could do was sympathize and be there for him, for counsel, for support . . . for sanity.

This was one of those times.

"They're *idiots!*" Sheridan raged.

They were in his office, except he wasn't in it so much as stalking it, like a caged animal. With them were the only two individuals in the entire galaxy he appeared to trust completely: Michael Garibaldi and Citizen G'Kar of Narn.

Neither of them truly worked for Sheridan. Once upon a time, Garibaldi had been Sheridan's chief of security. Those days were long past, and his responsibilities as a businessman occupied much of his time. His latest journey to Minbar was actually more of a stopover on his way to some other appointment. From the look on his face, Delenn suspected that he might very well be wondering whether the impromptu visit had been such a good idea.

G'Kar was another story altogether.

It was hard to believe that the tall, proud Narn had once been someone so insolent, so bellicose, that Delenn had literally had to bend him to her will via gravity rings. Since that time, G'Kar had become—there was no other way for her to say it—a creature of destiny. It was as if he knew that he had an important part to play in the grand scheme of things, and he was serenely and securely accepting of that role. Delenn couldn't help but suppose that it did, in fact, show some consistency. If G'Kar was an enemy, he was implacable. If, however, he was an ally, there was none more devoted.

On one occasion, Sheridan had referred to G'Kar as "the king's hand." This was a reference that completely eluded Delenn, and she had said as much.

"Ancient kings had men known as their 'hands,' " Sheridan had explained to her. "They would go out into the field and do the dirty work. The things that the king could not, or would not, get involved in. The hand was the most trustworthy and dependable of the knights."

"That is interesting to know, Your Highness," Delenn had said with open amusement, and bowed deeply. Sheridan had rolled his eyes, wondered out loud why he ever bothered to tell her anything, and taken the gentle ribbing in stride.

He wasn't in stride at the moment, though. His frustration had reached a boiling point and nothing that either G'Kar or Garibaldi could say would calm him. Wisely, then, they chose to say nothing, and instead allowed Sheridan to vent.

And vent he did, his neatly trimmed grey beard bristling as if it had a life of its own.

"I thought this was going to be it. This was going to be the one. Was there any planet more benign, less threatening, than Mipas?" He didn't give them time to answer. Instead he started ticking off responses on his fingers. "Bricarn 9. Shandukan. Harper's World. The list goes on and on! All helpless. All useful to the Centauri war machine, either for positioning, or raw materials, or even just sending a message to the Alliance that the Centauri are a force to be reckoned with. A message that the Centauri themselves thrive upon, becoming bolder with each unanswered strike! But every damned world they go after is a border world, far out at the edge of their interests, and making no move against the Centauri!"

"They're quite carefully selected, for maximum impact with minimal risk," G'Kar squeezed in, as an opinion.

Sheridan nodded vehemently. "Exactly. And the risk remains minimal because certain factions in the Alliance keep refusing to go up against the Centauri! Every time the Centauri take an aggressive action and succeed with impunity, they're that much more emboldened to keep to their course! A course that, over the past year, has brought us closer and closer to a costly, full-blown war!"

" 'Cost' probably has a good deal to do with it," a grim Garibaldi commented. "Not that I can prove it, you understand, but I suspect there's some serious greasing of palms going on."

"There are many who are happy to overlook long-term ramifications in return for short-term profits," G'Kar said. "It's been a pattern throughout history."

"Is that how it works, then?" demanded Sheridan. "Throughout history, the strong allow the weak to suffer so that they can obtain selfish goals?"

"Of course," G'Kar said reasonably. "Where have you been hiding?"

"That was the past," Sheridan insisted. "We're supposed to have advanced. We're supposed to have learned. Learned that you cannot allow thugs and monsters to have their way." He stopped at the window and gazed out as if he were trying to look past the Minbari horizon. As if he could spot Centauri vessels cruising around in the depths of space, looking for new prey. He shook his head, and when he spoke again he sounded discouraged and frustrated. "You would think that if we'd learned anything from the Shadow War, it was that even the most benevolent of races can become despotic, if they're allowed to exercise their might unchecked. Yet here we are again, facing an enemy who is building up strength, weaponry, and confidence, and the pacifists in the Alliance would have us do nothing."

"They don't think it affects them directly," Delenn finally spoke up. "The problem, John, is that your efforts with the Alliance have been too successful in other areas. Through the treaties you've overseen, the crackdowns on trade piracy, the assorted economic models you've introduced . . . through all of that and more, you've helped bring about an unprecedented sense of prosperity and economic stability throughout the system. When people are satisfied with their financial situation, when they want for nothing . . . it is difficult to get them to leave their comfortable homes and hurl themselves into the depths of space to fight wars. They have so much, they are not willing to risk losing it."

"If they can't get off their asses to fight the Centauri, they're sure as hell going to lose it," Sheridan said flatly. He leaned against his desk and shook his head, looking more discouraged and frustrated than Delenn could recall seeing him in years. "They keep being 'encouraged' to look the other way. They believe that if they simply let Centauri Prime take this world or that world, that it will be enough to placate them. They think things are going to settle down. They don't understand that it isn't going to happen unless we *make* things settle down . . . and that won't happen for as long as the Centauri think that they can walk all over us!"

Six more years. And this sort of irritation was all he had to look forward to, day in, day out? Delenn could not recall a time when she more despised Londo Mollari.

"I've spoken to the Brakiri. The Dubai. The Gaim. And on and on, a list almost as long as the list of worlds that have fallen to the Centauri," Sheridan continued. "No one wants to get involved. They come up with reason after reason why it's not a good idea, and you're right, Delenn, it all boils down to the same thing: It's not their problem." He shook his head. "If we had simply waited around until the

Shadows were ready to attack Babylon 5, it would be a seriously different galaxy out there. These damned pacifists . . ."

"Since when is peace bad?"

The youthful voice startled Sheridan out of his frustrated diatribe. They all turned toward the speaker, even though they all already knew who it was.

David Sheridan stood there, leaning against the door frame and smiling in that infinitely self-possessed manner that only adolescents could summon with facility.

"And here he comes . . . the great agitator," Garibaldi said with the air of someone who had been down the same road any number of times.

"Hey, Uncle Mikey."

Garibaldi emitted a pained howl, as if he'd just been stabbed through the heart. He staggered across the room, then suddenly lunged and snagged an arm around the back of David's neck. David let out a howl of anything other than anguish, as Garibaldi yanked on his long hair and snarled, "No 'Uncle Mikey'! I hate 'Uncle Mikey'! You *know* I hate 'Uncle Mikey'!"

"I'm sorry, Uncle Mikey!" David howled, choking on his own laughter.

"Punk kid. Get a haircut."

Garibaldi shoved him free, turned to John Sheridan, and chucked a thumb at the teen. "You got a punk kid there with no respect for his elders, including his beloved godfather."

"Tell me about it," Sheridan commiserated.

"David, I thought you were at your lessons with Master Vultan," Delenn said.

"I was. Vultan decided it was time to take a break."

"Meaning that he took his eyes off you for half a second and you were gone."

David shrugged noncommittally.

Delenn let out a sigh that was a familiar combination of love and exasperation. "He's your son," she said to Sheridan.

"How reassuring," G'Kar remarked. "There were those rumors . . ."

"Your sense of humor, as always, is not appreciated, G'Kar," Sheridan said with mock severity.

"True comic visionaries rarely are during their lifetime."

"A few more remarks like that, and I'll solve the 'lifetime' problem for you," Sheridan warned with that same feigned gravity.

"Sounds like you folks are all having a good time kidding around with each other," David observed wryly. "Kind of interesting, considering that when I came in everything sounded pretty damned grave."

"Language," Delenn said reflexively.

"Sorry. Pretty goddamned grave."

She looked heavenward for strength.

"You wouldn't, by some chance, be trying to change the mood in here simply because I'm around?" inquired David.

The adults looked uncomfortably at each other.

"It's all right," he continued, clearly not interested in waiting for an answer. "I was actually standing outside the last few minutes."

Garibaldi pointed at David and said to Sheridan, "That boy has a future in surveillance. Let me take him back to Mars and train him for a few years. You won't recognize him."

"If his hair gets much longer, I won't recognize him in any event," Sheridan commented.

"You didn't answer my question, Dad," David said, clearly not about to let his father off the hook. "You're angry with the pacifist factions who don't want to get into a full-blown war with the Centauri. What's wrong with pacifism? I mean, look at the Earth-Minbari war. Thanks to the aggressiveness of the Humans who fired on the Minbari, killing Dukhat, and the Minbari responding with pure rage, *there* was a needless interstellar war that cost millions of lives."

Delenn flinched inwardly. David *would* have had to bring that up. The fact was that it was Delenn herself who had made the fateful decision to attack the Humans, even as she had cradled the still-warm corpse of Dukhat. *They're animals!* The words, screamed in an agonized voice barely recognizable as her own, still rang in her head. But David had never learned that. It was a secret that she kept buried deep in her, a moment that she could never forget, no matter how much she wanted to.

"And then," continued David, unaware of his mother's inner turmoil, "the entire Human Homeworld would have been wiped out if the Minbari hadn't suddenly surrendered. The reasons were complicated, but the result was the same: a peace movement. So obviously, those who seek peace are right some of the time. When do you decide it's the right time for peace . . . and when it is time to go to war?"

"It's not an easy question," Sheridan admitted.

"Well, actually, it is an easy question. The answer's the tough part."

Sheridan glanced at Garibaldi, who had just spoken, and responded wryly, "Thank you, Michael, for that reassuring clarification."

"No problem."

Delenn stepped forward, and resting a hand on her son's shoulder, said, "It depends whether one is in a situation where a movement of peace is viewed as a benefit for all concerned . . . or merely a sign of weakness."

Sheridan nodded in confirmation. "There are some who use peace, not as a tool, but as a weapon. Something to distract or forestall opponents while they move forward with their plans for conquest."

"And how do you know when that's the case?"

"You have to look at the whole picture," Sheridan said. "You don't examine one action, or even a couple of actions. You look at everything they've done throughout their history, and get a clear idea of where they've been. Based on that, you can determine where they're most likely to go."

"In the case of Londo and the Centauri," Garibaldi said grimly, "where they're going to go is anyplace they want to. Right now they're the six-hundred-pound gorilla."

"The what?" David looked at him blankly.

"The gorilla. It's an old joke. Where does a six-hundred-pound gorilla sit? Answer is, anywhere he wants. Get it?"

"Kind of." David hesitated, then asked, "What's a gorilla?"

Garibaldi opened his mouth to respond, then closed it and sighed. "Never mind."

Easily turning his attention away from the joke that had left him puzzled, David said, "Londo . . . the emperor . . . you think that's what he wants to do? Go everywhere . . . anywhere . . . he wants?"

"I don't know. I don't know the man anymore," Sheridan said. He looked to G'Kar. "What do you think, G'Kar? You haven't been saying all that much. What's your opinion on Londo's intentions?"

"His intentions?" G'Kar shrugged. "I could not tell you for sure. But there is one thing I do know for certain: Londo Mollari is one of the most tragic individuals I've ever met."

"Tragic?" Garibaldi snorted. "Look, G'Kar, I once liked the guy. And then he went power mad, and now he sits there on Centauri Prime playing all sides against each other. And yeah, okay, I'll be honest . . . losing Lou Welch to those high-haired bastards didn't exactly endear me to the whole Centauri experience. I've heard them say, in their rhetoric, in their histories, that the emperor is the living incarnation of Centauri Prime. If that's the case, I have some major issues with the incarnation, because it means he's the living symbol of a planet that's gone straight down the tubes. So I don't exactly see, G'Kar, why I'm supposed to shed a tear for him and think of him as a tragic figure."

"Shed tears or not, as you see fit," G'Kar said with a shrug. "I know I shed none. Why should I? He was responsible for mass drivers being used against my people. For the deaths of millions of Narns. Do you know what would have happened if not for Londo Mollari?"

There was a pause. "What?" inquired David.

"Very likely the exact same thing," G'Kar told him. "It is my belief that Londo became swept up in circumstances that were beyond his control . . . perhaps even beyond his understanding. And by the time he did understand, it was too late. I believe he had hopes and dreams for his people, but only in the most ephemeral of terms . . . and others transformed those hopes into a harsh reality that he never contemplated in his wildest dreams.

"That, Mr. Garibaldi, is the tragedy of Londo Mollari: that he never had the opportunity to become that which he might have been had the vagaries of fate not caught him up. Do not misunderstand," he added hastily. "As I said, I shed no tears for him. In many respects he brought it on himself, and there were times he might have been able to stop it. Then again, perhaps not. We will never know. But whether he is pitiable or not, whether he is someone with whom we empathize or not, is beside the point. He remains a tragic figure nonetheless."

Sheridan was shaking his head and looking over at Garibaldi. "And here you said he wasn't talking much. See what happens? Now we can't shut him up."

"I won't burden you with my opinions if it's a problem, Mr. President," G'Kar said archly.

Sheridan waved him off.

"So what do we do, John?" Delenn said. "We remain stymied."

"We stay the course, that's all," Sheridan told her reluctantly. "I'm not going to unilaterally order the White Star fleet to attack Centauri Prime. I have to present an example for the Alliance, and what they do *not* need is an example of a leader who functions without giving a damn about the opinions and desires of his constituency. The Alliance refuses to pull the trigger. I can't go forward without them, so we remain together and stationary. And we hope that once the Alliance does come to its collective senses, it's not too late."

"That certainly seems the only way to go," Garibaldi agreed reluctantly. G'Kar simply nodded noncommittally.

Sheridan then gave Delenn a significant look, and she understood immediately what he wanted. "David," she said, "why don't we go for a walk?"

"Dad wants to be able to talk without having me around, right." Despite the phrasing, it wasn't a question so much as an affirmation.

"Nothing gets past you." Sheridan chuckled, but there was edginess in the laugh.

"Fine." David shrugged with feigned indifference and allowed Delenn to lead him out.

"He's a sharp boy, and he's growing up fast," said Garibaldi. "We probably could have kept talking in front of him."

"Let's let him be just a kid, at least for a while longer."

"I wouldn't say he's ever been 'just a kid,' Mr. President," G'Kar said.

"That's probably true." Sheridan seated himself back behind his desk. The back-and-forth with David had taken some of the ire out of his voice, but he was still clearly not happy with the situation. "The thing I find most disturbing about this is the business with the Drazi. One of their own people was murdered, and they simply let it go."

"The word on ISN was that it was a lone nut acting without the government's knowledge or consent," Garibaldi said. "They're even suggesting that it's a private group of saboteurs who're working to bring down the Centauri government by staging acts of violence designed to foster war with the Alliance. The new Drazi ambassador backed it up. Not that I necessarily believed it for a second . . ."

"You were wise not to," G'Kar said. "It was, in fact, the organized actions of a mob, performed with the full cooperation of the local authorities and Minister Lione's pet troops, the Prime Candidates. They tore the poor devil apart. His assistant was hurried away. I saw his picture on the same ISN broadcast that Mr. Garibaldi saw; he's the new Drazi ambassador. It seems his predecessor's misfortune was his own good luck."

Garibaldi looked at him suspiciously. "You're acting like you saw this as an eyewitness."

G'Kar said nothing.

Garibaldi looked from G'Kar to Sheridan. "Someone want to tell me what's going on? I mean, there's no way G'Kar could have seen it. A Narn on Centauri Prime? Impossible. They've banned all off-worlders . . . and even when off-worlders were welcome, Narns never were."

"I have ways," G'Kar said with great mystery.

"Mind telling me what they are?"

"I cannot, in good conscience, do so," G'Kar informed him.

"And you?" He turned expectantly to Sheridan.

But Sheridan shook his head. "I don't know, either. G'Kar hasn't told me."

"And you find this acceptable?" Garibaldi was openly incredulous.

"I'm learning to deal with it," Sheridan said.

"He is John's foot," Delenn, who had just reentered, said.

"His what?"

"Hand," Sheridan corrected her. "It's an old title . . ."

"Look, I don't care if he's your hand, your foot, or your lower intestine," Garibaldi said. "I don't like secrets being kept. Not among us. Not after everything we've been through together. Because secrecy under such circumstances leads to sloppiness, and the next thing you know, someone decides they're going to be a hero and they get themselves killed."

"That," G'Kar said, sounding not a little regretful, "is an occupational hazard for being a hero."

"And for being a martyr," Garibaldi reminded him, "I hope you're not aiming for that status for yourself."

"Why, Mr. Garibaldi . . . I didn't know you cared." He sounded more amused than anything else.

Sheridan turned to Delenn. "David squared away?"

"He's back with his teachers. He said he still doesn't understand who decides when peace is the right thing to do."

"What did you tell him?"

"I looked him right in the eye and said, 'I decide. And if I'm not around, your father decides.' "

"Really. And what did he say to that?"

"He said, 'As long as Uncle Mikey doesn't.' "

"I'll kill him," said Garibaldi.

This generated a booming laugh from Sheridan. Delenn loved hearing him laugh, because he did it so infrequently. With all his responsibilities, all the stress upon him, she wished that he could laugh more often. He needed to desperately. And she needed it, too.

Six more years . . .

Some days it seemed as if it was going to pass in an eyeblink. Other days . . .

Other days it felt as if it was going to be an eternity.

EXCERPTED FROM
THE CHRONICLES OF LONDO MOLLARI.
Excerpt dated (approximate Earth date)
March 30, 2275.

My concern about my memory grows.

Things that happened many years ago . . . these are clear to me. I can remember every word that was spoken, every nuance of every moment from ten, twenty, thirty years past. I can remember exactly what it felt like to run as a child, to fall and skin my knee. The twinge of the pain can be re-created in my mind with utter clarity.

I cannot remember what I had for dinner last night.

I have had to drink rather heavily in order to maintain some of the more sensitive entries in this journal, because I have not wanted my . . . associate . . . to be aware of some of the things I write. The problem is that I think it's starting to take its toll upon me. That and age . . .

. . . and the mirror.

I look in the mirror and I see reflections of a man I do not recognize . . . and yet, unfortunately, do. The image of me in my dreams . . .

My dreams . . .

Durla and his dreams. Now there is a subject . . .

It takes a great deal of effort for me to recall what happened at a ministry meeting yesterday. Durla was there, that I recall. He was in one of his wild-eyed moods, speaking once more about dreams that had come to him, images in those dreams, and he was presenting blueprints and descriptions of new and greater weapons.

The others looked upon his work and marveled at Durla the Visionary. That is what they call him: the Visionary. One of the greatest seers in the history of Centauri Prime. When he was elevated to the office of prime minister, he started claiming that he had been guided by his dreams for years. When he was a mere member of my personal guard, such statements would have garnered laughter. Now . . . now the others make appreciative noises and exclamations of amazement, and speak of the exciting time in which we live, that such a prophet walks among us.

It is ridiculous. Nonsense.

Except . . . those things that we produce tend to work. Or at least our scientists are able to make them work. The Centauri Republic is being crafted in Durla's image. Odd. It gives me a strange feeling of nostalgia. I see his designs for weapons, for ships . . . and I get the same chill I did when I saw the Shadow ships crossing the skies over Centauri Prime. Black and fearsome things they were, and to look at them was like staring into the very heart of madness. I wonder about these dreams, and their origins, but it is pointless to inquire. Durla would not understand, nor would he care.

No, two things occupy Durla's thoughts: his endeavors to build up our military might, and his desire to bring down the saboteurs who continue to frustrate and thwart him. They have done so in small ways and have not been able to truly stop the progress. For every munition factory they manage to destroy, there are five others. They can no more stem the tide than a coral reef can impede the ocean. But they are a presence and an irritant nonetheless, and Durla continues to be angered by their activities.

These matters will come to a head sooner rather than later, I fear. I do not like to think about whose head they may come to.

My memory . . .

I saw a lovely young woman walking the corridors the other day. I spoke to her, smiled at her, feeling for a moment like the Londo of old. Then I realized that she was Senna, the young woman whom I took as my ward some years ago. I had not seen her in quite some time. She remains without husband, and without interest in acquiring one. Instead she occupies herself by acting as an occasional nursemaid for some of the children of Centauri ministers and such. She is quite popular with them, so I understand.

Dinner!

Dinner the other night was with Vir. I recall now. I do not remember what we had . . . but he was there. Senna was there, too. They spoke quite gregariously with one another, I seem to remember. One would have almost thought I was not there at all.

Sometimes I think I am not.

3

Milifa, of the house of Milifa, burst into Durla's office, unable to contain his excitement. "Is it true?" he asked before Durla could open his mouth. "Is what I've heard true?"

Durla leaned back and smiled. Milifa was a man who virtually radiated strength. Remarkably charismatic, powerfully built, he was the head of one of the most influential houses in all the Centaurum. Even his excitement was carefully channeled, his dark eyes crackling with intensity as he said again, "Is it true?"

"Are you going to give me breathing space to tell you, my friend? Or will you simply keep asking?"

Milifa took a step back and a deep breath. "Do not toy with me on this, Durla. I warn you."

Virtually any other person who spoke the words "I warn you" to Durla would have been subject to harsh treatment. But from Milifa, Durla was willing to take it. "Yes. It is true," he responded.

Milifa sagged with visible relief. Durla had never seen the robust aristocrat so emotionally vulnerable. Even on the day that Milifa's son, Throk, had been killed, Milifa had managed to keep his rawest emotions in careful check.

"Four . . . years," he said incredulously. "*Four years* since the safe house of the Prime Candidates was destroyed. Four years since my son and his friends died at the hands of those . . . those . . . ." He trembled with barely contained fury.

"I cannot apologize enough, old friend," said Durla, "for the length of time it has taken us to apprehend one of these subversives. It is, frankly, an embarrassment. I do not know any other way to put it."

"An embarrassment, yes. Perhaps," Milifa said sourly, "your duties as prime minister have atrophied the skills you so adroitly displayed when you were minister of Internal Security."

"That is neither here nor there," Durla told him. He rose from behind his desk and came around it, clapping Milifa on the back. "He is being questioned even as we speak. Do you wish to come and see?"

"Absolutely," Milifa said. "After waiting four years to see the face of one of these bastards, I have no intention of waiting a moment longer."

Durla was pleased to see that the questioning was already under way. He was not, however, pleased to witness its lack of success.

The subject was strapped into an oversize chair, his feet dangling a few inches above the floor. He was rail thin, narrow-shouldered, and unlike most other Centauri of Durla's acquaintance, his hair was something of a mess. His head was lolling from one side to the other, as if attached to his shoulders by only the slimmest of supports.

Several members of the Prime Candidates were there, as well, looking particularly grim. Durla recognized one of them as Caso, a close friend of Throk's. Caso had suffered, to some degree, from survivor's guilt. A lung illness had kept him home in bed the day that the other Prime Candidates died in the explosion; had Caso not been bedridden, he would have died with the others.

"What is the vermin's name?" Milifa asked, standing just behind Durla.

"Lanas. Rem Lanas," Durla told him grimly. "He was found trespassing in one of our . . ." He paused, and then said, ". . . medical facilities, on Tumbor 2. He had counterfeit clearance identification on him. Quite well crafted, I might add. He was in the midst of endeavoring to rewire certain circuits that . . . if left unchecked . . . would have caused the facility to blow up. Fortunately, all he managed to do was trip an alarm. Our security systems have become increasingly sophisticated over the years."

"That is a fortunate state of affairs," Milifa said, "considering the alternative is leaving yourself open to being continually preyed upon by slime like . . . like this." His voice dropped lower on the last several words. He stepped forward and practically stuck his face into Lanas'. "Are you the one, slime? Are you the one who was responsible for killing my son?"

Lanas looked up at him without really seeing him.

"What's wrong with him?" demanded Milifa.

"Truth drugs, no doubt. Sometimes they take a while to reach full effect." Durla looked to Caso for confirmation. Caso, over the years, had apprenticed with some of the best interrogators in the Centaurum and had become quite skilled. He had personally requested the opportunity to handle the questioning of this latest subject, in the name of his departed friend. "How much longer, Caso?"

But Caso looked surprisingly uncomfortable. "Actually, Prime Minister, they should be at full effect by now. Before now, in fact. But he has been resisting all of our initial questions."

"Resisting?" Durla was astonished. "Are you certain you have administered them properly?"

"Positive, Prime Minister," Caso answered stiffly.

"And yet he resists? Increase the dosage."

"That may not be wise . . ."

Durla, feeling the quiet smoldering of Milifa next to him, said tightly, "On my authority. Do it."

Caso bowed deeply and put together another dosage. Moments later there was enough truth drug pumping through Lanas' veins to send a dozen Centauri pouring out every secret they'd ever held, all the way back to childhood.

Rem Lanas' eyes remained glazed. It was as if he was withdrawing completely into himself.

"I checked the records on this man," Caso said. "He was a worker on K0643."

"Was he now," Durla said. The excavation on K0643 had proven to be one of Durla's only unqualified disasters. He had been certain that there was some great source of weaponry there, but the entire excavation had been destroyed. There were wild rumors that technomages had somehow been involved . . . fleeting glimpses of them, but accounts of their numbers ranged from three to thirty. No one seemed sure of anything. He wondered if Lanas had been one of the workers who had been questioned. He leaned forward, and said, "What is your name?"

"Lanas. Rem Lanas." His voice was thick and distant.

"And are you part of an organization?"

Lanas' head teetered in affirmation.

"And what," Durla said with clear urgency, "is that organization? Tell me about it. Who is the head?"

"Minister . . . Durla."

A confused look passed among the Centauri in the room. Durla could feel Milifa's gaze boring through him, and he felt a faint buzz of danger. "Yes, I am Prime Minister Durla," he said, trying to discern whether the confused Lanas might simply be addressing him directly. "Who is the head of your organization?"

"Minister Durla," Rem Lanas said, this time with more conviction.

The blood drained from Durla's face.

But Caso looked suspicious, and said, "What is the nature of this organization?"

"Employment . . . workers . . . for excavation purposes . . ."

Durla put his face in his hands, partly out of frustration and partly to hide his relief. Such an absurd misunderstanding could have led to a world of trouble if left unchecked. "The Committee for Centauri Advancement," he said.

"Yes . . . organization . . ." Rem Lanas told them. He was half smiling, but it was such a disassociated look that it was clear he was thinking about something else completely.

Durla looked to Milifa, who seemed less than amused. "It's the association I created for the purpose of organizing Centauri workers for—"

"I do not care," Milifa said flatly. "I want to know about the bastards who killed my son. If he's one of them, I want all their names."

Durla nodded and turned back to Rem Lanas. "I am speaking of a terrorist organization. An organization created for sabotage. You are part of such a group, yes?"

Lanas nodded his head.

"Now we're getting somewhere," Durla said, smirking. Caso nodded approvingly. "How many people are in it?"

"All of them," Lanas told him.

"Don't spar with me, Lanas," Durla warned, becoming increasingly annoyed. He glanced up at Caso. "How is he able to do this?"

"I'm not sure," Caso said, looking a bit worried. "He should be unable to hold back anything. It should just all be spilling out of him."

"Lanas . . . who is the head of the organization?" Durla asked.

"The head?"

"Yes."

"The head . . . is our leader."

"Yes. His name. What is the name of the head of the organization?"

And his reply made no sense at all. "No. What is the name of the man on second base."

"Who?" Durla said, utterly flummoxed.

"No. Who is on first."

"*What?*"

"What is on second."

Durla felt as if he were losing his mind. In a harsh whisper he demanded of Caso, "This is gibberish. What is he saying?"

"I don't know!" Caso replied loudly.

"Third base," Rem Lanas intoned, as if by rote.

Durla was up off his chair with such force that he knocked it over. Caso was about to speak when an angry prime minister grabbed him by the front of his shirt and slammed him back up against the wall. "This is *idiocy!*" he said tightly. "What sort of game is this?"

"It's n-not a game!" Caso stammered, his veneer of Prime Candidate indifference wavering under the infuriated onslaught of the most powerful man on Centauri Prime. "It . . . it must be a fail-safe . . ."

"Fail-safe? What sort of—"

"Something planted in his mind. Imprinted. So that if he's being questioned or probed, instead of breaking through to the core of what we want to know, his mind automatically reverts to this nonsense. It becomes a loop that we can't get past."

"That's impossible!"

"No. It's not. I've . . ." He licked his lips nervously. "I've heard techno-mages can accomplish such things . . ."

"Now it's techno-mages!" Milifa bellowed. "Drugs! Children's stories about techno-mages! What sort of government are you running here, Durla!"

Durla rounded on him, suddenly not caring just how powerful a house Milifa ran. He pointed a trembling finger at Milifa, and said, "The kind of government that could strip you of name, rank, and property with a snap of my fingers! So watch yourself, Milifa, and show some respect for who and what I am, before I make you less than who and what you are!"

Milifa, wisely, said nothing, but the set of his face made it clear he was not happy.

Durla, for his part, felt shamed. And the notion that this scrawny no one was playing games with him and shaming him in front of a long-standing ally infuriated him beyond reason. "Forget the drugs," he told Caso. "Now . . . now we chat with him in the way we used to do these things."

Minutes later, Rem Lanas was upright and spread-eagled, his arms tied to the walls on either side of the cell. Durla stood several feet away, the lash in his hand crackling with energy.

"Prime Minister." Caso sounded respectful but nervous. "The

drugs in his system may impede his understanding if another element, such as extreme pain, is introduced into—"

"Then we shall give his system a chance to work the drugs out." He saw Milifa nod slightly in approval, took a step back and swung his arm around expertly. The lash slammed across Rem Lanas' back, shredding his shirt in a second. Lanas screamed, his eyes going wide, his body spasming.

"You felt that, didn't you," Durla said in a low voice. "Didn't you, Lanas."

"Y-yes," he managed to say.

"No one can endure more than forty lashes of that nature," Durla continued. "I do not suggest you be the first person to try."

"I . . . don't want to die . . ."

"At last, truth," Durla noted with satisfaction. "We don't care about you, Lanas. We want those in charge."

"In charge . . . of what?"

Durla did not hesitate. He swung the lash again, and again. Ten cracks of the lash crashed across Lanas' back, and each time the prisoner howled, until it seemed to Durla he could not remember a time when screams were not ringing in his ears.

"That," he said, "is eleven."

But Lanas didn't hear him, because he had lapsed into unconsciousness.

"Bring him around," Durla said to Caso.

Caso did so with brisk efficiency. Durla could see it in Lanas' eyes: When he came to, for a moment he didn't realize where he was. Perhaps he thought that what he had experienced was some sort of tortured dream. When he looked around, however, he realized the all-too-real nature of his predicament.

"Ask him who killed my son," Milifa demanded. "Was he himself responsible? Someone else?"

"Is your mind clear enough that you can answer the question?" Durla asked. Lanas glared up at him. "You see, we've figured out that when you lose control over your ability to keep information secret, you have some sort of . . . what was the word, Caso? Fail-safe. A fail-safe in your mind that prevents you from being forthcoming. It is my assumption that if you have possession of your faculties, then your free will holds sway once more. Employ that free will now. Save yourself."

"Tell me who killed my son," demanded Milifa.

Lanas seemed to notice him for the first time. "Who is your son?"

"Throk of the House Milifa."

"Oh. Him."

"Yes, him."

"He was the first."

"The first what?" Durla said. "The first victim of your organization?"

Rem Lanas took in a slow, deep breath. "Do you know who I am?" he asked.

"You are Rem Lanas."

"Beyond that, I mean." The pain in his voice appeared to be subsiding. And then, before Durla could reply, Lanas did it for him. "I am nothing beyond that. I am a nobody. A no one. I drifted . . . from one thing in life to the next. Used by this person, by that person. I have been a victim for as long as I can remember. No pride in myself, in my heritage, in my people. But I have been a part of something . . . that has made me proud . . . for the first time in my meager existence."

"So you admit you are part of an organization!" Durla said triumphantly.

"Freely," said Lanas. He looked like nothing. He looked like a weakling. But his voice was of iron. "And if you think that I am going to turn over those people who have helped to elevate me, for the first time in my life, to a creature of worth . . . then you can think again. And you, Durla . . . you think . . . you think you are in charge. You think you know everything. You know nothing. And by the time you do . . . it will be too late for you. It's already too late."

Durla suddenly felt a chill in the air. He brushed it off as he said, "If you know so much about me, why don't you tell me?"

"Because you would not believe. You are not ready. You likely never will be."

"Enough of this!" Milifa said, fury bubbling over. "Tell me who killed my son!"

"Your son . . ."

"Yes! Throk of the—"

"House of Milifa, yes. Your son . . ." He grinned lopsidedly. "Your son walked into his little hideout with a bomb in his hair. My understanding is that he realized it at the last moment and died screaming 'Get it out, get it out!' Very womanish, from what I've been told . . ."

Milifa let out a howl of agonized fury and grabbed the lash from Durla's hand. Durla yelped in protest and tried to grab it back, but Milifa was far bigger than he and utterly uncaring, at that moment, of Durla's high rank. He stiff-armed the prime minister, shoving him back. Caso caught Durla before he could hit the ground.

Milifa's arm snapped around, and he brought the lash crashing down on Rem Lanas. Lanas made no attempt to hold back the agony as the scream was ripped from his throat.

"Milord!" Caso shouted, trying to get the whip away from him, but Milifa, blind with fury, swept it around and drove Caso back. Any attempt to snatch it from Milifa's hand would simply have met with violence.

"Tell me—who!" And the whip snaked out.

"Who's on first!" shrieked Lanas, and the words were now pouring out of him, running together, bereft of any meaning. "What's on second, I don't know, third base . . ."

"Tell me! Tell me!"

"Get the guards!" Durla ordered Caso, and the young Prime Candidate did as he was instructed. Milifa was paying no attention. Four years' worth of anger, of rage, poured from him all at once, focused entirely on the helpless individual before him. Over and over he struck, and each time he demanded to know who was responsible for his son's death, and each time Rem Lanas cried out nonsensical comments about third base. Except he did so with progressively less volume each time, even the screams having less force.

The door burst open and half a dozen guards poured in, Caso bringing up the rear. They converged on Milifa, and he swung the lash to try to keep them back. But they were armored, and although they proceeded with caution, proceed they still did. Within moments they had Milifa pinned to the ground, the lash torn from his grasp. His chest was heaving, his face flushed, his eyes wild. "Tell me!" he was still shouting, as if he had lost track of the fact that he was no longer beating his victim.

Lanas' head was slumped forward. Durla went to him, placed his thumb and forefinger under Rem Lanas' chin. The head fell back. And he immediately knew what Caso confirmed only a moment later: Lanas was dead.

"Idiot," he murmured, and then his voice grew along with his frustration. "Idiot!" This time he turned to Milifa, who was being held on the floor by the guards, and kicked him savagely in the side. Milifa let out a roar of indignation, but Durla spoke right over it. *"Idiot!* He was our first, best lead in years! Years! And because of you, he's dead!"

"Less . . . than forty lashes . . ." Milifa started to say.

"It didn't matter! The threshold of pain isn't an exact science! Forty was the maximum! But look at him! He wasn't particularly robust! What in the world made you think he could endure that sort of sustained punishment!

"But no, you didn't think!" and he kicked Milifa again. "You just cared about your pathetic son!"

"How *dare* you!" Milifa managed to get out.

"How dare you interfere with an official interrogation! How dare you think that you can withstand my anger! Get him out of here . . . no! No, on second thought, shove him over there!" and he pointed to a corner of the cell. The guards obediently tossed him over into the indicated corner and stepped back. "You can stay here and rot . . . along with the corpse of your new best friend!" and he indicated the still-suspended body of Rem Lanas. "I hope you two will be very happy together!"

He stormed out, allowing the guards to follow and close the door behind him. The last thing the angry prime minister heard was Milifa's enraged shout of protest, before it was cut off by the slamming of the cell door.

4

Durla was impressed to see that Castig Lione had made it to his office suite before he arrived there. "Tell me it's not true," Lione, trembling with suppressed rage, said immediately.

Durla considered it mildly amusing that the conversation echoed the one he'd had with Milifa, so very recently. "That depends," he said calmly. With Milifa locked away and his fury at Lanas passed, Durla was actually able to handle himself with a considerable amount of sangfroid. "What are you referring to, precisely?"

"Do not fence with me—"

"And do not forget your station, Lione!" Durla warned. He was still calm, but there was definite menace in his tone. "Do not forget who is the power on Centauri Prime."

"Oh, I have known that for quite some time," Lione shot back.

Durla's eyes narrowed. "What do you mean by that?"

"You have put Milifa into prison! Do you have any idea how many friends the House Milifa has? How powerful he is! You need the support of the main Houses . . ."

"I have the support of the military, Minister Lione," Durla said. "The generals respect my roots. And they respect my long-term vision. They have helped to execute my inspirations, developing the technologies that will lead us to bury the Alliance. They have as little patience for effete, mincing heads of Houses as I do. They know that conquest comes from military might, and they know that only I have the strength of will to bring Centauri Prime to its true destiny."

"The Houses remain the foundation of your power, Prime Minister. If that foundation crumbles . . ."

"Why should I care what is below me, when my destiny is that which is above me?"

Lione leaned on a chair without sitting, and shook his head. "Madness," he muttered.

But Durla was studying him, like a small creature of prey sizing up something larger than he, trying to decide whether or not he could bring it down. "I have not forgotten your comment. Who is the power of Centauri Prime, as far as you are concerned?"

Lione regained his composure. "Why, you are, Prime Minister."

"Now you are the one who is fencing. What did you mean?"

"You do not desire candor, Prime Minister."

There was a deadly silence in the office for a moment. And then Durla said, "Lione . . . we go back quite a ways. Do not, however, assume that that lengthy relationship has weakened my resolve or ability to do what I feel needs to be done if I am being defied. Do not further assume that the fact that you head the Prime Candidates gives you a power base that is comparable with mine. If I were so inclined, I could order the military to annihilate every single one of them. The streets of Centauri Prime would flow with the blood of your precious Candidates, and parents might mourn, but otherwise life would go on."

"You would never do such a thing," Lione said.

Durla smiled thinly.

Suddenly the door opened and one of the most massive Centauri that Lione had ever seen walked in. He had to stop in the doorway for a moment, turning sideways slightly, in order to enter. Pure charismatic energy seemed to crackle around him. His neck was so thick that it seemed as if his head were jointed directly into the top of his torso. Furthermore, he had cut his teeth so that small fangs projected over his upper lip.

"Minister . . . you remember General Rhys. He's been overseeing a number of our construction projects on assorted fringe worlds. He also did a superb job leading the recent strike forces on Mipas and other worlds. General, it is good to see you."

General Rhys bowed deeply. But as he did so, he never took his eyes off Castig Lione.

"General," Durla said quite conversationally, as if discussing the weather. "I'd like you to do me a service, if you don't mind."

"Whatever you wish, Prime Minister."

"That sword hanging at your side . . . is it merely ceremonial?"

"Intended for ceremony, but it carries a killing edge, Prime Minister."

"Good. Kindly draw it and decapitate Minister Lione if he does not answer to my satisfaction."

Lione started to bark out a laugh, then the laughter choked off in his throat as smooth metal rasped against the scabbard, and he found the blade poised right against his throat. Rhys was holding it quite steady, not wavering in the slightest.

"You . . . you're insane," Lione whispered. Then he gasped as the blade edge pressed ever so slightly. That alone was enough to cause a trickle of blood to start running down. A small stain of pinkish red liquid . . . his blood . . . tinted his white collar.

"Look into my eyes, Lione," said Durla. The degree of calm in his tone was absolutely frightening. Lione found himself unable to look anywhere else. "I will be able to tell if you are lying. I have become quite sensitive to attempts at duplicity. One does not reach my station in life without acquiring that ability. Lie, and I will know. Now tell me . . . who do you think is the true power of Centauri Prime?"

"You."

"Ah ah ah," Durla said scoldingly, and Rhys—without having to be told to do so—pushed the blade ever so slightly more against Lione's throat. The minister gasped and sat bolt still, as even the slightest breath would cause the blade to drive into his throat on its own. "Did you think that I was joking? I am not. I do not joke. Ever. This is your last chance, Minister: Who is the true power of Centauri Prime?"

In truth, Durla was fully prepared for Lione to answer that it was the emperor. Durla was perfectly aware that there remained a handful of holdouts who believed that Londo Mollari still mattered in some way, shape, or form to the business of Centauri Prime. It was a quaint notion, of course. Truthfully, he would be surprised if it turned out that Lione was among those benighted few, but anything was possible.

What he was not expecting was the answer that Lione gave:

"The Lady Mariel."

For just a moment Durla's lips twisted in anger, and he was about to order General Rhys to dispatch Lione for good and all. If nothing else, it would prove to the other ministers that no one was immune to the ire and retribution of the prime minister.

But something in Lione's look stopped him, and he realized with a sort of bleak horror that Lione absolutely believed it.

"Mariel? My wife?"

Lione let out a slow breath. Clearly he thought he was as good as dead. That being the case, there was no point in withholding exactly what he believed, what he thought. "We are not fools," he told Durla with a nervous sneer. "Your obsession with her was known to all. Did you think that I was unable to tell? That none of us would figure it out? And then you wound up acquiring her in some pathetic game. What a startling coincidence."

"It was no coincidence," Durla replied hotly. "If you must know, Lione, the woman was attracted to me. Vir Cotto had no desire to try to hold on to her, since all she spoke of was me, and he was more than happy to see me secure her."

"Oh, was he now. And how very convenient for him. The chances are that he played you for a fool."

"Impossible. Cotto is nothing."

"He was in a position to give you that for which you hungered. He must have been *something*."

"He is nothing, I tell you. The Lady Mariel wanted me . . ."

"Let us say that she did. The reason is obvious. She wanted to be able to manipulate you. She was a spy in my employ, Durla, or have you forgotten that? I know just how much information that woman was capable of acquiring. She likely learned of your fixation with her and decided to use it to her advantage. Women, after all, have no power in our government. What better way for a clever and ambitious woman like Mariel to gain influence than by sinking her claws into a man who would accede to her every whim."

"Mine is the vision, Lione," Durla stated flatly, his considerable aplomb beginning to erode. "Mine is the direction for Centauri Prime . . ."

"Right, right. Your dreams, from which you garner impressive scientific developments. How likely is that, Prime Minister? As opposed to the thought that they are being fed to you by your beloved wife, who in turn is acquiring them from contacts she has managed to cultivate. We all know you dote on her, fawn on her. She is your sense of self-worth, your inspiration, your image, all rolled into one. You are nothing without the Lady Mariel."

"I had already achieved greatness before she ever became my wife," Durla reminded him. He was barely managing to keep himself from leaping across the room, grabbing the sword, and dispatching Lione himself.

"You achieved it in the hopes of impressing her. How pathetic a life is that?"

For a long moment, Durla said nothing. He fought mightily with himself not to betray a shred of the emotion roiling within him. Then, in a hoarse, choked voice, he said, "General Rhys . . ."

Lione braced himself for the killing stroke.

"Thank you for your assistance. Wait in the outer office please."

If Rhys was at all disappointed that he was not going to have the opportunity to lop off Lione's head and thereby provide some excitement to what was otherwise a fairly dull day, he did not show it. Instead he simply sheathed his sword, bowed slightly, and walked out.

Minister Lione sat there, clearly not quite knowing what had hit him. When Durla slowly came around to him, he automatically flinched as he saw a hand move toward him. But all Durla did was pat Lione on the shoulder, and say, "I appreciate your candor." He touched the pale, reddish liquid on Lione's throat. "You'll probably want to have that looked at." Then he walked out, leaving a dumbfounded Lione to wonder what had just transpired.

The Lady Mariel was most surprised to see her husband. He strode into their sumptuous quarters unannounced and unexpected. He had not been around much lately during the day; indeed, he had not been around that much at night, either. It was a situation that offered both pluses and minuses. Not having him around was, of course, rather nice, due to the fact that she did not love him. Oh, she feigned it masterfully. Then again, it wasn't hard to fake something when someone else desperately wanted to believe in it.

But if she wasn't a party to his goings-on, it made it that much more difficult for her to get information for her beloved Vir.

Vir, who was back on Babylon 5, putting the information she fed him to good use. She didn't know for sure, but she would not have been surprised if her wonderful Vir was somehow involved with the rebels who were causing so much trouble for Durla and his plans. This, of course, was something she would never let on to Durla. First, it would mean betraying the incomparable Vir, and second, her own duplicity would become known. It would mean death. Her death would be unfortunate enough, but Vir's death—*that* she simply could not risk. He was too glorious, too magnificent.

Not for the first time, she wondered why she felt that way about him.

Some part of her understood that she had not always embraced such depth of feeling for Vir. On some level, she knew the change had simply come over her, and she could not comprehend what had prompted it. Ultimately, though, it made no difference. Her Vir was her Vir, and that was all. However she came by her feelings, she knew they were honest and true, and every time she was with Durla, only her thoughts of Vir sustained her. At those times, things didn't seem as bad as they were.

"My husband," she said quickly. She had been carefully braiding the long lock of hair that was the fashion with her generation. She did not rise from the chair where she sat, in front of the makeup table. Instead she stayed where she was and watched herself in the mirror as she meticulously continued creating the braid. "Would you forgive me if I did not get up?"

"I will try not to allow it to put a strain on our marriage," he said, in an oddly stiff tone. "You look lovely today."

"And you, strikingly handsome, milord husband," she responded. She knew he liked it when she addressed him in the formal manner, and used it whenever she thought he might be in an expansive mood. It was usually enough to get him talking and spilling choice nuggets of information. "To what do I owe the honor of this appearance?"

He regarded her thoughtfully for a moment, and then said, "Do you love Vir Cotto?"

She allowed the question to appear to catch her off guard. In truth, she had anticipated his asking that at some point. Indeed, the Lady Mariel made it a point to try to anticipate as much as possible, so that—should the eventuality transpire—she would be able to re-act with a carefully crafted reaction and response.

At least, that was the theory.

"Vir Cotto," she said. "The ambassador? From Babylon 5?"

"Your previous lover," Durla said. There was a slight edgy sharp-ness to his tone. "I'm sure you have some familiarity with him."

"Yes, of course. But do I love him?" She knew full well that Durla fancied himself a true student of psychology. Often had he boasted to her of his ability to simply gaze into someone's eyes and, by that method, determine the veracity of what they were about to say. So she had long known that the only way she could glide past a poten-tially awkward situation such as this would be to look him right in the eyes and lie with confidence.

The thing was, the best way to get through the lie was to use as much of the truth as possible. "To be perfectly candid, my love, Vir was simply a means to an end. I used him as a means of establishing diplomatic contacts in order to supply information to Minister Lione. Certainly you must have known that. You were aware that I was in Li-one's employ."

"Yes. I was aware of that," he replied slowly. She continued to braid her hair. "You have not directly answered the question, though."

"I thought I had," she said carelessly. Once more she met his gaze, and this time she said flatly and with no lack of conviction, "No. I do not love Vir Cotto. I love only you, my great visionary."

It was the hardest thing she had ever said. Because the truth was that she did love Vir Cotto. The passing of years, the marriage to Durla . . . none of that had altered her thinking. Vir continued to be her sun, moon, and stars. She had agreed to the sham of Vir's "losing" her to Durla, had pretended that she had always secretly harbored a fascination for the prime minister, all because Vir desired it. She wanted to help Vir, to serve him in any way she could.

She hadn't lied about her original purpose for associating with Vir. Things, however, had changed. She had come to realize the full wonderfulness that was Vir Cotto. One treasured day, with a sudden burst of clarity, as if her previous life had been merely a dream, she abruptly had understood that Vir was the only man for her in all the universe.

She never doubted for a moment that, sooner or later, something would happen to Durla. Something nasty. Something final. Until that time, she would play the dutiful wife and think of Vir and provide him with whatever information she could garner. Because that was what Vir wanted.

Durla nodded and smiled at her affirmation of her love for him, as she had suspected he would. "You know of my dreams . . . my great visions," he said.

"Of course I do. Everyone on Centauri Prime does."

"Believe it or not, my love . . . in my dreams . . . it is you who comes to me."

"Me?" She laughed. "I am most flattered."

"As well you should be. It is not every woman who can serve as inspiration to the prime minister of Centauri Prime." He was walking slowly around her, his hands draped behind his back. "However . . . there are some who mistake this 'inspiration' that you provide me."

"Mistake? How?"

"They think that you control me. That I have some sort of . . ." He rolled his eyes and shook his head. ". . . some sort of obsession that unmans me in your presence."

"Ridiculous," she said vehemently, even as she finished braiding her hair. "You are Durla, prime minister of Centauri Prime. You answer to no woman."

"You know that. I know that. But they," and he pointed in the nebulous direction of the all-present "they," "they believe differently. And I fear that I must do something about it."

"I will support whatever actions you decide to take, beloved." She turned in her seat and smiled her most glowing smile.

He hit her so hard that he knocked her clear out of her chair.

Mariel fell back, striking her head on the floor. She lay there, stunned, feeling the blood welling up from between her teeth and trickling down from her nose. Her lower lip was already swelling, and her upper lip had gone numb.

She tried to stammer out something, anything, and then Durla hauled her to her feet. She tried to push him away but he was far too strong, and then he swung his hand around and struck her again. Her face reddened where he slapped her, and then he backhanded her and she went down again. Her lungs seized up with a coughing fit, and she spat out blood.

"There," Durla said.

"*There?*" She couldn't believe it. "Wha—what did I do? How did I displease you . . ."

"You haven't. Unfortunately we live in a world that is shaped by perception," he said sadly. "If the others think that I am unmanned by you . . . that I let you manipulate me in any way . . . then it can have a very negative impact on me and my fortunes. Even though it is not true. Therefore we need to make clear to any and all who are interested that I am my own man."

He kicked her in the stomach while she lay on the floor. She doubled up, curling almost into a fetal position, and then, with the side of his boot, he struck her in the face. Mariel, sobbing, rolled onto her back, her legs still curled up. She felt something small and hard in her mouth. She rolled it around on her tongue. It was a tooth. She spit it out and it made a faint *tik tik* noise as it bounced across the floor.

"Yes," he said with satisfaction. "Now any who see you will know that Durla is no woman's servant. No woman's slave. You may be my inspiration . . . but I have no compunction about treating you in the same way that I would treat the lowliest of the low. I do not play favorites. For you see, nothing, and no one, is more important than Centauri Prime. And only if I am strong can I help our beloved world attain its true destiny."

"Vir," she whispered, very softly, very hoarsely.

He hadn't quite heard her, because she said it just under her breath, and while he was still talking. "What did you say?" he inquired.

"Dear ... I said ... dear ... please ... don't hurt me ... any more ..." She didn't even recognize her own voice because it was so choked with pain.

"I need the full backing of all the ministers for the full military program that we have planned," he continued. He crouched next to her, and he spoke as if from light-years away. "Picture it, Mariel. Picture powerful warships, poised, ready. Needing only the final go-ahead from me to sweep across the galaxy like a black cloud of strength, reordering all the known worlds and uniting them under our rule. But it can only happen if the Centaurum is fully committed. To me. No hesitation, no reservation, no signs of weakness. I can take no chances that anyone think me soft. You understand, don't you?"

"Yes ... I ... I do ... I ..."

"Good."

Then he really began to hurt her.

And the thing that kept going through her mind was, *Vir ... Vir will help me ... he will save me ... Vir ... I love you ...*

Vir Cotto felt the world spinning around him, and he sagged to the ground, staring up in disbelief.

He was just outside the palace. The sun was hanging low in the sky, the rays filtering through the haze as the twilight approached. As a consequence, there wasn't much light with which Vir could make out the head on the pike in the garden. But there was just enough light to see, and the head was just familiar enough to recognize.

Rem Lanas stared down at him lifelessly. And yet, even in that lifelessness, there was accusation. *Why weren't you here for me,* he seemed to say. *Why didn't you help me? Why didn't you save me? I trusted you, became a part of your cause . . . and this is what happened to me . . . because of you . . . you . . .*

He hadn't expected such a sight. He had been told to wait in the garden, that someone would be along to escort him in for his meeting with the emperor. But he'd been caught completely off guard.

He wasn't sure how long Rem's head had been up there. The weather had not been kind to it.

Then a bird landed on it. To Vir's horror, it pulled experimentally at Rem's cheek, trying to dig out what it apparently thought was a particularly appetizing bit of flesh.

"Get away!" yelled Vir, and he clambered up on a stone bench. "Get away! Get *away!!!*"

The bird ignored him, and Vir, who was gesticulating wildly, suddenly lost his balance. He stumbled backward, struck his head, and lay there, unmoving.

He had no idea how long he lay there, but when he finally did open his eyes, he found that night had fallen. He wondered how he could possibly have just been left in the one place, unseen by anyone, for such a period of time.

Then he felt heaviness in his chest, and a distant buzzing of alarm in the back of his skull. Suddenly he began to feel as if someone had clubbed him from behind. Probably, he reasoned, some sort of residual pain left over from falling and hurting himself.

With effort, he looked up at Rem Lanas' head atop the pike.

It was gone.

His own head was there instead.

It looked rather comical in its way, and he would have laughed had he actually been able to get the noise out. Instead, though, there was simply an overwhelming desire to scream at the hideous sight. However, he couldn't get that to emerge either. There was just a repeated, strangulated coughing.

He turned and tried to run, tried to shout for help . . .

. . . and there was someone there in the shadows.

The darkness actually seemed to come alive around him as he stared, transfixed, at the being—no, the creature—that was moving slowly out of the shadows toward him. It fixed him with a malevolent glare, as if it had already destroyed him somehow and he simply wasn't aware of it yet. Vir knew it instantly as a Drakh, a servant of the Shadows. But he reminded himself that the average Centauri had never seen a Drakh, and the last thing he should do was blurt out what was on his mind.

"Shiv'kala," the Drakh said.

The word brought back awful memories. Years earlier, at the behest of the now-dead techno-mage, Kane, he had spoken that name to Londo. The mere mention of it had gotten Vir thrown into a cell. Later on, working in conjunction with another techno-mage, Galen, he had come to realize that the name belonged to one of the Drakh. Immediately he understood.

"You . . . are Shiv'kala," he said.

Shiv'kala inclined his head slightly in acknowledgment. "Names," he said, "have power. Power, however, cuts both ways." When he spoke, his voice was a gravelly whisper. "You mentioned my name once. Do you remember?"

Vir managed to nod.

"When you did so, it drew my attention to you. Why did you?"

"Wh-why did I . . . what?"

"Why. Did you. Mention. My name?"

Once upon a time, Vir would have panicked at a moment such as this. Confronted by a dark, frightening creature of evil, he would have been reduced to a trembling mass of disintegrating nerves.

That Vir, however, was gone.

Gone, but not forgotten.

Outwardly he was all terror and wide eyes, hands trembling violently and legs buckling at the knees, causing him to sink to the ground in stark-staring terror.

Inwardly, his mind was racing. For he was seeing this entity before him not as some overpowering, terrifying monster, but rather simply as a member of another race. Granted, an incredibly formidable race. But he had been responsible for the destruction of a long-lost Shadow vessel that the Drakh had craved. He had seen Drakh warriors killed before his very eyes. He knew they were not invincible.

They had limits.

And the question posed him by Shiv'kala revealed some of those limits.

In a way it was remarkable. A bare half-dozen years ago, the mere mention of Shiv'kala's name had struck a chill within him. Now he was facing down the owner of the name, and he was analyzing him with methodical precision.

The sight of his own head on the pole had been a nice bit of theatrics, but that had been sufficient to tell him that he was no longer in reality. He was in some sort of dream state, into which the Drakh had inserted himself.

But the Drakh was asking him questions.

Which meant the Drakh didn't know the answers. After all, if he knew the answers, then why bother to ask at all? To try to "trick" him for some reason? What would be the point of that?

So even though the Drakh clearly had some sort of advanced mental abilities, they were hardly limitless. They were apparently able to broadcast into someone's dream state, and were probably capable of receiving transmissions. But they were not readily capable of reading minds. Or, at the very least, they couldn't read a mind that wasn't cooperating.

Furthermore, Shiv'kala had waited quite a few years to come to Vir and start asking why his name had been bandied about. That indicated to Vir that their range might be limited, as well. Again, at the very least, it was limited where other species were concerned. Shiv'kala had had to wait until Vir was within reasonable proximity of the palace.

Why?

Because, as much as Vir's stomach churned just contemplating the notion, the fact was that the royal palace of Centauri Prime had become little more than a Drakh stronghold, a cover for the Drakh power base. Although Vir had strong suspicions that their true center of power was somewhere else on Centauri Prime.

But he had no desire to let the Drakh know that he had discerned so much, so quickly. Beings of finite power they might be, but there was no underestimating the ability of the Drakh to destroy him at their slightest whim. The only reason they had not done so by this point, he decided, was that they did not perceive him as a direct threat. If they *did* decide he posed a threat, however, he didn't stand a chance.

All of this went through his mind in less than a second, and by that point he was already back on the ground, "crumbling" at the mere sight of the formidable Drakh. He could tell from the Drakh's expression that Shiv'kala was by turns taken aback, appalled, and amused at the sight of this great, groveling oaf.

The thing was, he had to give some sort of answer that would throw the Drakh off track. He couldn't take the chance that Shiv'kala might figure out his connection to the underground. The only way to make sure of that was to present himself as a simple tool, a harmless foil who was about as capable of causing damage on his own as a wafting feather might be.

And the best thing of all was that he could tell reasonable amounts of the truth, which would be all the easier to sell to the Drakh. If there was one thing that Vir excelled at, it was sincerity. He wore sincerity as comfortably as other Centauri wore high hair.

"I . . . I was told to," he stammered out.

"By whom?"

"By . . . by . . ." He licked his lips. "By a techno-mage."

"Ahhhh . . ." Obviously it hadn't been the answer the Drakh was expecting, but neither did it seem to surprise him. "A techno-mage. And where have you encountered a techno-mage?"

"Back on Babylon 5. I first met them when I was serving Londo." The words were tumbling over each other. It wasn't really that long ago—a minor part of a lifetime, really—that Vir Cotto had been a bumbling, tongue-twisted, and perpetually anxious young man. Vir remembered that Vir-that-was almost nostalgically. At the time, life had seemed hideously complex.

He remembered quite clearly the man he had been, and had no trouble at all summoning the Vir from years gone by. He took that much younger Vir, slipped him on like a comfortable overcoat, and impersonated him with tremendous facility. "Londo, he . . . he wanted the techno-mages' blessing and . . . and . . . and . . . and . . ."

Shiv'kala nodded, and moved his hand in a slight clockwise motion as if to indicate to Vir that he should get on with it.

". . . and he sent me to them to tell them he wanted to suh-suh-see them!" Vir continued. "I thought that would be the end of it. But it wasn't. No. No, it wasn't. Because they came to me, and told me to walk into the palace and say your . . . that name. Why? Why would they do that? Please, tell me . . ." And he started to sob. It was amazing to him how easily the tears came. Then again, considering everything he had been through, all the horrors he had witnessed, perhaps the impressive thing was that he was ever able to *prevent* himself from crying.

He reasoned that the best thing to do was allow the Drakh, all unknowingly, to fill in the gaps himself. Shiv'kala, as it so happened, promptly did so.

"We have our suspicions" was all the Drakh would offer, although he did add, "You would be wise, Vir Cotto, not to meddle further with magic workers. You are merely a game piece to such as they, to be discarded at will. Do you know us?"

Vir shook his head fiercely.

Shiv'kala glanced upward in the direction of the head. "Do you know him?"

Vir looked back up, and he saw that the head of Rem Lanas was back in lieu of his own. As appalling a sight as Rem's head had been up there, he had to admit that it was better than his.

"His . . . his name is Rem Lanas," Vir managed to say, making the response seem far more of an effort than it was. "I . . . met him on Babylon 5. We had drinks."

"You have met a great many people on Babylon 5, it seems."

"I . . . I . . ." He tried to find something to say, and finally settled on, "I have a lot of free time on my hands."

The Drakh either didn't register the response, or didn't care that it had been made. Vir couldn't help but feel that Shiv'kala was assessing him right then and there, trying to determine whether Vir was indeed going to be a problem.

"You do know," Shiv'kala said softly, "that this is all a dream. It is not happening."

"I had been kind of hoping for that to be the case," Vir told him.

"Be aware of one thing ... we know of the predictions of the Lady Morella."

This caused Vir to freeze where he stood. Even though he was dreaming, even though he felt no normal sensations, he was still certain he could sense his blood running cold. "Morella?"

"Londo mentioned 'predictions' once," the Drakh said. " 'Both of us, protected by visions, protected by prophecy,' was what he said."

Vir remembered the exchange all too well. It had been in the cell that Vir had occupied for the high crime of mentioning Shiv'kala's name—at the urging of a techno-mage, that much at least had been the truth.

"I sought clarification from him as to what he meant. He was ... less than forthcoming. At first. But we can be most persuasive. He told us of how the Lady Morella made predictions, stating that one of you would succeed the other to the throne of Centauri Prime. Since he is still with us ... that leads us to believe that you will be the next ruler."

"It's just a prediction. It means nothing."

"Perhaps. But be aware, Vir Cotto ... should it come to pass ..." And the Drakh's mouth twisted into something approximating a smile, the single most horrific thing that Vir had seen in the entire encounter. "Should it come to pass ... there is much that we can offer you."

"I ..." He gulped. "I appreciate the thought."

"Our power is great. You can benefit by it ... or be destroyed. The choice, for the moment, is yours. In the end, it may or may not remain so."

And then he stepped back into the shadows, which seemed to reach out to claim him.

Vir stood there a moment, steadying the pounding of his hearts ... and then he noticed that the shadows were continuing to stretch ... toward him. Even though he knew it was a dream, even though he was certain he was not in any real danger ... nevertheless, he did not like in the least what the shadows portended, and he was loath to let them touch him. He backed up, and he bumped up against the pole on which he had seen his own head. He looked up involuntarily and let out a yelp of alarm.

Senna's head was there instead of his. It stared down at him, eyes glassy. And then the impact of Vir's thumping against it caused her head to topple off. The head fell, spiraling, and tumbled into Vir's arms even as he tried to do everything he could to avoid it.

And then, despite everything he'd been through, despite his being fairly inured to terrifying hardships, Vir found himself frozen, utterly paralyzed, unable to cope with what he was seeing.

He started to cry, tears running down his face, but without any heat. As grotesque and grisly a sight as it was, he clutched the head to him and the sobs crew louder.

And the head spoke to him. "Vir . . . Vir," came Senna's voice, impossibly, from the severed head. Then Vir was being shaken, and suddenly he opened his eyes, and the tears were very real and hot against his cheek.

Senna was looking down at him, her head securely back on her shoulders.

He remembered the first time he had seen her, more than a decade before, when Londo had taken her under his wing. There was no longer anything childlike about her. This was an adult woman, polished and intelligent, who looked as if she was already anticipating how she was going to respond to something you had not yet thought of saying.

She was dressed in a blue-and-white gown that was both simple and elegant. She had been wearing it the last time that Vir had seen her, about six months earlier, during a dinner with Londo that had quickly evolved into a rather pleasant evening. She had, in fact, salvaged the evening, because Londo had spent much of it getting quietly drunk—which was something Vir had not often seen Londo do. Drunk, yes, but quiet? Never.

She had been witty, charming, entertaining, and utterly captivating.

He had also heard from her from time to time during the interim, although usually it was about more . . . business-oriented matters.

"Vir . . . Londo sent me to fetch you . . . and you were here, and . . ."

"I'm all right, I'm . . . I'm all right," he said quickly, clambering to his feet. He glanced around automatically. Even though he knew that there would be no sign of the Drakh—that, indeed, the Drakh had most likely never physically been there—he found that he was peering into the shadows to see if any of them moved. "I saw . . ." Then he caught himself. He certainly didn't want to tell this young woman what he had experienced. There was no need to risk alarming her.

"You saw what?" she asked.

Slowly he pointed to the head of Rem Lanas, perched atop the pole.

"He was . . . one of yours?"

His head snapped around at those words. He saw it then, in her face, in her eyes . . . she knew.

"Not here," he said firmly, and tugged her arm. He started to pull her out of the garden, and she offered no resistance, but then he stopped, and said, "Wait . . . Londo will be waiting . . ."

"If he waits a few minutes more, nothing will happen," Senna said, and with that they departed. The unseeing eyes of Rem Lanas watched them go.

They wanted me to do something. How gloriously ironic is that?

The House heads were clamoring to see me. They were up in arms because Durla has jailed one of their own. They wanted to know what I am going to do about it, not only as emperor, but also as the head of a House myself

They all clustered outside my chambers, a flock of clucking birds, and at first Dunseny brought them in one at a time. But finally, at my instruction, he led in the entire group of them. Initially they comported themselves nobly, speaking in the sort of stately and pompous manner that I've come to expect. But soon one complaint tumbled into another, until they were all bleating about their situation. They tell me that, if this is allowed to continue, it is going to mean the end of the entire social and class structure of Centauri Prime. It will terminate life as we know it, everything that Centauri Prime is supposed to stand for and respect.

It is truly amazing.

Shadow ships darkened our sky . . . the Shadows themselves were given aid and comfort here on Centauri Prime . . . creatures who were the purest incarnation of evil ever known to this galaxy. That was not enough to be an end to life as we know it on Centauri Prime.

Nor was life as we know it threatened by Cartagia's mad reign, during which time the supposedly brave House leaders trembled in hiding, lest they truly lose their heads.

And now . . .

Well . . . truth be told . . . the life that we have come to know and cherish on Centauri Prime, the goals for which we have fought so diligently . . . these actually are in jeopardy. Not for the reason that the House heads claim, though. The heads of the Houses live in the uppermost branches of the tree that is Centauri Prime. When one is that high up, it is difficult to perceive that the true problem is root rot.

It took me a little time to discern exactly what has them so up in arms. Most interesting: Milifa, the father of the late and unlamented—except by him—Throk, spoke challengingly to our prime minister. One does not do so if one expects to live to a ripe old age. Milifa apparently forgot that, and is now imprisoned.

A rather foolish move, that.

Tikane came before me, of the House of Tikane. And there is Arlineas, and Yson, and a host of others. Persons who, after hiding in fear from the rampage of Cartagia, feel a greater sense of safety under my more "benevolent" rule. They have also been supporters of Durla, helping to smooth the way to his assuming the office and power of prime minister. I believe they are regretting that decision, and are hoping that I will rectify it for them.

"The Houses, Emperor," Tikane told me with a vast degree of pomposity, "are the underpinnings, the backbone, of your strength." The others nodded in accord.

My strength.

My strength.

What know they of my strength?

It is Durla who runs things, and I . . . I have been fighting political battles and games for as long as I can remember. For a time I thought that I was truly winning . . . except in this sort of game, to win is to lose. Durla feeds on this sort of business, the way a fire feeds on oxygen. The only thing I take comfort in is knowing that even Durla is deceived. He deludes himself into believing that he knows what is occurring . . . but he does not. He has no idea that he himself is a tool, of . . . others. Were I to tell him, of course, he would not believe me. He is far too taken with his own sense of self-importance.

Then it was Arlineas who spoke, and he looked a bit concerned. I have no idea how long I must have simply sat there, staring off into space, lost in my thoughts. Next to Arlineas was Yson—small in stature, but looming in charisma—who, as was his custom, said nothing. Very rarely did he speak. As a result, on the few occasions when he did, his words carried with them far greater importance

But it was Arlineas who spoke "Highness, are you—" he said tentatively

"I hear you," I answered him softly "I hear everything."

"Then certainly," Arlineas said, "you have heard the stories of the massive fleet buildup. Individual workforces, operating independently of each other, each assembling different parts of the whole, but no one person truly knowing its capacity—"

"Or purpose," Tikane said. "No one person except Durla   who now has virtually declared war on the Houses." The others crowded together, all bobbing their heads in agreement. "What does this say to you, Highness?"

"What does it say to me?" I replied. For the first time in a long time, I felt something other than lethargy running through my veins. "It says to me that you and your ilk were more than content to allow matters to progress to this state, when it suited your needs and egos. Durla has made no secret of his intentions. How many of you nodded dutifully and applauded his grand vision. And Vallko   Vallko, standing in the Great Square, preaching of Centauri Prime's great destiny, which any fool can see means nothing less than the annihilation or subjugation of every other world. How many of you shared his prayers to the Great Maker and sought the Great Maker's blessing for the very endeavors you now decry."

"We are simply concerned for the general well-being of our world, Highness," Tikane protested.

"Your own well-being, you mean. You reap what you sow."

They looked at each other in puzzlement. "We are not farmers, Highness," Arlineas pointed out.

I shook my head. "Never mind. I did not expect you to understand. But," I continued with renewed strength, "if you do not comprehend that, then this might serve instead. Something a Vorlon once said . . ."

"A Vorlon?" There were immediate looks, one to the other. Most of them had never had the opportunity to see a Vorlon, even one inside an encounter suit. I, of course, had not only extensively been in the presence of a suited one . . . but I was present that amazing day when Kosh Naranek, the Vorlon ambassador, emerged from his suit. Others reported visions of a great winged being, and I .   .

I saw nothing.

Actually, that is not entirely accurate. I saw . .   light. An overwhelming brilliance But it was shapeless, amorphous, and indistinct. For a moment, it seemed as though I perceived a hint of something, but that was all.

Sometimes I have wondered whether what others saw was some sort of mass delusion . . . or whether I was simply not deserving of the experience.

"Yes. A Vorlon," I said. "Understand, he did not say this to me directly, but to another. However, things have a habit of being passed around. And what he said was, 'The blizzard has already begun. It is too late for the snowflakes to vote.' Do you comprehend that, gentlemen?"

There were slow nods from all around. They understood all too well. They were not, however, happy about it.

"So . . . you will do nothing?" Tikane said. "You will simply allow Durla to do as he wishes?"

"Have you heard nothing I said?" I demanded. "He operates now using the power that your support provided him. He has grown beyond you. To him, you are all simple ground-dwellers. He no longer looks to the ground. He looks to the stars that he desires to conquer, and he has the backing of the military. And the people adore him . . . him and his ministers of religion and education and information. You, who have so much, cannot begin to comprehend how much those who have nothing appreciate such things as jobs and building toward a future of conquest. Since they have nothing, they consider it quite appealing, the prospect of taking that which others possess.

"You cannot stand against that, and I do not suggest you try."

"Then what do you suggest we do, Highness?" Arlineas demanded.

I sighed deeply and put a hand to my head. "I suggest you leave. My head hurts rather profoundly, and I would be alone."

They were not the least bit happy to hear that, but my personal guards did not particularly care about the feelings of the noble lords. They were escorted out. The last one to go was Yson, and I felt his rather malevolent gaze upon me even after he was out of the room.

"Leave me," I told my guards. They bowed and obeyed, closing the great doors behind them. The doors of my prison.

I rose from my throne and walked slowly across the room. Every movement these days feels labored and painful. In the past, at least my aches had been courteous enough to confine themselves to what is left of my soul; now they have actually intruded into my joints. Most inconsiderate.

I stood upon the balcony, holding tightly to the railing. I looked into the distance . . . and saw something that was most unexpected. There, walking across a field, were Vir and Senna. I had been wondering where Vir was; I had sent Senna to bring him to me, and yet there they were, walking away, speaking with each other like two old friends. Or more than that?

Then something else caught my eye, on another balcony, to the right and one level up. I knew it well; it was the residence and offices of Durla. The fact that he had acquired accommodations higher than my own was, I had always felt, a not-so-subtle message from him to me.

What I saw now, though, was not Durla. It was Mariel, and she looked simply awful. She was bandaged, as if she had taken a great fall. I did not have a chance to get a good look, however, because she spotted me looking up at her . . . and immediately darted back inside.

It was never like her to be clumsy. Then again, age begins to tell on all of us, I suppose.

"What make you of that?"

It was Shiv'kala. As always, I had not heard his entrance at all. Even after all these years of our .   "association". . . I still had no clear idea of how he achieved his comings and goings. I used to think upon it for extensive periods of time, scrutinizing the walls from which he emerged to see if there were hidden passages and such. If so, I never managed to detect them.

"Of them?" I pointed to Vir and Senna, mere specks in the distance. "How kind of you to care about my opinion."

"I have always cared, Londo."

I turned and looked into the face of the creature I hated above all others. If nothing else, his unchanging nature was aggravating. My face, my frame, reflected every minute of every day of my life, and not in an especially flattering manner. Shiv'kala, for his part, looked exactly the same now as he had then. "You say 'I' rather than 'we'? I had always thought you spoke on behalf of the Drakh entire."

"You have never truly understood me, Londo," Shiv'kala said. "Believe it or not, you have had no greater protector or friend than me."

"I will opt for 'not,' if it is all the same to you."

Shiv'kala looked at me with what seemed to be a perverse sort of paternal disapproval. "You have not been the best of servants, Londo."

"I grieve for my lapses."

"You do no such thing. Your little rebellions have been numerous, and usually ill timed. That you have survived them has been largely due to my sufferance. Fortunately enough, in recent years they have been fairly nonexistent."

Something about the way he said that caught my interest. "Why 'fortunately enough'?"

"Because," he said evenly, "matters will be coming to a head. And now would be a most unfortunate time to be . . . problematic."

I chuckled softly. "Are you not concerned that saying such things may provide a temptation for me to do exactly what you fear?"

"Fear?" The notion appeared to amuse him. "We fear nothing, Londo, least of all you. However, I have invested a good deal of time in you. The notion that the time was wasted would be displeasing to me."

"Of course . . ." I said, understanding. "You are concerned that I will be motivated by the complaints. That I will attempt to interfere in the plans of Durla, your chosen one."

"Any 'attempts' you make will be just that. You cannot stop this, Londo, any more than . . ."

"Than that vessel, Excalibur, was able to stop your plan to eradicate humanity?"

We both knew precisely what I meant.

"You grow old, Londo," he said after a time of silence. "You grow old . . . and tired. I can help you, you know."

"Oh, can you."

He stepped in close to me. Once I would have trembled inwardly. Now I was simply bored.

"We have our methods," he said. "You need not be a slave to your body. Options can be offered you . . . if your actions suit our desires. You can be young and strong again."

"I was never young," I told him, "and if I had ever been strong, I would not have allowed myself to get into this situation in the first place. I am not interested, Shiv'kala, in anything you might have to offer."

"When you are on your deathbed, you might have something else to say."

"You are likely right. And it will probably be something like this . . ." and I put my hand to my throat and produced a loud "Aaaackkkkkk!"

He looked at me very oddly, did the Drakh. "You have a curiously odd-timed sense of humor, Emperor Mollari."

"I have learned that life is short, Shiv'kala, and one must find one's amusements where one can."

He looked out toward Vir and Senna. I could not help but feel that he was studying them in the same manner that I might examine an insect before I step on it. "You have not answered my question, Londo. What make you of that?"

"What do I make of two people walking?" I shrugged. "It means nothing."

"Sometimes that which means nothing means everything."

"You speak like a Vorlon."

It was a passing, offhand remark. I thought nothing of it. But the moment the words passed from my lips, a massive jolt of pain surged through my skull. I dropped to one knee, refusing to cry out   a resolve that lasted for perhaps three seconds before a scream was torn from my throat.

Shiv'kala stood above me, looking down at me with that same crushed-bug expression. "Never," he said coldly, "say that again."

"Never   never   " I managed to get out. Then the pain ebbed, just like that, and I sagged to the floor, on my hands and knees, trying to prop myself up and stop the room from spinning wildly around me.

"And never forget who I am   what you are   "

"Never," I said again.

As if he had forgotten that I was there, he looked back out in the direction of Vir and Senna. "Cotto has been made a tool of the technomages. Are you aware of that?"

I shook my head, which was a mistake, because it made the room spin utterly out of control. My left elbow gave way and I crashed to the floor. Shiv'kala did not appear to notice.

"At least he has been in the past. Perhaps they were utilizing him again that day he was wandering the palace and almost came upon me. Well, Londo   what one group can turn to their advantage . another can, as well. And this we shall do   when the time is right."

"Don't hurt him," I gasped out from the floor. "He   is harmless."

"Hurt the next emperor?" He seemed astonished at the thought. "Unthinkable. He is our insurance, Londo. In case you become too troublesome, or decline to remain malleable . . . you can be disposed of, and Vir instituted in your place. And I strongly suspect that he will be far more compliant than you have ever been."

"I have . . . complied . . ."

"On most things, yes. On some, you have not. There should be no exceptions. It is not for you to pick and choose. It is for you to obey."

"Obey   yes .   I will   "

"See that you do," he said, and I could feel the temperature dropping significantly. "Otherwise Vir will step in where you leave off If you do not desire such a happenstance   then do nothing to bring it about."

"I shall do nothing." The pain was beginning to subside, but the lack of control, the sense of humiliation   these were wounds that stabbed far more deeply, and would never depart.

I waited for the response—some retort, some threat, some thing. But there was nothing. I looked up. He was gone.

I rose on unsteady legs and, as I leaned against the wall, I realized somewhat belatedly that I should have asked him if he knew the circumstances of how Mariel had come to be injured. For a moment, a demented moment, I thought that maybe Durla had done that to her. But then I realized that such a thing could not possibly be. He adored her. He doted on her. Amusingly, there were many who believed that she was the true strength behind the prime minister. I, of course, knew that it was the Drakh. But that was information that I had no choice but to keep to myself.

I have read back on what I have just written. My eyes are tired, and I feel myself growing fatigued. Vir and Senna came back later in the evening, and there seemed to be something in their eyes when they looked to each other . . . but they also appeared distracted, as if they had seen something that was bothersome to them.

. . . but I am an old man, and prone to imagining things.

What I have not imagined, however, is the concern expressed by the heads of the Houses. I do not care especially about their personal worries. Whatever ill fortunes befall them, they have more than brought upon themselves.

My memory of late continues to fade in and out, but occasionally I have times of starkly lucid clarity. And the extensive discussion of great vessels, fleets . . . these things, however, have caught my attention. Perhaps, despite whatever my "master" may desire, I shall see precisely what is going on, in detail. I likely cannot stop it; I am a mere snowflake, dressed appropriately for that status. However, I can at least provide a bit of slush, and see if Durla slips on it.

6

Senna had never seen Vir looking so shaken. He kept glancing over his shoulder as they retreated from the area of the palace. "Vir, calm down . . . you're moving so quickly, I can barely keep up . . ."

"I feel like we're being watched." They were the first words he'd spoken since she'd found him on the ground in the garden, and they were said with such intensity that she didn't even try to argue. Instead she simply quieted herself and followed him until they seemed to be far enough from the palace that he was satisfied.

She looked around at the hill where they had come to a halt, overlooking the city, and unbidden, tears began to well in her eyes. Vir, turning toward her, saw them and instantly became contrite. "I'm sorry," he stammered, charmingly vulnerable in his discomfort. "I shouldn't have been so abrupt with—"

"Oh, it's not you." She sighed. Even though she was wearing one of her more formal dresses, she nevertheless sank to the ground with another heavy sigh. "This place used to be . . . well . . . a teacher of mine and I used to come here."

"I had lots of teachers," Vir said ruefully. "I don't especially feel nostalgic for any of them. They had very little good to say about me. Do you ever see your old teacher?"

She looked heavenward at the clouds that wafted across the darkening sky. They were tinged bloodred, which was symbolic somehow. "Every now and again. Up there."

"He's a pilot?" Vir asked, totally lost.

She smiled sadly and shook her head. "No, Vir. He's dead. Long dead."

"Oh. I'm sorry."

"So am I." She looked Vir up and down appraisingly. "He would have liked you, I think. Because you're doing something about . . . about all of this."

"You mentioned that before. I'm not entirely sure what you're talking ab—"

Her gaze danced with amusement. "Don't try to lie to me, Vir. You're not very good at it."

With a heavy sigh he sat next to her. "Actually . . . I've not only gotten very good at it, I've gotten very *very* good at it. Which, on some level, kind of depresses me." He looked at her thoughtfully. "But not with you. You see right through me."

"As does the emperor, I suspect," she told him, and when Vir blanched visibly, she went on. "I don't know for sure. We've never actually spoken of it in so many words. I don't think he'd dare, for some reason."

"I can take a guess at the reason," Vir said darkly.

She wondered what he meant by that, but decided not to press the matter.

He seemed aware that he had said something better off not pursued, so he shifted gears. "I . . . did have some suspicions. All those times you would contact me, send me those chatty messages about something or other that Londo had said . . . and invariably, it was information that was helpful to me in my . . . endeavors. The thing is, I didn't know whether you were acting as Londo's mouthpiece, oblivious to what was going on, or whether you truly comprehended how the information you were passing along was being used."

"I see." The edges of her mouth twitched. "So you're saying you couldn't decide whether or not I was a blind fool."

"No! I . . . I wasn't saying that at all!"

She laughed quite openly this time. "Don't worry about it, Vir. You have a lot on your mind, I'm sure." At that he just stared at her, and began smiling. "What?" she prompted.

"I just . . ." He shook his head wonderingly. "You have a really lovely laugh. I never noticed that before about you." He seemed to shake off the digression and instead settled back down to business. "So all those messages you sent . . . they were actually at Londo's behest, because you felt you were aiding in the resistance movement."

"Partly."

"Partly?"

"Well . . ." She shrugged. "The truth is . . . I admire someone like you."

"You do?" He was genuinely curious. "Who is he?"

It took her a moment to understand his question, and then she laughed even more loudly. "You're so literal, Vir. Not really someone 'like' you. You. I liked communicating with you. I liked reminding you that I was around. Because what you do is so admirable.

"There are those who have a vision for this world that will lead us down a fiery path to total destruction. They pursue that path out of self-aggrandizement and ego and obsession with power. You, and others, try to stop them out of a pure sense of altruism. You care so much about helping others that you would risk your lives in order to do it."

"Not just *risk* lives," Vir said, glancing off toward the palace. From this distance, in the growing darkness, it was no longer possible to see the head that had been placed atop a pole.

She understood. "He *was* one of yours, then."

Vir nodded. "We have . . . all of us . . . certain 'safeguards.' A techno-mage aided us in conditioning our minds to resist truth drugs and such. But nothing is fail-safe. When I heard that Lanas had been taken, I immediately arranged a visit here, in hopes of being able to do something . . ."

"That was foolish."

He looked at her in surprise. "That . . . seems a bit harsh . . ."

"Yes. It is. It's also reasonable. Showing up here, timed with the capture of one of your people . . . you're drawing undue attention to yourself. You haven't fooled me, Vir; you've 'created' a persona for yourself, of a tongue-tied, fumbling bumbler—to convince others that you present no threat. You've done a superb job of acting."

"It's been less acting than you would think," Vir mused ruefully.

"Whatever the case . . . the masquerade has garnered you a certain amount of latitude. Despite the timing of your arrival, many will be willing to write it off as coincidence. You wouldn't exactly be the person they consider most likely to oversee an attempt to halt our world's military buildup.

"But all you need is for one person—the wrong person—to make the connection, and the next thing you know, you're the one whose resistance to truth drugs is being tested." She frowned. "You have to think of more than just yourself, Vir. People are counting on you. All of them," and with one sweeping gesture she took in the entirety of the city, "are counting on you, even though they don't know it. The emperor, though he can't say it, is counting on you." She hesitated a moment, and then added, "And I'm counting on you."

Vir looked at her wonderingly. He had seen her on any number of occasions, they had spent time together . . . but it was as if he was truly seeing her for the first time. "I . . . won't let you down," he said, and his voice was hoarse.

Senna had used her attractiveness, her vivaciousness, all as ploys to get people to talk to her. She had been particularly successful with the Prime Candidates, who vied for her attention because she was perceived as a potentially valuable acquisition. Indeed, the late and unlamented Throk had gone so far as to push for a marriage, a move that had been blocked by the emperor and was eventually rendered moot by . . .

"You were the one," she said suddenly. "The one who blew up the Prime Candidates' safe house. The one who killed Throk."

He looked away. The move spoke volumes.

She said nothing more for a time, and then she reached over and rested a hand atop his. "It must have been very difficult for you, Vir."

"It wasn't me," he said tonelessly. "It was someone . . . I don't know."

"But I thought . . ."

"We're in a war, Senna. We all become people we don't know . . . and wouldn't want to know . . . and in times of peace, people we would very much like to forget. I want to forget the person who killed him . . . very much."

She nodded, understanding, and then his hand twisted around and squeezed hers firmly. She interlaced her fingers with his, and she felt the strength in them, but also a faint trembling.

Senna had no idea what prompted her to do it, but she leaned over, took his face in her hands, and kissed him. She had never before kissed anyone sincerely. Reflexively he tried to pull back, but then he settled into it, enjoying the moment, kissing her back hungrily. There was nothing sexual in the contact; the need was far deeper than that. When they parted, he looked at her in amazement. "I . . . shouldn't have done that . . ." he began to apologize.

"In case you didn't notice, Vir, I did it," she said softly. She even felt slightly embarrassed, although she knew she shouldn't. "At the very least, I initiated it."

"But I'm . . . I'm old enough to be your . . . your . . ."

"Lover?" She was startled at her own brazenness. She couldn't believe she'd said it. At the same time, she was glad she had.

He looked at her for a long moment, and this time he was the one who initiated it. Her lips, her body, melted against his. When they

parted, he took her chin in one hand and studied her with both ten-
derness and sadness.

"Another time, perhaps," he said. "Another life. I can't obligate
someone else to me when I'm traveling down a road so dark, I can't
even guess at the end."

"I could walk down that road at your side."

"You need to keep your distance. Because the road tends to
branch off . . . and if I walk out on one of those branches, and the
branch gets cut off behind me . . . I can't take you down with me. I
couldn't live with that knowledge . . . for whatever brief period of
time I was allowed to live, that is."

It was difficult for her to hear, but she knew he was right. Or, at
the very least, she knew that what he was saying was right for him,
and that nothing she could say or do would dissuade him.

"Are you sure Londo knows? About me, I mean," Vir suddenly
said, switching gears. "And he's told no one?"

"If he had told someone . . . anyone . . . do you think you would
still be at liberty?" she asked reasonably.

"Probably not. I'd likely be up there with poor Rem. How many
more, Senna? How many more good and brave men are going to die
before this business is over?"

"There's only so much you can do, Vir. You must do your best,
whatever that may be, and pray to the Great Maker for strength in
dealing with the rest."

"I just wish I knew," Vir said grimly, "whose side the Great
Maker is on. Durla and his allies believe just as fervently as I do that
they are acting in the best interests of Centauri Prime. We can't both
be right."

"Perhaps," she said thoughtfully, leaning back, "you both are."

He looked at her in surprise. "How can we both be?"

She seemed surprised that he had to ask. "Isn't it obvious?"

"Not immediately, no."

"You have a destiny, Vir. I can tell just by looking at you."

"All creatures have a destiny," Vir said dismissively.

"Yes, but you have a great one. It's plain to see. The people of
this world are going to need you in ways that you cannot even begin
to imagine. And perhaps the Great Maker desires the actions of
Durla because he has plans for you. And those plans include your being forged into the man who will guide Centauri Prime to its future.
But you can only become that man by battling the plans of a truly
great enemy . . . and Durla has been selected for that purpose."

He stared at her. "You're saying that people are fighting, dying . . . that millions may be annihilated, if Durla has his way . . . all so that I can eventually pick up the pieces?"

"That's one way of putting it."

"It's not a good way, and I can't say I'm especially thrilled with the idea. It makes the Great Maker sound insane."

"Why should he not be?" Senna challenged. "After all, he made us in his image . . . and look at the terrible things we have done, as a race. Are we not insane?"

"That," Vir said, "makes a horrifying amount of sense."

They walked through the corridors of the palace, chatting agreeably about matters of little to no consequence. It was a rather pleasant change of pace from what they had been dealing with before.

At one point, Vir made a joke that Senna found particularly amusing, so much so in fact that she was seized with laughter, then had to stop and compose herself. Vir stopped, too, grinning amiably, and Senna took his hand in hers.

"Well, well! Looking quite friendly, are we?"

Senna and Vir stopped and turned. She still held his hand.

Durla was walking toward them with his customary swagger. Next to him was a woman that Senna could only assume to be Mariel. It wasn't possible to be sure, however, because she was wearing a veil. This was extremely odd: the only women who wore such things were the legendary telepaths who had once accompanied the emperor wherever he went. That, however, was a custom that had ended with the death of Emperor Turhan. Cartagia, proclaiming that he did not want women around who could peer effortlessly into his mind, had ordered them all killed. They were the first casualties of his bloody reign, and most certainly not the last.

Despite the fact that she was veiled, Senna could sense Mariel's gaze upon her, boring right through her. She reflexively released her hold on Vir's hand, doing so almost guiltily.

"I have known the lady Senna for quite some time," Vir said calmly . . . almost too calmly. "She is much like a beloved niece to me." Senna nodded in confirmation.

"Of course," Durla said with a polite smile. "Oh, and Senna, you of course remember Mariel. She is much like a beloved wife to me. Say hello, Mariel."

"Hello." Her voice was so soft as to be almost inaudible.

"Move aside your veil, dear. It is difficult for them to hear you."

"I . . . do not wish . . ."

"I did not ask you what your wish was in the matter," he reminded her in a voice so sharp that it made Senna jump. She looked to Vir, who somehow was maintaining a look of polite curiosity, but nothing more. "Move aside your veil so that you can greet our visitor properly." He looked at Vir apologetically. "She is being rude to you, perhaps out of some residual resentment over your losing her to me. But I do not tolerate rudeness. Do I, Mariel." It wasn't a question.

"No, husband. You do not," she said. And she put a hand to her veil and moved it aside so that Senna and Vir could see her face.

Senna gasped. She regretted doing so instantly, but it was an involuntary reflex, for Mariel's face was battered and bruised.

Vir gripped Senna's upper arm, also by reflex. He was holding it so tight that it hurt.

"What . . . happened?" Vir managed to get out.

"She is very clumsy, our Mariel," Durla said in a voice dripping with solicitousness. "She tripped over her own words." It had the sound of a remark that Durla had been rehearsing, in preparation for a question that he was longing to answer with smug arrogance.

"I must be more cautious in the future," Mariel admitted, and now she was looking to Vir. Her gaze flickered between Vir and Senna, and Senna saw in those eyes hurt that she could not even imagine.

Vir started toward Durla, and suddenly Senna knew beyond any question that if she did not do something, Vir would be upon him. There was no upside to such a confrontation. Durla had been a trained soldier. That had been some time ago, true, but the training remained. He might be a formidable foe. But if Vir, carried by burning rage, did manage to overwhelm Durla and beat him senseless, as was undoubtedly his intent, then his pretenses would be forever shredded. Senna might wind up proving uncomfortably prescient in her concerns over Vir being imprisoned and drugged up, even before the night was over.

Immediately Senna doubled over in "pain," crying out loudly enough to attract Vir's attention before he had managed to take more than a step or two. He looked at her, confused. "What's wrong?"

"Some sort of . . . of sharp cramp. Please. Would you . . . be so kind as to help me to my room?"

As this occurred, Mariel replaced the veil. Durla was looking at Senna with what seemed boundless compassion. "Attend to her, Vir.

I have known her for quite a while, as well. I knew her back when we all called her Young Lady. Quite a woman she has grown into. Yes, attend to her, Vir, by all means. I have a dinner with my ministry to attend."

"Perhaps . . ." Vir had barely managed to gain control of himself, and when he spoke it was in a voice that was vaguely strangled. "Perhaps . . . the Lady Mariel should . . . should be resting . . . do you think?"

"Oh, no," Durla said dismissively, "no, not at all. When one acquires a trophy such as the Lady Mariel, one is always eager to display her, even when she is feeling less than her best. And she is more than willing to accommodate my desires. Are you not, my love?"

"As . . . you say, my love," Mariel said, sounding like one already dead.

"There, you see? Enjoy the rest of your evening," Durla told them cheerfully. "And have a care with Senna, Ambassador . . . she is very precious to all of us."

Senna was holding Vir's forearm in a grip of iron. She surprised herself; she had no idea she was that strong. But desperate moments tended to prompt acts of equally desperate strength.

Durla headed off down the opulent corridor, the light seeming to dim as he passed. Mariel cast one more glance back at Vir and Senna, but the veil blocked any hint of her expression. Senna had a feeling that she could guess.

"That . . . bastard!" Vir spat out. "How . . . how could he . . ."

"I'll tell you how," Senna said with confidence. "She is his one weakness."

"His what?"

"His weakness . . . or at least she is seen as such. That's what I've heard from some of the chattier members of the Prime Candidates. And apparently he wishes to send a message to any and all concerned that he has no weaknesses at all."

"Naturally. Because if he'll treat someone he loves in that manner, then what mercy will he show for those he considers opponents?"

"None."

Vir was nodding in grim understanding. Clearly he wanted to say more, but he seemed to catch himself. That was probably wise. If there was one thing Senna had come to understand, it was that in

many ways, the palace had ears everywhere. She didn't quite understand the how and why of it . . . but she definitely knew the truth of it.

"Should we tell the emperor?" she asked tentatively.

"Londo?" Vir laughed in grim recollection. "He divorced her.
She tried to kill him. He's not going to give a damn about what happens to her. He'd probably have a good laugh over it . . . and that's
something I don't think I could stand to see. Better that we don't
bring it up." He looked in the direction that Mariel had gone, and
there was tragedy in his face. "I never thought he would . . . if I'd
known, I'd never have—"

"You'd never have what?" she asked with genuine curiosity.

"Nothing," he told her after a moment. "It doesn't matter."

Privately she resolved to mention Mariel's "condition" to Londo
in Vir's absence. Out loud, she said, "Vir—"

"I said it doesn't matter. What's done is done, and can never be
undone . . . no matter how much we may wish it." He squeezed her
hand gently, and said, "Let's go have dinner with Londo. It's best not
to keep the emperor waiting any longer than we already have."

EXCERPTED FROM
THE CHRONICLES OF LONDO MOLLARI.
Excerpt dated (approximate Earth date)
September 23, 2275.

For the first time in a long time, I had fun today I totally disrupted Durla's meeting   gave him a reminder of just who was in charge, for all the good that will do   and then had some excitement that resulted in a most unexpected reunion.

I am worn out from it and won't go into detail. Tomorrow, maybe. Hopefully even my occasionally faulty memory will suffice to hold on to the recollection until the morrow.

In case it is not   I shall jot down the phrase that will most stick in my mind, simply because Durla's expression was so priceless. The look on his face, as he spat words from his mouth that did not match the expression. "Emmmperor," he said, dragging out the first syllable as if it would go on forever. "How   pleasingly unexpected to see you   "

7

"Emmmperor . . . how . . . pleasingly unexpected to see you . . ."

Even as he spoke, Durla felt all the blood draining out of his face. He composed himself quickly, however, and rose. Seated around the table were Minister of Development Castig Lione, Minister of Information Kuto, and Minister of Spirituality Vallko. In addition, there was also General Rhys, next to whom Kuto—in his loud and amusingly self-deprecating manner—insisted that he sit. "Far easier than dieting," Kuto had chortled, slapping his more than ample belly. Not that Rhys was fat. But he was large enough and broad enough that he made Kuto look small in comparison, which naturally pleased Kuto no end.

"I believe this is your first visit to the Tower of Power, if I'm not mistaken," Durla continued. "Welcome, welcome. Minister Lione has been kind enough to arrange for these particular facilities to be used for ministry meetings. Hopefully you will find them up to your standards."

Rhys was at the far head of the table, and he was already standing and offering his chair to the emperor. Londo, with the omnipresent Dunseny at his side, nodded in acknowledgment of the gesture and took the proferred seat. He glanced around the table, bobbed his head in greeting once more, and then sat there with a slightly vacant smile.

"Highness?" Durla said.

Londo still didn't respond until Dunseny nudged him slightly, then he seemed to come to himself. "Yes. Good to see me. And it is good to be seen. I felt that I had not been doing that sufficiently of late." He leaned forward, and said in a conspiratorial voice, "I raised quite a fuss on my way over, you know. People in the street pointed, whispered among themselves. 'Is that he?' they asked. 'Is that the emperor? I thought he was dead!' " Londo laughed at that rather heartily, until the laughter suddenly turned to a violent, racking cough. It took a full thirty seconds for it to subside, and during that time the ministers looked uncomfortably around the table at one another.

Finally Londo managed to compose himself. Dunseny solicitously dabbed at the edges of the emperor's mouth with a cloth.

Durla found it difficult to believe that the old retainer was still at Londo's side. Dunseny had managed to outlive every member of the House Mollari who had been there when he started with the family. He seemed thinner, greyer, but otherwise no less efficient in his duties and attentions. For a time Throk had replaced Dunseny, as a means of keeping a perpetual closer eye on Londo, but Throk had come to a bad end. At that point, Londo had firmly reinstated Dunseny, and Durla had decided to let the matter go rather than press it. Somehow it didn't seem worth the aggravation.

"My apologies, Ministers. Old age is not exactly a blessing."

"Then again, it's preferable to the alternative, Highness," Kuto said in his booming voice.

Londo shot a glance at him. "Is it?" he asked.

There didn't seem to be any ready response for this, and Kuto didn't try to make one.

Londo's gaze focused on Lione. "Minister . . . where did you acquire that scar on your throat?"

Lione automatically reached up to touch it, but caught himself. Without looking at Durla, he said, "A mishap, Emperor. Nothing more."

"Yes. Most unfortunate. I hear tell from Dunseny that there seems to be a virtual epidemic of clumsiness going on in the palace these days. Your wife, I hear tell, suffered such a seizure," Londo said, swiveling his gaze to Durla. "Odd. When I was married to her, she was the most graceful and coordinated of all the women whom I called wife. Curious that she would become so accident-prone. Perhaps the process of aging has been no kinder to her than to me, eh?"

There was something in his look that Durla definitely did not like. So he cleared his throat a bit more loudly than was needed, and said, "Highness . . . you still have not graced us with the purpose for your visit . . ."

"The purpose. Ah, yes. It is my understanding, Durla, that this meeting was being held to discuss the current state of readiness for the Centaurum's reclamation of our great and illustrious heritage— presumably, over the dead bodies of those who would stand in our way."

"May I ask who told you that, Highness?"

"Certainly. General Rhys did."

Durla, stunned, looked to the general. Rhys returned the look blandly. "His Highness asked," he said by way of explanation. "He is my emperor, the supreme ruler and commander of this world. If he asks me a question about the status of military readiness, naturally it is my obligation to respond truthfully."

"Ah. Pardon my surprise, General . . . you had not informed me that the emperor had asked."

"You did not ask, Minister."

Durla cursed to himself. That was typical of Rhys. He was a brilliant tactician and an utterly fearless fleet commander. But he had a streak of individuality that he flashed every so often, apparently for Durla's benefit. Technically, he had done nothing wrong. He was indeed obligated, through oath and historical tradition of his rank, to answer first and foremost to the emperor, with *no* obligation whatsoever to report those discussions to others . . . even the prime minister. If Durla made too much of an issue of his actions, it would reflect poorly on him.

"Highness," Durla said carefully, "these are matters of an extremely delicate and sensitive nature. In the future, I would appreciate if any inquiries you might wish to make on these subjects come through my office."

"Are you endeavoring to dictate terms to me, Durla?" Londo asked.

There was an undercurrent of danger in the tone that brought Durla up short. Suddenly he was beginning to regret that he had not taken steps to dispose of Londo ages ago. Granted, the military supported Durla. There was no question about that, and there was intense loyalty from those who remembered Durla from when he himself was part of the rank and file. They perceived him as one of their own. However, ranking and highly regarded officers—such as Rhys—continued to show respect for the position of emperor. Not even aberrations such as Cartagia had diminished the military compulsion to stand behind whoever held the highest rank in all of Centauri Prime. Durla had no desire to make Rhys and other higher-ranking officers, for whom Durla spoke, choose their allegiances. Because he had no real way of controlling how those choices would fall.

So he put forward his most ready smile, and said reassuringly, "Of course not, Highness. You are Centauri Prime. I would no sooner dictate terms to you than tell the sun which way to rise."

"Don't underestimate yourself, Prime Minister. I have little doubt that—if you thought you might succeed—you might easily decide that the sun should rise in the west so that you can sleep in."

This drew mild laughter from the others. Durla nodded amiably at the small joke made at his expense.

"We have quite a military industrial complex under way, Prime Minister," Londo continued. "Many papers are brought before me for my signature and seal. I have continued to sign off on them, as an indication of my support. For I believe, as do you—as do all of you—that Centauri Prime has a great destiny to pursue. Although I doubt I could put forth the matter so eloquently or enthusiastically as Minister Vallko."

"I am honored and flattered that you would think so, Highness," Vallko said. "I have always felt that our positions complemented each other. That you attended to the well-being of the bodies of our people . . . and I to their spirits."

"Well said, Minister, well said," Londo said, thumping the table with unexpected vigor. "And since the bodies of my people are involved in the work that you are doing, I wish to know where we stand."

"It is somewhat . . . involved, Highness."

"Then involve me."

Durla started to offer another protest, but he saw the firm, unyielding look on the emperor's face and abruptly realized that—most unexpectedly—things had become uncertain. He had to remind himself that there was really no need to keep Londo Mollari out of the loop. It wasn't as if he could do anything to thwart their efforts. The people's taste for conquest had only been whetted by strikes Centauri Prime had made against worlds at the outer fringes of the damnable Alliance's influence. There was already momentum involved, and there was no way that anyone, even the emperor, could stem the tide.

And, of course, he had no intention of doing so. Durla was quite certain of that. This was merely an exercise in face-saving, that was all. When Centauri Prime achieved its destiny of conquest, Mollari wanted to be able to bask in the reflected glory. Understandable. Who wouldn't want to? But the people would know the truth, and the military—despite Rhys' knee-jerk compulsion—likewise would know it was Durla's vision that fired the Centauri movement. In the long run, Mollari's endeavors to attach himself to Durla's greatness would backfire. Durla was sure of that. He would be revealed for the posturing poseur that he was.

In the meantime, why risk alienating allies such as Rhys and those he represented just because he—Durla—was able to see through the emperor's pathetic maneuvering?

"Very well," Durla said simply.

And so he proceeded to lay out, in detail, all the up-to-date particulars of Centauri Prime's military buildup. All the outposts, operating under varying degrees of secrecy, that were assembling the Centauri fleet that would sweep out among the Alliance worlds and spread the ultimate dominance of the Centaurum.

"So we are not rushing into this," Londo said slowly, once Durla was finished providing the specifics.

"Absolutely not, Emperor. The initial strikes that we have made served a twofold purpose. First, we were testing the will of the Alliance members, and frankly, we are less than impressed. They have grown complacent in their prosperity and their sense of peace. To them, our attack on Narn was an aberration, a distant memory at best. We have managed, through a carefully orchestrated campaign of publicity and information, planned by Minister Lione and well executed by Minister Kuto . . ." and he gestured toward the pair, who nodded gratefully, "to associate those days—in the minds of the Alliance—with the reign of the mad emperor Cartagia. You, Highness, are seen as a very different animal."

"Certainly a less rabid one, I would hope," Londo said with a hint of irony. "So I am perceived as a comparatively benign, harmless ruler. An interesting epitaph, I suppose. 'Here lies Londo Mollari: a harmless enough fellow.' "

This drew a laugh from Kuto, who promptly silenced himself when he noticed that no one else was joining in.

Picking up after the momentary quiet, Durla continued, "We have further managed to pave the way, through backroom dealings, for key representatives of key governments to be . . . accommodating . . . to our attacks on assorted worlds. Furthermore, in launching the assaults, we have been testing the versatility and effectiveness of the vessels that we have assembled thus far. We are pleased to report that the tests of these prototypes have met with overwhelming success."

"Excellent." Londo nodded. Dunseny's head was likewise bobbing in agreement.

"There were a few places where ship performance could be improved." General Rhys spoke up. "Questions of maneuverability, and proper distribution of energy resources in weaponry. Problems that made no difference against small worlds that are relatively help-less . . . but could loom large when it comes to battles against the more powerful members of the Interstellar Alliance."

"We are attending to that, Highness," Lione quickly assured him. "I have scientists, technicians, going over all the specifics cited by the general and his board of advisers. Nothing is being left to chance."

"I have found, Minister, that 'chance' usually has its own feelings as to just what is being left to it, and has a habit of inserting itself into matters at its whim." Londo scratched his chin thoughtfully. "And it will come to a direct challenge to the Alliance, yes? I understand the reasons for concentrating on smaller worlds . . . but I cannot say I embrace it enthusiastically. It seems . . . beneath us, no? Considering what it is we wish to accomplish."

"The hard fact, Highness, is that the Alliance's attacks and stric-tures reduced us, militarily and technically, to a state of infancy," Durla said. Rhys looked as if he was bristling slightly, but he said nothing. Durla continued, "To that end, we must re-learn how to walk before we can run. There is really no choice in the matter."

"But it is merely a temporary condition, Highness." Vallko spoke up. "Nothing is more firmly written in the book of fate than that the great Centauri Republic will hold the stars in its palm."

The words, to Durla's surprise, seemed to jolt Londo slightly. "Is there a problem, Highness?"

"No. No problem," Londo assured him quickly. "Just . . . a re-minder . . . of an image I saw a long time ago. A vision . . . of just that. I think perhaps, Vallko, you are indeed correct."

"Of course he is correct, Highness," Durla said flatly. "Our timetable calls for, at most, another two years before a full fleet has been assembled. A fleet that will more than satisfy all the require-ments put forward by General Rhys and his advisers. A fleet that will cover the known galaxy as comprehensively as grains of sand cover a beach." His voice began to rise as he became more and more taken with the impending realization of his vision. "When the time is right, we will launch a multistage assault on the Homeworlds of many of the Alliance governments, taking the war to them directly." He saw heads bobbing around the table, and Londo's gaze was fixed upon him in fascination. "If we strike hard enough, we can immobilize them, and pave the way for full-scale assaults on their holdings that will leave them powerless against further Centauri aggression."

"The only problem," Vallko said with a touch of caution, "remains Sheridan. This is a man who faced both Shadows and Vorlons, and caused them to back down. There are some who say he is more than Human."

"With all respect, Vallko, we are definitely more than Human," Durla reminded him. "That makes us more than a match."

But Vallko's worries were not so easily dissuaded. "It is said he cannot die. Or that he is already dead."

And from the end of the table came a whisper from Londo. " 'You must not kill the one who is already dead.' "

Confused looks were exchanged around the table. "Highness?" Dunseny prompted.

Londo looked up at Dunseny and forced a smile. "Just . . . remembering old voices, Dunseny. At my age, I am pleased I can remember anything. Then again, you are older than I am by far, and you never forget anything. Why is that?"

"Because, Highness, at my age, there are fewer things worth remembering."

The exchange drew an appreciative chuckle from the ministers.

"Sheridan is just one man," Durla reminded them, bringing the conversation back on track. "Let us not forget that he was involved with three great campaigns in his life: the Earth-Minbari War, the Shadow War, and his assault on his own Homeworld. Let us also not forget how each of those disputes was ultimately settled," and he ticked them off on his fingers. "The Minbari surrendered; the Vorlons and Shadows voluntarily stood down and departed from known space; and his prime nemesis on Earth, the president, was considerate enough to commit suicide. Sheridan has never been in a position where he faced an enemy who would not back down. That is not the case here. Who here would back down from him? Which of you would tell me that—if faced with John Sheridan demanding your surrender—you would willingly do so?"

It was Rhys who spoke immediately. "Death first."

There were agreeing nods from around the table.

"He will be facing a very different creature when the full might of the Centauri Republic is unleashed upon him," Durla said.

"The people do not feel that way," Kuto said.

Durla turned and gaped at him. "The people? The people do not?"

"I am not saying they do not support you, Prime Minister," Kuto said quickly as the gazes of the others fell upon him. "But Minister Vallko is correct. The people rejoice in our achievements and call out their support publicly . . . but privately, my research says, they still fear Sheridan."

"We cannot have that!" Durla replied. "This is an alarming comment on the state of the Centauri mind . . . and it must be addressed at once. *At once!* Kuto—arrange for a public speaking display. Immediately, do you hear me! Lione, Vallko, assist him!"

The other ministers were caught off guard by the sudden change of mood in the room, the abrupt way that Durla's attitude had shifted. But they hastened to obey his orders. Londo said nothing, and merely watched silently.

Within moments, Durla and Londo were standing at a balcony on one of the lower floors of the Tower of Power. There were no windows in the Tower, which added to the mystique of the place. There was, however, the one balcony, which Durla had insisted upon for just such an occasion. The Tower had been well placed, for there was always a crowd of people around the base, just going about their business.

When Durla spoke, his voice boomed throughout the entire city, thanks to a multitude of hidden speakers. Not only that, but his oversize holographic image appeared throughout Centauri Prime, carrying his word far and wide. People on the other side of the world were jolted from their sleep by the unexpected intrusion of Prime Minister Durla. Londo, although at his side, was mysteriously absent from the projection. Only Durla's image loomed large, which he felt was as it should be.

"It has been brought to my attention," Durla's voice echoed throughout the assemblage, all eyes below turning up toward him, "that as Centauri Prime returns to glory, there are many of you who fear reprisals from John Sheridan. Many who think that this man, who formed the Alliance, presents a threat to our world! That our recent, successful endeavors to expand our holdings will be met with resistance, and that we—as many others have—will surrender to President Sheridan, simply because he will ask us to! And why not? The Minbari surrendered. The Vorlons surrendered. The Shadows surrendered. Why not we?"

And he received exactly the answer he was hoping for. Someone below shouted, "Because we are Centauri!" Immediately others took up the shout.

"Yes! We are Centauri!" Durla announced, receiving a resounding cheer in return. "And in those instances when we choose to exercise our might, we will achieve nothing less than victory! Victory at all costs! Victory in spite of all terror! Victory, however long and hard the road may be, for without victory there is no survival!"

"Victory!" the people in the street shouted.

"We shall not flag or fail!" Durla continued. "We shall go on to the end. We shall fight in the void; we shall fight on planets; we shall fight in hyperspace; we shall fight on the Rim. We shall fight with growing confidence and growing strength in space; we shall defend our Homeworld, whatever the cost may be. We shall fight in the asteroid fields; we shall fight in the nebulae; we shall fight among the stars—*we shall never surrender!*"

The roar that went up was deafening, and seemed to go on forever. Durla drank it in, a virtual sponge for the adulation he was receiving. He stepped back in off the balcony to receive the congratulations from the other ministers.

"Well done! Very well done!" burbled Kuto, and the others echoed the sentiments.

Only Londo seemed to have any pause. "And tell me, Durla . . . what do you think the reaction of Sheridan will be when he hears this speech of yours? How do you think he will react? Are you not concerned that he may be moved to strike first?"

"No, Highness, I am not," Durla answered firmly. "If he and his precious Alliance have not attacked because of our deeds, they will certainly not attack because of words. They will perceive it as saber rattling, nothing more. But our people—our people will know it for what it is. They will know and remember, and when the time comes . . ."

"They will know that we will never surrender," Londo said.

"That is exactly right, Highness."

"Let us hope—for your sake, if nothing else—that President Sheridan sees it the same way," said Londo.

The shouting continued, and Durla was only slightly soured to note that although many bellowed for him, the name of "Mollari" was being shouted with equal enthusiasm. But then he contented himself by recalling that the people in the square were truly only a fraction of the populace. Everywhere else it was Durla, and only Durla. And that was as it should be. Let the people call out for Mollari along with Durla, if it pleased them. Eventually they would come to realize who truly ran things.

Once upon a time, Durla felt as if no one would ever recognize him for his own achievements and his intrinsic greatness. Those days, however, were long past. He could afford to be generous, to share the wealth of the people's adulation. For the moment. Mollari looked weaker with every passing day. Certainly he had his robust periods, but his cough was becoming more and more pronounced. It was indicative of something deeper, more damaging to the emperor's health. But for some reason, Mollari seemed disinclined to seek out medical attention. And Durla certainly was not going to push the matter.

The shouting grew louder and louder. "Highness, they call for us," Durla said, bowing low in a gesture that was slightly mocking. "Shall we go back out and satisfy their worship?"

"I have never had any desire to be worshipped, Prime Minister," Londo said with a touch of amusement. "But if it will please you . . ." and he gestured that they should go back out onto the balcony. They stepped out and waved once more to the crowd. The people cried out almost as one, shouting their names, praising them to the skies so that the Great Maker himself would take note.

And that was when the shot rang out.

I did not hear it at first, because the shouts of the crowd were so deafening. Instead what I felt, rather than saw, was a sharp sensation across my forehead. I put my hand up to it to see what it could be, and when my hand came away it was tinged pink with blood. Then there was a sound, that of a ricochet, or of something striking nearby, and then a second.

I've been shot, I thought, and for a moment I felt—not concern or fear—but instead an almost giddy sense of accomplishment. So long had I been haunted by the image of G'Kar with his hands at my throat, I was almost resigned to it. If I was to die at the hand of an unknown assassin, then I had managed to thwart destiny. It was cold comfort to be sure, but given the comfort I had received of late, "cold" was almost a warming trend.

Before I could think or feel anything else, I was being hauled backward by my personal guards. Durla was likewise being hurried away from the balcony, General Rhys himself ducking Durla's head for him to make certain he was not hit. Below, the people were still cheering; they had not yet figured out what was happening.

"The emperor's been shot!" one of the guards cried out.

And then Dunseny was standing directly in front of me. He was saying loudly and firmly, in that no-nonsense tone that only the very old can successfully carry off, "Step aside. Let me see him." Amazingly, the guards halted in their ushering me away, and Dunseny inspected my forehead with clinical expertise. "He hasn't been shot," he announced sourly, and it was hard to tell whether his tone of voice was from annoyance at those who had pronounced me injured, or because he was aggrieved to discover it wasn't the case. He had a cloth out and was dabbing at the bleeding, which was already trickling off. "No burn marks," he said expertly. "It's a cut. A blast must have hit above or nearby him, chipped off a small piece of the building, and the flying debris cut across his head. See? It's stopping already."

"I am not surprised," I growled. "Blood circulates up there for the brain, and I have not been making many demands upon it lately."

General Rhys was already barking orders both to my guards and to his own security people. Although his authority extended only to the latter, everyone was attending to every word he uttered. "Get down there! Find the shooter or shooters! The emperor and the prime minister will stay here until the area is secured!"

"The crowd is huge, General, how will we—" one of his security staff began.

Rhys gave him a look that could have sliced him in half. "Move!" he bellowed with such force that his voice alone almost knocked the man off his feet.

The next hour was very confused, with mixed and conflicting reports being fed to us every few minutes. Durla, the other ministers, and I returned to the room where the briefing had been held, and there was great speculation among all of them as to who or what was responsible for this atrocious assault upon my sacrosanct person. The consensus seemed to be that the Alliance was behind it—Sheridan in particular. I did not believe it for a moment, and said so. "Sheridan may be many things," I told them flatly, "but an assassin is not one of them." They accepted my opinion with polite attention, but I suspected that they believed they knew far better than I about such matters.

Dunseny, meantime, expertly bandaged the wound on my head, although it was such a pathetic thing, really, that he needn't have bothered. I can only assume that he found that activity preferable to simply standing there and letting me bleed.

General Rhys disappeared, presumably to oversee the search-and-destroy mission personally. When he returned, he did not simply enter the room. Instead he virtually exploded into it, pushing the sliding doors aside since, apparently, they did not move quickly enough to suit him. "We have him," Rhys said without any preamble, and then added, "A more bizarre set of circumstances we have never seen." He turned, and shouted, "Bring them in!"

When I saw who was being led into the room, I was stunned.

Brought in side by side were Yson of House Yson, and another individual. Yson, burly and taciturn as always, was glaring. But no one was noticing; it was the person beside him who garnered all the attention.

"G'Kar?" I barely recognized my own voice. I didn't know whether to laugh or cry. "G'Kar?" I said again.

"The emperor remembers my name. I am flattered," he said.

Kuto was immediately on his feet. "Immediately," though, may be too generous a term. It took him long moments to trust himself to standing as his bulk fought gravity and won, but just barely. "What a magnificent day!" Kuto called out, apparently creating the release for the press even as he spoke. "Yson, one of our own nobles, fought to stop a vicious, bloodthirsty Narn from shooting and killing our beloved emperor!"

"No."

It was a young voice that had spoken, and then I saw that a number of the Prime Candidates had crowded in at the door. Clearly they had been in the midst of a struggle. Their hair was disheveled, and some of them had torn clothing. In the forefront was one I thought I recognized. But I could not remember his name if someone had put a gun to my head. I knew because, after all, someone practically had just done so, and his name still was not forthcoming.

"What do you mean, Caso?" asked Lione, graciously supplying the missing piece of information for me.

Caso pointed at Yson. "He was the one who was shooting. The Narn was trying to stop him."

"What?" Durla sounded horrified. "A Narn saved our emperor? And . . . this Narn?" The notion that a Narn might have had a hand in preserving my life must have seemed for him to go against the natural order. Imagine, then, his even greater astonishment when Yson himself spoke up.

"Not him," Yson said with great annoyance. "I wasn't shooting at the emperor. I was shooting at you, Durla."

One of the guards stepped forward. He was carrying a phased plasma gun. "Yson used this, Highness," he said, proffering it to me, as a hunter would deliver a trophy.

"I . . . I don't understand," Durla said. To my delight, he was stammering. It was a joy seeing him coming so close to losing his composure completely. "Caso . . . you claim that you saw it all?"

"Not all, Prime Minister," said Caso. For some reason, the others seemed to be tossing him unkind looks, but Caso did not let it perturb him. Or if it did perturb him, he did not let it show. "We were close enough to hear the first shot, despite the din of the crowd around us.

We fought our way through, and there discovered that Yson was struggling with his weapon, a red-haired Centauri in the process of try- ing to yank it from his hands."

"A red-haired Centauri? But then how did the Narn—"

"He has a name, Durla," I interjected, sounding far calmer than I ac- tually was. "Considering you apparently owe him your life, you could at least do him the courtesy of using it."

Durla looked ready to argue the point, but apparently decided it was not worth it. "How did . . . Citizen G'Kar . . . become involved? And where did he come from?"

"He . . . was the Centauri. It was apparently a holographic disguise of some sort. Whatever device was generating it was broken during the struggle, and the disguise dissipated."

Durla's eyes went wide. "A changeling net," he whispered. "They are illegal!"

"Arrest me," said G'Kar.

Slowly Durla rose from his seat. He was trembling with barely con- tained rage. "Oh, I will do more than arrest you! I will have you exe- cuted for . . . for . . ."

"Saving your life?" G'Kar was merely amused. I was not surprised. Af- ter all that G'Kar had endured in his life, it took far more than the ire of a Centauri politician—even a highly placed one—to give him pause. "Execution might not be such a terrible fate," he continued, sounding philosophical. "The fact that it took me as long as it did to dispatch this . . . person," and he indicated Yson with a nod, "is a bit embarrassing. I can only attribute it to the deleterious effects caused by extended use of a changeling net. Don't worry. Given time to recover, I'm certain that I will be sufficiently strong to take on anyone in this room if so inclined."

"I will have you executed," Durla said, reining himself in, "for tres- passing on Centauri Prime. Alien races are forbidden . . . or had you forgotten?"

"I forgot completely," G'Kar replied. "I wore the disguise only because I wanted to have hair. Tall hair."

Great Maker, I'd missed him.

"You wore the disguise to spy on us! You are a trespasser and a spy! For that alone, your life is forfeit."

"But it is not that alone, Durla," I said. I rose from my chair. My legs felt slightly unsteady, and I took a moment until I was certain that I could endure the simple act of standing. "That must be factored in with the debt that is owed him by you . . . and by me. Perhaps Yson's intent was to dispense with you, but I could just as easily have fallen within his target. Correct, Yson?"

Yson looked at me with utter scorn. "Durla is power mad. He has nothing but contempt for the Houses. For the traditions of Centauri Prime. But you . . . you are worse. For there is nothing worse than a weak emperor."

Slowly I nodded.

Then, in one motion, I turned and pulled on the ceremonial sword that General Rhys had in his scabbard. I admired the hissing noise it made as it slid out. Yson's expression of disdain was still on his face as I turned and swung my arm as fast as I could. The blade was as sharp as it sounded, and I was pleased to see that my arm still had some strength in it. Yson's sneer was frozen even as his head slid from his shoulders and thudded to the floor.

No one said a word.

I pointed the sword at G'Kar. His one eye glittered at me.

"Are you free for dinner?" I asked.

8

David Sheridan could see the eye, looking at him, and it seemed far less fearsome than when it had first appeared.

He still could remember exactly the first time that he had noticed it. He had just turned twelve, and had fallen asleep after a long day of celebration. In his dreams, he had been running, just running, across a great Minbari plain. He wasn't doing so out of fear, or pursuit. He was running simply for the pure joy of running, of feeling the youthful energy channeling through him, feeding him as if there was an endless supply that would carry him through an eternity of sprinting.

Finally he had stopped. It wasn't out of a need to catch his breath, but because he felt as if he should stop, because he was *supposed* to catch his breath. Then again, this was a dream, after all, and he was the one who set the parameters.

And then, for no reason he could discern, the world around him started to go dim. It was as if a total eclipse had suddenly and inexplicably sprung into existence. He looked up at the Minbari sun that had provided warmth and comfort for as long as he could remember.

The sun looked back down at him. A single great eye had taken up the entirety of it, and it was peering at him in silence.

He stared at it, transfixed. It blinked once, then again, and then it addressed him.

Hello, little sun, it said.

The scream had begun within the dream, but reached its completion when David sat up in bed. Unfortunately Minbari beds were upright slabs, and as a result David fell forward and hit the floor. He lay there, gasping, clutching the cool tiles, soaked with sweat and looking around as if afraid that the eye might still be upon him. Even though he knew that it made no sense, he ran to the window and looked to the moon, but found no eye peeking back.

Nevertheless he did not go back to sleep. He stayed there at the window, unmoving, waiting to watch the sun rise so that he could make sure for himself that the sun was as it usually was. He wasn't disappointed, for the sun shone that morning in all its normalcy, washing away the last dregs of that heart-stopping dream.

But he had not forgotten it. That would have been impossible . . . because every so often, the eye returned. Not very often; just from time to time, as if it was checking on him.

As terrifying as he had found it that first time, it became less so with each subsequent exposure. The eye never did anything harmful or threatening. It just watched him, occasionally saying a couple of well-chosen, nonintimidating words. He asked one of his teachers about it and was told that it undoubtedly represented either his mother or his father, or perhaps both. It was, they said, a subconscious desire to know that—when he was at his most vulnerable—his parents were watching over him and keeping him from harm. From then on, David gradually relaxed to its presence, seeing it not as a threatening image, but as a symbol that all was right with the world.

This particular night, the eye had returned, after an absence of many months. It did so, however, in a very odd way. David was dreaming that he was having dinner with himself. The "self" seated on the other side of the dining table appeared a few years older, and he possessed a look of quiet confidence. What was particularly odd was that he had a hair crest that was evocative of the Centauri. David couldn't for the life of him figure out why his older self looked like that.

"Do you like it?" the older David asked. "I'm not sure if it's me or not. What do you think?"

Young David shrugged.

"Good. No opinion. Not thinking," older David said. "Not thinking is what you'll want to do." And then his forehead blinked.

David stared more closely, having at first accepted the unreality of the moment without question. But now he was struck by the oddness of the fact that the elder David had a third eye. It was nestled serenely smack in the middle of his forehead, and it was staring at him. He recognized it instantly.

"That's my eye," he said.

There was a sudden rush of wings, and David jumped slightly. A bird, a crow of some kind, perched atop the elder David's head. He didn't seem to notice the weight.

"Does it offend you? If so, it can be plucked out," said the elder David. And then the crow stabbed its beak down and snatched out the eye from his forehead. David gasped as the orb was swallowed up effortlessly, and then the crow, or raven, or whatever it was, flapped its wings and took off.

"Are you all right?" he asked urgently.

More plates of food materialized in front of the older David. "Fine," he said. "See?" He pointed . . . and the eye was back. "It will always be there," he said. "Always. Waiting. Loving you."

The eye stared at him, stared through him, and David felt vaguely uncomfortable, but he couldn't quite determine why.

"Dammit!"

It was his father's voice, explosive and angry, and it was enough to snap David to full wakefulness. He blinked against the darkness, but saw that there was light filtering through the window. It was early morning.

His father had stormed past David's room, and for a moment David thought that his father was angry with him. But he continued walking, and behind him David heard his mother moving, as well. She said in a soft but rushed voice, "John, hush! You'll wake David!"

"That's the least of my concerns, Delenn," he retorted, but he lowered his voice nevertheless. They continued to speak, and G'Kar was mentioned, but he couldn't make out what they were talking about.

The timing of the sudden jolt couldn't have been better. The dream was still fresh in his mind, much more so than if he'd woken up on his own. He stepped down off his bed, reached for a robe, and pulled it around himself. Then he padded noiselessly down the hall, following his parents' voices.

Finding them presented no difficulty. They were in his father's main office, and he could tell from the way his father's voice came from one side of the room, then the other, that his father was pacing.

"We have to do something about this," Sheridan was saying. "We can't just let G'Kar sit there in Centauri hands!"

"It's not that simple, John . . ."

"Yes. It is. We go to the Alliance, or the Narns specifically, and say—"

"And say what?" There was a sharpness, a hardness in her voice that hadn't been there before. "That G'Kar was captured while on Centauri Prime? They will ask why . . . a reasonable enough question. After all, the Centauri have made no secret of the fact that off-worlders are forbidden. And you will tell the Alliance . . . what? That G'Kar was there because you and he had a tacit understanding that he was supplying you information about the Centauri? That he wasn't telling you how he was acquiring this information, and that you were not inquiring? That your 'hand' was caught in the cracker jar?"

Despite the seriousness of the moment, Sheridan laughed shortly. "Cookie jar."

"Who cares?" she retorted. "John, G'Kar knew the risks, as did you. You accepted those, as did he. And now he is dealing with the consequences, as you must."

"And I'm going to deal with them by getting him out. Fine, I won't go to the Alliance. I'll get him out myself."

"You'll be killed."

"It won't be the first time."

"How dare you."

Crouching, David peeked around the edge of the door frame. His father had stopped in his tracks and was staring at his mother. She was much smaller than he was, yet at that moment her anger was so great that it seemed to fill the room. *"How dare you,"* she repeated.

"How dare I? How dare I what?"

"How dare you recklessly and foolhardily throw away your life on a hopeless mission just to satisfy your ego."

"This has nothing to do with ego," he protested.

Before he could continue, she cut him off. "Yes, just as when you went to Z'ha'dum," she said, and clearly the very recollection of it was difficult for her. David had heard mention made of that dead world several times, and he knew that his father had journeyed to it. There were even tales that he had died there, but that was nonsense, of course. After all, there he was, clearly alive. "And at the time you went," she continued, "you were 'only' the commander of Babylon 5. We were not married. You had no son. You had no Alliance of which you were the president. You were young and cloaked with the banner of righteousness, and no doubt you thought you would live forever. None of those have been, or are any longer, the case. You have responsibilities to me, to David, to the other races in the Alliance."

"And my responsibility to G'Kar?"

"He is where he needs to be. They are not going to hurt him. Vir already passed that information along to us. He has been given humane, if Spartan, accommodations in the palace itself."

"And he's not being allowed to leave!"

"John . . . perhaps he is not supposed to," Delenn suggested reasonably. "Perhaps circumstances have conspired to put G'Kar right where he is supposed to be. Londo is cut off there, surrounded by many destructive forces. My guess is that, on that entire planet, he had not one ally on whom he could utterly depend. G'Kar is now that ally. Who knows what poisons have been whispered into Londo's ear. Who knows what dark forces may be shaping his thinking?"

"And you're saying G'Kar can undo that." He sounded skeptical.

"I'm saying he might be able to. He certainly has a far greater chance of doing so by being there. Those two . . . G'Kar and Londo . . . they are bound by fate, John. They circle each other, like binary stars."

"Binary stars," Sheridan reminded her, "allow no life between them. Their gravity wells crush whatever planets might start to form."

"Yes," she said. "I know. And that may well be the case with G'Kar and Londo, as well. They may well be destined to crush all life between them with the intensity of their will, until nothing is left. Perhaps not even them."

"Is that supposed to make me feel better somehow?"

"No. It is simply supposed to be a statement of what I believe. Unless my beliefs are no longer of importance to you."

He sighed heavily. "Of course they're of importance to me." He embraced her, holding her so tight that David thought he was going to break her. "It's just . . . when I think of G'Kar in that place, surrounded by enemies . . ."

"This is G'Kar we're talking about. He thrives on that sort of situation. Sometimes I think he's not happy unless he's surrounded by enemies. And he may be able to make a difference, John. He might very well be of far more service there than anywhere else."

And then David jumped—as a loud voice came from behind him. "And what have we here?" In an instant he was on his feet, turning at the same time. As a result he tripped himself up and landed hard on his own backside.

Master Vultan, his occasional teacher and frequent source of frustration, was standing right behind him, arms folded. "Spying, are we?" he asked in a stern voice, his bearded chin bristling with indignation. It was difficult for David to tell just how genuinely annoyed Vultan really was.

Determining the annoyance level of his parents, however, was no problem at all. When Delenn and Sheridan emerged from his office to investigate what the noise was about, they both stared down at their son and frowned. "How long were you hiding there, David?" his father demanded.

"Since you woke me up with your shouting," David replied.

This got Sheridan a dirty look from Delenn, which he did his best to ignore. "You shouldn't be hiding there, listening in on other people's conversations," Sheridan told him.

"You're right. Next time I'll find a better place to hide," he agreed, standing and dusting himself off.

His mother was not the least bit amused. "David . . . your actions were inappropriate."

He sighed heavily, and said, "I'm sorry, Mother." He was far slower to employ his sharp and ready wit on his mother. He just couldn't help but feel that he was far less likely to get away with it than he was with his father. He had a feeling that, secretly, his father was amused by his son's rebellious streak. That certainly made sense; after all, John Sheridan had practically written the book on rebellion. "I'm sorry, Father," he continued. "But when I heard you mention G'Kar . . . well, I've always liked him, and I hate to think about him being in trouble."

Sheridan sighed and seemed less irate than he had moments before. Now he just looked sad. "So do I, David. Your mom, too. But she's right: at this point, it's G'Kar's play. We have it on reliable authority that he is in no danger. On that basis, he may very well be able to do a lot of good, working from the inside, as it were."

Vultan looked from Sheridan to Delenn and back. "Are neither of you going to punish the boy? He eavesdropped. Certainly that behavior cannot be tolerated."

"You're absolutely right," Sheridan said firmly. "David: extend your left hand."

David immediately did as his father dictated. John Sheridan stepped forward sternly, looked down at the outstretched hand, and then slapped it once lightly on the knuckles. "Let that be a lesson to you," he said gravely.

"I shall never forget it, Father," David replied seriously.

Vultan rolled his eyes and shook his head in exasperation. "That child," he informed them, "doesn't need a teacher, or parents. He needs a keeper."

The moment he said that, something cold clutched at the base of David's neck. He trembled, and the look on his face caught his mother's attention. "David . . . what's wrong?"

Sheridan saw it, too. "What's the matter, son?"

"I don't know," David confessed. "Just the oddest feeling, that's all. It's like . . . like . . ."

"Like someone just stepped on your grave?" Sheridan suggested. "That's what my dad used to say when he'd get that look on his face."

"Yeah. Something like that," David agreed.

"I do not like that phrase," Delenn said curtly. "Please don't use it again."

"All right," Sheridan said, clearly not quite understanding his wife's reaction, but not wanting to argue. He turned his attention to David's teacher, and said, "Master Vultan . . . I think that David might be a bit starved for attention. I confess I've been somewhat preoccupied lately, and the boy has had to resort to tactics such as this just to get a crumb of attention. It's not right. If it's all the same to you, I think his mother and I would like to spend the day with him."

"As you desire," Vultan said, looking not the least bit upset over the prospect. He turned on his heel and departed, his long robes swishing softly on the polished floor.

"Go get washed and dressed, David," his father said. "Perhaps we'll take a shot at climbing the Mulkeen Heights today. Best view on Minbar, so I'm told."

"Okay, Father," David said. Then, recalling how disconcerted he'd felt just a short time ago, he quickly embraced his parents before running off down the hallway.

"He's your son," Delenn said, shaking her head as she watched him go.

"So you keep telling me," Sheridan remarked. "Part of me thinks you keep on saying so because you're hoping to establish some sort of alibi." Then he turned serious once more. "Do you really think G'Kar will be okay?"

"Vir is certain. The situation under which G'Kar was taken was quite unique. It's Vir's opinion that Londo is watching out for him."

"And Vir's opinion can be trusted?"

"I think so, yes. Don't you?"

He gave it a moment's thought, and remembered Garibaldi's description of the events surrounding that last visit to Centauri Prime . . . the one that had resulted in the death of Lou Welch. Michael had been uncharacteristically taciturn about the affair, but had managed to convey—through fewer words rather than more—that Vir Cotto had a handle on things. Sheridan even suspected, although he couldn't prove it, that Vir was somehow involved with the occasional acts of "terrorism" that the Centauri tried to ascribe to the Alliance.

So Sheridan said finally, "Yes, I think it probably can. It's hard to believe, considering how Vir used to be, that he is now one of the most dependable of all the Centauri."

"We've all changed, John, from what we used to be. Look at you . . . and me . . ." and she playfully pulled at his beard while running her fingers through her long black hair. There were a few tinges of grey in it.

"You're saying that we all have more hair?" he said. "Well, there's worse fates." Then, once again, he turned solemn. "We have more hair . . . but G'Kar has one less eye. And he lost it on that world where he is right now. If things turn ugly there, he could lose the other . . . and far more."

"That is the downside," she admitted. "On the other hand, there is always the bright side. Do you remember that urn?"

"Urn?" he asked, not certain what she was referring to.

"The vase," she prompted. "The one Londo gave us . . ."

"Oh! Yes. The last time we saw him. The one we're supposed to give David on his sixteenth birthday . . ."

She nodded. "With the waters from the palace river locked in its base. I found it in storage recently. It reminded me of how Londo was that day . . . the last day we saw him. He seemed so desperate just to have even the slightest hint of friendship . . . from us . . . from any-one . . ."

"And you think G'Kar will provide him that."

"We can only hope. Do you think that we should give the vase to David early? Before his sixteenth birthday?"

"Nah," Sheridan decided. "Let's honor Londo's request. The man who dropped that vase off was the closest thing to the Londo of old that I could recall. I miss him. There's no telling how this entire Centauri situation is going to play out. But on David's sixteenth birthday, whatever the outcome, he'll at least get a sense of the Londo Mollari that we once all knew."

9

The catacombs beneath the capital city were considered by many to be little more than a myth. Ostensibly, the great Emperor Olion had constructed them, centuries earlier. Olion, so legend had it, was absolutely paranoid over the notion of his people turning against him. So he had the catacombs constructed as a means of escaping any pursuit. Supposedly he was the only person aside from the actual creator of the catacombs—whom he subsequently had assassinated—to know the layout of the maze. The catacombs led from the city to the outlying regions and provided a handy means of getting in and out unseen, if one were so inclined, not to mention eluding pursuit.

But it was all the stuff of legend. The entrances certainly no longer existed. And even if they did exist, the tunnels would be so overrun with vermin that they would be virtually unpassable.

Years ago, however, when he was a young man looking for fossil remains of primitive Centauri cultures, Renegar—a heavyset lad even at that tender age—had literally fallen into myth.

Renegar had embarked on a one-man excavation on the outskirts of the hinterlands. The ground had given way, and he had fallen through into the catacombs of lore. When he had picked himself up, dusted himself off, and managed to push aside the mounting feelings of panic, he actually found himself rather taken with the place. True, the vermin population wasn't particularly appreciated, but the prospects of exploration proved too enticing for him to pass up.

Having almost no friends, and parents who displayed little interest in his comings and goings, Renegar wasn't about to share with anyone his new and exciting discovery.

He brought sounding equipment and other locator devices that hadn't existed centuries ago when the catacombs were first built. Over the course of many years, he managed to map the place rather

thoroughly . . . aided and abetted by the occasional explosive device.
Rock falls and other natural "disasters" had blocked some of the
paths, and Renegar quickly discovered that the judicious use of explosives could be tremendously helpful. The key word was "judicious," of course. The first time he tried, he nearly blew himself to
kingdom come. Necessity became the mother of invention, and his
familiarity with explosives and excavation came to serve him well in
later life.

The catacombs, as well, found new purpose.

Renegar made his way to the meeting area with sure, steady
steps, his knowledge of the catacombs by now so ingrained that he no
longer needed the maps he had taken such pains to create in his
youth. A rodent ran across his foot, and he kicked it out of the way.
It was fortunate that such creatures didn't bother him, else he never
would have been able to last in his exploration of the caves.

"Renegar!" The whisper came from up ahead, and he recognized
the voice instantly. "Is that you?"

"Of course it's me. Who else would it be?" he asked grimly. He
climbed over one more rise and came around a corner to discover the
others whom he had decided—insanely, he sometimes thought—to
trust not only with his life, but the future of his world.

Vir, naturally, was among them. So was Dunseny. There were far
more people Vir had managed to enlist over the years, but no one,
with the exception of Vir, knew everyone who was a part of the rebellion. That was probably wise, Renegar mused, but he couldn't
help but feel that it put a massive amount of strain on Vir himself.

The strain was beginning to show. Vir was looking more tired,
even a bit more despondent, than he usually did. But there was still
an air of grim determination about him, as if—having decided upon
the course he must follow—he had resolved that he would see it
through to the end, no matter what.

"You saw?" Vir said without preamble, and Renegar knew precisely what he was talking about.

"How could I not see? That damnable Durla was everywhere. Is
it true, though? That someone tried to kill them both? The emperor
and Durla?"

"Durla, for the most part. The emperor was simply at the wrong
place at the wrong time," Dunseny said.

"That might well summarize his life," Vir commented ruefully.
Then, in a more businesslike tone, he added, "But it's not going to
end there. Durla will never let it end there. If one House head en-

deavored to dispose of him, he's going to fear that all of them may form an alliance against him."

"You're saying he's going to declare war on the Houses?" asked one surly-looking but forceful fighter named Adi.

"Without a doubt. And that can only benefit us."

"How?" The question was echoed around the group, but it was Dunseny who answered.

"The House heads have resources. The military may back Durla, making his power unassailable, but the Houses have their own resources, ranging from personnel to weapons. Not only that, but there are key military personnel who owe ancient allegiances to the Houses, which supersede any way they may be beholden to Durla. In battling the Houses, in challenging the House heads directly, Durla may be sowing dissent within his own support system."

"He won't realize the danger if he thinks he's above them . . . which he does," Vir said. "It's the oldest danger in the world: arrogance becomes the enemy's undoing."

"Yes . . . including yours."

They turned to see who had spoken, and there was a collective and startled gasp from all of them.

A grey-skinned creature stood in the shadows.

Renegar immediately went for his weapon, and the voice boomed again from the monster. "It's too late. Whatever you do to me is of no consequence. Since I have seen you, I will commune with my brethren, and they will in turn seek you out. I've seen all your faces. You're finished. But first . . ." The creature paused dramatically. "I'm going to sing a few show tunes."

The others looked at each other.

"Juuuust me . . . and my shaaadow . . ." the creature from the darkness began.

"Tell me I'm dreaming," Adi said.

Vir was watching the entire scene with a severe lack of amusement. "Finian," he said sternly. "What sort of foolishness is this? I recognize your voice; I know it's you."

At that, the creature slumped to the ground in front of the incredulous group. It was at that point that they were able to see the wound that gaped in the back of its head, thick liquid coagulating around it. Clearly the thing, whatever it was, was dead. Then all eyes shifted as Finian, the techno-mage, stepped into view. "Did I scare you?"

"Yes," Vir said flatly.

"Good." This time it wasn't Finian who spoke, but rather Gwynn, another techno-mage who seemed to have taken an interest in the events that occurred on Centauri Prime. Finian, as always, maintained something of an open manner, with his round face and blue eyes that seemed incapable of any sort of deceit. Of course, that alone provided reason enough not to trust him.

As for Gwynn, her attitude was as imperious as ever. She looked at them as if she were observing them from a great height that made their concerns seem childish and irrelevant. Renegar didn't trust either of them. As a general rule of thumb, trusting techno-mages wasn't an especially advisable pastime.

"You have every reason to be scared," Gwynn continued. "We found him wandering the catacombs. He had a bit of an . . . accident. Rocks, even boulders, can come loose around here at the most unexpected times. If they strike unexpectedly enough, and with sufficient force . . ." She shrugged. "The results can be tragic, as you see."

"What is it?" Adi said, looking at it wonderingly.

"That," Vir told him, "is a Drakh. One of the creatures I told you about. Told all of you about," he said, raising his voice. Not that anyone was having trouble hearing him, his voice echoing there in the tunnels. "The creatures who brought a plague to humanity. The ones who are operating behind the scenes here on Centauri Prime. And, I believe, the ones who are truly responsible for the 'visions' that our beloved prime minister is always talking about."

"What's it doing down here?" Renegar demanded.

"We are not sure," Gwynn said evenly, "but he may or may not have followed you, Renegar."

Renegar turned deathly pale. "Impossible," he spat out. "He couldn't have known to follow me . . ."

"Perhaps not," Finian agreed. "He may have simply stumbled upon the catacombs on his own, and heard people talking. But I don't think so. I think the Drakh observe everyone, all the time . . . and something about Renegar's actions caught this one's attention."

The others looked accusingly at Renegar. He stepped back defensively. "I didn't know!"

Voices began to be raised in anger, but Vir shouted them down. "No one is blaming you, Renegar," he assured his fellow rebel.

"Then maybe someone should be," Gwynn responded. "This is not a game, Vir."

"Don't you think I know that!" Vir shot back at her. "I had one of these damned things in my head, Gwynn! I know what they're capable of!"

"Then know that you were most fortunate that we intercepted this one," Finian said. "We believe that although they have the ability to communicate telepathically with one another, it doesn't happen instantaneously. There is a procedure involved in which they sort of 'agree' to commune en masse. It takes some effort and preparation, and I doubt this one had the time to engage in it. As far as the Drakh are concerned, this fellow will simply have dropped off the face of the planet. They will keep an eye out for him, put their feelers out, and try to locate him. We will make certain that they do not succeed."

"We cannot keep covering for you, however," Gwynn said.

"We haven't been asking you to," Vir pointed out. "It's not as if we've been needing you to hold our hands. We've been doing fairly well on our own. We've managed to impede Durla's war machine . . ."

"Not enough." Again, it was Dunseny who spoke up. In quick, broad strokes he described all that he had heard at the briefing in the Tower of Power.

Vir was pacing by the time Dunseny was finished. "It's obvious that nothing short of total domination is going to satisfy Durla."

"Durla and the Drakh who support him," Finian said.

There were nods from all around. "It's clear what we have to do," Renegar said. "What we've been doing up to now is fine, as far as it goes. But we have to go further. We have to take on the Drakh, head-to-head. We have to drive these creatures off the face of Centauri Prime!"

There were shouts of agreement, but then Vir's voice carried over theirs once more. "If we take on the Drakh head-to-head, we'll be wiped out."

"You took them on," Renegar said. "You told me yourself. You blew up that death station that the Shadows left behind."

"Yes. I did," Vir confirmed. "And I got lucky. The majority of the Drakh weren't around when it happened; if they had been, the station would have been left intact. The problem is, the Drakh are *always* around on Centauri Prime. They're watching Londo, they're watching Durla, and they're watching me. Their agents and influence are everywhere.

"Plus, we still don't completely know what their influence over Londo is. There are too many pieces we don't have, too many things that aren't ready."

"We're ready for freedom!" Renegar asserted.

"But we're not ready for suicide," Adi said.

"Coward!"

"I'm no coward." Adi wasn't so easily riled as to react to insults. "I'm just not an idiot, either."

"He's right," Finian said, "as is Vir. You still don't have enough raw power backing you up, and you dare not confront the Drakh directly without it. You will have only one chance to do so, and if you are not fully prepared, they will annihilate you."

"So what do we do?" Renegar demanded.

"We do," Vir told him, "exactly what we've been doing. We prepare things slowly, methodically."

"And get killed?" Renegar replied. "The way Rem did?"

There was dead silence at that. The loss of Rem Lanas was still a gaping wound.

"Maybe," Vir finally said. "Or maybe we're ready when the time is right."

"The more time passes, the more ships Durla gets into place, the more the odds skew in his favor," Renegar said.

"Not necessarily," Finian said. "Your attacks on the construction efforts slow them ... while you continue to convert individuals or groups over to your cause. At the very least, you sow seeds of suspicion, so that when the full Drakh influence is revealed, the people will come flocking to your cause."

"Also, the Drakh will become overconfident," Gwynn said. "The closer the fleet comes to completion, the more sure they will be in their conduct. You see ... they have no glory of their own. They bask purely in the evil of the Shadows. The Shadows were far greater than their servants, but if the Drakh believe they are attaining the Shadows' purpose, they will assume an air of invincibility."

"And that will be a mistake," Vir said. "Besides ... we need their resources."

"What resources?" Adi asked.

"Don't you see?" Vir smiled in grim amusement. "The Drakh on this world ... they aren't the only ones. The entire foul race has contaminated everything good and noble there ever was about Centauri Prime. We don't just want to stop them. We want to obliterate them. We want them to pay for Rem Lanas ... for corrupting every office and every official of importance in our world, up to and including the emperor.

"They, through puppets such as Durla, are constructing engines of destruction. We impede the creation of those engines because we need time to build up our own assets. But ultimately, the fleet will be completed. It's inevitable . . . but it's also desirable . . ."

"Of course," Adi said, understanding. "Because once it's completed, we can use it against the Drakh themselves."

"Yes," said Dunseny. "They think that the fleet will go up against the Alliance . . . when in fact they're aiding in the creation of the very fleet that's going to be used to assault the Drakh."

"Exactly." There wasn't much light in the cavern, but what there was danced with almost hellish glee in Vir's eyes. "If we are patient . . . and thorough . . . and build up our forces . . . we will be triumphant. It *is* possible to take the long view. Once I met a servant of the Shadows. I told him that I longed to see his head on a pole and that, if it happened, I would wave to him like this." And he demonstrated, waggling his fingers in a manner that almost seemed comical. "It took several years . . . but that was exactly what happened."

"But how long can we sustain this?" Renegar asked. "Because if we are not careful, it'll be our heads up on poles, just as happened with poor Lanas."

"We will sustain it as long as is necessary," Vir told him firmly. "Remember, there are more, many more in our little movement. And we will get the job done. We have our connections. We will continue to get information, and use it well. But if we rush into anything, we'll be carried along in the tidal wave of events . . . and get swamped. We have to ride the crest of it and, in that way, stay above it."

"But we have techno-mages on our side," Renegar pointed out. "The two of you have stayed mostly in the background. Your disposing of this," and he nudged a toe into the body of the Drakh, "is something of a departure. Either you stay away or, when you do show up, you utter a few cryptic comments. But otherwise, for the most part, you keep to yourselves."

"That is because you are not our pawns," Finian told them. "You do as you wish, when and where you wish. We are, however, not averse to watching your backs every now and again." He indicated the fallen Drakh. "Case in point."

"Do not presume that we always will, though," Gwynn warned. "Your boundless enthusiasm is a disincentive. Plus, we have our own affairs to consider. So I suggest you do not try our patience . . ."

"For you are subtle and quick to anger?" Vir asked. When

Gwynn nodded, looking a bit surprised, Vir explained, "Londo once told me that a techno-mage said that to him, many years ago."

"It has not changed," Finian said.

Clearly deciding that the conversation needed to head off in another direction, Vir said firmly, "All right . . . here's what we'll do, then. All of you know people at different levels in the Houses. Talk to them. Feel them out. Get eyes and ears into any of the Houses where we don't have contacts. Durla is going to come down on them even more harshly than he has before. He's going to feel the need to either beat them down or eliminate them completely. We have to let them know that there is an alternative. That they do not simply have to roll over.

"In addition, our strikes at key construction points will continue. Siphoning the materials through deliveries at Babylon 5 has been an exercise in caution, but I've been using the station as a clearinghouse for the individual components of the explosives, so no one has been associating it with the completed devices."

The conversation went on for some time, Vir laying out the groundwork for how their resistance movement was going to continue to survive. The techno-mages stopped talking, simply listening and—remarkably—even nodding on occasion. Finally Vir said, "All right . . . are there any questions?"

"Yes. I have a question," Renegar said.

Vir looked at him expectantly.

"Are we going to win?" he asked.

Without a moment's hesitation, Vir replied, "Yes. And not only are we going to win . . . but the Drakh are going to lose. You've seen the face of the enemy," and he pointed at the fallen creature. "It's nothing unbeatable. They can be hurt. They can die. And if that's the case, then we can injure them and we can kill them. And we will. However many it takes in order to rid Centauri Prime of this . . . this cancer that's eating away our soul. That's what we'll do with our underground movement."

"Considering where we're meeting," Adi said, looking around, "I'd say 'underground' is definitely the right word for it."

This resulted in something very unusual for one of their clandestine meetings: a roar of laughter. For just one moment, they had a feeling of what it would be like to meet, not as coconspirators or desperate freedom fighters, but simply as men enjoying each other's company. Renegar wondered whether they ever would have that opportunity, to live relatively normal and unassuming lives. And he said as much.

Vir looked at Renegar skeptically and responded. "Renegar . . . if you had a normal and unassuming life . . . you wouldn't know what to do with it."

Renegar thought about that, then nodded. "You are very likely correct. But . . ." he added, "would it not be nice . . . to have the opportunity to find out?"

To that notion, Vir had no response.

EXCERPTED FROM
THE CHRONICLES OF LONDO MOLLARI.
Excerpt dated (approximate Earth date)
September 24, 2276.

Note to historians: Although naturally the Centauri year is different from an Earth year, we have taken the liberty of adjusting the date and having it reflect a parallel passing of time, vis-à-vis Earth time, due to Londo's passing reference to his anniversary with G'Kar, so as to avoid confusion for our Earth readers. We at the Centauri Historical Society are aware of the late emperor's fondness for inhabitants of Earth, and feel that he would approve of our efforts to minimize anything that might leave those readers in a quandary. For chronological purists among you, we thank you for your indulgence.

G'Kar stood at the door, in the same way that he always did. Straight, tall, looking directly ahead. And I, seated on the other side of the table, gestured for him to enter just as I always did. "One would think," I told him as he walked across the room, "that after all this time, you would see no need to stand on ceremony."

"Ceremony, Highness, is all we have. Without it, you are merely an oddly dressed Centauri in clothing that picks up dirt all too easily."

"You know what I like about you, G'Kar? You make me laugh."

"You did not laugh just now."

"So I didn't like you as much. Sit, sit." He never sits until I tell him to. I think he considers it a sort of odd game. "So . . . how was your day today, G'Kar?"

"The same as it was yesterday, Londo, and very much—I suspect—the way it will be tomorrow. Unless, of course, you decide to have me executed today."

"Why today?" I asked. I signaled for the wine steward to bring me a new bottle, and he went off to fetch it.

"Why not today?" he countered. "Sooner or later, my amusement value will reach its end, and then . . ." He shrugged and made a throat-cutting gesture.

"Is that how you think I see you, G'Kar? As only having 'amusement value'?" I shook my head, discouraged. "How very tragic."

"Of all the tragedies in your life, Londo, I truly think that my opinion in this instance rates fairly low on the scale."

"True. True." There was a silence then, the comfortable silence of two old acquaintances. I do not know if, even now, I dare use the word "friend." The new bottle was brought, glasses were placed in front of us, and the wine was poured. G'Kar raised his glass and sniffed its contents with a delicacy that provided an amusing contrast to his rough-hewn exterior.

"This," he announced, "is actually a good vintage."

"Is not all my wine of good vintage?"

"Not of this caliber," he said. "To what do I owe the honor?"

"It has been a year," I told him. "A year since you saved my life and came under my protection. A year since we began our weekly dinners together. I am surprised. I would have thought the date would be seared into your memory."

"There is a great deal occupying my mind at the moment, Londo," he said. "My apologies. This significant date must have been squeezed out of its proper place of importance. So if we are to celebrate this anniversary, does that mean you will be letting me go?"

"Why would I want to do that?" I asked. "Allow my most excellent friend, G'Kar, to simply depart? No, no . . . I am afraid I cannot, if for no other reason than that it would reflect poorly in the eyes of those who watch me most carefully."

"Because I am a potential tool that might be used in the event that the current situation deteriorates."

I hated to admit that he was right but, of course, he was.

"True enough," I said slowly. "My prime minister and his associates have made it clear to me that you will be allowed to live only if you do so here, under my protection. If I permit you to leave, it will seem as if I am granting you permission to violate the laws of Centauri Prime. Laws that ban visitors, that ban changeling devices. I cannot be seen as being lenient on criminals."

G'Kar had finished his wine. The steward moved toward him to refill the glass, but G'Kar, as usual, placed a hand over it to indicate that he wanted no more. "Why can you not?" he asked. "Be lenient, I mean. Certainly a quality such as mercy would be highly valued. Particularly when one considers the brutal actions taken by some of your predecessors. The people of Centauri Prime would likely regard it as a pleasant change of pace."

I laughed curtly at that. "It is a nice theory, G'Kar. But people do not want a change of pace, pleasant or otherwise. They want no more and no less than what they are accustomed to. Believe it or not, there are still those who believe Cartagia was the best emperor we ever had. That he harkened to a day when billions feared the Centauri because we were unpredictable. There are many who believe that I will indeed let you go, and they will eagerly use such a decision to undermine my authority . . . to undermine me. As fond as I am of you, G'Kar, I consider your freedom too high a price to pay for a crisis of confidence that could cost me my throne . . . and, of greater significance, my life.

"But you know, G'Kar . . . all of this is very much beside the point. We should ponder other matters. A new topic!" I announced, and I tapped my spoon repeatedly on my goblet as if I were addressing a crowded room of revelers.

While we had talked, food had been laid out for us, and it smelled excellent. I started to eat hungrily, having had very little over the course of the day. G'Kar, as always, ate little to nothing. It was completely beyond me how he managed to maintain the energy to function, considering the small quantities he consumed.

"What new topic would that be, Londo?" he inquired.

I allowed a moment to finish chewing my food. It would hardly have been dignified to send vegetables spewing out of my mouth like a multicolored fountain. "I think you should choose this time, G'Kar. I have done so the last few times. And they have been stimulating chats, to be sure, but I think it time that you seize the bull by the reins."

"The what?"

I waved dismissively. "An Earth saying. It is of no importance."

"No, that might be an interesting topic," G'Kar said. "Your fascination with all things pertaining to Earth. I have never quite understood it. You research them, you quote from them. Their achievements pale compared to those—laudable or otherwise—of the Centauri Republic. They are a relatively minor species. At least, they started out that way.

"Yet the Centauri saw something in them. Some spark, some potential. You must have. If not for the Centauri, after all, the Humans would not have acquired the jumpgate technology. Or at the very least, they would have lagged far behind in acquiring it. It might have taken them decades, even centuries more, to become a true power in the galaxy." Interest glittered in his one normal eye. "What was it about them, Londo? I have to admit, I didn't see it, nor did any of my people. What was the fascination?"

I chuckled. "It was a little before my time . . . a hundred years or so, you understand. So I cannot exactly tell you firsthand. But . . . I have been doing some reading. Comments, letters, correspondence from the emperor and the ministers at the time, that sort of thing."

"And what have you discovered?"

I leaned forward and gestured to G'Kar that he should do likewise, as if I was concerned that someone would overhear. He leaned closer.

"They thought," I said, "that the Humans would annihilate themselves."

"Really."

I nodded. "They saw the Humans as an opportunity for quick profit. And they thought that the Humans, once they had acquired the advanced technology, would move too quickly for their own good. My predecessors anticipated that there would be struggles and wars within the then-primitive Earth Alliance. Centauri Prime would secretly fund both sides, benefit from all concerned and—once the Humans had more or less obliterated themselves—the Great Centauri Republic would step in and pick up the pieces. It was a simple way to expand our control with no risk to ourselves, and nothing but profit to be had. It seemed the perfect arrangement."

"But it did not work out that way."

"Not exactly. They didn't wind up destroying themselves. Instead they managed to hang on long enough to offend the Minbari, and wound up almost being wiped off the face of existence. We predicted a war, yes . . . but the wrong war. They tripped themselves up, as we thought they would, but what a foe to do it with!" I laughed softly at the thought. "They wanted our help, you know. Wanted us to help them against the Minbari. If we had, the Minbari would have turned on us just as quickly. We knew we would not have had a chance against them. What would have been gained?"

"Did you not feel you owed it to them, as a race? If not for your giving them the technology, they would not have encountered the Minbari and gotten themselves embroiled in a war."

"Nonsense," I said firmly. "Responsibility only goes so far."

"Does it?"

He was watching me. I hated it when he watched me like that. "What is that supposed to mean?"

"If you do something to set events into motion, you owe something to those whom you have affected. You gave them the flame. They then burned themselves. You had a responsibility to try to tend to the wound . . ."

But I shook my head. "No. We gave them the match. It was they who chose to light the flame. It was purely their responsibility, wasn't it."

"Was it?"

"Bah!" I said in disgust. "We always get to this at some point or other. 'Yes, it is, no, it isn't.' No debate or discussion. Just rephrasing my question as another question. And then we go no further."

"So one who is given the match and chooses to light it . . . is owed no aid from anyone? No succor? Whatever the consequence or outcome, it is his responsibility and his alone to deal with?"

"That is correct, yes."

"And what of you, Londo?" His voice suddenly turned sharp, his manner alert. "You were given a match by the Shadows, were you not? By their agents? And you used that match to light a flame that wound up bringing a torch not only to my world, but also ultimately to your own. Yet now you want my aid to overcome that which you have thrust yourself into."

"Your aid? I have no idea what you're talking about."

"I do not know entirely myself, Londo." There was something about him, something that seemed to say that I could hide nothing from him. He exuded confidence. I almost envied him. "But there is something. Something you want of me. Something you are . . . saving me for. That is why I have been here for a year—that and no other reason. You could have me executed with impunity. You could find a way to allow me to depart, if you really wanted to. Instead you keep me here for your own purposes. I think you know what they are."

"Oh, really. And what do you think they are?"

And that cold confidence seeped over from him. It seemed to drain something from me as he said, "I think . . . you want me to help you escape. Not out that door. Not off this world. I think you want me to help you escape through the only way that will allow the pain to stop. To the only place where no one can ever touch you or hurt you again. I do not think, though, that you are ready for that. Or perhaps you feel that it is not a judicious moment. And so you wait. And we chat. And we have dinner. And we play at having polite discussions about matters both consequential and inconsequential, when the only thing you really wonder about is: Is now the time? Is there more that I can do?

Should do? Or should I ask my old friend G'Kar to do . . . what I myself cannot or will not do?"

Suddenly it was very, very cold. I felt it down to my bones, my blood . . . my very being. Whatever warming attributes came from the wine were gone.

"I think you should leave now," I said.

G'Kar inclined his head slightly, in deference, and rose. The guards were immediately at his side. What nonsense. As if they could have stopped him if he endeavored to attack me. He looked at one in curiosity, and said, "You are new. You are new to the guard . . . but I have seen you before. Where?"

The guard looked at me, seeking my permission to reply. I nodded absently, and he looked back to G'Kar. "My name is Caso. I was a member of the Prime Candidates."

"Of course. You were there that day, a year ago. You saw me stop the shooter. You are no longer a Prime Candidate?" He shook his head. "Why?"

He said nothing, but it was I who answered. "Because it was felt," I told him, "that he was wrong to reveal that you had saved Durla and me. The others pressured him to state that you yourself were involved, or even masterminded it. That way there would have been no reason not to dispose of you. And Durla is not pleased with the idea of being beholden to a Narn—any Narn—much less you."

"But you stuck to your principles," G'Kar said approvingly to Caso.

"I simply held to the truth," Caso told him. "It was not a difficult decision."

"Oh," G'Kar said, glancing at me, "you would be amazed how difficult a decision that can be sometimes."

Caso escorted him out then, leaving me with a bottle of wine that was not sufficiently full, and a soul that was not sufficiently empty, for what I needed to do.

10

Reality and fantasy were blurring for Durla. He was standing on a high cliff on Mipas, overlooking the ships that prepared to plunge into battle, and he could not recall for sure whether what he was seeing was really happening, or merely another of his visions.

"Magnificent," he said, and the wind carried his words away so that no one heard, save himself. Even so, the fact that he himself had heard it was enough.

Mipas was only one of the worlds where Centauri war vessels were being gathered, but it was a pivotal one, since it was within close proximity to the Drazi Homeworld. Fortunately, Minister Castig Lione had done a more-than-admirable job of greasing the right palms and making certain that the right people in the Drazi government asked all the wrong questions, thereby making sure that none of the Drazi would look too closely at what was going on. They knew Mipas was a hub of industry, but the Centauri insisted—with most convincing vigor—that the facility was simply being used as a construction project for the Centauri government to keep its populace gainfully employed.

And it was true that, at this site and at others like it, the Centauri had labored long and hard. And now the fruits of those years and years of labor were coming close to paying off. The ships looked so ready for battle—so powerful, that even sitting on the ground as they were, relatively helpless, they still appeared formidable.

It was, without question, the largest fleet that any one race had in its possession. Its creation had not come without cost, and it had required long years of experimentation and dedication.

"Magnificent," he said again. He wondered abstractly whether he had forgotten every other word in his vocabulary.

But it *was* magnificent, there was no denying. The ships were stretched all the way to the horizon, ready to leap into the air at his command. Not only that, but many already were up and flying. The sky was alive with activity, hundreds of ships, passing in perfect formation.

He stood there, arms stretched wide, and he could practically feel power from the ships themselves flooding into him. He felt as if he could, with a mere wave of his hand, send other worlds spiraling into oblivion. With his mighty fleet backing him up, he could shatter planets at his merest whim.

"Soon . . . very soon, sir," General Rhys said at his side. "Another two, three weeks . . . and we will be ready. At your hand, and your hand alone, will we strike."

It sounded good. Indeed, it sounded superb. "My hand," Durla said, sounding enchanted with the notion. "My hand will reach out. My hand will crush the Alliance worlds. They will not be able to stop us. Nothing can stop us."

And suddenly Mariel was at his side. She was smiling and perfect and glowing with that glorious inner light which, for some reason, he never saw when she was with him under other circumstances. "Sheridan can," Mariel said firmly. "He can stop you."

"Never!" Durla shouted.

"He stopped the Shadows. He stopped the Vorlons. He can stop you."

"I will eliminate him! Obliterate him! I—"

"I love you, Durla, you above all others," Mariel said. "And Sheridan shall be delivered into your hands. Sheridan and also Delenn."

"How?" Durla's eyes were wide in wonder. "How will you do this?"

"The son. The son is the key. Once you have the son, the father and mother will fall into line. He was born for one reason and one reason only: to become Sheridan and Delenn's greatest weakness. They will sacrifice themselves in order to save him. They will think, in so doing, that it is only themselves who are to be sacrificed, but in fact they will be sacrificing Sheridan's Alliance, as well. He has tried to create something greater than himself. He has not quite yet succeeded. He does not realize that once he is gone, his Alliance falls apart. When the Alliance worlds are assaulted by this mighty fleet you have created, they will turn to Sheridan for guidance, and they will find him gone. They will turn to each other and find only races that have let each other down. It will be glorious. It will be chaos. And it will be the end of the Interstellar Alliance."

"And I need do nothing?"

"Nothing." Mariel smiled. "Durla . . . do you know what you are?"

"Tell me."

"You are the greatest leader, the greatest thinker, the greatest Centauri who has ever lived. In the future, all will sing songs and say prayers to you. The actions you take in the coming weeks will grant you immortality. None will ever forget the name of Durla. You will be like unto a god."

"A god," he whispered.

"Even the Great Maker himself will pale in envy at the praise that will be sung to you. For the Great Maker possesses the abilities of a deity, which aid him in all that he would create. You, Durla, are a mere mortal . . . yet look at what you have managed to bring into being, through the sheer power of your will."

The sky was now so thick with ships that the stars were not even visible. Every so often they managed to peek through, ever so slightly, but for the most part it was a solid blanket of fighter vessels.

"All this, you have done. And for all this, you will be rewarded."

She reached for him then, her lips against his . . .

. . . and he awoke with a start.

In the darkness of the room, Durla felt flushed, breathing hard. It was that disconcerting sort of sensation that one always experienced when waking up in an unusual place.

The facility in which he was housed wasn't especially plush or fancy, but it was the best Mipas had to offer. It was only one night, though; the next day he would journey to another of the worlds that the great Centauri Republic had taken, and witness the final stages of the construction there.

It was a glorious tour, a validation of all his work.

His work.

The more he pondered, the more his suspicious mind began to work. And then he heard a soft moan. He glanced over and saw Mariel lying next to him, tossing and looking less than comfortable. Perhaps she had likewise been dreaming. But her vision wasn't remotely as broad as his, which caused him no little aggravation. After all, she had always been present in his dreams—an avatar of greatness. Certainly it wasn't her fault that the Mariel of the real world could never match up to that of the imaginary.

Nevertheless, it was a keen source of disappointment.

He shook her awake, and she sat up with a start, blinking furiously. The blanket fell away, revealing the sheerest of nightgowns.

Once upon a time, that sight alone would have been enough to inflame his blood. Now he barely gave it a glance. "Mariel . . . tell me what you think of me," he said.

She looked at him in confusion. "What?"

"Your opinion. Of me. I desire to know what it is."

"You are . . ." She licked her lips, still clearly befuddled, but game enough to try to reply. "You are my sun and moons, my stars, my everything. You are—"

"Stop it," and he grasped her firmly by the arms. "I need to know, because we stand on the brink of something great. On the brink of recapturing the lost glory of Centauri Prime. But it is important to me that you tell me what you think of this venture, and of me."

"Why . . . is it important?"

He took a deep breath. "It simply is. Now tell me. Am I a great leader? Will songs be sung about me?" When she didn't reply immediately, he shook her roughly and repeated, "Tell me!"

And suddenly her face twisted in fury, anger so palpable that he felt as if daggers were being driven into him through the ferocity of her gaze alone. "You desire to know what I think? Very well. I think you are mad. Insane. I think you are drunk with power. I think you tell yourself that all that you do, you do for Centauri Prime, when in fact you do it for yourself. I think you will bring death and destruction to our people. I think these 'great visions' you profess to have are nothing more than the delusions of a rotting soul making lengthy preparations for its own damnation. I think that if you have a shred of decency, you will halt this insane project before it goes any further. That you will refrain from bringing the wrath of the Interstellar Alliance down around our ears and instead work to create something good and prosperous and decent. Something that can stand as a symbol for a thousand years and say, *See here! We of the Great Centauri Republic accomplished this, and it benefited every sentient being everywhere.* And, Durla, if you persist in this course, then you will only lead others to destruction, and the only songs that you will inspire will be dirges. You wanted to know what I think? That is what I think."

It had all come bursting out of her in a rush, words spilling over themselves. She wasn't thinking rationally, or wisely. As had been the case with abused and downtrodden wives throughout the ages, she had been thinking at that moment about one thing and one thing only: to wound him. To get back at him in any way she could.

But always a woman of craft, intelligence, and deviousness, Mariel had suffered his wrath long enough. Before he could swing at

her, she whipped the covers off her body and leapt from the bed with
the force of a recovered predator. Something had at last awakened
inside her, a sense of dignity, of self-worth, a growing ember of the
respect she once held as a devastating lady of Centauri Prime.

Tonight she would get it all back.

Before Durla could untangle himself from the bedsheets, Mariel
ripped open the bedroom door so hard that it slammed into the wall.
She fled down the hallway, feeling him coming up fast behind her.
Only a few more steps to go; she could just reach the other room in
time. She grasped the handle of the door at the end of the hallway,
pushed, whirled, and closed it, throwing herself against the door and
locking Durla out. Forever.

As Durla pounded furiously against the door, Mariel leaned
against it and felt the blessed wood at her back, taking the brunt of
his anger for once. Across the room, there was a dark terminal. She
stared at it, realizing that she was trapped here only as long as she allowed herself to be.

Mariel crossed the room, touched her fingers to the side of the
terminal, and activated a call to Emperor Londo Mollari of Centauri
Prime. She was taking him up on his offer of help. She was going
home. And in a few moments, there would be nothing Durla could
do to harm her.

11

"Happy birthday, David!"

David Sheridan squirmed as his mother planted a kiss on his cheek. He wiped it off as quickly as possible, then howled in anguished laughter as Michael Garibaldi kissed him just as aggressively on the other cheek. "Uncle Mikcy!" he managed to get out as he quickly wiped the drool from his face. "Oh, *yuck!*"

" 'Oh, yuck'? Is that all you have to say?" Garibaldi asked him in mock offense. "And after the terrific present I've gotten you?"

They were gathered in Sheridan's den, a more private room for study and contemplation. It boasted an assortment of mementos from earlier in the careers of both Delenn and Sheridan, and the room overall had more of an "Earth" feel to it. At least, that's what David was told. Having never actually been to Earth, he could only take his father's word for it.

"Present? Is it the trip? Finally?" David asked.

Delenn rolled her eyes, as if this were a subject that had been broached a hundred times before . . . and indeed, perhaps it had. "David, we said eighteen . . ."

"What is the big deal about eighteen?" he demanded. Knowing that his mother was a dead end, he turned to his father. "Dad, I'm sixteen now. Would you please tell Mom that she's being paranoid."

"You're being paranoid," Sheridan told her promptly.

"So you're saying I can go."

"No, you can't go. But it's your birthday, so I figured I'd humor you."

David sighed in exasperation. He turned to Garibaldi, his court of last resort. "Can you believe this? They won't put me on a shuttle by myself to go visit you on Mars. To go anywhere! What the hell is going on?"

"Language," Delenn said primly.

"Sorry. What the bloody hell is going on?"

"Attaboy," Garibaldi said.

"A reminder here, David," Sheridan said. "You're 'sixteen' on a technicality. Minbari years are shorter than Earth years. By Earth standards, you've still got a ways to go."

"Okay, fine. But I've also got some Minbari blood in me, so that should count for something."

"Yeah. Don't get too attached to your hair, for one thing," Garibaldi cracked.

Delenn, who was busy slicing the white-and-chocolate cake that had been brought in minutes earlier, shook her head. "You, Michael, are precisely no help whatsoever."

"Thank you."

"You're welcome. Here," and she shoved a piece of cake at him.

"Look, I gotta tell you, the kid's got a point, that's all," Garibaldi said. He took a bite of the cake, then said, "Who baked this?"

"I did," Sheridan said. "I figured it's never too late to try something new."

"Well, guess what. You were wrong." He put the cake aside as Sheridan scowled. "It's just that . . . well, the kid's sixteen years old and he's never so much as flown on a shuttle by himself? Aside from a trip or two to Babylon 5, he's spent practically his whole life on Minbar. He should get out, have a chance to see the galaxy. My God, when I think what I was up to when I was sixteen . . ."

"The imagination fairly reels," Delenn said.

"It's a different situation, Michael, and you know it." Sheridan lowered his voice and glanced at David, as he said to Garibaldi, "And I don't know if now is the best time to—"

"Discuss it," David interrupted. He had finished his piece of cake, his teenaged taste buds apparently not the least put off. "God, I can't think of the number of times I've heard that. When is it going to be safe to discuss things in front of me, huh? How sheltered am I going to have to be?"

Sheridan looked to Delenn, but she shrugged slightly in a "What-else-can-we-say?" manner. "It's just . . . different," he said.

"How?" The question came from both Garibaldi and David.

"Because," Sheridan said patiently, "I'm the president of the Interstellar Alliance. And the fact is that there are people out there—some of them outside the Alliance, some of them, I hate to say, part of it—who might well desire to put pressure on me any way they can. To say nothing of the numerous people I've piled up over the years who have individual grudges with me. And my son would be a terrific prize to acquire in that regard."

"Wow, you really are paranoid," Garibaldi said.

"And so are you. Don't you remember? It's one of the things I've always liked about you."

"And paranoia has its time and place," Garibaldi admitted.

"That being all the time and every place," Sheridan replied.

"True enough. But don't you think there should be some balance? Like I said, when I was sixteen—"

"You were already bumming around the galaxy, I know. Snagging rides wherever you could, exploring colonies, getting into trouble. And it made you the man you are today."

"God help us all," Garibaldi said cheerfully.

"The point is," Sheridan continued, "David isn't you. You could do whatever you wanted, get into whatever trouble you wished, with relative anonymity. David had the bad luck to be my son."

"I don't think of it as bad luck, Dad." David sighed. "I wish you wouldn't put words in my mouth."

"Sorry."

"He's got so many of his own they just kind of spill out all over the place into other people's mouths."

"Don't help me, Michael," Sheridan told him.

"The thing is, you're right about one thing," David said.

"One thing." Delenn laughed. "My, my. That's an improvement of one hundred percent over most discussions you two have, John. You should be proud."

"Don't help me, Mom," David deadpanned. He turned back to his father. "The thing is . . . you're the president of the Interstellar Alliance. To all intents and purposes, you're the most powerful man in known space."

"A bit of a high-flown description, but I'll accept that," Sheridan said.

"But why is it, then . . . that the most powerful man in known space . . . has the most powerless son?"

Sheridan looked down a moment and sighed. "David . . . I wish the situation were different. I wish we lived in other circumstances."

"We live in the circumstances that we make, Dad. You can't create a certain set of circumstances, and then moan about it and chalk it off to the doings of fate."

"He has a point, John."

"*Et tu*, Delenn?"

"I'm not saying that your concerns aren't valid. Just that his are equally valid. There is no easy answer," she replied.

"When is there ever?" He thought about it a moment, and then said, "Maybe when you're seventeen . . ."

"Forget it, Dad," David said impatiently. "Just forget it. I'll lock myself in my room and come out when I'm fifty, and maybe that will be safe enough." Before Sheridan could respond, David turned to Garibaldi. "Okay, so what is your present, then?"

"David, you raised the subject; we can't just let it drop," Sheridan said.

"You know what, Dad? It's my birthday. If I want to drop a subject, then I think it should get dropped."

Sheridan put up his hands in an attitude of submission, whereupon David looked back at Garibaldi. "So? My present?"

Garibaldi reached into his jacket and pulled out a PPG. He handed it to David, and said proudly, "Here you go."

David took it and turned it over reverently, feeling its heft. "Wow," he whispered.

Sheridan's face was so dark that it looked as if thunderheads were rolling in. "Michael," he said stiffly. "May we speak privately a—"

"Oh, calm down, John. David, pull the trigger."

"David, you will do no such thing!" Delenn snapped.

"Will you guys trust me? After twenty-plus years, you'd think I'd've earned that. David, point it over in that direction and pull the trigger."

Before his parents could stop him, David did as he was told. He braced himself and pulled the trigger.

There was not, however, any of the expected recoil. Instead an image instantly appeared, floating in the air, materialized there by a steady stream of light from the end of the "PPG." It was a scantily clad young woman, life-sized and in glorious holographic 3-D, performing a dance that could only be described as extremely suggestive.

A grin split David's face. "Wow! Who is she?"

"God, I wish I knew." Garibaldi sighed. "Happy birthday, David."

Delenn cleared her throat loudly. "Michael . . . I don't know that it's particularly appropriate . . ."

"If you're going to keep the kid nailed to Minbar, the least you can do is let him get a view of what's out there. Am I right, John?" He paused. "John?"

Sheridan was staring at the holograph. With an effort, he blinked himself back into the moment. "Oh . . . right."

"John!" Delenn sounded almost betrayed.

"Delenn, it's harmless."

"Harmless! It teaches him to look upon women as physical creatures, rather than complete beings of spiritual and . . ." Her voice trailed off as she watched the gyrations. She angled her head slightly. "Are those . . . real?"

"Absolutely," Garibaldi said immediately. "You can tell."

"How? No, on second thought, I don't want to know," she amended quickly.

"That's probably wise," Sheridan said judiciously. Then a thought struck him. "Oh! One other thing."

He crossed to a cabinet and opened it. David watched in curiosity as his father delicately removed an urn. Walking carefully, as if afraid he would trip and drop it, Sheridan brought it across the room and settled it on the table in front of David where his other presents lay. David looked at it skeptically. "It's an urn," he said.

"That's right."

"Well . . . that's nice," David said gamely. "I was figuring I'd finish off the evening by having myself cremated, so . . . now I've got someplace to put me."

Sheridan laughed, and Delenn told him, "This is not just any urn. It was a gift from Londo Mollari."

"Before he became an asshole," Garibaldi added.

"Michael!" Delenn scolded.

"Okay, okay, you got me. He was an asshole already."

"Michael!"

"Oh, come on, Mom, it's not as if you speak highly of him."

"Ease up on your mother, David. And Michael, please . . . for once," and he made a quick throat-cutting gesture before turning back to his son. "David . . . I know that we've made some less-than-flattering comments about the Centauri in general and their emperor in particular. And God knows Londo has made some incredibly bad choices in his life. Then again . . . we all have."

"Not me," Garibaldi said. "Not a single mistake."

"Single, no. Numerous . . ."

Garibaldi clutched his heart as if stabbed by Sheridan's comment. Sheridan returned his attention to David. "The fact is that Londo brought us this urn before you were born. He told us that the Centauri tradition dictates that this be given to the heir to the throne when he comes of age."

"Like a Christmas fruitcake?"

Sheridan blinked. "What?"

David chucked a thumb at Garibaldi. "He told me that there was only one Christmas fruitcake ever baked. And no one wanted it. So it gets passed around from person to person, throughout history, every Christmas."

"You're just a bundle of information, aren't you, Michael."

Garibaldi grinned. "Boy's got to learn sometime."

"Yeah, well, hopefully what he'll learn is to stop listening to you. The point is, David, that—at that time, at least—we were the closest thing to family Londo ever had. He felt a . . . a connection to you. You were a sort of surrogate son, I guess. He was reaching out to you and, in so doing, reaching out to us, as well."

"And then he spent the next sixteen years trying to conquer the galaxy."

"I don't know how much of that is Londo, and how much of it is his advisers," Sheridan said. "In any event, they'll never succeed. We have some intelligence-gathering facilities of our own . . ."

"And they're not what they once were," Garibaldi said.

Sheridan glanced at him in amusement. "You mean since you left the job, it's gone downhill."

But Garibaldi obviously took the comment quite seriously. "If you want to know the truth: yes. You're depending on what other worlds are telling you. Except I know that palms have been greased, that people have found it to their advantage to look the other way, and no one truly believes that the Centauri are capable of trying what I think they're going to try."

"Londo may be many things, Michael . . . but he's not insane. Attacks on individual border worlds are one thing. But if the Centauri get it into their heads to make a full-blown strike at the allies, they'll be smashed to pieces."

"Londo may not be insane, but that prime minister of his is a few anvils short of a chorus," Garibaldi replied. "The problem is that he's ignorant and arrogant. Ignorance you can deal with. You can outsmart ignorance. Arrogance you can likewise get around. Arrogant people, you can appeal to that arrogance and set them up for a fall. Ignorance *and* arrogance is a deadly combination. Now, if the other members of the Alliance want to stick their heads into the sand, that's their choice, of course. But I'm hoping that you, Mr. President, aren't turning into one of those, or letting a gift from sixteen years ago soften you in your concerns toward the Centauri. Because I'm telling you: They're a threat."

"Believe it or not, Michael, I haven't lost sight of that," Sheridan said patiently. "But I also haven't lost sight of the fact that, once upon a time, Londo Mollari was our friend. God willing, he may be again someday. And in hopes of that time . . . here," and he slid the urn closer to David.

David picked it up, turned it over. "The bottom part is sealed," he noted.

"Yes, we know," Delenn said. "It's supposed to contain water from a sacred river that ran in front of the palace."

"It's kind of okay," David allowed. He turned the vase over. For some reason it felt . . . comfortable in his hands. Even though it was the first time he had seen it, he felt as if it had always been his. "It's nice."

"Kind of okay? Nice? From you, David, that is high praise indeed," his mother teased him.

He hefted the vase once more, then glanced at the leftover cake. "Mom, is it okay if I have another piece?"

"My God, he likes it," Sheridan said, amazed. "Absolutely—"

"—not," Delenn told him flatly.

David's "Mom!" overlapped with Sheridan's slightly less anguished, but just as annoyed, "Delenn!"

"You know how I feel about gluttony," she said. "Be satisfied with what you have, David. The rest of the cake will be here tomorrow."

"I sure as hell know I'm not going to take any of it," Garibaldi piped up cheerfully.

"I don't recall anyone asking you," Sheridan told him.

David found that, the longer he looked at the urn, the more trouble he had taking his eyes off it. "Dad . . . would it be okay if I sent a message off to the emperor? To thank him?"

"I think that would be a very nice gesture," Sheridan said. "You may have to jog his memory a bit. He never had the opportunity to meet you, after all."

"Who knows?" Delenn said. "If the situation changes for the better—perhaps you will have the opportunity to meet the emperor face-to-face someday."

"And won't that be wonderful," Garibaldi said.

12

When General Rhys met the prime minister for breakfast, he found Durla to be in a fairly somber mood. "Is there a problem, sir?" Rhys inquired.

Durla was holding a roll, staring at it. Then he placed it down carefully and looked at Rhys. "General," he said after a moment, "my lady wife, Mariel, will not be continuing with us. I wish to have her returned to Centauri Prime as soon as possible."

"Is she feeling ill?" Rhys asked solicitously.

"You can say that, yes."

"Ah" was all Rhys said.

"I believe she wants to go home. This surveying of our fleet is too strenuous for her."

"Ah," he said again.

"Furthermore," Durla continued, "I think it best if she be kept to herself for a while. I am concerned about things she might say and do."

"What . . . sort of things?" inquired Rhys.

Durla looked at him darkly and seriously. "Unfortunate things. Things that, if they were spoken by just any woman, would be considered disloyal enough. But spoken by the wife of the prime minister? They could serve to undermine my people's faith in me. I will not have it, General. I will not be undercut by her."

"That's very understandable, Prime Minister," Rhys said judiciously. But he was more than capable of reading between the lines . . . and was wondering, in a bleak manner, why Durla wasn't insinuating that the woman simply succumb to an "accident" on the way home. It was not a suggestion, however veiled, that Rhys was looking forward to receiving. He was not quite certain how he would react to such a thing. He was a soldier, not an assassin.

The question, however, promptly became moot when Durla

spoke again. "From whisperings I have heard, and things she has said
. . . I believe the emperor has taken an interest in her fortunes."

"I thought the emperor despised her," said a surprised Rhys.

Durla shrugged, clearly mystified. "Who can possibly intuit the
way in which the emperor's mind works . . . or even if it does work at
all." He laughed heartily at his little witticism, but when the general
offered little more than a slightly pained smile, he reined himself in.
Instead, all business, he continued, "So make certain that she is kept
to herself. I do not want her talking to others. I do not want her sending communications to others. She needs time, I think, to assess the
current state of affairs and come to terms with them."

"As you wish, Prime Minister."

Durla smiled. "There are times, General, when I think that you
alone fully understand my concerns."

"You wish to make Centauri Prime great again," Rhys said. "You
see our future as a great monument. Naturally you must chip away at
anything that is not in keeping with your vision."

"Yes, yes. Exactly." He let out a sigh, as if relieved.

Then he got up and walked over to the great bay window that
overlooked the field. There, in the morning sun, the ships gleamed.
Not as many as in his dream, no. But a considerable number
nonetheless. Besides, his dreams always looked to the future, not to
the present or the past.

In the distance, the construction facility was going full strength.
It provided him further affirmation that nothing could possibly stop
them. The future was in his hands.

His hands.

He looked over at Rhys. General Rhys, who, when he led the
troops into battle, would cover himself with glory. General Rhys, who
simply carried out the orders, but did not—should not—be the one
making the final decisions.

It was remotely possible that, once the battle began, it would be
Rhys who would be remembered. Despite the assertion of his
dreams, that it would be Durla whose name would be celebrated, he
nevertheless felt a degree of uncertainty.

He could see it now. *General Rhys led the attack, General Rhys
launched the ships, General Rhys paved the way* . . .

There had to be a reminder of just who was in charge.

"General," he said abruptly, "I have given the matter some
thought. Only one individual should have the final go-codes."

A flicker of uncertainty moved across Rhys' face. "Pardon, sir?"

"The final go-codes. The launch codes," Durla said matter-of-factly. "When all our ships have moved into position, the final encoded signal confirming the assault should come from me. Our fleet should answer to no other voice."

Slowly Rhys stood, uncoiling like a great cat. His gaze never left Durla. "Prime Minister," he said slowly, "with the greatest of all respect . . . those codes should also be in the hands of the fleet general."

"You mean yourself."

"Yes, I will be on site. You will not be . . . or at least, should not be, for you are too important to the future of Centauri Prime. Ideally, you should relay the go-order to me, and I in turn will inform the fleet . . ."

"Leaving the decision to strike, ultimately, to your discretion. I do not find that acceptable."

Rhys stiffened. "Prime Minister, I must ask . . . is there anything in my actions, or something in my conduct, that leads you to believe I am not trustworthy?"

"Not thus far," Durla said mildly. "But I do not intend to wait and find that I have misjudged. It is my vision, my dream that has brought us this far, General Rhys. It is my voice that the brave soldiers of our Republic are entitled to hear when they hurl themselves against our enemies in the Interstellar Alliance. And that is how it shall be."

Durla wondered just how much Rhys was going to object. He expected a fairly lengthy argument over it. He certainly hoped that he wasn't going to have to relieve Rhys of duty. He had proven too dependable an officer.

Fortunately, that dependability held up, for Rhys bowed slightly, and said, "If that is the prime minister's wish, then that is how it shall be."

"Thank you, General," Durla said, with a thin smile. He looked out once more at the fleet. "Marvelous, is it not?" He sighed. "To think that the foolish Houses of Centauri Prime thought I required their cooperation to create it. They did not realize how much could be accomplished in spite of them."

Rhys said nothing.

Durla turned back to him, feeling that the silence connoted disapproval of some sort. "Problem, General?"

"Since you are asking me, Prime Minister . . . I believe your lengthy campaign against the House heads, and the Houses them-

selves, has been . . ." He seemed to search for the right word. "Unfortunate."

"Indeed."

"Many are dead. Many more are in hiding. You have, I believe,
not done yourself a tremendous service."

"Perhaps," he said with a shrug. "Then again, I have shown them
that I play no favorites. They got in my way, General. Those who get
in my way . . . tend to come off badly."

"I shall remember that, Prime Minister."

"See that you do, General. See that you do."

And at that moment, half the field blew up.

Durla couldn't believe it. Even as the heat rolled around him,
even as the general pulled him away from the window so that no flying pieces of debris could injure him, Durla refused to accept what
he was seeing. "It can't be!" Durla shouted.

"The underground," Rhys snarled. "This treasonous act is of little consequence, though, Prime Minister. Only a handful of
ships . . ."

"And it could be more!" Durla howled. "Have your men search
the grounds! Make certain there are no more explosives! And if you
find anyone who might be a part of it, execute them!"

"Don't you wish them questioned?"

"No! I want them dead!" He thumped the wall in fury repeatedly.
"I want them dead! Their leader, dead! Their allies, dead! All of
them, *dead*! By my command, by my authority, anyone who is part of
these saboteurs will die in as grisly a manner as is possible! Now go,
General! *Go!*"

Rhys was out the door in an instant, and Durla looked back at the
flaming wreckage—all that remained of half a dozen beautiful vessels.

He wanted someone to die for this. Immediately.

Well . . . if the dream was right, David Sheridan would shortly be
in his hands. Which meant the father and mother would be, too. They
could all die together, as payment for this atrocity.

That was how his dreams would want it.

13

David lay back in his bed—or as "back" as the Minbari bed allowed him to be—and stared at the ceiling.

He had seen videos of Londo Mollari in action. The emperor had been addressing Centauri crowds in relation to some anniversary or something. David had been struck by the way the emperor had seemed bigger than life, somehow. He didn't speak so much as he had words explode from him. It was almost spellbinding to watch.

He would have liked to have the opportunity to talk to Londo. He could thank him for the urn. He would be interested to hear Londo's point of view regarding certain events he'd heard his father and mother describe. And he would love to ask just what the hell was going on with that hair.

Then he heard something.

It was some sort of rattling. David's eyes had grown accustomed to the darkness, so he wasn't entirely blind. He stepped down off the bed and looked around, listening carefully. There was silence for such a long time that he had almost convinced himself that he had imagined it. But then he heard it again, coming from the direction of the urn . . .

No. It *was* the urn. The urn from Centauri Prime was actually rocking slightly.

The first thing that occurred to him was that this was the beginning of a quake of some kind, but nothing else seemed to be affected by it. Then the next thing he thought of was that there was some sort of bomb inside the vase. But that made no sense at all. How could a bomb sit in a vase in his father's private study for sixteen years? No, that couldn't be it.

The vase's trembling seemed to have its origins at the base. David crouched closer, trying to make out what could possibly be causing it.

And suddenly the urn cracked open.

Reflexively David ducked back, but he was far too slow. From the small pile of debris that had once been an urn, something small and dark moved so quickly that he couldn't even begin to track it. It came right at him, and he batted at it helplessly, swinging through the air and missing it. There was some sort of moistness at the base of his throat then, and he tried to pull at it. His fingers felt something disgusting and protoplasmic, and he yanked his hand away from it. A wave of nausea seized him. It was as if some sort of huge tumor had sprung into existence on him.

He felt something snaking down the front of his shirt, sliding across his chest, and he opened his mouth to scream. Even as he did so, he staggered about the room, knocking over books and furniture as he tried to shake the thing off.

It's me.

The cry for help died before it could be fully born. There was no hesitation for David; he recognized instantly just who and what was upon him now. It was as if David had found a piece of himself that had been missing for as long as he could remember.

"You?" he whispered.

Yes. It's me, little sun.

He felt as if his world were spinning out of control. He tried to tell himself that he was, in fact, asleep. That none of this was happening.

Do not deny it, little sun. I have come here to help you. You have been waiting for me all this time.

David grabbed at the thing on his shoulder, and immediately a jolt of pain ran through him. He fell to his knees, gasping, trying to call out, but he felt his throat constricting. He couldn't get anything out, try as he might.

Why do you fight me when I have come here to help you? The voice in his mind sounded hurt. *I have spent so many years reaching out to you, becoming one with you. Why would you try to reject me now, when you and I have been together for so long?*

"What . . . are you?" David managed to get out.

I am everything you have ever wanted. Far more so than your parents. Your father, with his rules and restrictions. Your mother, with her moral harping. They don't understand you. They don't know what you need . . .

"I need you . . . out of my head!" David grated. He made no further move to pull the creature off his shoulder, however. He had learned better than that. His mind was racing, though, trying to summon the strength to call for help, trying to determine any course of action that would get this thing off him.

You don't want to do that. You know you want my help . . .

"I don't!"

You do. You want your chance to see the galaxy. You want to be out, exploring. You have the same desire to be a part of the great interstellar flow of life that your father had . . . except his father gave free rein to his desires, and yours won't.

He stopped. On some level . . . on every level . . . the thing was making sense. He knew it to be true, and this thing knew it, too. What was more . . . the fact that it knew it was comforting to him somehow. He felt as if he was sharing with it—in a way that he wasn't able to with his parents.

And then he tried to shout at himself—inwardly—that that was exactly what the creature wanted him to think. That he was falling into some sort of trap, as if this thing, this monstrosity on his shoulder, were his friend . . .

I am not your friend. I am your soul mate. I know you better than your parents know you. I know you better than you know yourself. And I can give you what you want . . .

"I want you off me!" But for some reason he noticed that his voice sounded a little less heartfelt this time.

You want off this world. What is there here for you? You have no friends. Minbari regard you with suspicion because of your lineage. You have private tutors, and in the rare instances where you have classes with other youths, you are far smarter, and they resent you for it. Your parents invited several guests to your birthday. They were all too "busy" or had other plans. Lies. They did not want to be with you.

You are neither Human nor Minbari, fish nor fowl. There is no place for you on Minbar. You want to see other places, to explore other worlds. To learn the truth about other races through firsthand experience. That is what you want. And I can provide you with that.

For a long moment, David said nothing. And then he spoke one word.

"How?"

His mind, however briefly, however momentarily, was open to the possibility.

From then on, it was only a matter of time.

* * *

John Sheridan couldn't sleep.

That bothered him a good deal. He usually had no trouble sleeping. In fact, it was one of the few things he wasn't having trouble doing these days. Lately he had been feeling the aches and pains more sharply than he wanted to admit. His reactions had slowed, his physical prowess was diminished. He felt as if his very thought processes were slowing down. As if there were a vague haze slowly descending.

He had the disturbing feeling he knew exactly why. The words of Lorien echoed more and more in his mind these days, even as he felt certain aspects of himself starting to . . . to dim. He knew that Delenn had to be thinking about it. *Twenty years*, Lorien had said.

At one point, a year or so earlier, Sheridan had joked that they should move to the Drazi Homeworld. Since a Drazi year was equal to 1.2 Earth years, Sheridan had jokingly reasoned that it seemed a quick way to pick up an additional four years of life. Delenn hadn't smiled when he'd said it; instead she'd immediately gone off to be by herself. He knew from then on not to attempt to deal with the subject by making light of it. In fact, since that time he hadn't dealt with it at all, at least not where Delenn was concerned.

They had both known that Lorien wasn't speaking in exact numbers, but rather in rough approximations. In the final analysis, they really could only guess how much time Sheridan had left.

Well . . . that was as it should be, wasn't it? Everyone had a finite time, when you came down to it. If one was going to look at it from a morbid point of view, birth wasn't the beginning of life; it was the beginning of a slow, protracted death. So Sheridan—unlike others—had a general idea of how much longer he had. That wasn't really such a bad thing, was it?

"Yeah. It is," he said to no one in particular.

Restless, he walked down a hall, without really having a destination in mind. It was a surprisingly chilly night for Minbar, and he had his robe tightly drawn around him. Maybe it wasn't so chilly at that. Maybe he was just feeling the cold more.

"Stop it. Stop feeling sorry for yourself," he scolded.

For the longest time, he had thought the thing he was going to regret the most was not having the chance to grow old with Delenn. But he had come to realize that he was wrong about that. At least he'd had the chance to grow older, to experience that gradual, easy comfort that two life mates have with one another. He might not have had the chance to consume an entire meal . . . but at least he'd had a taste of it.

Losing out on the chance to see David grow up, however, was really going to be hard to take. His son was sixteen, barely on the verge of manhood. There was so much Sheridan could do for him, so many ways he could try to provide guidance. But he wouldn't be there to do it.

And grandchildren; he would never have grandchildren. He would never have the chance to bounce a small continuation of his bloodline on his knee, one that would still be growing up when the next century turned. And perhaps feel his own father's voice in the back of his head, saying, "Well done, Johnny. Well done."

He would just have to be satisfied with what the cards had dealt him. After all, if Lorien had simply left him there to die, then David would never have been born.

Yes . . . he would just have to be satisfied.

Unfortunately, being satisfied had never been Sheridan's strong suit.

He stopped in his tracks. The light was dim in the hall, but still he saw someone at the other end. At first he was sure it was an intruder, but then he realized that it was David. Sheridan had been thrown for a second; something about David seemed a little odd. His body posture, the way he was carrying himself, was subtly different. Sheridan couldn't begin to imagine why.

"David?" he said cautiously. "Are you all right? You're up late." With a touch of levity that sounded horrendously forced, he added, "Still flushed with excitement from your birthday party?"

David said nothing. He walked slowly toward his father, and Sheridan realized that his son was fully dressed, in a loose-fitting shirt and slacks. He was wearing the new boots Sheridan had given him for his birthday.

"Are you going somewhere, David?" A hint of caution entered Sheridan's tone. He was becoming more concerned that something was awry. "David?"

David drew to within a foot of him, and Sheridan put a hand on his son's shoulder. He started to say, "David, what's wrong?" Then he felt a lump under David's shirt.

David's spine stiffened, his eyes going wide, as if Sheridan had just stuck a finger directly into his nervous system. "What the hell?"

Sheridan said, and even as David tried to take a step back, Sheridan yanked at the neck of the shirt, pulling it aside.

An eye glared balefully out at him.

Sheridan froze in place, his jaw dropping. He had no idea what he was looking at, but the surreal horror of it paralyzed him for just an instant. It was at that moment that David's fist swung, and there was no doubting just whose son he was. It was a powerful right cross, and even if Sheridan had been prepared for it, it would have done him damage. As it was, Sheridan wasn't ready for it at all, and he hit the ground like a bag of wet cement.

David stood over him, staring down at his father's insensate form with utter dispassion. He wasn't even fully aware that he was responsible for his father's current unconsciousness, and even if he had been aware, he wouldn't have cared. He knew who it was who was lying on the floor, of course. But for all practical purposes, he might as well have been looking at a stranger.

He turned and headed toward the nearest landing port. There was a private port not far away at all. That, of course, was to accommodate all the various dignitaries who came and went, visiting his father. There were several shuttles kept ready at all times, in the event that the mighty president of the Alliance had to get somewhere quickly.

David approached the port and slowed when he found another Minbari approaching him. He was a member of the warrior caste, and David could see that he was a guard. It was clear from the Minbari warrior's calm demeanor that he wasn't expecting any trouble. He didn't even have his hands near his weapon. He obviously considered this detail more for show than anything else. Who, after all, could really sneak in through the port?

"Young Sheridan," the guard said. "Odd hour for you to be out and about. May I help you with something?"

"Yes. You may put your hands over your head." And as he said that, the "PPG" given him by Garibaldi was in his hands.

The guard had no way of knowing that it wasn't real. It was possible, of course, that the guard might drop and pull his own weapon fast enough that he could shoot down David Sheridan. The positive aspect of that was that he would have done his job. The negative—and it was a sizable one—was that he would have just shot and killed the only son of John Sheridan and Delenn. It wasn't an option he was particularly happy about.

Slowly the guard did as he was told.

"Lie down. Flat," David continued mildly. He projected nothing but utter confidence. "Don't move, if you want to keep breathing."

He kept his "weapon" leveled on the guard even as he walked up to him. He placed it against the base of the guard's skull and pulled the guard's own weapon from his belt. For a moment he considered using the fake PPG to try to club the guard into unconsciousness, but he quickly dismissed the idea; it would be much too difficult, thanks to the guard's Minbari bone crest.

Shoot him. Kill him, the voice from his shoulder said.

David held the newly acquired genuine gun firmly and aimed it squarely at the Minbari's back. His finger twitched on the trigger. But that was all.

David . . .

"No," he said firmly.

The voice seemed to laugh in understanding. *Very well, then. Render him helpless, if you are more comfortable with that.*

Within minutes, David had bound and gagged the guard using strips of cloth torn from the guard's clothes. With that attended to, he walked quickly over to one of the shuttles and climbed in.

He looked over the control board. He actually had a good deal of practical flying time. His father had seen to that part of his education, at least. He remembered the first time he had taken a vessel into orbit, his father sitting proudly at his side, complimenting him on his handling of the craft and telling him that it seemed as if he was born to do this.

And Sheridan had been right. David *was* born to do this. By Sheridan's own admission, it was David's birthright, and his father and his mother had denied it to him. Of what use was it to live his entire life on one solitary planet, when the stars called out to him?

He brought the systems on-line, powering up the shuttle. For the briefest of moments, he wondered just where he was going to go. But then he knew—without having to consider it any further.

He was going to Centauri Prime. That was where he belonged. He didn't know *why* he belonged there, but he knew he did.

Sheridan felt himself being hauled to his feet before he had fully recovered consciousness. He blinked in confusion against the light that was streaming in through the skylight overhead. It was early morning, and Sheridan couldn't for the life of him remember why he was lying on the floor in a hallway.

"John! John, what happened?" someone was shouting at him. No, not shouting—just speaking forcefully, and with great urgency.

Garibaldi was staring at him, extremely concerned, supporting him by holding his arms up. "Happened?" Sheridan managed to get out thickly. "I don't—" Then it came back to him with the force of a hammer blow, and Sheridan shook off the confusion in an instant. "David! Something happened to David! There was this . . . this thing!"

"John!" It was the alarmed voice of Delenn this time. She was barreling down the hallway, followed by a Minbari whom Sheridan recognized as the sentry from the port. "John, David was at the port last night! He attacked this man and stole a shuttle!"

"It wasn't David," Sheridan said. When he saw the perplexed expressions of the others, he quickly clarified, "It wasn't David in control. It was something else . . . this . . . this thing on his shoulder, I've never seen anything like it. It looked like a lump of clay, but with an eye. It was controlling him. It had to be."

They ran quickly to David's room. Sheridan cursed himself for honoring his son's request for privacy by having his room set far apart from that of his parents. If he'd been nearby, he might have heard something earlier on, and been able to intervene before matters got out of hand.

Sheridan and the others looked in dismay at the wreckage. Whatever clues they might have found seemed hopelessly lost. Everything was smashed to pieces.

Sheridan leaned against the wall, sorting through everything he had seen. "Where could it have come from?"

"If it's as small as you say it was, it could have snuck in through any part of the house," Garibaldi said. He looked around. "David didn't go without a struggle, I'll tell ya. He tried to fight that thing off."

Delenn suppressed a shudder as she picked up the pieces of the Centauri urn, which had apparently been shattered along with other objects in the room.

"We've got to find him," Sheridan said furiously. "I want word sent out to all the members of the Alliance . . ."

"That might not be wise," Garibaldi told him.

Sheridan looked at him incredulously. "How could it not be wise?"

"Because it's everything you've ever feared," Garibaldi said. "If you advertise to everyone that your son's disappeared, two things are going to happen. First, knowing that he's off Minbar, every bounty hunter, every crackpot, every nutcase is going to turn out in force looking for him. They'll want to snatch him and use him to exert pressure on you. And second, any nut and his brother can claim that they have him and start making demands. Sure, they won't be able to prove that they have him, but you won't be able to prove they don't. You go wide with this, I guarantee you'll solve nothing, and create a thousand headaches you can't even begin to imagine."

"What would you suggest, then?" Sheridan asked icily. "Where would we start looking?"

"Centauri Prime," Delenn answered.

They looked at her. "What?" Sheridan said.

She was holding up pieces of the urn, pieces from the lower half of it. "Londo said that this held water from a sacred river? It's dry. There's no sign of its ever having been wet, not the slightest aroma of mildew or any smell that would accompany stagnant water. There's no moisture on the cabinet that it was on when it broke, none on the floor."

"It could have evaporated," Garibaldi offered uncertainly.

"It could have. But I don't think so. I think that thing John saw was hidden inside here, in some sort of hibernation. Waiting, all these years, for us to give it to David."

It made sense.

It made horrific sense.

"He said we would always be friends. Do you remember, Delenn?" Sheridan said. His jaw constricted with mounting fury. "Remember what he said the day he gave it to us? That that day in our company meant so much to him. Well, now we know exactly what it meant, the bastard."

"What do we do?" Delenn asked.

"We go to Centauri Prime," Sheridan said without hesitation.

But Garibaldi shook his head. "You do no such thing. You don't know for sure that it was Londo."

"Are you defending him now, Michael?"

"No, I'm trying to make sure you don't rush into something half-cocked," Garibaldi said. "I'm as furious about it as you, but I've got more practice than you do keeping myself wrapped up. If David was taken from here, it was for one of two reasons: either they're just going to kill him as a means of revenge, or they've got plans for him. If it's the former, you can't help him. If it's the latter, those plans will certainly involve you, and you have to sit tight until you find out what their next move will be. His kidnappers will contact you. At that point, you'll know for sure that it's Londo, or whoever, and *that's* when you can plan your strategy."

"My strategy is already planned," Sheridan said tightly. "It starts with killing Londo Mollari. After that, I'll improvise."

I cannot remember the last time I ran.

Not just ran. Sprinted. My personal guards actually had to run to keep up with me, and everyone we dashed past gaped at us. At me. And why should they not? My office is all about ceremony and posturing and maintaining dignity. The sight of the emperor charging down a corridor as if the hordes of hell itself were on his heels, well . . . I would have gaped as well.

I flung open the doors to Durla's private suite, the place that served him as both home and office. Durla was in a huddled conference with several of his ministers. Truthfully, I do not remember which ones. This has nothing to do with my recurring difficulties with memory. In this instance, I was simply so furious over the circumstances that had brought me here that I saw no one save for Durla.

He opened his mouth to make some oily inquiry as to why I had decided to grace him with my presence. I did not give him the opportunity to ask. "Get out," I snarled, and it was more than evident that I was referring to everyone but Durla.

And yet, incredibly, the ministers did not immediately leave. Instead they glanced at Durla, looking for confirmation. His. Over mine. The wishes of a prime minister over those of an emperor. Scandalous. Insanity. That such a thing could ever happen, and that I could be the emperor who had allowed matters to sink so low . . . it was a ghastly situation.

Trembling with rage, I said, "Now!" Just as I said that, Durla nodded, and the others rose and departed the room. I turned to my guards and said, "You, too."

"Highness, perhaps it may not be wise to—" one of them began.

"I am the emperor and you will do as you are ordered!" Whatever vestiges of pride and authority I might have had were obviously sufficient to get the job done, because the guards turned and walked out, leaving Durla and me alone.

"Is there a problem, Highness?" Durla inquired, unperturbed.

"Tell me how you did not do it," I said through clenched teeth.

"What 'it' would that be, Highness?"

He knew damned well, but if he wished to play his games for the few seconds longer I was going to allow him to live, so be it. "I have heard," I said, "that the son of John Sheridan is here. That you have kidnapped him. Yes? No?"

"No, your Highness."

"You deny that he is here?"

"No, I deny that he was kidnapped. Apparently he arrived here of his own free will."

"And why did he do this, eh?"

"Because we are Centauri Prime," he told me, "and it is our destiny to have all our enemies delivered unto us."

I could not quite believe what I was hearing. "What?"

"Highness," and he began to circle the room, and speak as if he were addressing a child. "His presence here is simply part of my grand vision."

"Not again." I had heard about his "vision" for Centauri Prime, and plans for the great Republic, all too many times.

"All this," and he gestured to the window that overlooked his balcony, "is because I envisioned it, Highness. When the great wave of Centauri vessels crashes upon the shores of the Alliance worlds, it will be the ultimate realization of my vision. I have willed it into existence. Because I have believed in it . . . it has come to pass.

"This is simply another example of the power of my belief. I believed that David Sheridan would come here . . . and he has. I must admit," and he leaned back against his desk, looking insufferably smug, "when Minister Lione informed me of young Sheridan's arrival, I was not the least bit surprised. Even Lione remarked upon how calm I was. Naturally. I could see it as clearly as I see you."

"And now that he is here, you will send him back, yes?"

"I will send him back, no," he told me. "You cannot be serious, Highness. This is the ideal opportunity to bend our greatest enemy to our will."

"You are insane! You would bring the might of the entire Alliance down upon us!"

"No. With his son's life at stake, Sheridan will bow to our will. It is inevitable. He cannot help himself. He is Human and, because of that, weak. In a way," and he laughed, "I almost feel sorry for him."

"Sorry for him? The Alliance fleet will bomb Centauri Prime back into the primordial ooze from which we crawled, and you feel sorry for him?"

"Yes, because he lacks the strength of dedication and commitment that even the lowliest of Centauri possess."

A door opened at the far end of the room before I could reply . . . and I gaped. I admit it. My jaw nearly hit the floor.

Mariel was there, emerging on unsteady legs. She was leaning against the door frame for support. There were faint discolorations on her face. Clearly she had been struck some short time ago. I knew that Mariel had not been seen as of late, but this . . . this . . .

I knew he had done it before. But now he had done it again, and what had seemed like an isolated incident became a pattern.

She had not heard me. I wondered if he had done internal damage to her. But she saw me and gasped, her hands automatically flying to cover her battered face. She ducked back into the other room, closing the door behind her.

Durla looked at me expectantly. He seemed to be wondering what other trivial matter I might bore him with at that moment. Forcing myself to speak clearly, levelly, I said, "You say . . . you have foreseen all this?"

"Much of it, yes."

"And have you foreseen . . . this?" And I drew back my fist and smashed him in the face as hard as I could.

It was likely a foolish move on my part, for Durla was an old soldier and still in battle-ready condition. I, on the other hand, had a flair for swords, but was older and much diminished. In a brief struggle, I might have been able to hold my own. In a prolonged fight, he could likely have done me great damage. Still, I was emperor, and there might still have been sufficient respect for the office to inhibit him from lashing out that aggressively.

None of that mattered. I struck him with no forethought, no care as to what might happen or how good an idea it was. All I knew, at that moment, was that I desperately needed to have my fist in direct contact with his face.

It was nice to see that I had not lost my punch, or at least was capable of recapturing it when the need arose. Durla went straight down, having been caught utterly unprepared. At that moment, I truly believe that I could have killed him with my bare hands.

And then the pain struck me.

14

Durla had been caught completely flat-footed. He had to admit that he had come to underestimate just what the emperor was capable of, and being knocked flat by Londo Mollari was a decisive reminder.

His head struck the floor when he went down, and just for a moment the world spun around him. He saw Londo standing over him, raging, and his hands seemed even larger as they descended, clearly ready to throttle him. Just for a moment, the normally confident Durla wondered whether he could actually withstand a concerted attack from the infuriated emperor.

And then, just like that, the threat passed. Because the emperor pitched back, clutching at his head. If someone had driven a spike through his skull, the reaction could not have been more pronounced. From the floor, Durla watched, utterly stupefied, as Londo staggered back. His eyes were tightly closed, and he seemed for all the world as if he wanted to do anything rather than scream. But then the scream came, and it was very loud and laced with agony.

It was more than enough to alert the guards outside that something was up. By the time they pushed through the door, Durla was on his feet, looking down at the writhing form of the emperor.

For a moment he wasn't entirely sure what to say. It wouldn't do for word to get out that the emperor had been so angry with Durla that he had assaulted him. It was hard to determine just how much popularity the emperor still possessed. Durla did not for a moment doubt that the people had come to love their prime minister, but the affection for the office of emperor was historical, tried and true. They certainly seemed to adore their figureheads, and the attendant pomp and circumstance.

"The emperor is having some sort of an attack," Durla said

quickly. "Have him brought to his quarters at once. Call a physician . . ."

"*No!*"

The word exploded from Londo as if torn from the depths of his dismay. And now Dunseny was at his side, propping him up. Londo's eyes were open wide as if there was agony still erupting behind them. "Highness, it's necessary," Dunseny said immediately. "I know your antipathy for physicians; you've not had more than the most cursory of examinations for over a decade. But in this instance . . ."

"In this instance," Londo managed to say, his voice still shaking, "I am still the emperor . . . and you are still . . . not." Whatever fit had taken hold of Londo seemed to be subsiding. "Help me up," he said in a vaguely commanding voice, and instantly several guards were at Londo's side, helping him to his feet.

One of them was Caso. Durla recognized him instantly. They exchanged a long look, then Caso helped the emperor to lean on his shoulders.

Durla had never been particularly impressed by Caso. He had struck Durla as faint of heart during the questioning of the traitor, Rem Lanas, and positively disconcerted upon the imprisonment of Milifa. When it had come time for Milifa to quietly die in prison, Caso had managed to absent himself to avoid taking part in that particular Prime Candidates function. His eagerness to clear the Narn, G'Kar, that day of the shooting, had not sat especially well with Durla, either.

Thinking of G'Kar and the prisons sent Durla's mind spinning in a particular direction, and he smiled faintly to himself. Without missing a beat, he turned to Londo, and said, "Highness . . . I hope you recover from your distress quite soon. And I shall remember our discussion for quite some time to come."

Londo was barely managing to lend any support to himself, but he still was able to summon enough strength to say, "I would strongly advise that you do so, Prime Minister . . . for all our sakes. Your treatment of young Sheridan, and of . . . others . . . shall not go unnoticed."

"No treatment shall," Durla replied, bowing slightly at the waist. His jaw was throbbing from where Londo had struck it, but he was not about to give Mollari the satisfaction of seeing him acknowledge it. "No treatment shall."

He waited until the room was empty, and then he turned and

went into the adjoining chamber. Mariel was sitting there, looking very concerned, and when Durla entered she immediately stood. "What happened?" she asked breathlessly.

"The emperor," Durla said evenly, "tried to attack me. In this instance, I did not have to hurt him. He was most fortunate. And it was your appearance, I think, that set him off. That was not appreciated, Mariel."

"I did not know he was there, my lord Durla." She bowed slightly. "My . . . hearing is not what it once was. I sustained an injury . . . in my clumsiness . . . that has reduced my hearing acuity. It is being treated, however, and a full recovery is expected."

The words were very carefully chosen and he knew it. He did not smile, merely nodded slightly. "For the duration, you will have to listen more closely," he told her.

"Yes, my lord husband." When she saw that he was heading out, she said, "Where are you going, my lord . . . if I may ask," she added quickly.

"I am going to visit an old friend with whom I have had some disagreements," Durla told her. He smiled. "I'm going to see if there's not some way we can't see eye to eye."

"That's very considerate, my lord."

"Yes. It is," he agreed. And just as the door closed behind him, Mariel let fly a spit of contempt. It landed on the door and ran noiselessly to the floor.

"Leave me," Londo managed to say.

Dunseny looked at him uncertainly. They had brought him back to his inner sanctum and helped settle him into a leaning couch. The manservant had been fussing over him for some time now, trying to make him comfortable and all the time wheedling him about having a physician brought in. Londo would not hear of it.

"Are you certain, Highness?" Dunseny asked solicitously. "Might it not be wiser to—"

"It might be wiser to do as I say," Londo told them. "Now go."

Seeing no other real options, Dunseny and the guards departed as they were instructed to do. Caso, the last one out, cast a glance over his shoulder in obvious worry. Then the door closed behind him.

"Well?" Londo asked, once everyone was gone. "What are you waiting for?"

The shadows moved, as he knew they would. In a moment, an all-too-familiar form was standing several feet away from him.

"How dare you," Shiv'kala said.

"How dare I?" Londo seemed amused. "How dare I know you would be there? I am so sorry. Did I ruin your surprise? Your flair for the dramatic?"

"You know what Durla is to us. You know what we have invested in him. He is our future, Londo." After his initial anger, Shiv'kala seemed relatively calm. "Not just ours . . . but yours as well."

"Is that so?" Londo was about to say something more, but suddenly he was seized by a racking cough. Shiv'kala waited patiently for the hacking to subside.

"Yes, that is so. I must admit to you, Londo . . . I am somewhat disappointed in you."

"I shall try to hide my extreme dismay over letting you down."

"I have spent many years with you now, Londo. I have explained to you the Drakh philosophies, the Drakh teaching. Tried to make you understand why we do what we do. Yet at every turn, you seem unwilling to embrace all we can do for you, bring to you . . ."

"You mean in the way Durla has."

"We have approached Durla differently than we did you. But yes, he shares our vision."

"He has the vision you implanted within him."

"No," Shiv'kala said, sounding almost sad. "Londo, how little you understand your own people. We have simply worked with that which already existed. We have unleashed the greatness that was within him, just as we have tried to do with you. Not just you, but your people as well. The Centauri Republic will be great, Londo—with you or without you."

"I had been hoping it would be both." Londo seemed rather amused by the comment.

Shiv'kala circled him. "Believe it or not, Londo, throughout the years, I have been your greatest ally. When others felt you simply were not worth the effort, I stood up for you. I spoke on your behalf. I argued that you could be brought around. That the time and effort being spent on you was not in vain. Then an incident such as this one occurs, and it leads me to wonder if the other Drakh were not correct."

"Meaning that I have let you down, and so you will kill me for it?" He seemed to consider this. "I do not see the threat. Death holds fewer and fewer terrors for me with each passing day."

"You say that now, when your life is not threatened," Shiv'kala commented. "It is always simple to laugh in the face of death when it is not facing you. In time, you may change your mind. This much, however, is certain, Londo. You will never lay hands upon Durla again. You will not threaten him, nor assault him. Nor will you attempt to dispatch any agents or cat's-paws to do likewise, because we will find out. And the pain that was inflicted upon you via the keeper today . . . will seem as nothing. If you do not trust my word in any other matter, I suggest you trust it in this: You will not survive."

"No one ever survives," Londo observed. "One just gets progressively worse opportunities to die."

There was a respectful knock at the door. Londo glanced at Shiv'kala, but the Drakh had already blended in with the shadows of the room. "Come," he called.

The door opened, and two members of the Prime Candidates entered. They carried between them a silver tray, covered with a cloth, which they placed on the table next to Londo. He looked at it with bleary curiosity. "Yes? What is it?"

"Compliments of Ministers Lione and Durla," one of the boys said. Then they turned and departed while Londo leaned forward and looked with curiosity at the covered tray.

A bomb, possibly. Or some sort of trap. At that moment, however, Londo didn't particularly care. He pulled off the cloth and gasped.

An eye was sitting on it, looking up at him.

Except it was no normal eye. It appeared to be solid, with a red tint to it . . .

"G'Kar," Londo whispered. There was a note on the tray next to it. With hands trembling, he picked it up and read it.

"The noble Citizen G'Kar is being forced to send his regrets. He is feeling somewhat put out at the moment, and will not be able to join you for dinner in the foreseeable future. Instead he will be undergoing an intensive, rigorous 'training program' to make certain he remains in good shape. We trust our meaning has been made clear, and will not be forgotten."

* * *

Londo started to stand, as if to go charging to G'Kar's aid. "Where do you think you are going?" Shiv'kala asked calmly. That was not unusual. He was calm most of the time. Icy, like a frozen planet, and with about as much chance of displaying pity or mercy. "Certainly you are not considering helping your pet Narn, are you?"

Londo pointed in fury at the eye. "This was your idea, I take it?"

"No, actually. We probably would have thought of it . . . but the truth is that Durla conceived of it all on his own. It will not go well for the Narn, I fear. But he will not die. Durla would not want that to happen, for if he dies, then he cannot be a source of ongoing torment for you."

"Bastards!" Londo spat out, and he started for the door.

Then the pain came again. Londo got only a few steps before it overwhelmed him, like an ocean wave batters a sand castle to bits. Londo staggered back and sank into the cushions.

"Some quiet time for you now, Londo, I think," Shiv'kala told him, as if addressing an angry child. "A day or so to contemplate your actions, and why it would be most unwise to repeat those actions."

"Must . . . stop him . . ."

"You cannot," Shiv'kala said. "You cannot stop any of this. It has gone too far. Within days now, the fleet will be launched. Durla will see to it. He has prepared for it extremely well. And you cannot—will not—do anything to stop it, Londo. Otherwise I will make certain that Durla does indeed go too far in his . . . what was the phrase . . . 'training program' for G'Kar. And that will be the least of the recriminations that await you . . . all in retaliation for anything you might try to do, none of which could hope to succeed.

"The only thing you will succeed in doing is injuring yourself . . . and others. G'Kar, Senna, even that absurd Vir Cotto, for whom you continue to have foolish affection. All of them will know the punishments attendant in your failed attempts to stop the unstoppable.

"Have we made ourselves clear, Londo?"

"Painfully so, yes." He managed to nod his head.

"As I told you, Londo . . . believe it or not, we have been merciful until now. Do not, at any time, mistake mercy for weakness. We are not weak. We are Drakh. We are of the Shadows. Is that also clear, Londo?"

This time he didn't even bother to speak. He just nodded.

"I am pleased we had this opportunity to chat, Londo."

And then, rather unexpectedly, Londo managed to get out, "The boy . . . the Sheridan boy . . ."

"What about him?" If the Drakh had had an eyebrow, he would have cocked it in curiosity.

"Bringing him here . . . is insanity. Crossing his father, crossing Delenn . . . the Earth fleet, the Minbari fleet will be brought down upon us. Even you cannot possibly think that we can withstand such an assault. The Minbari fleet alone could level this world."

"Very likely. But such an action would only result in the boy's death, and Sheridan and Delenn will not risk that. They will come here, alone and unattended. We know this for a certainty. And when they come here, you, Londo, will oversee their execution."

"On what grounds?"

"On the grounds that they are responsible for sending the Shadows away. They will pay for that with their lives."

"And the boy?"

"We have plans for the boy. With his parents gone, he will 'escape,' and live to serve our interests."

"Your interests?" Then he laughed bitterly. "Oh. Of course. The keeper."

"In the vase that you left, yes. Had you forgotten about that?"

"I tried to. Unfortunately, I seem to remember all the things I would rather forget, and forget that which I really should remember. When I brought the keeper in the urn . . . I hoped . . . it was for the purpose of spying. That was all. Influencing his father and mother on Minbar, perhaps. I never thought that this . . ."

The Drakh leaned in close to him. "Never forget," he said, "who is in charge. It will go badly for you if you do."

And with that, he left Londo sitting alone in his room—in a pain-filled silence enforced by the keeper—trying to determine just how things could possibly go more badly than they already were.

EXCERPT FROM
THE CHRONICLES OF LONDO MOLLARI.

EXCERPT FROM
THE CHRONICLES OF LONDO MOLLARI.
Excerpt dated (approximate Earth date)
December 3, 2277.

I had to call her.

I sat here, stewing for days, thinking about what I had seen . . . thinking about what that bastard Durla had done to Mariel, even knowing my protection extended to her after her return to the Palace. And I kept thinking to myself, At least your hands are clean. For all your crimes, for all that can be laid at your feet . . . at least you have never treated a woman in such a manner.

And then I thought about that some more, really thought.

I thought of Adira . . . my beautiful Adira. The dancer who elevated my past, haunted my present, and would never be a part of my future. When she died, I took certain . . . steps . . . which drove me down the dark road I currently tread.

I thought of Mariel, an appendage to that man, that monstrosity of a man. If I had never divorced her, she would not be in this position. I know, I know . . . to ensure her own future, she tried to kill me. But in a way . . . should I be entirely surprised? She observed the men in the society in which she was raised. My gender taught her the lessons to which she subscribed. If she was raised to be devious, to hold little regard for life . . . who am I now to condemn her? One who has led a stainless life myself? If I were not subject to coughing fits, I would laugh heartily at that.

I thought of Daggair, another wife of mine . . . eh. Well . . . I did not think of her too much. There is only so much guilt even I will feel.

And then there is Timov. Timov, whom I shunted away, for her own good. Making her believe that I do not, did not ever, truly love her. The thing is, she was a woman of boundless integrity and sharp wit. Had we ever truly been a team—Great Maker, the things we could have accomplished.

I felt the need to say this to her. To make her realize that I did truly value her. And—I have to admit it—to cleanse my own guilt, for in my own way I had abused her just as thoroughly as Durla had done Mariel. Abused her trust, abused her affection. I owed it to her, somehow, to make reparations for this.

Foolish. Foolish old man.

When my—small associate—freed me after a time of enforced "meditation," I resolved that I had delayed long enough. Too long, in fact. Years too long. I knew that she no longer resided on Centauri Prime but instead had relocated to one of the outlying worlds. It was not difficult for me to establish a real-time link with her. A woman whom I recognized as a longtime retainer to Timov answered my communiqué and looked most surprised indeed to see that she was being contacted by the emperor himself. She told me that her mistress would be right there.

Long minutes passed. I surmised that Timov was making me wait out of spite.

I was wrong.

When a wan and drawn woman appeared on the screen, for a moment I did not recognize her. There was none of the fiery robustness I had come to associate with the razor-sharp spitfire called Timov, but then I realized that yes, indeed, it was she.

She sat there, staring at me. Not saying a word. The only part of her that seemed to be truly alive was her eyes, and those blazed with the fire of inner vision.

"Timov," I said, surprised at the huskiness of my voice. I started to say, "You are looking well," but nothing could have been further from the truth, and we both knew it. So instead I cleared my throat and started to say her name again.

She cut me off curtly. "It's true. Are you satisfied? Obviously you're calling to see for yourself if whatever you've heard is correct. So . . . you're seeing. Good enough?"

"I have heard nothing," I said quite honestly. It may have been the most honest thing I'd said to her in years . . . if not ever.

"You haven't heard that I'm dying," she said with such contempt in her tone that it was clear she didn't believe it for a moment.

I have never taken quite as long to say a single, one-syllable word as I did at that moment. "No," I finally managed to get out.

"Mm-hmm." Still she did not believe. I could not blame her. "All right, then. Why, after all this time, have you called?"

"I . . ."

Everything I wanted to say to her flooded through my mind. But nothing came out.

She scowled in that way she had. "Londo . . . you chased me off Centauri Prime. You have treated me with disrespect that you would not show to your greatest enemy. You have exhibited contempt for me, you have—"

"I know, I know. I have done all these things. I know."

"I am the empress and have been dealt with as if I were the lowliest of slaves. And now, after all this time, what could you possibly have to say?"

"Why are you dying?" I managed to say.

"To annoy you. Anything else?" She seemed anxious to end the transmission, to do anything except talk to me, be anywhere except on a line with me. A hundred responses went through my mind, and only one emerged.

"I want you to know . . . I am sorry," I said.

She stared at me as if I'd lost my mind. The seconds passed like an infinity.

Then her eyes softened ever so slightly. "You should be. But not for what you imagine you're calling to apologize for."

"I'm afraid I—"

"You don't understand. But then you rarely took the time to understand, or even to consider your actions. You were impulsive the night you banished me from Centauri Prime." The effort of speaking took a great deal from her. She stopped to breathe, and I said nothing.

"I have been less impulsive and have had more time to speculate, given my current condition. Londo, I know about your dilemma."

"How could you possibly know?"

"Do you not remember Lady Morella? You asked her to tell you about your future."

"That was a private transaction."

"Mmm, everything important to a Centauri is a private transaction, hence everything important to a Centauri is open to public scrutiny. I'm your wife, Londo. Even in exile, I know almost everything you do.

"It comes with the territory." She did not say these words flippantly. In fact, her eyes burned brighter.

Ah, yes, Timov knew just as all empresses knew of their husband's good fortune and ill omens. I saw what she was saying now. She was implying that Lady Morella, previously a telepath somewhat stronger in psionic capability than the average empress, was granted special vision as the wife of Emperor Turhan.

Timov knew. As Lady Morella knew. I had to warn her. "It is very dangerous for you to speculate on these things. That is why you are kept in exile."

"I know that. You are surrounded in darkness, and it is a darkness I know better than to penetrate."

"I should go, Timov. I just wanted to call to say . . . many things. None of them expressible now."

"Good-bye, Londo," she said briskly.

I reached to cut off the transmission, and Timov abruptly said, "Londo . . ."

My hand paused over the cutoff switch. "Yes?"

"If you need me, call."

"I won't be needing you."

"I know," she said tartly. "That's why I made the offer."

The screen blinked off. And I knew at that moment that I would never see her again. But at least I had tried. Tried . . . and failed.

If I cannot achieve greatness, at least I can aspire to consistency.

15

Vir was hurriedly packing in his quarters on Babylon 5 when an urgent beeping at his door interrupted him.

"Go away!" he called.

"We need to talk," came a surprisingly familiar voice. And yet it wasn't entirely too much of a surprise. In fact, the main surprise for Vir was that it hadn't occurred sooner.

"Come," he called, his command disengaging the door lock.

Michael Garibaldi entered, looking entirely too calm. He glanced around. "Going somewhere?"

"Yes. You could say th—"

And then, before Vir could say anything further, Garibaldi was across the room. He grabbed Vir by the shirtfront and slammed him up against a wall, knocking over furniture.

"I don't think so," Garibaldi said, and he spoke with barely contained fury. "I think you're going to tell me exactly how you think your people are going to get away with—"

He stopped. There was a blade pressed up against his throat, the hilt gripped solidly in Vir's hand. And Vir was staring into Garibaldi's eyes with absolutely no trace of fear. Any resemblance to the Vir Cotto who first set foot on Babylon 5 was long gone.

"What I think," Vir said in a low voice, "is that you're going to get your damned hands off me. And then we will talk like the reasonable men I know that one of us is."

Very slowly, Garibaldi released his hold on Vir's shirt and stepped back, keeping the palms of his hands up where Vir could readily see them. "The only reason you got away with that," he said, "was that you were the last person I would have thought capable of doing it."

"That's how I get away with a lot of things these days," Vir told him. He slid the blade back into the scabbard that was hidden under his vest. He studied Garibaldi a moment. The former security chief was unshaven and glassy-eyed. "How long since you've slept?"

"Did you know about it?" Garibaldi demanded.

"About your not sleeping?" Vir was completely lost.

"About David?"

"David." It took Vir a moment to place the name. "Sheridan's son. What about him?"

"They have him."

Once again it took Vir a few moments to follow the track of the conversation . . . but then he understood. "Great Maker, no," he whispered.

"Great Maker, yes."

Vir walked around to the bar and promptly poured himself a drink. He held up the bottle to Garibaldi as an offering. Garibaldi took the bottle, stared at it a moment, then took a deep smell of the alcohol wafting from it before placing it back on the bar. "It's a good vintage," Vir said, slightly surprised.

"Maybe some other time . . . like when I'm on my deathbed."

"Tell me what happened. Tell me everything."

Something in Vir's voice must have convinced Garibaldi, for after only a moment's hesitation, he laid out the circumstances involving David's disappearance, in quick, broad strokes. When he mentioned the small lump of a creature on David's shoulder, Vir slowly nodded. "Drakh," he said.

"What? What about the Drakh?" Garibaldi said.

"Go on. I'll tell you in a minute."

So Garibaldi continued, and when he was finished, Vir simply sat there, contemplating his drink. "His parents are going out of their minds with worry."

"They have every reason to," Vir said. His eyes narrowed. "I think their friends are going a bit crazy, too."

"Sorry about . . . earlier," Garibaldi told him, gesturing to indicate his unexpected assault on Vir. "You said 'Drakh' before. Are you talking about the same Drakh who inflicted the plague on Earth?"

"The very same. That thing that you saw on David? Londo has one like it on him. It's how they control you, or watch you, or something like that."

"Are you saying," Garibaldi said slowly, "that the Drakh are somehow involved with Centauri Prime? With this kidnapping?"

Vir took a deep breath and let it out. "Yes. They have been for some time. They control Londo. I suspect they control Durla, to some degree. I also have reason to believe that a Drakh was involved in the death of Lou Welch."

"You told me it was the Prime Candidates."

"It was. But the Drakh apparently helped." He shook his head. "The plague they inflicted on Earth is not dissimilar from the plague they've inflicted on my world as well . . . except on Centauri Prime it's more covert."

"I don't understand. Why didn't you tell me this sooner?"

"I couldn't take the chance," Vir admitted. "These are agents of the Shadows we're talking about. I was concerned that if you knew they were on Centauri Prime, you would tell Sheridan, Sheridan would tell the Alliance, and that would have been all that was needed for the Alliance to come down on my people, attack without hesitation. The Centauri, after all, were seen as a beaten people. The Drakh would have been something that you would have gone after . . . but Centauri Prime would have suffered. You would have killed the patient in order to annihilate the disease."

"And you're not worried about that anymore?"

"Why should I be?" Vir said reasonably. "They have David. I doubt Sheridan's going to order a strike on a world when it would ensure the death of his son."

"Pretty damned cold-blooded of you, Vir."

"I've had to make some pretty cold-blooded choices in recent years, Mr. Garibaldi. You get used to it." He sighed. "Perhaps I should have gone public sooner. By allowing them to dwell in the dark, I've let them fester and grow. But exposing them might well have meant the death of my people. With any luck, though, we'll be able to have it both ways now. We've mustered enough resistance that the Drakh can be revealed for what they are without it amounting to a death sentence for Centauri Prime."

"You told me to trust you," Garibaldi said, stabbing a finger at Vir. "You told me to let you handle things. To let the Centauri solve the problems of Centauri Prime. And I've been doing that. But it's no longer just the Centauri's problem. It's John Sheridan's problem, and Delenn's."

"I'll handle it."

"*Vir!*"

"I said I'll handle it," Vir repeated firmly. "I'm heading to Centauri Prime right now. I've spent years—years of planning and preparing, of risking my neck and the necks of others—and it's all coming to a head. The fact that David was taken is just further indication of that. The Drakh want vengeance . . . but more than that, they also want insurance. But all the insurance in the world isn't going to help them against someone they don't know is their enemy. Someone they think of as a patsy, a fool."

"I'm coming with you."

"Now *you're* the fool," Vir said. He walked over to Garibaldi and put a hand on his shoulder. "We'll get David back for you, Michael. But we have to do it our way."

"Who is we?"

"The Legions of Fire."

Garibaldi looked at him oddly. "What?"

Vir smiled thinly. "I've found Earth history as interesting as Londo does. There are all sorts of end-of-the-world scenarios, did you know that? And one of them—from your Norse, I think it is—describes the world ending when a giant fire demon, Surtur, sweeps the world with his sword and cleanses it of all evil. That's what the Legions of Fire are going to do, Michael. We're going to sweep Centauri Prime clean of the blackness that's been upon it for so long. We're going to expose the Drakh presence to the rest of the galaxy. That way, we can point to those who are truly responsible for the fate of Centauri Prime. Prove that it's the Drakh who should be blamed . . . and that this prolonged campaign of resentment and aggression has been aimed at the wrong people. That it should be stopped."

"And you really call yourselves the Legions of Fire."

"Do you have a better name?" Vir asked, mildly annoyed. "We could call ourselves 'Vir's Victory Squad' or 'Cotto's Crusaders,' but that might tip off who's in charge."

"No, no, it's fine. Legions of Fire. Fine." Garibaldi took a deep breath, steadying himself. "Vir . . . he's my godson . . . and Sheridan and Delenn are my best friends in the galaxy . . ."

"And believe it or not, I'm your second best friend," Vir said. "I'll get the job done, and David home safely. You have my word."

"I didn't used to think that meant a lot," Garibaldi said, and then he shook Vir's hand firmly. "But now I believe it does."

By the time Garibaldi returned to Minbar, Sheridan and Delenn were gone.

16

Durla could not recall a time that he had wanted to cry tears of pure joy the way that he did at that moment. It was just as it had been in his dream. In fact, it was all he could do to make sure that he was not asleep.

There were ships everywhere. Everywhere. The skies above the spaceport were filled with them. The ground was likewise thick with ships preparing to take off.

They had come from all over, a few at a time, assembling on the only planet that seemed appropriate: the world designated K0643. The site of the failed excavation program had remained for him a stain on his otherwise perfect record. Now, however, he was prepared to erase that stain by using this backwater, nothing world as the jumping-off point for the greatest campaign in the history of the Centauri Republic.

The spaceport itself was nothing particularly wonderful. The buildings had been thrown together in a purely makeshift fashion. The command center, the barracks, all of them, shoddy construction. But they were serviceable, and that was the only important thing. All of the perfection of construction, all of the craft and abilities of the hundreds of workers who had brought this moment to fruition . . . that was what mattered.

General Rhys and all of his command staff were assembled, with last-minute checks being made, final preparations being completed. "The jumpgate has been fully tested and is on-line, General?" Durla asked.

Rhys nodded. "Absolutely, Prime Minister."

"No chance of sabotage?" he said darkly. "It will not go well for anyone, General, if anything should go wrong while ships are going through."

"I tell you, sir, it is impossible," Rhys stated flatly. "It cannot, *will* not happen."

"Well, then," and Durla nodded with approval. "That's heartening to hear." He looked around at the others, all waiting for his words. Surprisingly, he found himself thinking of his brother, the one whose death he had arranged out of a fit of jealousy. From time to time he had found himself wondering whether he had done the right thing. Now there was absolutely no question that he had. He had achieved the pinnacle of success, and if it was over his brother's dead body, well . . . so much the better.

"We all understand, then," Durla said. They all nodded. Naturally they did. And yet he couldn't help but outline the intent of the fleet again, simply because he loved the sound of it: the words, the plan, his own voice. All of it. "We intend to launch a multistage assault on the Homeworlds of ninety percent of the Alliance governments. The ten percent we are sparing are small and relatively helpless . . . and besides, we're going to need to get our new workers from somewhere, so we'd best leave a few worlds intact, correct?" He laughed at this, and the others quickly joined in. *They know what's good for them,* he thought grimly, and continued, "If we strike hard enough, fast enough, we can immobilize them and pave the way for full-scale assaults on their holdings. This plan of attack will leave them powerless against further Centauri aggression."

"Powerless," one of the captains echoed. "I like the sound of that." The others nodded in approval.

"We have," he said proudly, "over three thousand vessels at our disposal. They represent the result of almost two decades of slave labor. Oh, the Alliance has had its suspicions, the rumors have floated about. But in the end—an end which is coming quite soon—they were too lazy, and we, too clever."

"The Alliance does have more ships at its disposal," Rhys cautioned, clearly worried that his men might become overconfident. "The White Star fleet alone is a formidable one."

"True," Durla admitted, but then added, "however, we certainly have the single largest armada belonging to one government. We need not worry about intergovernmental disputes, or differences of opinion on the best way to attack. We will operate with one mind and one purpose, and in doing that . . . we cannot lose."

"Coordination is indeed going to be the key," General Rhys said. "Prime Minister, if I may . . ." Durla gestured for him to continue. "You all have been given predetermined points in hyperspace that will provide you access to each of your respective targets. Fail-safe points, if you will. You will stay on point until everyone is in place. Then we will launch full, simultaneous strikes on all the targets at once. You will attack military sites, the capitals, and communication centers, cutting off all the Alliance worlds from one another, instilling fear, and dividing them in panic. Since the Centauri fleet outnumbers any other single fleet, we will be able to hit our enemies in waves, one after the other, before the Alliance can organize its scattered members into any kind of cohesive force." He took a deep breath, and said, "On receiving the go-codes from the prime minister, you will launch your assaults."

There was a momentary confused look shared among the captains. One of them said, "Not from you, sir?"

"Do you not trust my judgment, Captain?" Durla demanded suspiciously.

"I did not say that at all, Prime Minister. It is just that, since this is a military operation . . ."

"And the military operation has been sabotaged repeatedly," Durla pointed out. "With all respect to yourselves, and very much to General Rhys . . . , the one person I know I can trust is me. It has been my vision, my drive that has brought us to this point, and my words will launch the attack. Is that understood? Do all of you understand that?"

There was a chorus of "Yes, sir" from around the table.

Durla nodded in approval. "Then, gentlemen . . . to work."

As one, they rose from the table, filing out of the room and stopping only to congratulate the prime minister on his momentous achievement. At the last, General Rhys hesitated. "Prime Minister . . ."

"It will be a masterpiece of coordination, General," Durla told him. In his mind's eye, he could already see it. "I am coordinating with Minister Vallko. He is going to be having one of his spiritual gatherings at the great temple. There, I will address the people, and speak to them of our capturing the glory that is Centauri Prime. We will stand on the brink of history . . . and then I will transmit the go-codes. And the rise from the great blackness will begin."

General Rhys looked as if he were about to say something, but then thought better of it. Instead he simply said, "It has been an honor to serve under you, Prime Minister."

"Yes. It has, hasn't it."

* * *

He was right. It was just like in his dream, a dream made into reality.

Durla stood on a cliffside, and stretched out his arms as the ships roared to life and took off, one by one. And as each one swung by him, throbbing with power, they banked slightly in acknowledgment. They bowed to him.

Just as everyone would. Sheridan and Delenn, who had by this point been informed of the whereabouts of their son, and were no doubt on their way to Centauri Prime. Once there, they would become public symbols of the humiliation that had been heaped upon the great Centauri Republic, and their fate would represent all the Alliance had to look forward to.

And Londo . . . well, Londo would probably decide that he had contributed all that he could to Centauri Prime. He would step aside willingly and name Durla as regent until such time that Londo's passing would ensure Durla's appointment as emperor. Then, of course, that time would come quite, quite soon.

The skies were so thick with ships that they blotted out the sun. It was as if night had fallen upon Durla. An endless night of glory, waiting to swallow him. And he fed himself to it willingly.

17

"You should not have come here," Senna said as the small vehicle took them toward the palace. "Vir, this was not a good time . . ."

"I had to," he said as the Centauri Prime spaceport receded into the background. "I stopped receiving communiqués from Mariel. I lost track of where Durla's plans stood. I was . . ."

"Concerned for her?" Senna asked.

He nodded. "And not just for her . . . also for you, and Londo. And now apparently David Sheridan has been added to the mix. You knew about this?"

She nodded, looking grim. "It's a terrible thing. He simply showed up. No one knew he was coming, not even Lione, and he was most upset about it. The only one who did not seem surprised was Durla. Sometimes I think nothing surprises him."

"Oh, I think we can arrange a surprise or two for him," Vir said grimly. "Can you get me in to see Mariel?"

"He's put her into seclusion. She's not allowed visitors."

"So you can't."

She smiled. "I didn't say that."

Senna strode up to the two guards who were standing outside Durla's suite of rooms, and said firmly, "The emperor wishes to see you."

They looked at one another, and then back to Senna. "Why?" one of them asked.

"I have known the man for nearly half my life, and if there is one thing I have learned, it is never to ask why. Lately, he does not take well to that . . . if you know what I mean." And she put a finger to her temple and mimed a weapon being fired.

The guards hesitated a moment. Senna crossed her arms and displayed her best look of impatience. "I do not think the emperor likes to be kept waiting."

Durla had ordered that a guard be kept outside his suite at all times. But Durla was not around, and Senna was well known to be trusted by the emperor. Somehow it seemed that ignoring the emperor's wishes, as relayed by Senna, might prove to have a negative impact on their life expectancy.

They bowed slightly to Senna and hurried off down the corridor.

The moment they were gone, Senna whispered, "Vir!" In response to her summons, Vir hustled down the corridor to her side. "The door is sealed," she told him. "So I am not quite certain how we can get in . . ."

Vir, looking utterly confident, pulled a small device from the interior of his jacket. He aimed it at the door, and it emitted a brief burst of noise. The door promptly slid open.

Senna glanced at the device appraisingly. "Where did you get that?"

"I move with an interesting group of people these days," Vir replied, and without another word walked into Durla's suite of rooms. Senna followed.

He took a few steps in and then stopped. There, on the balcony, looking out at the city, was Mariel. At least, he was reasonably sure it was she. Her back was to him. "Mariel," he called cautiously.

Mariel turned and looked at him, and it seemed as if she could scarcely believe what she was seeing. Nor could Vir entirely believe his eyes, either. The woman he had known, the vibrant, beautiful young woman, was gone. She had been replaced by someone whose face exhibited unending sadness, whose skin carried with it fading bruises that hinted of past atrocities.

"Vir," she whispered, and ran to him. She threw her arms around him, held him tightly, kissed him with such ferocity that he actually had to apply strength to separate her from him. "Vir . . . you've finally come to take me out of here?"

"Mariel, sit down."

"Vir!" She allowed herself to be guided over to a chair. "You don't know how long I've waited," she said. "Is it finally over? When do we leave? I do not care that I am still married to Durla, I will go with you, do whatever you want . . ."

She was speaking so fast, she was almost incomprehensible, and he gripped her firmly by the arms, kneeling so that they were on eye level. "Mariel . . . first things first. What is Durla doing? Where is he now?"

"I don't know," she said.

"What is his timetable? Where stand the ships he's been working on? How close to completion are—"

"I don't know, *I don't know!*" Her voice was rising, and Vir realized that she was rapidly coming to the end of her rope. "He doesn't talk to me anymore, doesn't tell me anything about anything! I don't know what his plans are, and I don't care anymore! I just want to be with you! The two of us, as it was always meant to be!"

"Vir, this isn't getting us anywhere. We should go," Senna warned him in a low voice.

"Vir, you can't." Mariel was clutching on to his arm, and all last traces of dignity, of strength, fell away from her. "Vir, you can't leave me here . . ."

"Mariel, it's not that easy. No harm will come to you, I promise, but I can't just take you out of here. We'll be noticed, we'll . . ."

"I don't care! Don't you *understand*, Vir? All that I have endured, I have endured for you! My love for you, it is boundless, it is endless. Please, Vir, I will do whatever you ask, whenever you ask! I have done nothing but dream of you, night after night. Whenever I was in his arms, it was yours I imagined. His lips crushing against mine, but I felt them to be yours and took comfort from that! You are my everything, my—"

"Stop it!" He felt as if what remained of his soul were being shredded. "Stop it, Mariel! You don't know what you're saying!"

"Yes, I do! I have heard it in my head, night after night, when I dreamt of you coming for me. It is all that matters, it is the only thing, it—"

"It's not real!"

He had not expected to say it. He had not wanted to say it. For years, the guilt he had carried within him had given him no peace, but he had still been sure that he would be able to contain the dark truth of what he had done. What was to be gained from telling her? Nothing. And yet when the words burst from him, he knew it was because his presence in her life was a lie, and he could not allow her to live it anymore. It was the only chance she had of divesting herself from the hellish existence that she currently endured. He had to try to undo the damage he had done to her.

She stared at him in confusion. "Not . . . real? What is not . . . real?"

"This thing you . . ." He took a breath and then turned to Senna. "Please . . . I need to talk to Mariel alone. Please."

Senna didn't understand, but she did not need to. "As you wish," she said, and she took Vir's hands in hers briefly and squeezed them. Then she walked quickly from the main room, the door shutting behind her.

Vir went back to Mariel, took her hands in his, and said, "You're under a spell."

"A spell." She repeated the words, but with no real comprehension.

"A techno-mage named Galen put it on you, at my request. I was . . . I was angry because I knew you had used me, to get in good with the other diplomats on Babylon 5. I knew you laughed at me behind my back. And I . . ." He looked down. ". . . I told myself that I had him do it to help the cause. So that I could bend you to my will, turn you back on the people who'd sent you to spy on me. But that was an excuse. I did it from petty revenge, and it was beneath me, and I've ruined your life, and I'm sorry. Great Maker, the words don't mean anything, but I am. I'm sorry."

"Vir . . ."

"Londo. Londo can help. He can grant you a divorce from Durla, and you can start over in a new life. We'll get you set up somewhere, I can—"

"Vir, it's all right."

He stopped talking and stared at her. "All right? How is it all right?"

"I saw. I saw the way Senna looked at you, and you at her. How she held your hand a moment before leaving. You think," and she laughed, "you think that I would not want to share you. That my love for you is so overpowering that I would be jealous of other women in your life." She stroked his cheek. "If you want both Senna and me, that is perfectly all right. Whatever makes you happy . . ."

"Mariel, I don't love you! Don't you see? I can't ever! Because any feelings you'd return for me were made for you by Galen!"

Her face flushed. "I don't know why you're saying these things. I know my mind! I know how I feel! No wizard put these thoughts into my head! You're just . . . testing me, that's it. Testing me . . . wanting me to prove my love to you, to—"

"No! I don't! It's—"

Suddenly the door at the far end of the room slid open. The guards were standing there, with Senna in between them.

"The emperor will see you now," Senna said gravely.

"He is not supposed to be in here!" one of the guards said.

"I heard her cry out," Vir said immediately. "I was outside and when I heard her cry of alarm, I thought that perhaps one of those saboteurs or someone like that was attacking Durla's wife. So I thought I would check, because there were, after all, no guards outside," he added pointedly. He bowed to Mariel, and asked solicitously, "Will you be all right, milady?"

Mariel, looking at him with limpid eyes, whispered, "I will prove my love."

Vir felt ill.

Vir looked ill.

At the very least, there were times when he had certainly looked better.

It is amusing the way things work out sometimes. There I was, speaking with Dunseny, saying to him, "You know what I desire more than anything? I would like to share a pleasant dinner with my old friend, Vir. Do you think that could be arranged?"

At that moment, in walked Senna with two guards. They stood stiffly at attention, as if they were awaiting orders. I had no idea what they wanted me to say. I looked to Dunseny, but he clearly had no better idea than I did. "Can I help you?" I inquired.

"We were told that you desired our presence, Highness," one of them said.

I didn't know what he was talking about. But I saw Senna standing behind them, nodding her head. Obviously this was some sort of childish prank and, to be honest, I thought it might prove amusing. I think I am someone very much in need of more childishness in my life. I found my head nodding in time to Senna's own. "Yes . . . yes," I said. "As a matter of fact, I would like you to bring me Vir Cotto."

The guards exchanged glances. "The ambassador to Babylon 5?"

"The very same," I said.

"I . . . believe I know where he can be found, Highness," Senna said. "He is actually here, in the palace."

I was astounded. Rarely do things work out for me as conveniently as that. "Escort him here at once!" I commanded the guards. As Senna led the apparently puzzled guards out, I turned to Dunseny, and said, "Have a meal prepared and brought up. Vir and I shall . . . chat . . ."

"At once, Highness," Dunseny said, and he went out to attend to my wishes.

The dinner was brought up mere moments before Vir arrived, escorted by Senna. "You will pardon me if I do not get up, Vir," I said. "My stamina is not quite what it used to be."

"Of course, of course," he said.

The food was laid out between us, and I gestured for everyone to leave us. Of course . . . I myself am never alone, but that is neither here nor there.

"So . . . Vir. What has brought you around?" I proceeded to eat heartily, displaying an appetite that was merely for show.

"Do I need an excuse to visit my Homeworld?" he asked. He wasn't touching any of the food in front of him. Perhaps he thought it was poisoned. If it were poisoned, I probably would have eaten it myself.

"Of course not. Of course not."

And we proceeded to chat. The conversation was strained at first, but as the time passed, the degree of comfort grew. He seemed guarded, even suspicious, and who could blame him really? After all, once before when we were together, I knocked him out and he wound up in a cell. For all he knew, this would be a repeat performance.

Really, it was not an important conversation, when one gets right down to it. Indeed, my memory is playing tricks on me. Much of what we discussed is gone from my head already. The drink, no doubt. However, there was one aspect that he seemed to find most . . . interesting.

"There is a Human work of literature that I stumbled over, Vir, that reminded me a bit of you and I."

"And what would that be, Londo?"

"The work of one Miguel de Cervantes. A book called Don Quixote. I'm in the middle of reading it, but it seems most fascinating. It is about a man with a most odd hobby. Do you appreciate odd hobbies, Vir? You have one or two yourself, I think."

He sat there for a moment, his face impassive. "We all have our hobbies, Londo, and each of them might seem odd to someone who doesn't participate in it."

"Oh, absolutely. But this fellow, this Don Quixote . . . I thought you might appreciate his particular hobby. I don't know why I did. But I did."

"And what would that hobby be, Londo?"

"He fights evil." I leaned forward. "He fights evil wherever he sees it. He even fights evil when no others see it. Even though he believes the odds to be hopelessly against him, he charges into battle against the forces of darkness. Many people in the book think him insane."

"Do they." There was no inflection in his voice.

"Yes. They do. But there is a handful of others . . . who do not."

"And who would these be?"

"One of them is his faithful squire—that is to say, assistant—Sancho. Sancho helps the intrepid Quixote on his missions, no matter how far-fetched, because he wants to help Quixote recognize his dreams. To validate them. To fight . . . against the forces of darkness."

"Yes . . . you mentioned those," Vir said slowly. "I . . . think I understand."

"And that reminded me of you . . . and even us. I think that once upon a time, Vir . . . I was Quixote. I had dreams of greatness, of what the Centauri Republic should be. And you . . . you were my Sancho," and I laughed and shook a fist. "At my side, supporting me in my efforts while at the same time trying to get me to see the reality of what I was doing."

"And when Sancho tried to explain reality to Quixote . . . did he understand?"

"Not really," I admitted. "Interesting the parallels that can be drawn, eh? And now, you know . . . I think that the roles have turned. I think, in many ways, you are the new Quixote, yes? You see a world that you want to be better than it is, and you fight the good fight to make it that way. And that would make me Sancho . . . trying to assist you . . . to tell you what is what. To tell you when dark forces are encroaching, and when time is running out."

"I think . . . in that respect . . . you would be an excellent Sancho."

"Good, good." I paused and took a deep breath. "Would you like to know . . . one of the ways in which the good Quixote fought evil?"

"Very much, yes."

I quaffed more of my drink, and said, "Windmills."

He looked at me oddly. "Windmills? What are windmills?"

"They were tall structures . . . very tall structures, and things were made inside them. Very tall structures . . . that seemed ordinary . . . but Quixote saw them as something else. He saw them as giants, and he attacked them. Charged at them with a long stick. It was called 'tilting.' He tilted at windmills."

"So he was insane, is what you are saying."

"Ahhh, but that is the test, Vir, you see. To look at tall buildings and say they are giants is, of course, insanity. But to look at towering structures and say they might be giants, why . . . that proves you a man of vision. A man who can see things when others do not, and act accordingly. That way . . . that way you can be prepared to do what must be done." I emptied my glass, poured myself another. "You might want to read the book, Vir. Reading is one of your hobbies, yes?"

"Yes. One of them."

"You should read it, then, definitely. Because it might have a very dramatic impact on your other hobbies . . . very soon."

18

Their voices were echoing throughout the catacombs, and it took all Vir's lung power to shout them down.

They had gathered quickly at Vir's summons; indeed, they'd been prepared for it ever since Renegar had filtered the word out that Vir was coming to Centauri Prime. Even the techno-mages had managed to show up, although how they knew to come—and why they weren't spotted when they moved about on the surface of Centauri Prime—was pretty much anyone's guess.

"I don't understand any of it!" Renegar said in frustration. "Windmills and Coyote—"

"Quixote."

"Whatever it is! How does this relate to—"

"He was speaking to me in a code," Vir told them. "I'm positive."

"What sort of code?" Adi asked suspiciously.

"The kind of code that only two people who've known each other for years could get away with. He was being watched and couldn't say anything overt . . . but he was subtle enough that I got it."

"Or you were misreading it," Finian suggested. "You could have been hearing what you wanted to hear."

"No," Vir said fiercely. "I heard what he wanted me to hear, and he was doing it to help." He started ticking off points on his fingers. "He knows I'm involved with the Legions of Fire . . ."

"The what?" they chorused.

"You guys. Never mind that now. He knows that I'm tied in with the saboteurs. He was trying to tell me that Durla is on the verge of making his move. That the Drakh are present in large numbers on Centauri Prime. That if we're going to do something about it, we're going to have to do it now."

"We don't know that for sure," one of the others said. "Perhaps the thing to do is wait, to—"

"*No,*" Vir said, stunning the others into silence. "You didn't see what I saw. You didn't see the look in his eyes, the desperation. He wants this stopped as much as we do. He knows that this insane plan of Durla's, this scheming by the Drakh, is only going to end in tragedy for all. We have to strike openly, publicly, and with finality. We have to turn over the rock that the Drakh are hiding under. It's the only way!"

"Londo might have been setting us up . . ." Renegar ventured. "If he's a tool of the Drakh, as you say . . ."

"Then why play games, huh? If he suspects that I'm involved with the underground, why not just tell the Drakh? Watch me disappear," and he snapped his fingers, "like that. You think the Drakh care whether I actually am a rebel or not? If Londo voices his suspicion to them, they'd obliterate me without giving it a second thought, just to play it safe. The fact that he hasn't . . . the fact that I'm still here, and not off in a dungeon being tortured or just being executed as a warning to others . . . that means something, I'm telling you! And the coded message he was sending me meant something, too! We have to stop them!"

"How?" That was, of course, the big question. It was Gwynn who had posed it.

Surprisingly, Vir had an answer.

"Now is the time," he said slowly, "to let everyone and everything know about the Drakh infestation on this world. Which means we reveal their headquarters. Londo has figured out where it is. I should have, too, to be honest. He kept talking about a tall structure that wasn't what it seemed . . ."

"The Tower of Power," Renegar said suddenly.

"Of course," Finian said, looking at Gwynn. "The structure with no windows. It makes sense."

"We've scanned it before, though, for signs of Shadow tech," Gwynn reminded him. "We came up with nothing."

"Probably because there was none when you first scanned it," Vir suggested. "Or so little that it was undetectable. No one could get inside, for a close scan, because the place is so closely guarded by the Prime Candidates."

"And it remains heavily guarded," Renegar pointed out. "If there are Drakh there . . . and we are going to expose them . . . how do you suggest we do it?"

"Simple," Vir said, with a surprisingly malicious smile. "We tilt."

19

In his cell deep beneath the palace, his body aching with a world of pain, G'Kar heard something faintly that sounded a great deal like cheering. As near as he could tell, it was some type of a massive rally. He had heard sounds like that before, and assumed it to be some sort of religious meeting. They liked their religious meetings, the Centauri did. It was a way to bolster the spirit of a people whose main occupation seemed to be endeavoring to dash the spirits of others.

Still, every so often, whenever he heard such things, he wondered whether he was eventually going to be made the subject of one. He could see himself being pulled out on a cart or some-such, to their great temple, bound from head to toe, being pelted by overripe fruit along the way. Once at the temple he would doubtless be subjected to assorted torture devices, hoping to wring a scream from him, as Cartagia had, before he died a hideous death. Curiously, he was certain at this point that he wouldn't mind such a fate. At least he would know where he stood. As it was now, the daily beatings and torments were wearing quite thin on him. The novelty was wearing off on his captors, as well; despite everything they had done, they had not been able to elicit the slightest sound out of him.

He wouldn't give them the satisfaction.

There was one thing he was at least grateful for: that John Sheridan had not done some damned fool thing, like sending someone to Centauri Prime in a vain effort to rescue him. Or even showing up himself. He knew Sheridan all too well, knew it was the kind of stunt he was likely to pull. But apparently he had not done so. He'd probably had the impulse, but cooler heads had prevailed. Thank G'Quan for that. The knowledge that Sheridan and Delenn were nowhere near this insanity brought him some measure of comfort.

In their cell beneath the palace, Sheridan and Delenn heard something faintly that sounded a great deal like cheering.

"Sounds like they're having a party up there," Sheridan commented. They were the first words he had spoken in some time.

"Do you think it involves us?" Delenn asked. She noticed some sort of vermin crawling around in the corner of the cell, and did her best to ignore it.

Sheridan noticed where she was looking. Without a thought, he walked over and stepped on it. "You mean do I think he's going to trot us out, his prize prisoners, and lord it over us? Is that what I think?"

"Yes."

"Yeah, I think that's what he's going to do." Sheridan looked haggard, as did Delenn, and for good reason. Their captors had not been especially kind to them, depriving them of food and water, endeavoring to extract information about the Alliance's armed might. Neither of them had said anything to that point, and they had no intention of doing so.

Yet Delenn couldn't help but be apprehensive. The Centauri efforts at extracting information from them had, thus far, been fairly mild. She was sure they could do a lot worse, and she had said as much to Sheridan.

"My guess," he had replied, "is that their more 'efficient' methods wouldn't leave us in especially good shape. Perhaps not even very recognizable as ourselves. And they may want the option of maintaining at least a semblance of . . . I don't know . . . mercy. Having a mindless shell of President Sheridan speaking out on their behalf isn't going to convince many people."

It seemed to make sense to her, but nevertheless she couldn't help but feel that something worse was going to be forthcoming. And when they heard the crowd noises outside, she began to wonder whether or not this might be it.

She said something softly, and Sheridan looked at her. "What? What did you say?"

"Nothing."

"Delenn." He sighed. "People don't mutter things under their breath because they don't want to be heard. They do it because they do want to be heard."

"You should not have come here," she said finally.

"What?"

"When that monster . . . Lione . . . contacted us, told us that they had David . . . that we were to come here at once, directly, informing no one, or else they would kill him . . . I should have come on my own."

"Don't be ridiculous," he said.

But she wouldn't be dismissed. "It is not ridiculous," she informed him. "I should have come here as an effort to try to convince them of the insanity of their actions. Try to reason with them. But you should have remained behind."

"Send my wife to do something that I'm afraid to do?" He shook his head fiercely. "Sorry, Delenn. Call me old-fashioned, but it just doesn't work that way."

"Why?" she demanded, her ire rising. "Because you're a man? A Human male? How typical! You have to throw yourself into the heart of danger when every reasonable assessment of the situation says that you should stay behind. John, it was foolishness! You're the president of the Alliance, and you delivered yourself to our enemies! The Alliance needs you!"

"You're the one who should have stayed, Delenn! You could do the Alliance far more good than I could. I tried to talk you into staying behind—"

"I'm David's mother, in Valen's name!"

"Hah!" he said triumphantly. "Now who's being typically Human! And you don't even have as good an excuse as I do! We both know that, if it's the Alliance you're so concerned about, you were the logical one to stay behind."

"How can you say that?"

"Because you'd be around longer! I've only got a few more years left!"

And there it was.

Delenn suddenly felt the coldness in the cell more than she had before. She looked down and away from him, because she knew it to be true. He had acknowledged the terrible truth that had preyed upon her, and somehow made it all the worse.

"I'm sorry, Delenn," he said softly.

And she turned and thumped him on the chest. It didn't hurt, but it startled him. The fury exploded from her.

"You're sorry? *You're sorry!* Don't you understand anything, John? I know I should have remained behind! That I should have let you do this on your own! But I couldn't refuse to come and risk condemning our son to death, because he's the part of you that will live on! And I couldn't be separated from you because, with the dwindling years we have left to us, every day—every second—becomes infinitely precious. Whether we live or die, all that mattered to me was that we did it together! How utterly, utterly stupid and shortsighted was that?"

He took her in his arms. "Completely," he said. "Can't you see how much I hate you for it?" He tilted her chin back with one finger and kissed her upturned lips. She returned the kiss as if it were going to be their last.

And then there was a rattling at the door. Several guards presented themselves and walked directly toward Sheridan.

"No!" Delenn cried out.

They grabbed Sheridan by either arm, forestalling any chance he might have at trying to pull away. She cried out his name, and he called back, "No, Delenn! Don't show them any weakness!" before he was hauled out of the room.

The door remained open. For a moment, Delenn thought that somehow they had actually overlooked the fact that she was still in there. Or perhaps they were so confident that it never occurred to them that she might make a break for it.

But as quickly as those hopes went through her mind, they were dashed when she heard footsteps approaching the door. And then she took a step back, startled, when a figure in gleaming white appeared. He looked almost heaven-sent in that aspect.

"Hello, Delenn," he said. He turned to the guards at the door and indicated that the door should be shut behind them.

"Highness, are you sure?" one of the guards asked.

"No. But one of the perks of being a highness is that people must obey your orders, even when there's no certainty in your mind at all. Do it."

The door closed, and he turned to Delenn.

"I felt you would be able to talk more freely if we were alone. Now then," he said. "Let us chat."

G'Kar heard a noise at his door and stood. He was certain that this was going to be it. And he steeled himself for the escape attempt he knew he would have to make, no matter how hopeless it was. Whenever they entered his cell, they always did so with enough restraints, shock prods, and such to control a dozen Narn. But today he would have to display strength on a par with more than that, for he knew in his heart that he would not have another opportunity.

But then the door opened only slightly, and instead of someone coming in to pull him out, a body was shoved in. It stumbled and fell, and the door slammed shut.

G'Kar squinted with his one eye. Only a small bit of light filtered through the tiny window in the door. The sounds of the crowd were getting louder, reaching a fever pitch, it seemed, only to get louder still. And then his new cellmate stood, steadying himself a moment, then trying to make out the other person he sensed in the darkness. "Hello? Who's there?"

G'Kar heard that distinctive voice and, to his own surprise, laughed softly.

Sheridan took a step into the meager light and peered into the gloom. "G'Kar? Is that . . . you?"

The Narn thought about just the right thing to say, given the circumstances.

"Please tell me," he said finally, "that you brought a deck of cards."

Londo simply stood there, regarding her for a long moment. "No hug?" he asked.

"Have you come here to gloat, Londo?" she asked icily. "Or perhaps you would like me to thank you, after sixteen years, for the lovely present you gave David."

"That won't be necessary." To her surprise, it seemed as if he couldn't look her in the eye.

"Were you pleased with yourself when you did that?" she asked. She knew this was precisely the wrong tack to take. Anything from pleading to wheedling would probably serve her better, but she was so consumed with fury that she could not contain herself. "Dooming a child not yet born, to a monstrous fate . . . was that something you did routinely, or was it specially reserved just for us?"

"You were my friends," he said.

"Then may the gods have mercy on your enemies."

"They actually seem to, now that you mention it," he commented thoughtfully. "My enemies seem to fare much better than my friends. Everyone I have ever loved, or felt close to, has come to a bad end, whereas those who oppose me thrive. Perhaps the gods are already carrying through on your wishes, Delenn."

"If they are, then David would be free, we would be gone, and you would all be punished for what you have done."

"It may very well be . . . that that can be arranged. The first two, at least. The third, well," and he rolled his eyes, "we will have to leave that in the hands of others, I fear."

For a moment, just one blessed moment, she felt hope stirring. "Are you saying . . . that David, John, and I will be freed?"

"David . . . yes. I believe I can arrange that. You and your husband, however," and he shook his head gravely. "You desired to be gone. Well . . . dead is gone. It will, at least, end your torment. That is the most I can offer you."

"You're the emperor," she said. "I would have thought nothing beyond your abilities."

"I would have thought that, too. Odd how things do not always work out the way one hopes."

"You said David could be freed. How? What do you get out of it?"

"Information."

She snorted. It was a most un-Delenn-like sound. "I knew it. Well, you will have no more luck with—"

But he was waving his hands, endeavoring to quiet her. "This is information you will part with, I think. It will not, in any way, compromise the security of the Interstellar Alliance. I would suspect that what I desire to know is so old that it can be of no use to anyone but me."

"Old?" She looked with curiosity at him.

"I am interested . . . in the beginning," he said. "The beginning of all . . . this," and he gestured around himself as if to encompass the totality of existence. "It started with the Earth-Minbari War. It started with your people, really. Yours and the Humans. I know our side . . . I know the Humans' side . . . I would like to hear your side."

"Why?"

"Because, Delenn," he said with the air of someone who was releasing a great weight from himself, "when one does not see much of a future for himself, one becomes more and more intrigued by the past. I wish . . . to know these things. To fill in the gaps of my knowledge. My recollections of recent times fade in and out. I keep a journal from time to time, and that is all that preserves me, because I look at the entries several days later and cannot recall the incidents that prompted them. But my memory of times long past, ah . . ." and he waggled a finger at her, "that remains, clear and pure. But it is only partial knowledge. I desire to know the rest. And you can tell me."

"And if I do this thing . . . then David is free."

"I will see to it. His main importance was to get you here."

"That . . . thing on his neck. That will be removed from him?"

He hesitated. "I suspect," he said, "that if I tried to lie to you now, you would know. So I will be honest with you: I cannot guarantee that, no. I will try. I will present a case, plead for it. Say that he has suffered enough. All I can promise you, though, is that he will be free . . . and safe. It is the best I can offer you, Delenn."

She wanted to ask him to whom he would present such a case, but she suspected that she would not receive an answer. Her mind racing, she weighed her options . . . and discovered that, in truth, she had precious few.

"What do you want to know?" she said finally.

"Everything."

So she told him everything. It took some minutes, and it seemed as if she had to keep raising her voice as the cheers and shouts from outside grew louder still. He nodded, listening carefully, asking questions here and there. Finally she finished and there was silence for quite some time, punctuated only by the crowd's huzzahs.

"You . . . were responsible," he whispered. He seemed overwhelmed by the idea. "You were responsible for the Earth-Minbari War."

"Not solely. But . . . yes. Had I counseled differently . . . had I not been caught up in the moment . . . it would not have happened. Then again—" she shrugged "—perhaps had I voted differently, others of the Grey Council might have changed their vote. Or the military might have staged a holy war, unapproved by the Council, out of vengeance. It is possible that it might have occurred anyway. But . . . in this reality . . . yes. The stain is on my soul. I have spent much of my life endeavoring to cleanse it. I do not know, even now, how successful I have been."

"You did what you thought was right for your people . . . and millions died because of it."

"Yes."

To her surprise, he laughed softly. "It may very well be, Delenn . . . that we have more in common than either of us has thought . . . or is ready to admit."

And suddenly an explosion from overhead nearly deafened them.

Delenn looked up in the general direction of the sound, and the screams that were accompanying them. "In Valen's name," she whispered, "what's happening?"

Displaying remarkable sangfroid, as if nothing was capable of surprising him anymore, Londo speculated, "I would guess that we are under attack. This may be your lucky day, Delenn," he said grimly. "The punishment you desired may well be upon us. You could wind up getting all three of your wishes sooner than you anticipated."

20

Durla stood next to Vallko, amazed and impressed that the minister of spirituality was able to work up the crowd to this degree of ardor.

Vallko, Durla, and other ministers were standing on the steps that led into the temple. The courtyard and the streets nearby were absolutely packed. It might very well have been that every Centauri in the capital city was there, for word had spread that this was not going to be just another spiritual rally. Oh, those were exciting and uplifting enough, of course, but the rumors flying throughout the city implied that some special announcement would be made, one that was to be a culmination of years of effort. Probably the only Centauri who were not present were the permanent guards stationed around the Tower of Power, some of the palace staff . . . and, of course, the emperor himself. Durla had informed him of the plans for the day, and incredibly, the emperor had elected not to come. "It is your performance, Durla," he had said. "I would rather not be seen as simply your assistant." That was fine with Durla. The more the focus was on him, the more he liked it.

Durla could not have asked for a better day. The sky was pure blue, not a cloud disturbing the vista. In the near distance, the Tower of Power stretched toward the sky, proud and unbending, as if pointing the way to greatness.

He knew that in hyperspace, even as Vallko spoke of the proud destiny that awaited Centauri Prime, the ships were waiting. By this time, they were at their stations, awaiting only the go-ahead from Durla to start their assault. But Durla had time. Standing on the edge of history, he wanted to savor the moment a while longer, as one studies a particularly succulent meal and appreciates it before carving into it. A worldwide communications web was, even now, transmitting this rally on a narrow-cast beam into hyperspace. There, in front of all of Centauri Prime, Durla would give the codes that would signal the attack. Once and for all, the people would indisputably link with him the coming greatness that was the destiny of Centauri Prime.

"For many years now, we have taken back what was ours, bit by bit," Vallko proclaimed. "We have done so through the sweat and endeavors of true Centauri." Again, for about the thirtieth time since he had begun his speech an hour ago, cheers and chants interrupted him. He allowed them to build and die down before continuing, "We have worked together . . . we have fulfilled the desires of the Great Maker, and we have shaped the destiny that is, by rights, ours!" More cheers, more waiting. "Because our work is pure . . . because the Centauri way is the right way . . . because we have resisted the impurities that other races would bring to us . . . we have been lifted up, elevated to a position that is unrivaled in our history!"

Durla nodded, smiling, but feeling a bit impatient. As if sensing his thoughts, Vallko said, "I leave it now to your beloved prime minister, Durla, to bring you to the next step in our history. For remember that it is his visions of what we should be that have guided us to where we are . . . and what we will become."

This was the loudest cheer of all, the welcoming cheer for Durla. At least, that was how he perceived it. He stood at the top of the great steps, his arms outstretched the way they had been when he had witnessed the ships departing for their glorious quest. The cheering washed over him like a physical wave.

"My friends . . ." he began.

He got no further.

The massive explosion ripped through the air, startling and terrifying the entire crowd. Then another explosion, and a third, and everyone looked to the skies, screaming, convinced that death was being rained down upon them once again.

It was Lione who saw it first. "The Tower!" he shrieked, and pointed.

Sure enough, the Tower of Power was crumbling. Charges blasted up from beneath, enveloping it, the lack of windows causing the force of the explosion to be contained. Smoke blew out of newly formed cracks, rubble flew, and then the entire upper section began to tilt even as the lower half collapsed.

"Impossible! Impossible!" Lione clearly couldn't believe what he was seeing. "There are guards . . . no one could get close enough . . . no one—"

Another explosion ripped straight up the middle, and the entire upper section was blown apart. Debris hurtled everywhere. People screamed, trying to run, unable to move because they were so packed in. Vallko's and Durla's cries for calm did nothing to stem the tide.

Then the first of the bodies fell to the ground, having been hurled a great distance by the force of the blast. Impressively, it was mostly intact, but that lasted only until it landed on the temple stairs with a disgusting noise. At that point the body smashed apart like an over-ripe melon. But even in that condition, everyone could see that it was not a Centauri body.

And more started to plummet from overhead, and they weren't even close to intact. Heads, arms, legs, torsos, all grey and scaly, cloaked in shreds of black cloth, spewing down from the skies as if a gigantic pustule had been popped.

A hole gaped in the ceiling of the catacombs, exposing them to sunlight for the first time in their history. The area directly above had once been the foundation for the Tower of Power; now there was nothing but the tattered remains of the ground where Renegar's ex-plosives had blasted apart the Tower from underneath.

Renegar clambered down from the surface and turned to Vir as the others held their collective breath. "Well?" Vir demanded. "What's happening?"

"It's raining Drakh," Renegar said.

"Good." Vir turned to Adi. "All right, Adi. Time for phase two. Tap into the broadcast web. Now."

What had seconds before been pure pandemonium had incredi-bly, eerily, fallen into silence, a silence that was even more deafening than the shouting had been. The Centauri were looking in wonder at the alien creatures who were suddenly in their midst, albeit in pieces.

"Wha—what is . . ." Kuto, the minister of information, couldn't comprehend what he was seeing.

Lione turned to Durla, kicking aside the remains of the body that had landed nearby. All the blood was draining from his face. "You . . . you said the upper portions of the tower were to be kept empty . . . for expansion . . . no one was to go up there, not even me . . . Were these . . . these . . ."

"Quiet!" Durla said urgently. "I have to think . . . I . . ."

That was when a gigantic hologram appeared before them, much like the one of Londo some fifteen years earlier, and Durla far more recently. But this was someone whom Durla had not remotely expected. Whom no one had expected.

"Cotto," Durla snarled.

"My fellow Centauri," the gigantic image of Vir boomed throughout the world. "I am Vir Cotto. I am the leader of a resistance movement called the Legions of Fire. We have known for some time that it is not the leaders—specifically, the prime minister—of Centauri Prime who have been shaping your destinies. It is these beings . . . the Drakh. Servants of the Shadows. Monstrous beings."

"This is broadcasting everywhere!" Durla practically howled at Kuto. "Shut it down! Find a way!"

"The people of Centauri Prime have been used. Duped. The Drakh played upon our nationalistic feelings in order to use you—to use us—as cat's-paws to strike against the Alliance. An Alliance that goes against everything they want to see happen in known space. They are a disease that has been slowly rotting us . . . and we did not even know that we were sick. But now you know. It has not been Centauri Prime for Centauri. It has not been the clear vision of a people, or even of the 'visionary' prime minister. He has been duped. You have all been duped.

"And to all the member worlds of the Alliance, know that the aggression you have seen from Centauri Prime has been nothing but the cold, manipulating tactics of an evil race. We are as much victims as you. We are—"

At that moment, the image of Vir Cotto blinked out. And then something monstrous came through the sky, something black and frightening, and—in the heads of everyone below—there seemed to be something akin to a scream as it flashed past.

The ship drove straight toward the vast hole that had been created by the explosion. Then, from the vessel, a small army of Drakh descended, heading right for the now-exposed tunnels.

The Drakh poured into the catacombs, weapons at the ready. And when they arrived, they found no one there. At least, no one at the point of entry.

"Spread out!" the order came down, and the Drakh moved every which way through the catacombs, searching for Vir Cotto and the others, certain they were facing a small force of people who could quickly be obliterated.

They were wrong.

For suddenly, from every discernible direction, Centauri came charging forward. They were servants and soldiers attached to the Houses. They were scholars. They were poets. They were subversives, philosophers, writers. But under the direction, planning, and supervision of Vir Cotto, they were warriors all. Moreover, they were warriors who had thoroughly familiarized themselves with every twist and turn of the catacombs.

The split troops of the Drakh were cut off from one another. In what could only be considered the height of irony, they were lost in the dark.

And then there was much screaming. Amazingly, little of it involved Centauri voices.

21

Mariel watched in amazement from the balcony. She had heard the explosions, the same as everyone else. She gaped in astonishment, watched the Tower of Power disintegrate. She saw distant, non-Centauri bodies falling through the air in assorted bits and pieces. Something smacked against the wall just to her left. It was a single small piece of grey flesh. She stared at it in wonderment as it hung there.

And then she heard the voice—that magnificent voice, that powerful voice—and the image, like a vision from the Great Maker himself. Vir—her Vir—speaking to the people of Centauri Prime, telling them what was happening, stepping forward into the position of leadership that she had always known he rightly deserved.

Then she saw the dark ship descending, and terror descended upon her, as well. Instinctively she knew who and what they were, and what they intended for Vir. She saw them stream down into the blast point.

There was no way to help Vir. Nothing she could do.

Then she realized that there was. She ran quickly into her bedroom, closed the door behind her, dropped to her knees.

"Please, Great Maker," she whispered, "I will give anything, do anything, sacrifice anything, but please let Vir be all right. Save him. And save Londo. I tried to do him ill and, in so doing, upset Vir, and I repent of that. I repent of it all, please . . ."

That, and similar sentiments were all she voiced for some minutes, until she heard shouting from the main room. First and foremost came Durla's voice, and then she heard others, as well. She heard the voices of Castig Lione, and Kuto, and there was Vallko, and Munphis, the minister of education. They were all talking at once, and it was difficult to make them out, until Durla shouted them down.

"This cannot be!" he bellowed. "It is a trick! A hideous trick!"

"You saw!" Lione shouted back. "We all saw! The Drakh. Great Maker, Durla, the Drakh!"

"You will address me as prime minister!"

"How can it be a trick?" It was Vallko, and he sounded like a broken man, someone whose faith had been shattered. "We saw . . . that ship, the Drakh, here in the heart of the city . . ."

"A trick, I tell you, put together by Cotto!"

"Prime Minister, it makes no sense!" That was Kuto speaking. "We saw them! We saw the Drakh attack! Drakh bodies falling from the Tower, Drakh warriors from the skies . . . it's . . ."

"Face it, Prime Minister . . . you've been used. We all have," Lione said.

Durla's voice was trembling with fury. "You will not stand there and tell me that my vision for Centauri Prime was something manufactured by an alien race!"

"Great Maker take your visions!" Lione snapped. "I'm telling you, we've been used!" There were mutters of agreement.

"I have trouble believing that you are my cabinet. My ministers, those I trusted." Durla's voice sounded like a mixture of disgust and sorrow. "That you would turn on me now, at our moment of greatest triumph . . ."

"Triumph! A war on the entire Alliance that was planned by a race who were servants of the Shadows!" That was the normally reticent Munphis speaking up. "Who knows what their long-term plans are! It could very well be that they're looking to us to smash the Alliance for them . . . and they, in turn, will conquer us!"

"We are Centauri Prime! We will never be conquered again! And I will not allow the trickery of the 'Legions of Fire,' and Cotto, and these imaginary Drakh to dissuade me from my course! I have planned this for far too long, done too much, to let it end here and now!"

She heard footsteps then, quick movements. "Durla, what are you doing?" It was Vallko's voice. He sounded as if he was starting to come out of his shock.

"This is my backup transmitter. We had to shut down the world web to take Cotto's rants off-line, but this will still get me directly to the ships. The attack will go on as planned."

"You're insane! We can't! We have to wait, to get this sorted out—"

"That's what they want us to do, Lione! Wait! Because time is on the side of the Alliance! Cotto has convinced them, just as he has you, that we are the tools of a malevolent race! They will erect defenses against us! Be ready for us!" There was a tone of mounting desperation. "Besides, if the go-codes are not given within the next seventy-two hours, the fleet will stand down! They will think that something is wrong—"

"Something *is* wrong!" Vallko was getting more strident. "It may well be that nothing is what it has seemed! I have spent years, Durla, telling the people that the future of the Centauri people is in our own hands. We have seen evidence today that that may not be the case!"

"And how much of that did you know, eh?" Lione demanded. Their voices were moving around, making it clear that they were circling each other. "Why did you instruct that the upper floors of the Tower remain off limits? 'Reserved for future expansion.' You knew, didn't you. You knew that our symbol of destiny was . . . infested with those creatures!"

"I knew no such thing! It was part of my vision, I tell you—"

"A vision given you by the Drakh! Open your eyes and see the truth, Durla!" Lione shouted. "You've been used! Your power stems, not from any divine vision, but from notions planted in your skull by the Drakh! It's the only answer!"

And suddenly there was a deathly quiet. When Durla spoke again, it was with a soft and frightening conviction. "There is," he said, "another answer."

"Durla, put that down," Kuto said warningly, although Mariel had no idea what he was referring to.

"And that answer is that you're all in league with Cotto. I should have seen it earlier. All of you, trying to tear me down. Jealous of me. Planting those fake bodies, getting in league with those . . . 'Drakh' . . . to discredit me. Yes . . . jealous of me. And traitors, all of you."

As one, the ministers shouted out, and then Mariel heard the blasts. She clapped her hands to her ears, crying out, as the death screams and the sounds of weapon fire filled the air. It seemed to go on forever, although, in truth, it lasted only a few seconds. And then there was silence once more.

Very tentatively, afraid of what she would see, Mariel opened the door.

Durla was standing there, and contrary to what she had expected, he looked exceedingly calm. His hand was at his side, holding a plasma charge blaster. The floor was light red, thick with blood, and the bodies of the ministers were strewn about. Several of them had their eyes open, and they all seemed quite surprised, yet for all their astonishment they were no less dead.

Slowly Durla turned and saw Mariel standing there. Without a word he raised his weapon and aimed it at her. "Do you," he said steadily, "stand against me, too?"

She shook her head.

He smiled. "That's good. That's very good, my love. I would have hated if you had." He looked around at the carnage with a sort of distant sadness. "I was afraid this would happen. That's why I sent the guards away. I had hoped it would turn out differently but . . . not everything can. They didn't understand. None of them did."

She saw the transmitting equipment nearby. She stepped delicately over the fallen body of Lione, and said softly, "I understand. I didn't used to but . . . now I do." She was within six feet of him . . . five . . . walking slowly, almost slinking . . .

"That's good. That's very good. Would you like to watch, Mariel?"

"Watch?" She froze at four feet.

"Watch me transmit the codes that will launch the attack."

"Of course, my love."

He turned back to the transmitter and began to manipulate the controls.

Three feet . . . two . . .

Suddenly he turned and aimed his weapon at her. "I don't believe you," he said, and fired.

At point-blank range, he should not have missed. But Mariel twisted out of the way, the bolt barely grazing her hip, and then she was upon him. She grabbed at the gun with both hands, shoving it away from her, trying to shake it out of his hands, as Durla struggled against her. He shoved her away, tried to aim quickly, but slipped on the blood. Mariel leaped desperately, landed full on top of him, momentarily knocking the wind out of him, and they rolled across the floor. The gun fired wide, ricocheting harmlessly off the wall.

Durla managed to get to his feet, and Mariel clung on, like a spider holding on to a wind-tossed web. They were away from the blood, moving toward the balcony, and Mariel had a better grip on his gun hand this time. But Durla grabbed her trailing length of hair, twisting it around his free hand. She let out a howl of pain but did not let go.

"Stupid cow!" he howled as they staggered about. "I remade the world for you!"

"But I won't let you end it for me!" she cried out.

Her strength, her resolve, momentarily lessened, and then she thought of every time he'd struck her, every time she'd submitted to his abuse, and a fire of fury boiled through her veins. Mariel pushed back, as hard as she could, one desperate shove.

Durla's back hit the balcony railing, and he overbalanced, flipping over. An eight-story drop yawned beneath him. He let out a shriek of alarm, his fingers still firmly entangled in her hair. He dropped the gun and clawed at the air, and then he tumbled over the edge of the balcony. And Mariel, entangled in his grasp like some sort of perverse lovers' embrace, went with him.

As she fell, she felt some small degree of pleasure that he was screaming and she was not.

Londo . . . Vir . . . look! I'm flying at last was the final thought across her mind before the ground rushed up to meet them.

EXCERPTED FROM
THE CHRONICLES OF LONDO MOLLARI.
Excerpt dated (approximate Earth date)
January 1, 2278.

"Shiv'kala. Not dead, I see? Pity."

I have no idea what prompted me to sound quite as jovial as I did. It was probably the sight of the Tower of Power lying in ruin and rubble out in the town.

Shiv'kala, for his part, seemed positively disconcerted. How long I had waited to see him that way. He was covering it as best as he could, to preserve what he fancied as his dignity and mysterious reserve. But we had been "together" too long. I could tell that he was trying not to panic, and only barely succeeding.

He had appeared, as always, out of the shadows in my inner sanctum. I still did not know how he had gotten there and, frankly, had stopped caring. "No, Londo . . . still not dead," he whispered. "And not for want of trying by your . . . associates."

"Are you implying that I had something to do with this?" I demanded. "How would you suggest I did that? Your little friend watches me at all times. If I were helping to run an underground rebellion, I think you would have known."

He advanced on me, his red eyes burning into me. "You always keep certain thoughts buried just below the surface, Londo. The keeper senses it, even if he can do nothing about it. I suspect they may have to do with your 'associates' . . ."

"Again that word. I am emperor. I work with any number of people. I remind you that your precious Durla is as much my associate as Vir."

"Not anymore. Durla is dead."

That brought me up short. "Dead?" I whispered. "When?"

"Moments ago. After he annihilated his ministry. He fell to his death off a balcony, locked in combat with his wife."

I had been standing, but suddenly the strength went from me. I sagged into a chair and for just a moment I had a mental picture of Mariel when I first saw her. Young and beautiful, and even though it was an arranged marriage and I wanted to hate her out-of-hand, I was transfixed by her comeliness. I could not have known the future, of course. Could not have known what she would become . . . or what I would become. And now . . . now . . .

"Mariel," I whispered.

"She stopped Durla before he could issue the go-codes to launch the strike against the Alliance," Shiv'kala said, sounding rather bitter. "You must attend to it."

It took me a moment to focus on what he was saying. "I must attend to . . . what?"

"You must order the ships to launch against the Alliance worlds. The invasion can still go forward . . ."

"Are you mad? Yes, I think you must be. Shiv'kala . . . it is over." I managed to stand, because for this I wanted to be on my feet. I wanted to be eye to eye with him, not backing down. "Your involvement with our affairs, your manipulation . . . it is all out in the open now. The people of Centauri Prime will never support—"

"They will support what you tell them to support, Londo. With Durla gone, with the ministry gone, it is you to whom the people will turn. Rudderless, they will be looking for a captain to take control of the ship of state. You are the emperor. You are still sealed in their minds as the one who freed them from Cartagia, the one who subjugated the Narn, at least for a time. The people will follow you. The ships will attend to you. Even though you do not know the specific passwords and codes, the military will still respect your authority. You can order them to move and they will obey . . ."

"And what of the revelation of the Drakh involvement?" I said bitterly. "How do I explain that, on a world of Centauri Prime for Centauri?"

"We were your secret allies."

"You controlled us! Controlled me!"

"Lie, Mollari. It's what you're good at. Duplicity is the single most prevalent product that Centauri Prime exports. Say that you sought us out. Say that we offered our services. Say whatever you wish, but say something—"

"You want me to say something? Very well. I will say something," and I advanced on him. "Leave my world. You have done enough damage."

"Have we?" His eyes narrowed. "Have you forgotten the further damage we can do?"

It was at that point that my instincts as a card player kicked in. Because I knew precisely what he was referring to. I knew he was speaking of the bombs that he and his people had claimed to have planted throughout Centauri Prime. Bombs that they had been holding over my head to keep me in line all these years.

But I was certain at that point that Vir and his people had found them, defused them. He had been so thorough in so many other matters. Either that . . . or they had never existed in the first place. It was the latter that I was becoming more and more convinced of—for, as I said, my card-playing instincts told me Shiv'kala was bluffing.

"You must realize," I said carefully, "that it is indeed over. That this cannot continue. You can flood me with pain until I cannot stand, you can isolate me so that I cannot speak. You can use me as your public face and puppet ruler, but really . . . what is to be accomplished by this? It will not even work on the surface, for if you subsume my mind, turn me into nothing more than a shell who is your mouthpiece . . . the people will know.

"They know how I speak, how I carry myself. They will be alert to further Drakh manipulation. If I am not myself . . . either they will know, or at the very least they will be sufficiently suspicious that they will not heed me.

"And then there is your own presence. Knowing that you are here, at the very least the Humans will come for you all. Even as we speak, they may well be assembling a fleet for an assault. After all, you did introduce a plague into their Homeworld. The surviving Humans are not gently disposed toward you. And if you think that they will be worried about the prospect of some Centauri dying during an assault on a Drakh-held world, then you'd be well-advised to think again."

He actually looked away. He was unable to hold my gaze. I sounded conciliatory—an impressive feat—as I said, "You have always struck me as a race who does what needs to be done, but no more. You are not bloodthirsty. You are not barbarians. You have a purpose to serve, and you serve it. Annihilating my people simply out of a fit of pique, in the face of a hopeless cause . . . it makes no sense. It goes against the grain of the Drakh."

And he looked back at me with grim amusement in his eyes. "After all this time," he sighed, "how little you know us."

It was at that horrific moment, a moment that will always be frozen in time for me, that I knew I had badly miscalculated.

I was not even aware of the explosion when it actually occurred. All I knew was that one moment I was standing, and the next, I was on the floor. There was a ringing in my ears, and even though my eyes were wide open, all I saw was whiteness. I was flash-blinded.

Then a wave of heat swept over me, blasting in through my balcony, and wind so furious that it knocked everything off my walls and pushed me halfway across the floor.

I staggered to my feet, reaching out, trying to find something to hold on to so that I could get my bearings. A hand grasped mine. It was gray and scaly and cold to the touch, and I yanked it away quickly. I heard a low laugh, and I knew it was Shiv'kala's.

"You . . . you bastards . . ." I whispered.

My vision was starting to clear, and what I saw was beyond horrific. Fully half of the capital city was in flaming ruins. It was as bad as, if not worse than, when we had been attacked years earlier. A charnel smell wafted on the wind to me. The sky was already black with smoke, flames licking up toward the obscured clouds.

I reached out, as if somehow I could scoop up my people in my hand, preserve them, save them, turn back the hands of time and make it not have happened. And I heard voices crying out to me, Londo, Londo, why have you forsaken us? I could not tell if they were real or if they were imagined, but beyond question, they were my fault, my responsibility, on my head.

I had gambled with their lives, and I had lost.

"That," Shiv'kala said in a voice from beyond the grave, "was one third of the bombs we have planted. What you see here before you is merely representative of what has occurred throughout your world. Here is what you will do. Are you listening, Londo?"

"Yes," I whispered.

"You will bring Sheridan up here. You will show him the damage that was done, and you will make clear to him that these are crimes for which he and he alone bears responsibility . . . because he has been working in concert with the Legions of Fire."

"You intend . . . for me to blame this destruction on Vir?"

"Of course," said Shiv'kala. "He has already taken credit for destroying one monument. It is obvious that he will go to any lengths to satisfy his hatred of us, regardless of the cost. Next . . . are you listening, Londo?"

I nodded. I tried to hold my breath against the smell of burning flesh, and when I was unable to, I dry-heaved. Shiv'kala did not appear to notice, or care.

"After that, you will have Sheridan executed. Then you will have Delenn executed. I want the executions done separately, since I've no desire for people to see them drawing strength from each other in their last moments. Then you will find Vir Cotto, if he still lives, and execute him. And then you will inform the fleet that the assault against the Alliance is to be carried out.

"You are right about one thing, however: If we remain, there will doubtless be a strike launched against Centauri Prime. So we will make a show of departing, to put the Alliance off its guard. But once the Alliance is in disarray, we will return, to make Centauri Prime the cornerstone of the new Drakh Entire."

"Not Vir," I whispered.

He looked at me most oddly. "What?"

"I will not execute Vir. Nor will you. I will not stand in the way of what the people do, but he will not die by my hand, nor at the hands of the Drakh."

"Now you are the insane one, Londo." His voice rose. "Look at your city! Look at your world! It lies in ruins because you misjudged us, and you would still dictate terms?"

"You will grant me this," I said tightly, "or Mariel and Durla will not be the only ones who die off a balcony this day."

He seemed ready to argue it, but suddenly became impatient. "Very well," he said. "Do as you have been ordered, and Cotto will be spared. The odds are that he is dead anyway. And if he is not, well . . the people will attend to him soon enough."

"Thank you," I said.

"You see, Londo? Even under such extreme circumstances . . . you cannot say that the Drakh are totally without compassion."

He said a few things more, but I was paying no attention. Instead my thoughts were elsewhere, nearly twenty years gone, to the words of the techno-mage, Elric. "I see a great hand reaching out of the stars. The hand is your hand. And I hear sounds . . . the sounds of billions of people calling your name."

"My followers," I had whispered in awe.

And in a voice like ice, he had replied, "Your victims."

I had always thought—always assumed—that he had been referring to the Narn. I now realized that he had not. That it was my own people, here and now, crying out for aid from an emperor whose misjudgment had resulted in widespread slaughter. I did not plant the bombs . . . I did not trigger the bombs . . . but, Great Maker, I did not stop them, and my people have paid for it.

I wanted to fly away. To be able to step to the balcony, change into a winged creature, and fly off to someplace where there was no death, no destruction. No voices calling my name, and no Drakh. I had waited sixteen years to feel fear and desperation from Shiv'kala, and I had managed it. But my people had paid a terrible, terrible price.

I had never wanted to be with Mariel at any given time as much as I did at that moment.

22

Vir gazed in horror at the smoking ruins of the city. A number of his followers stood at his side, likewise stunned by what they were seeing.

They had emerged from the far end of the catacombs, using as an exit the place where Renegar had first discovered the tunnels so many years ago, several hundred members of the Legions of Fire, looking ragged, exhausted, but also grimly triumphant. They had left a sizable number of dead Drakh below them, and with any luck those few that remained would wander hopelessly, lost in the maze.

But any satisfaction the rebels might have taken from their triumphs paled next to the aftermath they were seeing now.

"The Drakh," he whispered. "They must have done this. It could only have been them . . ."

"It certainly redefines the concept of 'sore losers,' " Renegar said.

"There may be more bombs," Finian said grimly. "If you'll excuse me, I'm going to go find them."

"Now? *Now* you're going to find them?" an incredulous Vir asked. "Why didn't you find them earlier, before this damage was done?"

"We'd always been seeking out Shadow technology. As near as I can tell, these explosives were of a more mundane nature. Even I cannot locate that which I do not know exists," Finian told him. "Leave it to me now."

"But—"

"I said leave it to me," he repeated firmly. And with that, he walked away.

"There may be bombs planted all over Centauri Prime," Renegar said. "How can he get to all of them . . ."

"He's a techno-mage," Gwynn said airily. "He may be a

supremely annoying one, but he is a mage nonetheless. Don't underestimate us."

Vir stared off into the distance, and said, "Gwynn . . . I'm heading into the palace. You've got to get me in there."

A chorus of "*What?*" came from all around him.

"I have to see Londo. Have to speak to him. Make sure he's all right."

"Your concern for his safety is laudable," Gwynn said, "but illtimed."

"No, it's the perfect time. Renegar, you'll be with me, too. You'll coordinate with Dunseny and help get David Sheridan the hell out of there. The rest of you," and he turned to his followers, "get to the city. Help where you can. Mount rescue operations, tend to the wounded, bury the dead. Gwynn . . . you're going to help us get inside."

"How?"

"You're a techno-mage. I don't underestimate you."

She smiled, but it looked more like a pained grimace.

The door to the cell opened, and the guards came in for Sheridan. He quickly got to his feet, and demanded, "What's going on out there? It sounds like a damned war zone!"

His only response was a quick club to the head, which caused him to sag in their grip. G'Kar took a step toward them threateningly, but half a dozen shock prods suddenly formed a barrier between him and the guards.

"Try it, Narn. Just try it," one of them said.

G'Kar didn't take him up on it, as Sheridan was dragged out of the cell. But while the door was open, just before it slammed, G'Kar could smell something wafting down the corridor, very faintly.

It was the distant aroma of burning flesh. It was a smell he knew all too well. It had hung in the air around Narn for months after the Centauri had attacked them with mass drivers.

"Do unto others," he said softly.

EXCERPTED FROM
THE CHRONICLES OF LONDO MOLLARI.
Excerpt dated (approximate Earth date)
January 2, 2278.

I had such dreams. Such dreams.

I dreamt of power and glory and followers. I dreamt of protecting my Home-world from dark invaders. I dreamt of restoring my great republic to its former glory. I dreamt of a noble death in battle, with my hands at the throat of my greatest enemy. I dreamt of love and I dreamt of redemption.

Such dreams. Such dreams.

Sheridan looked as if he were in a dream when they brought him before me some hours ago. I have known John Sheridan for longer than I would have thought possible . . . and never have I seen him with such an air of confusion.

The guards held him in front of me, bracing him firmly. He was shaking his head, as if he was uncertain of where he was. I looked to one of the guards and, my face a question, mimed a blow to the head to ask them if they had somehow beaten him severely, possibly concussing him. The Human skull is such a fragile thing. But the guard shook his head that he had not, and I had no reason to doubt him. I am, after all, such an infinitely trusting soul.

He looked up at me then and seemed quite surprised. I do not suppose that I can blame him. I have, of course, seen better days. Still, such a look of shock on his face. One would think he had not seen me for twenty years. The room was fairly dark, the only lighting provided mostly by the flames of my city dancing like ghouls outside.

". . . Londo? What . . . am I doing here . . . where . . ."

I smiled at him grimly. "Welcome back from the abyss, Sheridan. Just in time to die. Your timing, as always, is quite exceptional."

I did not think any single being could be as perplexed as that man. Then again, the Human capacity for bewilderment seems a virtually bottomless fountain.

"Londo . . . what am I doing here   " he said again. "What're you . . "

It was necessary to be as forceful as possible. I needed everyone . . . and everything . . . to know of the certainty of my forthcoming actions. "What I'm doing is what someone should have done a long time ago," I told him. "Putting you out of my misery." I coughed slightly, mildly amused at my equally mild attempt at humor, and then growled, "Fitting punishment for your crimes."

Wide-eyed, he said, "What crimes? I don't—"

The man was beginning to annoy me. Naturally I understood his desire to avoid any sort of blame. Why not? I, who have been blamed throughout my life, whether justified or not, could easily comprehend a desire to avoid once, just once, recriminations being heaped upon me unjustly.

Nevertheless, I could not let such disingenuousness pass. I nodded to my men, and one of the guards punched Sheridan hard in the solar plexus. Sheridan went down on one knee, gasping. I stooped and looked into his eyes. I spoke as if I were playing to an audience, and in a way, I was . . . but it was none of the people in this room.

"The crime of neglect," I told him. "The crime of convenience. During your little war, you drove the Shadows away, oh yes, but you did not think to clean up your mess. If a few of their minions, their dark servants, came to Centauri Prime, well, where is the harm in that, yes? Hmm?"

He stared at me blankly. He seemed to have no idea what I was talking about. I began to comprehend just how this man, in becoming president of the Alliance, had formed himself into the most successful politician in the history of his race. Apparently his capability for self-denial knew no bounds. If I did not know better, I would think he had never heard of the Drakh, was unaware of the outcome of the Shadow War . . . that, indeed, everything I was saying was news to him.

And here I thought I was the foremost practitioner of self-delusion of our age.

"You want to see the harm? Do you?" I asked. Not waiting for an answer, I indicated to the guards that they should bring him to one of the windows. It used to be that I never had the curtains drawn. That I could not get enough of the view of the city that my station had afforded me. Now, of course, heavy drapes blocked the view. Drapes that the guards pushed aside so that Sheridan could see for himself the damage that had been wrought.

He stared in astonishment at the remains of Centauri Prime that flickered through the long, dark night. Ruined spires half thrown down, smoke rising from distant fires. Overhead a vehicle passed, dark and sinister, bristling with needlelike points. A Drakh escape ship; the last of their kind, one could only hope, making their way off the world that they had secretly run for so many years.

"There is the legacy of your war, the price we paid when you abandoned us to the enemies you managed to escape," I told him. "Forgive me if I do not share the view . . . I have seen it enough."

Sheridan was pulled back in front of me.

And he began to babble.

"But this couldn't happen, not in this amount of time . . . the time stabilizer . . . it was hit . . . what year is this?"

I stared at him incredulously. If he was trying to pretend that he had some sort of amnesia, then he was failing miserably. "It is the last year and the last day and the last hour of your life. Seventeen years since you began your great crusade . . . seventeen years since . . ."

And I faded.

My mind goes in and out. The moments of confusion, of depression, of total loss of where I am and what I am doing, become more and more frequent.

"I'm tired," I said. "Take him back to his cell." I fixed Sheridan with a glare, and said, "Make your peace with whatever gods you worship; you will meet them the next time I send for you. I cannot change what is . . . cannot recall my world from what it has become . . . but I can thank you . . . properly . . . for your role in it."

The guards pulled Sheridan out, half-dragging him as they went. For me, his presence was already a part of a distant past that I was anxious to forget, and would likely do so all too quickly. I walked back to my throne, touched it . . . not with pride, or possessiveness . . . but disdain. For this thing, this thing to which I would never have thought I coudl aspire, was something that had been tied around my neck, long ago, and was now crushing the life out of me.

I walked over to the window, glanced out in spite of myself. Then I drew the drapes closed.

I hear laughter as I write this . . . laughter from nearby. Who could laugh at such destruction?

Children. Yes, of course, children. At least two. I hear their rapid footsteps, their gleeful chortling, as they are running through the halls of the palace.

And then I hear an adult voice, a woman. She is calling with extreme urgency, "Luc? Lyssa! Where are you?" The voice—musical, softly accented—is unfamiliar to me . . .

No . . . wait . . .

I know . . . yes. Senta, was it? No . . . Senna, I think her name is. She is . . . a nurse or child attendant around here, I think. Or perhaps . . . yes . . . a retainer to one of our Houses . . .

I drink in the sound of their laughter, a man parched of emotion, with a soul as dry and shriveled as my skin. I hear them clattering about in the very next room.

Perhaps they will come in here. If they do, I will talk to them. I will tell them of how Centauri Prime used to be, of the greatness to which we aspired . . . in the beginning . . .

And then . . . then I will say my good-byes. To Sheridan and Delenn, to Vir and Londo . . .

Shiv'kala. He is the one to whom I would most want to say farewell. To be rid of him, quit of his influence, has been my fantasy for nearly fifteen years now. I suspect, however, it is not going to happen. Not only that, but his ego is so great that I fear—no matter what—that Centauri Prime will never rid itself of him or his influence. He fancies himself something more than a simple minion, a creature of darkness serving masters long-gone. He thinks himself a philosopher, a student of behavior. He thinks he is so much more than he is. Here, at the last . . . I pity him in a way. For he will never truly understand or know himself for the pathetic monstrosity that he is. Because of that, he is very predictable.

Whereas I know myself as that all too well. There is something to be said for self-awareness. It strips away your illusions and makes you unpredictable. That is the one great weakness that the Drakh have, and I am going to exploit it for all that I can . . .

23

Delenn sat in the dank cell, her legs curled up under her chin, rocking back and forth while softly chanting a prayer, and certain that she would never see her husband alive again.

"We're bringing him down," a guard had growled. "We know how much you'd like to have a last moment with him." From the tone of his voice, it seemed to suggest that there was some cruel surprise in store for her, and she was sure she suspected what it was.

When the door was yanked open, she was positive they were coming for her. That first they were going to bring in John's corpse as part of their perversity, allowing them "one last moment." Or perhaps they would present her with his head or some other identifiable body part—just so they could see her reaction. Perhaps they hoped that she would break down crying, sobbing, into a hopeless mess, wailing Sheridan's name and cursing her captors. If that was their plan, then they would be sorely disappointed.

Then, to her astonishment, Sheridan was thrown in, and the door slammed shut behind him. At first she could scarcely believe it was he. The fact that it was hard to see did not simplify matters, for the only illumination in the cell was a pale light coming in from a grated high window. Sheridan looked around as a man befuddled, leaning against the wall for support. Then he squinted into the darkness, and said, "Who . . . who's there?"

She could hardly speak. She was almost afraid that, if she said something, her own voice might break the spell of the moment. "John?" she managed to say.

She emerged from the shadows, and Sheridan turned and looked at her.

Every year she had dwelled on the dwindling time available to them. She had cursed it, cursed the fate that had given them so little time together. Now . . . now the three or four years that remained seemed an eternity. She would sell her soul just to have the opportunity to live out even one of those years by his side, instead of ending in this horrid cell. She rushed to him, embracing him with all the fervor of her passion for him.

"Delenn? What're you doing here?"

Yes, he was definitely confused. Perhaps a blow to the head had robbed him of some of his memory. But all she had to do was remind him of what was happening, and it would all come clear for him. "I didn't tell them anything. They tried to make me ... but I didn't. There's nothing they can do to me. They know that now. They're allowing us one last moment together, before ..."

She tried to finish the sentence, and couldn't. So instead, with determination to present a brave front, she managed a smile. "It's all right, John. I accepted this fate a long time ago. They cannot touch me. They cannot harm me. I'm not afraid. Not if you are with me. Our son is safe. That's all that matters. John ... I love you."

And she kissed him.

He seemed startled, as if she had never kissed him before. But then he returned it, as if it was something that had always been meant to happen.

Then Sheridan gently pulled her away and looked earnestly into her eyes.

"Delenn ... listen to me," he said intensely. "This may not make any sense ... but I'm not supposed to be here ... I'm not really here ... the last thing I remember I was on Babylon 4, and my time stabilizer was hit, then suddenly I was here."

She was thunderstruck. Could this be? She stepped back further, studied him for a moment, and gradually the truth sank in. It was so absurd, and yet so obvious, that she almost wanted to laugh. Here she had been producing a tortured rationale as to why he seemed so disoriented ... and yet she should have realized it instantly.

In the latter half of the year 2260, the lost space station, Babylon 4, had appeared like a gigantic phantom in space. Swept up in all manner of temporal flux and time anomalies, several people had braved that mysterious and ostensibly doomed station and found themselves caught in a bizarre unfolding vision of the future. Among those people had been Delenn, Sheridan ... and Jeffrey Sinclair, the first commander of Babylon 5.

One dark night, long after they were married, and after Londo had risen to the post of emperor, Sheridan had told Delenn most of what he had experienced. He had been vague about the details of the encounter. Now she was beginning to understand why. How could he have told her that they would be trapped together in a Centauri prison, facing almost certain death?

In an amazed whisper, she said, "In Valen's name . . . it is true, isn't it? I can see it in your eyes. You told me, long ago, that you had seen this moment. But until now, I never really believed . . ." She was overwhelmed. There was so much she wanted to say to him. So many things . . . and her mind recoiled from the possibilities. One wrong word and her entire reality might come unraveled.

More than twenty years ago, she had held the fate of humanity in her hands. With the fallen body of her beloved mentor in her arms, and explosions of shorted circuitry all around her, it was she who had cried out in pain, *"They're animals! No mercy!"* Thus had the Earth-Minbari War begun. On her head. On hers.

Now, once again, the fates of untold millions were hers to do with as she wished.

Don't go to Z'ha'dum, she wanted to scream at him. He wouldn't know what she was talking about. *You'll die there! You'll come back, but changed, and your life will be reduced to but an instant!*

But she reined herself in, knowing that she did not dare.

"Oh, John . . . there is so much ahead of you, so many changes, so much pain and grief . . ." She shook her head, still finding it hard to believe. "I look in your eyes now, and I see the innocence that went away so many years ago. But then . . . you don't know any of what's happened, do you?"

Like a man trying to catch up with a play, though he had walked into the middle, Sheridan said, "From what Londo said, I get the impression that we won the war . . . but not completely."

She shook her head. "The war is never completely won. There are always new battles to be fought against the darkness. Only the names change." She saw that there was a bleak sense of despair creeping onto his face. She couldn't let him return, thinking that their grand endeavor had failed—*would* fail. "We achieved everything we set out to achieve . . . we created something that will endure for a thousand years . . ." she said proudly. "But the price, John, the terrible, terrible price . . ."

Don't go to Z'ha'dum!

She bit her tongue, kept the words in. "I didn't think I would see you again, before the end."

There were footsteps approaching briskly down the hall, moving with purpose. He pulled her close and spoke to her with a ferocious intensity that had within it hints of the man he would become. "Delenn . . . is there anything I can do to prevent this? There's still a chance . . ."

"No," she said forcefully. "No. This future can be changed only by surrendering to the Shadows, and that price is too high to pay."

The door opened. She knew that it was their time. She knew they were going to be brought to their execution.

"But we have a son . . ." Sheridan said. There was a touch of wonder in his voice.

"Yes. David . . ."

"Out!" the guard barked. "Now!"

She held him close, and then they faced the light. They walked to the door and through it, out into the hallway. Sheridan held her close . . .

. . . and staggered.

"John?" she said, and then more alarmed, "John!"

He collapsed, and at that moment, another guard—a more highly ranked one—strode down the hall and called out in annoyance, "New orders. The emperor said to wait an hour!"

"Why an hour?"

"Who knows?"

There was some muttering that Delenn couldn't quite make out, although the words "crazy old man" might have been bandied about. At that moment, though, she cared about nothing except her fallen husband. "Please . . . he needs help," she said.

"Why? You're both going to die soon anyway," one of the guards pointed out, but they helped Delenn and Sheridan back toward their cell.

At that moment, Sheridan suddenly roared, *"No!"* His eyes were wild; there was nothing but confusion in them. And for a moment she thought she actually saw some sort of glow around him. Instantly she realized what was happening; it was some sort of temporal backlash. The Sheridan of the past and the present were, in some way and on some level, colliding. They were struggling for possession of the one form.

And it was nearly tearing them apart.

Sheridan's knees gave out, and he collapsed to the floor of the cell. Delenn instantly fell at his side, pulling him to her, but he had passed out. "John . . . it will be all right . . . I swear to you, it will," she whispered over and over again as the cell door slammed behind them, their destiny postponed a short time longer. And as she kept assuring him that all would be fine, she thought bleakly, *Who says Minbari never lie?*

EXCERPTED FROM
THE CHRONICLES OF LONDO MOLLARI.
Excerpt dated (approximate Earth date)
January 2, 2278 (final entry).

Note to historians: This is the one entry of the emperor's chronicles that is not strictly from his physical chronicles. It is a combination of written notes he was making at the time that he dictated his history of Babylon 5, and audio records that were made secretly, by the emperor himself, at the time. It is believed that, knowing his final hours were upon him, he was taking extensive pains to leave as thorough an accounting as possible. That would be in keeping with the character of Londo Mollari, who—as anecdotal evidence indicates—had dreamt of this moment for so large a portion of his adult life that he likely considered it the defining moment of his existence. We of the Centauri Historical Institute believe that what follows is an accurate depiction of the emperor's state of mind. It has been approved by Emperor Vir Cotto for inclusion into the historical records, and we wish to believe that Londo Mollari himself would likewise have endorsed it as accurate.

I looked at the lady Senna, and in a low voice, a voice that might once have been alluring when spoken by a young and handsome man, I said to her, "Dear lady . . . I would love to walk with you on a beach . . . somewhere. For just five minutes." I felt tears welling in my eyes, and I fought them back. It was the single greatest battle of my life. "How strange . . . to have come this far, and to want so little."

I turned away from her, for I did not know how much longer I could keep my eyes dry. A dear, sweet woman. Two lovely children. They could have been mine. They are the life I turned away from—the life of a different man . . . a lucky man.

"Children." My voice was low and hoarse. "Will you remember this story? Will you remember me?"

"All my life, Majesty," Luc said in wonderment.

I nodded. It would have to suffice. "Then go."

But Luc suddenly seemed less than willing to depart. "What happened to Sheridan and Delenn?" he asked. "What about the end of the story?"

"Sheridan," I said slowly, "became the president of a great alliance, Delenn ever at his side. And the story . . . is not over yet. The story is never over. Now go."

Senna took one child in each hand, and she started to head out of the room. Then the girl, Lyssa, stopped, and inquired, "Did they live happily ever after?"

"Lyssa!" Senna said in surprise.

"Did they live happily ever after?" she repeated more insistently.

"That . . . remains to be seen," I said after a moment.

And as Senna ushered them out . . . I remembered her. For a brief moment, I remembered who Senna was . . . and then it was gone.

As was she.

I used a spy device to watch Delenn and Sheridan in a tearful reunion down in their cell. Very moving.

Not everything was in place, though. Not everything was ready. Everything had to be done just right.

I picked up a bell and rang it. Moments later, I said to the guard standing there in response to it, "I need another bottle. I will need several more bottles. Then wait one hour . . . and bring the prisoners here."

He nodded and left me alone . . . a state to which I have become accustomed. Sometimes I think I have been alone my entire life.

I had a bit of one bottle left, and I emptied the contents into a glass. I raised it and said, "To the future . . . my old friends." And I drained the contents.

I heard footsteps, and I recognized the stride. How could I not? After all these years, it was impossible for me not to. I looked up and there he was, holding several bottles on a tray. I waggled my fingers, and said, "Come here."

Vir approached me. He had obviously encountered the guard returning with the drinks and decided to bring them to me himself. Whether the guard had turned the drinks over willingly or not, I did not know . . . or particularly care at that moment.

There was so much to be said between us . . . but it was necessary to concentrate purely on matters of historical record. "You will drink with me, Vir?" I asked.

"No, if it's all the same to you," he said. I think of the old days; when his voice always seemed to have a slight tremor to it. No more. Now he speaks with confidence . . . and just a hint of perpetual sadness.

"I have decided to work on a history, Vir. And I have decided that you will write it with me."

"I will?" He seemed most surprised. Of all the things he probably thought we would discuss, I doubt this was listed among them.

"Oh, yes. It will be quite comprehensive. Unfortunately, I do not think I will have overmuch time to complete it. I would like your help in achieving that. You were there for most of it. I think you are fit to do the job. If you wish, you may put your name first in the credits. For I strongly suspect, you see, that it will be published posthumously."

"I see," he said.

"I shall spend the next hour," I told him, as I proceeded to pour a drink, "giving you some details . . . some highlights . . . for I have been discussing it at length recently, and it is all fresh in my mind. You may record it however you wish. Expand upon it, put it into chronological order at your convenience. Then you will leave me, for I will meet with Sheridan and Delenn."

"Are you . . . are you . . ." He could not even frame the words.

I shook my head. "I . . . do not wish to discuss it, Vir, for reasons I cannot explain at the moment. For I am watched, you see, all the time . . . even here. So let us instead discuss matters of scholarship . . . and let the rest sort itself out.

"And Vir . . . you will let the people know. Let them know there was to be more than a world in flames. That there was supposed to be . . . should have been . . . greatness. With all the sacrifices, with all the people who have died, you would think we were entitled to that.

"You will carry on for me, Vir. It will be among the last orders I give. You will carry on and tell the story to others. It will be uplifting . . . or a warning . . . or simply a rather Byzantine adventure, depending upon how it's told and who is listening, I would imagine. And in this way, the story will never end. You will do this thing for me, Vir?"

With true tragedy in his voice, he replied, "Of course I will."

"Thank you," I said. "Thank you, my old friend." I patted him on the hand and leaned back, feeling the warmth of the liquor already beginning to fill me.

I shall drink myself into oblivion . . . and shortly thereafter, my soul will follow.

Vir waited for me to speak. He had found a recording device, and held it in his hand. "Where . . . where do you wish to start?" he asked.

Where to start? Where else, of course? In the beginning . . .

I looked out upon the burning remains of Centauri Prime, steadied my hand so that I could permit the liquid to cascade down my throat . . .

. . . and I began to speak. "I was there, at the dawn of the Third Age of Mankind. It began in the Earth year 2257 with the founding of the last of the Babylon stations, located deep in neutral space. It was a port of call for refugees, smugglers, businessmen, diplomats, and travelers from a hundred worlds. It could be a dangerous place, but we accepted the risk because Babylon 5 was our last, best hope for peace . . . It became a dream given form . . . a dream of a galaxy without war, where species from different worlds could live side by side in mutual respect . . . a dream that was endangered as never before by the arrival of one man on a mission of destruction. Babylon 5 was the last of the Babylon stations. This is its story . . ."

I had such dreams. Such dreams . . .

24

His clothes were tattered . . . one eye was missing, replaced by a black cloth . . . and he had been beaten so thoroughly in recent days that almost every step was agony. And yet G'Kar carried himself so tall, so proudly, that one might have thought at first glance that the guards surrounding him were at his service, rather than acting as his captors.

But G'Kar was nothing short of astounded when the guards led him to the throne room . . . then stopped at the door. Under normal circumstances they would be flanking him, front and back, to make sure there was no way that he could spring at the emperor in some improbably fit of fury. But this time, it was not the case.

They were allowing him to go in unescorted.

One of the guards saw the puzzled look in G'Kar's good eye. "Emperor's orders," he said, matter-of-factly.

G'Kar nodded and stepped through the door. He had no idea what to expect. For some reason he thought that perhaps there was going to be a firing squad on the other side. The shooters would yell, "Surprise!" and then open fire, and that would be that.

He was, however, quite wrong. Instead there was the throne room, utterly devoid of retainers, guards, and such . . . except for two people. One of them he had expected to see. The other he had not.

There was a small table set up, and seated at it were Londo Mollari and Vir Cotto. There were several empty bottles and glasses on it. It seemed a phenomenal amount of alcohol to have ingested, even by Londo's standards. There was still a partially filled bottle. There was also a bowl of fruit, half consumed. Londo had just finished saying something about Delenn, and suddenly he was seized with a racking cough. Vir, for his part, didn't even seem to notice. Instead, he looked up at G'Kar and nodded slightly in greeting.

G'Kar hadn't quite recognized Vir at first. He looked so much older and so careworn. G'Kar made the traditional Narn gesture of greeting.

"That," Londo said, coughing, "is what we need."

Vir looked at him in confusion. "What is, Londo?"

"A way of saying hello. The Narn, they have that business with fist and chest . . . the Minbari, with their fingers as triangles . . . what do we do?" He waggled his fingers. Then he shook his head. "Pathetic. Truly. Perhaps we deserved our fate on that basis alone. Sit, G'Kar. Sit. Vir . . . I need you to do two final things for me."

"Whatever you need, Londo." G'Kar saw such sadness in Vir, he could barely conceive what it must have been like for him.

"I want you to go to my private chambers. There is a hidden place, behind my writing desk. In the wall. Volumes are stored there. Chronicles of my life as emperor. I think you will find them . . . illuminating. Combine them with what I have told you and . . ." He stopped and coughed for a full thirty seconds before he managed to pull himself together. His voice was hoarse and scratchy; he sounded as if he had been speaking for hours. Every word sounded as if it was taking effort. ". . . combine them . . . and tell others of me. Because otherwise I will be forgotten . . . and I do not think that I would like that."

"Because your heroic efforts deserve to be immortalized?" G'Kar could not resist asking.

But Londo looked up at him with a baleful stare that carried with it not a hint of irony. "No. Because stupidity as monumental as mine should be enshrined so that others may learn. Vir . . . the second thing . . ."

"Yes?"

"Once you have them . . . leave. Leave and do not look back. Do not return until it is safe . . . if ever. And watch the shadows . . . sometimes, when you're not watching . . . they move. I have struck a bargain of sorts to preserve your life. If I had not, you would have been dead moments after you set foot in my presence. But I do not expect that it will be honored beyond my death . . . which, I suspect, will come soon."

Vir nodded, and G'Kar wondered if he understood what Londo was talking about. Vir started to head out, and G'Kar wanted to say something, because he had the oddest feeling that he was never going to see Vir again. "Cotto," he called out.

Vir Cotto turned and waited politely for G'Kar to speak.

G'Kar gave it a moment's thought, and then said, "Never mind. It will come to me later."

Vir laughed softly at that.

And then he was gone.

It was just the two of them.

As Vir made his way hurriedly down the corridor toward Londo's private chambers, he ran into Senna coming in the opposite direction. They stopped, facing each other. For a moment, there seemed a gap between them that no amount of effort or emotion could possibly bridge.

And then, before either of them even realized it, they were in each other's arms, and he kissed her hungrily. He held her tightly, as if she were a lifeline.

"Come with me," he whispered. "At least for a little while. Until we know it's safe."

"I will . . ."

"The children . . . do you need to bring—"

Senna shook her head. "Luc and Lyssa's parents picked them up a few minutes ago. They have a bunker they built some time ago that they're taking the children to. They'll be perfectly safe."

"I have to make a quick stop at the emperor's private study . . ."

Her face was a question mark. "Why?"

"I have to get his legacy," he told her grimly.

Londo slowly leaned forward and clearly tried to focus on G'Kar. It seemed to the Narn that Londo was seeing less with two eyes than he, G'Kar, was seeing with one.

"Can you see it?" he whispered.

G'Kar made no effort to hide his confusion. "See what?"

"Ah. You have answered my question, thank you."

"Have I?"

"Oh yesss," Londo told him, slurring the words. "Because if you could see it, you would not have to ask what it is you are supposed to be seeing."

"I see."

"Sit, sit. You have become my regular dining companion, you know. I would not want to cheat you of a final meal."

"A final meal?" G'Kar sat opposite him and picked up a piece of fruit. He took a bite of it, wondering if it was going to be poisoned. If it was, it certainly tasted sweet. The juice ran down his face, and he made a token effort to clean it off with his sleeve. "Are you planning to kill me, then?"

"I? I make no plans. They require too much . . . planning." He took a deep swig of the contents of the bottle and, for some reason, glanced at his shoulder. "I have been giving matters . . . much thought. And I have decided . . . that all of this . . . was about me."

"All of what?" G'Kar was genuinely curious.

"Everything. Babylon 5 . . . the Shadow War . . . the fate of Centauri Prime . . . all about me."

"Very egocentric," G'Kar observed.

"That does not make it wrong," Londo pointed out. He seemed to be enjoying the effect that the alcohol was having on him. All his words were slurring, one into another, and it was with difficulty that G'Kar was able to understand what he was saying. "It was in her predictions, you know. The one about the man already dead . . . that was easy. That was Sheridan. She also told me that I had to save the eye that does not see. Until an hour ago, I thought that referred to you."

G'Kar was completely lost, but he was not about to admit it. "But now you no longer think that."

"No. I think I misheard her. I think she referred, not to the 'eye' as in orb, but rather 'I' as in 'I, myself.' Because I had all the hints, all the warnings that I needed. It was all there, right in front of me. Morella tried to warn me . . . and the techno-mage . . . and Vir, Great Maker knows, over and over again . . . they all tried to make me see. But I did not. I did not see where my path was taking me. In order to avoid the fire that awaits me at the end of my journey, I must first save . . . myself."

"It sounds like a bit of a tautology," G'Kar pointed out. "To save yourself, you must save yourself? Not very useful advice."

"It is useful if I put it to use . . . which is likely also a tautology, yes? But I am emperor, and so have that prerogative." He drank deeply again. Then he leaned forward, and said conspiratorially, "So . . . do you see it yet?"

"I suppose I do not," G'Kar admitted.

"Soon enough. Where was I?"

"Saving yourself."

"Ah, yes! Thank you, my good friend, G'Kar." He seemed to find that phrase rather amusing. "My good friend, G'Kar. Who would have thought such unlikely words would be paired, eh? Almost as unlikely as Emperor Mollari. No . . . not my good friend. My . . . greatest friend," and he clapped G'Kar on the shoulder. "And my greatest fear."

"I am flattered on both counts," G'Kar said, "that you—"

"You should be able to see it now," Londo suddenly said, sounding somewhat annoyed. "I don't understand why . . . oh. Oh, of course. I am still wearing my mantle. Naturally . . . naturally, you do not see it, because I am covering it. Here . . . hold on." He shrugged off his ceremonial cape. G'Kar leaned forward, confused. There seemed to be some kind of lump visible now, a tumor of some sort . . .

Then he gasped and tried to stand up so quickly that the chair he was sitting on tumbled back with a clatter. He almost stumbled, but righted himself at the last moment.

The creature situated on Londo's shoulder literally reeked of evil and foulness. It apparently had an eye of some sort, but the eye was just in the process of closing. G'Kar could barely make out tendrils that were extended down into the emperor's pure white clothes.

Londo was utterly unperturbed. "You see it, yes?"

G'Kar managed to nod, but just barely.

"Very stylish, eh? Soon everyone will be wanting one, I think."

"What . . . is it?"

"My conscience," Londo told him. His thick eyebrows knitted as he tried to pick up the thread of the conversation. "Ohhh . . . yes. Yes, I remember. All about me. That is what this has all been."

"Londo . . ." A stunned G'Kar was pointing at the creature on Londo's shoulder.

But Londo was paying it no mind at all. In his own mind, the conversation had moved on. "All of this . . . has been one great epic about the loss of a man's soul . . . and its eventual recovery and redemption, but only at a terrible price. As an epic story, it has potential . . . do you think?"

G'Kar managed a nod.

"The thing is, G'Kar . . . that at this point, the Drakh—believe it or not—need me. Even as some of their number depart this world, others desire to stay. They still see me as their instrument of revenge . . . their puppet, to be danced with for some time to come. Without me . . . they have nothing. And without Sheridan and Delenn . . . they do not even have revenge. They hate Sheridan and Delenn, you know. Because they told the Shadows to leave . . . and the Shadows did. In some ways, the Drakh are like . . ." He fished for a comparison and then smiled. ". . . they are like children. Children abandoned by their parents and taking out their anger on the world. I can almost find it within me not to hate them. Almost. But not quite."

"You said . . . 'without Sheridan and Delenn.' Are you saying that you intend to let them go?"

Slowly Londo managed to nod, though not without effort. "That is my intent. It will be . . . somewhat involved. The Drakh do not want them to leave. The Drakh want them dead. And in recent days, it has become rather important for me to do things . . . other than the way the Drakh desire."

Suddenly so much of everything that had happened became clear. How long had Londo not been responsible for his actions? How long had one of those creatures sat on his shoulder, watching him, manipulating his moves? All the way back to the beginning of the War? Had the creatures told him to bomb the Narn Homeworld? Betray G'Kar? Was Londo, after all this time, genuinely an innocent man?

"If Sheridan and Delenn can leave . . . so can you, Londo," G'Kar said with sudden urgency. "We all can. We can escape . . ."

But Londo shook his head. "No . . . no. Sooner or later, my small . . . associate . . . would awaken. The instant that happened, the Drakh vessels would come after us and blow us to hell."

"Then let me kill that thing . . ."

"If it dies, I die. Besides, G'Kar, some things are preordained. Trust me on that. This is the only way."

"But if that . . . thing . . . controlled your actions . . ."

"Ahhh . . . I see what you think. No, G'Kar, no. In the grand scheme of things, this," and he indicated the creature, "is only a recent acquisition." He leaned forward, coughed several times, and then said raggedly, "Would you like to know . . . what sort of person I was? After I arranged for the bombing of the Narn colony in Quadrant 14 . . . the emperor, Emperor Turhan, with his last breath, told me that my associates and I were damned. And I announced that instead he had condoned and applauded our actions. And do you know what else, G'Kar, old friend?" And he half smiled. "Given the exact same opportunity . . . I would do it again. I would figure out some way to spare my people this . . . this debacle," and he gestured to the smoking ruins of Centauri Prime. "But what I did to your people . . ." And he snapped his fingers. "Like that, once more, given the opportunity."

G'Kar bristled, his blood thudding in his temple, and it was all he could do not to leap for the smirking face right then . . .

And then he figured it out. He realized that Londo was just trying to get to him . . . to enrage him . . . to get him to . . .

Attack him? Kill him?

Of course. Kill him. That had to be it.

And then, before G'Kar could say or do anything further, there was the sound of voices approaching. Stern guards were saying, "Keep moving!"

Londo stood on uneven legs and, with more willpower than actual strength, thrust himself toward his throne. He caught himself on it and swung himself to a seated position, allowing the shadows to cloak him.

"Hide," he told G'Kar. "Now. Hurry. There is a small dressing chamber over there," and he pointed. Even that movement clearly pained him. "Go there."

"Why?"

"Because time is running short, and the minutes it would take me to explain to Sheridan and Delenn why things must be done, these lost minutes might well prevent our being able to do them. Do as I say."

"As you command," G'Kar said with a deep sense of mockery. He stepped into the room Londo had indicated and softly shut the door behind himself.

And then he waited . . . for his final instructions.

25

Londo did not sit forward on his throne, because the pain was too great. His conversation with G'Kar had taken the last of his strength from him. He did not think he had any reserves left.

One of the guards came in first and walked toward the throne. He did so hesitantly, as if he wasn't sure if Londo was even there. That was how well hidden in the shadows Londo was. "Highness?"

"Yes."

Having affirmed for himself that Londo was there, the guard said, "Sheridan had passed out for a short time, but he seems to have recovered."

"Oh, good," Londo said dryly. "We wouldn't want him to be anything but awake for his final moments. Bring them in."

Sheridan and Delenn were ushered before his presence. They squinted in the dimness of the room; Londo preferred it dark these days. It was as if he had surrendered totally to it. The guards stepped out, leaving them alone. Sheridan and Delenn seemed puzzled, as if wondering whether they were alone.

Suddenly Londo's hand went numb. Even he had lost track of how much he had had to drink. The glass, which he had totally forgotten he was holding, slipped out of his grasp and clattered to the floor. Delenn jumped slightly. Sheridan did not. For some reason, Londo found that interesting.

Delenn and Sheridan slowly began to walk toward him, squinting.

"Close enough," Londo said softly. He spoke hardly above a whisper, and the words were slurred. He barely recognized his voice. He felt as if he were viewing the world through a haze.

He tried to stand and discovered that his legs and brain were no longer on speaking terms. If he did manage to get to his feet, he would most likely topple over, and how dignified would that be? It wasn't fit that he spend his last moments—and they were his last, he was quite convinced of that—flat on his face.

"You will excuse me if I do not stand," he managed to say. "You see, I have had considerable to drink . . . it is the only way we can be alone. We do not wish to wake it."

Sheridan looked at him in confusion. Technically, he looked twice as confused as he should be, because Londo was seeing two of him. "Wake what?"

Londo cocked an eyebrow, which was the only part of him capable of movement. "Ah, then you do not know. We all have our keepers, you see . . ." He chuckled softly. "Oh, they make us think we have free will, but it's a lie. I gave a very good performance, yes?"

He saw understanding beginning to dawn on Delenn's face. Sheridan still looked befuddled. That made sense to Londo. He had long suspected that Delenn was the true brains in the family. "It was satisfied," he continued. "It doesn't care why I do what I do as long as I do it . . . as long as you are dead."

He managed to find enough strength to lean forward. Delenn's face remained impassive. It was as if she was expecting to see the creature there. But Sheridan looked totally stunned, and that confused Londo even further. Londo knew that he had spotted the keeper on his son's shoulder, when he had endeavored to stop the boy from leaving Minbar. Now, though, Sheridan acted as if he'd never encountered one of them before.

"It cannot hold its liquor, you see," Londo explained. "I learned that if I drink just enough, I can put it to sleep for a few minutes . . . a few minutes where I am in charge of myself again . . ." He took a deep breath. Putting together understandable words, coherent sentences, was a tremendous effort for him. "But the minutes have been growing shorter and shorter . . . so we do not have much time."

He leaned back, once again at home in the shadows. And why not? He had been living within them for so long, he no longer had anything to fear.

"My life is almost over. My world, all I hoped for . . . gone. You two are my last chance . . . for this place, for my world . . . for my own redemption." He steadied his voice, glad that the alcohol had so numbed him that he was no longer capable of feeling any emotion; merely observing it from a distance, as if in a dream. "You will find a ship hidden behind the palace. My personal guard will take you. In exchange for your lives, I ask that you and your allies help free my world. I can do nothing more for them."

Sheridan seemed touched, and still a bit bewildered. "Londo . . . if there's anything—"

Londo shook his head. "No. There is nothing. Now go, quickly. You don't have much time. I can . . . feel it starting to wake up. Hurry. Go," his voice got louder with the last words.

Sheridan and Delenn looked at one another, and then turned and left. He knew that Dunseny and Caso would be right outside, as they had been instructed. That they would carry out his final orders.

Alone, again, as always, Londo waited for the creaking of a door that he knew would come. "You are there, my old friend?"

G'Kar entered the room, watching him, looking at the keeper balefully. "Yes," he said.

"They will never make it out alive, unless . . . ." He took another breath. "You see, my keeper will awaken any second. It will alert the others . . . and my only hope will die. And I will die soon after. They do not take betrayal lightly."

And at the last . . .

The words of Lady Morella floated to him across the years.

. . . you must surrender yourself to your greatest fear . . .

He wondered if that was strictly true anymore. Because in a way, his greatest fear was that he might continue to live.

. . . knowing that it will kill you.

He paused, an infinity of time passing in a second, and said the words that he had known, for as long as he could recall, that he was destined to say. "We have unfinished business between us, G'Kar. Let us have an end to it, quickly, before it stops me. I am as tired of my life as you are."

G'Kar came at him. His hands clamped around Londo's throat, and it did not seem right somehow, because in the vision he had always been fighting back. But he had no desire to do so. He just wanted it over, done, finished. He marveled at the Narn's strength, wondered what it would have been like to battle G'Kar hand to hand, man to man, back in his prime, back at a time when anything seemed possible.

And then the keeper awoke.

G'Kar could not count the number of times that he had thought of this moment. There were times when he had, for his amusement, speculated what it would be like to sink his fingers into Londo's fleshy throat, feel the pulse beneath his fingers, feel it slowing, feel it stopping. He had wondered how long he would actually stand there, once there was no life, and still keep squeezing, just enjoying the life-lessness.

And that day—that terrible day, when he had learned of Londo's duplicity, drinking with him in friendship while Londo sent ships to kill thousands, millions of innocent Narns—he had gone berserk that day. When he stormed down the corridors of Babylon 5, howling for Londo Mollari's blood, he would have done more than strangle him. He would have ripped his living hearts from his body, held up one, and consumed the other while the life flickered from Londo's eyes.

Now . . .

Now he had him. Londo wasn't putting up a fight. He was . . . he was sacrificing himself. Surrendering to G'Kar, telling him to get it over with, so Delenn and Sheridan could escape.

Sheridan. "The king." And he was the hand of the king, and those hands were wrapped with murderous intent around the throat of a true king, an emperor.

The Narn named G'Kar who had imagined this moment, the Narn named G'Kar who would have reveled in it, had died years ago, replaced by a philosopher who was revered throughout the Narn Homeworld as G'Kar the wise, G'Kar the thoughtful, G'Kar the scholarly. His writings were endlessly studied, examined for the slightest nuance. Students who sat at his feet repeated his teachings, statues had been built to him, songs sung, stories written. They wor-shipped him as a man of peace even more than they had revered him as a man of war. Some called his writings the most important since those of G'Quan himself—a claim he had always considered to be a tad overblown, but there it was, and he wasn't going to deny it.

G'Kar the wise had forgiven Londo his trespasses. Had come to appreciate him, not for the man he was, but for the man he could have been . . . and might yet be.

The hand of the king was going to have the blood of the emperor on it, and G'Kar's will faltered. He saw Londo surrendering to what he recognized as his fate, and something in G'Kar recoiled at the very notion. There had to be some other way. Sheridan and Delenn had to escape, yes. But there had to be a way for Londo to escape as well, something that would not cost him his life. It couldn't simply end like this, with cold-blooded murder . . . even if it was at the request of the victim. He was not an executioner. He was G'Kar, son of G'Qarn, scribe, sage, both teacher and student of the universe, and he could not, would not, do this thing.

And in deciding this, he began to ease up, ever so slightly, on Londo's throat.

And then the keeper awoke . . .

We are threatened! We are being assaulted! It is trying to kill us!

The keeper howled in anguish and fear. It saw its host was in danger, saw its own life threatened, because they were bonded, one to the other. A keeper could disengage, but it was a lengthy process, one that took time . . . time the keeper did not have. It did, however, have defensive capabilities.

In the early years of their relationship, the keeper had simply been an observer. But as time had passed, the keeper had insinuated itself so thoroughly into Londo's nervous system that, in times of stress, it could take over the body entirely for short periods.

Stop them, Londo! We love you! We care for you! We will never leave you!

The creature had never been so terrified, not since its spawning. When Shiv'kala had removed it from its nourishment pouch, it had feared the Centauri. Feared it so much that it had trembled in Shiv'kala's keeping. But the Drakh had assured it that all would be well, and it had been.

And now it wasn't.

Protect us, Londo! Protect us! Save us! Love us!

And Londo's arms flew up, not of their own accord, but at the keeper's command. They grabbed on to G'Kar's throat, clamping in with ferocity.

26

"I am Dunseny, and this is Caso," Dunseny said by way of hurried introduction as they proceeded down the corridor. "I tell you that so that, if this does not go well and we die, you will know whose name to curse with your final breath."

"Very considerate," Delenn said. She cast a worried glance at Sheridan, who was suddenly starting to look a little uncertain on his feet. Dunseny hurried on ahead, Caso behind him, leading the way for Sheridan and Delenn. His hand hovered near his weapon, just in case some sort of resistance might be met.

Suddenly Sheridan's legs began to buckle once again. He leaned against the wall, supporting himself. Delenn took his arm, her face a mask of worry. "What is it?"

Sheridan tried to fight off whatever had a hold of him, but was unable to. "I'm . . . being pulled back again. Go on, hurry, don't wait for me."

"No. I won't leave you," she said firmly, shaking her head.

He tried to take a few more steps, got halfway down another corridor, and then the pain overwhelmed him. "It's no good . . . I can feel time pulling at me . . ."

She held him tightly. "Then take these words back with you to the past: Treasure the moments you have. Savor them for as long as you can, for they will never come again."

She knew that was all she should say. That she could take no chance of disrupting the past. Who knew what she might change? If she said the wrong thing, David might never exist, or the Shadows might triumph, or . . . or anything. There was simply no way of knowing, and every instinct, every fragment of common sense she possessed, warned her to keep her mouth shut . . .

And then she heard her own voice blurt out, "John . . . listen to me, do not go to Z'ha'dum. Do you understand? Do not go to Z'ha'dum . . ."

She held him desperately, wishing she could shield him from
harm with her own body, and suddenly Sheridan tore away from her,
slamming against the wall as if in the grip of some vast invisible fist.
He convulsed once more, his head snapping this way and that, and
then with tremendous effort he focused on her.

"Delenn..." he whispered. "I...I blanked out, I..." He
looked around the corridor in utter astonishment. "How did we get
here? How did..."

Caso had stopped, and was standing there. He was looking
around with barely controlled nervousness, clearly concerned that
someone might show up. Realizing that they had halted, Dunseny
came back to them and gestured urgently. "What are you waiting
for?" he demanded.

Sheridan looked in confusion from one to the other. "Are you...
taking us to Londo?"

"We were just there," Delenn told him. "John...we can't stop
here and discuss this. Later. Later we can—"

Suddenly his hand clutched her arm so hard that pain shot up to
her shoulder. Then he realized what he was doing, and eased up.
"Babylon 4," he whispered. "The time flux...this was it..."

"Yes," she said, relieved that she wasn't going to have to explain.

"I *thought* I was suddenly having déjà vu," he said, looking
around.

Urgently she suddenly inquired, "Z'ha'dum...did you—"

"Go?" He nodded. "Yes." He sounded almost apologetic, because obviously he remembered her breathless advice...and had
felt constrained to disobey it anyway.

She felt an awful mixture of relief and pain, all at the same time.
Relief because she had allowed a moment of weakness to jeopardize
everything that was, or might ever be...and nothing had come from
it. And pain because it meant that, in three years at the most, John
would be lost to her. The time given him as a reprieve against death
would be running out. If he had not gone to Z'ha'dum...

"Ifs," Sheridan had said to her, years before. With an amused
grin he had explained, "My father used to say 'If ifs and ands were
pots and pans, the world would be a kitchen.' " She hadn't been entirely certain she understood it, but the message was clear.

"Mr. President," Dunseny said with extremely forced politeness,
and he indicated that the hallway awaited them.

Without any further discussion, Sheridan and Delenn bolted
down the corridor. A series of quick turns and they emerged through

a door of the palace. On a pad nearby, there was a shuttle waiting for them.

"It's the emperor's personal landing pad," Dunseny informed them. His attitude seemed to carry the message that for the emperor to provide such a service for them was a singular honor. They were, to Dunseny's mind, probably not acting with sufficient awe or gratitude. "He wished me to convey to you his hope that the shuttle will sufficiently accommodate you."

"What about David," Sheridan said urgently. He turned to Delenn. "Where is he?"

She rested a hand on his arm, and said firmly, "Londo assured me that David would be safe. That he would be gotten off-world. Londo said he himself would attend to it personally. Come." And she was pulling him toward the shuttle.

Had he not been so groggy and confused, Sheridan would have put up a greater struggle. As it was, he was arguing nevertheless, dragging his heels, not petulantly, but with determination. And each word or phrase was matched by a small stomp of a foot. "We aren't . . . leaving . . . without . . . David . . ."

"It has been attended to, sir," Caso offered. He led them over to the shuttle. "Now you have to leave . . ."

Clearly Sheridan was getting his usual fire and composure back, because standing just outside the shuttle, he rounded on the guard, and said, "Listen, sonny. We don't 'have' to do anything that gets in the way of what's important: namely, getting our son back." His hand was trembling, and he was shaking a finger at Caso. "If he doesn't turn up—"

"John!" Delenn's voice was a cry of alarm, flooded with relief. "Look!"

Sprawled in the center of the shuttle, like a large bag of produce, was David. Delenn ran to him, checked him over. She was relieved to see that his chest was rising and falling in a wonderfully normal manner. "David . . . David, wake up . . ."

"That would not be wise. Nor feasible," Dunseny said. "He's asleep because we drugged him."

"Drugged him!" Delenn said in alarm.

"Well . . . drugged his food, technically."

"What have you done to my son?" Sheridan demanded angrily.

If Sheridan's anger was intended to intimidate Dunseny, it didn't work. The faithful retainer looked at him with only the mildest of concern. "Nothing that wasn't necessary."

Suddenly Delenn understood. She pulled back the edge of his shirt, around the throat. The small mass of protoplasm—the thing called the keeper—was still attached, its single, fearsome eye closed. It slept as soundly as David.

"In Valen's name . . ." she whispered.

"As you see," Dunseny said mildly. "We did to him what the emperor did to himself, but on a far more extreme level. As I said, necessary. If his—associate—were to see the two of you, it would put an end to your escape." His face twisted in disgust. "The Drakh may be in the process of abandoning this world, thank the Great Maker. But if the keeper were in working order, you can rest assured that one of their vessels would still find the time to blow you out of the sky."

"He should be out for some time yet," Caso told them. "Perhaps not quite long enough for you to get to Minbar . . . but far enough, at least, to be safe in deep space, several jump points away."

"At that point, if he awakens, don't tell him your position. We're hoping even the keeper can't send information to the Drakh that his host doesn't possess." Dunseny looked around apprehensively once more. "Standing here talking is counterproductive. Leave. Now."

Sheridan quickly moved forward to the cockpit of the shuttle, Delenn staying by David's side, caressing his hair gently. Some part of her couldn't quite believe that he was with them again. She looked to Dunseny, standing outside the shuttle, looking in unflappably as the door irised shut. The skyline of the burning city was visible behind him, in the distance. Just before the closing door cut off her view of his face, he said—without the slightest trace of irony—"Thank you for visiting beautiful Centauri Prime. We do hope you've enjoyed your trip. Please come again." And then the door closed.

27

Far, far away from it all . . .

The female Centauri lay on her deathbed.

The women who tended her were moving around like moths, flitting about, dabbing her head that was burning with fever, trying to keep liquids in her, and taking care of her needs. She did not pay attention to any of them, did not seem to know that any of them were there. She stared at the ceiling, although since her eyes were glassy, it was difficult to know just how much she actually saw.

In a way, it seemed that she was not looking at the ceiling . . . but through it. Through it to a place light-years away, to events that she could not see, could not possibly know about . . . and yet, somehow, she did . . .

The moment G'Kar felt the fingers tighten on his throat, he knew there was no backing out. He knew that he was in the fight of his life . . . a fight *for* his life. But he wasn't looking at Londo as he redoubled his efforts to crush the emperor's throat. His focus was entirely on the eye that was peering back at him . . . the single, unblinking eye.

He saw terror in it, and from that terror, he drew strength.

Harder, Londo! Save us! Save us! We do not want to die!

Londo saw the fearsome red eye of G'Kar, and it was looking to his side. He realized that, at the last, G'Kar's battle was not with him, but with the thing on his shoulder. Londo's mind was almost detached from what was happening. In a way, it was symbolic. The keeper was the incarnation of all the dark, background forces that had made Londo their puppet for so many years.

And even as he thought that, his efforts increased, his death grip on G'Kar's throat redoubled. Strength flowed from the panic that the keeper fed into him, and he wanted to scream *Faster, G'Kar!*

Faster! End it before it's too late! But he could say nothing, for his windpipe was already crushed. He had no chance, and still he fought on.

Londo! You can stop him! You can kill the Narn and we can live on, and it will be much better, you will have more time for yourself, we can do this thing for you, we will treat you better, and the Drakh will make things better, love us, Londo, stop him!

Londo had heard that, when one is dying, one's life flashes before one's eyes . . .

As G'Kar's fingers burrowed deeper, his mind further disassociated, and he waited, and saw nothing . . . and there was still nothing, and time stretched out and continued to warp around him and there was nothing . . .

Nothing . . .

Londo . . . fight . . . fight . . . help us . . . Shiv'kala . . . Drakh, masters of shadow, help us . . . do not flee, do not run, help us, help your servants . . .

Words . . . so many words . . .

It was incredible to G'Kar. He had been a warrior, with no patience for words, and yet words had become his weapon, cutting more deeply than any blade, smashing down more doors than any strength of arm. Words, words came floating back to him . . .

No one here is exactly what they seem . . .

I did not fight to remove one dictator just to become another myself . . .

There's someone else out there, Na'Toth . . .

The future isn't what it used to be . . .

These and hundreds of others tumbled around, fighting to be noticed, to be remembered and treasured and cherished one final time, one final moment before sliding off into oblivion.

He shoved forward, tumbling to the floor, his hands still wrapped around Londo's throat, his eye still fixed on the malevolent creature staring back at him. He desperately wanted to hear the mouthless creature scream. He thought, in some way, he actually heard it doing so. Not hear it . . . feel it . . .

Feel it . . . feel it all . . .

Feel the agony of seeing his father hanging from a tree, telling his son with his dying breath that he was proud of him . . .

Feel the warmth of the blood splattering on him . . . the blood of the first Centauri he killed . . .

Feel the pain of Delenn's gravity rings crushing him . . .

Feel the loss, the humiliation, the betrayal of his people at the hands of Londo Mollari . . .

Feel the ignominy of being forced from the council after the Narn had fallen . . . and the swell of desperate pride as he made his exit speech . . .

Feel the agony of the eye being torn from his face . . . that was as nothing compared to Cartagia's lash upon his back . . .

Feel the momentary glory of triumph, breaking free of his bonds in Cartagia's throne room, seeing the shock of his Centauri captors as they realized just what it was they were facing . . .

Feel the serenity of his writings . . .

Feel the friendship for Londo that he never thought could occur . . .

Feel the pride in accomplishment . . . the softness of a woman's skin pressed against him . . . the smell of fresh air . . . the warmth of a sunrise . . . the coolness of a sunset . . . *the hands around his throat . . . the pain . . . receding . . . the job . . . not done . . . not quitting . . . wetness . . . on his hands, Londo's tears flowing, sobbing at his fate, tears on G'Kar's hands . . . the hand . . . of the king . . . saving the king . . . saving the realm . . . saving . . .*

Londo! Do not stop! You can save us! The darkness . . . there are things in it . . . I am afraid of the darkness . . . Londo . . . love us . . . Londo . . . Londo . . .

Nothing . . . there was nothing . . . he was . . .

I saw nothing . . . not a thing . . .

When Kosh emerged from the encounter suit . . . to save Sheridan that time . . . Londo had been standing there . . . and the words, the whispered wonderment . . .

Valeria . . . Droshalla . . . G'Lan . . .

They all saw . . . something . . . and Londo, squinting against the light . . . saw . . .

I saw nothing . . . not a thing . . .

Nothing . . . the nothingness of an empty soul . . . the nothingness of the damned . . . the nothing . . .

* * *

Londo! Save us . . . save . . . save . . .

Save . . . save us . . .

Save me . . .

And then . . .

. . . then the mental picture that he had snapped of that moment, buried in his head for all these years . . . suddenly developed . . . the detail fleshing in, and he saw . . . he saw . . .

. . . a being . . . a great being, with wings outstretched, looking up . . . no, down . . . down at him, smiling, and the face, a female face, flickering, shifting, and it was Adira, smiling at him, telling him that there was nothing to fear, and she stretched her hand out to him . . . he reached for it . . . and tears began to flow, tears of joy . . . and behind her, a beach seemed to shimmer . . .

Black tendrils, snared around his arm, pulling him back . . .

. . . he fought against them, the final fight, the only fight, the only one that mattered, and his fingers were almost brushing against hers . . .

Londo . . . you cannot get away . . . you will always be ours . . . you . . .

I will be my own man, *he howled in his mind, and he lunged for her, for the warmth, for the beauty of that winged and glorious creature, and his fingers brushed against hers. The moment they did there was a crackle of energy, and it filled him, and exploded within him, and then the world turned to pure white . . .*

Far, far away from it all . . .

The female Centauri focused, for the first time in a long time, on those who were tending her. And in a voice surprisingly strong and firm, she said, "Oho. *Now* he needs me. Typical . . ."

. . . and then her eyes closed in repose, and Timov, daughter of Algul, empress-in-exile of Centauri Prime, passed away . . .

28

Renegar and Gwynn were standing at Vir's shuttle, gesturing frantically for him to come aboard. Gwynn seemed to be assessing Senna, casting a critical eye up and down. Senna didn't seem to meet with her approval. Then again, very little did. So instead she turned her attention to the skies, obviously anticipating the possibility that one of the Drakh might detect them somehow and take their revenge. But as Vir approached, he suddenly slowed, then stopped.

"What the hell are you doing?" Renegar demanded.

Senna turned to look back at him in confusion. "Vir?"

Vir was holding a large satchel clutched in his arms, like a child. Suddenly he shoved it into Senna's arms, kissed her quickly on the cheek, turned, and headed back for the palace.

"I'm going back to help Londo."

"You can't help him," Gwynn said flatly. "You can only destroy yourself."

"Destroy myself?" There was a flat, disbelieving tone in Vir's voice. "You still don't get it, do you, Gwynn. Everything that was good about me is long gone. Everything that I used to despise about myself, I now realize was the best of me. I can't destroy myself; Vir Cotto was destroyed long ago. I can only end myself, and believe me, at this point, I don't much care about that."

He turned and bolted for the castle. Behind him, Renegar shouted, "You're being a fool!"

"Long practice," Vir shouted back.

Renegar watched him go in disbelief, and then shaking his head, he turned to the techno-mages. "Do we wait for him to come back?"

"Only if we are as great fools as he is," Gwynn shot back. "Come." She headed for the shuttle, then stopped at the door ... knowing without even needing to look that Renegar hadn't budged from the spot. Neither had Senna.

"Leave without me if you want. I'm waiting here," Renegar informed her.

"As am I," Senna echoed.

Gwynn let out a long, frustrated sigh, and then said, "No. We're not. We're taking off, right now."

Renegar turned away from her and then felt her hand on his arm. The other hand touched Senna's arm. They tried to pull away, and Gwynn muttered some words, and they each felt a tingling sensation that quickly moved up into their heads. Then just like that, Gwynn was pulling them along and they were unable to prevent her from guiding them into the shuttle.

There was deathly silence in the throne room when Vir entered. Somehow, before he even walked in, he knew what he would find. They were lying there, G'Kar and Londo, hands wrapped around each other's throats. There was, to the scene, a sense of completion, of closure, as if this was somehow always meant to be.

The great seal of the emperor lay nearby. Slowly Vir crouched and picked it up. He turned it over and over, felt the weight of it, shaking his head as he did so. He felt as if he held the entire weight of all the expectations of Centauri Prime, all the dashed hopes, all the shattered promises of the future.

His eyes were dry. He had no more tears to shed.

He looked down at Londo, the life gone from him. His final expression, incredibly, was a smile.

He looked over to G'Kar, into his eye . . .

The burning red eye . . . which moved. Twitched ever so infinitesimally.

"Great Maker," Vir breathed, scarcely able to believe it. "G'Kar . . ."

G'Kar's eye focused momentarily on Vir, then glanced away . . . glanced . . . at something . . . toward Vir's feet.

Vir reflexively looked to see what G'Kar was looking at . . . and took a step back, gasping in horror.

The creature appeared to be in extreme pain. Its tendrils were whipping about noiselessly, its single, hideous eye crusting over. There was a gaping hole in its side, like a hornet having torn its stinger away to pull itself free. But it was inches away from Vir, and it was not done yet, hanging on with determination that bordered on the supernatural.

The keeper looked up at Vir, although it might not have seen him so much as sensed him.

And Vir screamed, but it wasn't a sound of terror. Instead it was blind fury, such as he had never known. And gripping the seal of the emperor, he smashed it down upon the keeper. It made a vomitous squishing sound, and he was certain that somehow he heard a screech in his head . . . impossible, certainly, since the thing had no mouth, but he heard it just the same. He was positive it wasn't his imagination. Even as he raised the great seal up, he saw the mass on the floor still twitching. It wouldn't have mattered if it had been moving or not, for he was so seized in a fit of fury that he would have brought the seal crashing down again even if the creature hadn't been moving so much as a centimeter.

And then a third time, and a fourth and a fifth. He lost count. He lost track of time and lost all reason. He was astounded to realize that he was sobbing, the tears that he hadn't thought he possessed opening up. He hurled every invective he could think of at the creature and all that it represented, every profanity in his vocabulary, words that he had never uttered and never thought he would. The empty throne room rang with the clanging of the great seal of the emperor, which became more dented and twisted with every impact.

Finally, his fury expended, he backed up and assessed the damage he had done. The keeper was nothing but an indistinguishable pile of goo on the floor. He tossed aside the seal, not caring about its tradition or sacred meaning. It lay on the floor like some worthless piece of scrap metal, which—as far as Vir was concerned—was all it was.

He looked over at G'Kar, and he knew instantly that the life was gone from the great Narn. Indeed, he wondered whether he had even been alive at the last. Whether that twitch of his scarlet orb was deliberate, a mute warning . . . or just some after-death spasm simulating a last act of heroism. He couldn't know, nor would he ever.

"Tell your masters," Vir snarled at the smear on the floor that had once been alive, "that their time is over. Centauri Prime for Centauri."

"Tell us yourself."

The words were a hoarse whisper that came from behind. He whirled and saw half a dozen Drakh directly behind him. One of them he recognized instantly.

"Shiv'kala," he said.

"Vir Cotto," Shiv'kala replied. "Finally . . . we are face-to-face . . . true enemies revealed at last."

"You won't control me," Vir shot back.

"You know so little," the Drakh snarled. "But you will learn."

They advanced on him, and Vir backed up as fast as he could. They were coming in from all sides, circling him, and the only avenue left was the window, facing out onto a drop that would kill a hundred Virs.

Vir did not hesitate. He clambered up onto the window, poised in the sill. The night air, heated from the flames in the distance, swept around him.

"I've nothing to learn from you," he said defiantly, "except the lengths that someone should be willing to go to, just to live free in mind and spirit."

He took a look down, getting ready to make his fatal plunge. And then his eyes widened as he saw . . . a shuttle. No, not just any shuttle: his shuttle. It was approaching rapidly from below, coming straight toward him with a roar of engines.

The Drakh came at him, and he was out of time and options. Vir leaped through the air, feeling anything except graceful, and he landed atop the shuttle. He cried out, having landed badly, pain shooting through his right knee. He thought he might have torn a ligament, and then he started to slide off the top. It was smooth, giving his desperate fingers no purchase upon which to grab. But then the doors irised open, and Renegar was there, catching Vir as he slid by. "Hang on, I've got you!" he shouted, and hauled the flailing Cotto into the shuttle as if he weighed absolutely nothing.

Vir heard a screech of rage from the Drakh even as he tumbled into the shuttle.

Then he heard the sound of weapons fire.

He scrambled to his feet and what he saw through the window was enough to make his hearts sing. Guards, led by Caso, had come pouring into the room, heavily armed. The Drakh had turned to face them, a dark and fearsome last stand against the rather unexpected forces of light. The guards were opening fire on the Drakh. The grey servants of the Shadows were putting up a struggle, but it didn't seem likely they were going to survive for long. In a city reduced to smoking ruins thanks to their evil, at least one group of Drakh was undergoing what could only be described as a desperate last stand. He envisioned a throne room littered with Drakh bodies . . .

. . . and then couldn't help but remember that one of the bodies littering that throne room was that of he who should, by all rights, be sitting in that throne.

"Are you all right, Vir?" Senna asked. She was by his side, and he realized she was checking him over to ascertain whether he had sustained any sort of damage. "Are you unhurt?"

"That's . . . two different questions, really," Vir said ruefully. "I'm unhurt, yes. As for my being all right, though . . . I don't think I'll be all right ever again."

"Londo . . . were you able to help him?" Renegar asked . . . and then he saw the expression on Vir's face.

Senna did as well. "You mean . . . he's . . ."

"He died at G'Kar's hands, as did G'Kar at his."

"But why?" Senna asked desperately. "I don't understand. I don't understand any of it. Why would they kill each other?"

"I have some guesses on the matter," Vir said thoughtfully. "I don't know that we'll ever know for sure."

Senna began to sob. She seemed unable to find words to express the grief she was feeling. Vir reached for her and held her close to him.

"He tried. He tried so hard to be the best emperor he could," Senna managed to say.

"He did the most that anyone could—"

"Excuse me," Gwynn cut in, sounding a bit annoyed. "Can we save the maudlin eulogizing for a more appropriate time? There are other matters to be attended to."

"Shut up, Gwynn," Vir shot back. "You're a techno-mage, and I know perfectly well that there's a huge amount of things that you know about that I couldn't even begin to understand. But there are some things that you know absolutely nothing about, and this is one of them, so I'm telling you again, especially when it comes to Londo: Shut the hell up. Got that?"

Dripping with sarcasm, Gwynn bowed slightly, and said, "Of course, Vir Cotto. After all, I'm only the one who brought this vessel around, using my skills to find you, and saved your life. It's not as if you owe me the slightest bit of gratitude."

Vir allowed the remark to pass, partly from disdain and partly from the fact that he knew, deep down, that she was right. But she was so damned annoying that he couldn't quite bring himself to show his appreciation. So instead he changed the subject. "The remaining bombs . . . are we sure we've got them all?"

Renegar nodded. "Once we knew they existed—although it would have been great if we could have discovered it through some other method than having them be set off—Finian was able to tap into their energy signatures and locate them quickly enough. They were cloaked, but you can't cloak something from a techno-mage if they know what to look for."

"He never told anyone," Vir said in amazement. "Never trusted anyone . . . trusted me . . . enough to tell me . . ."

"Can you blame him?" Senna asked. "He must have thought that you would find them on your own. And he must have been afraid that, if he did say something, the Drakh would detonate the bombs as punishment. Afraid." She said the word again as if she could not quite digest its full meaning. "How many years must he have spent living in fear."

"I don't know that you can exactly call that living," Vir said. "Where are the bombs now?"

"Finian has them," Gwynn said immediately. "He was anxious to get them off-world, away from possible Drakh influence. He's defused them, but he felt it best that the Drakh be given no opportunity to use them for further mischief."

"Where is he now?"

"In another vessel."

"Can you communicate with him somehow?"

Gwynn nodded. "Absolutely. Where do you want them brought? Truth to tell, he'd be more than happy to be rid of them, sooner rather than later."

Vir didn't even hesitate. "To Minbar. I'm going to turn them over to Sheridan. A little gift in advance . . . for the help he's going to give us."

"What help are you talking about?"

"I suspect," Vir said, patting the satchel that was lying on the floor—the satchel that held Londo's memoirs—"that these words of Londo's are going to be very instrumental in letting the Alliance know just how involved the Drakh were in much of what has been blamed on Centauri Prime. The Alliance isn't going to appreciate being played for fools, and as for Sheridan . . ." He shook his head. "Let's just say that he has the most finely tuned sense of moral outrage I've ever seen in a Human. Now that the Drakh are in disarray, it shouldn't be too difficult to convince the Alliance to join forces with the Centauri fleet. Right now our ships are all sitting on station, waiting for someone to gather them in . . ."

"And that's going to be you?"

Vir nodded.

"How do you figure that?" Gwynn asked.

"For starters," Vir said slowly, "the fleet commanders have now been made to understand that what was supposed to be an initiative of Centauri origin was actually a massive manipulation at the hands of the Drakh . . . including the manipulation of the much-beloved, much-attended-to Prime Minister Durla. Durla's vision was actually Drakh vision, and that's not going to sit too well for men whose mission once seemed so clear-cut.

"I can guess that, even as we speak, there are counsels going on among the military leaders, trying to figure out what will happen next. Some will struggle for dominance. The ships may even be fighting each other. As soon as a new leader is announced and affirmed, the chances are that the fleet will fall into line eagerly, just so it can have a genuine purpose, for the first time in its existence."

"And you still think that leader will be you?" Renegar asked. "How do you figure that?"

"For starters, my connection with unveiling the Drakh is well known. And second, Londo once moved heaven and earth to try to get an endorsement from a techno-mage, because he felt that such an action would be a tremendous boost for his own chances at the throne. I know, because he enlisted my aid in trying to make things happen. Me . . . I'm going to have the endorsements of *two* techno-mages. That can be arranged, can't it, Gwynn?"

Gwynn was at the controls of the shuttle, guiding the vessel with speed and certainty away from the burning world below. She grunted in response. "Don't bet on it."

Without hesitation, he continued, "I'm also going to have the influence of the extremely influential General Rhys. I contacted him shortly before the revelation of the Drakh, informing him of what was going to happen. That was a gamble on my part, but the interaction I'd had with Rhys told me that he, of all people, would be the most outraged over the pervasive Drakh influence. He was loyal to Durla; when Durla proved less than trustworthy, Rhys needed someone to whom he could switch allegiance. I suspect that I will be that individual, and when that occurs, he'll bring the rest of the key military personnel along."

"Unless Rhys chooses to grab power for himself."

Vir shook his head. "Not Rhys. Believe it or not, he's not the type. He's old school, and believes that his allegiance is, and always must be, to the emperor. But the title of emperor is one that has traditionally always passed to those of higher birth. Rhys is lowborn, and proud of it. He's not going to want to reorder all of Centauri society just to accommodate some sort of power play.

"Now I . . . I'm of higher birth . . . no matter how much my parents would have liked to deny it," he added as a witheringly accurate self-portrayal. "Also, I believe that John Sheridan, president of the Alliance, will support my claim as well, as will most of the remaining Centauri nobility."

"You've been giving this a great deal of thought," Renegar observed.

"I learned from the best," Vir replied.

"But why?" Senna asked.

He looked to her, not quite understanding. "Why what?"

"Why would you want to be emperor? The responsibility, the danger, the—"

"The need," Vir said. "I see . . . a need. I've been doing that for years now, Senna. I see a need that has to be filled, and I . . . well . . . I just do it. Ever since I first came to Babylon 5, really. Londo needed an aide, I was his aide. He needed a conscience, and I was that, too . . . although I don't know that I did such a good job of it. The Narns needed someone to help them get to safety, and I was there for them. Centauri Prime needed someone to—"

"I need you to be quiet," Gwynn said tartly. "Am I going to get my wish?"

"Am I going to get the endorsement I need?"

"Anything for you, Your Highness."

Vir nodded in exaggerated gratitude. But despite the moment of levity, he still couldn't erase the image of the fallen Londo from his mind.

And on some level, he didn't want to.

I should be trying to figure out some sort of memorable opening words to this, but nothing's really coming.

Londo had such a way with words. Him and G'Kar. When I think of the two of them lying there, hands around each other's throats, I'm kind of struck by the irony of it. Two people who had the greatest gifts for words of anyone I've ever met, aside from John Sheridan. And the source of that strength, their words . . . cut off. What were their last thoughts, their last feelings? G'Kar . . . well, in many ways, I never really understood him, even at the end.

As for Londo, I can only think that it was probably something like relief.

I should introduce myself, I suppose. I am Vir Cotto, once the embarrassment of my family. I was considered to be such a joke that I was basically "exiled" to a station called Babylon 5.

It's a funny thing about that space station. In order to generate artificial gravity, it turned, like the center spoke of a great wheel. Sometimes I think that Babylon 5 was the hub of our universe, turning in the center of it while the rest of events circled around it.

That's good. I like that. Deep thoughts, descriptive phrasing . . . yes. Yes, that's definitely the type of thing that these journals should be filled with. I don't know if that's really me . . . but it's what people have come to expect. And every so often, you just have to knuckle down and give the people what they want.

In any event, I was packed off to Babylon 5, to serve as the aide to a lower-level politician named Londo Mollari. No one could possibly have known that the association would wind up leaving me in the highest position of power in all of Centauri Prime. Selfishly, I wish my family had survived the bombs to see it. Then again—and I know this will sound cold, but it's also true—if my family had lived to see me attain this height, they would have been perfectly capable of planting their own bombs outside the palace, to blow the whole thing into orbit. Anything would have been preferable to allowing such a humiliating joke of a person as myself to assume power.

What can I say? That's just the kind of loyalty I inspired in my family.

Following the escape from Centauri Prime, my arrival on Minbar was greeted with some suspicion by the local residents. I can't entirely say I blame them. After all, the Centauri had been painted as mad-dog killers for so long, the Minbari probably couldn't help but think that I had some sort of sinister motive planned. Sheridan and Delenn, who arrived at roughly the same time, however, intervened in this potentially sticky situation. They paved the way for my setting up a temporary "exile headquarters" on Minbar.

From that point on, the rest was simply a matter of organization. Word was sent out to the remaining heads of the Centauri Houses. Some came to Minbar curious, others came in anger, still others came seeking answers, while still others desired power. The point was . . . those who survived, came.

I managed to keep the debate under control. There was some initial resistance, but I was backed up by the techno-mages, the Alliance in the person of John Sheridan, and the awareness on the part of the House heads that the fleet was still floating around out there, looking for a target. If matters continued in a disorganized fashion for too long, someone in the military might have taken it into their head that Centauri Prime itself was ripe for military rule. Either that, or we might have had various leaders go rogue and decide to start attacking the Alliance on their own initiative. That, of course, would have been suicidal. What little of Centauri Prime was still standing wouldn't have remained standing for long, once the Alliance started fighting back.

Thanks to the agreement that has come to be known as the Minbar Accord, the following was worked out:

The House heads have recognized my claim as emperor.

The military is being recalled to Centauri Prime, with new instructions and directions being given them. They will have the target they so desperately need to validate their fleet's existence. That target is the Drakh. Many of the escape vessels were tracked and targeted. A number of Drakh were also captured and were . . . shall we say, forthcoming . . . about certain Drakh interests and strongholds. The Centauri fleet, in tandem with the resources of the Alliance, is going after the Drakh with a vengeance.

Sheridan has been good enough to put telepaths at the disposal of the Centauri and Alliance fleets. Telepaths capable of detecting both the Drakh and their keepers, should any more of those vile little creatures try to spread their influence.

What has been most impressive during all of this, I must admit, is Senna. As if she has been watching, waiting, and preparing for this her entire life, she has been dealing with the House heads, the remaining ministers . . . all of them. They are surprisingly—even to themselves, I think—comfortable discussing such things as military, financial, and governmental matters with her. It's unusual, considering that women are held, if not in low esteem, at least in less-than-impressive regard in our society. Perhaps it is because she has been around for so long that many of them know her and feel at ease.

Perhaps, as the daughter of Lord Refa, the ward of Londo Mollari, and the beloved—yes, I'm afraid it's that evident—of the next emperor, they see her as a connection to the far and near past and to the future. It would be premature, maybe even absurd, to think that she could one day hold a position of authority in our government. Then again, this is a time of possibilities, and why shouldn't something such as that be possible? Such things do not happen overnight.

Sheridan and Delenn have been remarkably supportive. At one point, Delenn looked me straight in the eye, and said, "Vir . . . you're a living symbol of everything that is positive about Centauri culture." Hard not to be flattered over something like that. Sheridan has likewise been forthcoming with his help, support, and insight. I very much doubt whether I could have held matters together in the initial stages if his presence had not sent a very distinct message.

Their son, David, on the other hand . . . well . . . that is another matter . . .

29

David pulled once more against the restraints, his face twisted in fury. For Delenn, watching from the edge of the room, it took every amount of strength and self-control she possessed not to let her grief be displayed. Those monsters might be watching her at this very moment, peering through the hideous eye that sat unblinkingly upon her son's shoulder, at the base of his neck.

Nude from the waist up, David had absolutely no chance of tearing free of the straps that held him firmly to the chair. That did not, however, stop him from trying.

The keeper remained inscrutable, but it was his actions they were viewing. Delenn was quite sure of that.

A score of Minbari doctors and scientists had been through the medical facility, studying the situation from every possible angle. They were the best that the Minbari had to offer. Yet the man next to whom John Sheridan was now standing, the man who had just gotten done examining David—he was someone whose medical expertise Delenn trusted above all others, including that of her own kind.

"What do you think, Stephen?" Sheridan asked.

As dire as the situation was, Stephen Franklin would not be rushed. He put up a hand to quiet Sheridan as he finished studying readings he had taken.

Delenn looked at her son once more, her heart aching for her inability to help him. She knew that if anyone could, it would be Dr. Stephen Franklin. David, after all, was a unique hybrid: mostly human, but with a few Minbari traits. And he had a creature spawned from the black pit of Shadow and Drakh technology bonded to him.

Franklin's knowledge covered all the bases. He had been an expert on Minbari physiology at a time when the Minbari were busy trying to exterminate Humans altogether. He had been squarely in the middle of the Shadow War, and his detailed research into Drakh capability during the time of the Great Plague gave him insight into the bio-organics that that insidious race was capable of.

"If anyone can help, he can."

The hushed voice next to her, verbalizing the words in her head, startled her. She turned and let out an automatic sigh of relief when she saw Michael Garibaldi standing beside her. He had barely slept since David's return. If he had not been consoling or giving moral support to Delenn and Sheridan, he had been by David's side, trying to reach the boy, help him, as if he could get the teen to rid himself of the Drakh influence by willpower alone. He had been awake for so long that Sheridan had personally threatened to knock him cold just to make sure he got some sleep. Reluctantly, Garibaldi had gone off to bed, promising he'd sleep until he felt rested. That had been forty-seven minutes ago, yet she couldn't find it in her to scold him.

"I know," she said softly, patting him on the cheek. His three days' growth of beard was scratchy.

Sheridan started to say "Well?" again, almost out of reflex, and then stopped himself with visible effort and waited.

As for David, he said nothing, as he hadn't for some time. It was as if the creature had some sort of lock on his speech center. In a way, Delenn was grateful for that. What if the keeper had so subsumed his personality that he began spitting out curses and defiance, like some demon-possessed shell? Or worse . . . what if his own personality held sway, and he was crying out for her help? The prospect of standing there, listening to his cries, knowing she could not aid him . . . it would have been beyond excruciating.

Franklin finally looked up and indicated with a gesture of his head that they should reconvene outside the room. They walked out, Delenn bringing up the rear and casting one last, sad look at her son. It was hard to tell whether he was even aware of it.

"Look," Franklin said slowly, "I have to admit, my ego, if nothing else, would love to be able to come in here, take one look at the situation, and say that there's some simple answer that everyone else has overlooked. But there's not. That thing is like . . . it's like a parasite that's literally eaten into him on a neurological basis. It didn't happen overnight, either. The . . . keeper, you said it's called?" Sheridan nodded. "The keeper, as near as I can tell, has been establishing a psychic bond with him for a number of years now. It had the opportunity to intertwine itself with him on a far more comprehensive and profound basis than it could have with an adult, because it connected with him at such a young age. For all I know, it's been influencing him on a low-level basis of some kind since birth."

Delenn let out a choked sob but managed to pull herself together quickly. Coming apart now wasn't going to benefit anything. Instead she let the cold, burning fury that she felt for the monsters that had done this come to the fore.

"The creature's tendrils have wrapped themselves around David on a basic neurological level," Franklin continued. "If we tried to remove the thing by force, it would be the equivalent of tearing out his central nervous system with a chain saw."

"We can put it to sleep," Delenn suggested. "Londo told us that alcohol numbed its awareness."

"It's awareness, yes, but not its influence. If its life is threatened, no matter how incapacitated it is, it will fight back, and David will likely be the battleground. The chances are that, even if David manages to live, there will be nerve and brain damage so extensive that whatever is left won't really be David anymore."

"There has to be a way."

Franklin took a deep breath. "As near as I can tell—based on brain-wave readings I've gotten off the keeper—it draws a sort of strength from its point of origin."

"Point of origin?" Garibaldi sounded confused.

But Delenn understood instantly. "The Drakh that made it."

"Made it, nourished it, sustained it . . . however you want to describe it," Franklin agreed. "That Drakh, whoever and wherever it is, is the keeper's foundation. As with any house, remove the foundation, and the structure collapses."

"Is there a way to generate some sort of scrambling field so it can't communicate with the Drakh?" Sheridan asked.

Franklin shook his head. "Even if we could manage it, it would just trigger the keeper's self-defense mechanisms, and David would suffer for it. The only thing I can suggest is finding a way to terminate the signal from the other end, as it were."

"You're saying we have to find the Drakh who did this . . . and kill it," Sheridan said grimly.

"In essence . . . yes."

"How in Valen's name can we possibly do that?" Delenn demanded.

"I wish I had an answer for you . . . but I don't."

* * *

Slowly, Garibaldi walked toward David. His determination to struggle against his bonds seemed endless. During every waking hour he kept it up; only when he slept did he cease his struggles, and he only slept because he had exhausted himself so thoroughly that he couldn't move anymore.

Garibaldi focused all his attention on the keeper, staring straight into that hideous eye. "Whoever . . . wherever you are," he said intently, "if you're seeing me . . . sensing me, whatever . . . I'm telling you right now: I will find you. And when I do, the only thing that's going to be on your side is that you'll die quick and easy. Trust me: I'd rather prolong it. Make you feel every second of agony, for as long as possible. But I don't want you influencing this boy for an instant longer than necessary. You got that, you disease-ridden piece of filth? I . . . am coming . . . for you."

The keeper didn't seem especially perturbed by the prospect.

Dinner that evening was a less-than-festive affair. Vir and Senna had joined Delenn, Sheridan, Franklin, and Garibaldi around a table that had more than enough food to accommodate everyone. Unfortunately, much of it was left uneaten, since no one seemed particularly hungry.

Franklin, in short order, brought the two Centauri up to speed with what he had already told the others. Vir didn't seem especially shocked to hear it. "I can't say I'm surprised," he told them. "You know of how I found G'Kar and Londo . . ."

"With their hands at each other's throats," Sheridan said grimly.

"There was no way . . . no way . . . Londo was trying to fight G'Kar off on his own. He wanted to make certain that the two of you escaped, and he was willing to sacrifice his life to make sure that happened. Any resistance given to that end was entirely at the keeper's control."

"Is that supposed to make us feel better about the guy?" Garibaldi demanded.

"Michael . . ." Sheridan tried to rein him in.

But Garibaldi wasn't listening. He put down the fork that he hadn't used to pick up any food for twenty minutes, and leaned forward. "You're sitting here telling me that, after he was responsible for the deaths of millions, all long before the Drakh got their hooks into him, we're all now supposed to feel sorry for Londo Mollari and take pride in him because he sacrificed himself to save three people? Granted, three people whom I myself would crawl through hell over broken glass to help, but three people nevertheless? Is that somehow supposed to balance the scales?"

"No," Vir answered softly.

"Then don't try to make him out to be some sort of grand hero, at least not while I'm around."

Once upon a time, Delenn thought, Vir would have been intimidated by the ferocity and intensity of Garibaldi's outburst. Instead he just looked a bit tired, and said, "You know, Mr. Garibaldi . . . Londo was endlessly fascinated by Earth and its inhabitants. He stepped in whenever he could to help you. Did things behind the scenes, positive things, which your people never knew anything about. He read over Earth culture endlessly, always researching, always trying to understand. I asked him occasionally why he was so intrigued by all of you, and he never really managed to give me any sort of satisfactory answer. But you know what? I think I've figured it out. I think that, in many ways . . . he was far closer spiritually to any of you than he was to any of us. He had a clear vision of what he wanted, a vision that exceeded his grasp at every level, but he never stopped reaching, despite the inherent character flaws that pulled him down. Londo Mollari was not a hero, Mr. Garibaldi. What he was . . . was all too Human."

There was a long moment of silence, and then Sheridan turned to Vir. "Well spoken," he said.

Garibaldi rolled his eyes. "Sometimes I don't get any of you people."

"That's quite all right, sir," Senna spoke up. "I don't 'get' any of you, either. And I'm speaking largely as an outsider. But what I do see," and she looked around the table and actually smiled, "is a group of people who would very much prefer to like each other . . . but have been through so much, they don't know if they can."

"This is quite a perceptive young woman you have here, Vir," Delenn remarked. "You would do well not to let her get too far."

"Thank you," Vir said. "I'll see that she doesn't. Oh . . . Senna. Do you have the drawings?"

"Drawings?" Sheridan asked.

"Senna's been busy," Vir said, by way of explanation. "She has untapped talents."

Senna had unrolled several large sheets of paper, and she handed them to Garibaldi. He endeavored to maintain his surly attitude, but in spite of himself, he raised an eyebrow upon seeing the illustrations. "Fairly decent likenesses of Londo and G'Kar," he said. "I like the way they're standing there, with their backs to each other. Seems symbolic."

"It's quite rough," she said.

"What's this area between them?"

"That's the city. I told you it was rough."

"The city?" Then he understood. "These are statues. Designs for statues. My God, they're huge."

"Statues?" Sheridan leaned over, as did Delenn. Franklin got up and came around the table to get a better look. "You're thinking about building statues to Londo and G'Kar."

Vir nodded. "At either gate of the main city. Part of the rebuilding of Centauri Prime." He shook his head. "Hard to believe. It seems that just yesterday we had to rebuild from the Alliance attack. Now we're looking to the Alliance to help us recover again."

"The Alliance will be there to help," Sheridan assured him. "That much I can promise you. And this . . ." He shook his head and tapped the drawings. "If you'd told me twenty years ago that there would be a statue of G'Kar . . . of any Narn, for that matter . . . built right on the edge of the city . . ."

"It is a most remarkable concept," Delenn said. She tapped the paper. "I am curious, though. Why are they both faced away from the city? It almost seems to say that they have turned their backs on the Centauri people."

"No, Delenn, not at all," Garibaldi told her. "Takes an old security warhorse to understand: they're standing guard. You can't stand guard if your back is to your enemies."

"That's exactly right," Senna said. "Although it's also more than that. Londo . . ." She seemed to know what she wanted to say, but had trouble putting it into words.

Vir stepped in. "We have Londo facing away from the capital that he inhabited for so long . . . obsessed over for so long . . . that it was all he could see. He didn't look to the long-range results of his decisions, because he was so blinded by his poor decisions."

"So instead," Senna said, "we're positioning him the way I think he would have wished he had been. He's looking away from the city and, instead, to the horizon."

"Very nice," Sheridan said. "And something tells me that G'Kar would have appreciated the irony of protecting the capital city of what were once his enemies."

Garibaldi commented, "And the way that you have them positioned . . . they're really watching each other's backs."

"As they did in life," Delenn said. "It has a symmetry to it. Well done, Vir and Senna . . . very well done."

"I just wish they could have lived to see it," Sheridan said.

She put her arm through his, linking them. "You know, John . . . I think, in a way that we'll never understand . . . they did."

Senna and I returned to Centauri Prime today. The reception was muted, which is to be expected. We are still burying our dead, and naturally it's a little difficult to get all worked up over the arrival of the man who has been promised to be the next emperor.

The fires have long been put out, but the damage remains. The smell of burned flesh still hangs in the air; if I take a deep breath, my gag reflex kicks in. Upon my arrival, the first thing I did was walk through the streets of Centauri Prime, surveying the damage. It was as if I were wandering through a ghost town, except the ghosts were out and about. People looked at me with haunted, almost vacant expressions. Despite my brief holographic appearance, they likely didn't know who I was. I have not yet taken to wearing the white. I don't know when I will. I think there's a long way for our world, our people, to go before we start assuming the outward vestments of the past.

The palace, of course, remains untouched. Naturally. For the Drakh, it was a symbolic stronghold of their influence, second only to the Tower of Power they engineered. Sheridan showed me a picture of a tower on an Earth desert, constructed by insects and swarming with them. That's what the Tower of Power was: an infestation. We exterminated that infestation. But, like any number of insects, the inhabitants of the Tower turned around and stung us. It will take us a long time to recover from such a severe stinging.

On the shuttle from Minbar to here, I brought some acquisitions that Sheridan and Delenn were generous enough to give me. Books and some assorted pieces of furniture, including several tables, chairs, and a large wardrobe. All very old and crafted in the Minbari style. Their generosity is amazing.

I have had initial discussions with my ministers. I intend to make General Rhys minister of Internal Security. He told me he didn't want the job. That's more than enough reason to give it to him.

When I arrived at the palace, Dunseny was waiting for me, as were Caso and Renegar. Renegar handed me a crystal that, when I played it, revealed a communication from Gwynn and Finian on it. Both of them looked . . . tired. As if the events that had transpired had taken a lot out of them. I couldn't really blame them, I guess. I think we all felt that way. But the fact that they were techno-mages should have . . . I don't know . . . protected them somehow.

"It's over, Vir," Finian told me. "But it's also just started. And Gwynn and I both want you to know . . . that if an emergency ever presents itself . . . if there is ever some catastrophe facing you as you proceed on your path as emperor of Centauri Prime, trying to pull together the shattered remains of your republic . . . in short, if there's ever a situation in which the talents of the techno-mages are required . . . then both Gwynn and I want you to know . . "

"That you can forget it," Gwynn completed.

I actually laughed out loud at that as the picture blinked out. One had to credit them: techno-mages habitually spoke in a manner so oblique, so indecipherable, that it was a pleasure to see that they could say exactly what they meant when they put their minds to it.

As the day drew to a close, I held Senna close to me and watched the sun turning red on the horizon. So much to do. So many things that needed attending to. And I found my thoughts turning to Timov, the former wife of Londo. Word had reached us that she had passed away quietly, of illness. Apparently she had hung on for far longer than the doctors had believed possible. She died on the exact same day that Londo did. On the one hand, there is certainly no reasonable way she could have known. On the other hand, considering the formidable woman she was, it might be that she was simply so stubborn that she felt she had to outlast Londo, no matter what.

And naturally, thoughts of Timov turned me to Mariel.

We all carry our sins upon us. Mariel will always be mine. I was working to save a people . . . and in doing it, destroyed one woman. I can justify it as much as I want. I can make myself believe that she had it coming. That it was necessary. That it was any one of a hundred things. But what I keep coming back around to is that it was wrong, and it's something that I can never, ever fix. Not ever.

I felt a frost upon my spine, feeling as if a shadow had touched me, and held Senna closer as the night chill began to fill the air.

30

"Do you want me to sleep with you tonight?" Senna asked.

Vir considered it a moment, but then shook his head. "The time . . . isn't right." He sighed. "I don't . . . I can't . . . I . . ."

She put a finger to his lips and hushed him. "When the time is right, then." Her lips brushed lightly against his. "Good night then, Vir."

"Good night."

He went to his quarters then. He had selected something simple for himself, nothing ostentatious. He couldn't bring himself to take over the private quarters that had once belonged to Londo. Too many ghosts that had not been laid to rest, and quite possibly never would be.

As the door slid shut behind him, he glanced around the room approvingly. The things he'd transported from Minbar had been brought there and set up just as he had specified. There was the desk, and the chairs. And the wardrobe, polished and ornate, big as a man and twice as wide.

It was late; he'd had a long day, and he had a series of meetings scheduled for tomorrow that were going to be pivotal in his decisions as to what direction Centauri Prime should go. Yet with all that, he could not bring himself to sleep. Instead he sat down at a computer and recorded another entry in his chronicles. There were many ways in which he had no intention of following Londo's example, but the concept of keeping a journal was a good idea. For an emperor owed it to more than himself to try to keep his thoughts orderly, try to maintain a record of his achievements, or lack thereof. An emperor owed it to whoever followed him in the office. A blueprint, a template, for what to do right . . . and what to avoid.

"I felt a frost upon my spine, feeling as if a shadow had touched me, and held Senna closer as the night chill began to fill the air," he said, and was about to continue when another chill struck him. That was odd, however, because when he'd been with Senna, they'd been standing on a balcony. Here, however, he was in a room that had been warm only moments before.

The room also seemed darker somehow, and the shadows were—impossibly—starting to lengthen.

Slowly Vir rose from his chair. He appeared for all the world as if he wanted to cry out, but he could not.

A form separated itself from the shadows and stood facing him in the middle of the room.

"Shiv'kala," Vir managed to say. "You're . . . not dead."

"In that ambush? No." When he'd encountered Shiv'kala in the past, he'd always been struck by the calm, level tone of the Drakh. Now, however, Shiv'kala sounded as if every word from his mouth was laced with rage. He couldn't be sure, but it looked as if Shiv'kala was actually trembling. "No, I was able to make my escape . . . for all the good it did me."

"Good?"

"I," the Drakh growled, "have been shunned. Shunned by the Drakh Entire. Because of Londo. Because of you."

"I . . . don't understand . . ."

"Of course you do not," he snarled. "You cannot understand. Cannot know what it was to commune with the Entire. But our hold on Centauri Prime has disintegrated, my people are in retreat. The mighty fleet we helped construct now seeks us out to destroy us . . . and they blame it on me. They say I did not treat Londo harshly enough. I attempted to educate him, you see." He was circling Vir, exuding anger. Vir was rooted to the spot. "Tried to teach him our purpose. Our reason for existence. Tried to get him to understand the rightness of our cause. Instead he mistook compassion for weakness, and betrayed us in a way that he never would have if I had treated him appropriately. I did not break him sufficiently. I will not make that mistake again.

"My people have abandoned me along with this world . . . but I will get them to understand. I will show them just what I am capable of. I will bend this world to the way of the Shadows, single-handedly if I must. And the Drakh will see my accomplishment, and return. If it takes a century, it will not matter, for we have nothing but time, despite all your ships' pathetic attempts to track us down and annihilate us. But it will start with you, Vir Cotto."

"You mean . . . you . . ." Vir gulped. "You're going to try to break me the way you didn't with Londo?"

"No," the Drakh said, speaking so softly that Vir could barely hear him. "You . . . I am simply going to kill. I will deal with whoever follows you . . . but you I will not suffer to live."

Vir licked his lips, seeming to summon his courage. "No. You won't kill me. Instead . . . you're going to tell me where I can find the Drakh that spawned the keeper on David Sheridan."

It was hard to believe that a Drakh could look surprised, much less as surprised as Shiv'kala did just then. "I had thought," he said slowly, "that you simply acted the fool, in order to throw suspicion from yourself. But I was wrong. You truly are a fool."

"Tell me," Vir said, as if somehow he had the upper hand.

"You want the Drakh who produced David Sheridan's keeper?" He spread his arms wide. "He stands before you." And then his hands came together, and he advanced on Vir.

Vir didn't budge. "Thank you. I figured as much. And it's all I wanted to know."

Shiv'kala had taken only two steps toward Vir when the door of the Minbari wardrobe cabinet banged open. He spun, staring in confusion.

Standing inside the cabinet, a PPG clenched securely in both hands, was Michael Garibaldi. There was a lopsided, wolfish grin on his face and a glitter of death in his eyes.

"What's up, Drakh?" he asked.

Shiv'kala let out the howl of a damned soul, and his arm moved with a blur. But Garibaldi didn't give him any time. He squeezed off two quick shots, and both struck home, one in the Drakh's stomach, the second in his chest. The impact lifted him off his feet and slammed him against the far wall, even as a pointed steel rod flew from Shiv'kala's sleeve. It thunked into the wood six inches to the right of Garibaldi's head. He didn't even flinch, or seem to notice.

Shiv'kala flopped about on the floor like a beached whale. The only sound issuing from his mouth was a sort of incoherent grunting, and his chest made a wheezing, sucking noise that Garibaldi knew all too well. The floor beneath him became dark and stained with the awful liquid that passed for the creature's blood.

Garibaldi stood over him, aiming the PPG squarely between Shiv'kala's eyes. "The first one was for David . . . and the second was for Lou Welch. And this . . ."

"Mr. Garibaldi," Vir said sharply. Garibaldi looked to him, and Vir extended his hand, a stern expression on his face. "I can't let you do that. Give it here. Now."

Slowly, reluctantly, Garibaldi handed it over. Vir held it delicately, hefted the weight, clearly impressed by the lightness of it. Then he looked down at the fallen Drakh. "In the end . . . Londo had you pegged," he told the Drakh. "He said you were predictable. And you were. Your ego had to bring you back here, make you vulnerable. To get away, all you had to do was leave. We'd probably never have found you. But you had to stay around, to have your vengeance. You refused to admit that the time of the Drakh on Centauri Prime is over. A lot of creatures that walked or swam or flew this world's surface didn't realize when their moment passed. But it's strange: Nature doesn't care whether they knew it or not. Nature just got rid of them. Turned them extinct. Oh . . . and by the way," he added, almost as an afterthought, ". . . this is for Londo and G'Kar." And with that, he blew Shiv'kala's head off.

David Sheridan's shriek was so loud that many Minbari within a mile radius claimed to have been able to hear it.

Sheridan and Delenn were there in seconds, neither of them having even bothered to pull on robes. They had no idea what they were going to find when they entered the room, although neither of them would have been surprised to discover their son's corpse.

Even faster on the scene, amazingly, had been Stephen Franklin, who had opted to stay on Minbar for a time, to monitor the boy's condition as best he could. He was already there when Sheridan and Delenn arrived, and his body blocked their view of their son. "Stephen!" Sheridan cried out. "David! What's wrong with David?"

Franklin turned around, and said with an absolutely unreadable expression, "Wrong?" Then he stepped aside.

They saw with astonishment that Franklin had just finished unstrapping the teen, who wore a pale and wan expression. Sheridan immediately looked to the keeper . . . except it was no longer there. There was a severe reddish mark indicating where the creature had been, but it was gone. Instead he saw Franklin crouching and picking it up with a pair of forceps. Its tendrils were hanging limply. Its eye lay wide open, but was glassily blind. It seemed about as threatening as a clump of seaweed. Clearly the creature was dead or dying. Franklin opened a large specimen jar and dropped the thing in, and it landed with a sickening little *plop*.

Delenn and Sheridan moved instantly to their son's side. Delenn was running her fingers over the area where the keeper had been, shaking her head in wonderment.

"Lemme guess," David said, in a voice that was hoarse and croaking. "Uncle Mikey?"

"I suspect so," Sheridan told him. "He volunteered to go on 'stakeout,' as he called it, on Centauri Prime. Something tells me he hit pay dirt far more quickly than we could have hoped."

"Oh, David," Delenn said, stroking his face repeatedly as if unable to believe it was him.

"It's okay, Ma . . . really. I just . . . I'd like to know one thing . . ."

"Anything, son. Just name it," Sheridan said.

"Okay." He took a deep breath. "Can I have that second piece of birthday cake now?"

Sheridan and Delenn looked at each other, then burst into joyous laughter, holding their son tight.

"More than that, David," Sheridan said fiercely. "If there's one thing I've learned, it's that hiding you here can't protect you from the galaxy. So we might as well go out there and take it on. When you recover, I'm taking a break from the presidency . . . Michael goes on vacation from his business . . . and Michael and I are going to take you on a tour of known space. Hitch some rides, grab some freighters, go down and dirty—the real worm's-eye view. Just us guys."

"Really?" David looked in amazement at Delenn. "Mom . . . that's . . . that's okay with you? You won't feel left out or—"

She laughed. "*Someone* has to run things while your father and godfather are gallivanting about in the throes of their second childhood."

He embraced both of them, and as he did, Delenn breathed silent prayers of thanks to Vir, to Garibaldi, to Valen, to Lorien. To whoever and whatever beings, real, spiritual, or imagined, had given her back her son. She would never again bewail the dwindling amount of time she had left with her husband, because at least they would all be able to enjoy it.

"So . . . Vir . . . well done," Londo's voice growled in my ear. "Look where you've come, eh? Who would have thought?"

We sat drinking together on a beach, the wave washing up along the shore. The sun shone down upon us, bathing me in a pleasant warmth. I had read in his final memoirs how he would have given anything to walk upon a beach for a brief time . . . and here it appeared he was going to have an eternity of time to do so. He looked just as I remembered him when we first met. I never realized how young he was. Great Maker, how young we all were.

"Who would have thought," I echoed.

"Look at you. Remember the days when you would get drunk on one glass alone?" He chortled at the thought. "I'll be honest with you, Vir. When you first came to Babylon 5, I gave you three months. Six months at the outside. I didn't think you'd last. Who could know that you would last . . . and I wouldn't?"

"You lasted a good long time, Londo," I assured him. "You had a good run."

"Did I?" He laughed softly. "I suppose I did. A low-level ambassador assigned to a space station that was considered a joke. They called it 'Sinclair's Folly,' you know. It wasn't exactly a stepping-stone to greatness. It was considered more a dead end. Who knew that it would lead to the throne."

"It didn't lead there, Londo. The path was very crooked, and you cut it yourself."

"I was led," Londo said firmly. "The Shadows and their agents, and their agents' agents, led me. But make no mistake. I'm not tossing aside responsibility. It was I who walked that path, and walked it willingly. Perhaps . . . perhaps at the end, that was what mattered. I took that final responsibility . . . and preserved a future that didn't include me. Does that make sense?"

"I suppose it does." I looked around. "Too bad G'Kar couldn't join us."

"He had another engagement in Na'Toth's dream. Even he can't be everywhere. On the other hand, there are always unwelcome visitors. Hold on a moment, please . . ."

Suddenly there was a sword in his hand. I flinched automatically, but he turned away from me and, in one smooth motion, threw the blade with unerring accuracy. It thudded into a grove of bushes nearby. There was a grunt, and then the impaled body of a Drakh fell from darkness into the red-tinted sunlight that was just filtering through from the sun on the horizon. The moment the rays struck it, it evaporated into dust.

"If he had been expecting that," Londo said mildly, "he could have stopped it. That's what you always have to do with forces of darkness, Vir. You have to catch them by surprise. Emissaries of evil tend to think very far, and very deep, but not very fast. Are you writing this down, Vir? That was a good one. You should remember that."

"I will."

"And never stop watching the shadows. You never know."

"But the Drakh are gone from Centauri Prime, Londo. In full retreat. Our people are safe, they—"

"Vir," he said patiently. "You started out as an aide to a low-level ambassador and you wound up emperor. What does that say to you?"

"You never know."

"Exactly."

"I'll watch the shadows, Londo, just in case they decide to watch me back."

"That is good. That is very good." He took a deep, final drink. "I think, Vir, it is time for deep, thoughtful, and profound words of wisdom that will explain the entire purpose of the universe and guarantee a life of accomplishment and prosperity."

"And they would be . . . ?"

Londo rose and walked across the sands. Standing there was Adira, smiling, her arms open to meet him.

Then I heard a steady, measured tread, a "splish splish." And there came Timov . . . walking across the surface of the water. "Londo!" she called sternly with a smile. "It's getting late."

Londo saw her, rolled his eyes, and, inclining his head, said, "She always has to show off."

She stepped out of the surf and they regarded me warmly, although Timov was watching Londo with the patient air of someone who had evaluated all of Londo's flaws and simply decided to find them charming.

"The words of wisdom, Londo?" I prompted.

"Oh, yes. Of course." And in a booming voice, Londo said, "Make love as often as possible." And with that, Londo and his women, one of passion, one of conscience, walked away, leaving no prints on the sand. His deep laughter echoed down the palace halls and carried me into wakefulness.

The sunlight of the new morning beamed through the window at me. I glanced at the corners of the room, but the light was thorough and revealed nothing of any threat hiding there.

I shrugged on my robe and left my quarters to find Senna and heed Londo's advice. I think he would have wanted it that way.

ABOUT THE AUTHORS

Peter David is famous for writing some of the most popular of the original *Star Trek: The Next Generation* novels, including *Imzadi* and *A Rock and a Hard Place*. His original works include the Arthurian novel *Knight Life* and the quirky werewolf story *Howling Mad*. He single-handedly revived the classic comic book series *The Incredible Hulk* and has written just about every famous comic book superhero. He collaborated with J. Michael Straczynski on the *Bablyon 5* comic book series, and with Bill Mumy, he created the Nickelodeon television series *Space Cases*. In his spare time, he writes movie screenplays, children's books, and TV scripts (including *Babylon 5*).

J. Michael Straczynski is one of the most prolific and highly regarded writers currently working in the television industry. In 1995, he was selected by *Newsweek* magazine as one of their Fifty for the Future, described as innovators who will shape our lives as we move into the twenty-first century. His work spans every conceivable genre—from historical dramas and adaptations of famous works of literature (*The Strange Case of Dr. Jekyll and Mr. Hyde*) to mystery series (*Murder, She Wrote*), cop shows (*Jake and the Fatman*), anthology series (*The Twilight Zone*), and science fiction (*Babylon 5*). He writes ten hours a day, seven days a week, except for his birthday, New Year's, and Christmas.